THE PIÑON NUTS

TOM BISHOP

All images and design by Tom Bishop
Cover photo: Chef's Knife And Piñon Nuts
Back Cover Photo: Rainy Sunset Over Pikes Peak

www.TOMBISHOP.biz

Any similarity to real persons living or dead is probably beyond my skills,
but if someone should by chance take offense to any portion of this work of fiction,
please accept my sincerest apologies and just get over it.

For Ev, Robert, and the whole Gang,
without whom this book would not have been possible
and without whom my life would have been immeasurably diminished.

PART I

...O...O...O...

My mind yearns for the high places. Whenever I drive through the mountains of the American West, I find myself longing to abandon the highway, to drive a rutted gravel road all the way to the end, and then to get out and start walking. I re-create myself on those wild summits. Their eternal youth transports me back to my own youth, rambling through the Colorado Rockies. But all too often I've had to make the next town, the next gig.

It figures, I suppose, that an old musician, like an old song, should just slowly fade away. Before I slip quietly into the anonymity of a normal job and a regular life, though, maybe I'll haul out some of my old war stories about life on the road.

I never got fat singing for my supper but I hit the road more in search of stories than money anyway. Gigging is great for that: lots of free time, meeting new people every night, drinking for free most of the time. Stories just fell into my lap.

I used to play the tiny resort town of Saratoga, Wyoming. One night an ancient cowboy caught my sleeve as I walked to the bar on a break. He didn't even want to chat. He just had to tell me this story:

It seems a man had a cat for which he had no particular affection, and the feeling, or lack of it, appeared to be mutual. He didn't want to take it to the pound. No one wants a grouchy old cat. Besides, neither he nor anyone else would ever truly own this cat, which seemed, as do most cats, quite self-sufficient.

So the man resolved to let the cat choose its own fate. With some mutual cursing and scratching, he put it in his truck, drove to the edge of town, and set it free. But he hadn't been back home long enough to drink a beer before the cat meowed at the door.

Obviously he hadn't driven far enough. This time he drove way out into the country, shooing the cat from the truck near what looked like a rodent-rich old barn. By supper-time the cat once again scratched at his door.

Now it had become a challenge. The next morning he wrestled the cat back into the truck and started to drive, grim determination on both their faces. He drove past the old barn, across the river, along the railroad tracks all the way to the spur, through a valley he'd never seen before, over a mountain pass...

In fact, he drove so far he had to follow the cat back home.

My years on the road have left me lonely, weary, and poor. For ten years now, I've lived in Seattle between gigs, longer than I've lived anywhere but Colorado, and I still feel like I'm on the

1

road. In fact, as far out and lost as I feel, I may need to follow two or three cats back home, and God only knows how they'll find the way. But before I hit the highway, one more time, exit singing—

Off we go, into the wild blue yonder…

August 8, 1999

Amanda Black loved to soar. She loved to fly, free of the noisy, turbulent tow plane, free of the flat, unforgiving earth. She loved the rush of the wind across the streamlined body of the glider, the gentle tug of the stick. She loved catching a thermal from the mountains to the clouds, lifting her faster and farther than the tow plane and doing it for free.

Maybe this love amounted to no more than escapism but sooner or later everyone seeks some alternative to the usual dreary reality. Amanda had lived all of her four dozen years in Colorado Springs. Today, for the first time, she didn't feel like going back. She wished she could just soar beyond the rainbow to that land where troubles melt like lemon drops.

In front of her and below, she saw the pilot of the tow plane waggling his wings and she realized he had been waggling them for some time now. She pulled herself from her daydream. Joyce, her partner at Earthworks who owned the glider, had reminded Amanda to stay in the moment at this time of year because conditions could change in a heartbeat. But that's true of life itself, Amanda thought, and if Joyce knew what had happened earlier, she would have forgiven Amanda's momentary distraction.

She pulled the tow rope release toggle twice and felt the vibrations from the plane's motor cease. As soon as she saw the free end of the rope whipping in the wind, she pushed the rudder pedals and eased over on the stick to bank the glider up and to the right. The tow pilot banked left to fly back to Kelly Air Park in Black Forest. Colorado lay at Amanda's feet.

Puffy white cumulus clouds gathered above the Rampart Range, meaning Amanda could count on plenty of updrafts this afternoon. Joyce had gone camping, leaving Amanda free to soar to her heart's content as long as she could stay aloft. Amanda had flown solo just a couple of times before but she had piloted for Joyce often enough that they both had confidence that she knew what she was doing.

The glider's variometer indicated she had caught a thermal and she felt her stomach flip as the glider rose. Far below, the dark green of the piñon and juniper forest on the red dolomite of the Rampart Range undulated into the distance, north and south. Beyond the clean, austere, geometrical buildings of the Air Force Academy, the broad, raw scar of the rock quarry appeared bony and dead. From this height the cluttered grid of Colorado Springs looked hazy, theoretical, two-dimensional.

She and Joyce had earned their get-aways this weekend. Earthworks, the craft store they owned in Broadmarket Square, had seen nothing all week but cranky tourists and idle housewives with a thousand questions about a single spool of hemp twine. Joyce's boyfriend Ben—*boy*friend? he would be eligible for Social Security in ten years—had just learned his company planned to transfer him to the Atlanta office. Amanda's troubles centered, as usual, around her daughter May.

May's jail term for her DUI had ended, somewhat unexpectedly, at the beginning of the summer and she needed a place to stay until she got back on her feet. Amanda, trying hard not to make the same mistakes she felt her own mother had made, gritted her teeth and offered to put May up in her little bungalow in Cheyenne Cañon. May, to her credit, had worked double shifts at the Waffle House on the weekends to pay off the fine she still owed for the DUI but that saddled Amanda with a lot of baby-sitting, caring for May's 14-month-old daughter Libby. Libby's father, Paco, technically had full custody of the baby but he liked to go out and get drunk on the weekends.

Libby had developed an ear infection last night while May was at work. Amanda couldn't get her to sleep until almost two and then she woke up again at first light. Rather than try to go back to sleep herself, Amanda had decided to get up and get busy. For years she had intended to refinish her old rocking chair. This seemed as good a time as any.

But memories blind-sided her. When she unfolded the dusty old canvas drop-cloth that had been in the utility closet since her parents bought the house 30 years ago, she saw a small, reddish-brown bloodstain among the caked spatters of paint, a memento of the end of Amanda's childhood. Before she could repress them, memories of May's father came back in a flood of tears.

Amanda had struggled with menopause lately. Her periods lasted three weeks and her emotional swings made the ups and downs of the glider seem tame. But this morning's tears had come from her heart, not from some hormonal imbalance.

Topping the Rampart Range, she could see a castle of cumulonimbus building above Pikes Peak. A moving column of air has to rise to pass over a mountain, creating not only a cloud but a wave of lift that a good glider pilot could catch and ride, like a surfer catching a wave. Other than smaller Almagre Mountain to the south, 14,110-foot Pikes Peak stands virtually alone, the only fourteener in a radius of nearly a hundred miles. Some gliders soared as high as 40,000 feet on its wave.

Around 9:00 this morning, the sound of both Libby and Amanda crying woke May, understandably grouchy after her 16-hour minimum-wage work day on Saturday and before the eight hours she had to put in tonight. May had flipped on the television, groaning when she got some Sunday morning news show.

The tag story concerned the 25th anniversary of Richard Nixon's resignation. May wanted to flip to cartoons for Libby but Amanda insisted on watching the old footage of Nixon boarding the helicopter at the White House, his suit coat buckling, his jowly grin jarring with the circumstances, waving his arms above his head, the first two fingers of each hand held up, signifying what? peace when there was no peace? victory when there was no victory? Nixon had achieved his promised "just and lasting peace" in Vietnam only by conceding defeat, symbolized by the ignominious airlift from the roof of the American Embassy in Saigon nine months later. And what could have gone through Nixon's mind as he gave that sign, having just resigned the presidency under not just a dark cloud but a massive thunderhead? How could the man even conceive of using a symbol of victory in those circumstances?

May couldn't be bothered with it. Amanda tried to explain what her generation went through to get rid of Nixon and the war he spent so many years—so many lives—losing. People at home too gave their lives, sacrificed their freedom, left their country, to end the absurdity.

"Those things are just so trivial," her daughter shot back, "compared to the problems I have right now. I miss Libby more than you can imagine."

"Oh, yes," Amanda retorted, "it must be horrible not to see your daughter for months or years on end."

May knew quite well that Amanda was referring to the years May had spent incommunicado, lost, but she responded only by shouting at Libby to quit crying. For a moment Amanda found herself wishing May would just disappear again.

By circling back over the Rampart Range a few times, Amanda had gained enough altitude to make it over to the wave of Pikes Peak. Throwing caution to the wind, she turned the stick. She swooped through the trough of Ute Pass and gained the foothills that led to the peak. Ahead rose the hump of crumbly red granite, dwarfed by the anvil-shaped battlements of cloud above. Banking up onto the wave, Amanda looked back over the undulating mountains toward the plains to the east. She found herself singing what always came to mind when she saw this view:

> Oh, beautiful for spacious skies, for amber waves of grain.
> For purple mountain's majesty, above the fruited plain…

Katherine Lee Bates wrote those lines at Colorado College after a trip to the top of Pikes Peak. From here, the beauty and majesty of America stretches to the horizon. Here, all the petty concerns of work and family should fade away. But Amanda's mind couldn't let it go.

In the midst of all the morning's caterwauling, Deb McCleary, Amanda's oldest and dearest friend, called from Seattle. For such close friends, their lives couldn't have turned out more differently. Amanda felt that she, in her own meek way, had carried the torch of the counterculture of the 1960s while it seemed to her that Corporate America had swallowed Deb whole. It shocked Amanda when she learned that Deb remained blissfully unaware of the World Trade Organization meeting scheduled for the end of November right there in Seattle, a meeting to negotiate trade deals that might end up subverting American labor and environmental protection laws which people like Amanda had worked very hard to put in place. Deb spent so much time on her pet charities and projects like the Japanese Garden and the Seattle Symphony that she never even noticed the bigger issues anymore.

The afternoon had grown darker but out the window Amanda could see a golden eagle doing the same thing Amanda was doing: riding the thermal up to the clouds, the pinions of the eagle's wings feeling for every nuance of current. She often saw hawks and eagles doing this, certainly for recreation, since even their sharp eyes couldn't possibly spot a vole or a pika from this altitude. The powerful lift of the updraft felt exhilarating. This is better than sex, she thought. The same soaring ecstasy without the questions, the sloppy physicality, the emotional weight. The children.

Earlier, Amanda and Deb had argued about children. Deb had no children of her own and over the years had often put in her two cents' worth about May, which Amanda generally appreciated. But today, Libby's crankiness, May's short temper, and Amanda's own emotional vulnerability made Deb's counsel to show May more patience sound irritating.

"Easy for you to say," Amanda had snapped. "You haven't been around to pick up the pieces every time May goes down in flames."

To which Deb had said something so shocking, so unbelievable, that Amanda, for the first time in their lives, hung up on her. Deep in her heart she wanted desperately to call Deb back and straighten things out but the feelings of betrayal and outrage were still too raw. Even now her stomach was in knots.

Something banging as loud as a pistol shot on the canopy of the glider jerked her out of her daydream. Her last circle over the northwest shoulder of the Peak had carried her into the ragged edge of the clouds. She should have come back out by now. Another bang, like the sharp crack on a car's windshield when a truck throws a stone, and she realized that the thermal had pulled her into the storm system. The same cloud that can lift a glider can throw it down much harder. Hailstones as big as marbles clattered on the flimsy shell. Terrified, Amanda checked the compass and the artificial horizon but the readings made no sense. Fighting to regain control of the glider though the dark fog, Amanda saw a blinding flash of light and then everything went white.

. . . O . . . O . . . O . . .

Idle conversation used to land me in a standard dialogue. I've grown weary of it over the years but I suppose I ought to set it down for the record.

"So what do you do?" the barber, the car mechanic, the doctor, the lady at the party would ask.

"I'm a musician."

"Really!" the person would say, sounding impressed. "What do you play?"

"What instrument?" I'd ask. "Or what kind of music?"

"Instrument" usually came first.

"Several, actually," I'd explain. "I'm a one-man band. I play guitar, keyboard, and harmonica on stage, but I also play bass and drums and percussion in my own small studio. I record all the parts of a band and use the tracks as my back-up band on stage."

"Wow. That sounds like a lot of work."

"It takes about two days of work for every minute of music," I'd estimate.

"What kind of songs?"

"All sorts of things, since people ask a solo act for nearly everything. Mostly covers: oldies, rock and roll, country. Originals too."

If the person didn't already know my name, he or she would ask. When I'd say it, I'd get a blank stare.

"So where do you play?"

"Around Puget Sound," I used to say. Or the Great Northwest, if I was out of state. Or just the West if I was far from home. Wherever it was, it was almost never somewhere the person was likely to see me perform. And that generally wrapped it up.

I guess I've always been an explorer of sorts. Columbus probably had similar wearying dialogues with his sail-maker and the salted-meats guy. They'd admire his guts but consider him a bit loose in the flue. "You wanna sail where? The Far East? By sailing west?"

Like Columbus, I've kept a journal of my travels, for my own sake if nothing else, not knowing whether anyone would ever read what I wrote. When I played in Alaska nearly a decade ago, I whiled away the time describing the different characters peopling the Last Frontier, including this third-person description of myself:

"Slender and weak compared to most Alaska men, his boyish looks and demeanor belie his 40 years. He has thinning hair, intelligent blue eyes, a ready smile and quick wit, but an air of preoccupation that borders on gloom. Like a lot of people here, he has a varied background and has to be versatile and self-sufficient just to survive. Unlike most, he doesn't smoke cigarettes and rarely drinks. He seems out of place.

"People gravitate to him with requests, jokes, offers, stories, and criticisms. He weathers most of it with a smile and polite response. A few women have made blatant passes at him. He seems to go along with them for a while out of curiosity, but he sleeps alone. His looks, talent, and personality make him easy to like, but his intelligence and aloof air make him hard to understand."

Unlike Columbus, I don't really have a home to go home to. Or maybe, like another famous traveler, Odysseus, I won't recognize the place when I get there.

October 12, 1999

The rocker lies upside down on the canvas drop cloth. May is painting the rose on the back of the headrest, dipping the brush into the red paint. A few drops spill across the wood. Wearing just a T-shirt and some old ragged panties, May slips off her panties to wipe up the paint.

"Oh, man," he says.

May didn't realize he was there. She doesn't know him at all. But he looks nice.

"Do you want a beer?" she asks him.

He smiles.

She gets up self-consciously and walks through the empty bungalow to the kitchen to wash her hands. The paint looks like blood and won't come off. She gives up and gets a couple of beers from the fridge. She wants to open them but there doesn't seem to be a pop-top on either end. The phone rings. She struggles with the cans.

The phone rang again and woke her up. Shaking off her doze, she got up from the still un-refinished rocking chair, picked up the phone, and said hello.

"May?" her grandmother asked.

"Hi, Nana."

"Are you busy, child?"

She snorted. "What have I got to be busy with?"

"Oh, quit feeling sorry for yourself," Nana said in her quavery voice. "I'm coming over to cheer you up whether you want me to or not."

May sighed. "I guess you can try."

It would take her ten minutes to get there. Might as well get the dishes done, May thought, walking into the kitchen of the bungalow. She set a blunt stack of heavy crockery into the sink and pulled the string to turn on the light. The weight on the end of the string was the thin gold band and small stone of her wedding ring. She got more use from it now than she had during her worthless marriage to her worthless husband, Paco. And when May desperately needed cash to buy Libby new clothes, the guy at the hock shop, looking at the ring, had laughed at her.

It obviously never meant much to Paco, whom she found, less than an hour after he slipped the ring on her finger, flirting with Maleeka, her maid-of-honor.

Then, after all the years and all the crap May had gone through for him, Paco decided a couple of years ago that he was bored. For a few months he got drunk and beat her. After that he got drunk and left for days at a time, leaving her to wipe the drool and food and shit from their beautiful daughter.

Oh, but Libby was *so* beautiful. Just this morning May had heard on the radio that scientists had designated a baby born in Bosnia as the six billionth person on the planet. But as far as May was concerned, no baby born after Libby really mattered. From her father, Libby had inherited her short temper and lack of impulse control; from May, her lusty voice that cried too much. Where the curly blonde hair came from was anybody's guess.

May still couldn't believe the judge had taken Libby away from her. May had only been in one other car accident in her life, way back in 1986. In fact, the worst charge against her in that accident, involuntary manslaughter, subsequently had been overturned. The incident shouldn't have been on her record any more. This time she didn't refute the coke, the dope, or the beer, but their effects had long since worn off by the time that jackass swerved in front of her. The jackass gets the ticket, May gets the time.

With the understandable exception of those dreadful weeks in August after her mother's death, May had been clean since she got out of jail in June. In fact, the only time she'd gotten really drunk was with her mom one hot night last July.

Meanwhile, Paco and his live-in floozy, Shirley, got trashed every other night. Since Paco had custody, they used Libby as a bargaining chip, bringing her over any time they wanted to go on a bender, knowing May would do almost anything to see her daughter. Two weeks ago Paco actually had the *cojones* to hit her up for twenty bucks. But he didn't own a car and Shirley did nothing but smoke and watch soaps all day, so they didn't get traffic tickets. Model parents in the judge's eyes.

May batted the wedding ring again just to watch it spin. Her fingers groped for forks and spoons. Her eyes fell on a framed poem on the wall. For whatever reason, her mother had kept this poem over the kitchen sink. Steam had warped the mat and blurred the edges of the spidery calligraphy that had proven a mercifully short interlude between her mother's macrame and stained-glass periods but May still could make out the words:

May

August took my love away
And left me stranded on the road.
It scorched the fragrant flowers of May.
It changed the song to minor mode.

The new year dawned with hope so bright
It blinded me to lines I'd crossed,
But fall will bring the early night
And memories of things I've lost.

If I had to choose which two
I miss the most, I'd have to say
My home and all the friends I knew
And love, whose month is ever May.

A life's story begins with choosing a name. Her mother had given May the same name as the poem but May could never see why. She was born in February, after all. February, on the other hand, truly would have sucked as a name; the month of May at least had better weather. The grammatical uses of "may" mingled doubt ("It *may* not happen") with permissiveness ("You *may* leave the table now"). Doubt and permissiveness: her life in a nutshell.

Not until that night in July when they got drunk together did her mother ever tell her where the poem had come from. It always had struck May as kind of a gloomy thing, anyway, and knowing it had come from her father didn't help.

Bill Black had never been much of a father. The ritzy house on Portales Road near the Broadmoor screamed money on the outside but inside it looked smarmy and cold. He spent all his waking, cheerful, sober moments at his car dealership and usually didn't stagger home until after his wife and daughter had gone to bed. He treated Amanda with contempt and ignored May.

Until the summer May turned 15. One Saturday while Amanda went shopping, May caught her father staring at her through the window as she lay tanning on the deck. When she slipped a robe over her bikini and went inside, he blocked the doorway to her room. The sour smell of bourbon on his breath, the trembling ash of his cigarette, his greasy, graying hair—the image hadn't dimmed.

"Remember how I used to play Suds Monster with you in the tub?" he'd asked. His leering, gold-flecked grin, the way his eyes pried into the cleavage of her robe, the feel of his strong fingers on the bikini top—she still shuddered to think of it.

Six months later, after May had moved to Buena Vista, her mom finally called it quits with Bill and moved into this little bungalow in Cheyenne Cañon. Within months of the divorce, Bill married a cocktail waitress he'd patronized for years at the Pink Lady, a titty bar down on 8th Street. Ten years had passed since Bill had even bothered to call on May's birthday. May didn't much like her married name, Mendoza, but she sure didn't miss her maiden name of Black which, she realized one night after too much beer, sounds just like someone barfing.

Her mother never cared much for the bungalow, with its brown-stained shake, green eaves, dusty screens, and rattling old furnace, but Nana and Poppa Harve Tyree had bought it as a rental property years ago so they charged Amanda a very reasonable rent. All too often, though, Amanda's artsy-craftsy doodads failed to bring in even that much but she had developed almost an aversion to money. She was certainly too proud to let her parents or ex-husband help support her—not that either had offered.

May heard her grandmother knock. She dried her hands on a towel and went to open the screen door.

"Isn't it a lovely night?" Nana asked, lingering on the porch.

The temperature had reached the 80s in the afternoon. Colorado had enjoyed a classic Indian summer the last few days, the golden cottonwoods along Cheyenne Creek becoming reminders of the Cripple Creek Gold Rush days a century before. Now, at dusk, the evening air hung still in the small cañon, redolent with barbecue smoke and the tang of the ponderosa needles. In the distance, children squabbled in play and dogs barked joyfully. Up on Cheyenne Mountain, the clarion chimes of the Will Rogers Shrine of the Sun rang the half hour.

"Doesn't the chill bother your back?" May asked as her grandmother came in.

"My back only hurts when I'm walking, standing, sitting, or lying down," Nana said, unwrapping her paisley shawl and handing it to May, retaining the packet she carried. "The rest of the time it's fine."

Cynthia Tyree still cut an imposing figure. Though last year's spinal fusion had left her an inch shorter, it had reinforced her ramrod-straight posture and, if anything, strengthened her iron will. Her silver hair fell in elegant waves and her green eyes could bore right through May. Only Nana's diaphragm had betrayed her, leaving her deep voice sounding uncharacteristically uncertain.

"Can I get you anything?" May asked her.

Her grandmother, as usual, settled into the rocking chair by the small bay window in the living room. The rocker always reminded May of that awful day last August when her mother had started to refinish it. So far May hadn't plucked up the courage to complete the job. In fact, she hadn't even tried sitting in the rocker until this evening and after her odd dream, might not try that again for a while.

"For a ceremony like this we ought to have Champagne," Nana said, "but I'd prefer a stiff gin-and-tonic. I don't suppose you have either of those."

"I thought the doctor..."

"To hell with all doctors! We should celebrate. What about some of that pot you had?"

May blushed and laughed nervously. "You know I'm not supposed to..."

"Just testing," Nana chuckled. "And you passed. In any case, we should celebrate. You must have something we can toast with."

"I think there's still a bottle of Gewurtstraminer that Mom bought."

"Well, don't just stand there."

May got down the dusty bottle and rummaged through the kitchenwares drawer for a corkscrew. "What are we celebrating, anyway?" she called out to the living room. She certainly hadn't expected a celebration. She assumed that Nana just wanted to remind her that she wasn't even keeping up with her mother's modest rent payments.

"That's right, bring some matches with you too," Nana called back.

While May set down the wine with a couple of glasses, Nana leafed through the bundle of papers she'd brought. "Here it is," she said, pulling out a yellowing, official-looking document.

"What is it?" May asked with dread, pulling the cork from the bottle.

"It's the mortgage on this place," Nana said, handing it to her. "I intended to do this yesterday but they closed the banks for Columbus Day, even though Columbus Day is really today. I wish we could go back to the days when the government only lied to us about corruption."

May's heart sank as she looked at the mortgage. "Nana, I know I told you I'd make at least the September payment this month but the tips at the Waffle House have just been—"

"Hush up. Read the date on it. Flip to the back page and look at when it was signed."

"December 16, 1969," May read, feeling puzzled.

"And how long a mortgage is it?"

"Let's see—oh, thirty years," May said, handing her grandmother a glass of wine. "What does that mean? Do I have to pay the full amount by then?"

Nana chuckled. "Don't be silly. It means it would have been paid in full this December 16th."

"Except that...?"

"Except that I went down to the bank today and made the final four payments. Hand me those matches."

With a steady hand she held the mortgage by one corner over a metal wastebasket and lit the bottom edge. Bright flames quickly consumed the old paper and she dropped it into the wastebasket, then picked up her wine glass and tapped the rim to May's.

May drank half the glass of wine but it didn't calm her the way she'd hoped. "So does this mean that you can keep the rent payments I make to you?" she asked.

"Silly girl!" her grandmother laughed. "You won't be making rent payments to me any more."

"So are you going to sell the house then?" May asked despondently.

Nana groaned as she pushed herself to her feet. She walked over and sat on the couch next to May. "Honey," she said, her age-spotted hand on May's arm, "the house is yours now."

May's head hurt. "Nana, I know you're going to think I'm hopelessly dense but I don't understand. Who do I make the rent payments to?"

Nana patiently decided on another tack. She pulled an envelope from the sheaf of papers. "Here, write down who you'll send the rent to." She waited while May got a pen. "Okay.

May Mendoza, 969 Ridge Road…"

May quit writing and looked at her grandmother skeptically. "You're saying I don't have to make payments any more?"

Nana smiled. "Oh, I never said that. You still have to pay the utilities, the insurance. Oh, and the taxes. Can't forget the taxes."

May shook her head. "You can't just give me this house."

"I can if I want," Cynthia Tyree said firmly. "I'll have Stu Martin draw up the papers tomorrow."

"But I didn't pay you anything for it."

"Why do you have to make everything so hard? All right then, I'll sell you this house if you can meet the asking price."

Sometimes, after a couple of days on a boat, sea-legs can make a person feel seasick on solid ground. May felt almost relieved to be back in her life's usual white-capped waves and sickening troughs. "How much is it worth?" she asked with trepidation.

"Now? Or when we bought it?"

"Um, both, I guess."

Nana rummaged through the papers. "What did Harve tell me? I think it was eighteen-five. It would say on the—" She dropped the papers and laughed until she coughed and then had to drink her wine to quiet the cough. "It would say on the mortgage I just burned! But I think Harve got them down to eighteen-five."

"Is that $18,500?" May asked, watching another dream fly away.

"In 1969, yes. But we've done quite a bit of work on it over the years. Replaced the roof, the water heater, paved the driveway. And property up here has gone through the roof. That's right, I probably have a tax assessment in here." She went back to rummaging through the papers. "Yes, here, in 1998 it was assessed at $135,000."

The amount staggered May. The creaky floors, the torn screen door—she never dreamed it could be worth this much. She gulped the rest of her wine and poured another glassful.

Nana looked up from the assessment and saw May's expression. "But I thought I'd offer it to you at a discount," she added.

"So how much?" May asked, bracing herself.

"I'll sell it to you for one dollar," Nana announced. "And another glass of that wine. You can pay me the dollar when the papers are drawn up but I'm afraid I'm going to have to insist on the wine now."

May sat dumbfounded until Nana handed her the empty wine glass.

"Now, child," she insisted.

May hastened to refill the glass but said, "This is too much."

"A dollar's too much?" Nana asked. "Though this Gewurstraminer is quite good, even warm. Your mother was a better judge of wine than of men, I'm afraid. Not that I always gave her the best advice on either score, I suppose."

"I mean, how could I ever repay you?"

Nana looked meditatively at the small bubbles in her wine glass. "You may not believe this but I have no intention of living forever. Sooner or later—and God help me, I sometimes pray for sooner—the bulk of my estate will pass to your uncle Peter. But it was always my intention that your mother would inherit this house. Now that she's gone, it should belong to you. You know, when your grandfather suggested she move in here, he told her he wouldn't charge any rent. Your mother always covered the mortgage payments because she was an obstinate, impractical, honorable woman. She made up her mind when she divorced your father that there's no such thing as a free lunch. Nobody ever gives you something without expecting something in return. She knew that if she accepted money from Harve and me that I'd want to stick my big fat nose into her affairs and she wanted none of that."

Here it comes, May thought. Pay-back time. "I'm sorry, Nana. I know I've screwed things up bad."

"May, honey, it's hard for me to be proud of what you've done with your life. I mean, seriously, Pedro?"

"Paco."

"Whatever. You're a pretty girl and smart enough in a pig-headed sort of way. You can make something of yourself if you'll just…well, just quit being your own worst enemy. As a homeowner, you could take out an equity loan on this place, consolidate your bills. Find a better job. Prove to that judge—and to me—and to *you*—that you're the best person in the world to care for that beautiful great-granddaughter of mine."

May's tear fell right in her wine. She set the glass next to her grandmother's and hugged her until Nana had to back away and straighten up.

"I'll do things differently now," May promised.

"Just promise to try, that's all I ask."

She sniffed and nodded.

"Now," Nana said before another sip, "you call this a party? It's pretty damp in here for a party, isn't it?"

A laugh forced its way up through May's tears. "You're right. I'm sorry."

"Stop apologizing. For such a party girl, you sure can be a wet blanket. You know what might be fun? Your mom left some things in the safe deposit box that we could read."

"What are they?"

"I have no idea. She left this manila envelope in there around the time we bought this house and evidently we all forgot about it. I ran across it today when I got out the mortgage. I assume it's chock-full of juicy old love letters and the polemics against the unjust world that your mother and her friends used to take so seriously. She'd be mortified if she knew we read them. But now she'll never know, will she?"

In recent years Amanda had abandoned her "hippie-drippy" pastimes, as Nana used to refer to the calligraphy and macrame, for more visceral thrills. Joyce had introduced her to gliding a couple of years ago. Amanda had fallen in love with it and soon earned her license. Then, every weekend, whether Joyce was in town or not, Amanda headed out to the air park in Black Forest. May could picture her perfectly in the cockpit, her graying hair bound in a loose ponytail, her jeaned legs bouncing with excitement, her atonal voice singing a soundtrack to each wind-whistling, cloud-banked soar.

But last August, while literally trying to catch the wind over Pikes Peak, she had been caught in an afternoon thunderstorm that pelted Colorado Springs with hail the size of golf balls. Search and Rescue had spent thousands of hours combing the wooded slopes and raw ravines of the Peak and had found scattered shards of the flimsy glider in a large snow field above the Crags on the northwest slope, but not a trace of its pilot.

May and her grandmother both fought back sniffles as they went through the contents of the manila envelope on which Amanda had written her name. But soon nostalgia and curiosity prevailed.

"Here's her diploma from Cheyenne," May said.

May herself had attended Cheyenne Mountain High School for a couple of years before dropping out. A fine college-prep school, it had demanded discipline of her that she couldn't muster.

"Here's her letter of acceptance from Colorado College," Nana said.

"How long did she go there?" May asked. "Mom never talked about it much."

"Just the one year," Nana told her as she read the letter.

"What happened?"

Nana looked up at her. "You."

"Oh."

"Here's her birth certificate," Nana said, leafing through the papers. "And your birth certificate too."

"Who are the Piñon Nuts?" May asked.

"Let me see."

On a sheet of paper made to look like parchment, in Amanda's flowing but pre-calligraphy hand, was written:

We the Undersigned
The Exclusive and Permanent Members of
The Pinon Nuts
Hereby Pledge
On Pain of Dismemberment, Excommunication, Ridicule, and Worse
To Assemble Again On This Very Spot
Thirty Years Hence
The Dawn of the New Millennium
Come Hell or High Water

It was dated December 31, 1969, below four flamboyant, nearly-illegible male signatures.

Nana chuckled. "Heavens, I'd nearly forgotten those boys. Friends of your mother's from high school. The Piñon Nuts was some sort of dinner club they put together. They'd take over one of their parents' homes for the evening, prepare their concept of a gourmet dinner, and spend the rest of the evening gorging themselves and intoning about how one day the world would dance to their tune."

Attached to the back of this pledge by a rigid loop of dry scotch tape was a fading, greenish Polaroid photo of four young men, dressed surprisingly formally in sport coats and loud ties. One, with short sandy hair, stood tall and lean in the center, looking serious. Beside him stood another, a shock of thin curly red hair receding from his forehead, holding his fingers in a peace sign and his face in an expression of lofty bemusement. To the other side stood an athlete, judging by his muscular build and very short hair. The last sat in a chair in front of the others turning toward the camera, wild blonde curls hiding much of his profile.

"What does this have to do with Mom?" May asked, trying to glean insight from the momentary expressions on the faces.

"What do you think?"

"Which one did she like?"

"See the one sitting backwards, looking over his shoulder?"

"It's not a very good picture but from what I can see he looks kind of cute," May confessed, intrigued. "What was his name?"

"Jason Walker."

May could tell by Nana's tone that there was more to the story. "Well?"

"Oh, she and Jason went to school together. She always talked about him as a friend but I could tell there was more to it than that. This was about the time your father came along."

"I wish my father hadn't come along," May said bitterly.

"Now, honey, don't speak ill of the dead."

May looked up at her in surprise. "My father's not dead. Is he?"

"I'm just warning you in advance. Nobody lives forever."

May laughed. "So what happened to this Jason?"

"You know, I'm not really sure. There was some sort of trouble. He died or ran away or something. I don't think I ever did hear whether he turned up again."

"Who are the others?"

"The one with the very short hair is John."

"Uncle John?" May asked, looking closer. "I haven't seen him since I was a little kid."

"He's not really your uncle, of course."

"I know. That's just what Mom used to call him. What happened to him?"

"The last I heard he was working for the newspaper up in Estes Park."

"And the other two?"

"I don't even remember their names, dear. It's been a long time since I thought about any of them."

"What do you think the chances are that they'll defy hell and high water to get together on New Year's Eve?"

"God help us all if youthful promises count. What's that?"

"I don't know," May said. "A letter I guess."

"Who's it from?"

"It's just signed 'J'."

"Jason?"

"I don't know. What do you think?"

On a sheet of lined, three-ring-binder paper was scrawled:

chinook

thurs

man—

not much left of me. walking the knife's edge. i guess you know i couldn't stay.

toss the poem if you like. last line's uncle willie's anyway. it, and this, and me, headed for oblivion, i'm sure. there's no room for me in anybody's life anymore. thought i might be somebody. thought there might be a beginning. looks like the end instead. i always said it doesn't matter. but it does.

ring, rang, wrung you. try try try. fbi. fmi. i am fucked. but the quaker s.o.b. will never catch me. nix nix nix. gentle as a lam. on on on. going quietly. disappearing, in fact. like tom huston, the man with the plan. taking a breeze. scot free.

i assume matt didn't get you in time. man, you did what you had to do. i don't blame you. put your mind at ease and put the load on me. king midas in reverse. right now, both our futures lie beyond the borders of this kingdom.

don't worry. i'm gone to stay this time. i have to do what i have to do, too. it's for the best. tell the piñon nuts good-bye for me. nothing but bad choices as far as the eye can see. like the old chief said: i will fight no more forever. from here there's no turning back.

same for you. don't look back. don't go black. no baby's worth that bill.

oh, but i miss my baby angel. eggs with wings. unseen things. nature abhors a vacuum.

but right now, dangerous hot nasty summer, this big fat hairy ball can't take that one last straw. it doesn't need a billion ewes. just one you. zero me. had to be.

maybe a tomorrow will come to me. maybe at the end of time, maybe just the century. till then, bon chance, bon ami. i won't forget may. but you'll forget me.

j

The J had three small circles instead of a single dot above it.

The two women read this in silence, May squinting, Nana shaking her head.

"Who's 'man'?" May asked when she finished. "Or is that just some sort of hippie language?"

"Those boys always called your mother 'Man' or 'Manny'," Nana said. "I used to get so angry. If 'Amanda' was too hard, couldn't they at least call her 'Mandy'? *We* called her Mandy."

"Then who's Tom Huston? Is he one of these Piñon Nuts?"

"Honestly, child, I don't recall," Nana said, shaking her head. "That all happened 30 years ago. I'm sure I've forgotten most of it. What's on the other page?"

Under the letter was another sheet of paper.

"It's that poem!" May exclaimed when she looked at the page of backwards-slanting scrawl. "The one Mom did!"

"The one your mom did?"

May jumped up, ran in the kitchen, and grabbed the old framed calligraphy from above the sink. She handed it to Nana.

Nana held the warped frame and tilted her head back to inspect it through her bifocals. "I never much cared for your mother's calligraphy," she said. "It made even a shopping list look important."

"But this *is* important!" May insisted. "It's the same poem, right?"

"What of it?"

"Last July, after I got out of jail and came back here, Mom and I got drunk one night." She caught Nana's stern look and responded a little defensively. "It helped. We hardly ever talked but we talked that night. And she told me she got that poem from my father. I asked her about it the next day but she never wanted to talk about it again. But look! That's Jason's handwriting, not Dad's. I didn't think it seemed like Dad's style," she added, rereading it.

Nana reread it too. "Your father hasn't got the sensitivity it takes to copy a poem like that out of a book, much less write it."

May went back to the letter. "Look at this paragraph where it talks about black and bill. My father's name is Bill Black." She thought about it and felt chills run up the back of her neck. "At least I thought it was. But maybe Bill Black isn't my father."

"Honey, it's late," Nana counseled. "We've had some wine and we're both tired. Don't get too caught up in all this. Your mom's passed away and you never did get along with your father too well. I think maybe you just want to find some alternative to the way things are for you right now."

May didn't acknowledge the advice. "I wish I knew when this was written. When did Mom meet…um, Dad?"

"Oh, they knew one another in high school."

"Was he part of this Piñon Nuts thing?"

"No, Harve and I knew the Blacks socially."

"When did she put this stuff in the safe deposit box?"

"Oh, my word, who knows?"

"Did she put it in all together in this manila envelope?"

"I suppose. The envelope was still sealed."

"And didn't you say my birth certificate was in there?"

"That's right," Nana recalled. "Right after you were born your mother asked what she should do with your birth certificate and we told her she should put it in the safe deposit box. She must have included these things as well."

"So that would have been in early 1971. And doesn't the letter say something about summer?" She turned back to the letter again. "See? The line about 'dangerous hot nasty summer'? So maybe this was written in the summer of '70. When she was pregnant with me."

Nana wrinkled her brow at her granddaughter's growing intensity.

"What's the line about the baby?" May went on. "'No baby's worth that bill.' If by the bill he means my father…"

"May, I think you're reading more into this…"

"But then he says 'miss my baby angel.' *His* baby angel. 'Eggs with wings'," she went on, her voice increasingly bleak. She turned to her grandmother. "Nana, if you know the answer to this, will you please tell me?"

"The answer to what, honey?"

"Did Mom try to have me aborted?"

It took a lot to shake Cynthia Tyree but this did it. She slumped back onto the couch, her eyes unfocused, her lips trembling, lost in thought.

May awaited the answer anxiously but took some comfort in the deliberateness with which her grandmother seemed to frame her words.

At last Nana pulled herself up again and resumed her rigid posture. "Sometimes I miss your grandfather more than a drowning person misses air," she began, her voice shaky but her resolve firm. Harve, a cigar aficionado, had died of throat cancer six years before. "Other times I envy his distance from this vale of tears. But always, at times like these, I wish I could hear what he had to say, because he would say it well and you would feel better.

"May, child, the honest answer to your painful question is that I don't know. Your mother certainly never confided in me about such a drastic thing. But, as you know yourself, there comes a time in a young woman's life when she feels her problems are beyond her mother's wisdom and guidance. Mandy and I never suffered the kind of rift that you and she went through when you quit school and moved away. But for a time there before you were born, she went her own way and made her own decisions. It wasn't until I could be more a grandmother than a mother that she and I began to talk to one another again.

"Now I don't doubt that she did some things in her late teens and early twenties that she came to regret. Some of the things you've done in the past may be difficult to explain to your own daughter when she grows up. I must confess that had I known that that envelope would lead to this sort of question I might have left it where it was, at least until you get yourself on your feet again.

"I do know that your mother and her friends lived through some traumatic years and that they did drugs and other things that I didn't know about at the time. I also know that your mother loved you very much and that she never regretted having you in her life, even when you did things that must have hurt her very much.

"But regardless of what you find out—and from the look on your face, you're going to try to find out all you can—try to remember that what seems right one day, one week, may look entirely different years later. And should you come to doubt it, just remember Pedro."

"Paco, Nana."

"Whatever. Now, it's late and I'm old and you have to work in the morning. I'll expect that dollar house payment at closing."

May realized, as she had a few other times in her life, that her Nana was her guardian angel. She hugged her tightly and whispered in her ear, "I'd be lost without you. Thank you for everything."

<h1 style="text-align:center">...O...O...O...</h1>

Walt Kelly, creator of the Pogo comic strip, had many ways of breaking the frame, like having a character lean against the border of the panel. In the strip published the day I was born, Kelly gives a glimpse of the man drawing the cartoon. Seminole Sam, the shyster fox, asks Albert, the otherwise not-too-bright alligator, if he'd like to sell his memoirs. Albert replies, "But I uses them myself...goin' over 'em at night an' tryin' to win."

One of the hazards of writing a memoir is the temptation to use the perspective of hindsight to justify or glorify past actions. I could never write skillfully enough, accurately enough, nor in enough detail to let the reader see my past even from the fog-shrouded vista of my memory. What I choose to include—and what to delete—will have to suffice.

When I first moved to Seattle, the clerk at the driver's license bureau mistyped the year of my birth, allowing me, if I chose to keep it, to do something that Rosemary Woods, Richard Nixon's secretary, did for him: lose a chunk of time. Like Nixon did, I suppose, I find some of what happened in the late '60s and early '70s too painful or embarrassing to want to recall. So maybe I'll shelve the original road trip and write about what's happened between then and this last trip. After all, unlike Nixon, I never got caught. Maybe it's best to let sleeping dogs lie. Sometimes the child must die for the man to live.

October 15, 1999

John Kaufman decided to play hooky. He headed up US 36 to the Beaver Meadows entrance to Rocky Mountain National Park instead of back to Estes.

"Hooky," in this case, meant merely a quick drive of the Deer Junction loop through the Park. Depending on traffic, maybe a 45-minute vacation. But how often does even that much freedom come along?

In summer the "park" in Estes Park became not so much a description of the place as what it was you spent most of your time trying to do. But now that the hikers and tourists had subsided and the Scottish Festival had wheezed the last strains of "Lord Lovatt's Lament," a drive through downtown Estes Park could be accomplished before either the ice cream or John's patience melted. Today, an extraordinarily short line at the Post Office and at the bank got him out to the Dunraven Inn so early he fully expected to find Jack Lambert either out or not ready with the copy for the Dunraven's ad in the *Trail Gazette*. But Jack was there, his ad looked flawless, and now John had the better part of an hour to do with what he pleased.

As he drove past the Park's visitor's center he reached into the glove box of the Subaru

Outback and took out a small tin. From it he took a venerable wooden pipe with a hinged lid. He opened it to find he had indeed reloaded it last time. The tin contained a lighter as well which he used to light the pipe. It wasn't the premium quality smoke of years gone by but it was decent commercial-grade dope and it filled his lungs neatly.

To say that life was good would be going too far. But at the moment, life offered him a brief respite from pummeling him about the head and shoulders. It had taken most of the summer and much of the skin on his knuckles but he had managed at last to complete an extravagant jungle gym/play house for Alice, his younger daughter. The fact that the weather soon would turn too cold for her to play on it didn't diminish John's relief at being done with the damn thing. Last summer he had injured his back, which still hurt, helping his mother, Kate, move back to Ramah, the little town on the eastern Colorado plains where she had grown up. He felt good to know she had happily settled in with all her old friends close by. And over the weekend he had managed, with a minimum of cursing and only a half a dozen trips to the hardware store, to replace the old kitchen faucet with a new retractable sprayer, which his wife Susan had insisted constituted a basic requirement of even the most rudimentary kitchen. (Traded the original rigid faucet for the soft, low-pressure hose, huh? Paging Dr. Freud.) So far at least, no one had come home to a flooded kitchen floor. Even at the *Trail Gazette*, articles now concentrated less on airlifting hypothermic campers and more on school policy and the best times and places to catch the elk bugling.

He took another toke, which always helped to broaden his view, allowed him to see things from a different angle. But maybe that wasn't it. Maybe just finding a brief lull in the constant din of modern life, which was the only time he could afford the luxury of getting even slightly high, increased his perspective, altered his viewpoint.

God knew the view was pretty broad from here on Deer Ridge. Long's Peak had a dusting of snow and the imposing facade of the Continental Divide beckoned to him, as always. The bull elk, leaving shreds of bloody velvet in fresh scars along the already blackened aspen trunks, had the Midas touch: the currency-green leaves had been converted to trembling gold coins, soon to be spirited away by the light-fingered fall wind.

He hadn't ventured even this far into the Park since June, when he had taken Alice and Anne on their first overnighter without their mom.

"This is pathetic," he said to himself, to the Park. "Isn't this why I came up here to live?"

Estes had seemed like such a tiny backwater when he moved here 25 years ago. With nothing to do in town, the theory went, he could spend as much time in the Park as he wanted. And spend the rest of the time writing.

But over the years both Estes and his family had grown. His schedule now bulged with making lunches before breakfast, trying to catch the network news just for the Denver weather, driving the kids to school, dropping off last night's videos before work, writing copy, blocking ad space, proof-reading, meeting with clients at their convenience, soothing egos, gossiping, listening to Susan's daily tribulations while hashing together dinner for four different tastes, appetites, and schedules, struggling to make homework more important than "Dawson's Creek," and then struggling to make bland sleep more appealing than the thousand enticements of Life in America.

He had come to Estes to write. He had wanted to get closer to the people involved in the stories than writing for a big paper would allow but he found that writing the repetitive local interest stories that made the townsfolk favor the *Trail Gazette* over the *Rocky Mountain News* quickly lost its thrill. When coordinating the ad space devolved to him, he realized that unless someone competent and community-minded sold the space, there wouldn't be a local paper in which to write anything. And now the *Trail Gazette* had been sold to the *Denver Post* and the concomitant muddle had grown so thick that he couldn't trace his way back to what he wanted to write about in the first place.

The Outback rounded the broad curve into Horseshoe Park. A few cars clustered around some bighorn ewes. He waited patiently and then pulled around the cars and sped away. One of the highlights of those tourists' trip to the Rockies proved just another traffic clog to him.

Had he become complacent about the natural wonders all around? Or was there really a bigger story than just this local color?

Originally he had dreamed of writing The Truth About America. From the perspective of idealistic youth, that meant exposing the hypocrisy of the Establishment. Now that he had become entrenched in that same Establishment, he realized that not only was the hypocrisy inevitable, writing about it without radical alteration of his life would be just another level of hypocrisy. The struggle became not to eliminate hypocrisy but to maintain some solid moral core untainted by its stained veneer.

Still, the glorious Indian summer afternoon made all that seem petty. As he pulled into town, he checked his eyes, his face, in the rear view mirror. His hazel eyes looked clear, no more bloodshot than usual. His hair and beard had reached a temporary equilibrium. In summer he grew his thinning curly hair to protect his scalp from the ever-increasing ultraviolet found at 8000 feet; in winter the hair was shorn to fit more neatly under a cap but he let the beard grow out to save his chin from the biting frost. His gut sagged in his shirt more than he would have liked but all in all, not bad for pushing half a century. Ready for most anything.

o   o   o

He walked into the *Gazette* office beneath the green awning that still read, ironically, Estes Park Newspapers, Inc. He crossed to the reception desk, which featured the brass silhouette of a bugling bull elk, the paper's logo. Behind the desk the police scanner crackled excitedly and instantly John could feel the buzz. Hattie, the receptionist, and Gloria, who somehow made sense of the computer system, huddled in intense conversation.

"What's up?" John asked.

Hattie glanced at a young woman waiting in a chair in the small lobby and said, "Come here." She led John back to his own cubicle.

"You know Wayne Giles, don't you?" she asked him.

He set his briefcase on his desk. "Anne does. He's in her class."

Bruno Giles, Wayne's father and a local developer, sat on the school board, irascible, indomitable, ultra-conservative.

"Ready for this?" Hattie asked rhetorically. "One of the other boys—well, you know him, Terrell Haskins, who had such a great year with the basketball team last year—was evidently taunting Wayne, so Wayne pulled a pistol out of his locker and threatened to blow his head off."

"What!?" John exclaimed, adrenaline shooting through him.

Hattie confirmed it with an excited nod.

"Was anybody hurt?"

"Thank God, no," Hattie said, to John's great relief. "But the gun went off. He ended up holding Terrell and some others plus a male teacher hostage in the gym for an hour. Eventually the teacher managed to calm Wayne down enough to get the gun away from him."

"Holy mother of pearl," John said, shaking his head. "So they arrested him, I assume."

Hattie confirmed it. "And get this: when they took him home and searched his room, they found not only another gun and some ammunition but apparently a bag full of marijuana."

"Jesus," John said. "Bruno Giles is going to shit. Do people still die of apoplexy? Cause Bruno is going to be apoplectic."

"Tim went over to try to interview him. How about that for a plum?"

Tim, the longtime editor of the paper, had an easy-going, liberal personality that rarely offended anyone. He and Bruno had locked horns a few times about school policy and about politics in general so he would be having a field day with the pompous ass. Disgusted with the sale of the paper, Tim had already sent out resumes to other papers and had little left to lose in Estes.

In any case, this story would rock Estes Park. In a town where placing a new traffic light on a downtown street could mean endless debate and furor, a story like this, in light of the Columbine massacre in Littleton in the spring, would set tongues wagging for months. For that matter, the state, even the national, media might pick up on it. Bad news for the town, great news for the paper and those who wrote for it.

"So much for the 'off' season," John said to Hattie.

"Tim wanted me to ask you if you'd be willing to stay late tonight, help write this thing up."

"Sure. I'll call Susan and tell her she'll have to pick up the kids after all. I was supposed to meet the new G.M. at the Stanley Hotel later tonight but under the circumstances I think I can beg off." He picked up the phone.

Hattie left the cubicle but popped right back in. "Oh, also, there's someone here to see you."

"Who is it?" he asked as Susan's phone began to ring.

Hattie shrugged and said, "I'm sorry. I'll send her back."

Susan, in the midst of coordinating a banquet for an electrical contractors' convention at the Holiday Inn, had already gotten the story from Anne who, shaken and nervous, had to tell someone. As John gleaned more hearsay from Susan's account, the young woman who had been waiting in the lobby came into the cubicle. John motioned to her to take a seat.

Susan had a few more details and a lot more opinion and reaction to relate but they had been married long enough that he could absorb all she had to say with only part of his brain engaged. The young woman, trying not to eavesdrop, idly inspected all the print matter covering his desk and the walls of the cubicle. John, like many another middle-aged married man, knew well how to appreciate discreetly an attractive and evidently single young woman, betraying neither his interest nor his marriage in the process.

About thirty, she wore a tank top, evidently without a bra, under a frayed, over-sized jean jacket. She had gathered her thick auburn hair into a ragged bun with a clippy. She had a bit of a pug nose, a strong chin, and her teeth, if a bit irregular, added up to a warm smile. Wire-rim glasses made her sea-green eyes look smaller than they were and dark circles hinted at troubled times of late. Her body language said sensual but wary, nervous but determined.

Susan, given these sensational circumstances, could talk indefinitely, slipping easily into speculation when she had exhausted facts and opinions. John gracefully steered around to her picking up the girls and mentioned that Tim had requested that he stay late. She decided the best thing for all concerned would be for her to take Alice and Anne down to Loveland and grab some dinner, maybe see a movie with them to get their minds off the events at school.

After he hung up the phone, John apologized to the young woman. "We had a bit of an incident at my daughter's school."

"So I gather," she replied. "I hope she's all right."

"I'm sure she's fine, thanks. Sorry to keep you waiting. What can I do for you?"

"I don't suppose you remember me?" she asked.

She did look vaguely familiar but he shook his head.

"My name is May Mendoza. I'm Amanda Black's daughter."

"Of course you are!" he exclaimed, extrapolating back a quarter century to her childhood features. "Boy, it's been a long time! Last time I saw you, you were just a toddler." He gazed at her affectionately.

"I think I was about five," May said. "I remember you gave me a pony ride on your leg."

"Good Lord!" he said, trying to keep the twinkle in his eye as avuncular as possible. "I hope you're not here for a repeat."

"I think we're both too old for that," she said.

"Ouch!" He gave a mock wince. "Thanks at least for including yourself."

"I didn't mean you were old," May said with a slight blush. "You're the same age as my mom, aren't you?"

His levity vanished. "May, I can't tell you how sorry I was to hear about your mom's accident. I would have come to her service but I had a family vacation that we had been planning for months. I really wanted to pay my respects, though. I know she and I didn't talk as much as we should have in the last few years but I considered her one of my best friends. She tried as hard as anyone I know to live up to her ideals and the world is worse for her loss. I miss her very much."

"So do I," May confessed. "At least she died doing something she really loved."

"I had a great time visiting with her at the 30th class reunion for Cheyenne last summer. She went on and on about the glider, about how free she felt floating through the air. 'I can just leave the world behind,' she told me."

"She left it far behind," May admitted. "I envy her sometimes."

John looked sympathetically at May's down-turned eyes. "She said you were going through a rough patch."

"If you call losing my mom, my marriage, my baby, my job, my apartment, my driver's license, and going to jail for three months a rough patch, then yeah, I guess I am."

"She didn't tell me about all that," he admitted.

"She was never the kind to brag," May said bitterly.

"Actually, if it's any consolation, she thought you were just carrying on a family tradition. She went through some rough times herself, you know."

"That's part of the reason I came up here to talk to you." From her purse she took a manila envelope from which she pulled a *faux* parchment document with a photo stuck to the back. She handed it to him. "My grandmother and I found this among some of my mom's papers last week."

"How is your grandmother, anyway?" he asked as he unfolded the paper. "She always scared the bejeezuz out of me."

"I always thought she hated me," May admitted. "But maybe losing my mom softened her a little. And she absolutely dotes on Libby, my daughter. She's letting me keep Mom's house."

"Great!" he said distractedly, reading the parchment. "Oh my God! I had completely forgotten about this! I haven't thought about the Piñon Nuts in years."

That wasn't strictly true. He hadn't thought about the dinners he and his friends had put together but he often thought about the guys. And, just a minute ago, he'd thought about their word-play the night the Piñon Nuts came into being, using the homonym "pinion" to imply that their nuts were shackled, their wings clipped. They had joked about it back then. Now the shackles of his marriage and kids and job reminded him that the joke was on him. But he couldn't very well say anything about that to May.

He turned the Piñon Nuts pledge over to look at the photo. "That was an interesting night. One of many interesting nights I had with those guys, actually."

"Who are they?"

"Believe it or not, I'm the skinny one with the short hair."

"Nana remembered you but not the others."

"The one with the curious look and the loud tie is Russ. The tall guy in the middle, looking considerably more conservative, is Matt."

"And the guy sitting down?"

"That's Jason," he said, gazing fondly at the face from long ago.

"Where are they now?"

"Let's see. Russ owns a restaurant in Manhattan. And Matt works for some biotech company in Seattle."

When he didn't go on, she prompted him: "And Jason?"

He thought about his response a moment. This subject hadn't come up in years. When in doubt, always revert back to the easy default answer. "Jason died not too long after that picture was taken."

"Oh."

She looked and sounded surprisingly upset at this news. They both looked at the picture awhile.

When he looked up to hand it back to her, there were tears in her eyes.

"Are you okay?" he asked.

"Oh, fine. Just fine." She jammed the parchment back in the envelope and the envelope back in her purse. "Well, thanks for your time," she said, standing up.

"Wait!" he cried. "That's it? You came all the way up here just for that?"

"Well, no," she admitted. "But maybe the rest doesn't matter now. I don't want to take up any more of your time. I know you're busy."

He picked up the phone and rang Hattie at the front desk. "Has Tim called in?" he asked her.

"Not yet," Hattie said.

"I don't suppose he gave you any idea when he'd be back?"

"God alone knows," Hattie said. "Why?"

"The young lady back here is the daughter of a dear old friend. I'm going to ask her to have a drink with me."

He looked the question at her and she reluctantly nodded.

"Hattie, page me when Tim gets in. We won't go far."

He stuck his pager in his belt and they walked out through the lobby and the front door. The high peaks already had cut short the afternoon sun, the last rays lingering up on the Twin Owls on Lumpy Ridge, and the air had begun to cool. They walked down the tree-lined, brick sidewalk along Moraine to the malt shop and took a left on Weist toward Lonigan's, a hopping rock-and-roll bar in the summer, a local hang-out now.

They went in the back way, past the dark stage where bands played on weekends and across the dusty, echoing dance floor, now occupied by a ping-pong table. The round-cornered sunken bar, lit only by neon beer signs, featured, above the standard array of liquor bottles, three TVs, one showing a rodeo, another interviews with various Denver Bronco players, the last CNN.

A few bleary patrons sat at the bar, lost in desultory conversation about the trouble with the world at large and the Broncos in particular. John and May picked a table and, catching the waitress's eye, ordered a couple of beers.

"Talk to me," he urged May while they waited.

"I don't know what else to say," May said.

"You didn't come all the way up from Colorado Springs just to show me that pledge and that picture, did you?"

She bit her lip. "It just seems stupid now."

"You know, I don't want to boast," he said, determined, if at all possible, to cheer her up a little, "but I'm something of an authority on stupid stuff. I've been doing stupid things since long before you were born. Maybe you should let me be the judge of what's stupid." He smiled at the waitress when she brought the mugs of beer.

Reluctantly May took the envelope from her purse again and took out a letter. She looked at it briefly and handed it to him. "Nana and I found this too."

It was addressed to "man." He drank half his beer while he read it.

"Wow," he said, scratching his short beard, thinking about Jason and all he went through back then. "I sometimes forget what strange days those were."

"What does it mean?"

"Your guess is as good as mine on a lot of this stuff," he said. "What have you come up with?"

"Well, Nana said that you guys used to call Mom 'man,' and she also said that she had some kind of a relationship with Jason. Isn't the letter signed with a 'J'?"

"Oh, yeah, that's definitely Jason's 'J.' He certainly developed his own unique style toward the end. What in particular did you want to ask me?"

She took the letter back from him. "It's this part: 'don't look back. don't go black. no baby's worth that bill.' And then he goes on: 'miss my baby angel. eggs with wings. unseen things.' Do you know when he wrote this?"

John thought about it. "It must have been in the summer of 1970. Right before his disappearance."

"My mom was pregnant with me then."

This shook him. He held out his hand and she handed the letter back to him. "'Eggs with wings,' huh? Boy, I wouldn't have thought of it that way. What are you saying?" He didn't want to jump to a conclusion she had missed.

"Did she try to abort me?"

He had jumped that way, too. "I don't know," he said honestly. "And I'm not sure this is enough to prove anything. But I can see what you're saying."

"Okay," she went on. "Was I Jason's 'baby angel'?"

"In other words, was he your biological father?" he clarified.

She nodded.

"Again, I can't say that for sure."

She quickly turned away.

"But I must admit," he added, "he might have been."

She turned back to him. "Really?"

"I know he and your mom were, ah, physically intimate."

"He told you?"

"They both told me."

She seemed to brighten a little at this.

"But I have to point out that for all I know your father—Bill, that is—was intimate with her as well around then."

Her gloom returned.

"You seem disappointed to hear that."

"Who would you rather have as a father?"

"You barely know anything about Jason."

"Do you know…Bill, my father so far?"

"Well, yes," he admitted. "I admit that's not who I would choose as a father."

"And you should choose your parents carefully, right?"

He laughed. "Hard to argue with that. But," he continued more soberly, "Jason certainly had his flaws as well. And even if he was your father, what would you gain?"

"All I'm looking for is the truth."

"Is that all? Well, that shouldn't take more than another lifetime or two."

She looked back at the letter. "According to this, I'm lucky just to have this one."

"Listen, even if what you're assuming really happened, your mom and Jason probably had what they felt were good reasons to do what they did."

"Good reasons."

"Okay," he backtracked, "maybe it's hard to justify abortion."

"Maybe there are good reasons for abortion," she conceded. "I'm not saying that. All I'm saying is that for some reason my parents didn't want me to exist. How should I feel about that?"

"You're making too much of this," he said, backing away from that bleak precipice. "Maybe your mom and Jason, young as they were, considered an abortion. Evidently they changed their minds. At least your mom did. You're living proof of that. And I know for a fact that your mother never loved anything or anyone more that she loved you. Except maybe her new granddaughter."

"You knew both my mom and Jason," she said. "Do you know why they would have wanted to abort me?"

"Obviously, I never thought about this until today," he admitted. "But I could probably come up with a list. They weren't married, for one. Jason was in a lot of trouble at the time.

"For that matter," he went on, gaining momentum, "they—we—ingested our fair share of illegal substances back then. You know those three little circles where the dot should be on Jason's J? J stood for joint too and those were his version of puffs of smoke."

"So?"

"So we did more than smoke pot. One of the most prominent rumors going around about LSD was that it was teratogenic, that it altered your genes and could cause birth defects. If your mom and Jason really did consider an abortion, they may have wanted to prevent something like that."

"Maybe that's what's wrong with me," May said despondently.

"'Our faults lie not in our stars but in our selves'," he quoted Shakespeare.

"What's that supposed to mean?"

"From what your mom told me it sounds to me like you created a lot of your own problems. I wouldn't rush to blame your parents, whoever they are, or some predetermined fate for your own mistakes. That makes you a slave to determinism. It's only when you take responsibility for your choices that you begin to exercise free will. Determinism is what got you here, free will is what happens next."

"Mom used to talk about stuff like that."

"I know," he said. "I used to love talking about that sort of thing with your mom and the Piñon Nuts. Of course, sometimes we were stoned enough that we couldn't really tell if it made sense."

"Could those drugs have made mom and Jason want to abort me?"

"How much do you know about psychedelic drugs?"

"I've smoked pot," she said. "And blown coke."

"Those really aren't the same sort of thing," he cautioned. "But in any case, I don't think any of those substances can make somebody do something they really don't want to do."

"Maybe I should find out for myself."

"You mean take acid or something just to see what it's like?"

"What have I got to lose?"

"For one thing, aren't you still on probation?"

Her look was enough of a reply to that.

"In any case," he went on, "hallucinogens aren't the same as marijuana or cocaine. You really need to be in the right circumstances, in the right frame of mind, with the right people. If you're in a good place, it can make things very interesting. If you're depressed or anxious, it can be very frightening."

"I can't seem to do much about my frame of mind," she said, and then looked him right in the eye. "But maybe you could help me with the right circumstances and the right people. Uncle John."

He felt like his hair caught fire. "Me? Holy crap! I haven't done anything like that in years."

"So?"

He chugged the last of his beer. He sure as hell hadn't seen this coming. Out of the question was his first inclination. But another part of him, a voice he hadn't heard in years, refused to dismiss it out of hand. The tradition of the master assisting the novice who sought alternate reality, like Carlos Castenada's Don Juan, still meant a lot to him. A certain ethic seemed to be at stake. Wouldn't denying that add yet another layer of hypocrisy?

Nevertheless, if the townsfolk of Estes saw him with May, they would associate him with a different Don Juan.

"Come on, May," he pleaded. "Isn't life complicated enough already?"

"Sure, I understand," she said, refolding the letter and putting it back into her purse. "You've got better things to do."

"Oh, jeez, it's not that…"

"What about Tom Huston? Would he know anything about this stuff?"

"Tom who?"

"Tom Huston. Jason mentioned him in the letter."

"Oh, yeah." John racked his brain. The name had a very familiar ring to it but he couldn't put a face to it. "I have to admit, I can't recall Tom Huston at all." Just then, his pager offered him a reprieve. Saved by the beep. "Hey, listen, I've got to get back to work," he said, settling up the tab. "Thanks so much for coming all the way up here to see me and I'm sorry I couldn't be more helpful. Where can I reach you? I'd like to keep in touch."

"I'm at my mom's place. Same address and phone." She stood and shouldered her purse. "So I guess I'm still on my own when it comes to figuring out why I exist at all."

He winced.

"But let me ask you this," she went on. "What are the chances that at least you and Russ and Matt will honor your pledge to get together New Year's Eve?"

"My gut reaction? About the same as the Broncos winning another Super Bowl this season," he admitted. "But I tell you what. I'll call Russ in New York and see if he remembers any more about what all happened thirty years ago. Maybe he'll remember Tom Huston too. I haven't talked to Matt in probably twenty years but I'm sure Russ has. In fact, let's stop at the office. I'll make a copy of the pledge so I can fax it to Russ. If nothing else, he'll get a good laugh out of it."

She smiled tentatively. "You'll really do that?"

He hugged her awkwardly. "I'll really do that," he promised. "And I'll even think about how I could show you what those drugs were like. If nothing else, I'd like to try to get together with you again to talk about your mom and Jason and the events back then. Russ and Matt might feel the same way. You deserve to know more than you do. But in the meantime, do me a favor?"

"What?"

"Take it easy on yourself. Life is a gift. Enjoy it."

...O...O...O...

Dreams play an odd role in our language, in our collective psyche. Scattered bits and splinters of waking reality fashioned into a new and often startling narrative, they seem utterly captivating while we're dreaming but "only a dream" when we wake. And yet we can survive longer without food than without dreams. At the same time, the most fantastic thing we can hope for—the dream job, the dream date—is to an extent just that: a fantasy, an illusion.

Two of the most important dreams of my life have been playing music and writing. Even as a kid scribbling in a journal, I dreamed of someday becoming a writer, at least after the music petered out. So far writing has brought in a total of $27. So maybe I'm a failure. That's not for me to judge. I like to think it preserves my amateur standing, leaving me free to write what I like to read.

Sometime in my teens I realized I could hear all the parts that made up a popular song and I dreamed of recording all the instruments and vocals for a virtual back-up band. I've lived that dream. But people seem to think that I've been living the American Dream, the way that Andrew Carnegie or Elvis Presley lived the American Dream: Born in humble circumstances with dreams of Making It In The Big Time, the hero never flags in his pursuit of his vision until at last fame and fortune drop the dreamer into the velvety lap of luxury.

I started out humble enough and I've been down to nothing a few times since. I put everything I could spare back into the solo act, buying instruments and studio equipment, and living off my meager savings when the gigs dried up so I could stay home and record new backing tracks. And performing isn't always easy. I've played and sung with cracked ribs, a broken heart, a sprained ankle, a back so far out of whack I couldn't stand up straight, screaming fevers, and a tube sticking out of my side to drain a post-operative infection. The worst, of course, seems trivial to non-singers: a throat infection, which is the equivalent of making an athlete perform with a sack of red-hot potatoes tied to her leg. I even sang just a week after an operation on my vocal cords.

But those things only hurt my body. I've heard so much bullshit I don't believe much of anything anymore. I've been the target of insults, threats, come-ons, beer bottles, and, once, a rubber chicken. I've driven in conditions that made the mailman stay home. On one trip, I lost a wheel off my old car while sailing down the highway at 50 miles per hour.

For all my pains and expenses, I made less money most years than I would have made flipping burgers at McDonald's. "But you love what you're doing," people would argue when I'd complain. So everyone who enjoys his job should make minimum wage?

But none of that explains why I've abandoned my dream and taken a day job. I can illustrate that best by an incident that happened at one of my last stints in Canada. I played just west of the four contiguous national parks, at a resort called Fairmont Hot Springs. It was a decent, family-

oriented place but dull as dishwater. The patrons not only didn't clap, they didn't even make eye contact with me. One night a group of young dudes came in and enjoyed themselves: they had a few drinks, requested songs, even sang along with me. Just when I thought I had finally succeeded in entertaining someone, the management kicked them out. I couldn't wait to get back to the States.

But lethargic, self-absorbed audiences, even here in the Wild West, have become the rule, not the exception. People like to think that they're the stars of the show. Hence the karaoke craze. I no longer cherish any illusions of stardom. But maybe it's time I woke up from the American Dream and accepted the American Reality.

June 30, 1969

Nothing seems different. Just another oppressive afternoon, thunderheads building over the Front Range, magpies quarreling in the scrub oak.

John looks out the window. He's at his rich aunt Beatrice's sprawling house that tops a hill above Cheyenne Mountain High School. He can see the entire panorama of the mountains. Waiting.

The smell of burnt popcorn. Russ, Jason, and Gina, Russ's little sister, are playing Monopoly around Beatrice's pool: "I'm the boot, fool." Waiting.

Then it comes. Brighter than pain, hotter than sun. It bursts above the mountains, it burns away the clouds. The beginning of the end.

Somehow unsurprising. "Come here, look!" The light obliterates shadows, ends all secrets. It hangs suspended above the mountains. Impossible to look away.

He can feel Russ look at him. "Shouldn't we leave?"

"And go where?"

Not minutes, seconds. Then came another, another, and another. The genius of multiple warheads. The shock palpably approaches.

Gina rolls the dice. Russ looks for his car keys in every conceivable place. "Where's my mind?"

From this hilltop John can see the buffalo horns of Cheyenne Mountain, right below the blasts. As the fireballs meld into one, the rocks begin to glow, then to flow. The re-igneous slumps and sags, brightens to the yellow-orange of flame. The approaching impact sounds like a buzz growing louder and closer—

A bee hitting the open window jerked John awake. For a moment the apocalypse of the dream lingered as he slumped back into the pillows and threw off the sheet. Ugh.

The dream left him a raging hard-on. Rockets maybe. But he had the morning off. No point in wasting it.

Who then? Joanna Pettit in *Casino Royale*, that skimpy top. Goldie Hawn in a bikini. What lucky bastard got to paint those jokes on her? What about Julie Christie? The figure, the grace, the spun gold hair and sultry eyes, the lips that smiled because she knew…what?

What about Manny? At the restaurant night before last her blouse had puckered enough that he could see the bottom of her bra. Nothing wrong there.

But already it had wilted in his hand. Dream boners never last.

In a way the same thing happened with Manny the other night. Parked in her driveway, she had rested her head on his shoulder. They both knew the moment had come. But when he leaned to kiss her, they both cracked up. They ended up talking about games they had played in the sandbox when they were little. How can you put the moves on that sort of history?

Something else remained unresolved this morning. A tiny motion in the corner of his eye reminded him: across the cool concrete of the basement floor walked the biggest, hairiest bumblebee he'd ever seen.

The first thought that went through his mind, of course, was that he lay on the bed wearing nothing but his old gray gym shorts and that this bee's day had started badly. He pulled the sheet back over himself.

The bee buzzed futilely against the floor a couple of times but couldn't get airborne. So it trudged toward the bedroom door. It took a full five minutes to make it to the hall.

John got up and slipped into a faded Broncos T-shirt and some flip-flops. He went to the door and looked around the corner. The bee walked straight for the light coming through the screen door at the top of the stairs.

By now whatever fear John had felt had changed to curiosity. He walked up right behind the bee and squatted to look closer. Dense yellow and black fur covered the fat body and saddlebags of pollen clung to the shiny black legs. Reticulated iridescence shone from the smoky translucent wings.

Coming to the bottom of the steps, the bee rested. John could see the abdomen puffing in and out. Finally, its fragile wings snapping on the linoleum, the bee mustered up the effort to fly up the first step. It walked four inches, rested, then made it up the next step. Soon John knelt on the stairs, his face just inches from the bee, urging it on.

He actually cheered when the bee made the twelfth step and wearily plodded for the door. John held the door open for it when the time came and it walked across the sill and out onto the sunlit stoop. Flexing its wings in the morning sun it paused only briefly before its body temperature rose enough to allow it to fly away and go on about its morning chores.

No such obligations troubled John. Tomorrow he'd be back at the Cheyenne Mountain Zoo, mucking out the pens for the ungrateful rhinos, giraffes, and elephants. Today, though, looked free.

His mother had left early for her tennis lesson and to lunch with his aunt but before she left she had poured him a bowl of cereal and a glass of juice. John rummaged about in the cabinets, not looking for anything in particular, scooping a fingerful of chunky peanut butter from the jar.

A car pulled into the drive. Through the window he could see that it was the Tank, Matt's 1956 creamy green Pontiac with the chrome-and-amber hood ornament. From it stepped Matt himself, dazzling in the bright summer sun, wearing a tight white T-shirt, white bellbottoms and sneakers.

"The man of the hour," John greeted him through the screen door.

"So you're up, Jacque," Matt surmised.

John's middle name was Otis, so his initials were JOK. Matt, with his peculiar sense of formality, had franked everyone else's "Jock" to "Jacque."

"Not up enough."

"Didn't sleep well?"

"'I have had a dream'," said John, an English major, "'past the wit of man to say what dream it was.' A midsummer night's dream, my friend, a week late."

"Have you broken your fast?" Matt asked, coming in.

"Just about to."

"Don't," Matt decreed. "We've got to get going."

"Where?"

"To clean you up," Matt said, surveying John's rumpled hair and wispy sideburns. "At least sartorially. Then we're off to Russ's."

"For?" John asked reasonably, following Matt back down to his bedroom.

"The ultimate breakfast," Matt informed him, rummaging through John's hanging clothes.

"Why?"

"Ours is not to reason why," Matt said. "They sent me out for this stuff when I got to Russ's." He handed John a list, written in Jason's cramped scrawl, including things like papayas, smoked oysters, and Darjeeling tea.

"Did your orders include money for all this?" John asked.

"We'll split it four ways," Matt told him, handing him a faded Madras-plaid shirt and a pair of jeans that John's mother Kate ironed, creased, and put on a hanger.

John put on the shirt and jeans but balked at shoes. Matt frowned at the flip-flops but acquiesced when presented with the option of zoo boots, and they were off.

"Is there an occasion for this breakfast?" John asked as Matt drove up Cheyenne Boulevard.

"Well, Russ is leaving for New York in a couple of days," Matt told him. "Who knows when he'll be back?"

"That's right, his father's already out there, isn't he?"

Matt turned left on Cresta. "Jason said you had an interesting time at the Denver Pop Festival night before last."

"Did he tell you we got tear gassed?"

"What!? What did you do?"

"We didn't do anything. We were just minding our own business, watching the Flock— or was it Big Mama Thornton? I don't remember—and this brouhaha breaks out in the south stands of Mile High. I found out yesterday that they oversold or somebody counterfeited tickets or something because there were like 15,000 people who'd paid their six bucks and they wanted in. They were trying to push over the chain link fence so somebody called the police. The brilliant Denver cops get there and find a riot in progress and they figure, what the hell, what's a riot without tear gas?"

"Bad show."

"Which got worse when the wind shifted and this ugly acrid cloud drifted over the stands. It burned like hell. We had to get out."

"Did they call off the concert?" Matt asked, pulling into Russ's driveway.

"Naw. The tear gas didn't hit the stage. In fact, the band kept playing. By the time the breeze blew away the rest of the tear gas and we got back to our seats, Barry Fey decided just to let everybody in so there wouldn't be any more incidents. The people of Denver weren't too keen on having 30,000 hippies looking for a place to crash as it was."

"So who else played?" Matt asked as they got out and gathered up the groceries.

"Oh, the Mothers!" John exclaimed, picking up a couple of bags. "God, Matt, you should have seen Zappa. I mean, the other Mothers were a regular freak show, decked out in their full hippie regalia. But Zappa was *so* hot. At first I thought he was some sort of giant because his guitar looked so tiny. But somebody told me he plays a mini-Strat and a mini-Les Paul so his fingers don't have to work so hard. God, he was fast." John demonstrated by singing falsetto and making "biddle-iddle-iddle" noises with his tongue, holding the neck of the air guitar near his own neck, like a cello. "And the sounds he got from his equipment blew me away. And get this: he played at least as much keyboard, mostly a grand, as he did guitar."

"You're kidding!" Matt said. "That sounds incredible."

"Yeah but Hendrix played there last night. I really wish I could have seen him. They announced that he and a bunch of other name acts will be at some festival they're putting on in New York in August."

"Maybe Russ will be able to go to that one."

O   O   O

Russ's house bustled and clattered and from the stereo in the living room the Beatles sang "Good Morning." As John and Matt set down the sacks of groceries, they could hear Russ singing in his wispy voice: "Good morning, good morning, good morning—guh!" He pulled stacks of china from the breakfront in the dining room and set them on the table. Russ's mother Ellen sang out a friendly greeting to the late-comers as she swirled an electric mixer through a bowl of pancake batter. Jason sliced a plastic tube of sausage into patties. Beside him at the stove Russ's grandmother, universally known by Ellen's appellation "Mother Jones," stirred a pan of ham gravy from the drippings of last evening's dinner.

John gave Ellen a peck on the cheek while Matt spread out the groceries.

"They had no Darjeeling tea," Matt informed Russ, "so we got something called Lapsang Soujong instead."

Russ cracked the plastic wrap on the box and sniffed critically. "Interesting," he declared. "Smoky or something. In any case, 'twill serve."

"What should I be doing?" Matt asked.

Russ, his hands full of the tea, cups and saucers, and a creamer, shouted back over his shoulder, "Cut the papayas!"

"How?" Matt asked, looking askance at the unfamiliar fruit.

Russ came back in carrying a waxy glass candelabra. "Lengthwise once, scoop out the seeds," he told Matt. "And a quarter of lime in each. Time is of the essence! Slice like your life depended on it!" He set the candelabra on the small breakfast table, the brilliant morning sun streaming through the fanlight above the tall, east-facing window. Holding the candelabra over the wicker trash basket, he chipped away at the old streams of wax. "How's the ham gravy, Mother Jones?"

Mother Jones, who had Southern manners and a bit of a dowager's hump, didn't reply, concentrating on blending the drippings into the flour water.

Jason, now cooking the sausage patties, vouched for her. "She let me taste it," he said to Russ. "It is the nectar of the gods."

"Are you ready for the pancakes, honey?" Ellen asked her son.

"We're ready for everything!" Russ ruled. He picked up a box of fresh strawberries and sang, now that *Sgt. Pepper's* had finished, "Let me take you down," and then popped one in his mouth.

Ellen handed the pancake platter to John and asked him, "Did you invite Amanda?" Unlike her mother-in-law, Ellen was tall and graceful with a broad smile and an easy, congenial laugh, but she shared with Mother Jones the southern sensibility about observing the proprieties and the importance of relationships.

"I only heard about this half an hour ago," John hedged.

"You're throwing a party without inviting a single girl?" Ellen chided Russ.

"It's not a party," Russ insisted, waving away his mother's concerns. "It's just having some guys over for breakfast." He lit the candles on the clean candelabra.

"Unless you and Mother Jones would favor us with your presence," Matt added politely as he wrapped a dish-towel around the biscuits Mother Jones had taken from the oven.

"Oh, no," Ellen demurred. "Mother Jones and I are going to sit in here and gab while you young men carry on. Oh, but I want to get a picture!" She went upstairs for her camera.

Jason, having drained the sausage patties on a paper towel and gathered up the ham gravy Mother Jones had poured into a gravy-boat, joined the procession of platters and dishes and trays into the dining room.

The Jones house stood at the corner of Mesa and Cresta, just a couple of blocks from the blushing tan tower of the Broadmoor Hotel, the world-class resort where Jason worked on the grounds crew and Matt jerked sodas in the drug store. The Jones's large, two-story, gray stucco home had a slate roof and featured four large bedrooms on the upper floor, a living room and solarium in addition to the foyer, dining room, and kitchen on the main floor, a big detached garage, and even an elevator installed in the solarium for a partially-disabled previous owner. The dining room window overlooked the expansive sunlit lawn and a hedge of overgrown blue spruce that provided some privacy from the intersection.

Ellen's damask tablecloth covered the oval oak table and a panoply of the Jones family china, which had accompanied Mother Jones on her train trip out, was carefully arranged in four elaborate place settings. Sweating ice-water glasses, cut-crystal wine goblets, and the cream-colored candles in the candelabra gave the scene sparkle. Eric Satie's *Trois Gymnopedies* replaced *Sgt. Pepper's*.

As Ellen came back down with her Polaroid, four heavy dining room chairs slid out across the hardwood floor. Russ stood on the long east side of the table looking out the window, John to his left, Matt across, and Jason on the north end. Russ, having filled the goblets with sparkling grape juice, held his own aloft while still standing, striking a pose, as did they all, for Ellen's camera.

"Gentlemen, a toast!" Russ proposed. "To the day when all questions will be answered!" He clinked his glass to Jason's to his right.

"To the end of the world then," Jason offered, clinking Matt's.

"To the beginning of the next," Matt added, clinking John's.

"And the women who loved them!" John exclaimed irrelevantly. They all chuckled and sipped, then sat.

"Where do we start?" Matt wanted to know, surveying the feast.

"Papaya first," Russ said, squeezing lime juice onto the tender orange flesh.

"I dreamt about the end of the world," John mentioned, passing the biscuits to Jason.

"How was it?" Jason asked, trading him the ham gravy.

"Colorful," John said. "Terrifying in an inevitable sort of way."

"Sounds realistic enough," Matt said, slopping real maple syrup on a short stack of pancakes.

"Which colors?" Jason asked.

John, taking no prisoners, had already stirred the crumbled shreds of sausage patty and scrambled eggs into the ham gravy and he meditatively chewed an overloaded forkful while he tried to recall the fading images. "I remember the mountains melting. Lots of reds and oranges. The sky turned white."

"That's the amazing thing about dreams," Matt put in, topping a precise slice of biscuit and gravy with a smoked oyster. "You can do anything you want. Even end the world."

"Didn't Freud say that dreaming is wish fulfillment?" Russ asked.

"I don't want to end the world," John said. He thought about what had happened when he first woke up. "Besides, if my dream had been wish fulfillment, there would have been a woman."

"What about Manny?" Russ asked.

John, chewing another mouthful, gazed out the window. "I don't know. Maybe we've known each other too long. She just seems like a friend, like one of us."

"Man's fantastic though," Jason pointed out. "She's got beauty, brains, personality, money. What do you want?"

"More gravy," John said.

"I don't blame you," Matt said, passing the gravy-boat. "Who wants fantasy when you can have reality?"

"Ham gravy is reality?" John wondered, though Mother Jones had outdone herself.

"Well, one man's reality is another man's cold broccoli," Jason said. "I think Amanda Tyree is a peach, whereas John evidently looks at her and sees, what? Cold broccoli?"

"I think I specified ham gravy, actually," John defended himself. "And I dare anyone to cast aspersions on Mother Jones's ham gravy."

"To Mother Jones and her ham gravy!" Matt said, raising his glass and his voice. There were no dissenters.

"Thank you, boys," came Mother Jones's quavering voice from the kitchen.

"Let's get back to reality," Russ said.

"Fat chance," John ventured.

"Seriously," Russ said. "Is Jason right? Is one man's reality another man's cold broccoli? How can two people look at the same thing and see it so differently?"

"Isn't it just as amazing that two people ever agree on anything?" Matt wondered. "I mean, there's three billion people on this planet with three billion different points of view and yet we all agree on some things."

"Like what?" Jason asked.

"The sky is blue," Matt offered.

"Not in my dream," John said. "The Bomb turned it white."

"Dreams aren't reality," Matt contended.

"They are to the dreamer," Russ said.

Matt, his mouth full of biscuit, grunted his doubt.

"This coming from someone who's dreaming that the New York Mets will go all the way this year," Jason said, siding with Matt.

"You're kidding," John said to Russ.

"It all comes down to pitching," Russ observed.

"But that's a mighty unlikely reality you're pitching," John said. "I mean, the Mets spent last winter in the cellar."

"Are there different kinds of reality then?" Jason asked.

"What do you mean?" Russ asked back.

"I mean, Matt's point was that most people agree that the sky is blue. It's blue almost by definition. But, at least in his dreams, for John the sky was really white."

"And it seemed frightfully real at the time," John said.

"Okay, there's obviously some sort of individual reality," Russ conceded. "And each of us has to find a way to deal with that. But only madmen and dreamers think the sky is something other than blue."

"Or that the Mets will win the Series," John retorted.

"What about somebody who's color blind?" Matt pointed out. "Wouldn't he claim that the sky was something other than blue?"

"Steve's partially color-blind," Jason pointed out, referring to his older brother. "They almost wouldn't let him into Nixon's army because of it."

"I'll bet Vietnamese blood and American blood both look red," John said. "Even to someone color-blind."

"I hope he doesn't get a chance to find out," Jason said. "There's been enough bloodshed over there already."

"'Only the dead have seen the end to war'," Russ quoted Plato.

"Besides, what's war without bloodshed?" John asked.

"Politics," Jason said.

"The point is," Russ went on, trying to herd them back to the subject, "does the sky look blue to Steve?"

"He always said it did," Jason said.

"But is the color he sees when he looks up into the clear day-time sky the same as the color John sees?" Matt asked. "What would happen if you put John's brain into Steve's head?"

"It'd rattle around a lot," John said.

"What it comes down to," Russ theorized, "is that no matter what color the individual sees, everyone agrees to call it 'blue'. So there's some sort of individual reality which may vary from person to person but there's also a reality that everyone shares."

"Except us madmen and dreamers," John put in.

"But until a few hundred years ago," Matt said, "everyone thought the world was flat."

"Okay, so there must be a difference between the reality everyone agrees to and ultimate reality," Russ conceded, pouring some Lapsang Soujong tea into Jason's proffered cup.

"Another reality rears its ugly head," John pointed out.

"Yeah, but 'ultimate reality' has a nice ring to it," Jason said, sipping the hot tea carefully.

"So you're claiming that there are three levels of reality," Matt said to Russ. "IR: individual reality; UR: ultimate reality; and whatever that other thing is that everyone agrees to, at least till they find out differently."

"Duh, I are individual reality," John said in a stupid voice, though proudly.

"You are ultimate reality," Russ assured him.

"But what's the other one?" Matt wanted to know. "CR: common reality? ER: everyday reality? Maybe AR: average reality?"

"AR, mateys," Jason said in a pirate's voice.

"Ar, ar, ar," the others chimed in.

For the past year and a half they had been performing together as a band, Jason playing his Gibson guitar and singing, Matt lugging around an old Wurlitzer electric piano, John playing bass and singing too, and Russ playing his Slingerland drums. They played parties and the Tin Can, a teen club held first in an old Quonset hut (hence the name) and then in the basement of a church, making barely enough money to pay for gas. Since Jason sang most of the leads and had a wild shock of curly blonde hair (known thereafter as the Golden Fleece), they called themselves Jason and the Argonauts. The "ar, ar, ar" thing had become a band trademark.

Gina, Russ's younger sister, came home from spending the night at a girlfriend's house while the pirate ARs still rang. She took a look at the demolished brunch, rolled her eyes, and went up to her room.

"In any case," Matt said, stacking his plates and saucers, "MR, My Reality, says that I've got to finish filling out those scholarship papers by this afternoon. They have to be in Seattle by Tuesday."

"Not till after the Toilet Bowl," Russ pointed out, referring to their long-running touch-football rivalry.

"Oh, jeez, I don't know," Matt said.

"Oh, come on, you can be on the Icons this time and I'll be on the Toads," Russ offered. The Icons, the American Football League representative, had copied Broadway Joe Namath and the upstart Jets and led the N. F. L. Toads in the ongoing series. The players frequently switched sides but the game went on.

"Besides, what do you want to go up to the University of Washington for, anyway?" John asked him, crunching a last slice of bacon. "What's up there? Rain? Slugs? The Space Needle?"

"Yeah, what've you got against good old Colorado schools?" Jason said as he gathered up the cloth napkins.

"Say, JC," Russ said, "did you ever send in that dorm thing?"

"I'm sure there are other places to live in Boulder besides the dorms," Jason pointed out.

"Like the streets," Matt said.

Ellen, hearing the sound of china banging on china, came in to help clear the table. "How did your breakfast turn out?" she asked them.

All four declared their fast broken beyond repair and traipsed into the kitchen to pay homage to Mother Jones, who took it all with a blush and a smile.

"Mother," Russ informed Ellen, "we're off to play the latest round in the on-going Toilet Bowl."

"We're not playing anything yet," Matt insisted. "We've got to stay and clean up this mess."

"Matt, you're just as sweet as can be," Ellen said with her broadest smile. "But Mother Jones and I will clean up. We're enjoying our visit. You boys go out and play your football game."

"Are you sure?" Jason asked. "Because you've gone above and beyond the call of duty in hosting this thing. We don't mind staying."

"Go on," Ellen insisted. "Who knows how many more times you'll get a chance to do this?"

"Where are my keys?" Russ wondered, walking around looking in every conceivable place.

...O...O...O...

I don't gamble, at least not the way most people gamble. The average, non-problem gambler lives a normal life, works hard most of the year, saves up for that big trip to Vegas for a week of slots, booze, and shows. I, on the other hand, have gambled my life and time on the long-shot, inside-straight of Show Biz, which not only satisfied any urge I had to gamble, it also left me with no disposable income to gamble with. Nevertheless, I've always felt a certain kinship to gamblers, so when I had a chance to play a gig in Nevada, I jumped at it.

Of course, I didn't play Las Vegas or Reno. I played the Mizpah Hotel in Tonopah. Jammed into a barren arroyo, Tonopah is the only town I've ever seen where no two homes looked even remotely similar. "Great," I thought to myself. "This place ought to provide some unique characters."

Wrong. The management had arranged the lobby of the Depression-era Mizpah so that a person could not sit down without facing the business end of some gambling device, mostly flashing video poker machines. From the raised stage behind the bar, I got a bird's-eye view of the patrons and discovered that the gambling so absorbed their attention that they completely ignored their surroundings, including me. Any unique characteristics the people walked in with disappeared as soon as they became tethered to a machine.

Two things make people gamble. One is the random nature of the reward. If you paid gamblers a regular wage to sit in front of video-poker machines and try to guess random, computer-generated card combinations with nothing at stake but the satisfaction of a job well done, they would soon find it the most mind-numbing, pointless job on the planet. Even though they would be guaranteed to come out of it money-ahead, almost all would quickly walk off the job.

The other reason to gamble is the tantalizing prospect of winning the huge jackpot that (theoretically) puts an end to all money woes. In that respect, I am as susceptible to Gold Fever as any other American. I once dreamed of striking it rich in Show Biz. But I wanted to succeed based on my merits, not just on some lucky break. State-sponsored lotteries, unheard of when I was a kid, seem to have changed the concept of money from something you earn to something you win. The lottery results, in fact, have become part of the evening newscast. Just once I'd like to see the smiling anchorwoman say, "Today, 60 million people threw away worthless lottery tickets."

Actually, I did buy a bag of snack-size Snickers bars once that told it like it is. As part of some ad-executive's get-rich-quick promotion, each wrapper (at least in the bag I bought) had the following message printed on the inside: "Sorry. You are a loser." Like I needed to be reminded. Snickers indeed.

A few years ago I played a reception for the true lottery winners, held in a grand hotel and featuring Olympic Gold Medalist Bruce Jenner, whose only duty was to smile and have his picture taken with people. The lottery winners were, of course, the people who sold the tickets, not the ones who bought them.

With a few, rare exceptions, we're all winners of a lottery of sorts: conception. The mother contributes just one egg, but the father throws hundreds of millions of sperm in its direction, each with a slightly different version of the father's genome. Some, naturally, are deficient in some fashion and don't stand a chance. But many are hearty enough to find the egg and vie for the honor of fertilizing it. The one that persuades the egg to let down her guard and allow penetration may have some superior characteristics but it's mostly a matter of pure chance. And the winner takes all.

My sperm are reflections of their progenitor: hardy, willing to go that extra mile, but ultimately unlucky. Three of them have drawn winning numbers but didn't come away with the jackpot. One succeeded despite an IUD, another made it all the way up a fallopian tube, and the third was the victim of some really bad timing.

God, on the other hand, hasn't had to depend on luck. (No great surprise there, I suppose.) After all, Mary's is not usually considered a case of true parthenogenisis so much as some sort of cosmic fertilization and it seems unlikely that hundreds of millions of God's silver-tipped sperm went to waste. But did He have just the one seed for man? Has He been impotent for 2000 years? Or is there a blessed Mary out there right now heavy with Child, still starry-eyed over her fling at the end of March? Will ours be the generation lucky—or cursed—enough to witness a rebirth of God's commitment to mankind? This would be the year. A second coming for a Second Coming. Would we recognize the second Son of God? Or would He be "just a slob like one of us, just a stranger on the bus trying to make his way home," to quote a current song?

October 17, 1999

CTRL+SHIFT+D for drive? Russ tried it. No, nothing. CTRL+SHIFT+S for shift maybe? The screen shifted to some sans-serif font. No, ALT+EU, undo. That's not it. CTRL+SHIFT+A maybe? *Voila!* Now, FILE OPEN on drive A. Somewhere near the bottom of the list of hundreds of things to do came reorganizing and relabeling those macros.

As Russ scanned the file names, Bob Murphy, the Mets' long-time radio announcer, imparted the ominous news that Atlanta's Bret Boone had just hit a hard double to left field. Shit, Russ said to himself. The Mets had already fallen behind the Braves, three games to one, in the National League Championship Series and even though they had a two-run lead, the Braves had all faced the Mets' starter Yoshii and might already have his number. This could be the beginning of the end.

Russ couldn't see the calendar on the list of file names so he popped the diskette from the laptop. Well, no wonder. This diskette held the accounting files; the calendar would be on the F&B diskette. He found that one, put it in, hit ESC, then ALT FO again. Okay, CAL99.DOC. Now: what weeks remained unbooked?

While he looked over the calendar, he heard the heavy clomp of Rolando's black shoes coming down the stairs. The clatter of dishes paused briefly while Rolando and Miguel, the dishwasher, chatted briefly in Spanish, then the ruckus resumed and Rolando came into Russ's tiny, cluttered cubicle.

"Whatcha doin', boss?" Rolando asked, sitting on the stack of liquor boxes next to Russ's cluttered desk and looking at the screen of the laptop.

"Going over the entertainment schedule for the rest of the year," Russ told him. "How did Lacey do last night? Did you get many people?"

"Lacey's hot, man," Rolando said. "Looks great, sings like an angel."

Russ picked up the folded, rubber-banded cash register tape and looked at the bottom line. "You z-ed out at just seventy bucks more than we usually make on a Saturday. I paid her more than twice that." He looked at his night manager, a pudgy, fat-faced thirty-something.

Rolando used up all his white teeth in one big smile and shrugged. "Maybe she sang so good, people forgot to drink."

On the radio Murphy's bleary voice broke the news that the dreaded Chipper Jones had doubled to left as well, driving in Boone and shrinking the Mets' lead to a single precarious run.

Rolando broke into Russ's gloom by asking, "Did you finish the liquor order yet?"

"No. Why?"

"Don't forget that Glenmorangie."

"Didn't we just get two bottles of that?"

"Single malts are the bomb, boss." With that, Rolando got up and left, stopping for a few more quick words to Miguel as he climbed the stairs.

Russ thought about digging out his old liquor orders to see when he had last ordered Glenmorangie but then Brian Jordan singled to left and tied the score. His gloom deepening, Russ decided to blow it off and get back to the entertainment.

As he thought, he had only the last two weeks of the year left to book. The Stilton Agency had sent him a stack of a dozen solo artists' promo packages, which would take hours to go through. Booking live music already seemed like more trouble than it was worth. Can there really be that many hungry musicians out there begging for work? How many of them can be any good at all if they're still trying to find work for New Year's Eve, 1999, arguably the biggest date of the millennium? But Tweak had to offer something to compete with every other nightclub, restaurant, bus kiosk, and phone booth that offered some sort of Turn of the Millennium Gala.

Tweak, his corner restaurant in Greenwich Village, had been booking musicians for four months. He had hired live entertainment years ago at another nightclub but a lot had changed since then. Already he'd dealt with double bookings, no-shows, losers. Three weekends ago, singer/songwriter Martin Panghorn's girlfriend, the pharmacist's assistant, had filled a jar with various mood-altering drugs from which Martin sampled freely before his brief, disastrous set. The skinny Vietnamese singer (what was her name? Tran?) had numbed the few who stayed with her whiny warblings of old Leonard Cohen songs. Even the good ones tended to be catty, self-centered, unreliable, weird.

He drifted through the stack again. So far he had found three main contenders for New Year's Eve. Jack, the big cheese at Stilton, raved about a fellow called Tragore who managed to blend synth-pop with traditional Indian raga riffs and nasty guitar. Rolando lobbied for Crazy Fred, who would take his cordless microphone around the room and stir up some sort of excitement among the otherwise complacent and self-absorbed Tweak regulars. Russ's own hunch had been Lacey, a slender pop singer who seemed not only talented but sexy as well; however, last night's receipts looked surprisingly anemic.

Russ heaved a sigh of relief as Mets coach Bobby Valentine lifted Yoshii in favor of Orel Hershiser who, though getting long in the tooth, had impeccable credentials in play-off games.

The phone on his desk rang. He dug through the stacks of mail, computer print-outs, back issues of *Sports Illustrated*, and the like until he found the phone, into which he said,

"Tweak."

"Russell?" his mother Ellen asked.

"Hi, Mom," he said. "How's everybody up on the farm?"

"Just wonderful. Your father's doing his exercises on his stationary bike and guess who I just talked to."

"Gina," he guessed.

"She thought you and Syl might be up here this weekend. Are you watching the game, honey?"

"I'm listening to it on the radio here at work. Was Gina excited?"

"Well, of course, except she said that Atlanta had caught up. She called them the Borg. I didn't know what that meant so she told me to ask you."

Russ laughed, thinking about Glavin, Maddux, and Smoltz. "They're the Borg all right, Mom. I'll explain another time. Hang on."

Bob Murphy, in his slightly inebriated-sounding voice, described how John Olerud had thrown to Hershiser covering first to put out Walt Weiss, ending the Atlanta fourth with only two runs scored.

"Yes!" Russ exclaimed.

"Did the Mets score?" Ellen asked.

"No, but they got out of the inning tied. It could have been much worse. So, did you take Tiny Cat to the vet?"

Louie, long retired as a producer of television commercials, and Ellen lived in an old farmhouse in upstate New York with three cats: Big Cat, an old calico matron, Little Cat, who, when a little yellow kitten, deserved the name more than he did now that he was bigger than Big Cat, and Tiny Cat, a little tiger stripe who was the latest addition and who had had an appointment to be neutered.

"Yes, we got him snipped and he's just fine. You know what your sister said?"

"I can only imagine."

"She said, 'There goes the last chance to hear the pitter-pat of tiny feet in our family.'"

"Yeah, ha, ha," Russ said mirthlessly.

Gina and her long-time partner Louise had long ago abandoned the thought of children and Russ and Syl, so far at least, had none, though not from lack of trying.

"How's Big Cat?" he asked, changing the subject.

"Big Cat is as fine as frog hair," Ellen said. "She kind of creaks when she gets up in the morning but yesterday she caught a butterfly in mid-air. In fact, she's sitting in her usual place on the window sill right now. Do you want to say hello?"

"No, Mom, I really better get back to work. We'll see you next weekend."

"Bye, honey."

Russ embraced several contradictions. For someone who professed such faith in reason and logical argument, he often willingly, gladly, let himself be ruled by superstition. For one thing, he felt deep in his bones that somehow the Mets, those miracle Mets, would find a way to become the first team in baseball to fall behind three-games-to-none in a seven-game series and come back to win, maybe even play the Yankees in a subway World Series, every New York baseball fan's dream. He also believed, perhaps with more justification, that as long as Big Cat sat on that window sill, God was in his heaven and all was right with the world.

Growing up, Russ had the usual appetites: sports, girls, food, the finer things in life. His philosophical discussions with Jason, John, and Matt, though, had served only to whet another appetite: delving into big ideas, figuring out what life means. So it made perfect sense to him to pursue those subjects in college.

It made no sense to his parents. Ellen, in particular, could see no practical use for a degree in philosophy with a minor in religion. Would some wavering soul, having just spotted an actual fire in a crowded theater, stand up and shout, "Is there a philosopher in the house?"

But Russ graduated college with, if anything, more questions than ever. Admittedly, he had a much broader view of the world of ideas but he felt he'd never had the kind of spiritual teacher who could guide him to a deeper level of understanding of himself and of the world around him. He also continued to struggle to make sense of Jason's disappearance and the events that led up to it.

Shortly after he graduated and went back home to Colorado Springs, a friend of a friend told him of a spiritual teacher who led a small school in Monument, just north of the city. Russ felt the hand of fate. He called the teacher, an older, charismatic woman named Sonja Weinstock, and she encouraged him to attend one of their meetings. At the meeting she likened human existence to a carriage: the coach itself, the physical being; the horse, the animal being; the driver, the intelligent being; all are necessary to support the master, the rider, the enlightened being who integrates all these different levels of existence. This resonated so strongly with Russ that he dove in head first.

Sonja's teaching was related to the Work, derived from the writings of George Gurdjieff and Peter Ouspenski. It centered around the concept of self-remembering: trying to rid the mind of the everyday clutter and noise so that the more enduring, meaningful aspects of one's life and soul could shine through. People get lost in small emotions—bitterness, jealousy, ennui, wistfulness—and don't take to heart all the contradictions in their lives and thereby achieve wisdom. According to Sonja, being self-critical but self-forgiving was the first step to a civilized society based on what Gurdjieff referred to as "organic shame." The impulse to be harsh, unforgiving, and conflicted about ourselves and those around us robs us of those better aspects of human nature: self-knowledge and compassion.

Soon Russ's life revolved around the school. There he found some new, close friends, and even his first wife, Becky. Together, the small group planned most of the events of their lives: trips, weddings, even a relocation, *en masse*, to Bend, Oregon. He supported himself waiting tables, tending bar, selling computers.

But as the years went by, he became disillusioned. Sonja died and the woman who took her place didn't have the same spark. He felt that the group kept going over the same ideas *ad nauseam*, that they had an unwarranted pride in themselves and their spiritual accomplishments. The members, though adults, nevertheless ended up in a sophomoric competition for the attention of the teacher. He gradually became aware of a lot of restrictive, unwritten rules about how one should think and feel and function, which seemed completely contradictory to the explicit teachings of the Work.

After a decade and a half of deep involvement, Russ's disillusionment spread beyond the school to the rest of his circumstances: a dead-end job, a failing marriage, life in a small town. In one of those rare but vital moments of insight, he woke up one morning and realized he needed to leave the school and take control of his life.

Ellen, who had always considered the school a cult, made no secret of her relief and implored him to come live with them on the farm while he decided what to do next. He acquiesced and moved his few possessions back east.

For a while he wandered around the wooded acres of the old farm like a recovering amputee, fighting off the phantom sensation that he was still part of the group, explaining to them, rationalizing to them, why he no longer was attached to them. Louie, who, at Ellen's insistence, had kept his usual gruff opinions to himself, ended up breaking the spell by asking what seemed like a relatively simple, innocent question: had Russ dropped out of the school or graduated?

Certainly, as far as the school was concerned, Russ had dropped out. But then, like a church, the school had no recognized mode of graduation: once you joined, you were expected to stay. As far as he was concerned, he had gleaned the last kernel of insight from what they had to teach. But to what end?

Big Cat gave him the answer. The two-story farm house had a roofed front porch, up the side of which ran a rose trellis. Big Cat, at that time young and spry and the only cat patrolling the grounds for those pesky squirrels, one day climbed the trellis to the porch roof. Reluctant to climb or jump back down, she sat on the window sill of the sewing room until Ellen saw her and opened the window to let her in. That became Big Cat's spot and in all but the coldest, blusteriest weather, there she'd sit, her calico fur flattened against the wavy glass, looking out over the huge sugar maples in the front yard, the ridge road, and the tranquil valley beyond.

One fall day, Russ came upon her in this meditative state and it reminded him of a story he'd read years before. According to the story, cats evolved a sophisticated civilization many eons ago. In fact, philosophical and religious matters came to so dominate their lives that they became almost catatonic at times, neglecting practical matters like finding food and shelter. Fearing a catastrophe, the feline leaders concatenated their greatest thinkers by the cataract under the sacred catalpa tree. Some venerable Cato suggested training a lesser species to cater to their practical needs, leaving cats free to seek catharsis through their ancient catechism. They decided to domesticate a category of ape, admittedly crude and quarrelsome but possessing the unique ability to stand upright. That freed the naked apes' opposable-thumbed hands to build cozy homes, pick the burrs from a busy cat's fur and, ultimately, operate a can opener. The rest is history.

It occurred to Russ, watching Big Cat contemplating the mysteries of the universe from her window sill, that it was high time at least one crude ape emulated his mentor. He decided that he too could sit and stare out the window and philosophize and go Big Cat one better by writing it down. That way he could feel he had graduated from the school.

Not that such a noble purpose kept him from enjoying his other interests. As now: while ostensibly reviewing the promotional materials for the musicians wanting to play Tweak on New Year's Eve, he focused mainly on the pitching duel that had evolved between Hershiser and Atlanta's Greg Maddux. Already in the seventh inning, the score remained tied at two.

His phone rang again. It was Sylvia.

"Where are you, love?" he asked her.

"Les Deux Gamins," she told him, sounding bubbly.

"I thought you were going to get a reading from Zena."

Zena, Clairvoyant, had a tiny shop where Bleeker ran into 7th Avenue. Russ didn't put much stock in such things but knew that Sylvia occasionally found comfort and guidance from Zena's insights.

"That was hours ago, darling. Then I ran into Michelle and we ended up here. But now you have to come rescue me. Please?"

"Rescue you from what?"

"From this dreadfully heavy discussion," she said, and he could hear her companions laugh and jeer. She lowered her voice and confided, "I'm getting a little worried, *cher*. Some of this is starting to make sense."

"Why don't you just leave?" he asked. Les Deux Gamins was just a few blocks away.

"I forgot to bring an umbrella," she confessed. "You wouldn't want me to melt, would you?"

"It's not raining, is it?" he asked, surprised. He hadn't heard Bob Murphy mention it but his work had distracted him.

"Really, darling, you must come up for air once in a while. How long have you been languishing in that dreary dungeon of yours?"

"Since half-time of the Jets game," he said, looking at his watch. It was now past six. "Is it really raining?" He didn't relish the thought of the Mets having to finish a rain-out opposite Monday Night Football.

"It's sprinkling or dribbling or something. Besides, I miss you. Please? I'll give you anything you want."

What he wanted was to catch the end of the baseball game but that's not legal tender in the economics of marriage. He had to want something she had to give. And he knew, once he saw her, he would. He sighed. Les Deux Gamins didn't have a TV but maybe somebody there had a radio.

"I'll come as soon as I can," he assured her.

"Words no woman wants to hear," she teased. "Don't forget the umbrella."

He stuffed all the promo materials back into the file folder as a lost cause, shut down the laptop, switched off the light and the radio, and closed and locked the door to the cubicle.

He glanced around the fragrant, sweltering kitchen. "I'm going to take off, Buzz," he called to his lead cook.

Buzz, a tattooed, bald, goateed Gen-Xer, looked up. "What do you want to do for tomorrow's special?"

"What are we long on?"

Buzz checked the cooler. "Skate," he said. "Hanger steak, maybe."

"Do the steak," Russ decided. "See you."

o   o   o

Upstairs, Tweak seemed busier than the typical Sunday afternoon but a light drizzle had indeed begun to fall, forcing indoors the habitués of the Village's sidewalk cafes. A good hour before the usual dinner rush, Russ could spot few empty seats.

Open just a couple of years, Tweak had already become something of an institution. Prime location, on the corner of Christopher and Bleeker, didn't hurt. The rough edges left over from its years as a sporting goods store hadn't been polished completely, giving it a lived-in feel. The wood floors had been stripped but not varnished, the original brick of the old four-story building had been exposed wherever possible, the classic tin work along the back wall painted black. A partial wall divided the space into two rooms. The larger corner room, where the stairway led up from the kitchen, held a dozen small tables, the musicians' tiny corner, and the brushed-copper bar, big enough for just half a dozen stools. The other, smaller room, which had a separate storefront, featured tiny round tables where they served mostly coffee, tea, and pastries. The muted lighting throughout came primarily from the individual spots shining on the original artwork that provided most of the wall decor. The tea room, in fact, doubled as a gallery. Soft jazz and light pop CDs completed the warm, comfortable ambiance.

Oscar, Tweak's taciturn, middle-aged bartender, beckoned to Russ as soon as he came upstairs. Russ walked to the corner of the bar, which functioned as the serving hub, where Oscar and Christine, Tweak's lead server, stood, obviously concerned about something.

"What's up?" Russ asked them confidentially.

"We got stiffed," Oscar said.

"How much?" Russ asked Christine.

She checked the tab. "Seventy five bucks."

The phone rang and Oscar answered it.

"They just walked?" Russ asked.

Christine sighed and looked out the window. In addition to being an excellent server, she also was one of the most beautiful women Russ had ever seen. She had short blonde hair and playful blue eyes, a clear, Julie-Andrews-type complexion and smile, and absolutely stunning breasts. They weren't so much bodacious as they were elegant, perfectly proportioned. Of the multitude of distractions Russ faced every day, they were by far his favorite.

"I was helping Karen," she said, turning back to Russ, who brought his eyes back up to her face. "I guess I just lost track." Karen was new.

"You're sure there wasn't a credit card or a bill stuck to a plate or something?" Russ asked.

"I checked twice and even went down and asked Miguel."

"Get this," Oscar said, hanging up the phone. "It's our seventy-five-dollar party. He claims he left a hundred dollar bill on the table and wants to know if he can come in for the change we neglected to give him. He's on his way to talk to you."

Russ shook his head in disbelief. "Well, that's a new and interesting scam. Talk about *cojones*."

An elderly woman approached and interrupted their confabulation. "Excuse me," she said to Russ. "Are you the owner?"

"For a few more minutes, at least," Russ said.

"I hope you don't mind my asking," she said politely, "but is that an original Guy Ellis?" She indicated the painting above the musician's corner.

"His first name rhymes with 'key,' but yes, ma'am, it is," Russ told her, always happier to talk about art than commerce. Ellis, who was French and a mainstay of the Village art scene, became so frustrated with Americans mispronouncing both his first name and Henri, his middle name, that he eventually went solely by his last.

"Oh, I just knew it!" the woman exclaimed, nodding eagerly to her companion, another elderly matron. "I recognized the signature. Oh, my, it's just absolutely lovely!"

"Thank you," Russ said. "It's one of my favorites."

He may have understated it. He couldn't think of a painting he loved more than this one, which Ellis titled simply "Fall." It depicted the Pond in Central Park on a clear autumn day, the cerulean sky swept with mare's tails, the tall trees and brilliant foliage reflected vaguely in the cat's-paws on the water. In the distance, just a hint of the canyon of buildings beyond the park made the natural space seem that much more inviting. The style was impressionistic, the shapes indistinct. Two details gave the canvas motion and vibrancy: the slew of colorful leaves the breeze teased from the trees, and the solitary figure on the walk. With just a few careless-looking strokes, Ellis had created wind-tossed black curls, long, slender legs, and a shocking pink dress with just a hint of white slip along the fluttering hem. Although the woman's figure was small and squiggly, everything else in the broad canvas seemed to revolve around it, at least to Russ. In the corner was the trademark slanted *L* that Ellis, known to his Village friends simply as "Ell," used as a signature, along with the date, 1986. Relatively conventional by Ellis's usual standards, it often drew comments like this.

"This is our first time in New York," the woman went on, pleased to chat with an actual denizen of the city.

"Where are you ladies from?" Russ asked politely.

"Omaha," she replied. "We're doing a tour of the art museums but I must say, you have some very beautiful works on display right here."

"Well, Tweak's becoming a non-profit institution even as we speak," Russ said dryly.

"It's none of my business, I know, but just out of curiosity: how much did you pay for that Guy Ellis painting?" She pronounced the first name correctly this time.

Russ smiled. "It's on loan from the owner and is not for sale. But what else have you seen around town? What are your favorites?"

"Oh, we just loved the Museum of Modern Art," she gushed. "They have a Guy Ellis there, too, you know, as part of their century retrospective exhibit. That's how I happened to recognize the signature."

"Which one are they showing?"

"I think it was called 'Metamorphosis.' Are you familiar with it?"

"Oh, yes."

"Metamorphosis" had created something of a stir in the art community, especially here in the Village, though, at first glance, it was hard to see why. It was a large, portrait-shaped acrylic that depicted nothing more than a young man's naked torso, waist to shoulders. Lit by a startlingly rich, afternoon light, the slender torso seemed to rise above the canvas, seemed to beg to be touched. Though not exactly androgynous, the figure was graceful, the skin smooth and glabrous, the breasts contracted and erect, the paint of the nipples actually rising life-size from the canvas. The posture, with the arms raised above the shoulders, looked languid, like a stretch after just awakening. Behind the figure was the clear blue sky and an odd-shaped cloud, looking vaguely like a clearing storm.

But looking closer, one saw that a shadow fell oddly across the ribs on the left side, not necessarily a wound but perhaps a gap, an opening. And the cloud, on examination, seemed feathered, almost like wings. The painting, which Ellis was working on at the time of his death, seemed rough around the edges, possibly incomplete. But the gay community fell in love at first sight, claiming the combined images of crucifixion and male sensuality represented a reconciliation between gays and the Catholic church. Ellis was Catholic.

"I don't suppose you knew Mr. Ellis?" the woman asked Russ.

"No, ma'am, I didn't."

"I was just fascinated by the story about his losing his right arm in Vietnam and then teaching himself to paint with his left. It's sort of like what Leonardo da Vinci went through at the end of his life, don't you think?" she asked.

"I hadn't thought of it that way."

"You know, the blurb they had at the museum mentioned something about an 'alternate lifestyle'." She leaned closer to him conspiratorially, even though Christine and Oscar had long since gone about their business. "Do you think he was gay?"

"That's a question for his widow," Russ said, spotting a man coming toward them sheepishly. "But thanks for all your interest and for stopping at Tweak."

"Oh, thank you!" she said, rushing back to her companion.

"Mr. Jones?" the embarrassed gentleman asked. "I'm afraid I owe you an apology. I called earlier to complain that your waitress failed to bring me my change. Well, right after I called I found my hundred-dollar bill still in my vest pocket! I'm so sorry for the misunderstanding and please keep the change." He handed the bill to Russ.

"I'll pass it along to Christine," Russ told him. "I'm sure she'll appreciate it."

"Incidentally, the chicken and roasted pepper sandwich," the man went on, shaking Russ's hand, "was superb." He turned and left.

Oscar had come back over. "On the phone he complained about the food," he said in his soft voice. "Funny how things taste better when you're in the wrong."

Russ handed him the bill and said, "Here. Make Christine's day. I've got to go. See you tomorrow."

O   O   O

Outside, the sidewalks were wet but the rain had stopped. Couples of various styles and genders bustled along. Russ skirted between a taxi and a delivery truck stalled in traffic and ducked into the small 327 Bleeker Grocery.

"Hey, Sid," he said to the young guy behind the counter.

"Russell, my man!" Sid said. "I got those Panda licorices in."

"Maybe tomorrow," Russ said. "What's the score?"

"Still tied at two," Sid told him. "Bobby Cox just called a suicide squeeze with Maddux at the plate but Maddux missed the ball and Hershiser tagged Klesko comin' home. Double play. They didn't get nothin'."

"Amazing!" Russ cried, then waved and headed down Bleeker. The rain brought out the colorful palette of odors he had once heard euphemistically described as "musky": the Mediterranean pastries of Village Delight, the carbon tetrachloride from the dry cleaners across the street, the over-powering fragrance from the scent shop Enflourage, the stale urine of dogs and bums, the acrid exhaust of the traffic, the enticing aroma from the tobacco shop and all the other restaurants crowded together here. New York assaults the senses, sometimes brutally, but it's never dull.

Turning left on Grove, he decided to check out the entertainment competition. The usual quiet jazz at 53 Grove brought out the usual quiet bourgeoisie. Rose's Turn featured a Fred Astaire tribute followed by some gay dove magicians. In Arthur's Tavern some guys from Brooklyn cranked out some blues/rock from Alabama. At Maria's Crisis Cafe Judy Garlands and Frank Sinatras, spirits more alcoholic than ethereal, sat next to the piano, hoping to breathe new life into some old standard when the mike was free. Russ, as part of his ritual whenever he passed this spot, kissed his knuckle and touched it to the plaque commemorating Thomas Paine's death here at 59 Grove. Most things in life fall in that broad gray area between the sublime and the ridiculous.

Russ always cringed when he had to leave the peaceful enclave of the Village to cross Seventh Avenue, the never-ending traffic bleating and the subway entrances busily swallowing some people and spitting out others. But Christopher Park seemed to blot all that out, with its tall trees and odd collection of statuary: General Sheridan, coated with pigeon droppings and verdigris, gazing serenely at the pale gay and lesbian couples. Across Grove, the Monster, as usual, was packed to the gills, the piano swamped by the crowd, and Russ even spotted a couple of people who might actually have been women.

Les Deux Gamins, across Waverly from the old Northern Dispensary, made Tweak look vast. Also on a corner, it had one small room with a couple of steps up to an even smaller one. The decor was simple, eclectic, inexpensive, the menu a little more upscale than Tweak's. Americans like crowded places but, oxymoronically, they like to sit as far away as possible from other people. But force them to sit next to one another and they end up chatting and schmoozing and enjoying themselves. At tiny Les Deux Gamins, sitting far from others wasn't an option and a camaraderie often developed between the patrons.

The most conducive spot for this was next to the tiny wine-label-papered bathroom, below the big mirror framed by wine corks. A built-in wooden bench provided seating for three small tables and as usual the occupants of these tables already had broken the ice and seemed embroiled in a spirited discussion. Wine bottles cluttered the small tables, some, without labels, serving as water carafes, others, with labels, nearly empty.

At the center table of the three, Russ recognized Sylvia, her back to him, her long black hair shiny against her black pea coat. He walked behind her and put his hands on her shoulders and kissed the top of her head, her perfume, Magie Noir, lightly scenting her hair.

On the bench, next to the door to the restroom, sat the only other person he recognized: Michelle, a model Russ and Sylvia knew well.

Sylvia didn't look up at his touch. She did place her hands on his and she rubbed her cheek against his fingers. But the discussion went on.

"She wouldn't have the same mind as me, would she?" Michelle asked the others.

"She'd have the same brain," the man sitting by the window contended.

"Not even the same brain," said the Caribbean-looking man sitting across from Michelle. "At best, a faithful reproduction."

"That's not reproduction the way most people think of it," said the woman in the center of the bench.

"And I'm not sure faith has much to do with it," Sylvia said as Russ pulled up a chair behind her. "We're discussing clones," she explained to Russ. "Specifically, whether we should clone Michelle. Oh, this is Collette and Paul," referring to the woman across from her and the man by the window. "You know Michelle and this is her friend Carlos."

Michelle smiled when Russ greeted her. He would have been hard-pressed to find a better candidate for cloning. In her early 20s, she had long blonde hair, deep-set blue eyes, broad cheekbones, and a practiced grace. She had modeled for Sylvia several times, though most of her other work had been photographic. The only reason Russ considered Christine the most beautiful woman he'd ever seen (after Sylvia, of course) was that Michelle looked almost too perfect. He had trouble seeing her as a real person.

"Sexual procreation certainly isn't accurate reproduction," Paul said. He looked like a smaller, thinner version of Sean Connery: short gray hair, dark eyebrows, a mischievous glint in his dark eyes, an easy smile, simple but stylish clothing. "If you really wanted a reproduction of Michelle," he went on, smiling over at the original, "—Lord knows, *I* do— who would you put your faith in: God, in his infinite whimsy, or the lab tech in his white coat?"

"I'm pretty sure," Michelle said, unabashed, "that Sylvia was talking about a different kind of faith."

"Isn't faith, true faith, what a person actually believes?" Paul asked.

"Some people really do believe in God," Collette pointed out. She looked forty-ish, with green eyes and thick auburn hair piled in a loose bun on top of her head. She had painted her close-lipped mouth red and it punctuated a sensitive, sorrowful face.

"But how many people go to church believing that their lives will be tangibly better for it?" Paul asked, looking around the group.

No hands went up.

"How many people buy lottery tickets?"

Still no response.

"But many people do," Collette said, helpfully, hopefully. She seemed taken with Paul.

"This is not the average group of Americans," Carlos pointed out.

"I'll bet more people in this country play the lottery than go to church every week," Paul ventured. "That shows where their faith lies."

"You get the results of the lottery sooner," Sylvia conceded.

"I think we're on to something," Carlos said, inspired. "Screw bingo! Start a church lottery. Why deny churches the kind of dough the states rake in?"

"Replace the donation basket with scratch tickets," Paul suggested whimsically.

"Instant redemption!" Collette fantasized.

"Take a chance on a special dispensation from the pope," Paul added. "Rich people, of course, would have a better chance, the same as always."

"Our Lady of Perpetual Moola," Carlos said.

"The Father, the Son, and the Holy Numbered Ping Pong Ball," was Collette's version.

"What do you think, darling?" Sylvia asked Russ.

Normally, this type of discussion was right up Russ's alley. But at the moment he could hear the faint, distinctive sound of a sportscast on a transistor radio. Absently, he said, "You gotta believe."

"I'm afraid his mind is more on Mets than metaphysics," Sylvia apologized to the others. "I'd better get him home to a TV set."

"We should go, too," Michelle said to Carlos. "We need to get those proofs to Barry." She stood, a glimpse of belly showing between her low-slung, hip-hugging jeans and her tight shirt. She gathered up her appointment book and purse.

Russ could feel an elaborate set of farewells coming so he decided to take a chance. He walked up to the smaller room and pushed open the door to the kitchen. From the radio, the crowd cheered. "Did we win?" he asked.

The two cooks shrugged and shook their heads, not understanding him. The bartender, bringing in a bottle of liqueur for some glaze or sauce, said in a heavily French-accented voice, "Benitez shut zem down in ze tenth."

"*Merci*," Russ said to him and went back to the other room, where Michelle and Carlos had already left and Collette and Sylvia hugged. Outside, it was raining again.

"Is it over?" Sylvia asked Russ.

"Still tied, bottom of the tenth," Russ said. "Ready?"

"Where's the umbrella?"

Russ looked around blankly. "Damn!"

"Here," Paul offered, handing his own umbrella to Sylvia handle-first. "I just live a couple of doors down the street."

"Oh, we'd better not," Sylvia demurred. "How could we return it to you?"

"I come here for breakfast nearly every morning," Paul said, still holding the umbrella out to her. "Just drop it off sometime."

Sylvia relented, saying, "If you ever saw me with frizzy hair, you'd know what a favor this is. I've got an appointment in the morning but I'll bring it by here tomorrow afternoon."

"And if you don't," Paul said, standing, "it's just an umbrella. All I ask is that you think of me the next time it rains. It was nice meeting you, Sylvia, Russ."

Shaking Paul's hand, Russ suddenly became quite conscious of how thin his own hair had became, how portly his belly, how stiff his movements. He and Sylvia thanked Paul again and went out to the sidewalk, popping open the umbrella.

"See?" Sylvia said, putting her arm around Russ's waist as they walked back along Grove toward home. "Wasn't that discussion completely out of control? Thank you for rescuing me."

"I think Paul did more to rescue you than I did," Russ said. He almost never felt jealous of Sylvia but something about the way Paul had looked at her rankled in him. "Do you know him very well?"

"I used to work with him a long time ago," she said, contentedly resting her head on Russ's shoulder. "Anyway, you're my hero, my shining *chevalier*."

He looked down at her and smiled. He knew he could be forgiven the occasional pang of jealousy. While not possessing the sort of glitzy beauty that had put Michelle's face and cleavage on the cover of *Cosmopolitan*, Sylvia, a model too at times, looked great. Tonight she wore high-heeled black boots beneath her tight, faded jeans, a high-collared lacy shirt under her lavender sweater, and the calf-length wool pea coat. She had inherited her thick black hair, olive skin, and Roman nose from her Italian parents. Her deep brown eyes that glinted with flecks of gold, though, and her lips that changed expression nearly every moment, were distinctly her own. But those qualities barely scratched the surface. Sylvia's beauty, and Russ's love, ran much deeper. She had the most intriguing soul of any woman Russ had ever known.

o   o   o

They had met almost a decade ago. Russ had completed a rough outline and about 80 pages of the book Big Cat had inspired when he decided, once and for all, that living with his parents, despite the love all three felt for one another, was simply intolerable. The nicer they acted, the more encouraging they became, the more he resented feeling beholden to them. Further, his philosophical work had bogged down in anecdote and rhetoric. And, last but not least, the quiet twittering of the birds around the farm just couldn't compete with the siren song of Manhattan.

Over Ellen's protests, he searched the classifieds of the *Daily News* until he found a studio apartment to sublet on the Upper West Side. The tenant, a photojournalist, had gone to the Mideast to cover the Gulf War, leaving his furniture for Russ to use. There being no shortage of restaurants in Manhattan, Russ easily found work, and his computer skills and management experience made him indispensable to businesses trying to upgrade their accounting systems. Within weeks, his life-long fantasy about living and working in the City became a reality. True, living in Manhattan proved so expensive that he could rarely afford to do the things that drew him there in the first place. But he got by, taking the subway out to Flushing to see the Mets play, catching the free concerts in the parks, going to the museums only for special exhibits.

One such special exhibit was a Jackson Pollack show at the Museum of Modern Art. He got there early and savored not only the Pollacks but also the Klees and Miros as well as the new tribute to Guy Ellis. About midafternoon he'd had to take a break. Gravitating as usual to MOMA's peaceful cul-de-sac that contained Monet's big water-lily triptych, he sat next to a young woman dressed all in black. She had short wavy black hair, sad furtive eyes, and what appeared to be the weight of the world on her shoulders. Using nothing more than his native goofiness, he succeeded in making her smile. In the decade since, he'd gotten pretty good at it.

In fact, she smiled up at him now. "Do you realize," Sylvia said, "that's the first time I've ever seen you go by that Thomas Paine plaque without doing your knuckle kiss?"

"Shows how much you know," he said in mock derision. "I did it on the way over."

"I thought you had to do it every time."

He had a thorough, arcane set of rules governing all such things that baffled even Sylvia. "I have to knuckle-kiss it any day that I walk by it but once I do it, it's done for the day," he explained patiently.

She stopped and turned her face up to his for a kiss. "You know why I love you?" she asked, her voice soft amid the patter of rain on Paul's umbrella.

It was a stock question, over the years eliciting responses from Russ such as "Brain lesions," "Somebody has to," and "Cary Grant's dead." Tonight he quoted S. J. Perelman: "Because before they made me, they broke the mold."

She always agreed with his response and she did so again, waiting for the traditional second kiss. Then she tugged his arm down Bleeker. "I need to get some hose," she told him.

They walked half a block to the Strawberry Fields Market. While she searched through the plastic eggs, he noticed the tiny black-and-white TV by the check stand. To his amazement, the Mets game was still on, Bobby Bonilla pinch-hitting for somebody.

"What inning is it?" he asked the checker, an older Asian woman.

"No idea," she said, glancing apathetically at the TV. "Chou left it on."

"I can't believe they're playing in this rain," Russ said but realized no one else cared.

When Sylvia found and bought her hose, they opened the umbrella and started for home, passing a "One Way" sign on Bleeker on which the "One" had been taped over and "Your" written in its place.

"Do you know why I'm so happy?" Sylvia asked him.

"Because you're a little drunk, you have brand new pantyhose, the Mets are still alive, and your husband's handsome, virile, and wealthy," Russ guessed.

"Half of that new gallery they're opening in Dia will be my paintings," Sylvia said, Dia being a relatively new, cutting-edge group of galleries on the Lower West Side. "They're opening New Year's Eve."

"That's wonderful!" Russ exclaimed. She had been trying for this for months.

"Come with me," she pleaded.

"God, New Year's Eve," Russ said, thinking about what a night that was shaping up to be. "I'll try. What time? Midnight?"

"I don't know. I'll ask them tomorrow."

"Is that where you're going in the morning?"

"Yes. I'm meeting Colin at ten to discuss which paintings."

"What about Paul?"

"Who?"

He raised his eyebrows and bobbed the umbrella.

"Oh, that's right," she said. "No, remember? I told him I'd bring it by in the afternoon."

They stopped to key in the code to open the heavy wrought-iron gate at Grove Court. It clanged shut behind them as they walked across the mossy brick courtyard. Formed-concrete planters overflowed with thick ivy and bedraggled impatiens. Overhead an ivy-covered ailanthus tree dropped a few small yellow leaves along with the rain. The summer, unbearably hot and dry, had proven a record-breaking drought and then in September Hurricane Floyd had dumped a summer's worth of rain in a few days. New Yorkers couldn't even hope for the usual brilliant fall; they just prayed the few trees outside the park would survive.

Formed by the bend in Grove Street, Grove Court is a three-story block of half a dozen brick townhouses separated from the quiet street by this triangular courtyard. Built in 1854 by a man named Samuel Cocks, it soon had acquired the disreputable name "Mixed Ale Alley." With the gentrification of the Village, though, it had become a rather exclusive address, although, since it fell between 10 and 12 Grove, it technically had no address at all.

Russ and Sylvia went in the entrance and Russ got the mail while Sylvia shook the rain from the umbrella and folded it up. They went up the two flights of stairs, jiggled the key in their old front door, and were home.

Typical of New York, what made the townhome exclusive was the location, not the size. It consisted of a small living room, a cramped kitchen to the rear, and two bedrooms, one facing the street, where Sylvia kept her studio, the other in back where they slept. Their furnishings suited the place: his black leather-upholstered easy chair, her over-stuffed couch, the small entertainment center by the window. The walls, not surprisingly, displayed quite a bit of original art, mostly Sylvia's, of course, but also pieces by other prominent Village artists, including some eye-catching abstracts by Guy Ellis.

Samuel Cocks had constructed Grove Court well but inexpensively and the hot water heat, unnecessary until this first real storm of the fall, had come on with a vengeance. Russ flipped on the TV and then closed the valve on the radiator and opened a window.

Sylvia took off the pea jacket and asked him, "Did you get dinner?"

Russ, stunned to find the Mets game still on, didn't reply. Mets manager Bobby Valentine brought in starter Octavio Dotel as the ninth Met pitcher, leaving just yesterday's and tomorrow's starters in the bullpen. It looked like Dotel's game the rest of the way. Russ leafed through the mail.

Sylvia, assuming Russ's lack of reply meant that he hadn't eaten, brought out half a sandwich on a plate and a bottle of Guinness and set them on the TV stand next to the easy chair.

"What's this?" Russ asked, taking her hand.

"I got a smoked salmon sandwich at Gamins and couldn't eat it all."

The sandwich, one of his favorites, made his mouth water: smoked salmon, thin-sliced hard-boiled egg, wilted basil, and some *pesto alla genovese* on a French roll. "You know why I love you?" he asked Sylvia, kissing her knuckles.

"Because, without me, you wouldn't last two days," Sylvia said, without fear of contradiction. She sat on the arm of the easy chair and pulled the sweater over her head. "Any mail for me?"

"Something from Idant Laboratories," he said, handing it to her.

She looked at the envelope without opening it. "Is it that time already?" she asked herself.

"Something important?" he asked her absently, watching a replay of Dotel's pitch sequence.

"I'll deal with it later," she told him, slipping the envelope into her pocket.

"That's a pretty blouse," he said, taking a bite of the sandwich now that a commercial interrupted the game. "Is it new?" Something about it…

The blouse was cream-colored silk with a high lace collar and *faux*-ivory buttons. "Would you like it?" she offered, unbuttoning the top two buttons. She wore nothing underneath and her firm dark nipples showed plainly, enticingly, through the silk.

"I thought you ovulated next week," Russ pointed out. Ever since they had started trying to get pregnant, sex seemed to have an ulterior purpose.

"This is now," she said, leaning down to kiss his neck.

As usual, he wanted what she had to give. Two things stood in the way of his taking it right now: he still had a mouthful of sandwich and the game came back on. Swallowing, he said, "This is bound to be over soon. The Mets are out of pitchers."

"Maybe I'll go paint for a while," she said, kissing his forehead.

Atlanta manager Bobby Cox had gone deep into his bullpen as well but the looming figure of John Rocker still warmed up vigorously. The Mets better do something soon, Russ thought, because there probably won't be much later.

The phone rang and Sylvia answered it on her way back to the studio. Within moments she was laughing. He could tell from her voice it was someone she spoke to rarely but fondly. Russ closed his eyes and luxuriated in the happy sound.

"It's John Kaufman," she said, handing the cordless phone to him.

"*Jacque, mon frere,*" he said, pleased, sitting up. "*Comment allez vous?*"

"I haven't been called 'Jacque' since the last time I talked to Matt," John said, amused.

"Sorry. I'm eating French bread."

"How is Matt, anyway?"

"He sounded fine when I called him last summer," Russ said. "How are you? I saw Estes on the news last night. Are the girls okay? Was the incident at their school?"

"Yes, Anne and Alice are both fine," John said. "It did happen at Anne's school but she wasn't involved."

"Thank goodness," Russ said. "What's with all the school violence lately? Is this some extension of the Black Trenchcoat Mafia?"

"Not exactly but this is already the biggest story here in Estes since the dam broke," John said. "Boy, Russ, school's changed a lot since we went to Cheyenne Mountain thirty-odd years ago. In some ways you're lucky you don't have kids."

"But I might someday, who knows?" Russ said, hedging. He hadn't broached the subject of their fruitless efforts outside his family. "So what happened?"

"Well, as I said, this isn't exactly like Columbine but there are some similarities. And you know, after they just arrested one of Harris and Klebold's classmates for threatening to 'finish the job,' the authorities aren't taking any chances."

"Oh, yeah, I saw that in the *Times*. So what happened up there in Estes?"

"I guess Terrell Haskins, who is the star of the basketball team and a good student—and according to Anne, a pretty decent guy for the most part—was teasing another student named Wayne Giles, who is a bit of a misfit, from what I've heard. So Wayne pulled a gun from his locker and threatened to blow Terrell away."

"Jesus," Russ said. "I didn't exactly run with the in-crowd when I was in school but it never crossed my mind to do something like that. In fact, you were a jock and a socialite and yet you and I were good friends."

"Gimme a break," John said. "I don't know that you were that much of an outcast, as you proved at the reunion. And I certainly wasn't that much of a jock, despite my initials."

"Don't you still hold some swimming records?"

"In any case," John said, breezing past it, "jockdom has changed a lot since we were in school. I mean, if Michael Jordan decided to unretire from basketball again, he could make more for missing a free-throw than Bill Bradley made for a season. The big kids in school, the ones who are good at sports, have always had advantages socially and now, if they're good enough or snazzy enough, they can count on incredible financial success as well. Terrell Haskins already has a scholarship to Duke and if he continues to improve—he's already an excellent forward—he may end up in the NBA before he graduates. Wayne Giles, on the other hand, smart as he is, may struggle just to stay in the upper middle class like his parents, making one percent of Terrell's starting salary. It sure adds to the tension."

"It's the jock version of the lottery," Russ agreed, thinking about the earlier discussion, watching hyperactive, highly paid John Rocker dash onto the field at Shea.

"I've been thinking about that lately. The state-run lotteries reinforce the same message, broadcast as news on TV: success in our society is often nothing more than just dumb luck or brute strength."

"You sound pretty worked up about this."

"Oh, I could write volumes."

"Why don't you?"

"Actually, I am writing one part of this story but not that. Tim's writing up the gun-related issues and I'm covering drugs, since they found marijuana in Wayne Giles's room."

"That should be interesting," Russ said, knowing John's continued use of same.

"I may want to discuss that with you sometime," John said. "But how are things in Gotham, anyway? Sylvia says she's fine; we didn't waste our time talking about you."

"Sylvia is beyond fine," Russ said.

"You've got a lot of honey there."

"I feel like a bulimic bee," watching her walk into the kitchen.

Despite the open window, the townhouse still felt close. Sylvia, now wearing just the blouse and her panties, had gone to the refrigerator and taken a fudgesicle from the freezer. She sat on the arm of Russ's chair again, sliding the confection across her lips as she idly watched the game. Noticing that Russ watched her more than the game, she unbuttoned the silk blouse all the way and left fudgesicle trails across her sternum and belly.

"But how are you doing?" John asked. "Did I catch you at a bad time?"

"You caught me at a great time," Russ said, closing his eyes as Sylvia rubbed her sticky hand across his crotch.

"I could call back later if you like," John said, hearing Sylvia's sultry chuckle.

"Wouldn't help," Russ told him. "Sylvia will be fine later too, I assure you."

"Well, give her a little tweak for me, you old Tweakster," John said with a chuckle. "How is Tweak, anyway? Have you got it tweaked just right yet?"

"The restaurant cooks right along. It's doing so well, in fact, that I've added a new wrinkle: live music."

"Excellent!" John said. "Live bands? Could this be a gig for the Argonauts?"

Russ laughed. "I don't know what your bass playing is like but I'm no kind of a drummer anymore. Besides, I can't afford the space, the volume, the hassles, or the money for a band. I'm just hiring solo acts and that's already complicated enough for me. And the only Argonaut that could pull off a solo act is long gone."

"He's part of the reason I called."

"You know, he's been in my thoughts a lot the last couple of months," Russ said wistfully. "It's only natural, I suppose, with Amanda's passing."

"I saw your names on the list of donors to the World Wildlife fund," John said. "Man would have liked that, I know."

"I doubt if anyone but you knew who Russell and Sylvia Jones were, though," Russ said. "I wish I could have made it out for the service but after coming out for the reunion just a month before, there was no way I could get away again."

"I didn't get to the Springs for it, either. I've just been swamped lately."

"Her passing affected me more than I thought possible, I must admit," Russ went on. "Partly because I found after she was gone that I respected her greatly. It's so easy to take it for granted that someone like that will always be there, that one day you'll get around to expressing how you feel. But partly it's because of the really odd coincidence in where both she and Jason disappeared. Did they ever find her body?"

"Not that I heard," John said. "And she and Jason disappeared on opposite sides of Pikes Peak, actually. Many miles apart."

"Still, it's odd. And it's odd to have to hold a service without a body. And then holding it on the last total eclipse of the millennium too. Weird. How's her daughter taking it? What was her name?"

"May," John said. "And to tell you the truth, she's not taking it very well."

"Manny was always pretty thin-skinned, too. May must be more like her mother than her father that way."

"That's where the plot thickens. Manny left behind a bit of a mystery."

"Just one?"

"May came up here to Estes on Friday to talk to me."

"Wow. What's she like? I haven't seen her since she was a toddler."

"Well, she's all grown up now, with a daughter of her own," John said. "She's got a lot of grown-up problems, too. Manny tried to solve one of them and created another. She left her the house up in Cheyenne Cañon but along with it came a couple of interesting documents, one of which you signed."

"Wait a minute," Russ said, his heart sinking as he watched the dreaded Chipper Jones hit a double off Dotel. Keith Lockhart hoofed it around the bases from first only to run right into Mike Piazza guarding the plate for the Mets, Piazza limping back to the dugout but the score still tied.

"Are you sure I didn't catch you at a bad time?" John asked.

"Oh, I'm watching this doggone Mets game, which is like four-and-a-half hours old. Sorry. Anyway, you were talking about some document I signed? Is this a legal document?"

"I'll fax it to you, along with the incriminating photograph. You can judge for yourself whether it's legally binding."

"What the hell are you talking about?" Russ asked, intrigued.

"Let me ask you this: what are you doing New Year's Eve?"

"I don't know. Going crazy. Why?"

"Because according to this signed document, we're getting together in Colorado Springs on New Year's Eve."

Russ chuckled, then guffawed. "You must be joking. I could get away from Alcatraz easier than from Tweak that night. What are you talking about?"

John read him the text of the Piñon Nuts pledge.

"That's a riot!" Russ said. "Oh, the callowness of youth!"

"That may be," John pointed out. "But you did sign it and failing to meet the pledge puts you at risk of 'dismemberment, excommunication, ridicule, and worse.' Is the mere survival of Tweak worth the risk of failing to show?"

"Seriously, John," Russ said in his adult/business voice, "I couldn't possibly get away, much as I would love to see you and Matt again. Have you talked to him about this?"

"I don't even have his number anymore. I tried information, but it's unlisted. I was hoping you'd call him."

"Oh, he'd get more of a laugh out of this than I did. You know what he's been working on at Novagen? At least when I last spoke to him?"

"What's that?"

"The Y2K bug! It's not like he'll have anything to do that day."

"Holey moley!" John laughed. "I knew you guys would find excuses not to do this but this is above and beyond."

"It's too bad," Russ admitted. "An Argonauts reunion is out of the question, of course, since you and I at least haven't got three licks left between us. But the Piñon Nuts—well, I think we would all still know how to eat. And all too often I find myself cooking again."

"Oh, I'm sure we could put on a hell of a spread," John said. Then his voice turned serious too. "But even if we don't get together in person, there's something we ought to discuss. Along with the Piñon Nuts pledge was a letter from Jason to Amanda."

"No kidding. What does it say?"

"Well, as you know, Jason wrote a formidable letter and this definitely ranks up there with the classics. Much of it I can't make head nor tail of. But May thinks one passage implies—and I can see her point of view—that she's actually Jason's daughter and that Amanda tried to have her aborted."

Russ sat slack-jawed and speechless while this news sank in. "What did you tell her?" he asked at last.

"I said it was theoretically possible. Isn't it?"

"I suppose. Only Amanda would know for sure. Has May had any kind of paternity testing done?"

"Well, she just found this stuff last Tuesday. And I counseled her not to get her hopes up too far. In fact, I don't see much advantage in her being Jason's daughter. I mean, what does it get her?"

"Well, if nothing else, a far different heritage than she's assumed was hers so far."

"Yeah, but Jason left almost nothing behind. I don't even know if his mother's still alive.

Do you?"

"I wouldn't have the foggiest notion. But speaking of theoretically possible, what about Jason himself?"

John sighed. "You're not still holding out hope for that."

"That's the difference between you and me. For me, hope is a thing with feathers," Russ said, watching the battered Mike Piazza stride to the batter's box once more.

"But do you want to get May's hopes up based on that?"

Russ thought about it. "No, I guess not."

"May's got enough problems as it is. Even if she's not Jason's daughter, she is Amanda's daughter and I'd like to think there's something we could do to help her out."

"Like what?"

"At least fill in some of the blanks about what her mother went through back then, what we all went through back then."

"John, that all happened thirty years ago. I don't know about you but I'm having trouble remembering last week."

"All the more reason we should get together and pool our knowledge."

Russ laughed. "I'm not sure the three of us combined could muster more than a puddle of knowledge."

"Just the fact that we got together and talked about it would mean a lot to May, I'm sure."

"You're still lobbying for a New Year's Eve Gathering."

"You did sign the thing."

"You know, ironically, we really could have it at the old house."

Russ's father, Louie, did much of his television production work on the East and West Coasts but had decided to raise Russ and Gina in the more normal, middle-American community of Colorado Springs. When Louie bought the house at Mesa and Cresta, it came with a zoning variance that the previous owner, who had a partially-disabled child, had procured in order to install the elevator. Even after Louie and Ellen moved to New York, Louie held on to the house, planning to expand the variance to make it a commercial property. The nearby Broadmoor Hotel raised hell with the zoning commission but since the hotel itself, a decidedly-for-profit enterprise, was owned by the non-profit El Pomar Foundation at the time, a special act of the U. S. Congress was required to maintain the Foundation's tax-free status. The zoning commission, despite the pressure of the hotel's powerful lawyers, didn't appreciate the pot calling the kettle black and sided with Louie. He converted the home into an exclusive, intimate restaurant called Crestwood which, despite the inevitable problems of having local management but out-of-state ownership, prospered. In 1985, when he retired, Louie sold it to a Houston conglomerate that owned several landmark Colorado restaurants. They expanded the basement into more kitchen space and storage, retrofitted the elevator to serve all three floors, redecorated, and reopened, retaining the Crestwood name. It continued to thrive.

"You think we could get a table in the same room, the old dining room?" John asked.

"Well, let's see. Last I heard, Eric Van Deutch was still managing the place. My mother and Lucy Van Deutch still exchange Christmas cards so I probably could get a hold of her that way. Maybe she could put in a good word for us. There's just one thing we better watch out for."

"What's that?"

"Flying pigs."

John laughed. "How so?"

"Well, I'm sure when Tweak runs so smoothly I can take off the busiest night of its existence—*and* I can somehow get out of attending Sylvia's gallery opening that night—*and* when you and Matt can disrupt whatever plans you have—*and* when Crestwood struggles to book their finest room for this New Year's Eve—surely by then pigs will be flying."

John laughed again. "Hey, you and Matt may have to fly but this little piggy can drive all the way there."

Gloom soaked the feathers of Russ's hope for the Mets. In the top of the 15th, Keith Lockhart exacted his revenge for being thrown out at the plate in the 13th by driving a triple to right center, scoring Walt Weiss from second. Trailing by a run, the Mets would need another miracle.

"Listen, John," Russ said, depressed, "it's your dime but right now I don't see any way of getting out of here alive for months, and especially that night."

"At least call Matt and tell him about this stuff. Maybe fax that Piñon Nuts pledge to him too."

"I'd be glad to talk to Matt. We haven't spoken in a while anyway. But like I said, his schedule could prove even more prohibitive than mine. So don't get your hopes up. Or May's, for that matter."

"Hope springs eternal, my friend."

"That's what I hear," Russ said. At the moment despair had taken hold of him.

"Boy, I'm sure there was something else I was supposed to ask you," John said in the pause. "Anyway, I'll let you get back to the game. Give my best to the beautiful Sylvia."

"Mine will have to do."

"Take care."

"You too."

O   O   O

Russ hung up and went to the bathroom. When he came out he peeked into the studio to check on Sylvia.

Slightly larger than their bedroom, the studio was cluttered with her art supplies: boxes of paints, thinners, brushes, charcoals. Her sturdy work table, broad, tilted slightly, and butted up against the window sill, held an agglomeration of preliminary drawings, doodles, correspondence, and pictures torn from magazines, as well as the lacquered steel shell-casing she used as a brush holder. A wooden bin overflowed with rolled-up, unstretched canvases and square frames. Various paintings hung on the walls, some, merely sketches, haphazardly tacked up, others, completed and framed, placed with care. One such, in the center of the long wall, was an early, magnificent Guy Ellis abstract entitled "Stonewall," a blue and steel-gray square surrounded by slashes and streaks of bright fundamental colors: red, black, yellow, orange.

In addition to the smell of oil paints, Russ could smell marijuana smoke. Sylvia, echoing recently released memoirs of the late Carl Sagan, felt marijuana freed up her mind, allowed her to find creative artistic solutions that didn't seem to come to her otherwise. Getting high also made her horny.

Russ had smoked dope back in college days but hadn't touched it in decades. He liked the effect it had on her a lot more than the effect it had on him: it made him sleepy, dull, and morose. But he had come to relish the smell of it nonetheless. It gave him a sort of contact horniness.

Beneath her unbuttoned silk blouse Russ could make out the vertebrae of Sylvia's spine as she worked. When she got high, she painted with a single-minded intensity to the exclusion of the world around her. But he knew that if he made just one slightly suggestive remark, she would drop the paintbrush in an instant.

Fifteen years younger than he, she longed for a baby. For eighteen months they'd timed their love-making to correspond to her ovulation, so far without result. No, results galore: fabulous love-making that left them both panting and limp. Just no pregnancy.

Maybe he was shooting blanks. Her gynecologist could find nothing obviously wrong. Six months ago Russ's doctor had counseled them to keep trying a while longer, saying that babies come from magic and chance more than science, and that if a few more months of determined effort proved fruitless he would test him. Russ's annual check-up came up in a couple of weeks and Russ had already phoned the office to make sure they would test his fertility.

Sylvia's first marriage had ended without children, but she told Russ that they had "never really tried." His own first marriage, to Becky, who had two children from a previous marriage, had bogged down in raising her kids, paying the bills, and participating in the school. Toward the end they had made an effort to conceive, hoping that children of their own might give them unbreakable ties. But, as the Mets could attest, there's no such thing in this world as an unbreakable tie.

Without saying anything to Sylvia, Russ went back into the living room to watch the end of the game. He felt discouraged. For the first time in his life, having a baby really felt like the right thing to do and now he couldn't seem to do it. He had already braced himself that parenthood would mean even less sleep and even more work and an infinite amount of love. When they had broached the subject to Ellen, she had joked that he probably would have to bypass having children and go right to having grandchildren. The other new parents he knew were half his age. He didn't care. He wanted to do this.

Now the only question was how. Had he waited too long? Had that ship sailed without so much as a toot of its horn?

He sighed and sat back down in the easy chair. It looked like the Mets' season was coming to a close too. Shawon Dunston, who hadn't been able to reach Lockhart's drive that put Atlanta ahead, led off the bottom of the 15th, already the longest game in post-season history. The wily veteran fouled off six pitches in a row with the count 3-2, then managed to eke out a single. Bobby Valentine pinch-hit for Dotel, meaning the Mets would almost have to recruit someone from the stands to pitch the 16th if they somehow managed to tie the game. Then a walk and a sacrifice put men at second and third, and another intentional walk to John Olerud loaded the bases. A double play at any of the bases would end the Mets' season. But then the Braves' pitcher Kevin McGlinchy did the unthinkable: he walked pinch-hitter Todd Pratt to retie the game.

Russ sat up in his chair. If the Mets didn't score here, God only knew how they could even put nine men on the field for the next inning. But, for the moment at least, there was hope. Robin Ventura came to the plate. He ran the count to 2-1 and then launched a rocket that sailed over the fence and out of the park, a grand slam home run.

The place went berserk. The Mets poured from the dugout and mobbed Ventura before he made it to second, the winning run having already scored. They got so carried away, Ventura never made it around the bases, making his hit possibly the longest game-winning single in history.

Russ had never seen anything like it. There had never *been* anything like it. "Yes!" he shouted, jumping to his feet. "Yes, yes, yes!" It felt like a sign. It *had* to be sign. But what did it mean?

"Did we win?" Sylvia called from the studio.

In a flash, he knew exactly what it meant. He strode purposefully down the hall.

Sylvia, still wearing just the blouse and panties, sat curled up where her work table met the window ledge of the studio, staring out at the rain pelting the silent courtyard below. He smiled, thinking of her as his Window Syl. Many an inspiration for a painting had come while she sat thus.

Sylvia's favorite Guy Ellis watercolor, "Pensive," hung just behind her. It caught Russ's eye and then stopped him dead in his tracks.

Modest in size and subject compared to most of Ellis's other work, nothing else he ever did better displayed the subtlety of his technique. His brush, in applying the watercolor to the paper, seemed rather to have drawn the color from it. It depicted, in the soft tones of early spring and in the soft light of this same window, Sylvia, sitting almost exactly the way she sat now, wearing this same cream-colored, lace-collared blouse.

The day Russ met her at the Museum of Modern Art, her black apparel represented not a fashion statement but widow's weeds for her late husband, Guy Ellis. She had come to the museum that day in December of 1989 to approve the exhibit of his work on the first anniversary of his death.

Everything Russ knew about Guy Ellis that day he had learned from the captions on the paintings in the exhibit. One thing he knew about Sylvia from the moment they met was that Ellis's death had utterly devastated her. Even though a year had passed since his death, Russ sensed that her heart had taken refuge deep within her like some timid forest creature hiding in its den. With great patience and tenderness he had gradually drawn her out, succeeding where her other friends from the Village had failed largely because he had no association with Ellis. But, as a consequence, Russ knew less than many other Villagers about Ellis and his marriage to Sylvia, since at first she hadn't wanted to talk about it and, after enough time went by to heal the wounds, neither of them wanted to dredge up difficult memories.

When Russ and Sylvia married, they discussed moving out of the Grove Court townhome Ellis had bought in the 1960s but neither could imagine a place they would rather live. Sylvia assured Russ that she felt the place was hers as much as Ellis's; Russ, for his part, assured her that he didn't believe in ghosts.

But now a ghost had popped up. Russ had never seen her wear that blouse before. He didn't realize she still owned it. Why wear it now, today? What had changed? Could their unsuccessful struggle to have children, to realize their union in a way she and Ellis never had, have left her nostalgic for the immense spirit that still pervaded this place?

Those doubts soon faded, though, overshadowed by desire. If "Pensive" described the mood of the subject in Ellis's watercolor, "desire" described the mood of the artist, and now of the observer. As fascinating as Ellis's portrayal of Sylvia unarguably was, the real person, sitting there with her knee tucked under her arm, her blouse casually falling open, was a hundred times more appealing.

She sighed, turned, and saw Russ standing there. "Did we win?" she asked again.

"Yes," he said, sitting in the chair at the work table, running his finger along her smooth calf. "We pulled off another miracle."

"So, do you want this blouse now?" she offered, slipping the silk from her shoulders.

He took it from her, allowing himself a lingering look at her pale breasts, then looking down at the creamy silk in his hand. "How come I've never seen you wear this before?" he asked, glancing at the watercolor on the wall.

She looked at "Pensive" too. "He painted that the day we decided to marry," she told him.

"I didn't know that," he said. "But…"

"I went to Zena to talk about Ell and she asked me to bring something that reminded me of him, so I wore this."

"What did you talk about?" he asked her. "What did she say?"

She looked into his eyes for a few moments but then went back to gazing out the window without a reply.

"I'll tell you what," Russ said. "When you're ready, you'll talk about it. But if you ask me, I think a part of you is still holding onto Ellis and just can't let go."

She turned around and said, "You know something? You're right." She kicked out her foot, brushing the Idant Laboratories envelope from the work table. She slid her bottom down onto the cluttered table, then pulled her panties down from her hips, past her legs, and tossed them aside.

Russ looked at her naked body stretched out on the sturdy work table. "But what about —?"

"Tonight's the night," she said.

He stood to unbutton his pants. This might be an artless, animal urge but it felt right. "Tonight's the night," he agreed.

...O...O...O...

The Fourth of July doesn't conjure up my best memories. For one thing, I suppose, I often end up working that night, so I miss the fireworks. Actually, sometimes I miss the fireworks even when I don't work. One year I had Independence Day off in Billings, Montana, so, along with the rest of hoi polloi, I marched over to the municipal stadium and plunked down my hard-earned cash to see the big Fourth of July extravaganza.

Now, I don't know a soul in Billings, so when I scanned the bleachers, I saw just my fellow Americans: blue jeans, T-shirts, athletic shoes, baseball and cowboy hats, cigarettes, beer, and soft drinks, with corporate logos plastered over everything. Parents reined in the kids, young couples made out, babies squalled, old folks smiled, serene in the knowledge that all of that folderol was behind them. Plop me down in almost any crowd in any town and ask me where I am, I'll only be able to say, "America."

But this much I'll say with dead certainty: not one of those folks in the bleachers had a part in planning that fireworks show. When at last the summer dusk faded and the big yellow moon rose from the Montana plains, the Fireworks Wizards took the field and began igniting the assembled rows of mortars, which exploded with ear-splitting noise, flinging their charges high into that Big Sky.

Unfortunately, the bleachers in Billings are covered. So we could feel the thunderous explosions high above our heads and bask, I suppose, in the reflected glory of the dazzling display. I'm sure the highly-paid Wizards on the field got an eyeful of their own spectacle. The rich folks in the big houses up on the bluff probably sat on their porches, sipped their drinks, and admired the show. But hoi polloi in the bleachers couldn't see a thing.

Not that I begrudge the rich folks their success. The American concept of luxury leaves me cold anyway. One of my greatest disappointments about my own generation is how similar our definition of luxury is to our parents' definition. SUVs have replaced big-finned Cadillacs and instead of lighting a cigar with a $100 bill, the rich use a platinum Master Card, but the effect is the same. The word "luxury," once a pejorative term, is related to "luxate," to put out of joint or dislocate. I agree with Hamlet: The time is out of joint.

But as the non-profit prophet said, "My people love to have it so." And like him, I wonder, "what will ye do in the end thereof?" But enough of my Jeremiad. The rich will have their houses on the bluff. The poor in spirit, I hear, have dibs on the kingdom of heaven. The rest of us, the poor in fact, will be stuck in the covered bleachers.

July 4, 1969

Russ's worst nightmare came true.

The original plan for this summer had been to accompany his father to New York, where Louie hoped to shoot a TV commercial for Lucky Strikes. The company, though, got wind of a rumor of a ban on commercials for cigarettes and decided to cancel the spot. So two weeks ago, Russ, yielding to Ellen's ever more insistent reminders, had taken a job bussing tables in the main dining room at the Broadmoor.

The main dining room was pleasant enough, with the north wall mirrored and a large round yellow-glassed skylight in the center of the room lighting a fountain surrounded by variegated philodendrons. Chairs of *faux* bamboo with an imitation needle-point floral pattern on the cushions complemented the formal white tablecloths and flowers in crystal bud vases and white china with black stripes and a gilt Broadmoor "B" constituted the table settings.

None of the fine surrounds made the work any easier, though. It was bad enough making scrawny wages for hefty work, bustling about silently, deferentially, in a busboy's dorky black waistcoat. Worse was the dread that someone he knew from high school would come in for dinner and see him working there.

The sun, about to set, still toasted the seats by the west-facing windows and as he cleared the table he could feel drops of sweat coursing down the back of his neck. The seemingly endless stream of diners, most over-heated and surly from celebrating the Fourth, had become just a faceless blur. So as he whisked the last few wrinkles from the white table cloth and straightened the forks, he muttered to the couple waiting, "Enjoy your dinner." His worst dread was realized when it turned out to be Bill Black pulling out a chair for Amanda Tyree.

Bill Black played varsity sports at Cheyenne and drove a new Mustang from his father's dealership. He and Russ had had the same gym period senior year and Russ vividly recalled him drying off his muscled naked body in the locker room, singing, presumably of God, "He's got the whole world, by the balls," *u. s. w.*

Russ knew Amanda only through Jason and John, who had gone to school with her for years, John since grade school. Russ didn't find her as pretty or outgoing as some of the other girls in their class but he nevertheless shared his friends' opinion that her wit, intelligence, and integrity put her in a class of her own. So he felt a little dismayed at seeing Amanda out with Bill Black, a rich insensitive boor, in Russ's opinion.

But his dismay ran deeper than that. One of Amanda's casual friends, Leslie Adamson, represented, in Russ's eyes, God's best effort to date in creating the perfect woman. Even though making something happen with Leslie amounted to nothing more than a daydream, he knew that having Amanda report to her how dorky he looked working as a busboy certainly wouldn't help his cause. Even though his cover had already been blown, he nevertheless turned on his heels and fled the dining room.

He skulked around in the kitchen awhile, letting the other busboys handle the floor as much as possible, so he wouldn't have to go out and face Bill and Amanda again. By the time they left at 9:30, the dining room had quieted down and he could clear their plates in relative peace.

What a way to spend his Fourth of July. He silently cursed his fate as he gazed through the window at everyone else leisurely enjoying the evening.

He couldn't spot an empty chair out on the terrace overlooking the small lake. His shift wouldn't end till ten, after all the legitimate fireworks displays would long since have drifted away. The only fireworks display he would see this year consisted of some prissy young girls prancing about twirling red and green sparklers. Oh, and some geezer with a fat cigar and a copy of the *Wall Street Journal* using his gold sparkler as a baton to direct "The Stars and Stripes Forever," which wafted out through the open doors of the Terrace Lounge. Dex Walker, Jason's father, played the piano in the lounge. A large crowd had gathered around the table where Dan Rowan and Dick Martin, *Laugh-In* on summer break, sat joking and doing schtick the night before they opened across the street in the International Center. Russ missed it all because he had to clean up other people's slop.

Amanda had ordered the shrimp Madras. She couldn't finish it all and evidently couldn't bring herself to ask for a doggy bag so she had left the rice and a few shrimp in a corner of the plate with her knife and fork across it. Bill, on the other hand, had stubbed out his cigarette in the fat outer portion of his prime rib, which Russ found revolting but completely in character for Bill.

He hoisted the full tray onto his shoulder and carried it into the kitchen. He set it on the racks outside the steamy cubby hole where Lucky Lowe, the dishwasher, rinsed the dishes and rammed them into the machine, singing, to the tune of the bridge of "Zippity Do Dah:"

> I've got elbows on my fingers
> It's my tooth, it's fractured
> Gotta get some manufactured

Russ liked Lucky, found him an interesting character. He stood a head shorter than Russ with a sagging beer belly, arms like Popeye's, a flattop haircut, and an odd rolling gait when he walked. He sported a crooked grin of teeth so rotten they regularly dropped out when he used a toothpick and a husky voice which, when not being used more prosaically, invariably belted out some upbeat tune with the words badly mangled.

"How goes the battle, Lucky?" Russ asked him.

"Making a dollar a minute!" Lucky bragged, barely breaking stride from the song. "How you doing, young fella?"

"Life sucks."

"Don't it though?" Lucky agreed, looking at Bill Black's cigarette-stubbed prime rib. Mr. Calderone, the kitchen manager, had instructed Lucky to throw any decent-looking meat scraps into an old pickle can for his pampered Airedale. "The dog eats better than we do," Lucky had complained to Russ but he saved the scraps anyway. Bill's prime rib, with its cigarette butt, went in the trash.

"Ever had a worse Fourth of July?" Russ asked him gloomily.

"Oh, hell, yes," Lucky said. "Had a rough one 25 years ago."

"What happened?"

Lucky pulled the trash can from under the metal sink. "I'll tell you if you'll help me with this trash. In fact, I'll show you something I just got a couple of days ago, something I'll bet you've never seen before."

Russ hated the task but he wanted to hear the story, so he helped Lucky hoist the heavy can onto a wooden cart which he pulled to the service elevator.

"Ever hear of a place called St.-Lô?" Lucky asked, pushing the button for the bottom floor. "Over in France."

Russ shook his head. The service elevator clunked into motion.

"I parachuted in there with the Rangers on D-Day. Thought we'd stir up some rear-action trouble for the Krauts, keep their minds off the beaches. But the ack-acks blew half the flight squadron out of the sky and scattered the rest. We ended up in the woods miles from the target, miles from the rest of the battalion."

The heavy door of the elevator rose and they pulled the wooden cart toward the service landing under the hotel. Russ hated it down here in the bowels of the hotel: noisy, smelly, dark.

"So what happened?" Russ asked Lucky.

"The Germans spotted us before we even jumped. Clay pigeons is what we were. Clay pigeons. And they had machine guns."

He no sooner said it than they heard a gunshot. Russ just about jumped out of his skin. Lucky helped him halt the cart's momentum.

"Hey, Marvin!" Lucky shouted onto the landing. "Hold your fire! We give up!"

Marvin had worked maintenance at the hotel for thirty years and he moved pretty slow, Lucky explained. One of his pet projects was to bring his .22 rifle down here and try to shoot the rats infesting the garbage cans.

Marvin fired once more and then shouted, "Awright, Lucky, come on. I missed the bastard anyway."

Russ helped Lucky roll the cart across the greasy uneven concrete and they pulled the heavy can from the cart, replacing it with an empty. Russ looked around uneasily, not sure whether he had more to fear from the rats or from the man trying to shoot the rats.

"How many you got today?" Lucky asked Marvin.

"Not a damn one," complained Marvin, graying, tall, stooped. "Rats are smarter than people."

"How do you figure?" Russ asked him.

"They got no pride, no principles," Marvin said. "They'll do anything to stay alive. They know better than anybody that once you're dead, you're nothing but rat food."

"Young Russ here," Lucky said, draping his arm around Russ's back, his sweaty shirt smelly and damp, "thinks life sucks."

"It just proves my point," Marvin said. "Good lookin' boy like you, with your whole life ahead of you, and you're pissin' and moanin'. Meanwhile, that rat I missed is home right now braggin' to the wife and kids about how he out-foxed old Marvin again."

"You'll get him tomorrow," Lucky said as they hauled the cart away. "You mind helping me get some ice while we're here?" he asked Russ.

"Why not?" Russ acquiesced. "Might as well find out why the rats like it so much."

"It's not so much the rats as the spiders and roaches you gotta worry about through here," Lucky assured him.

They went through a door and entered a long concrete tunnel that connected the hotel proper to the power plant. The tunnel was a hundred yards long and lit by three bare light bulbs, a fourth having burned out. Overhead, rows of pipes brought hot water and power to the hotel, making the tunnel as hot as the outskirts of Hell. Water dripped into the dark undrained midpoint of the passage, leaving a pool of water twenty feet long and four inches deep to wade through. All around him Russ could hear little scurrying sounds but couldn't tell if it was creepy-crawlies or just the pipes expanding.

"So what happened?" Russ asked Lucky, trying to distract himself.

"Howzat?"

"When you parachuted into France."

"Well, first off, like I said, we ended up parachuting into the woods, which is real bad cause the chute gets caught in the trees. Me and this guy named Rosco from the 89th end up twenty feet off the ground in this great big old oak tree. Rosco's got his arm all tangled up in the cords and I'm hanging there trying to tell him how to get out of it when a jeepload of Nazis drives by and spots us. Watch your step here."

They stepped gingerly through the warm black puddle in the low point of the tunnel.

"What'd they do?"

"Shot the hell out of us. Got Rosco right in the nuts."

"What about you?"

"They got me in the legs. That's how come I walk so funny. I lost three inches from my right leg and an inch from my left. Pull it in here."

Russ guided the wooden cart into the ice room. In one portion were stored the empty ice buckets, big enough to hold ninety pounds, with tapered metal sides and removable heavy mesh bottoms to let the ice drain. Since the metal handles let them nest only part way, a stack of half a dozen buckets was taller than Russ. The other portion of the room held the freezer, where heavy cans held twenty gallons of water till it froze, and the cutter, which sliced the heavy blocks into one inch cubes.

Someone else already had cut four buckets of cubes. Russ and Lucky lifted two onto the cart.

"Isn't it kind of unsanitary walking around in here in our dirty shoes and putting the buckets on the cart we took the garbage out on?" Russ asked.

"What they don't know won't hurt 'em," Lucky said. "Two's enough this late. Let's go."

They maneuvered the cart back into the tunnel and Lucky let Russ pull it while he limped along behind.

"Was there a lot of pain?" Russ asked.

"Tonight wasn't too bad," Lucky said wearily.

"I mean when you got shot."

"Oh, Jesus," Lucky said. "Well, actually, not at first, cause I passed out. Saved my life. The Krauts figured I was dead and went to shoot some more sitting ducks like me and Roscoe. I must've been out the rest of the day and most of the night cause it was pitch black when I woke up. I thought I was dead. Couldn't see nothing, couldn't hear nothing, couldn't feel much below my waist. Couldn't even sing."

"What did you try to sing?"

Lucky's husky bar-room tenor echoed in the hot, dark tunnel: "Amazing grace, how sweet the sound…"

"What about Roscoe?"

"He didn't say nothing so I figured he was dead. And he was. When the sun came up I could see him there, pitched back in his harness, all the blood gone from his face so he looked like a spook. His guts had made a puddle on the ground."

"What about your legs?" Russ asked, stepping gingerly through the black puddle in the tunnel again.

"Anything that could hurt on my legs hurt so bad I couldn't stand it. At first I was afraid to make a sound for fear they'd come back and finish me off. But by about noon I started crying like a baby, afraid maybe they wouldn't. Cause about then the flies found us. The weather had turned hot and muggy and pretty soon Roscoe was just covered. My right boot filled up with blood dripping down from my leg. Doctor told me later that if it hadn't been for the parachute harness cutting off my femoral artery, I'd of died for sure. And the flies got onto my leg too. I figured I was going to spend my last few hours on earth looking at Roscoe hanging there dead as a mackerel and feeling the maggots wiggling around inside my boot."

Russ shuddered at the image but couldn't think of anything to say.

"Around dinner time," Lucky went on as they got back to the elevator and wrangled the cart in, "an old French farmer came around scrounging C-rations from the dead GIs. I tried to call out to him but my tongue was so swollen I couldn't make much sound. When he got up underneath the tree I just started bouncing around the best I could, shaking that old oak tree till he saw me."

"How'd he get you down?" Russ asked as they pulled the cart from the elevator into the kitchen.

"At first I didn't know if he would. He stood there yammering in French for a while and then walked off. So I set about thinking about what I wished I coulda wrote to my folks. And you know, bad as my legs were, what really got to me toward the end there was just breathing. Hanging there like that, just lifting up your ribs gets to be too damn hard. Maybe that's why Jesus didn't have more to say in that situation."

"Maybe," Russ said. "I hadn't thought of it that way."

"Anyway, before I got much past my 'Now-I-lay-me's' the old farmer comes back in this rusty old stake-bed truck. He pulls the cab up under me and gets out and climbs up on top. He pulls a tree lopper out of the bed and sticks it up and cuts through the parachute cords one by one till finally I fell down onto the truck roof. He slid me down onto the hood and drove me real slow back to his old bombed-out farmhouse, and he and his daughter patched me and kept me going till a battalion of Australian light artillery come through a few days later. They got me on a plane back to London but I got blood poisoning in the hospital. That Fourth of July, which don't mean much over there anywho, I was outta my head with fever, the room spinning and sinking like a roller coaster. Bad as some of my Fourths have been since, not one compares to that."

They unloaded the ice buckets and parked the cart. Lucky went back into the steamy little dishwashing cubicle and Russ stood leaning against the doorway, watching the strange little guy slam the dirty dishes into the dish rack before spraying them off and sliding the rack into the dishwasher.

"Can I ask you something, Lucky?"

"Fire away, laddie," Lucky said without turning around.

"Where'd you get the name Lucky? I mean, with all the bad shit that's happened to you…"

Lucky turned around. "You didn't hear a word Marvin said, did you? Hell, I'm damn lucky just to be alive. Who do you think's luckier, me or Roscoe?"

"You are, I suppose," Russ conceded. "Though it'd be hard to ask Roscoe."

Lucky chuckled. "Yeah, maybe old Roscoe's flittin' around on some cloud somewhere, strummin' his harp and feeling sorry for me that I ain't there with him."

"What were you going to show me, anyway?"

"That's right!" Lucky said, fishing through the pockets of his stained and frayed jacket hanging next to the garbage can. "Ever seen one of these?"

He handed a clear plastic case to Russ. Inside was light blue satin ribbon. From it hung a gold star surrounded by a wreath with the head of some goddess in the center, the star suspended from a spread eagle holding a gold bar that read "Valor."

"Wow, it's beautiful!" Russ said. "What is it?"

"That, my boy, is the Medal of Honor," Lucky said proudly.

"You just got it?"

"Coupla days ago. My company commander applied for it right after the war but I guess my paperwork got lost somewhere. I imagine they got a lot of applications back then."

"Well, anybody that went through what you did deserves it."

"What, at St.-Lô?" Lucky said. "Naw, this isn't for that. That was just a big screw-up. I did get a Purple Heart for it though. The Medal of Honor was for blowing up a tank in

North Africa in '43."

"What happened there?"

"Oh, the tank killed a buddy of mine and then ran right over him. But that was their mistake, cause they got me riled. I rolled a grenade into their tread and when they came stormin' out I shot the bastards."

"See, I can't picture myself doing something like that," Russ admitted. "I think I'd chicken out."

"Don't sell yourself short. When the time comes, you'll do what you gotta do, you'll see. May get your chance pretty soon, too. They're still drafting guys for that Veet Nam. You got your own war to fight."

"It's not a war, it's a police action," Russ corrected him sardonically. "And I have no idea why we got dragged into that."

"That ain't for you to figure out. When you get the call, you just do what they tell you."

"I don't think the guys in charge know what they're doing in this war either."

"Don't kid yourself," Lucky admonished him. "The guys upstairs know exactly what they're doing."

"I've got my doubts," Russ said, shaking his head. "But thanks, Lucky, for showing me that medal, for telling me about the war you were in. How come a guy like you has to wash dishes for a living?"

"Ain't a whole lot of money in the heroing business," Lucky said. "I gotta do what I gotta do."

"Well, I'm done doing what I've gotta do for today," Russ said, peeling off the waistcoat and hanging it up. "I'll see you tomorrow, Lucky."

"I'll be seeing you," Lucky sang, "in all the light fantastic spaces…"

o o o

When he got down to the hotel drugstore, Russ sank wearily into the blue vinyl booth and waved to Matt. Someone had left today's *Free Press* lying on the seat of the next booth. On the front page was the story he'd heard on the radio the night before: Brian Jones, recently forced out of the Rolling Stones, had drowned during a solitary, late night swim in his pool. He read the whole story again. It didn't seem possible that someone so young, so vibrant, so famous, could die so easily, so senselessly.

To get his mind off of it, Russ turned to the sports section. The *Free Press* didn't have the coverage that the *Gazette Telegraph* had but it would have to do. He still followed the Tigers, who had first captured his imagination when he lived in Michigan years ago, but they had played catch-up to the Orioles all season. But his miracle Mets had turned into the team to watch. If he had gone to New York as planned, he could have been watching Seaver and Koosman pitching the rest of the National League into the dust.

He fidgeted through the box scores, wondering how the rest of the night would go. He and the other Argonauts had pulled the old switcheroo. He had told Ellen that he would spend the night at Jason's. Jason had told his mother that he and Matt were going camping. Matt told his mom he would be at Russ's. John had told his mom that he and Jason would spend the night at Matt's. Every mother thought she knew where her boy was and most likely none of them would check. On this Independence Day, they had their independence.

Russ rarely lied to his mother and he felt guilty. Even more, he felt nervous. He had only known Jason a couple of years, the others less than that, and sometimes he still felt like the new kid on the block. He had no idea what they had planned. He knew only that they had all resolved to stay up all night, not for any particular reason, just because.

He still wore his black pants and white shirt and as he read the paper he rolled back the sleeve cuffs.

Matt, who had manned the fountain at the drugstore the summer before too, finally caught up with his other customers and brought Russ his usual: a hot fudge sundae with lots of Spanish peanuts and whipped cream. He too wore black pants but with a white tunic like the pharmacists wore, to assure the customers that their sundaes met the same exacting standards as their prescriptions. After seven hours though, streaks of strawberry syrup, cherry juice, and chocolate ice cream made Matt's tunic more abstract expressionist than reassuring. The hectic pace of the day meant that he still had most of his clean-up to do before closing at eleven.

"Where are the others?" he asked Russ, leaning on the back of the booth to ease his tired feet.

"Beats me," Russ said. "I thought they'd be here already."

"Are you ready for this?" Matt asked, referring to the all-nighter.

"As ready as anyone, I guess."

John had had to work too, since no one could persuade the zoo animals to quit defecating for national holidays. Only Jason had the day off.

"Speak of the devil," Matt said.

John and Jason wandered in, looking scruffy for the Broadmoor. Jason wore threadbare jeans and a jean jacket over a Colorado Buffaloes T-shirt, John his clunky zoo boots and jeans and a bulky yellow sweatshirt.

"Remember," Jason cautioned John under his breath as they sat down opposite Russ. "Pretend like we're nornal."

John snickered and looked at him, squinting. "I don't have to pretend," he said. "I am nornal."

"Nornal?" Russ asked Jason.

Jason giggled. His eyes were red and shiny, like he had hay fever. "Nornal?" he asked John. "Why don't you explain nornal? You're the one who is."

John's eyes looked about the same as Jason's. "Nornal," he said, pulling himself up in the booth and sounding authoritative. "N-o-r-n-a-l. Existing in a condition, state, or region of nornality. Nornish or norn-like. Top o' the norn to ye. More than beamish, west of south. Nornal."

"What's the matter with you guys?" Russ asked them.

"Matter?" Jason asked, looking to John for corroboration. "It's a matter of energy, isn't it?"

"Energy," John said, "being a square emcee."

"Indeed," Jason concurred, nodding. "And word."

"What are you talking about?" Russ asked them.

"Words," Jason said.

"And deeds," John added. "Like matters."

"What matters?" Russ asked.

"Nothing," Jason smiled cheerfully.

After serving malts and banana splits to the after-movie crowd that had straggled in, Matt came to their table. "What'll you gents have?"

John ordered a frosted Coke, Jason a butterscotch sundae, both stumbling over their words.

Matt smiled at their befuddlement but asked, "So is everybody square with their parents?"

"As an emcee," John assured him.

As Matt walked away, Russ saw Jason retreat inside himself, the change in his mood more drastic and sudden than usual.

"Are you all right?" Russ asked.

"His handcuffs chafe," John explained, referring to Jason's parents.

Dex and Nora Walker lived in what Dex referred to as "Shanty Broadmoor," straddling the boundary between the luxurious homes and mansions of the posh neighborhood that surrounded the hotel and the more average dwellings beyond. The couple, well-liked both by their neighbors and by Jason's friends, didn't always get along with one another.

Two weeks ago they had grounded Jason for missing a curfew and for arguing its fairness with his mother. "Don't you set foot outside the house this weekend," Nora had warned.

That Friday, Matt and John had kidnapped him, coming into the kitchen where he sat talking with Nora, lifting him up and carrying him out to the Pontiac—carrying him, in fact, everywhere they went that night so that he never set foot outside the house. The whole thing amused Nora too much to intervene. But she extended his grounding to a week when he got back.

"It's gotten worse since Steve left," Jason said hollowly.

"Do they fight?" Russ asked *soto voce*.

"With me, yes. But they barely talk to each other," Jason said. "In the morning they compete to see who got less sleep. In the evening Mom sits in front of the TV, sipping her wine and pretending that everything's fine. Dad plays most nights, doesn't get home till after I go to bed. We don't see a whole lot of him. I think that's what bugs her the most."

"Has he thought about giving up the music?" Russ asked.

"If he gives it up, he can't send me to college, making his younger son eligible for the draft too," Jason said gloomily. "But no pressure there." He put his hands on the table and his chin on his hands. "He doesn't think she can see his side of this at all."

"Women," John said.

"Can't live with them…" Jason said, and didn't go on.

Matt set the frosted Coke and the butterscotch sundae in front of them. "Anything else?" he asked wearily.

John slurped the frosted Coke too fast to talk, slaking what appeared to be a Saharan thirst.

The butterscotch sundae captured Jason's full attention. He carefully wove the end of his spoon through the swirls in the paper-lined dish. "This is the most incredible thing I've ever seen," he gushed to Russ. "Look!"

Russ looked: a butterscotch sundae. "What are you not telling me?" he asked, feeling a bit betrayed, a bit left behind.

"Everything," John said.

"There are more things in heaven and earth," Jason said, destroying the swirls to wolf down the sundae.

When they finished, Matt gathered the dishes and set them behind the counter. He tossed his rag into the bleach bucket and his tunic into the hamper. "Let's get out of here," he said to the others. "Marianne can do your dishes in the morning."

"Where to?" Russ asked.

"Go west, young man!" John said, pointing north.

They walked north from the drugstore into the hotel proper, turning left at the lobby and taking the spiraling steps of the Italian marble staircase two at a time to reach the mezzanine. Jason, leading the way, turned right at the top and headed east instead of west, leading them out onto the portico above the entrance to the hotel.

"Isn't this a dead end?" Matt asked as they stopped by the low wall.

"Yeah, but I always liked this spot," Jason said, looking beyond the fountain—a cherubim's cornucopia trickling water across geese, mermaids, and spouting horses—to the row of junipers framing the lily pond, the three tall flagpoles, the folded roof of the International Center, and the broad, straight expanse of Lake Avenue. "I like to picture myself as Teddy Roosevelt standing out here, haranguing the multitudes. 'We have nothing to fear—'"

"Wrong Roosevelt," John pointed out.

"And maybe we ought to fear those guys," Russ said, jerking his head toward the doormen staring up at them.

"Things are not always as they seem here," Jason told him, putting his finger to the side of his nose. "Follow."

He led them past the top of the stairs and the service elevator into the sitting room of the mezzanine, which had a fireplace at one end, paintings on the walls, and cut-glass chandeliers and frescoes on the ceiling. Matt stopped to tinkle a couple of melodies on the grand piano.

"What's wrong with this picture?" Jason wanted to know, gazing at the Maxfield Parrish painting of the Broadmoor hanging in a nook.

"What do you mean?" Russ asked.

"This is some other reality."

Russ looked too. "Huh?"

"Which way are we looking?" Jason asked him.

"East."

"I mean in the picture."

"Oh. West."

"That's the thing about Colorado Springs," Jason said. "The mountains are always to the west. And look, he's captured the mountains well. There's North and South Cheyenne Canyon, and Almagre Mountain. Right below that you can almost see where Jones Park is. Have you been to Jones Park, Russell T. Jones?"

"Uhh—"

Jason couldn't wait. "And then there's the hotel, of course, in all its splendor. And in front of the hotel here is the lake."

"Wait a minute," Russ said, scrutinizing the painting. "It goes hotel, lake, mountains. Not lake, hotel, mountains."

"The guy should have his artistic license revoked," Jason said.

"Finally," John said, staring at the paintings on the ceiling. "A worse dancer than me."

The ceilings of the mezzanine level were hand-crafted by Italian workmen right after World War I. This room featured cherubim frolicking with angels.

"Which one's the worse dancer?" Russ asked, looking up too, feeling like a rube.

"That one," John pointed. "The one with his feet on backwards."

Sure enough, one of the angels had been painted with a left foot where a right belonged and vice versa.

"That's my guardian angel," Jason confided to Russ. "Clumsy bastard."

By now, hotel employees kept a wary eye cocked in their direction.

"Let's blow," John said.

They walked by the escalator onto the now-empty terrace and past the Terrace Pool.

"Where are we going?" Russ asked again.

"West," John said again, pointing west this time, toward the mountains.

"Golgotha," Jason specified gloomily.

"Insane," Matt muttered, shaking his head.

"But we're making great time," John assured him as they started walking around the lake.

O   O   O

Broadmoor Lake was roughly kidney-shaped, about three quarters of a mile in circumference, and lined with full-grown silver maples and blue spruce. In the north end, connected by a short bridge to the sidewalk around the lake, was a small island where waterfowl like wild ducks and even some domesticated black swans from New Zealand nested. The Argonauts chose to walk around that north end of the lake, past a pipe spewing steamy effluent from the laundry and power plant into the water.

They couldn't have picked a better night to ramble outside. An afternoon shower had settled the dust and freshened the smells of flowers and earth. Bushels of stars glittered across the night sky and a waning gibbous moon hung suspended at its zenith. Only the sound of the carillon chimes from the Will Rogers Shrine up on Cheyenne Mountain disturbed the peace, tolling the half hour with Westminsterian solemnity.

Just as Russ opened his mouth to comment on the pleasant night, a bright flash lit the small island, followed by a tremendous thunderclap which seemed to reverberate forever between the tall hotel and the horseshoe-shaped stadium on the opposite side of the lake.

They all froze.

Russ found his voice first. "What the hell was that?" he asked in a terrified whisper.

"Something blew up on the island," Matt said.

"It's the Fourth of July," John reassured them coolly. "Somebody just set off an M-80 or a cherry bomb."

"Whoever comes to check on it will think we did it," Jason pointed out.

"Then let's get the hell out of here," Matt said. "Run!"

As they sprinted toward the exit at the cog railway station, Russ gasped, "If they see us running, it'll look even more like we did it."

"Then you can walk and explain it to them," John said, picking up the pace as he ran by the stuccoed wall of Pauline Chapel.

They ran a half mile west on Mesa Avenue before Russ and Matt had to pull up. They all kept walking west, panting.

"What about the Tank?" Matt asked when he could, referring to his Pontiac.

"We'll get it later," Jason assured him. "Let's just walk."

"Tell the truth," Russ said to John and Jason. "Did you guys plant that cherry bomb?"

"Fuck, no!" John replied.

"How could we?" Jason asked. "You were with us."

"Besides," John went on, "we're not vandals."

"What's the challenge in that?" Jason asked.

"Well, there is a lot of spelling," John pointed out, "if you get into the spray paint side of it."

"Precisely," Jason said. "I don't want to waste my time farting around with that sort of crap. You know why I'm taking all those science classes, biology, physics?" he asked Russ.

"Because you're good at it?" Russ guessed.

"No," Jason said. "That's why Matt takes that stuff. He's going to learn everything there is to know and take over the world. I take biology to figure how a flower works. It's the study of life. That's why I love reading my Uncle Willie too. I want to figure out what's important, what matters."

"What matters?" Russ asked. He felt like he'd done this before, like he was just setting Jason up, but he didn't really care because he liked the timing of the response.

"Nothing," Jason smiled cheerfully.

"That's his latest thing," John explained. "Nothing really matters."

"It works amazingly well," Jason said. "Try it. Name something you think matters."

"Philosophy," Russ asserted.

"Words," Jason countered. "Hot air. To be or not to be. It doesn't really matter. Either you is or you ain't. Arguing about it won't change a thing."

"The electromagnetic spectrum," Matt offered.

"Rainbows," Jason said. "You're going to tie me down with rainbows?"

"The New York Mets," Russ said.

Jason dismissed it with a snort. "You're joking, right?"

"God," Matt offered, which struck Russ as odd since Matt never seemed to show much interest in religion.

Jason had to think about this one. "God is the color of the wind," he concluded. "Irrelevant. He's like a gentleman farmer. Owns the place, shows up when he's got nothing better to do. Sits on the veranda with his seegar and his julep, watching the rest of us doing the dirty work. 'Say, boy,' sez he, 'How's about a sprig of that mint for my drink here?' 'Why, yassir,' you say, getting up from your knees to jump right to it. 'Yassir, comin' up!' You flatter yourself that you matter to him 'cause otherwise you're just another sweating slave fresh off the boat from Africa, just another beast of burden. He chuckles and gives you the occasional pat on the head—'Good work, son'—because otherwise, what's he got? Fallow fields and an unlit cigar."

They walked in silence awhile. This had turned into a serious challenge.

Russ's mind sought a stronger entry. He knew that Jason often just winged it on things like this, that he wasn't defending a serious philosophical position. But he often managed to pull Russ from the well-trod path of conventional thought. The sparring honed Russ's philosophical skills as much as a formal course would. And as usual, Jason had picked a position easy to defend, if not too appealing. Russ could anticipate Jason's arguments on a dozen different topics.

"Death," Russ settled on at last, thinking of Brian Jones.

"Two things come to mind," Jason said after a little pause. "One is that death is inevitable anyway, so what does it matter? No one gets out alive. The other is that any meaning death has is completely dependent on what precedes it." Anticipating Russ's corollary, he went on, "And life, being temporary at best and arguably pointless in any case, doesn't really matter much in this universe. Otherwise there'd be more of it out there," sweeping the cosmos with a wave of his hand.

"Told you," John said to Russ and Matt.

"I haven't heard you try," Matt said.

John looked around the quiet street they walked. "Love," he said.

Jason looked around too and then at John. "That's dirty pool."

They already had walked almost to the end of Mesa. Behind a three-railed wood fence the last housing lot before the upsweep of the mountains held the white Tyree home, relatively new and not elegantly designed but conspicuously expansive, with multi-paned windows, dormers, and a shake roof. Set above the street, it overlooked a couple of acres from which most of the native ponderosas had been removed, replaced with a huge lawn studded with a few bedraggled crabapple and poplar trees and a flagpole. Facing east, above the woodbine trellis, the bedroom on the second floor belonged, John had told them, to Amanda Tyree.

"All's fair in love and war," John said. "But does love matter?"

"Obviously, not to you," Jason said, "because you can afford to pass it up. And why should love matter to me? It's not like I can do anything about it."

"You haven't even tried," John pointed out, shoving him toward the drive.

"I've known Manny about as long as you have and you said the reason it didn't click for you two was because you'd known each other too long. What makes you think she'd look at me any differently than she looks at you?"

"I've seen her look," John said.

"Besides, it's an uphill battle," Jason said, discouraged.

"Her parents," John explained to the others, "weren't all that keen on me either. They think she should go out with some cotillion snob, someone like Bill Black."

"He's a jerk!" Matt cried.

"He's a rich jerk," Jason said despondently.

Russ, not wanting to break the news to Jason that earlier he had seen Manny and Bill together at the hotel, decided to stick to the subject at hand. "So money matters?"

"Not to me," Jason said. "But to the Tyrees? Yes."

"And you don't think love can overcome that?" Russ asked him.

"Love conquers all," Matt said.

"I don't want to be conquered!" Jason shouted up at the sky. "I want to be free! I don't want to be *in* love. I want to be *from* love."

Now that they had walked well past the Tyree home, Russ felt free to applaud Jason's performance. "Nicely put!" he cheered, clapping. "Did you actually mean any of that?"

Jason shrugged. "It comes and goes. Let's go down Evans here."

Straight ahead lay South Cheyenne Canyon, a pleasant stretch of scenery that led up to Seven Falls, a series of cascades over the granite bedrock. It had been developed into a tourist attraction with the falls lighted at night and a wooden staircase up the side, an aerial tram and a snack bar, all closed at this time of night. By contrast, most of North Cheyenne Cañon was a park, with the Cub, a curio shop/snack bar, a few miles up by more modest and natural Helen Hunt Falls, and a small group of summer homes and cabins above that. Since the residents needed access, the road here remained open, even if the park was technically closed.

They walked silently up the narrow, deserted blacktop, knowing they crossed a boundary not only into the park but also away from homes and street lights and man-made laws. The canyon walls were steep and the moon had slid far enough down that often times they had to navigate the road by just the moonlight reflected from the cliffs above.

The cooler air by the small noisy creek made Russ regret leaving his jacket at home but the willows and cottonwoods had a warm comforting smell. He hadn't done much hiking in these mountains and had never hiked at night but the other three had lived around here all their lives and he trusted their judgment. His peace of mind flew out the window, of course, when he spotted the eerie light reflected from the eyes of a raccoon in the chokecherry bushes. The others laughed unmercifully when he shied away and stepped in a puddle.

"Jesus, where are you taking me, anyway?" he demanded.

Jason put his arm around his shoulders. "We can take you anywhere you want to go," he said. "Do you want to go back?"

"It's not that," Russ said, calming down. "I just had the impression that you guys had a destination in mind."

"Do we have a mental destination?" Jason asked John.

John pulled up the right sleeve of his yellow sweatshirt and struck a pose pointing up to the far reaches of the universe. "To boldly go where no man has gone before!" he proclaimed.

"Which means virgin territory," Jason explained to Russ. He laid his hands on Russ's temples. "And since we're talking about mental destinations, do you have any virgin territory in here?"

"A fucked mind is a fertile mind," John said.

"Ahh," Russ said, realization dawning. "Did you get that weed from Dan?"

"Indeed we did," John said. "It's been very interesting."

"That's why you acted so strange in the drugstore," Russ surmised.

"That butterscotch sundae started it!" Jason said defensively. "It's all Matt's fault."

Matt had walked ahead of them for much of the way, quietly taking in the conversation. "Just taking orders," he told Jason.

Russ felt relieved to have an explanation for their odd behavior. "You guys have been creeping me out all night."

"Oh, we weren't even trying to creep you out," Jason said. "Matt, tell him about the ghost train."

"Oh, Jesus," Russ said, knowing they would tell him, knowing he would listen, no matter what.

Matt dropped back to talk to Russ in his low, steady, rational voice while John took his place in the lead.

"You know the Gold Camp Road, right?" Matt began, pointing to the slash of roadway far up the mountainside.

Russ nodded.

"Well, it started out as a railroad. They built it to carry the ore from the mines up at Cripple Creek down to Old Colorado City and the smelting plants. So the people who live in those houses up above Helen Hunt Falls got used to the engineer blowing the steam-whistle before every turn and tunnel."

"Are you okay, Russ?" Jason asked. "You're shivering. You want my jacket for a while?"

Comfort beat pride. He slipped on the old jean jacket which smelled like Jason's sweat and patchouli oil.

"So anyway," Matt went on, "when the mines petered out they took out the railroad tracks and converted it to a road. Well, a few months after they took out the tracks, a couple of guys from a local radio station decided to play a Halloween trick on the folks up in the canyon here. They got hold of a recording of an old train chugging along and blowing its whistle and they hooked it up to their sound truck that had some broadcast speakers on it. They came up here on that dark windy Halloween night and drove along the road playing those train sounds. Got everybody's hackles up. People called the sheriff and the F.B.I. and everything. I heard about one lady whose dog lost its voice howling at that ghost train."

"What happened to the guys who did it?" Russ asked. "Did they get caught?"

"Actually, no," Jason said, picking up the tale from Matt. "The night turned out to be so dark and so windy that they missed that hairpin curve right above us. The truck plummeted down that steep gravel slope, throwing them both out and killing them. Some people claim that their ghosts still haunt this canyon."

The words had barely left his mouth when they heard a low moan from the bushes up ahead. Russ, caught up in the story, took it for the voice of the unsettled dead. He stopped in his tracks, the hair standing up on the back of his neck. "Jesus Christ!"

"Whoa, Russ! It's not the Second Coming," Jason said, clapping his hand in Russ's shoulder. "I just made that last stuff up. That moan came from John peeing in the mountain maple bushes."

John emerged zipping and chuckling. "Way to go, JC! I've never heard that story told better."

Russ, though rightfully aggrieved at first, finally came to see the humor in the situation. "God, you guys! What are you trying to do to me, making up stories like that?"

"Everything I told you was true," Matt said.

"My moan was completely sincere as well, for that matter," John pointed out. "That piss felt great."

"Meanwhile, we're here!" Jason said, pointing up at a rocky spire looming far above them.

"Ah, the very place," John concurred.

They crossed the road and climbed a gravel path and a short flight of metal stairs. At the top was a simple amphitheater of wooden benches focusing on a small platform. Across the canyon, they could see the bulbous-topped rocky pinnacle flanked by a smaller spire. Darkness crept up the canyon walls, swallowing the skim-milk light that the moon, dipping toward Mt. Cutler, poured down. They could hear nothing but the murmur of the creek and the slight breeze through the narrow-leafed cottonwoods below and the Douglas fir and ponderosas all around.

Russ, warmer now after the climb, gave the jacket back to Jason. "What is this place?" he asked, looking around.

"Rocker's paradise," John said cryptically.

"The soldiers from Ft. Carson come up here to practice mountaineering techniques," Jason explained. "A couple of days a week they put on a rock climbing demonstration for the public, ropes and pitons and all that."

"Didn't Steve do that?" Matt asked.

"Damn near got himself killed over there," Jason said. "This rotten granite can give way at any time. He only slipped about ten feet before his harness caught him but it gave the crowd a hell of a thrill. That was a year ago, before he went to Nam."

"Did he ever take you up there?" Russ asked. He was a little acrophobic anyway and wouldn't dream of doing anything on that sheer precipice.

"Me? Naw," Jason said. "He's a lot crazier than I am. He takes risks with his body. I only take risks with my mind."

"Speaking of which," John said, holding out his hand. In it, barely visible in the pale moonlight, lay a hand-rolled joint, the ends twisted closed.

"May I?" Russ asked. John handed it to him and Russ felt its uneven shaft and tapered ends. He sniffed it but couldn't smell much. "Do we each get one?"

John took it back. "Jeez!"

"John and I smoked just part of a thin one earlier," Jason explained, "and you saw how we were."

"Wow," Russ said, duly impressed.

"Besides," John said, taking out a box of wooden matches, "there's kind of a camaraderie involved in passing it around." He lit a match and burned the paper from one end, then put it to his lips and drew on it while holding the match to the end. The acrid smell of the burning cigarette paper gave way to the pungent odor of the cannabis. Holding in his hit, he passed it to Russ.

Russ held it gingerly. He had smoked cigarettes once in a while, pilfering Ellen's mentholated Kools from her purse, so the action wasn't completely foreign to him. As casually as possible, trying not to betray his inexperience, he took the long deep draw that cigarette smokers take.

The smoke caught in his throat and lungs and he immediately coughed out most of what he had taken in. He handed the joint to Jason.

"Are you in on this?" Jason asked Matt before taking a more moderate, carburetted drag.

"Maybe I'll just be an observer this time around," Matt said, passing the joint back to John.

"Thank you, my friend," John said. "Being new at this ourselves, it wouldn't hurt to have someone around who had his wits about him. Look at Brian Jones."

"How are you doing?" Jason asked Russ, who still coughed. "We can't afford to lose our drummer."

"It's stronger than I thought," Russ said, watching carefully John's technique. "What'll this do for my warts?"

John laughed out his hit. "Sometimes you are so-o-o fucking funny!"

Jason watched Russ take a milder hit. "It may not do anything for you. When John and I did it the first time—the only other time—neither one of us got high."

Russ let out the smoke through his nose. It tasted weedy but not unpleasant. He felt a little light-headed and his mouth was dry but no profound change overtook him. He could tell, though, that John and Jason once again felt the effects.

"Rocker's paradise!" Jason said, nudging John, as though he just got it.

"Okay, stoner's paradise," John said with smoke, making Jason giggle. "You are what you smoke, J."

Russ had one more hit, the other two two. He got the shivers again as he watched the moon brush the tops of the trees on Mt. Cutler.

He could feel Jason looking at him. "How's your head?" Jason asked creepily, the way Vincent Price would.

"Yeah, Russ," John joined in, putting the roach into a small waterproof cylinder he had used in Boy Scouts to keep matches dry. "See any more…ghosts?"

Jason put his hand reassuringly on Russ's leg. "Don't worry," he said soothingly. "If you start to freak out, we'll have Matt tie you to a tree until the men in white get here."

John tried to add to the creep show by humming and whistling odd intervals at the same time.

"Actually," Russ said, shivering again as the moon slipped behind the trees, "I was thinking of a T. S. Eliot line:

"Between the idea
And the reality
Between the motion
And the act
Falls the Shadow."

When he said the last line, both Jason and John looked over their shoulders at the moonset and the rising shadow.

Matt chuckled. "Score one for the new guy."

"Okay," Jason conceded. "But the quote has 'reality' in it and Russ owns the reality franchise."

"Oh, God, no!" John said. "Not tonight! Anything but reality."

"Sorry," Russ said with a laugh. "Blathering on. So when does the show start?" He looked around the empty amphitheater, still not sure he could tell any difference in himself that corresponded to the change he saw in his friends.

"Whenever you're ready," Jason said to him, waving him toward the presentation area at the focal point of the amphitheater. While Russ got up and cleared his throat, the others moved back a few rows and spread out to seem more like an audience.

Now that he had their attention, Russ felt self-conscious and the yawning canyon behind him seemed very dark indeed. "What should I do?" he asked, straining to see their faces in the dark.

"Give us a song, luv," John said in a pretty fair Liverpool accent.

Russ thought about it a moment and then tipped his head back and closed his eyes, his right arm held aloft. "'To dance beneath the diamond sky with one hand waving free,'" he sang, gracefully turning a circle, not knowing, or caring, whether it was he or the earth that turned.

"Ringo sings better than you do, Johnnie," Jason beatled to John.

"I've been trying to tell him that," John beatled right back. "He won't listen."

"Maybe he can't hear you over the singing," Matt guessed.

Russ sat down to great applause. "Who's next?"

"John," Jason said, "give us the Seven Ages."

John walked to the center of the semi-circle and turned around. "Boy, I haven't tried this since we had to memorize it for Miss Herrick's class in 8th grade." He saw Jason walking up the benches to the last row. "Where are you going?"

"I get to be the heckler in the back row," Jason said.

John drew himself up and took a breath. "'All the world's a stage—'"

"Louder and funnier!" Jason called.

"'—And all the men and women merely players'," John said. "Then something, something, something, exits and entrances, and then the seven ages. Starts with the infant, of course."

Here Jason made a surprisingly accurate imitation of a braying mule that trailed off in barfing noises.

"'Mewling and puking in the nurse's arms'," John remembered, "thank you very much. Then the whining schoolboy, creeping like a snail unwillingly to school. I remember that from my own creeping days."

Jason sighed theatrically.

"Okay," John said. "The lover, sighing like a furnace, writing ballads to his mistress' eyebrow. But he's drafted, right? Becomes a soldier?"

"Goddamn fucking son of a bitch!" Jason shouted.

"'Full of strange oaths'."

Jason popped his finger from his mouth and then made the sound of an explosion.

"Oh, yeah, 'the bubble reputation even in the cannon's mouth.' And the next one was the castrated cock, right? The judge with the capon in his stomach."

"Voo-vah, voo-vah," Jason said

"That's right, 'wise saws and modern instances.' Damn, you remember this better than I do, Jason."

"Dance more!" Jason requested. "Show some leg!"

"For what I'm getting paid? Not a chance! Oh, wait, it's coming back. Something about the old guy with his 'shrunk shank.' How's it go?"

"Hell, I don't remember that one that well," Jason said, coming back down from the back. "I just remember the demonic devices we made up. Uncle Willie would kill me."

"Isn't the last stage second childhood?" Matt asked.

"Like we'll have to worry about that," John said. "If the Russkies don't get us, the army will."

"Actually, that's the only part I still remember," Jason said. "It ends with 'mere oblivion, sans teeth, sans eyes, sans taste, sans everything'."

"Sans grim to me," Russ said.

"Just you wait, my pretty!" Jason said, rubbing his hands together like the Wicked Witch of the West.

"Okay, hot shot," John said, sitting down. "Your turn."

Jason stood up and walked to the front, clumsy in the fading moonglow. From the bottom of the canyon came the sound of a lone car wending its way down the winding road, its headlights raising a ghostly glow.

"'In the beginning'," Jason began in stentorian tones that echoed from the rocky cliffs, "'God created the heaven and the earth'." His voice dropped to a whisper and his posture to a crouch. "'And the earth was without form, and void'." Then he rose and turned, his arms grandly encompassing the inky void above and below, even seeming to halt the car: "'And darkness was upon the face of the deep. And God said, Let there be light'!"

And there was light. Suddenly the rock spire across the way lit up with the wandering rays of a searchlight.

It struck them dumb. Jason stood stock still, mouth agape, until the light swung across the canyon and began to play on the cliffs above the amphitheater and the large white firs behind it.

"Jukes!" he cried and he and Matt scrambled to get below the benches. Russ and John quickly followed suit.

The light came to rest on the rocky spires above and behind them but left the benches dark. Then flashing red and white lights joined the searchlight.

"It must be the cops!" John whispered.

"Shh!" Jason whispered back. "They'll probably just go away."

Russ cowered behind the bench. His knees ached from resting on gravel and the cool damp concrete made him shiver. His fear felt like a bowling ball in his gut.

The silence of the deep canyon was shattered by the sound of the police radio on a loudspeaker, tinny, harsh, unintelligible. They heard the car door slam and the searchlight momentarily disappeared when the policeman walked in front of it. His boots slowly crunched across the gravel and up the hollow-sounding metal steps. He halted at the top of the stairs and the beam from his flashlight played across the amphitheater, stopping where Jason knelt behind the first row of benches.

"Who's there?" the policeman asked, his voice deep, tense.

"It's just me, officer," Jason said from beneath the bench, his voice muffled and shaky.

"Stand up slowly with your hands in the air."

Jason carefully did as he was told. "Don't shoot," he said. "I'm not armed."

"Come over here where I can see you, son," the cop said. "Keep your arms above your head."

Jason stepped over the bench and walked into the searchlight beam. Russ could hear the cop patting him down.

"The park is closed at night," the cop informed him.

"Oh," Jason said. "I didn't realize."

"What are you doing up here, anyway?"

"Shakespeare?" Jason offered doubtfully.

Despite his terror, or maybe because of it, it took every ounce of will Russ could muster to keep from giggling.

"What's your name, boy?" the cop asked, less than amused.

Jason hesitated, then said, "Bill Black, sir."

Only a supreme act of fear-enhanced self-control prevented a laugh at this.

"Bill Black?" the officer repeated. "That would make you the son of Bernie Black, as in Bernie Black Ford?"

"Yes, sir, it would."

"Well, Mr. Black, you better come with me."

"Am I being charged with something, officer?"

"How about loitering? Throw in trespassing too if you like, maybe destruction of public property. I'd like to run a check on you."

Russ wanted to protest but John beat him to it.

"That's not fair!" he said, standing up.

The cop shoved Jason to the ground and drew his gun again.

"I'm unarmed too!" John declared.

"You just stay where you are," the cop said. "Are there any more of you hiding up here?"

Russ and Matt cautiously stood, their arms held high.

"That's all, I swear!" John told the cop.

The cop left the gun pointed at John's chest while he pointed his flashlight into each face in turn. Apparently their abject fear convinced him they weren't much of a threat and he eased the pistol back into its holster.

"How about you all come down here into the light with your friend where I can get a better look at you?" the cop said. "Nice and easy."

They walked gingerly down into the beams of the searchlight, the cop watching them closely.

"Can I get up?" Jason asked, still lying where he'd been pushed.

The cop extended his hand to help him up. In the harsh light Russ could tell that Jason had skinned his chin when he fell and he dabbed at the blood with his hand.

"Have you boys been drinking?" the cop asked.

"No, sir, we haven't," Matt said with conviction.

The cop looked around. "I thought I smelled smoke. You're not starting any fires up here, are you?"

"No, sir!" they all insisted.

"How did you get up here? I didn't see a car."

"We walked," Jason said.

"Walked? From where?"

"The Broadmoor," John replied.

"I've got my car there," Matt explained.

"Just how were you planning to get back?"

"Same way we got here," Jason said.

"Do your parents know what you're up to?"

No one answered.

"Uh-huh," the cop said. "Maybe you guys better come with me."

"Are we under arrest?" Russ asked, dreading the answer.

"Do you want to be?"

"No!" they all insisted emphatically.

"Then I better see some cooperation."

They trooped meekly down to the police car where the cop found a bandage for Jason's chin in the trunk of his squad car. Jason put it on and the others stood around awkwardly while the officer radioed his status to base.

"What does 'jukes' mean, anyway?" Russ asked quietly.

"Matt knows," Jason said, kicking a large boulder next to the police car.

"It was a game we played as kids," Matt said, sounding calmer than the others. "Actually, it was a game within a game. We used to get all the kids on the block together after dinner and play Hide And Seek or Red Rover. Whenever a car would go by, though, whoever saw it coming first would shout 'Jukes!' and everyone would dive for the shadows. If the light caught you, you lost and had to freeze like that."

"Well, I sure as hell froze," Russ said. "I've never been so scared in my life. How did you do that, Jason?"

"Do what?"

"Time it like that. 'Let there be light'."

"Magic, my friend."

The officer had been jotting notes on his clipboard. He got out of the car again and looked at Jason. "What did you say your name was?"

"Uh, Bill Black, sir."

"Why did he just call you Jason?"

Russ's heart sank. No one said anything.

"Is your name Jason Walker?" the officer asked.

Jason cleared his throat. "Well, actually, yes, sir. I was just playing a little trick on my good friend Bill Black."

"And a good one it was," the officer said. "I played one on him myself last week when I stopped him for speeding. Now, you boys want to get into the car?"

"I thought you said we weren't under arrest," Russ pointed out.

"I'm just going to give you a ride back to the Broadmoor to make sure you don't get sidetracked along the way somewhere. You three get in back. Jason can ride up front with me."

Russ had never been inside a police car before. It smelled of coffee and cigarettes and the radio chirped sporadically. The handles for the doors and windows had been removed and a heavy metal grate separated the back from the front. The officer took off his hat and entered some more notes in his shift log before putting the car in gear.

"You seem like smart kids," he said as he drove down the winding canyon road. "I didn't hear any Shakespeare but the Bible quote sounded pretty authentic."

"My Shakespeare wasn't as good," John admitted.

"Smart kids like you," the officer went on, "ought to know what a risk you took tonight. Were you afraid when I came up to the amphitheater?"

"Oh, yeah!" Russ acknowledged.

"So was I," the officer confessed. "I could have shot one of you."

"Thank you," John said, "for your restraint."

"Aside from that," the cop went on, "I could still make your lives pretty miserable. Trespassing and loitering, which you probably scoff at, could be on your records for years to come, could make it hard to get a good job or to get into a good college. And for that matter, smoking marijuana is a serious crime but I'm sure you had the good sense to get rid of any traces of that before I got there. Right?"

"Oh, yes, sir!" John said, making sure the match container was deep in his pocket. "I mean, no, sir, we weren't…uhh…"

The others kept silent.

"In any case, I'm sure your parents will give you enough grief when you get home," the officer said soberly.

"How did you know my last name?" Jason asked.

"Your father's been looking for you all night."

"Really?" Jason said, sounding genuinely surprised. "I didn't think he cared what happened to me."

"You may find out tonight that he cares more about you than you ever dreamed."

They rode the rest of the way in silence.

By the time they drove up to the Broadmoor, the eastern sky showed the first pale streaks of dawn. Dex Walker's black-trimmed white Chevy Impala sat in the valet parking area.

Dex got out and waited while the officer let the boys out of the squad car. "Thank God,"

Dex said dully. "Where did you find them, officer?"

"North Cheyenne Cañon, sir," the officer said.

"What the h—?" Dex began, looking at his son in bewilderment, rubbing his temples. "Oh, never mind. What are they charged with?"

"Not a thing, sir," the officer said. "I just gave them a ride back to their car."

"Are you all right, Jason?" Dex asked his son. "What happened to your chin?"

Jason looked at the officer but said, "Aw, nothing really. I just tripped in the dark, skinned it. But what are you doing here?"

"Looking for you," Dex said wearily. "Your mother—"

"Dad, we weren't doing anything wrong," Jason interrupted defensively. "We were just out walking and talking."

"You shouldn't have lied," Dex said.

"You're right, I know," his son admitted. "I shouldn't have lied."

Dex looked haggard and grim and everyone could tell he was upset. But it seemed to Russ that there was more to it than just Jason's disappearance.

"Dad, I'm sorry I did it," Jason offered when his father didn't say anything. "But I'm all right. What's wrong?"

Dex stared at the pavement. He sniffed. "I guess there's just no easy way to say it," he said. "Jason, your brother Steve's been killed."

"Oh, God, no!" Jason said. He went to his father and hugged him but Dex's arms hung limp at his side.

"Let's go home," Dex said hollowly.

They got into the Impala and drove away.

Russ and the others stood in shock for a moment. Finally the officer broke the silence, asking, "Can you boys find your way home?"

"We'll be okay, sir," Matt told him. "Thanks again for the ride."

He got back into the squad car and slowly drove off. The fountain in front of the hotel sounded loud in the early morning stillness and a few early birds chirped meditatively.

"Poor Jason," Russ said, having a hard time fathoming this news. He watched the Walkers' Impala round the three flagpoles at the entrance to the hotel and head east on Lake Avenue into the dawn of a new day.

...O...O...O...

My parents, for all their differences, agreed that their kids should get to know the American West, taking us on a series of summer vacation trips to the great national parks and monuments: Yellowstone, Yosemite, the Grand Canyon. The last I took with them was a houseboat trip on Lake Powell in Utah.

Since much of the lake is unfathomably deep, the houseboats don't carry a traditional anchor, just a lighter metal wedge to set in the sand on the rare pockets of beach. Glen Canyon Dam had been completed just a few years before our visit and the lake was still filling, submerging the little beaches of the year before and creating new ones from the sandy hollows once atop the canyon walls. So in order to tie up the boat, we had to find a suitable spot that wouldn't appear on a map.

One evening we came to a promontory in the convoluted lake, a peninsula by virtue of a low strip of bare sandstone. The other side of this narrow isthmus seemed a likely spot to tie up for the night so I suggested that, rather than ride around the promontory with them, I could just swim ashore and walk to the other side of the isthmus, ready to set the anchor in the sand when they arrived.

The lake is deep and cool but the desert begins at the water's edge. By the time I had scrambled to my bare feet, my hair had almost dried. I watched the houseboat chug slowly out of sight, out of earshot, around the promontory.

I found out later that my mother, either as a prank or as one of her tough lessons about independence, told my dad to cut the motor and they just let the boat drift awhile. I stood for perhaps half an hour on that sun-drenched isthmus wondering what had happened. If they had lost their way in that labyrinth of flooded canyons, there I would be, naked but for my swimming trunks, caught between the vast expanse of open water and the endless merciless desert. I'll never forget the feeling of relief when the boat finally chugged around the other side of that promontory. I'll also never forget that first taste of being utterly alone.

October 23, 1999

First comes that luxurious, butter-smooth feeling of release. The head nods, the eyelids become transparent, the other, easier sequence resumes.

Under foot, the rocky path. Above, granite crags catch the evening sun. A brook tumbles down the valley. It's like you've been here before but when would that have been?

Turn around. Look back. See how far you've come. Drink in the unfamiliar vista, the undiscovered country, the last frontier.

He's here with you, as he often is. You ask him something technical, like what do we do when we reach the ridge. He replies...

Matt's head nodded too far forward and he woke with a start. The shutter fell; the other reality slipped away.

Who was with him there in that dreamscape? Sometimes it seemed like an amalgam of former friends and hiking buddies. Other times it seemed like a denizen, a figment, of the dreamscape, as elaborately fictional as the rest of the scene. Either way it felt good to be with him again.

Back to work. The sun had dipped closer to the horizon, the aurora it conjured from the sea-mist tangled in the firs on Ozette Island. Tonight's sunset probably wouldn't hold a candle to last night's.

Last night's sunset had been perfect. It completely justified the five-hour drive west from Seattle, the two-hour hike into Olympic National Park on the boardwalk, the freeze-dried dinner, the long night on the hard ground. It had even softened the blow of meeting some other lone, middle-aged hiker who, coming upon Matt taking a macro of the iridescent bubbles in the seafoam, greeted him as "a fool with a camera." Matt had seen that sunset photograph in his mind for years now and finally the fates conspired to let him capture it.

Near the campsite down at Sand Point, one of the innumerable small streams long since subsumed by the Sitka spruce of the forest surfaces briefly when it reaches the wide beach. Since the uniform texture of the beach sand lends its flow no definition, the stream manifests itself only as a patch of wet sand as long and wide as a tennis court but only skin deep. The direction of its flow, just south of west, made it ideal for Matt's purpose.

Given some early fall rain—which had just ended Wednesday—plus a clear dry evening —which yesterday's had been—and the rich tones of the autumn skies and cirrus clouds, he could set up his camera on the low tripod at the emergence of the small stream and capture a portrait shot of the sun and surf reflected in the undulating ripples of wet sand. With the telephoto lens to maximize the sun's disk and the luxury of plenty of light to allow slow-speed film, he could get a shot that would enhance the depth of color while softening the motion of the waves. One exposure even included the spray from either a gray whale or, more likely, a rocky outcrop offshore.

At least he thought that would be in the shot. Single lens reflex cameras are like quantum physics: you can see everything but the picture you actually take, the way you can know a subatomic particle's momentum or its position, but not both. Then the additional filters of processing and development would add to the print interpretations he never intended. And how many artistic media include a delay of days or weeks or months until you can find out exactly what you created, if anything?

But the challenge of capturing that perfect moment, that tiny fraction of a second, made any frustrations tolerable. And, through the lens at least, last night's sunset looked perfect.

Tonight's, though, not so much. A gray haze robbed the blue from the sky and here at Cape Alava the receding tide exposed the unphotogenic bony ribs of the intertidal zone. Matt took one last shot of a lonely great blue heron silhouetted against the slate-gray surf.

Boy, that doze sure felt good, though. Some people fantasize about sumptuous surroundings or passionate love or fine cuisine as the ultimate luxury. Dreamers know the truth: nothing on earth beats the release from mundane consciousness and the renaissance of the dream.

The sun slipped behind a bank of clouds. Time to pack it in.

He grunted himself away from the beached log against which he'd been sitting and slowly stood, unwinding the kinks from his back. He had reached the age when he could look back fondly to the days when only his back hurt. Now it seemed like he had an ache for every joint. He still managed, though, to strap on the old internal-frame pack, the camera and the tripod, and hike out to the beach or, once in a while, up a peak. He'd even lost a little weight lately. Must be doing something right.

He went back to the campsite. Everything seemed in order. He had gotten used to the standard bear precautions: tying the food in a tree, keeping odors to a minimum in camp. But here the raccoons and ravens matched wits with the cleverest of campers. The raccoons had figured out how to climb a tree up to a bear wire, tight-wire it out to a vertical rope, shinny down the rope, and rip through the heavy material of a pack on the chance that it might hold something tasty. At the campsite any food left unattended for more than a few seconds disappeared.

Not that he begrudged anyone the food. His appetite wasn't what it used to be and he often carried back half of what he brought. But he begrudged the wild critters the loss, no matter how willing, of their independence.

He sat down on the 20-gallon plastic paint can he used to foil the coons, which doubled as a camp stool. He took out the old pipe he smoked once every six months or so. He packed some tobacconist's best efforts—this was called "Sunset"—into it and lit up. Since he bought the little white-gas camp stove, his pipe served as his campfire. The fragrant smoke wreathed his head.

Cape Alava would leave Horace Greeley speechless. The only way to hike farther west in the Lower 48 would be to wait for an exceptionally low tide and hop the slippery rocks out to Ozette Island. America's compass has always pointed west, making this the end of America. Destiny made manifest. Protected not only by Olympic National Park and Cape Flattery Marine Wildlife Refuge but also by miles of winding roads and months of extreme winter storms, it is a place of great beauty, solitude, and an almost mystical calm. The perfect place to wrap up the hiking season.

This year, for the first time, he was almost glad to see it go. Work at Novagen somehow had become both boring and stressful and the implacable deadline—the end of the year, the century, the millennium—loomed larger with every passing day. He felt beat, worn out.

And, not surprisingly, he had to pee. Between the lattés on the way over yesterday and the beer with dinner tonight and the bathtubful of water everyone advised him to drink daily, he felt like he hiked outhouse to latrine to porta-potty now. It had gotten to the point that he kept an old juice bottle with him just in case.

Since the bottle was already half-full, he brought it with him to empty it in the latrine before getting into the tent for the night. The little one-man tent was cramped but it weighed a third as much as the two-man, so unless he could persuade Deb to come along, he just brought the little one.

When he had the pad squared away beneath him and the sleeping bag zipped up, he lay on his back with his head on his hands and listened. One other campsite held a young couple with a small child; other than that, he had the place to himself. He could hear nothing but the hushing of the surf.

Sharing a campground with even one other party didn't happen often. Most of the time he camped alone. He almost always hiked alone, often going to places where a badly sprained ankle would mean not only death but dismemberment by the coyotes before a search party could find the body.

Not that that bothered him much. He always figured he'd die alone, which even to him seemed strange considering he'd been married for 27 years. Maybe it just represented his preference.

At his father's funeral the minister had contended that death was something to be overcome. "The last enemy to be destroyed," and all that. But Matt's father Hank had died by degrees, slowly wasting away from emphysema. After all that long slow uncomfortable dying, death became a blessed release. Much as Matt missed him, he would never have wished another year on him. Matt felt certain that, had she been alive, his mother would have agreed.

The phrase "tragic death" has become cliché. But how many deaths are truly tragic? Most are average, some are unfortunate, many are more prolonged and less dignified than in the past, a few are untimely. They often bring sorrow and misfortune and anger to those left behind. But tragic?

And the phrase "escaped death" means nothing. The best one can hope for, physically at least, is to postpone it. And postponing it has become very profitable for the medical community. Ten years ago, Matt's grandmother, in her early 80s, had suffered a burst appendix. Had it happened just a few decades earlier it would have meant a painful but mercifully quick death. As it was she lived several more years with little quality of life and a prolonged expensive death. Death in our culture has become something to be avoided at all costs.

But for all our technological postponements, not even the most optimistic person would claim any sort of victory. If we can make it past the childish chant of "We don't want to die!" maybe we can reconcile ourselves to the inevitable and try to envision how we *do* want to die. How do you define the good death?

Even mentally Matt could feel his knees creak and his back grind as he bent to pick up that gauntlet. Okay, here goes:

The Good Death—

Caveat: At the time of his death, his affairs would be in order, as they usually are. Deb would mourn his passing, of course, but she hardly depended on him.

Grandview Peak in the Olympics. A gloriously beautiful day in July, a few puffy clouds in the sky, just to give context to the pictures of Mt. Olympus. A light breeze blows from the southwest.

Matt invented and for years has practiced a fertility ritual. (He had always found the usual American rituals—Santa Claus, tailgate parties, church weddings, political conventions, and the like—vacuous and commercialized.) Finding a suitably private spot on the summit of a peak or some other wild place, he strips down, kneels, and spills his seed upon the ground, Onan-like. At first the mere thought of it aroused him. Lately he's required visual aids to get started. The best is a picture of Deb wearing nothing but a ribbed tank top and a pair of paisley silk boxer shorts. Sometimes she would spritz some of her Zen perfume onto the back for him before he left. He had more revealing pictures of her but this one captured her feisty, randy quality that never grew old.

And there on a rock his hapless, haploid DNA would rest, yielded up to the capricious transformations of the mighty thunderbolt, scattered with the dust in the autumn wind, pervading the very source of the waters that ever sought the cradle of the sea. Or something along those lines. A sort of Pangaean renewal ritual. Eccentric perhaps but innocent enough.

Then maybe lunch. Alder-smoked turkey thigh, Jarlsberg cheese, sesame crackers, Henry Weinhardt's Cream Soda, red globe grapes, toll house cookies.

Take one last picture of the glaciers on the Olympic massif. Strap on the headphones and listen to the Brandenburg Concertos. On the trail down the ridge, the breeze flowing up the steep slopes carries the scent of the countless flowers below. In this wet climate the flowers rely on visual cues more than ephemeral scents to attract pollinators so none smells that sweet by itself, but taken together they fill the air with the breath of angels. The air itself contributes: on this first rise from its long salutary sojourn over the open Pacific, it is arguably some of the freshest on earth.

Plodding along, his feet set to Trailmatic, he's completely lost in that one idiosyncratic asymmetry in the first concerto, the ritard in the allegro movement, when the female mountain lion catches a whiff of the Jarlsberg on his fingers. She follows him a little ways and then, without warning, leaps on his shoulders. With one swift chomp to the back of the neck, she severs Matt's spinal chord. Death comes within a minute, totally out of his control, virtually painless, the work of a consummate professional. What the big cat might do with his body and the Jarlsberg may upset some but it would matter not a whit to Matt. And the nutrients of his body, rather than being left six feet under ground to rot, would sustain the mountain lion's cubs.

So there you have it: his definition of the Good Death. But the newspapers would cover it as a tragedy and the mountain lion most likely would have to die as well for her assistance, probably leaving her cubs to starve.

What jolly thoughts to usher one into Slumberland. Not that he would spend a lot of time there anyway before he'd wake up to commune with the juice bottle. He rolled onto his side, trying to get the ache in his back to hurt differently for a while. He heard the first tiny ticks of the drizzle on the rain fly.

He reached into the pocket of the tent and took out his small flashlight and the plastic storage bag in which he kept the picture of Deb. In some Hindu sects the devotee worships not the idea of the god but the image of the god. He loved Deb but she was complex, changeable, impossible to grasp. This picture, though, captured the aspect of her he absolutely revered: playful, teasing, easy to use, impossible to use up. Like all idealizations, it captured just one small facet of her but we grow impatient with complex gods. Just this will do. With the delightful image of his own goddess foremost in his mind he soon felt the buttery-smooth sensation of release.

O   O   O

In the bleak morning he wrapped up the night's drizzle in the tent, walked through the drizzle to the Volvo, drove through the drizzle to the highway. Along the road the vine maples peppered the uniform green of the secondary-growth firs with the first fiery bursts of fall color.

When he stopped to take a leak and buy a cappuccino in Port Angeles, his pager beeped. He checked the number: area code 212. It must be Arnie Farquhar from NyChem with his Y2K compliance estimate. Back to reality.

He drove half an hour savoring the cappuccino, going over all the details that Arnie would want to talk about. He must have hit a snag to be calling on the weekend but the end of the year loomed and things must be dealt with now. Reluctantly letting go of his mini-vacation before even getting home, Matt dialed the number.

A man said hello. Somewhat informal for a big firm like NyChem but it was Sunday after all.

"Arnie Farquhar please," he said.

"Arnie Farquhar?"

"Is this NyChem?" He checked the readout on his cellphone to make sure he had dialed the number from the page.

"No, I'm sorry."

"Well, I'm sorry too," he said, feeling awkward. "I got a page to call this number and I assumed it was NyChem."

"Well, it's not, Matt," the man said. "But I could try to call them if you like."

"Oh my God! Russell?"

"I have my doubts that I'm your god," Russ said. "And you're welcome to go back to calling me Arnie Farquhar if you want. It's certainly a more memorable name than Russell

Jones."

"I'm so sorry!" Matt said. "I was expecting a call from New York and I guess I just assumed… So, how the heck are you?"

"Better than nothing. And other than confused, how are you?"

"About as well as you can expect for an old geezer. Well, I'd much rather talk to you than to Arnie Farquhar any day. And I'm up to here with Y2K compliance estimates. I confess, though, that one of the little treats I look forward to when I call you is when Sylvia answers the phone. What's she up to?"

"Gathering momentum as a painter," Russ said. "She's got her work hanging not only here but at several other galleries around town."

"I'd love to meet her someday. She's such a creative person."

"That she is," Russ said thoughtfully. "Although perhaps not as creative as she'd like to be."

"What else could she hope to do?"

"I haven't told anyone outside my family this," Russ confided, "—but what the hell, who are you going to tell?—Sylvia's hoping to become a mother."

"What? Are you guys trying?"

"Trying, yes. Succeeding, no. And everybody's getting a little antsy. I'm starting to wonder if my little salmon have what it takes to swim upstream. I thought maybe a stud like you could give me some pointers."

"Hey, don't ask me," Matt said. "My little salmon are still swimming around hoping to find a fish ladder."

"What do you mean?"

"Oh, Deb had her tubes tied right after we were married. We decided early on not to have kids. We figured our species had exceeded the carrying capacity of the planet and that was three billion people ago."

"Well, that's a noble sentiment. Then no regrets?"

"Only that the world won't see any more like Deb."

"All too true," Russ agreed. "I assume she's still setting an example for us all."

"Yeah, still doing the volunteer work at the Japanese Garden and down at Children's Hospital. She's also become a lot more active in some of her environmental causes the last few months, something I've been just too busy to do. She's been working with a group called Earthjustice on putting together some sort of demonstrations here in Seattle next month for the World Trade Organization talks. I think Deb works harder now than she did at Microsoft."

"But gets paid less, I assume."

"Every time Regis Philbin bellows, 'Who wants to be a millionaire?' Deb yawns and says, 'Been there, done that.' That stock just keeps going up, my friend."

"Even with the pressure from the Justice Department?"

"Listen, don't tell anybody where you heard this," Matt confided conspiratorially, "but rumor has it Gates is considering a hostile take-over."

"Again? Who is it this time?"

"The Government of the United States."

"President Bill?"

"Are you kidding? He just wants to run it, not be president. He'd have to take a cut in pay. Besides, we already have our hands full with our current President Bill."

"Well, I don't, but I suppose some young intern does."

Matt laughed. "Hey, if you're going to do schtick, you better get out your drums for the ba-doom-boom—tchishhh!"

The cell phone got fuzzy as he went across the Hood Canal Bridge.

"You're in your car," Russ realized. "Isn't this costing you a fortune?"

"One of those one-rate deals," Matt said. "Not to worry. It's great to hear from you. Sorry about your Mets not making it to the Series. What a tough way to lose." The Mets lost Game 6 of the National League Championship Series when the Mets' Kenny Rogers walked in the winning run in the bottom of the 11th. "But those Yankees look mighty good."

"I wish I was a Yankees fan," Russ said. "Anyway, there's something else we should probably discuss. When did we talk last?"

"In August, I guess. When you called to tell us about Amanda," Matt said somberly.

"Oh, that's right," Russ said. "Sorry once again to have been the bearer of bad news."

"Thanks for letting us know. If you hadn't told us about it then, you might be breaking the news to me now."

"I thought Manny and Deb were still pretty close."

"They were still good friends," Matt said. "Close? I don't know. You know how it is. You tell yourself, 'I ought to call so-and-so,' and you mean to, but then the car breaks down and the horse gets sick and there's a brand new symphony hall in town. Pretty soon six months or a year go by and you get the preprinted Christmas letter. You slap your forehead and swear you'll do better next year. Hell, you and I are the same way. You called about six months ago about the reunion, as I recall. I'm not sure we would have spoken since if it hadn't been for Man's death."

"You may be right."

"How was the reunion, anyway? We never talked about it, what with the other news. I assume you and John made my excuses to everyone."

"We told a bunch of jokes at your expense, if that's what you mean. But seriously, a lot of people asked about you, wanted me to say hi."

"Did Manny come?"

"Yeah," Russ said fondly. "She looked radiant as ever."

"I wish now we'd made the trip, I must admit. Twenty-twenty hindsight. You can never tell when you'll see someone for the last time, I guess."

"Did you guys make it back for the service?"

"You know, Deb took Manny's death even harder than I thought she would. I guess she and Manny had an argument over the phone the day Manny died and I think Deb's been flagellating herself about it ever since. I urged her to fly back, thinking it might help her come to grips with the loss, but she told me she would be too upset. She sent some beautiful flowers and a wonderful note and made a big donation to something—"

"World Wildlife Fund."

"Yeah. Anyway, she was just devastated. She rode her poor horse practically to death for weeks after that. I'm not sure she's over it yet. So you and Syl didn't make it either?"

"I got hung up at Tweak," Russ said. "And I had gone to the reunion just a couple of weeks before."

"Did you hear any more about what happened to Man?"

"Nope. As far as I know, she just fell out of the sky."

"Well, if you've got to go…"

"At least she was doing something she really loved. That's the best you can hope for."

"Yes," Matt agreed. "The good death. How's May taking it? Have you heard?"

"According to John, she's struggling. In a way, she's lost both parents."

"Something happened to Bill too?"

"No, it's more complicated than that. Let me ask you what John asked me."

"Shoot."

"What are you doing New Year's Eve?"

The question seemed so incongruous he had to laugh. "I don't know. Watching the end of the world?"

"Seriously."

"Seriously, we've got tickets to see Beethoven's Ninth at Benaroya Hall. No wait, our tickets are for the 30th. Oh, of course, I remember now. Deb's been working on the big Millennium Moonlight Ball so I'm sure that's what we'll be doing. Why?"

"Because you have a prior commitment."

"Say what?"

Russ read the text of the Piñon Nuts pledge to him.

"And I signed that?" Matt asked.

"In a bold hand," Russ said. "Matthew McCleary."

"How in the world did you remember that?"

"I didn't," Russ confessed. "John faxed me a copy of it. I guess May found it in some of Manny's effects."

"I didn't realize John was still that close to Amanda. Or to May."

"He wasn't. May went up to Estes to see him."

"What, to give him that pledge? What does she care if three old fogey friends of her mom's get together on New Year's Eve?"

"Well, there's more to it than that."

Matt saw the sign for Kitsap Memorial State Park. "This sounds like it may take a while. Mind if I stop and take a leak?" he asked, turning in.

"Not a bit," Russ said. "But you're welcome to call me back when you get home if you like."

Matt pulled into the parking lot by the johns. "Well, you've got me intrigued now. Sorry for the interruption. Has this started to happen to you?"

"What?"

"Stopping to pee every five minutes?"

"I don't do too bad," Russ said. "I get up at night sometimes. Have you talked to your doctor about it?"

In the restroom Matt cradled the phone on his shoulder so he could unzip his fly. "Actually, I did have a little scare a couple of months ago. When they did the blood-work part of my regular physical, it came back with an elevated PSA count. I went back a couple of weeks later and got the dreaded DRE."

"DRE?"

"Digital rectal exam. Don't you just love those?" gaily lisping the s's. "Separates the men from the boys."

"Up yours."

"Don't tease me now," zipping back up. "Anyway, my doctor couldn't feel anything and when they ran the PSA test again it wasn't elevated. So I'm supposed to go back in monthly for a while to check it, though I missed last month—no, wait a minute. That was in July. So I missed, let's see… this is what, October? Wow, I ought to call him." He got back into the car and drove out of the parking lot.

"Yes, you should."

"I've just been so busy. This Y2K thing…"

"How's that going?"

"I have to keep reminding myself that this is a real problem and not just an elaborate practical joke."

"It is like a virus."

"No, it's genetic. What those programmers thirty years ago didn't take into account was how easy it would be simply to copy their work into meta-programs. They probably figured, hey, let's get a working version of this up and running as quickly and cheaply as possible and five years from now somebody will come along and catch our mistakes and correct them. But people just kept building on them. Now going through the whole system is like working with palimpsests, layer upon layer of code with date-dependent functions hidden in the oddest nooks and crannies."

"I thought you were working on that AIDS-testing kit."

"I was. I am."

"How's it coming?"

"Great! We've got accuracy up above 97% and the cost down significantly."

"Weren't you having trouble getting FDA approval?"

"In a way the test works too well. Since it can be self-administered using just about any bodily fluid, the FDA is afraid people might not get the appropriate counseling and make rash decisions. But 30 million HIV-positive people outside the U. S. don't have the luxury of counseling and complicated treatments. For them it's a choice between dying alone or bringing a bunch of people with them."

"So where does the Y2K bug fit into that?"

"All our reagents are date-sensitive. Novagen needs to have all our suppliers on a steady track in order to get the kits out. Paychecks, bank accounts, all that stuff is linked together by computer now. Hell, if the Airborne Express machine in the shipping room goes down, people in Thailand and Botswana infect more lovers and kids with HIV. Or worse."

"What could be worse?"

"Antibiotic-resistant TB. It thrives on AIDS victims and is an airborne pathogen. In a way we were lucky with AIDS: infection required intimate contact of some kind. With TB a sneeze can infect a room full of people."

"Isn't it a matter of just developing a new antibiotic that works on TB?"

"You know, Russ, decades from now, the medical community may refer to this half of this century as 'when antibiotics worked.' Bacteria are so adaptable that they can do an end-run around an antibiotic within a human generation. But Novagen is working on it anyway. That's my next project, if we survive the end of the year."

"Well, I already told John that getting together for New Year's was nigh on impossible."

"Oh, that's right, you were telling me about May. I'm sorry, I got yakking on about my problems."

"That's all right. It turns out May found something else along with the Piñon Nuts pledge: a letter to Manny from Jason."

"That's who it was!" Matt exclaimed.

"Scuse me?"

"I'm sorry, Russ," he explained. "I sometimes dream with the recurring theme of being up in the mountains. I had one yesterday evening and I couldn't figure out who was in it, who I was talking to. That's who it was: Jason."

"Really! How odd."

"How so?"

"Because May and John both thought that one passage of the letter seemed to imply that Jason was May's biological father."

Matt had driven the old Volvo so many years that it had become second nature. Sometimes he would swear the car could smell the garage the way an old horse could smell the oats in the barn. He would just give the Volvo its head and it could find its own way home. While his eyes and hands automatically dealt with the two lanes of traffic going a mile a minute, his mind wandered through the dusty corridors of long ago.

That last dreadful night in Jones Park came flooding back. Jason, as distraught as Matt had ever seen anyone, had implored Matt to do one thing for him: get back to town first thing in the morning and get a hold of Amanda, no matter where, no matter what the cost. All he wanted was to beg Amanda not to do it, though he didn't specify what "it" was. When at last the morning came and Jason was gone, John counseled Matt to honor that last wish, which Matt, against his every instinct, had done. Whether that one long distance call to Texas had made any sort of difference or not, Matt had never known. But maybe the news Russ had just told him represented another piece in the puzzle.

"Matt?" Russ asked when he didn't reply.

"Oh, sorry. I had to pay attention to the road."

"Did you hear that last bit about Jason and May?"

"Oh, yes. And I was formulating an answer."

"Anyway, John and I agreed that it was theoretically possible. Would you agree?"

"Yes, I would," Matt said pensively.

"For that matter, I've always thought it possible that Jason didn't die that night."

"You weren't there," Matt pointed out. "The condition he was in, the kind of night it was —I don't see how he could have walked out of there."

"He was a hell of a walker."

"He was in a lot of trouble too, though."

"The thing with Nixon?" Russ asked. "I think some of that was a figment of John's imagination."

Matt paused. "Okay, one thing is clear: some of what happened back then isn't resolved."

"True."

"Well, what's your situation? How are things at Tweak?"

"I tried to convey that to John," Russ said. "Tweak is doing so well, I've decided to add some live entertainment."

"So you've added 'impresario' to your list of accomplishments. What kind of entertainment?"

"For New Year's, I booked a young lady named Lacey Tremaine. I haven't seen her but I've read her reviews and heard her CD and I think she'll do a great job. The only negative comment I've heard about her is that she tends to be a bit flighty."

"What? A flighty musician? Hard to believe."

"Ha, ha. Anyway, I'm going to have my hands full here that night."

"So you couldn't do this Piñon Nuts thing regardless."

"I don't see how," Russ said. "Why, do you think it's even a possibility?"

"You know, maybe we do owe May some sort of explanation about what happened back then. It wouldn't hurt us to talk about it."

"Boy, I didn't think there was a chance in hell you'd even consider it."

"What would it take to put it together?"

"Wow. I don't know. Some phone calls for starters."

"Want me to do anything?"

"Hmm. I don't know yet. I tell you what, let me put out some feelers and see what I come up with."

"Fair enough."

"Hey, listen, thanks for calling me back. It's good to hear from you."

"And you. Say hi to Sylvia."

"Give my best to Deb and I'll try to call you back in a few days."

"And maybe see you in a couple of months."

...O...O...O...

My love life hasn't played much of a role in what I've written so far. But love has influenced most of the major decisions of my life. Cupid's arrow first pierced my heart with a quivering thunk! when I was in the sixth grade. A new girl came to our school, a blue-eyed blonde with freckles who quickly proved much smarter than I. I found myself at the mercy of emotions I had never felt and couldn't control. Far too shy to actually talk to her, I wrote a song—the first I ever wrote—that a friend and I sang to her in an anonymous phone call.

One day I discovered that the green rubber eraser in my desk, on which I'd written my name, had a line in red ink under the name. Convinced, for reasons that escape me still, that the little yellow-haired girl had put that line there to acknowledge our secret passion, I treated that eraser as a sacred talisman. When my friend realized what a powerful effect that single red line had on me, he drew half a dozen more. Shocked that he could desecrate such a precious relic, I found some new friends. But, even though I went to school with her for six more years, I never did talk to the girl.

Since then, Cupid has riddled my heart with holes. Love sent me on, and brought me back from, my longest, strangest road trip.

A decade ago I carried the torch for a woman to whom I'll refer by the title her father undoubtedly gave her as a little girl: The Princess. She convinced me that if we moved to Seattle together, life would be a dream, sha-boom, sha-boom. Within months we lost the house and split up. She moved in with someone else and I took what I will call euphemistically my Princess Cruise (I actually drove the whole way) up to Alaska to try to dig myself out of debt, hoping someday to recapture her heart by supporting her in the style to which she wished to become accustomed.

I played first in Valdez during the summer when Stevie Ray Vaughn died and Saddam Hussein invaded Kuwait. This was a year after the Exxon Valdez oil spill and the whole town seemed grateful for a little peace and quiet.

One night, as sometimes happens, an attractive woman came in and insisted on singing with me, rubbing her breasts against my left elbow as I played my guitar. After the set, she introduced me to (drat!) her husband Dick, who owned the Gateway Lodge in a little junction town up the pipeline called Glenallen. They wanted to know if, after I finished in Valdez, I would be interested in playing the Gateway's bar, Dirty Dick's Saloon. After getting their assurance that I wouldn't be living in another scuzzy leaky trailer like the one in Valdez, I agreed, having, I thought, nothing much to lose.

When I got to Glenallen, I found out that I would be staying in scuzzy prefabricated Atco temporary housing with three other people in three other 12-foot cubes, mine, the fourth, being the one that had been used for a drunk tank. It had bullet holes in the door and the rancid stink of the brandy a couple of passing Czechoslovakians had puked all over the mattresses. The Atco didn't have a bathroom so we were all forced to use the restroom in the rundown lodge, when it was open, and to bathe in a communal shower in the storeroom that hadn't been cleaned in so long that the scum would have to be scraped off with a putty knife.

Chief among the motley characters at Dirty Dick's were Dick himself, a retired sea captain best played by Humphrey Bogart, and his young wife Shelley, a knock-out by Alaska standards with "a steady scowl that takes over whenever lighter emotions aren't animating her face," as I described her in my journal. I befriended a few other victims, er, employees as well: Karen, the night bartender, just up from Oregon, short and stocky with "a large bust one customer refers to as campaign buttons" who "wished she knew how to flirt;" Cosmo, the cook, rangy, freckled, intelligent, and wild, who could drink more alcohol and smoke more dope than anybody I ever saw and still throw a rowdy drunk clean over a parked car; and Rick Hartman, an ex-boxer straight out of a Jack London story, who kept himself in pocket money selling drugs and tending bar, serving drinks mostly to himself.

About a week after I started at Dirty Dick's, Dick found Hartman and Shelley doing the horizontal bop in the parking lot and in the ensuing mayhem Hartman and Shelley admitted they'd been having an affair for some time. Dick 86ed them both from the bar but sank into a deep depression. Sunday morning Shelley ran into the lodge screaming that Dick had the barrel of a gun in his mouth, threatening to blow his brains out in front of their tow-headed son. Karen went over and managed to get the gun away but, needless to say, things got a little tense after that.

A few nights later, Karen and Cosmo, knowing I was as unhappy as anybody and their only hope for entertainment other than the soap opera that is Glenallen, took me to another lodge and got me staggeringly drunk and stoned. After a while I teetered out into the parking lot for some fresh air and to watch the Northern Lights shimmer across the stars. Karen, who found me attractive by Alaska standards, joined me. We got talking about Shelley and Hartman and I told her frankly about how Shelley had come on to me in Valdez and that I couldn't believe either Shelley or Hartman were wasting their time with one another.

What I didn't know was that Hartman was lurking in the shadows, listening to every word. Plastered himself, he decided my face was out of alignment and offered to rearrange it for me, and I, in a drug-and-alcohol-induced hallucination of sobriety, decided not to let him. Cosmo, knowing Hartman usually had a weapon and often a gun, intervened, which may be why I'm alive to write this now.

Karen kindly brought me back to my drunk-tank home and proceeded to use her campaign buttons to lobby for better relations between us. Having had way too much of everything by this time, I bolted out into the morning and resolved to head southeast to the Northwest at the first opportunity, where the Princess, as it turned out, awaited my return with a happy-ever-after that lasted nearly four months before she split for Los Angeles.

Ah, love.

July 21, 1969

"Houston, the Eagle has landed," John said, dropping his pack frame and flopping down beside Bear Creek in Jones Park.

Without a word, Jason stripped off his sweat-soaked pack and leaned his beat-up guitar against an aspen trunk. He kicked off his tennis shoes and waded into the icy water.

Matt, sweating as much as the others in the early afternoon sun, stood by patiently, contemplating what to do next. "Maybe I'll take the stuff up to the cabin and get settled in," he said at last.

When neither responded, he picked up the other two packs and headed up the trail.

This last quarter mile always seemed the toughest, even though the trail leveled out somewhat from the three steep miles up the Seven Bridges Trail in North Cheyenne Cañon. Matt followed the fork by a small tributary creek and in a few minutes the cabin came into view.

It wasn't much to look at but to Matt it felt like coming home. His parents had moved every few years in the course of his growing up and he had never felt completely at home in any of the houses they had chosen. But this dilapidated one-room log cabin, which belonged to anyone willing to hike in for a night or two, belonged to the three of them this Monday.

He walked up the two rickety steps and clomped across the wood porch to the door and knocked for the sake of discretion. Hearing no response, he pushed open the battered wood door and went inside, setting all the packs onto the built-in wood table covered with carved initials and dust and candle wax. Some generous soul had improved the cabin's only window, above the table, with the addition of a sheet of more-or-less clear plastic reinforced with some rabbit wire. With the ventilation more restricted than when the window frame stood empty, the smell of bacon grease and wood smoke lingered stronger than ever. As he loosened the ropes holding the packs, sleeping bags, and jackets to the Army-surplus pack frames, he heard footsteps coming up the gravel trail and onto the porch.

"So this is the fabled Jones Park," John said, squinting in the dim light of the cabin after the bright sun.

"I'm boggled to think you've never been here before, Jacques," Matt said, untying his own sleeping bag and tossing it onto one of the bunks.

"Jase always talked about it when he and I would hike up at St. Peter's Dome or Cathedral Park but I guess I assumed this place belonged to the two of you alone."

"Nothing could be further from the truth," Matt contended. "How's he doing?"

"Hasn't said much. I figured I'd give him some time to himself. So why don't you give me the tour?"

"Well, you can tell at a glance that the focus here in Happy Aspens is on necessities rather than amenities. Obviously we have the table and bench with these two log stumps for portable stools as well. Over here—watch your step; a couple of the floorboards are loose— we have the wood stove, which must have required a mule to haul up here."

"Who built this place?"

"A guy named J. C. Jones, who owned this whole area a hundred years ago. I guess he started a little mountain resort, built some summer cabins up here that people from the Springs could rent. This one was sort of a stagecoach way-station."

"Stagecoach?" John asked. "From the Poor Farm down there on 21st Street to the middle of nowhere?"

"This was part of the old Bear Creek trail, the first route up Pikes Peak. Lake Moraine is just a few miles farther. There used to be a hotel up there."

"Well, no offense to J. C. Jones, but this isn't much in the way of luxury accommodations," John said, looking at the dilapidated stove pipe.

"The stove works," Matt said.

"Really?" John asked, opening the rusty door of what looked like half of an old metal drum. From the rear of the chamber the dented stove pipe ran up a few feet, made a right turn, and exited the cabin through a hole in one of the logs.

"It better work or this won't do us much good," Matt said, hefting the two-pound lump of hamburger, still frozen in the center, he'd carried up in his pack.

"Skillet provided, I see," John said, looking at the blackened cast-iron pan that hung from a nail.

Matt handed him a couple of sleeping bags. "You want to put these where you want to sleep? I stuck mine on one of the bunks but you have your choice of anywhere. Check out the loft."

The bunks, built onto the log walls, consisted of wide wood slats with a three-inch edge to keep the active sleeper from rolling out of the narrow frame. A ladder attached directly to the wall and made from two two-by-fours with one-by-four steps led up to the loft, which extended about half the length of the cabin and provided sleep-space enough for several, depending on how they lay and how intimate they wished to be with their fellows.

"This is cool up here," John said, rolling out the bags and looking over the log edge down at Matt.

"Actually, it's warmer up there than down here at night if you keep the stove going," Matt said, unpacking the food and candles. "But where it stays fairly cool is down below the floor boards by my bunk."

On his way back down from the loft, John looked under the bunk, where a hole in the floor gave access to a primitive root cellar. He pulled out a couple of disappointingly empty beer cans.

"Do you put food down here?" he asked.

"Sometimes," Matt said. "Though it's pretty hot out today. It'd be good to keep the meat as cold as possible. Maybe I'll stick it in the stream."

"Did everything make the trip okay?"

"Most of it. The bread got squished," holding up a crumpled loaf of Wonder.

"That's only going to build strong bodies six or seven ways now."

"But the graham crackers made it okay."

"Smores?"

"Course."

Through the open door the hot summer air bore the faint strains of Jason's guitar, drowned out occasionally by the swish of the breeze through the aspen leaves or the grating call of a magpie.

"What's he playing?" John asked.

"Sounds like Dylan, maybe," Matt said, listening too. "'Masters of War'?"

"Maybe we ought to go talk to him."

O   O   O

By the time they got down to the creek Jason had quit. He and his guitar lay side by side in the tall grass, face up to the sky where harmless herds of white clouds wandered by.

"How you doing, big guy?" John asked, standing over him.

Jason looked at him and shrugged. Pale streaks ran from the corners of his eyes.

"You know," Matt said, sitting down next to him, "it's okay to cry."

"No, it's not," Jason said, sitting up and wiping his dusty cheek on his sweaty T-shirt. "It hurts to cry. I should know, having done it a lot the last couple of weeks."

"But it gets it out of your system," John pointed out, sitting on his other side.

"No, it gets right back into my system and pretty soon I'm crying again. When I was a little kid I could get my way if I cried long enough. Now I don't get my way no matter how much I cry."

"You want to talk about it?" Matt offered.

"Words won't bring back the dead."

"They might help keep the spirit alive," Matt said.

"What, am I going to forget about him?" Jason asked. "He was my brother. As long as I'm around, he'll be around in spirit."

"He was a heavy-headed dude," John said.

"And I'm not sure I'm up to carrying the load," Jason said. "I'm not as strong as he was. I have enough trouble keeping myself going."

"So you'll rise to the challenge," John said. "Look at what Bobby Kennedy did when his older brother got shot."

"Got himself shot?" Jason asked sardonically. "What are you saying, that I should join Nixon's circus like Steve did?"

"Okay, bad example," John conceded.

"There's always Teddy," Jason went on cynically. "I could do what he did in the Chappaquiddick the other night. Managed to get himself out of his car seat, managed to keep himself in his Senate seat. Wouldn't his big brothers be proud?"

"He's no John Kennedy," John admitted.

"You think Jack Kennedy was above a little hanky-panky?" Matt asked.

"No, I think he was smart enough not to get caught at it," John said.

"Well, he was dumb enough to get us bogged down in this Vietnam mess," Jason said. "Johnson couldn't get us out. Nixon wants to get us out by getting us in deeper. The only one to figure out a way to get out of there is Steve and he came home in a box."

"At least he died bravely, fighting for what he believed in," John said.

"I'm not sure he believed in this war any more than I do," Jason said. "I think he just liked the adventure, the challenge, the chance to play with guns and fly in helicopters. He didn't care who runs the government in Vietnam. Nobody does. We're killing half the people to save the other half. Let the commies have it. In twenty years, when their bogus economic system collapses, they'll decide they want to be friends with us again."

"I didn't know Steve was that caught up in the soldier thing," Matt said.

"He didn't used to be," Jason told him. "He used to love nothing more than to come up here with this guitar and hang out for a weekend. He's the one who turned me on to this place."

Matt and John both looked with new eyes at the guitar. It had grown beyond a beat-up $30 Silvertone acoustic with flat frets and a warped neck and had become a relic.

"I forgot he played," John said. "What kind of stuff did he do?"

"Mostly folk," Jason said, picking up the guitar and strumming a G-chord. "'Tom Dooley,' 'Where Have All The Flowers Gone,' that sort of stuff." He went to the C and sang, "This land is your land, this land is my land…"

The thin sound of the cheap guitar trickled through the dell. Jones Park consists of a few acres of relatively flat park land along meandering Bear Creek below Almagre Mountain, Pikes Peak's southerly lieutenant. Aspen trees, with their dusty white bark and tremulous leaves, form the canopy, with an understory of shrubs and grass and summer-blooming wild flowers: shooting stars, Queen Anne's lace, columbines, and roses. Long since absorbed into Pike National Forest, truly "this land was made for you and me."

Jason made it only that far into the song before quitting to attempt once more to get the guitar in tune.

"Did he teach you that song?" Matt asked him.

"I don't know. Maybe," Jason said, twisting the loose B-string peg as carefully as possible only to have the string jump up half a step at once. "He certainly taught me how to play the basic chords, using this guitar, which is like learning to lift weights by lifting pianos. If you can play a bar-A on this guitar, you can play it on anything."

"So play something with open chords," John suggested.

"Like what?" Jason asked, abandoning the tuning as a lost cause.

"Your choice," Matt said.

"My choice would be to play with the Argonauts," Jason said.

"Hey, I don't leave for over a month," Matt said defensively. "And I'll be home on breaks."

"Naw," Jason said pessimistically. "You'll get up in all that rain and grow roots. We'll never see you again."

Matt didn't know what to say. He could see that Jason felt forsaken but there was nothing he could do. When Jason went back to fiddling with the guitar and wouldn't look up, Matt just shrugged and looked away.

"Listen," Jason said, relenting, "I'm sorry. I just feel like everything's going wrong all at once. I'd feel better if I knew I had my buds around to see me through it."

"Russ'll be up in Boulder with you, right?" Matt said. "You guys got a place, didn't you?"

"As far as I know," Jason said. "But it's been hard to make plans with him going to New York this summer after all."

"Well, I'll still be in the Springs, 90 miles away," John said, who had been accepted at Colorado College.

"Besides," Matt added, "I thought you wanted to be a writer. So write. Write letters to me and John. You always said you could come up with even better stuff if you sat down and thought about it first."

"I know," Jason admitted. "I'm down, that's all."

"Well, your brother just died," the other two said together.

"It's not just that," Jason said. "I feel totally disconnected from my parents too. Mom can't seem to deal with Steve's death at all. The doctor had to conk her out with sedatives the first week. And now, if anything even remotely connected to Steve comes up, she breaks down in tears. I think she always had a tender spot for him. Me, I've always been self-sufficient, mature for my age. Steve needed Mom to get him out of all the scrapes he got into. She's proud of me, but she loved him."

"I'm sure she loves you too," Matt assured him but it sounded hollow.

"How's your dad taking it?" John asked.

"You know my dad," Jason said. "He's always got to make sure everything's done right, all the proprieties observed. Everybody else's needs come before his. Which is great, don't get me wrong. But I feel like he keeps me at arm's length. I know all this is tearing him up inside but he won't let any of it show. So I feel like I shouldn't let any of it show either. Gotta be a *man*."

He punctuated this by whanging an E-chord on the guitar.

"Is that all that's bothering you?" Matt asked.

"Jeez!" John said, frowning at Matt's insensitivity. "Other than that, Mrs. Lincoln, how did you enjoy the play?"

"I just meant," Matt said, backing, "maybe he had other things he wanted to get off his chest."

Jason lay back down face up, still holding the guitar. "What do you want, a list? I'm busting my butt doing a minimum wage job so I can help pay for a university I don't really care about so I can bust my butt to get a better job I don't really care about. The only alternatives, it seems to me, are Canada or Vietnam. College, Canada, or Cong. Plus my band's breaking up, my friends are scattering, and I can't get a woman to give me the time of day."

"It's almost 3:30," John said helpfully, looking at his watch. He and Matt lay on their backs as well, staring up into the sky.

"So it's over with Chris?" Matt asked.

"Last time I talked to her, which was like a month ago," Jason said, "she told me I was too complicated."

"She's more the simpleton type," John said.

Jason just kept up a solid 4/4 on that E chord.

"So did it help?" Matt asked him.

"Did what help?"

"Getting that stuff off your chest."

"Hell, I can't even get this guitar off my chest. I'm trapped."

"So play something," John suggested again.

"Same old shit?"

"Not necessarily," Matt said. "Write something."

"I don't even feel like I can do that," Jason lamented, still hitting the E. "Even my muse has deserted me."

"The bitch," John said.

"Who needs her, anyway?" Matt agreed, looking up at the bright white clouds. "Just pull something out of the clear blue sky."

"That sky is mighty blue," Jason said.

"I wish I had a good camera," Matt said.

"You'd take a picture of the clear blue sky?" John asked.

"No, I'd use it as a background for the greens and tans of the aspen leaves and the whites and grays of the trunks and clouds. And if you use a circular polarizer, you can filter out a lot of scatter, tone down the sky. It makes the blues look good."

"There you go!" Jason exclaimed. "Can I use that?"

"Use what?" Matt asked as Jason's little finger began to rock the A-string B up to the sixth on the backbeat.

"Use that line for a song," Jason said, the E-chord taking on a slow shuffle. He sang, getting a good growl in his voice, "Oh, baby, you're making the blues look good."

"I thought you said your muse deserted you," John pointed out, taking a round Sir Walter Raleigh tobacco can from his back pocket.

"She did," Jason said, moving up to the A for a bit. "That's who I'm singing it to. She ran out on me—no, here you go" singing again "You ran out on me just like I knew you would" back down to the E "Oh, baby, you're making the blues look good."

"Except it should be at the end of the twelve-bar, shouldn't it?" Matt asked.

"Yeah, you're right," Jason said. He went up to the B7, avoiding the bar chord, for the first line and down to the E for the hook. "You know, that's not bad."

"Maybe that's your lot in life," Matt said.

"What? Singing the blues?" Jason asked. "I'm not sure I want a life that inspires nothing but the blues."

"Maybe you don't have any choice in the matter," Matt said.

"It's predetermined?" Jason asked. "It's my fate? The blues are my destiny?"

"Not necessarily having the blues," Matt conceded. "But maybe to be the one who puts his feelings and frustrations into words and music for those who can't."

"So you're saying it's out of my hands," Jason concluded, his hands still following the cycle of the twelve-bar blues. "I have no choice in the matter."

"It sounds like the old free will/determinism debate," John said, rolling a pinch of crumpled marijuana bud between thumb and forefinger to eject the seeds.

"With Matt coming down on the side of the determinists," Jason said.

"Well, I wasn't really thinking of it in those terms," Matt said, watching John carefully distribute the green powder along the crease of a cigarette paper.

"What do you think, John? Do I have a choice?" Jason asked.

John carefully licked the glue strip on the paper and rolled the joint closed. "Just one, it seems to me," he said, holding up the finished product.

Jason took it and grabbed one of the loose kitchen matches from the tobacco tin. He struck the match on the back of his jeans and lit the joint, drawing carefully until the paper had burned away. He held his hit and offered the joint to Matt. "Don't feel obliged," he said to him with the smoke.

John seconded him on that. "Matt, you are so wigged out anyway that you don't need any sort of artificial enhancement. Feel free to indulge if you like but certainly don't feel pressured in any way."

Matt had never smoked anything before. He held the smoldering joint thoughtfully, smelling the acrid smoke. "What's the difference between having only one choice and having no choice at all?" he asked and, remembering Russ's first drag, took a conservative hit before passing it on to John.

The smoke burned the back of Matt's throat and lit up his bronchial tubes but didn't taste strong or even bad. It tasted weedy but natural, not appealing the way pipe tobacco or incense smells, but not disagreeable either. As he exhaled he could feel his heart rate quicken slightly and everything else around him seemed to slow, as though the day had become more deliberate. He noticed the smell of the aspen leaves and the damp warmth of John's fingertips as he carefully plucked the joint from Matt's.

"That was a good question," John said before taking his hit. "Don't ruin it with your answer," he said to Jason, passing the joint.

"Well, it seems to me that's at the heart of the free will/determinism debate. A choice is an option. It has to have at least two alternate outcomes, doesn't it?" He took another hit.

"But the way John said it," Matt said, taking the joint again and holding it while he thought of his response, "it sounded like there was only one possible outcome." He took another small hit, the action, in fact, everything around him, seeming familiar and odd at the same time. He passed the joint back to John.

"I guess that's what I meant," John agreed. "If you say, 'There's only one decision to be made,' you usually mean only one possible course of action, don't you? I mean, possibilities have to come at least in pairs. Otherwise it's a certainty."

"Or how about this?" Jason said, waving the doobie. "Do we just have the illusion, the sensation, of having a choice before what's destined to happen anyway happens anyway?"

"I think I know what you mean but give me an example," Matt said, waving off the doobie.

"Boy, choices come in all sizes, I suppose," Jason said. He picked up an ant from the ground. "Is it this ant's destiny to be squished between my fingers today? I have the sensation of having a choice in the matter right now but do I really? Do I have to live up to my destiny, whether it's squashing the ant or letting it go, as much as the ant does?"

"In other words, when we feel like we're making a choice do we actually change the future or just predict it?" Matt paraphrased.

"We need Russ," John said, putting the half-smoked joint into the waterproof match container.

"You got a jones for a Jones in Jones Park?" Jason asked as he watched the ant, a small quick black one, run around his hand and fingers before setting it back on the ground.

"So the ant was destined to be set free," Matt concluded.

"Or Jason made the other choice," John pointed out.

"Same choice, different outcome," Jason corrected him. "Did you choose to be a determinist?" he asked Matt. "Or was it your destiny?"

"Did you choose to have free will?" Matt countered. "Or was it your destiny?"

"I choose not to choose," John said.

Matt laughed. "I knew you'd say that."

Jason laughed too and lay back down to gaze up at the sky, quite possibly squashing the little black ant in the process. He plucked a seed head from a clump of grass and stuck the sweet pale base of the stem into his mouth. "Sometimes I at least *feel* like I have a choice," he ruminated. "And I usually feel better when I think I can choose. There are times, you know, when it's more comfortable to just drift with the tide and accept your fate. But I feel more alive when I feel like I'm manning the tiller."

"Or maybe it's like cross-country skiing," Matt said, sitting cross-legged, fending off a horsefly that had found them. "When you follow the regular trail, you find yourself in the same old rut as everyone else. You find the path of your skis is predetermined. But when you get into the soft powder snow up in one of those open bowls, your skis are free to go anywhere you will them to go."

"I want to try that sometime," Jason said. "Teach me."

"Christmas break," Matt offered. "I'll take you up to my uncle's cabin in Breckenridge."

Jason dug into his pocket and pulled out a lemon drop. He unwrapped it and stuck it in his mouth.

"That stuff made my throat dry," Matt said. "I don't suppose you have some more of those lemon drops."

Jason, rolling the candy with his tongue, dug into the pocket again. "Just one," he said, pulling it out.

"I'll flip you for it," John said dryly, digging into his own pocket and pulling out a nickel. He thumbed it skyward.

"Heads," Matt called.

Heads it was. John got up to retrieve the canteen from the stream while Matt unwrapped the lemon drop, which tasted extraordinarily good for some reason. Tart and sweet and fresh. His whole mouth felt yellow.

"You know," Jason said around his lemon drop, "you guys just took the discussion to a new level."

"How so?" Matt asked.

"Rather than exercise your free will, rather than make a conscious choice about who would get the lemon drop, you let chance decide for you. But chance has nothing to do with a coin toss. The final resting position of the coin, heads or tails, is absolutely determined by Newtonian physics, right? What makes it seem like an element of chance is actually ignorance: the tosser isn't skillful enough to flip the coin a certain number of times and the caller can't count the rotations well enough to predict the outcome."

"Did he just call us ignorant?" John asked Matt, passing the canteen to him.

"Duh, maybe," Matt said slowly. "I'm too ignorant to know for sure."

"Now I don't feel so bad about running out of lemon drops," Jason said.

"No, I know what you mean," Matt said. "Theoretically it would be possible to invent a machine that could either accurately toss a coin or accurately calculate the outcome based on rotation and trajectory and stuff."

"In which case," Jason said, "you wouldn't use a coin toss as a way of letting chance or fate or whatever decide. It's our ignorance of the future that makes it seem like chance or fate."

"Although even seemingly random events reveal patterns," Matt said. "The laws of probability and all that."

"As an English major," John said, "I'd just like to say: huh?"

"Just that," Jason explained, "there's a one in two chance of heads coming up in a single toss of a coin. But the chances of throwing ten heads in a row are like one in a thousand."

"One in 1024," Matt specified, shooing the horsefly that had returned.

"So?" John said.

"Just that improbable things rarely happen in the universe," Jason said.

"Improbable things happen," Matt clarified. "They just happen rarely."

Just then something improbable happened. The horsefly attracted a couple of horses.

o   o   o

The three friends had been talking next to the chattering stream a short way from the main trail and hadn't heard the cantering hooves until they got disconcertingly close. In just a few moments the horses would be upon them.

John, having learned to be more discreet from the cop in the canyon, quickly tightened the lid onto the tobacco tin and shoved it back into his pocket.

Matt, having assumed that they had the place to themselves and feeling frightened about, and the effects of, the marijuana, wanted to flee. "Should we hide or something?" he asked the others.

"Why?" John said coolly. "We have as much right to be here as anyone."

So the three of them sat with awkward smiles watching the dense aspens to see who rode up the trail.

The riders of the horses slowed as they approached the short side trail that led to the shallow ford where the three sat. When John made eye contact with them, he waved.

"Manny," he called. "What a treat!"

Amanda Tyree rode the lead horse, a chestnut mare, followed by another girl Matt hadn't seen before, who rode an Appaloosa. Amanda wore old blue jeans and a sleeveless denim shirt with pearl snaps, cowboy boots, and a white straw cowboy hat. The other girl wore tan pants with a white shirt knotted at the waist over a swimming suit top, boots, no hat but a bandanna tied at her throat. Both were laughing and out of breath, dusty and sunburned.

Amanda rode right to the creek, the mare putting her front hooves in the water and bending to drink. "I knew you could do it, Queenie," she said to the horse, bending to hug her neck before looping the reins around the saddle horn and dismounting. "Hey, John," she said, hugging him too since he had stood to greet her. "Hey, Jason, hey, Matt."

"So you two having a race?" John asked.

"She started out ahead," the other girl said. "I just wanted to see if Cochise could catch her."

"You remember Deb, don't you?" Amanda asked John. "I think you met at Heather Cooke's party."

"Sure," John said to Deb as she swung from her saddle. "It's good to see you again."

When it became obvious that John was content to stand and watch Deb get Cochise squared away next to Queenie, Amanda continued for him, "Deb, let me introduce the others. This is Jason Walker and Matt McCleary. Jason, Matt, Debra O'Donnell."

Matt watched Jason to see if he would stand to greet Deb, planning to follow suit. He didn't, so Matt didn't, which was fine because Matt suddenly felt very awkward.

"Hey, Deb," Jason said. "Nice to meet you."

"Mandy's told me a lot about you," Deb said.

"Lies!" Jason protested. "All lies!"

"She said you were smart and funny and a good musician."

Jason pretended to slide the guitar out of sight behind him. "Well, I guess I can't deny being a musician," he admitted.

Amanda went over to him and knelt, facing him. She touched her hand to his cheek. "I just wanted to tell you again how bad I felt about Steve."

Jason looked down. "Yeah, me too."

"Are you okay?" she asked gently.

"No."

"So Deb," John said, letting Jason and Amanda have a moment to themselves. "Come here often?"

Deb smiled and looked around. "Where's here?"

"Jones Park," John said. "Have you ever been up here?"

"Nope," Deb said. "Never have."

Matt, meanwhile, felt as conspicuous as a beached whale. Everything about him, his arms, his feet, his head, seemed brobdingnagian. His mouth, already dry, felt like the surface of the moon. He grabbed the canteen and took a quick swig, which made him cough. He wished these were side effects of the marijuana but he knew better. It was the girls.

John, a decent halfback and a good swimmer, qualified as enough of a jock to be the closest thing the Argonauts had to a socialite. He always seemed relaxed and confident around girls. And Jason had that quality of vulnerability and creativity that attracted girls, at least for a while.

Matt, tall, thin, quiet, felt he had nothing going for him. He was polite and thoughtful and earnest but he tended to fade into the background. Which was fine with him since he was painfully shy.

He had known Amanda about as long as John and Jason had but had done little more than exchange pleasantries with her at school. He remembered her as a gangly kid with a prominent nose and an easy frank smile. Now that she had grown, gangly had become svelte, her tight jeans accentuating curves he hadn't really noticed in the skirts she'd worn at school. She'd gathered her long hair, as straight and shiny as Queenie's mane but a couple of shades darker, into a loose pony tail and her eyes, as green as the aspen leaves, held the promise of intelligence and compassion. A formidable package.

But Deb completely paralyzed Matt. He looked at her every angle, her every gesture, and couldn't spot a flaw. A bit smaller than Amanda, she looked perfectly proportioned. The sun had lightened her wavy blonde hair, toasted her petite nose, teased a few freckles from her cheeks. In the gap between her knotted shirt and her braided belt, he could see her tanned midriff, which he felt guilty even glancing at, as though he were peeping, but he couldn't seem to help himself. The corners of her mouth curved up naturally, the way a dolphin's do, so she was never far from smiling. But when she really smiled, as she did at John's pleasant small talk, it made Matt wish with all his heart that he could think of a way to keep her smiling always.

He felt so dazzled he didn't notice that she had asked him something until she and John both had been waiting expectantly a few moments. "I'm sorry, what?" he asked.

"I just wondered how long you and Jason have been coming up here," she asked again, smiling again, dazzling again.

"Uh, ten years maybe," he said.

"You two hiked up here when you were eight?" she asked, arching her eyebrows.

"Oh, no, when we were twelve, I guess," he corrected himself. Somewhere just beyond the periphery of his dazzlement, the mathematician in him protested. "So then six years," he added lamely.

"But this is your first time up here too?" she asked John, redirecting the brilliant beam of her attention away from Matt, to his great relief. He wiped the sweat from his upper lip onto his shirt sleeve.

"Yes," John said, scooching over so she could sit down between him and Matt, "you and I are both Jones Park virgins."

Deb glanced down at the ground, smiling. Matt couldn't tell if her face, already glowing from the sun and wind, blushed. The audacity of John's use of "virgin" astounded him but her reaction seemed not so much flustered as discreet.

Amanda had sat next to Jason, holding his hand. They hadn't said much to one another but Matt could tell from the way Jason leaned his shoulder against hers that the gesture comforted him. Amanda idly picked up the burnt wooden match that Jason had stubbed out in the dirt in front of him. "I didn't know you smoked," she said, sounding a little surprised but not accusatory.

The question caught Jason off guard. He glanced at John. "Well, I, uh…"

Usually pretty glib, the best John could muster at the moment was, "What makes you think that's our match?"

Both girls smiled at the boys' obvious befuddlement. The dope and the situation once again made Matt feel panicky, but fortunately the girls focused on the others.

"Are you little boys playing with matches up here in the woods?" Amanda scolded teasingly.

"No," Jason maintained defensively. "And we weren't smoking cigarettes."

"Then what were you… Oh." Amanda saw the light. "Oh, well, isn't that interesting?"

"Actually, yes," John admitted. "Why? Are you interested?"

Amanda and Deb looked at one another. "What do you think?" Amanda asked her.

"If you're talking about what I think you're talking about," Deb said, looking to John for confirmation and getting it, "I've never tried it. Have you?" she asked Amanda.

"No," Amanda admitted. She looked sternly at John. "Are you trying to induce some sort of reefer madness in us poor innocent girls? Take advantage of us?"

"Drat! They're on to our clever little scheme," John said to Jason. "Now what?"

"What choice do we have?" Jason said ominously, looking at the two girls. "We'll have to kill them to prevent them warning the others."

"Orrr…" John said, pulling the tobacco tin from his back pocket, "we could just try to get them high enough that they'll laugh at our jokes."

"How much is in there?" Deb asked.

"Not nearly enough to make you laugh at *our* jokes," John said, opening up the tin, taking out another cigarette paper, and crumbling some more cannabis into the crease.

"Why?" Deb asked. "What are the jokes like?"

"Uh, let's see," John said, licking the edge of the paper. He carefully rolled the joint between his thumbs and the first two fingers of both hands but having everyone watching him made him nervous and the paper creased, leaving the joint lopsided but serviceable.

"Okay," he said to Deb, "What's the difference between lighting a joint and setting the woods on fire?"

Deb smiled, both at the question and at his fumbling, and shook her head. "I don't know."

"Okay, then you light it," John said to Amanda, handing her the joint and a match. "Sorry," he said to Deb, "we just can't take the chance."

She laughed.

"And if you're already going to laugh at my jokes," he went on, "you don't need to smoke any of that vile weed."

Deb stifled her laughing for a moment but then started again.

Amanda, like Russ, had drawn too strongly the first time and she coughed. Jason gently pounded her back and handed her the canteen before taking a hit himself and passing the joint to John.

"A word to the wise," John said to Deb as he held the joint to his lips. "Don't take in just the smoke. Draw in some air along with it" carburetting a lungful "and hold it in," he added in a small voice.

Deb tried and succeeded, handing the joint to Matt. "How am I doing?" she asked him.

He hadn't spoken in a while and he tried clearing his throat, which worked only part way. "You're doing great," he croaked, then got flustered and passed the joint back to Amanda without taking a hit, on the theory that discretion is the better part of valor.

"So is this what you guys do?" Amanda asked. "Hike up here and get high and tell jokes and play guitar?"

"When we're not busy solving the riddles of the universe," Jason said. "Actually, this is the first time we've gotten high up here."

"So Jason, you play the guitar," Deb said. "And John, I guess, must be the one who tells the jokes."

"Such as they are," John said.

"So what do you do, Matt?" Deb asked, turning to hand him the joint again. "Are you in charge of solving the riddles of the universe?"

Her eyes, sapphire blue, penetrating, infinitely interesting, held Matt's eyes a moment before he had to back down. He was afraid his voice would crack again if he tried to answer her and besides, his mind had gone completely blank. He decided to take another hit after all, just to have an excuse for not being able to respond.

Mercifully, John answered for him. "Jason and I come up with our own little theories about the universe. Matt just steps in to correct our mistakes."

"For instance," Jason said, "until today, I suffered from the delusion that my destiny was in my own hands. Matt informs me that my fate has been preordained and there's not a thing I can do about it."

"What fate is that?" Amanda asked him, putting her sun-tanned arm around his shoulders.

"To sing the blues," Jason said.

"Is that a good thing or a bad thing?" Deb asked.

"I don't know," Jason said. "It's just reality, I guess."

"But what sort of reality?" John asked, fashioning a roach clip from a paper match by splitting the heavy paper down the center. He offered the delicate structure to Deb, who demurred, as did Matt, as did Amanda, leaving Jason to take the last toke.

"I didn't know there were different kinds of reality," Amanda said. "Like different flavors or something?"

"Well, there's individual reality," John said. "Everybody has their own version of that."

"What do you mean?" Amanda asked.

"I'll give you an example," Jason said. "One time Steve and I were walking up Cresta Road in Skyway Park and we almost stepped on this huge snake. It must have been fifteen feet long, like a boa constrictor or something. Scared the crap out of us. But when we got home we couldn't convince anyone that we'd actually seen something like that. Now, with Steve gone, I guess it's just part of my individual reality that no one else shares and that can't be proved or disproved."

"And then there's a kind of everyday reality," John said. "Maybe it's just a common sense sort of thing. It's what most people believe."

"But it's not necessarily right," Jason added. "For instance, most people used to believe that the earth was flat."

"Or that man would never walk on the moon," Amanda said.

"Wasn't that amazing?" Deb said. "Watching the pictures on TV yesterday of those astronauts bouncing around in the Sea of Tranquillity on the moon. It's still hard to believe they're really up there."

"They must be on their way home by now," John pointed out.

"Boys and girls," Jason said, "that is a long way home."

The afternoon sun beamed over the shoulder of Almagre Mountain, the air cooling down a little and the shadows lengthening, bringing out the colors in the aspens and the wildflowers, where Queenie and Cochise grazed contentedly in the knee-high grass. Overhead, a mountain bluebird, as blue as the clearing sky, sang to its mate high in the branches. To the east they could see the moon, almost to its first quarter, peeking above the horizon.

"It's that moon right there, isn't it?" Deb said quietly.

"There's ultimate reality," Jason said.

"Uh-oh," Amanda said. "Another reality."

"And God only knows what ultimate reality is," Jason said.

"God and Matt, from what you said about your destiny earlier," Deb pointed out.

"I hadn't looked at it that way," Jason said. "Is destiny the same as ultimate reality?"

"Maybe ultimate reality is known only to God," Deb said.

"But don't you think it's possible that God changes her mind once in a while?" Amanda asked.

"Well, if God is indeed a woman," Jason said, "I'd be stunned if she didn't change her mind once in a while. But what are you trying to say?"

"I don't know," Amanda said. "Maybe there's just some form of alternate reality."

"You mean I'm not necessarily destined to sing the blues?" Jason asked, searching for her meaning in Amanda's green eyes.

"I think you could do anything you set your mind to," Amanda said. "I thought you wanted to become a scientist."

"Yeah, Matt, I could be a scientist," he said, playfully thumbing his nose at his friend. "I don't have to sing the blues my whole life."

Matt shrugged. "Forget I said anything."

"You haven't said much," Deb pointed out.

"Maybe that's just as well," John said. "How many of us really want to know what the future holds?"

"Which explains," Deb pointed out, "why Tiresias was such a wet blanket at parties."

At that point the two couples carried on simultaneous conversations, thus:

"Great reference!" John said to Deb. "Where did you go to school, anyway? You didn't go to Cheyenne, I know. I would have remembered you."

"Benet Hill," Deb said.

"What's Benet Hill?"

"It's a Catholic girls' school out east, by Austin Bluffs. My parents thought it would keep me from getting too involved with boys."

"Did it work?" John asked.

"I'm not involved with anyone, if that's what you're driving at."

"Just wondering."

"In any case, didn't you take Mandy to Heather Cooke's party? I thought you two were a couple."

John glanced over at Amanda talking quietly with Jason, plucking a flower. "She goes out with other guys too, like Bill Black. Man and I are just friends. We tried dating a few times but we just didn't click that way. Maybe we've known each other too long."

"She's known Jason about as long as she's known you, hasn't she?" Deb asked.

"Yeah, I suppose," John said, then lowered his voice so the other two wouldn't overhear. "Why? What are you driving at?"

"Oh, nothing, really."

John elbowed her ribs. "Come on. Tell me."

"I just get the feeling," Deb said confidentially, "that Mandy wishes she could get closer to Jason."

"I didn't know you and Man knew each other that well."

"Her house is just a couple of blocks from ours. She and I go riding a lot."

"How did you get up here, anyway? Did you ride all the way from Manny's house?"

"Oh, no, we trailered the horses up to Captain Jack's on the High Drive and rode up the ridge trail."

"Do you do this very often?"

"Usually just shorter rides from home. And gymkhana, barrel racing."

"You know," John said, "I've met several

"I always thought you were really good at biology," Amanda said to Jason. "I was so impressed when I borrowed your notes for that week I was out with the flu. Couldn't you get into something like that?"

"Yeah, I've thought about it," Jason said. "I've always liked flowers. Maybe I could get into botany."

"Aren't you working on the grounds-crew at the Broadmoor?"

"How did you know that?"

"I thought I saw you dragging hoses across the street to water the flower-beds in that traffic island by the Broadmoor greenhouse. We honked but I guess you didn't see us."

"Who were you with?" Jason asked, looking down.

"Bill."

"Oh, yeah. Russ said you two were going out."

"Just a couple of times."

"Do you think you could be serious about him?" Jason asked cautiously.

"Oh, I doubt it," Amanda said, twirling a little purple aster between her fingers. "Going out with him was actually my parents' idea. His father sold my father our car and my father sold his father their house so they know each other pretty well. Mom wishes we'd get together because eventually Bill will take over the Ford dealership from his father."

"He'll be a wealthy man someday," Jason admitted. "Is that what you're after?"

"Money doesn't mean much to me *per se*," Amanda said. "But I sure wouldn't mind having the freedom that money can bring."

"If you had your druthers, what would you like to do?"

"Oh, read and draw and travel and ride," Amanda said. "Stuff like that. Just be free as a bird. In fact, I wish I could fly."

"What about kids? Do you want to raise a family?"

"Someday, maybe," she granted. "But they would have to have a really special girls who got into the horse thing as teenagers. What is it about horses, anyway?"

"Mandy says that when she's out with Queenie, they can just roam free. Maybe it's a girl thing."

"What about you and Cochise?"

"What about us?"

"Well, for instance," John said, "is he a gelding?"

Deb looked at him and laughed. "Jealous?" she asked him. "Come on, I'll introduce you to the man in my life. Mandy, John and I are going to check on the horses."

father."

"Special how?"

She just looked down, smiling inscrutably. "Bill's been as sweet as he can be to me," she said without looking up, sounding slightly defensive.

"Hmm," Jason said, looking for clues in her eyes. "That was a pretty non-committal answer. Could there be some sort of alternate reality in your future as well?"

Amanda raised her eyes to Jason's. Some questions are best answered without words. Even Deb's statement failed to break the spell.

Obviously, Matt had trouble following both conversations and the imperfect bits he caught of each convinced him that he had become a fifth wheel.

Besides, sitting next to Deb drove him crazy. He could smell her hair: not just her shampoo, which was delightful, or her cologne, which was elegant, but also the fresh air and sunshine and sweat from the ride up. It intoxicated him. Every so often her knee would touch his and it felt like a low-voltage electrical current ran through his entire body. The thought of trying to meet and hold her azure eyes again made his palms sweat. He was almost relieved when she and John got up and Matt excused himself as well.

He crossed the creek on a couple of rocks and wandered upstream far enough to give Jason and Amanda their privacy, far enough that he could gather himself out of Deb's presence.

"What the hell's wrong with me?" he asked himself aloud as he walked, oblivious to the scratches the goose-currant bushes left on his bare calves. He had never felt this way about a girl but he had never been stoned before either. The cannabis did have a way of intruding into each moment, the fascination of the sensory environment making it difficult to focus on cold, rational thought.

But there was nothing cold or rational in what he thought about Deb. If he had devised specifications for the ideal woman, she would fit them perfectly. Her eyes, her hair, her smile, her petite, perfect proportions—each alone would have attracted him. Together, they bowled him over.

And what had been his response to meeting this ideal woman? Had he been the debonair gentleman he fancied himself those rare times that he succumbed to idle teenage fantasies, suavely introducing himself to her, Bond-like: "McCleary. Matt McCleary"? No. He had galumphed along like a drunken buffalo, sitting cross-legged long after his legs had begun to ache, just so he wouldn't call attention to the fact that their knees were touching, croaking out unintelligible responses to simple questions, forcing John and Jason to pass off his tongue-tied silence as a mark of superior intelligence. Duh, 18 minus 10 equals 12, right? Jesus.

He found some consolation in the shy person's default position: he didn't stand a gnat's chance in a hurricane to begin with. When humiliating defeat is what you've come to expect, its arrival is hardly a shock. He softly sang to himself the chorus of the Donovan song: "Ah, but I may as well try and catch the wind."

Or try to catch one of those brook trout, he thought, noticing out of the corner of his eye the quick dart of the small fish as he walked along the stream. He stopped and searched the rippling water to try to spot it again. These wild fingerlings were as shy and elusive as any creature on land and didn't share the languor and momentum of their larger brethren. Matt squatted, then knelt, then lay beside the burbling creek. For about as long as he had been fascinated and defeated by girls, he had been fascinated by these little darters and defeated in his attempts to hold his arm still enough, long enough over the rushing water to lay hands on one. He lay parallel to the stream on the bank and held out his arm like a dead branch, upstream from his body because the fish always faced that direction and wouldn't be as likely to spot him.

While he lay with his head on his other arm, his eyes searching for the brown and green speckled trout, he could feel his heart beating in his chest against the cold earth. He took a deep breath and sighed it out, trying to alleviate the ache in his chest, but it didn't help. A bruise to the heart lasts as long, and hurts as much, as any other bruise.

He thought his eyes detected the tell-tale lanceolate shape of a four-inch brookie in the swirling frigid water. If so, it was within the sweep of his hand. Sure enough, it briefly became an S before returning to a quivering I. Whether he changed the future or merely fulfilled his destiny, he reached the moment of choice and decided to swoop. He thrust his hand into the water.

Two rare, improbable things happened in quick succession. First, he felt momentary contact with the slippery scales of the trout as his hand scooped both it and a broad fan of water from the stream. Then he heard a high-pitched, startled gasp.

He had been so intent on the fish he hadn't noticed Deb come up beside him, leaning forward to watch in silence what he did. Not only did the fan of icy water drench her, through some quirk of fate the fingerling found its way inside her unbuttoned white shirt. She immediately jumped back to her feet, squealing as the trout wriggled around against her bare midriff.

The exaltation Matt felt at finally laying his hand on the trout quickly turned to horror as he watched Deb, water dripping from her face and blonde hair, dance around in circles trying to get a hold of the fish, which had wriggled its way to the back of her shirt. He jumped to his feet and ran to her.

"Oh God, I'm so sorry!" he exclaimed. "What can I do?"

"Get it out! Get it out!" she screamed, wriggling around as much as the fish.

She had knotted her white shirt tightly at her waist and the water had made the fabric stiff and impossible to untie. He unbuttoned the shirt as far as he could and thrust his hands around her waist to try to grab the fish but it still proved too lively and too slippery to hold. Somehow, in trying to corner it, he inadvertently unfastened the hook on her swimsuit top, the elastic fabric falling limp, hanging from the straps tied behind her neck.

Still concentrating on his hands behind her back struggling to secure the elusive fish, he couldn't prevent his eyes from falling on her unconfined breasts, which looked as perfect as he would have imagined, had he dared to imagine he would ever see them: small but lovely, pale against her tan, contracted from the splash of cold water.

Praying fervently for God to strike him dead at this moment of supreme chagrin and bliss, he struggled gallantly on. After two or three seconds, which were the closest he would ever come to experiencing eternity, he managed to pinch the fish's tail between thumb and forefinger and then to grab its body with his other hand. Pulling his hand from behind her back, he held it out for both to see. Slender and slick, its body trapped in his grip, its gills gasping desperately, Matt wasn't sure if he should bless or curse it. Either way, he had to let it go. He chucked it back into the creek.

"Is it all right?" Deb asked.

"I'm sure it'll be fine. Are you all right?"

She laughed, to his great relief. She demurely pulled the swimsuit top back over her breasts but found that she couldn't fasten it without letting go of it again and couldn't fasten it through the shirt in any case. "Well, mister," she said. "You figured out how to unhook that so I guess you can figure out a way to hook it back up."

"Oh, I'm so sorry," he said again. "What can I do?" He looked over her shoulder but couldn't see a way to hook it through her shirt either.

"I guess you'll just have to put your arms around me inside my shirt again," she said, looking up at him.

He gingerly sought the unhooked ends of the top and pulled the stretchy fabric taut behind her back, pulling her closer to him. He gazed down into her eyes, the fact that she had placed herself in his hands bolstering his confidence. Her smile, though no less dazzling, now reassured him. The only thing standing in the way of his getting out of this more or less gracefully was that he didn't have the foggiest notion of how the swimsuit hook worked. He had never unhooked a girl's bra, at least intentionally, and hooking one is still more complex.

After fumbling with it awhile to her evident and growing amusement, he finally asked, "What am I doing wrong?"

"Maybe you're trying too hard," she said, relaxing in his arms. She left her head tilted back but closed her eyes.

The next thing he knew he was kissing her, their lips barely touching at first, her breath soft and sweet. She didn't seem a bit surprised and soon she returned his resolve, his tenderness, his passion, with grace and joy. His hands quit fumbling with the top straps and caressed the warm skin of her back. His right hand, finding a will of its own, explored its way around her side and up her ribs to cradle her still damp, chilled breast. Still kissing him, she murmured and melted into his arms. Matt, certain that this was just a dream, hoped with all his heart that he would never wake.

But sooner or later reality, in one form or another, intrudes.

"Debra?" Amanda called through the trees.

Deb and Matt shook themselves from their trance and looked with surprise into one another's eyes. They had no time to exchange romantic words: they could hear the horses' hooves. And the swimsuit top remained undone.

Matt went to work, determined to accomplish at least this small gallantry. Three tries, and three kisses, later, hook found eye and the top was resecured.

Not a moment too soon. Amanda rode up on Queenie, Cochise's reins in her other hand, just as Deb managed to rebutton the bottom buttons of her shirt.

"Is everything all right?" she asked them, noticing their flushed expressions and the damp blotches on Deb's clothes. "We heard a commotion."

"We're fine," Deb said. "Matt just surprised me, that's all."

"We ought to get going," Amanda said, handing Deb Cochise's reins.

"So soon?" Matt said, watching Deb lift her boot into the stirrup and swing herself up onto the Appaloosa.

"Yeah, already?" John said as he came up to them through the trees, Jason right behind him with Steve's guitar slung over his shoulder. "Why don't you stay for dinner? We've got plenty, right, Matt?"

"Oh, easily," Matt said, willing if necessary to go hungry himself.

"Thanks for the invitation," Amanda said politely, "but we really need to get the horses back and into the trailer before it gets dark."

Even now, the sun had slipped behind Almagre Mountain and the quarter moon offered just half light. Matt, his heart overruling his natural realism, wished that he could, like

Joshua, bid the sun and moon halt their inevitable progress, at least long enough to secure, if not victory, at least a beachhead.

"Well, Man," Jason said, setting the guitar on the ground and putting his hand affectionately on Amanda's thigh, "I can't tell you how much it meant to me to run into you up here today. Through your eyes my life looks less bleak. And Deb, I really enjoyed meeting you."

Cochise, anxious to hit the trail, nervously turned a couple of circles. "Thanks, you guys," she said, reining him in. "I had a great time."

"I'll get your number from Manny," John said to Deb, watching her tighten the bit in Cochise's mouth to settle him down. She finally pulled him up between John and Matt.

"Have a good trip home," Matt said to her, not knowing what else to say.

"There's no place like home," Deb said to him. "And like Dorothy, all I have to do is click my heels to get there. But she can have the Scarecrow. I think I'll miss the Tin Man most of all."

He hadn't thought of himself that way but like the Tin Man, he knew he had a heart because he felt like it was breaking to see her leave. But looking up at her on the horse, he found himself speechless once again.

She leaned down to him and asked, so no one else could hear, "Do you want to see me again?"

Matt found his tongue. "I will see you always," he whispered to her.

She smiled happily and clicked her heels. Cochise was off like a thunderbolt, leaving Amanda to spank Queenie's flank to try to catch up.

Jason sighed as he watched them gallop down the dusty trail. "Gents," he said, "there go a couple of real beauties."

"And the *girls* aren't bad either," John said. "How did Deb get wet, anyway?" he asked Matt. "What were you doing?"

Matt smiled as he watched Deb disappear around a bend in the trail, still three lengths in front of Amanda and Queenie. He looked at John and said, "Fishin'."

"Well, you might want to check your bait," John said with a grin, "cause Deb and I have a date."

PART II

. . . O . . . O . . . O . . .

"A sad tale's best for winter," quoth the Bard. "I have one of sprites and goblins."

Many trailheads now have a sign that reads: The mountains don't care. Meaning: If you get in trouble, if the weather turns bad, you're on your own up there. But I often feel a presence in the mountains, a mischievous sprite who tempts me to exceed my limitations just to get a peek at her ineffable beauty. Maybe being single for so long has made me more susceptible to those prankish spirits.

That mountain sprite introduced herself to me the first time I ever stood atop a peak. Oddly perhaps, considering how many years I spent in Colorado Springs, the only time I ever went to the summit of Pikes Peak was when I was five years old. A friend's father played some small role in clocking the Race to the Clouds one Fourth of July. My friend and I got to be runners, running the times for each car from the official scorekeepers to the Summit House, where the results were tallied and broadcast on the radio. To my amazement, right after the race began, it started to snow. I got so excited running through the snow on the Fourth of July on the top of Pikes Peak that I got sick as a dog. I threw up all over the back seat of my friend's dad's Mercury as he raced like one of the Unsers down the mountain to get me home.

Since then I've found myself at the mercy of that mountain sprite many times. Tempted by the delicate, fragrant flowers or the spectacular view to go too high or to stay too long, I've been beaten by the hail, blistered by the sun, lost and frozen just short of frostbite in summer blizzards, caught in impenetrable darkness, and slammed by the concussion of the thunder before the lightning bolt faded. You're never far from dying up in the mountains. You're always on the knife's edge, especially if you're alone.

Don't get me wrong. I don't flirt with danger. But sometimes that dangerous sprite flirts with me.

One June, between gigs in Great Falls and Miles City, Montana, I camped and hiked in the Little Belt Mountains. I had just bought a compass and, dying to try it out, I parked on an abandoned logging road and picked a north-northeast bearing toward Baldy, the highest peak of the Little Belts, resolving to keep to that bearing if I could. Along the way, in the middle of an ordinary slope in the dense forest, I came upon a tiny spring, no bigger around than a large pumpkin. It wasn't even a spring, really, since it didn't have an outlet. It was just a tiny segment of an underground stream, with no sign of surface water either up or down the slope. Three steps in any direction and it disappeared entirely. I felt I had come upon a water sprite there in the woods. It tempted me to linger but I had a mountain to climb.

I had the pate of Baldy to myself that day. The mountain sprite persuaded me to strip to my shorts, to roam barefoot across the pink alpine phlox and the tiny cloud-white to sky-blue forget-me-nots. The warm breeze lifted great clouds of chartreuse pollen from the lodgepole pine forest below. The only hint of danger was an old crumpled plane wreck.

When at last the shadows began to lengthen, I headed back down the ridge, easily finding the place I'd marked when I'd topped the ridge in the morning. Reversing the bearing on my compass, I wondered how close I could retrace my steps through the dense, unrecognizable forest. To my delight, I once again came across the tiny spring I'd found in the morning, again not spotting it until almost stepping in it. I stopped and bathed my face in the cold clean water.

Perhaps the water sprite took offense. Perhaps, more prosaically, there was an unknown toxin in the water. Perhaps it was just all the pollen from the trees. In any case, within minutes my windpipe began to contract. By the time I made it to my car, my uvula, the little punching bag in the back of my mouth, had swollen to three times its normal size and it slithered up and down my throat with every breath. If that sprite continued to tighten her grip on my throat, she would strangle me in hours, maybe minutes.

Driving seemed both hazardous and unavoidable. Weeks might pass before anyone came up that logging road. So I drove. Gasping for air, I managed to drive 60 miles to the nearest village, White Sulfur Springs. At the tiny medical center the emergency room guys got me breathing again with a massive dose of diphenhydramine, the active ingredient in both Benadryl and most over-the-counter sleep aids. It knocked me on my ass. I had to sleep off the shot in the shabby motel next door.

My uvula has reacted the same way two or three times since, under far different conditions, with no warning or known cause. Maybe that water sprite never left me.

November 1, 1999

Was this supposed to be a date? John wondered. If so, maybe he was too old and too married for this sort of thing.

He sat scrunched down in the Subaru Outback in the parking lot of the visitor's center east of the Beaver Meadows entrance to Rocky Mountain National Park. That sunny day when he had played hooky, he pulled out his old dope pipe as he drove by here. Could that really be just two weeks ago?

Among other things, the weather had changed. La Niña, which had bombarded the Rockies with a snowy spring and a stormy summer, had till now granted them a warm dry autumn. But this morning a high haze blanked the sky, the sun shining through feebly and the snow-powdered peaks of the Continental Divide dull and harsh looking. Not the sort of day he had hoped for when he planned this.

This day, intended to be a lark, had required a ridiculous amount of planning. And bullshitting, for that matter. He couldn't tell if it constituted a cosmic commentary or not but just this morning, for the first time in his twenty-odd years in Estes, he had found right behind his car a convoluted lump of dark brown bighorn sheep shit. The elk had graced his yard many a time with their little dented pellets but the bighorns never had.

For years the only lying he had done had been the sort of white lies that prevent the unraveling of the social fabric: No doubt having a hypnotist will make the Fireman's Ball extra-special this year but I'm afraid we have church camp that weekend. The kids picked out this video, thinking a movie called *Sirens* would be a police drama; without ratings, how were we to know? Oh, yes, Mrs. Creach, your Timmy's really got a knack for that violin.

But he only gave as good as he got. What about the One-Hour Photo place that never had his photos done in less than three hours? What about Ed McMahon assuring him that he'd won ten million dollars? Did the president really not have sexual relations with that woman? Or inhale?

And speaking of marijuana, how could he write an article containing the truth about dope that the local readers would accept? He felt like Jack Nicholson: "You can't *han*dle the truth!" Americans don't even *want* the truth. We pay good money to be lied to: professional wrestling, karaoke microphones, breast implants and other artificial additives and fillers, the false promise of inflationary progress, virtual reality. But if he wrote just what people wanted to hear, what would that be? Non-non-fiction?

In any case, other than his share of innocuous fibs, there had been no reason to impugn his credibility for years. And having good credibility makes lying so much easier.

One particular lie had served well both at work and at home: he was going to spend this Monday researching his marijuana article in the C. S. U. library in Fort Collins, probably wouldn't be back till very late. Neither Tim, his trusting boss, nor Susan, his trusting wife, had reason to doubt it.

The sleepy retiree manning the desk at the two-story brown Brynhaven Inn for the off-season hadn't batted an eye at the story John told while filling out the guest registration card: his wife's niece May Mendoza had popped in to visit for a couple of nights, catching them in the middle of repainting and carpeting the guest room. But even the off-season rates made John wince.

May had no reason to question his story about the Brynhaven's having advertised in the *Trail Gazette* and gladly comping him a room for a night this time of year in return for the great results they got from the ads they placed in his paper. Or that he had just happened to run into an old chum, a freak from John's wilder days, who just happened to have some nice shrooms for sale; would May by chance be interested in coming back up to Estes to do them with him, in light of their recent conversation?

The one about the shrooms was actually the biggest whopper. He had put out discreet feelers all over town with no result: all his old connections had long since cut their hair and found real jobs. The guy who sold John his semi-annual half oz. of dope had no interest in dealing anything else. Purely on a hunch John had managed to score the shrooms by approaching, sweating profusely, a couple of young bored snowboarders watching "Futurama" in the Wheel Bar.

But maybe the biggest lie was to himself. Was he really dipping back into the drug culture to lend verisimilitude to his article? Was he really upholding some old tradition of helping to guide a novice through the labyrinthine mysteries of psychedelia? Was he really trying to honor the memories of a couple of dear departed friends by befriending their only daughter?

Or was he just a randy old geezer with too much stress at home and too many compromises at work, trying to skip past a mid-life crisis holding the hand of an attractive young woman?

Ugh. He couldn't tell.

Regardless, his bowels were in an uproar. Normally a man with an iron-clad constitution, his meals had been making it through his system in record time for a week now. He had just resolved to visit the restroom in the visitor center once more when a rusting red Fiat X1/9 pulled into the space next to his and he watched May stub out a cigarette.

He hadn't remembered her smoking. Actually, he knew almost nothing about her. Was spending time with this virtual stranger really worth jeopardizing his marriage, his family, his reputation?

But did he really expect to bring her back to the Brynhaven, strip her naked, and make wild monkey love to her? Hardly, though that's what the wagging tongues of Estes Park would assume he had done if they found out he spent the day with her and got her a motel room. He wasn't sure he would get involved with her sexually even if she offered. But the offer sure would be a tremendous ego boost.

The last time he and Susan had made love was Labor Day. Despite having the day off, he was up at the crack of dawn, too early and too horny. Susan had allowed him all of five minutes to do what he needed to do; then she bolted for the shower, tacitly reminding him of how little he could do for her in a mere five minutes.

May smiled and waved from the X1/9 and finished gathering up her things. If she got into his car, he crossed a threshold. He had reached the point of no return.

She tapped on the window to remind him to unlock the door. He reached over and flipped the latch. No turning back.

"Hi there," she said breezily, slinging her day-pack into the back seat. Into the car with her came the smell of fresh air, cigarette smoke, coffee, and something vaguely feminine, though not necessarily perfume.

"Hi, May," he said. "So you made it okay."

She settled into the seat. "No problems. But I wasn't flying. Did you hear about that plane crash back east?"

"Yeah, that Egyptian plane, right? What a drag," he said, relaxing a little with the small talk. "It's good to see you again. How are you?"

"Better than the last time I saw you," she said. She did look a little better: less stress around her sea-green eyes, less grim determination around her mouth. "I really want to thank you again for talking to me last time I was here. And for taking time off to spend the day with me."

"My pleasure," he said sincerely, starting the Outback and pulling out of the parking lot. "Thanks for coming all the way up here again. Did you find your way around town okay? How's the motel?"

"Drove right to it," she said. "The room is dinky and a little drafty, but what do you want for free, right?"

"Right," he said, looking forward to his Visa bill. "So, are you ready for this?"

"I think so," she said.

He looked her up and down. She wore a bulky white wool sweater and an old leather jacket, jeans, and Doc Martens. Tiny braids, bound on the end with red beads, hung from each temple; the rest of her dark brown hair had been pulled back in a French braid. Not enough Gortex to be enviro-chic, but adequate.

"Let me see your socks," he said.

Puzzled, she pulled up a pant leg. A good thick sock peeked over the top of the Doc Marten.

"Looks good," he said, watching the road again. "I've got an extra poncho if we need it. Hopefully we won't."

"What's the weather supposed to do?"

"There's a front coming in tonight but today looks pretty good."

"Where are we going again? Lake Hiawatha?"

"Lake Haiyaha," he corrected her. "It's just a couple of miles up from the Bear Lake trailhead. It's a good little day hike. Pretty lake, nice view of the peaks. I brought some lunch and snacks. Did you get breakfast?"

"I'm not a breakfast person," she said. "Just coffee."

He hadn't eaten either but that was mostly due to stress. Now that the die had been cast, he felt a little calmer but still pretty shaky. He slowed at the entrance station to show his park pass and then relaxed a little more.

"So how are things in the Springs?" he asked her.

"The house is officially mine," she said proudly. "Nana and I went down to the bank and signed the papers on Thursday."

"Well, that's great! How does it feel to own a home free and clear? That's something I may never do."

"It's kind of scary, actually. I've always been able to just pack up and leave if I got tired of living somewhere. Now I can't do that. And if anything goes wrong, it's up to me to get it fixed. No more running to Mom or Nana."

"How's Nana?"

"She's been doing great. I think she's finally about healed up from her back surgery. When I talked to her yesterday, though, she said she might be coming down with a cold or the flu or something."

"Well, give her my best when you see her again," he said.

He turned left onto the road to Bear Lake. He had hoped the aspens would still be in fall foliage but the wind had stripped most of the branches, the bare trees looking like static patches of smoke among the ponderosas and Douglas firs.

"What's your little girl's name again?" he asked.

"Libby."

"How's Libby doing? Have you seen her?"

"Paco and Shirley let me take her last weekend."

"That's nice."

"Well, they just wanted to get rid of her so they could get drunk."

"Jeez. Have you talked to the judge about regaining custody? Maybe owning a home will make a difference."

"That's what Nana thought too. And now I can get a home equity loan to consolidate my debts, which will help get the creditors off my back. But the judge is going to want to see me in a better job before she's convinced I've really turned things around."

John smiled to himself. He had some news on that front that she might find interesting but he decided to bring that up later. "How old is Libby now?"

"Sixteen months. Actually, 17 months today. She's coming up with new words all the time: 'ball' and 'cup' and of course 'mama.' But she calls Big Bird on TV 'dada.' It drives Paco crazy. If I didn't know better I'd think she did it on purpose just to get to him. He'll slap his chest and go, 'No, baby, me dada! Me dada!' and she just grins and points to the TV: 'Dada!'"

"'How sharper than a serpent's tooth to have a thankless child'," he said.

She chuckled. "Where do you come up with this stuff?"

"I got that one from another old fool of a father with daughters who give him nothing but grief."

"That's right, you have daughters of your own, don't you? How are they doing?"

"Remember the incident at the school when you came up here a couple of weeks ago?"

"Oh, yeah, the kid with the gun that held a teacher and some other kids hostage. I read more about it in the paper the next day. Your daughter wasn't one of the hostages, I hope."

"I think I would have preferred that," John said glumly. "Actually Anne was more of an accomplice."

"Oh no!"

"Oh yes. And what makes it worse is the way she deceived us. At first she pretended to be as shocked and traumatized as all the other kids. And Susan and I went for it hook, line, and sinker. It wasn't till a week later, when she and Alice had one of their daily spats about some unbelievably trivial transgression, that Alice let slip to Susan that Anne was more than casually acquainted with Wayne Giles. It turns out that Anne has been skipping drama club after school to have make-out sessions at Wayne's house while Bruno and Barbara were at work."

"Uh-oh."

"Indeed. She not only knew he had a couple of guns but she had heard him say that if the other kids didn't quit pushing him around, he was going to blow somebody's head off. And she didn't tell anybody!"

"Well, nobody wants to be a snitch," May offered.

"She was smoking dope with him too!" John went on, incensed now. "I can't believe she didn't feel like she could talk to me about *that* at least. I've always made it clear to both my daughters that if they had any questions or problems with drugs, they could come to me."

"Do they know you smoke dope?"

"Well, I don't just light up around them. Susan would kill me. But knowing the era I grew up in, Alice and Anne must assume I've had some experience along those lines. I've talked to them about it before. Hell, they know I'm writing an article for the paper about marijuana."

"Really?" she asked. "What are you going to say?"

"God, I don't know," he lamented. "Both Tim and Susan think I'm down in Ft. Collins researching it today. But all the research in the world isn't going to produce the article people around here want to read."

"I hope my coming up here isn't interfering with your work."

"There's research and then there's research," he said, reaching into the glove box. "Would you care to join me?" he asked her, taking out the old wooden pipe.

"I thought we were going to…"

"Oh, yeah, we will," he assured her. "I just like to prime things with this. Please forgive my shitheadedness. It's been a rough couple of weeks and I really need to leave it all behind for a little while."

She watched him light the bowl. "Do you think I should?"

"You know," he said, exhaling, "on second thought maybe you shouldn't. You ought to experience the psilocybin alone to really assess what it does."

She watched him take a second toke. "Can you write an unbiased article about marijuana if you use it yourself?"

"Probably not," he admitted with the smoke. "But then wouldn't you find prejudice in an article about alcohol written by a teetotaler? Or one about sex written by a nun? Abstinence brings a different kind of bias."

"Are you going to admit you use it?" she asked.

"Probably not," he said again, putting the pipe back into the little tin. "I'll probably say what so many people, including the president, have said: I experimented with it years ago. That's one of my deep disappointments with Bill Clinton, that he never really cleared the air about a substance that he admitted using himself."

"What would happen if you did confess to it?" she asked.

"Legally, probably nothing—as long as I got rid of my stash. And if Wayne Giles hadn't been involved in guns, his father probably could have gotten him off of the drug charge easily. As it is, he'll probably do community service and have regular pee tests and psychological evaluations and be on probation for a couple of years. But if he were Black, and his father weren't head of the school board, and they caught him with crack cocaine, the consequences would be far worse than that."

"What about Susan and your kids?" May asked. "How would they react?"

"If I got busted for possession? I'd be in deep shit. Tim might have to fire me rather than have the paper suffer the bad publicity. Susan probably would dump me and take the kids. She hates dope and even though she knows very little about my use, she considers it one of my many serious problems. On the other hand, I think smoking dope has enabled me to quell my anger over the years and preserve what's turned out to be a less-than-perfect marriage.

"But if I admitted having a 'problem' and sought help, no matter how hypocritical a ploy that might be, most people, maybe even Susan, would admire my honesty and character. At least that's how it works with celebrities and politicians. As long as you're a victim, as long as you don't choose to do it, as long as you claim not to like it, you're okay."

"Are you addicted to it?" she asked him.

"I love getting high," he admitted. "But only as long as it doesn't interfere with whatever else I'm doing. As far as that goes, I love eating ice cream too. Sometimes when things get hectic I forget about smoking dope for days or weeks. Last winter I went for three months without smoking. But I hardly ever go three days without ice cream. What about you? Which would you find easier to give up: dope or cigarettes?"

"Oh, I never fiend for dope the way I do for cigarettes. I can't imagine bumming a joint from a stranger the way I would bum a cigarette."

"And what about your DUI? That was for alcohol, right?"

"And coke," May admitted. "I went out partying with some friends to try to forget about Paco for a while and got careless on the way home."

"Alcohol makes me careless too," John said. "I just literally don't care what happens. But dope always makes me more paranoid, more afraid something bad will happen. I usually drive slower if I'm a little high. But too much definitely can be distracting. Of course, if you're impaired by anything—dope, coke, booze, Benadryl, sex, lack of sleep, whatever— you shouldn't be driving."

"So why do you think marijuana's so illegal?"

"Lots of reasons, some of them going back a long way. Like William Randolph Hearst protecting his interest in timberland as a supply of pulp for his newspapers by demonizing a cheap, easily grown, renewable source of fiber. Nixon picked drugs as part of his law-and-order campaign too, going so far as to use a different formula on the same raw data to make it appear that drug use went up 800% in two years. But I think the reason it still scares the establishment so much is that it grows almost anywhere with little care and requires almost no processing. Just dry it and ingest it. Very few other drugs are so potent in their natural form. If it were legal to grow, think of all the middle men who would lose their profits. So the drug dealers are just as adamant about keeping it illegal as the government is. Back in college I used to fantasize about becoming Johnny Hempseed, wandering through the countryside sowing hemp from a bag slung across my shoulder, until eradicating it would be impossible, until it would be free for the taking. It would become an uncontrollable controlled substance."

She laughed. "Wow, what a thought! Anybody could get stoned any time they wanted."

"But, you know, I don't think that would happen. Even if dope were legal and relatively cheap and readily available, how many people do you know who would become dope fiends? Probably a lot of people who have never taken a toke might try it but most of the people who don't smoke marijuana now have reasons for not smoking it that wouldn't go away: they wouldn't care for the sensation, they'd find it too distracting from their jobs, they'd prefer a different kind of buzz, like a drink. Those people are in the majority now and they'd probably stay in the majority if it were legal. Most of the people who enjoy marijuana already smoke it, despite its illegality. Besides, legalizing something is not the same as advocating its use. Alcohol and tobacco are legal but I don't think the government is trying to imply that people ought to drink or smoke cigarettes. In fact, if, when prohibition was repealed, the government had imposed more stringent guidelines for the reasonable use of alcohol and imposed stiffer penalties for its abuse, like the one you suffered, millions of people would never have died in car accidents over the years."

"Well, I'm still driving without a license," May pointed out.

"Driving drunk?"

"Oh, hell, no."

"There you go. It works. I doubt if anybody thinks marijuana *abuse* should be legal."

"But wouldn't people abuse it?" May said. "I'd be tempted to."

"A lot of people already do, depending how you define abuse. Although, as far as that goes, we've been doing unsupervised human tests on marijuana for three or four decades now and not only don't you see a marijuana ward at the hospital, now some states have brought cannabinol into the pharmacopoeia.

"Some people are going to find a way to abuse themselves no matter what," John went on. "I've known people who severely limited their mental capacities sniffing glue, or gasoline. Making something illegal makes it less likely that people who have a problem with it will seek help. The money we spend fighting the war on drugs could be better spent on treatment and treatment would be more successful in an atmosphere of acceptance. For that matter, we not only spend huge amounts of money on enforcing drug laws, we also screw ourselves out of a huge tax revenue that could be used to treat people with problems. The reason the price of marijuana hovers around the price of gold is almost entirely due to the outrageous, untaxed mark-up between the grower and the consumer. Even imposing a gigantic sin tax on legalized marijuana would probably bring the price down and net the government billions."

"You make some great arguments," May said. "So why is it still illegal?"

"*Cherchez la* buck," John said. "Money doesn't just talk in this country. It dictates. How many hundreds of thousands of people die from tobacco-related diseases every year? How many thousands die of alcohol abuse, and poisoning, and even overdose, something that has never happened with marijuana? On every tobacco-lobbyist's key-ring, next to the one for the Lexus and the health club where he's going to meet the guy from Seagrams or the traveling Prozac sales-rep, is the key to the chamber doors of the Senate of the United States."

"Obviously, you're really worked up about this," May pointed out. "Why don't you write about it?"

"If I write what I just said for the *Trail Gazette*, I'll be fired more surely than if I admitted smoking dope. It's a funny drug. The people who hate it and don't use it see the users as lazy and weird, qualities they can't stand. Dopers, being lazy and weird, tend to just accept other peoples' judgment of them. If you imposed the same laws on tobacco as we have on marijuana, there'd be armed rebellion. And some of the laws have become pretty outrageous. If you're convicted of growing a certain number of marijuana plants, whether you've actually sold any or not, your house, your car, all your possessions can also be tried and convicted of selling marijuana, confiscated by the police, and sold, with the same police who busted you keeping the profits. Even rapists and murderers don't suffer that."

"Maybe you should have become Johnny Hempseed after all," May said. "All this absurdity would have gone up in smoke. So why didn't you?"

"Jason convinced me that it would be an ecological disaster."

With the mention of Jason's name, John could feel May's eyes focus sharply on him.

"We'll talk more about that stuff later," he promised. "But now we have work to do."

While he had been talking, they had skirted the base of two large moraines and followed

Mills Creek up a wide valley, the last mile a series of switchbacks leading up to the bench that held Bear Lake. He pulled into the big parking lot. Thankfully, only a handful of cars clustered around the trailhead. He found a relatively isolated slot and shut off the car.

"We're here," he said.

"Now what?"

He pulled a film container from his shirt pocket. "You've never done this before?" he asked, opening the container to show her the contents: a few dried, ragged caps of tan, gray, and gold mushrooms, with a half-dozen scraggly stems and some powdered caps and gills at the bottom.

She shook her head. "It really is just mushrooms," sounding surprised, picking up piece of a cap. "We just eat them? Do they taste bad?"

"They taste more or less like mushrooms. But is that all you want to ask?"

"Did you do this with my mom and … Jason?"

He thought back. "I'm not sure we ever did actual shrooms together. But we did similar things."

"Was it worth it?"

That'd teach him to ask for questions. He bought some time. "What do you mean?"

"If you had it all to do over again, would you leave out this sort of thing?"

"Psychedelics?" John asked and she nodded. "I might not do as much as I did. I'd do things differently, for that matter, with different people. I'd, uhh…"

There was really only one way to answer the question. He fished out a small cap and popped it in his mouth. She did the same.

He hadn't done this for a long time. He had forgotten how dry and chewy and then slimy they were. He'd forgotten the way his jaws tightened slightly as his body detected the drug. He'd forgotten that, far from being an escape, this represented a commitment, that whatever happened to him in the next few hours would happen in the context of this altered state, no matter what.

"You know," he said to May, watching her turn the mushroom over in her mouth, "there's no turning back."

"Then we'd better press on," she said, chewing a stem too.

When they had finished about half of the shrooms in the film canister, they washed the remnants from their mouths with some apple cider John had brought just for that purpose. They pulled their packs from the back seat and got out and locked the car.

o o o

At the trailhead John excused himself for one last visit to the restroom. His colon still felt jittery but everything that could be evacuated was already long gone. As he sat there thinking about what lay ahead, he said aloud to whatever part of his brain prompted him to pull crazy stunts like this, "Another fine mess you've gotten us into." But actually, it felt good to be up in the mountains and he enjoyed May's company. He spent too little time anymore with people with whom he could be open and honest. With whom he could get high, for that matter.

When he rejoined her, she whispered to him, "I don't feel anything. Do you?"

He touched his face with his fingers. "Oh my God! I've gone completely numb! Can't feel a thing!"

She hit him on the arm and they started walking past the lake.

Bear Lake is the last of a string of paternoster lakes along the ancient bed of a glacier between Flattop Mountain and Hallett's Peak. One of the most accessible destinations in the park, the lake's encircling trail had been renovated during the summer to offset the wear and tear of countless footfalls. They took the less-used trail to Nymph Lake, though, each of them lost in personal thoughts, getting used to the walking and to the day. About mid-morning now, the sun made more of an effort to pierce the high haze, with little luck. A cool breeze slid down the valley, invigorating the hikers' lungs and tweaking their noses and ears.

Nymph Lake is little more than a pond but from here they got a better view of Long's Peak and the Keyboard of the Winds. They stopped for a breather.

"This is beautiful," May said, taking in the tall subalpine trees and the ripply water and the larger view.

"In the summer, the lake is covered with water lilies," John told her.

She looked at the few brown and shriveled husks that hadn't yet sunk. "The summer's gone," she said wistfully.

John looked at the sad nymph as she gazed into the dark water. "You probably want to know how Jason died," he said softly.

She looked up at him. "I guess it would help."

"I wish I had an easy answer for you but Jason wasn't an easy person," he said as they started walking again, May in front so she could hear what he said. "To tell you the truth, even his good friends still disagree about what actually happened. Maybe someday, maybe even New Year's Eve, Matt and Russ and I can get together and give you our separate opinions. But rather than influence you with my own bias, maybe I should just tell you what it said in the papers. Fair enough?"

"Fair enough."

"Okay, here goes: In the summer of 1970, while camping in an old cabin in a place near the Springs called Jones Park with friends, namely Matt and me, Jason went out to take a leak and disappeared in the middle of a cold, stormy night. Despite an extensive search, his body was never found."

"That's it?"

"For now," he said, not surprised she felt short-changed but reluctant to open a 30-year-old can of worms. That could take all day and he wanted to deal with more positive aspects of Jason's story first. "Like I said, opinions differ about the cause of his disappearance."

"Isn't it kind of weird that both he and my mom disappeared up in the mountains near Colorado Springs?"

"Russ wondered the same thing. Is it an odd coincidence? Yes. Is it more than that? I don't think so. It's impossible to search every inch of these rugged mountains. And frankly, what with mountain lions and coyotes and bears, dead bodies don't stay put too long. That may be the reason your mother's body was never found."

She looked around at the woods nervously.

"I said dead bodies," he assured her. "That's why we're going stay alive today."

"But…"

"In all the years I've been up here, I've never had a problem with those animals. But just to make sure, let me give you one simple rule: Shy means tasty."

"What does that mean?"

"Just that animals that are good to eat, like deer and rabbits, tend to be shy. They run and hide and stay quiet. Animals like porcupines and rattlesnakes, which aren't very good to eat, or are dangerous to try to eat anyway, aren't very shy. So act in the woods like something not very good to eat. Make plenty of noise, talk loud, look confident. And try not to sneak up on anything. No one likes to be surprised that way."

"Maybe you should go ahead of me," she suggested, stopping.

"Actually, the first in line is more likely to surprise a bear but the bears are all asleep now.

Mountain lions are more likely to attack a smaller individual trailing behind. So why don't you lead the way? Besides, I'm really enjoying the view from back here." He was, too. She filled out her jeans nicely.

She looked at him and blushed.

"Now what did I just get through telling you? Shy means tasty," he kidded her.

She rolled her eyes and led on.

Whether it was the bit of flirting or the mushrooms or the stress, by the time they reached the outlet of Dream Lake John felt a little queasy. May, breathing hard from the hike, didn't mind stopping to take in the view.

Dream Lake lay long and skinny in the valley. A shelf ran around the shoreline, the crystal clear water revealing the rocky bottom; the deeper, darker water in the center looked opaque and impenetrable. From here they could see the sheer cliffs that the glaciers had carved in the flanks of the peaks. Fresh snow on the summits hinted at the coming winter and here the wind grew stronger and chillier. Rather than head up to the dead end at Emerald Lake, they took the fork in the trail that led across Tyndall Creek and past Lake Haiyaha toward the Loch.

The trail steepened and before too long May had to stop to breathe. John thanked her, having graduated from queasy to nauseated.

"Are you okay?" she asked him, looking at his pale sweaty face.

"Uhhh…" he said, bent over and panting with his hands on his knees. "This happens sometimes."

"What do you mean?"

"The mushrooms have this effect sometimes when they hit your system. You don't feel anything?"

"My stomach's a little upset," she admitted. "But you really don't look very good."

"That's because…"

But before he could go on, he dropped his pack on the trail and bolted down into the trees. Slumping over a stump, he felt his gorge rise and he knew he had to throw up. Sweat popping out on his brow, he closed his eyes and yielded himself up to the inevitable.

Fortunately or otherwise, the fact that he had ingested only the mushrooms and the apple cider this morning meant that he had very little to throw up. After a couple of gut-wrenching heaves, he produced only a little stream of sour liquid flecked with bits of mushroom. Exhausted, he lay over the stump a few moments until she called to him.

Well, now, isn't this humiliating, he said to himself. Damn good thing May brought along an experienced mountain man/trip guide. Aloud he said, "I'm all right. Hang on, I'll be there in a second."

He struggled back up to the trail, feeling slightly better in his stomach but having the sensation in his mouth of what he imagined flamingo shit would taste like after it had gone bad.

"Is there anything I can do?" she asked him, her concern suffusing her face. "Can you make it back to the car?"

He smiled crookedly and swallowed painfully. "I don't suppose," he managed to choke out, "you have a breath mint?"

She searched his face and when she realized he was serious, she searched her pack, coming up with a ragged, stuck-together roll of tropical fruit Life Savers. She pried off a mango and gave it to him.

He sucked on it gratefully. "How can I ever repay you?"

"Do I need to go for help?" she asked urgently.

He picked up his pack. "Oh, no, I'll be fine. How about you? You're still okay?"

"My stomach's a little upset still but I'm—" She too had bent to pick up her pack. "Wooo, that was weird. The little red beads on my braids. When they swung down, it seemed like…"

"Like they left trails?"

"Yeah! Exactly! Is that what…?"

He nodded sagaciously. "Welcome to the wonderful world of color."

"And there's no turning back, is there?"

"Then we'd better press on," he said, pointing up the trail.

"Are you sure you're going to be all right?"

"I'm going to be better," he said with confidence, waving her on.

The trail rose unrelentingly and they established a cycle: They walked until they had to stop to breathe, John's weakened condition matching May's inexperience and smoker's lungs. They stopped, panting, giving May a chance to search his face for signs of incipient gangrene. That gave John a chance to invent ever more drastic facial contortions portraying his imminent demise. Both reassured, they cast their eyes about the thick dark forest on this north-facing slope, acclimating to the ever more interesting distractions of the hallucinogen. Then the trail beckoned again and they walked some more.

At last they topped the ridge and suddenly things changed. The trail leveled, making walking a joy instead of an effort. The forest became much smaller and more open, affording views of Long's Peak they hadn't seen. The milky haze in the sky had curdled, creating an intricate pattern of clotted gray clouds separated by patches of blue sky. The shelter of the deep forest gave way to the rush of the chilly breeze flowing down from the high passes.

May, encouraged by the flat ground, plunged enthusiastically along the trail, hopping a couple of rocks across a stream. He called a halt and she spun around, taking in the grandeur of the place.

"This is fantastic!" she cried.

"You know what's more fantastic? We're here!"

While it's impossible to dispute a statement like that, she nevertheless cast about her. "Isn't there supposed to be…?"

"The lake's off the trail, up here. Follow the stream. It's the outlet."

"All my life I've been looking for an outlet," she said, gladly abandoning the trail, caught up in the liberation of choosing her own path.

Within just a few steps, though, she stopped short, staring at the ground. Coming up next to her, he saw what stopped her: on the ground lay the skull of an elk with a full four-point rack of antlers still attached.

He saw the fear on her face again and tried to dispel it, whispering, "Lions, coyotes, and bears. Oh my!"

"That's not funny!" she said, looking around.

"Okay, first of all, it must have died sometime last winter, since the antlers are still attached. Look," he said, pointing to striations in the smooth white bone. "You can see where the squirrels and shrews have sharpened their teeth and added some calcium to their diets."

"But whatever killed it…"

"Is long gone, if it was killed by a predator," he said. "But it most likely died of old age or hypothermia or starvation or a fall. Or maybe a rival killed it during the rut. There aren't any other bones around, so probably the coyotes dragged just the skull down."

"So it's not a bad omen?" she said, running her finger along the smooth, yellowing antler.

"I think it proves that life thrives in abundance up here," he said.

"It is beautiful," she admitted, lingering over the elegant forked symmetry and blunt, bleached points.

"So is what's coming up next," he told her, pulling her away.

Sure enough, across a small rise they came upon a still pool of crystal water studded with lichen-encrusted stones. "Is this the lake?" she asked him.

"Disappointed?" he asked.

"No! It's wonderful!"

"This is what God does when he's by himself, walking in the garden in the cool of the day. Keep going," he suggested.

The stones in the pool were placed in such a way that one could easily find a path across the water without ever touching it. Some large boulders, the size of haystacks, defined the upper end. Finding a way through them, she topped another small rise and found herself on the shore of Lake Haiyaha.

When he caught up with her, she turned to him, her face alight with wonder and awe. "It's just…just incredible!" she cried. She threw her arms around his neck and hugged him.

"I'm glad you like it," he said. His jangled nerves had left him feeling like all his bones were out of joint but the pressure of her hug seemed to knit everything back into place, the way smoothing a ruffled feather restores it.

She turned him loose to resume her delight in the panorama: the clear but choppy water, the stunted trees ascending the slopes, the vast empty gorge above the lake, the indomitable peaks towering above it all. "How high are we?" she asked.

He reached over and pretended to wipe something from her earlobe. "I don't know how to break this to you but it looks like your brains are starting to leak out."

Her consternation quickly turned to exasperation. "No, you know what I mean."

"Let's see," he said, surveying the shrinking trees. "Timberline here is around eleven-three, eleven-four, so we must be at around eleven thousand feet."

"Wow, I don't think I've ever been this high," she said, whirling just in time to scowl him away from wiping her ear again.

"It's a brave new world, isn't it?" he said, delighting in her delight.

"I don't know. It looks really old somehow."

"The rocks are old," he conceded, looking up at the sheer cliffs. "But the valley is, geologically, quite new, just a few thousand years old, going back to the last ice age."

"So glaciers did all this?"

"See those snow overhangs in those high couloirs?" he said, pointing up at the vertical cliffs along the ridge line. "Those are glacier seeds. Add water and pretty soon this whole valley disappears under hundreds of feet of ice. Just by putting one flake on top of another, you can move mountains. The glacier carved out the lake bed and left behind all those boulders in Chaos Canyon."

She looked where he pointed. "It's not really called that, is it? It sounds like something out of a fairy tale."

"It is called that and the name is apt. I went up there with a hiking buddy of mine once. Most places in these mountains can be reduced to a human scale. Even roping up the Shark's Tooth, or the Diamond on Long's, you do two or three feet at a time. But Chaos Canyon is just a jumble: boulders as big as semis down to rocks the size of bowling balls. All thrown together at random. There's no sense of surface. It's all up and down, scrambling and sliding."

"Chaos Canyon sounds like it should have monsters," she said.

He thought about it. "It does. They have black bodies decorated with fluorescent green Christmas trees and eight black legs and eyes. They are the major predator up there."

She looked up at him skeptically. "Uh-huh."

"Okay, so they're spiders but, in terms of biomass, they're still the major predator, snagging skeeters in their webs. When they see something as big as a person coming, they drop and roll, curling their legs around themselves and becoming a ball that rolls down between the rocks and out of sight."

She squinted at his veracity.

"If I'm lying, I'm dying," he said, raising his right hand.

"And that's Mount Everest," she said.

"Actually, that's Hallett's," he said. "And that's Otis Peak on the other side."

"How did you find out all this stuff?"

"I learned everything I know," he said, putting his arm around her shoulders and turning her around, "from this old guy right here."

"This old guy" was a gnarled, ancient limber pine growing just a little way from the water's edge. Only some twenty feet tall, it was nevertheless the oldest, most substantial tree in sight. The winter winds howling off the flat of the frozen lake had twisted and convoluted its several trunks into a fantastic, complex puzzle. Far from being defeated by the harsh conditions, it seemed to thrive on the adversity, the occasional broken limb offering an opportunity for some young sprout with a better idea. Its dark green needles, flagged by the wind, sprung bold and vigorous from the sturdy, stubby twigs.

"Oh, he's wonderful!" May exclaimed, wrapping an arm around a thick horizontal trunk and stroking the rough bark. "Is he a piñon?"

"He looks like one, doesn't he? Actually, he's a limber pine. You can tell by his nuts."

She ignored his crudity. "He reminds me of Yoda. Will he talk to me?"

"If you're wise enough to listen," he told her, admiring the ruddy glow in her face.

She tilted her head back and gazed up at the fretful brows of needles, at the ribs of dead wood as white and smooth as the elk skull, at the knobby knees of root crossed over the unyielding bedrock. "What can you teach me?" she asked it. "Something about survival, I'll bet."

"What doesn't kill us," John said, as much to himself as to her or the tree, "makes us stronger."

"You can't kill something that was never born," she said. "How could a seed grow in such stony ground?"

"It depends on the seed."

She caressed the sturdy trunk. "He must have had great parents."

"Or he learned early how to adapt."

She looked around. "The tree that his seed came from must be long gone." She patted his thick bark. "You must have survived without much help from your parents. What's the trick, Yoda? How do I avoid falling prey to my dark side?"

John scrunched up his voice *a la* Frank Oz. "May the forest be with you."

She laughed. "I want to live here with this old guy," she proclaimed.

"You do live here," he pointed out. "But you know what we need?"

"A wookie?"

"No. Lunch."

The wind swept as hard and straight as a broomstick across the lake, forcing them to seek shelter behind one of the large boulders by the rock pool. He spread his large black poncho on the ground and unwrapped the lunch from a thick towel. Using the towel for a cushion, they sat shoulder to shoulder, leaning their backs against the boulder.

For lunch he'd brought a thick ham-and-Swiss sandwich on sturdy rye bread with plenty of mayo and mustard, some barbeque-flavored chips, a couple of Cokes, and for dessert some Oreos and pine nuts, just because. He set it all out in front of them, along with a notebook and pen.

"How's your stomach?" she asked him.

He looked into her blue-green eyes, dilated and brilliant in the daylight. "Everything is better, as promised," he said.

It was true. One of the things he'd forgotten about shrooms was the feeling of absolute well-being that chased all memory of any discomfort the drug may have caused earlier. The feeling seemed to emanate from his spine and it extended to the farthest extremities of his being. Some of it came from purely physical comfort: the boulder shielded them well from the probing fingers of the wind. The sun, when not blotted by the clouds, felt warm and reassuring.

But the effect of the psilocybin was far more than simply a happy glow. Even though he may have lost some of the expected potency by throwing up part of the mushrooms, the drug still worked its way into every crevice of his consciousness. Every movement, every color, every sensation sparkled with newness, as though all previous experience had taken place in a muddled dream from which he was now freshly awakened. Each trivial action, hitherto just another chit in the humdrum log of daily life, now seemed imbued with special meaning and purpose. Blake came to mind, unbid:

> To see a world in a Grain of Sand,
> And a Heaven in a Wild Flower,
> Hold Infinity in the palm of your hand,
> And Eternity in an hour.

May, too, seemed fascinated by minutiae. She picked up the bag of piñon nuts, took out a couple, and popped them in her mouth.

"What do you think?" he asked her.

"Not bad," she said, taking a bit of something from her mouth. "What are these little chewy things?"

"That's the germ, the seed's embryo."

"Will these grow?" she asked, looking at the bag of nuts.

"Now?"

"They're baby plants, aren't they?"

"I think they're cooked or something," he said. "They wouldn't grow around here anyway. Now they're lunch."

She looked at a creamy seed. "Baby angel," she said to it. "Never had a chance to grow."

He cringed to hear Jason's phrase. "Now it can help you grow," he suggested gently.

"I'm already grown," she maintained.

"To quit growing is to die," he said. "Up here, at this time of year, you have to eat."

She looked at what was spread before her. "I can't eat all this."

"I know. Eat half."

"Of everything? Cause I'm not eating half of that notebook."

"I'll eat the notebook and the pen. You eat half of everything else."

She took a desultory bite of the sandwich. "What's the notebook for, anyway?" she asked after a sip of Coke.

"Notes."

"Like musical notes?"

"Whatever. I just thought it might be nice to have in case anything interesting happens."

"*Every*thing's interesting!" she exclaimed.

He handed the book to her. "Then this belongs to you."

She set down the sandwich, took the pen and book, and scribbled something on the page. He couldn't see what she wrote but the way she wrote it, the way she held the pen, conveyed earnest intent and creative joy in the act of writing. He hadn't seen anyone write that way for a while. It looked familiar, refreshing.

The mushrooms dulled his appetite too but he knew they had to keep their energy up for the hike back. He urged her to take another bite.

"You sound like my mother," she said, complying.

"I'm sure she said things like that because she loved you."

"I know," May said. "She told me. She told me once she loved you too."

"And I loved her," he said reflexively.

She looked up from the notebook. "Did you?"

Spotting a caution sign, he took another bite of sandwich to formulate a response. "Well, sure," he said. "She and I knew each other since grade school. She was a wonderful, kind person and a great friend."

"Did you go out with her?" she asked.

"Actually, yes, we did go out a couple of times right after we graduated from high school."

"Did you…?" She looked the rest of the question at him.

"Did we…? Oh. Oh, no. We never did."

"Well, when did she meet Jason then?" she asked, jotting another note.

"Ah," he said. "Actually, she knew Jason about as long as she knew me, though he went to a different grade school than we did. But I did something that helped get them together. I never told the others about this."

"Well?"

"Okay. The summer before Jason disappeared, his brother Steve was killed in Vietnam. Matt—remember? from the photo?—and I thought the best thing to get Jason's mind off of it would be to take him up to Jones Park, the place I mentioned to you earlier. (This was a different hike than the one I mentioned earlier.) Well, I called your mom the night before and told her confidentially that we were taking Jason on this hike, just in case—hint, hint— she might want to take her horse for a ride up in the mountains."

"Oh, yeah, Queenie. She used to show me pictures of her."

"So she and a friend of hers rode up and joined us, as though it were a total coincidence. I knew that if I asked, Jason would say he wanted to be up there with just the guys but I also knew that having your mom around would console him in a way that Matt and I couldn't do."

"Did they spend the night up there with you?"

"In our dreams," John said, with a chuckle. "We asked them to stay for dinner, though. But it turned out to be just as well they didn't."

"How come?"

"Well, we had brought up a bunch of hamburger, enough for everybody if they'd stayed. But Matt took what he thought was the wise precaution of sticking the hamburger into the stream to keep it cool. When we went to fish it out, we found— Are you sure you want to hear this?" he asked, watching her munch an Oreo while she scribbled something else in the book.

"Course!"

"Well, we'd wrapped it up in plastic but somehow they got in anyway."

"What did?"

"Leeches."

"Eeewwwwwww!" She set down the cookie.

"Our reaction exactly."

"What did you do?"

"Well, as I said, we had plenty of hamburger so we just scraped off the outer layer and made up burgers with what was left."

"Eww, ewww, ewwwww!" she said. "What did they taste like?"

"Actually, leeches inject an anti-coagulant to keep their host's blood from clotting. It acts like a tenderizer. Boy, those were some tender hamburgers!"

"You're right," May conceded, shaking her head. "It's just as well Mom didn't stay. She was kind of vegetarian anyway. If she'd been there for that, she and Jason might never have gotten together, and then where would I be?"

Ignoring the conclusion she had jumped to again, he said, "They did make a connection that day though. I think they both had wanted to get to know each other as more than just friends for a long time and her being there to console him about his brother gave them the opportunity they needed. But actually, they weren't the ones who fell in love that day."

"What do you mean?"

"Remember your mom's friend who rode up with her? Her name was Deb."

"Oh, Deb and Matt McCleary. They sent some beautiful flowers and a nice card when Mom died. And you know what? Now that I hear her name again, I think I remember her from one of Mom's Queenie pictures. She was really pretty."

"That was the day they met and fell in love," John said. "They shared a private moment up there and something happened that he would never tell anybody about. But from that day on, there was no one else in the world for him. They married about three years later. As far as I know, they're still living happily ever after in Seattle."

She clapped. "I love a love story with a happy ending!"

"Me too," he admitted.

"I miss love," she said, scribbling again.

"Me too," he said, without thinking about it.

"What about your wife?" she asked, looking up.

At first he regretted the inadvertent revelation but then realized he could talk openly with May in a way that he couldn't with anyone in Estes. "I don't think Susan misses love that much," he said.

"How married are you?"

"Why?"

"I just wasn't sure why you asked me to do this with you."

"Me neither," he said noncommittally. "I'll tell you this: I've enjoyed rubbing shoulders with you."

She smiled and affectionately rubbed her shoulder against his. "So how married is Susan?"

"Why?"

"Earlier you made it sound as though she's prepared to leave you at the drop of a hat."

He struggled to draw words that made sense from the background of startling imagery the drug induced. "Susan loves being married," he said carefully. "I'm just not sure she loves being married to me."

"And if you two should split, the girls would go with her?"

"Without a doubt."

She touched his scraggly beard. "Well, if they decide they don't want you anymore, I'll take you."

This came so close to the ego boost he had hoped for that all he could do was to look down at his empty hands with a disbelieving smile.

"What's sex like?" she asked, writing again.

He thought about it. "Remember that elk skull?"

"Yeah?"

"That poor bastard had only one chance a year to have sex and he had to fight tooth and nail and butt heads to get it. He was so hard up he grew horns."

She snickered. "So?"

"So I can relate." To himself he added, I just hope I don't lose my head over it like he did.

"Actually," she said, "what I meant was, what's sex like when you're doing shrooms?"

This was a far different question and a loaded one at that. He decided to answer in a general way. "All the unusual sensations can be distracting."

"What do you mean?"

"Hmm. Okay, I'll tell you what. Close your eyes." She did. "What do you see?"

He could see her eyes moving under the lids. "All sorts of nothing in particular."

"Is it moving?"

"Very much."

"Okay, follow one thing for a ways." He could see her face relax and her concentration increase. "Now tell me what happens when I do this." He brushed her cheek ever so lightly with his finger.

"Oh, my! Oh God, oh God, oh God! That's incredible! It changed from green to…no, it didn't, it split into…oh wow, there's so many—" Her eyes popped back open. "What did you do?"

"Touched your cheek."

"That's phenomenal! Amazing! Want me to do that to you?"

"You don't have to," he said. "I'm enjoying turning you on to it."

"Then do me again!" she insisted. She pushed aside the notebook and the remains of the lunch and lay at his feet, eyes closed, knees up.

He waited until she sank back into the infinite fractal permutations that her mind invented when not supplied with actual visual stimulation. This time he touched just the tip of her nose, then gently stroked her eyebrow, then carefully touched her forehead, both cheeks, and chin simultaneously. Each touch elicited an ever more awed response.

This is why I asked you to do this with me, John thought to himself. Tripping like this creates a *tabula rasa*, opening in the adult mind the wonder and awe of the child. The experience can be both liberating and disorienting, making it possible to see past, or impossible to see, the usual labels and categories for people on which the everyday mind relies: culture, age, even gender.

May tested that last distinction. "You need a bigger blackboard," she told him. Without opening her eyes, she reached down and pulled up her white sweater, pausing to hook her fingers under her bra and pulling it up as well.

John took it in stride. In other circumstances, in another frame of mind, this would be enticing, provocative. Now, though, seeing things from her point of view, he took it as an invitation to play more than a sexual overture.

Not that it didn't take him a moment to adjust. He hadn't been this close to any woman's naked breasts other than Susan's since they'd married 19 years earlier. May's were smaller than Susan's, the areolas dark, the nipple rapidly wrinkling in the cool air. Her slender waist lay flat, her navel deep, and he could make out not only Libby's stretch marks but also a Cesarean scar. He ran his fingernail down May's sternum to her solar plexus.

Her entire body shivered at the sensation. He paused to make sure there were no objections but she urged him, "Don't stop now!"

Some of the touchy-feely games John had played long ago on other children's backs came back to him: the Ice Skater, the Galloping Horse, the Spider Doing Push-ups. The last works particularly well on a breast, since the spider's light legs rise to a focal point, as does a breast. May's goose-bumped right nipple rose along with the spider, contracting to a mere point. She let out a trembling sigh at the sensation.

She let go of the sweater and bra with her left hand and grabbed the wrist of his other hand. He froze, thinking he had gone too far. To the contrary, she pulled his reluctant hand down between her thighs. He felt reluctant to move it, deciding whether he wanted to take this next step. She decided for him, opening her eyes just long enough to look into his and say, "Please?"

The crotch of a pair of jeans contains the intersection of four seams, creating a thick, square button of denim. The way she lay, the way her jeans were cut, this button lay atop her clitoris. With his middle finger he pressed lightly down on the thick fabric and moved it ever-so-gently in a small circle.

It affected her profoundly. Her entire body seemed to melt. Her head fell back and her mouth fell open. Her right hand lost its grip on the bra and the elastic sprang back down, trapping the spider's legs beneath it. From deep within her a low, sweet moan welled up.

A moment later her moan, transformed and amplified, seemed to echo throughout the huge valley. Simultaneously, what looked like small bits of Styrofoam littered her prone figure.

"Oh my God! What on earth are you doing?" she cried out as the Styrofoam bits melted and ran down her ribs. "Silver fire! Golden horns!"

John had been so caught up in what he was doing it took a moment to pull himself back to reality. He looked around. The Styrofoam was easy enough to explain: small pellets of snow had begun to fall. The golden horn had him stumped until it resonated through the woods again.

"It's a bugle," he said, "heralding the snow."

She opened her eyes and pulled her sweater back into place. "Wow, it is snowing!" she said, watching the light pellets ring the still water of the rock pool. "But what do you mean a bugle?"

"It's an elk bugling," he explained, watching her pick up the notebook again. "The bulls do it during the rut to advertise their sexuality."

The elk bugled a third time, the deep-in-the-gut bellow rising and falling on the discreet harmonics of his long windpipe, ending in some spasmodic grunts. It was a lonely sound of primal urgency.

But John realized the snow represented the greater urgency to them. "We've got to get out of here," he told her, watching her jotting notes.

"One second," she said, intent on capturing her impressions.

As he watched her write, John had a startling revelation. It wasn't just the intensity of her concentration that seemed familiar to him.

"Have I ever seen you write before?" he asked her.

"I don't think so," she said without stopping.

"I don't think so either," he said. "But I have seen someone else write just like that."

She shielded the page from him. "I didn't know you were reading this."

"I'm not," he said. "I don't mean what you write, I mean the way you write, physically. You know who it was?"

He had her attention now. "Who?"

"Jason," he told her with conviction. "He's the only other person I've ever seen who held a pen that way."

"Are you sure?" she asked, looking at the pen in her hand.

"Positive. I don't know how something like that could be inherited but I can't explain it any other way."

"So you really think…?"

"Seeing that, it's going to take a lot to convince me you're not his daughter."

"This is incredible!"

"Maybe so but we still have to get the hell out of here."

By now, the pellets of snow pelted them thickly, ricocheting off the rocks and hazing the view. He quickly gathered up the lunch leftovers and wrapped them in the towel and repacked his pack. She closed the notebook and handed it to him and he stuck it on top.

"Boy, it's really coming down!" she said, strapping on her pack.

"Yeah," he agreed, putting on his. "Go, go, go!"

The rocks of the pool, wet and dotted with the snow pellets, were now trickier to negotiate and a slip, even though it would mean just a dunking, not a drowning, would certainly mean a soaking they could ill afford in this weather.

She made it to the other side ahead of him and paused to look back. "Good-bye, Lake Haiyaha. How do you spell 'Haiyaha' anyway?"

He spelled it for her as he caught up and looked back too, not at the lake but up to where the clouds obscured the peaks.

"Do you know what 'haiyaha' means?" she asked.

He chuckled in spite of his concern. "It means Stone Lake. What better place to bring you for this?"

"I can't imagine a better place on earth," she said.

"Yeah, yeah. Get going," he told her. To himself he thought, Unless you want this to be your last place on earth.

He had fucked up. Between the drug and the company and the Spider Doing Push-ups, he had committed a cardinal sin of hiking: he had lost track of the time and the weather.

It was only a little after 3:00, which day before yesterday wouldn't have been too bad. Yesterday, Halloween, had been the first day after Falling Back to standard time. The extra hour's sleep had been nice and he hadn't noticed yesterday how much earlier it got dark because he had gotten so involved in putting together and then taking pictures of Alice's Queen Amidala costume. This afternoon, with the heavy clouds, it felt like it was getting dark already. He had a small flashlight with him that he always kept in his pack but if they should somehow lose the trail, it might prove impossible to find again in the snow.

The snow had come sooner and thicker than he anticipated. Already the ground began to blanch. The only emergency gear he had with him consisted of the ponchos, which would help keep them dry but not warm, a lighter to try to start a fire, which would be damned hard to do with wet wood, and the remains of the lunch plus some trail mix for food. If they couldn't make it back to the car, they might not survive the night. To hell with lions, coyotes, and bears; hypothermia was the real threat.

Some small comfort was the fact that May seemed blissfully unaware of the danger and he didn't want to betray his concern to her if he could help it. So he thanked his lucky stars when she spontaneously skipped into a jog on the steep downhill of the first part of the trail. He gladly followed suit and they made good time until his foot slipped on a wet root and he took a header onto the rough gravel, skinning the heels of his hands and muddying his knees, disconcertingly close to the place where he had thrown up earlier.

"Are you okay?" she asked, coming back up the trail to help him up.

He dug the little rocks from his palm and said, "As usual, the only real injury is to my dignity. You're setting a good pace there."

"I'll slow up a little."

"Not on my account."

By the time they reached Dream Lake again, the deep azure of twilight made the lake look like steel and the tree trunks like coal. In a sort of photonegative effect, the ground, dark earlier, now looked light covered by an inch of snow. Where it was protected by the trees, the trail remained clear and obvious; in the openings it was anybody's guess. The grade leveled here too, making the footing better but the going slower.

By Nymph Lake his summer hiking boots were wet and the muddy slush stuck in clumps to the soles. The snow, coming down now in thick clusters of flakes, didn't stick to their clothing too much but May's French braid, like the branches of the subalpine firs around them, had collected little snowdrifts in the level spots. Even the twilight had faded but the thick low clouds reflected light from somewhere, maybe from some hidden moon. He hesitated to use the flashlight: it lit what it was pointed at quite well but made it impossible to see anything else.

The peak of the psilocybin had passed and the intensity of the conditions left little time for the frivolities of the drug. As they stood for a quiet breather at the small lake, though, a silent gray form floated through the falling snow above the dark water.

"Did you see that?" May whispered to him, still breathing hard from the hustle.

"I'm still seeing it," he said, watching the fleeting wake of colors his brain invented to supplement the original image.

"It looked like a ghost, didn't it?"

"Maybe a goblin."

"It wasn't though, was it?" she whispered. "I don't believe in ghosts."

"Do you believe in owls?"

"I do now."

o o o

Bear Lake, of course, was deserted and only one other car remained in the parking lot. The snow had separated to individual flakes but they slanted sharply as the wind picked up. The temperature had fallen considerably as well. His stubby mustache was soaked with snow and condensation and snot and it required all his effort to bend his fingers enough to pull the car keys from his pocket and open the door for May. Her hair had frizzed from the braid and held a jeweled net of droplets. She shivered uncontrollably. When he finally managed to pull the handle on the car door, she insinuated herself into his arms, her own clutched to her breast. He held her trembling body close and kissed the top of her head. He relished the myriad points of wet against his face and the fresh clean smell of her hair.

"Now get in," he urged her. "Let's get the heater going."

He got in and started the car. The blast of cold air from the fan made her squeal.

"I'm sorry," he said, shutting off the fan until the motor warmed up. "In fact, I'm sorry for everything."

"What are you talking about?" she asked through chattering teeth.

"Oh, just everything. The lousy motel room. The long hike. Ralphing my cookies on the way up. The lunch you didn't eat. Losing track of the time. Falling on my face. Nearly freezing you to death. I just hoped it would turn out better, that's all."

She put her hand on his to keep him from putting the car in gear. "John, listen to me." She waited until he turned to her. "This was the best day of my life. No one has ever made such an effort to show me a good time. Plus, you may have given me a different father than

I thought I had. I wouldn't trade today for anything."

"So your first time on shrooms wasn't so bad?"

"It was great! I see what you mean: there's no comparison to dope or coke or whatever. It's a whole different thing."

"Nicely put," he agreed. "A whole different thing indeed. So did tripping make you do anything you didn't want to do?"

"Oh, no!" she said, letting him put the car in gear. "I loved the way you were touching me."

"That was certainly a highlight for me, too," he said, glancing at her, catching her blushing a little. "But that's not what I meant. The original reason I planned this was to show you that these kinds of drugs may make things seem awfully weird but they don't often make you do things you wouldn't do otherwise."

"I suppose," she agreed, nodding to get him to go on.

"You and I originally got on the subject of psychedelics talking about your mom—your parents—possibly trying to abort you. And what I'm saying is that they wouldn't have made that decision or taken that action while tripping like this. Of course, what you and I did today wasn't the same as a full-blown acid trip by any means but the principle's the same."

"I see what you're saying," she agreed. "That's not a decision you'd make on a whim. And she—they—must have had other good reasons even to consider it because the shrooms made every living thing seem special to me."

"Well, I, for one, am glad you were born," he said, patting her knee. "So does this mean you're going to be doing shrooms all the time now?"

"I can't imagine doing them with anyone else," she said. "And I know that I'll probably never do this with you again."

"But would you mind seeing me again?"

"God, I hope I see you again!" she said. "Other than my Nana, you're probably the only real friend I have in this world."

"Don't be too sure," he said, pulling out of the parking lot. The snow, already a couple of inches deep, squeaked beneath the tires.

"What do you mean?" she asked, bouncing in the seat to keep from shivering.

"Russ called me on Saturday."

"He's the one in New York?"

"Right," he said, carefully negotiating the switchbacks. "He said he talked to Matt in Seattle a week ago and it turns out they're both interested in talking to you about your mom and Jason and what all happened back then."

"Are you kidding? You mean the three of you might stage another Piñon Nuts Gathering on New Year's Eve after all?"

"For one thing, it would have to be the four of us since you would have to be there to represent your father. And your mother, too, for that matter, since she was there when that picture was taken."

"She was?"

"Who do you think took the picture?"

"I didn't know that."

"On the other hand, New Year's Eve would be really tricky. Russ would have a devil of a time getting away from the restaurant that night and Matt's working on the Y2K bug so he's bound to be busy as well. Plus, it could prove the worst weekend ever for traveling."

"What about you and Susan?" she asked. "What are your plans?"

"Traditionally, we go down to Phoenix for the holidays to let Alice and Anne's grandparents spoil the hell out of them. We haven't really talked about it specifically but I imagine that's what Susan is planning."

"What about the other wives? Didn't you say that Matt's married to mom's friend Deb? And is Russ married?"

"That's another issue. Russ and I talked about it and I think we all feel that if we ever do this, adding the wives would make it impossible to do what we really need to do: rehash this stuff about Jason. And the three of us getting away from the wives on the turning of the millennium would require one of history's greatest feats of diplomacy."

"Well, I wouldn't want to see you go through all that just for my sake."

John sped up as the road leveled out. The snow had let up a little down in the valley. The heater, now that the engine had run awhile, threw out a blast of hot air that steamed the damp from their clothes and made the numb tips of John's fingers ache.

Having thought about her last statement, he said, "We wouldn't do it just for your sake. We'd do it for ourselves as well. Jason, with all his strengths and weaknesses, was what we all had in common. He was the glue that held us together. I must admit, when I called Russ and read him the Piñon Nuts pledge, I figured the glue had long since disappeared. I think he felt the same way when he called Matt. But I guess, even after all these years, Jason still holds us together. And it's not just our disagreement about what happened to him. It's what he meant to each of us, which was something different for each of us, that helped make each of us who he is today. I think we would all agree that we're better for having known him."

She sniffed, not necessarily from the cold. "You make me wish I could have known him too."

"Well, maybe you can get to know him a little through us."

"Whether it's New Year's Eve or not, I hope I can be there when you get together."

"Okay, that's another thing. If we can somehow work it out to do this New Year's Eve, we'll need a place to get together."

"Wouldn't you just do it where you took the picture? Where was that?"

"It was taken at Russ's house but his parents don't own it any more. You know where Crestwood is?"

"Sure. At the top of the hill on Cresta. I used to go by there on my way to the Hatchcover when I tended bar there."

"Have you ever eaten there?"

She snorted. "I've never been able to afford it. And Paco's idea of a night out was a combination meal at Taco Bell and getting wall-eyed on Stolys and Coronas in the parking lot outside the liquor store."

"How did you end up marrying a guy like that, anyway?"

"When we first met he treated me like a queen. And he's really good looking. And an excellent liar. So I'm a fool. What can I say?"

"Anyway, that picture was taken at Crestwood."

"I thought you guys did your Gatherings at somebody's house."

"We did. At that time Crestwood was somebody's house. Russ's parents', to be specific."

"Really? I'm impressed."

"I never thought about it being impressive. When you're a kid, you take things like that for granted. You probably never thought that much about your father's—I mean, Bill's—house, did you?"

"Everything about my father is going to take some getting used to."

"It's a wise child who knows his own father," John pointed out. "So anyway, the building is now owned by a big corporation but the restaurant is managed by Eric and Lucy Van Deutch, some friends of Russ's parents. Russ mentioned putting together a Piñon Nuts Gathering to his mom, who spoke to Lucy, and it turns out we may be able to get reservations there for New Year's Eve."

"That's great!"

"There's a catch, though. We may need to have some pull with one of the hostesses."

"Why wouldn't—?"

"Hear me out," he interrupted her. "Russ said that you're supposed to make up a resume, put on a nice dress, and go in and talk to Lucy Van Deutch about being that hostess."

"You're kidding."

"If I'm lying," he said, raising his right hand but then quickly putting it back on the wheel to round a slippery curve. "In any case, it's just hostessing to start. But it would be a step up from the Waffle House, wouldn't it?"

"Anything would be better than the Waffle House," she said. "And if there's a chance I could become a server—well, they must make two or three hundred a night there."

"So you'll consider it?"

"I'll call tomorrow afternoon. Her name is Lucy Van Deutch? Oh, I can't thank you enough!"

"Don't thank me. This is Russ's doing."

"Well, I'll just have to thank him then."

"It's going to require some changes on your part, you know."

"What do you mean?"

"You're going to have to quit spending your days off doing drugs with low-life scuzzballs like me."

"I'm going to take Nana's advice," she said, smiling. "I won't promise I'll change. But I promise I'll try."

"Good advice," he said as they approached the Visitor's Center.

"Did you ask Russ about that other guy?"

"Other guy?" John asked, hoping it wasn't…

"Tom Huston," she said. "The guy who disappeared in Jason's letter."

That's what he was afraid of. "No, I spaced it," he said. "But I did remember him finally."

"Who was he?"

John had no short simple answer to that short simple question. He would have to discuss the draft, the state penitentiary, the anti-war movement, the FBI, and the sinister machinations of Nixon's White House. Tom Huston amounted to a very small tail to pin on that large and amorphous donkey—or elephant, in this case.

"You know what?" he said as he pulled into the deserted parking lot next to her Fiat and shut off the engine. "That's a long story and I only know a portion of it. We'll discuss it in detail at the Gathering, I'm sure."

"Why didn't you mention it earlier?"

"I thought about it but you know what? I didn't want to ruin a perfectly good hike talking about Tom Huston. But if you want to ruin a perfectly good dinner…"

"Don't you have to get home?"

"I told Susan I wouldn't be home till late. I want to make sure my pupils are undilated," checking them in the rear-view mirror. "How does pizza sound?"

"Now I'm hungry," she said. "That sounds great."

"Bob and Tony's is pretty good," he said. "We'll have to do take-out, you know."

"I understand," she said. "That's fine. No point in feeding the rumor mill."

"But I'd be glad to drive you around, show you the town while we talk."

"I'd like that. So you want to follow me back to the motel?"

"Okay."

She pulled her pack from the back seat. "Once again, I just want to thank you for all you've done. It's been a great day."

"I've enjoyed it too, except for the throwing up and falling down and almost freezing to death."

"Picky, picky, picky," she said. "See you at the motel."

As she got squared away in her car, he pulled his pack from the back seat too and got out the pipe tin, which he hadn't taken out of his pack on the hike. Lighting the pipe, he watched her. It had been easy to see Amanda in her face, her eyes, her behavior. But the more he saw her, the more he saw Jason: the shape of his nose, his need to explore, his urge to write.

The notebook slid from the pack. That's right, she hadn't kept her notes. He wasn't sure he should read them, but they were in his book and curiosity got the better of him. He opened the cover and read:

> High? Yeah. Hah!
> Tough nuts, stony ground.
> High, mom, I'm home!
> I'm with your father.
> Eat, grow, live, die.
> Haphazardly ever after.
> In a rut.
> Silver fire, golden horns.
> Horny as an elk, lonely as a train.
> May…Be.

The acorn doesn't fall far from the tree, he thought with a smile.

o   o   o

Even before they got to the Brynhaven, he could see the dazzle of emergency flashers. The police had cordoned off the motel parking lot so John and May parked down by the miniature golf course and walked back up to stand by the yellow "Do Not Cross" tape. Smoke poured from the roof of the motel and firemen lumbered in and out of one of the rooms.

"Is it your room?" he asked May.

"No, mine's a couple of doors down."

"Well, thank God for that."

"Yes, lucky you," a woman's voice said frostily.

John turned to find his wife, bundled in a down parka, her frosted hair tied back severely, looking May up and down.

"Susan! What are you doing here?"

"I suppose I could ask you the same thing," she said haughtily. "If it weren't so obvious."

"I mean why—?"

"When the motel owner couldn't find the room's occupant, they tried to contact the person who had registered. You didn't leave a number, clever you, but they looked up our number in the phone book."

"It's not what you think," John said but she paralyzed him with a withering glance.

May stepped into the breach. "Mrs. Kaufman?" she said, braving Susan's icy glare. "I'm May Mendoza, Amanda Black's daughter. Maybe John told you that my mom was killed a couple of months ago. Anyway, I remembered Mom saying that John lived up here so I called him this morning to see if he could recommend a place to stay and to see if he wanted to get together to talk about Mom. He got me this motel room and then took me for a hike up in the mountains."

"I should have called you, I know," John said as glibly as possible. "She caught me just as I was leaving for Ft. Collins."

Susan listened to this in stony silence, looked at him with utter contempt, then turned on her heels and walked away.

"Oh, John, I'm so sorry!" May said to him.

"It's not your fault," he said, dread sitting like lead in the pit of his stomach. "Thanks for trying."

"You need to go to her," she said.

"Yes, I do," he said. "But you and I have some unfinished business as well."

"Listen, if you never speak to me again, I'll understand."

"I'll call you."

...O...O...O...

Sometimes people compliment my singing by saying I can "really wail." The line is thinly drawn between grief and joy at times.

I remember when the concept of mortality first hit me. When I was about eight, our next door neighbor, a test pilot for the Air Force, flew his plane into some power lines and crashed, killing him instantly. My parents told me his wife and young son would need their privacy, that a terrible thing had happened to them, and that the little boy's daddy wouldn't be coming home anymore. I understood the awful magnitude of death but it remained accidental and it happened to someone else.

A couple of weeks later, though, I sat alone in the basement room my brother and I shared, listening to my family talking and laughing around the dinner table upstairs. Perhaps I wondered what it must be like at the neighbors' house with one of the voices missing, gone forever. Suddenly it came home to me that death is no accident, that someday it would come to my parents and eventually to me and my brother too.

I quietly began to cry. At first I cried for my own sake and from deep in my heart. But children cry, as they should, to draw attention to themselves, to let their parents know something's wrong. When no one came downstairs to check on me, I cried louder. Still no response. I had to really wail before I heard Dad's footsteps on the stairs.

"Something wrong?" he asked.

"Well, yeah," I said, a little miffed. "Didn't you hear me crying?"

"Sorry, son," he said. "We thought you were singing."

Having sung professionally most of my life, I can testify that you can die singing too. In fact, one gig in particular may have been the death knell of my solo act.

A few summers ago I took a job from an agency I hadn't worked with before, playing in the small remote dusty town of Challis, Idaho, the "Gateway to the Frank Church Wilderness." The name of the bar, the Custer Saloon, should have tipped me off, I suppose. But I desperately needed the money and really wanted to please these new agents.

Custer did better at the Little Big Horn than I did at his saloon. The place was a hot smoky dive, the patrons rowdy and rude, the bartenders sullen and cold, the agents amateurs. The "accommodations" my contract promised consisted of a hell-hole of a trailer that hadn't been cleaned since it was new and hadn't been new since Nixon was president. The summer sun got the trailer hot enough to melt the candles in my backpack. On the Fourth of July, we all staggered out onto the main drag (in Challis, you can get your drinks to go) to watch the fireworks, which consisted of a couple of guys setting off a few Roman candles on top of the hill above the town, which lit the grassy hilltop on fire.

Since I wasn't quite miserable enough, I developed some sort of sinus/lung infection which made breathing difficult and singing nearly impossible. Unable to bear Sunday and Monday in the trailer, I decided to drive down to the Sawtooth Range between Challis and Sun Valley and hike up to Sawtooth Lake, the biggest lake in the wilderness.

At the end of the long hot hike I found that the Sawtooth Range had suffered one of the worst winters ever, the snowdrifts still 15 to 20 feet deep and the lake still frozen. I set up my tent on one of the few spots of open ground, finding some small consolation in the hope that all that snow might keep out the mosquitoes and the other hikers. Wrong. Clouds of hungry skeeters, out for blood, trapped me in the cramped tent. And a group of young, loud hikers arrived with an old dog wearing a bandanna for a collar. The dog had probably started out as a yellow lab but it looked almost white with age.

After dinner this group of young bucks took the dog up the ridge above the lake to watch the full moon rise. They came back to camp without the dog. Pretty soon the dog began to howl. The guys would whistle to it once in a while but they didn't try to rescue it and the dog didn't seem to budge. As the full moon slowly drifted across the night sky, the howling grew louder, then more desperate, and eventually began to weaken. It occurred to me as I tossed in my bag that perhaps the guys had brought the old dog up there to die, that they might even have hiked back out already, leaving me and the dog alone.

My infection kept me barking most of the night too, so finally, before sunrise, I gave up trying to sleep and decided to hike up the ridge to try to escape the bugs. The dog had fallen silent. Gasping and coughing up things I never dreamed my body could produce, I topped the ridge at moonset. Much newer mountains than the Colorado Rockies, the Sawtooth Range is largely just a pile of rubble and I soon found myself stuck on a crumbling ledge, fighting off the mosquitoes that proved much hardier than I and listening once again to the old white dog, who woke up at sunrise and began once more to wail away the last of its strength. Suddenly I found myself howling too, my cries echoing the dog's, reverberating across the wide, frozen bowl above the lake.

That's when I decided that, before I'd take another gig like the Custer Saloon in Challis, Idaho, before I'd end up dying like an old dog, I'd get a normal job of some kind. I worked my way off the ledge, slid down the rain-troughed snowdrifts, and headed back to town. Down by the trailhead, I ran into the other hikers and trotting along with them was the old white dog. "Hope he didn't keep you up," they told me. "Sometimes he just likes to wail at the moon."

August 16, 1969

John got shocked first, and worst, at least physically.

It happened near the end of "Bad Moon Rising," on the line, appropriately enough, "Hope you are quite prepared to die." His Silvertone bass amp, six 10s in a squat, vinyl-wrapped cabinet, had a separate head that tucked into the rollered box when being moved but sat on top when in use. The Argonauts were playing loud enough, and the linoleum floor was flimsy enough, that the head, responding to the vibrations it had created, walked itself off the cabinet below. He didn't notice it until he glanced at Russ, who gestured violently with his head, his hands and feet occupied with playing his drums. John turned around just in time to see the front feet of the head slide off the cabinet and the whole thing teeter on the edge. He jumped back and caught it just as it fell but unfortunately what he grabbed turned out to be the square metal transformer.

Every nerve in his body boogied briefly to the 60-cycle jitterbug. The heavy head slipped from his hand, breaking the circuit, and dropped face down onto the floor with a thick thud. John cursed it roundly.

Jason, trying to sing over the cacophony, turned to glare but quickly realized what had happened by the dazed look on John's face and the fallen amplifier. Jason made eye contact with Matt and Russ and they ended the song without repeating the chorus.

"You okay?" Jason asked John.

"Boowahgajordaplangchudorf," John said, his arm still tingling, his head still trying to reorient itself in the room.

"Did you bust it?" Jason asked, looking at the face-down head.

John played his E-string and the amp and chord both still worked.

"Can you play?" Jason asked as John set the amp back onto the cabinet.

John squatted to grab the pick he'd dropped, his knees still rubbery from the shock. Standing back up, he gripped the pick in his stiff right hand and played a few notes. "I guess," he said, his voice sounding hollow in his head from the ringing of the shock and the volume they'd been playing.

Jason turned to Russ. "You up to some Iron Butterfly?"

Russ, who had flown in from New York just a couple of days before, still felt the effects of being back at 6000 feet: migraine, bloody nose, nausea. He sat on his drum stool looking pale and disgusted. "Like McWatt said just before he flew into the mountain, 'Oh, well, what the hell!'"

Jason looked at Matt, who shrugged and launched into the opening riff of "In-a-Gadda-Da-Vida," a *faux*-Bach arpeggio. The record's fat, ominous Hammond organ part sounded tinny and spry on Matt's out-of-tune Wurlitzer electric piano. Tuning the piano required dropping liquid solder onto the ends of the metal tines and filing the blobs down until each tine vibrated at the desired pitch. Every time they moved the piano, some of the solder blobs fell off, so dissonance was more the rule than the exception.

The song lurched forward when the rest of the Argonauts came in, the dreary unison guitar and bass parts competing with John's lead vocal. His voice, gloomy enough with the ponderous melody, sounded in his head like Boris Karloff on freon. Still dazed, he mumbled his way through the words, no great loss, until Russ's extended drum solo offered him a reprieve.

Customarily, he and Jason and Matt left the stage to give Russ the spotlight for his solo. Actually, they didn't own a spotlight, just four colored floods attached to a four-foot length of one-by-six that sat on the floor in front of the stage, controlled with a homemade switchbox. Jason left on the red light that pointed at Russ and his drums. They had no stage either, just an open spot along the outside wall of the bathroom, so the three of them trooped into the john.

"How did you get this gig again?" Matt asked Jason, taking a leak in the filthy toilet.

"I told you, my dad told this agent he knows about the Argonauts and she called me up to see if we were interested."

"Did anybody ask the crowd if *they* were interested?" John asked, still vibrating from the shock. "These guys hate us and they have no interest whatsoever in white bread music."

"Good thing we're paisley," Jason said.

The night before, John and Jason and a couple of other friends had gone up to a big rock on the face of Cheyenne Mountain to smoke a joint. The rock had a deep crevice in its center up which they climbed, scrambling up to a flat spot on the top that offered a spectacular view of the Front Range and Colorado Springs and, to the south, the big yellow banana that Ft. Carson resembled from this height. It also offered an interesting challenge when it came time to scramble back down in the dark, stoned.

While on the top, though, they had attracted the attention of a couple of girls, from Texas, judging by their accents, perched on another, smaller rock a hundred yards away. John shouted an invitation for the girls to join them on the bigger rock.

The girls talked it over quietly a moment. Finally one of them drawled, "Y'all dawgies?"

The soldiers at Ft. Carson were often referred to derogatorily as "doggies."

Jason did a pretty fair impression of a coyote howling at the moon but John hit his arm to make him quit. "No, we are not doggies," John called over to them, a little galled at their attitude but not yet losing hope that they could find common ground and perhaps lie upon it together before the end of the night.

They could hear a hasty confab on the other end and then the girl's voice called out, "Y'all colored?"

This tacky question so clashed with the pleasant high they had achieved that for a moment no one knew how to respond. Finally, John dismissed them by shouting, with much conviction, "Colored? We're *paisley!*"

John peeked around the corner of the men's room now like a commando calculating the survival odds on a suicide mission, wishing he could trade that paisley for camouflage. Which was a bit ironic, since the enemy in this case was the U. S. Army.

They were playing the Doghouse, an enlisted men's club on post at Fort Carson. The building had been slapped together out of cheap lumber at the end of World War II, back when the base was still known as Camp Carson. Built on short stilts over the hot dusty hardpan, the building was a long rectangular clapboard affair with little more than a few windows, some fluorescent lights, and the one-hole men's room behind the stage area. Designed as a general purpose building, it had no air conditioning, no central heat, not even a bar, just a long folding table with a keg of 3.2% beer and stacks of paper cups. An oscillating fan churned the thick air. Even though the sun had long since set, the room felt like a sauna, stinking of cigarettes and stale beer and sweat.

When John saw the source of the sweat stench, he felt grateful for the paper cups instead of beer cans or bottles. If the audience threw paper cups, the Argonauts would just get soaked, not cut and bruised. For that matter, some of these guys brought their automatic weapons. John and the others had faked their way through requests they'd never even attempted to play before. These guys had to be the lowest echelon of the Army, cannon fodder who couldn't afford to go off base to get drunk on a Saturday night. Mostly draftees, they came from all over the country, almost all poor, many Black and Hispanic. All struggled with an overdose of testosterone.

Till now, the Argonauts had played just the Tin Can, the teen club in the basement of the church, and some private parties. They had always played for well-mannered, enthusiastic, middle- and upper-class white teens. Nothing had prepared them for this.

"This isn't what I signed up for," John said to Jason.

Matt was blunt. "I hate this. Don't you?"

Jason looked at his bandmates' worried, dismal faces. "Did you ever hear the one about the Catholic, the Jew, and the Christian Scientist in hell?"

"Aren't you a Christian Scientist?" John asked.

"That's how we were raised," Jason said. "At least that's where the folks would drop us off on Sunday mornings."

"I always thought the term 'Christian Scientist' sounded oxymoronic," Matt said.

"Just because I'm dumb as an ox—" Jason began.

"Just tell the joke," John said impatiently.

"Okay, so these three guys are talking about how they happened to end up in hell. The Catholic says, 'I lived a good Catholic life. Went to mass on Sundays, gave freely to the priests and the poor, confessed most of my sins. But I'm a meat-and-potatoes man and, boy, I just couldn't abide that pasty fish on Fridays.'

"And the Jew says, 'What was I, a bad Jew? I know the Torah back to front, I closed the liquor store on Saturdays, I even had a moil circumcise the dog. But it was a pig brought me down. Pork chops, ham, bacon! Oy! Couldn't resist.'

"When he finished the two of them looked at the Christian Scientist, who stood there smiling. So the Catholic says to him, 'What's your story?'

"And the Christian Scientist, still smiling blithely, says, 'I'm not here.'"

"Yeah, ha, ha," John said. "Any advice for those of us who *are* here?"

"Well, it can't get much worse," Jason said. "At least we're getting paid."

The Argonauts' best paying job to date had been a prom they had played in Moreland, Kansas, a town without a traffic signal near where John's aunt and uncle lived on a farm. The town had feted them as foreign dignitaries. The kitchen table never lacked some new temptation to a growing boy. The Argonauts put on their matching ties and played in the muggy gym, where the decoration committee had realized the theme, "Apple Blossom Time," with miles of crepe paper and thousands of tissue blossoms. After one set, most of the farm kids went out to their parents' trucks and got drunk, prompting the vice principal to call off the rest of the dance. Had they not spent it on burgers and souvenirs, the Argonauts would have brought home $15 apiece for the job.

Of late, as more of their fan base trickled away to jobs and college, the pay had shrunk, until a few weeks ago at the Tin Can they had actually had to chip in out of their own pockets to help pay the security guard. In fact, at that point they had unanimously agreed to disband the Argonauts, lured out of retirement only by Jason's promise of $30 apiece, after he paid the agent's commission of $22.50 and Jason and Matt each took $3.25 for gas.

"You think we're going to live to see any of that money?" John asked.

"We've just got to figure out what they want," Jason said, peering out at the soldiers sitting in clumps at the unfinished banquet tables, talking loudly over Russ's drum solo.

"They want to kill us," Matt said.

"Then we'll just have to launch a pre-emptive strike," Jason said. "Let's go."

They all noticed that Russ's solo was losing steam. Normally, he rushed it, straying from the unit pulse of the original to throw in jazz and modern percussion licks they'd used in band in school. John, Jason, and Russ had all played drums in high school band, John on bass drum, Russ on snare, Jason specializing in whatever odd percussion part the score called for. Jason and Russ were both good drummers but Jason played some guitar too, so when they formed the Argonauts, Russ became the drummer. Most nights he quickly grew bored with the thumpeta-thumpeta of the In-a-Gadda-Da-Vida solo but tonight even those primitive rhythms lagged a little.

They got back to their instruments and finished out the song to no applause at all. Jason immediately kicked on his fuzz tone that, through his little Fender Vibralux amp, made his Gibson SG sound like a chain saw. He slid into the F-G-G-F-G of the intro to "You Really Got Me." By the time they finished the song the crowd seemed, if anything, even less interested.

"So how many of you are here for the big Apathetics Anonymous convention?" Jason asked them. No one responded at all. "Great! Anything you apathetics want to hear?"

"'The Tennessee Waltz'," shouted a thick Oklahoma accent.

"Anything by the King," insisted an Elvis fan.

"Otis!" "Sly!" "Aretha!" came a chorus of impatient Soul fans.

"'Mustang Sally'," Jason called to the others. Russ clicked it off with his drumsticks.

This went over a little better, Jason succeeding in getting a few guys to clap along and even sing the "Ride, Sally, ride" part. They jumped into "Good Golly Miss Molly," which mollified the boys from Georgia. Gaining a little confidence, they tried Cream's version of "Born Under A Bad Sign." This didn't go as well.

"We already *got* the blues," one forlorn voice moaned.

"Pick it up, man!" somebody else insisted.

Then came some guesses about what sign it was Jason had been born under.

"Bet it was Stop!"

"Slow!"

"Children Playing!"

"Dead End!"

Russ always struggled with the paradiddle between right foot and left hand at the heart of Ginger Baker's drum part and tonight all the bounce had left his leg. John tried to sing a harmony part, which turned out to be too high for his voice. Matt had the ninths down on the piano but Jason was nobody's idea of Slowhand.

"Come on, you guys!" Oklahoma demanded when it was over. "You're rockin' us to sleep."

"Play something good!" one of the Georgians suggested, in case that hadn't occurred to them.

"They're doin' just fine," one of the black guys, who was on crutches, maintained, and the others clammed up.

"You want to try 'Fire'?" Jason asked, looking at Russ.

Russ looked pooped. "Let me stand next to your water," he said to John, who passed him a full paper cup. He gulped it down greedily and then nodded to Jason, who played the pick-up notes. Russ did his best in trying to keep up with Hendrix's frantic tempo, filling between the A-C-D-D figure with his best imitation of Mitch Mitchell's hot licks but his bass drum foot still lagged behind.

Jason had trouble syncopating his voice correctly against Russ's vague drumming. John, still dazed and very hot, also struggled to keep up the driving tempo. Matt had nothing to do but copy the A-C-D-D figure and sing the unison refrain with John.

The crowd didn't buy it. "Play something black!" the Georgia boys pleaded during a lull in the song.

Jason looked over to John, who could only shrug his shoulders and keep playing. They came to the key change for the instrumental and John could see Jason contemplating something he'd tried one night at the Tin Can. Since Hendrix's lead consisted of just a few bent notes on the top E-string, Jason had used the mike stand as an improvised slide, adding a little bit of razzle-dazzle that the crowd ate up.

It turned out even more dazzling this time. The ungrounded power cord from Jason's amp was plugged into a different outlet than the P. A. amp, setting up a ground loop. When the string touched the chrome of the mike stand, the inverted A. C. ran through the thin nickel of the string like lightning, making it glow red-hot briefly before the string broke and the two ends burst into yellow flame, jiggling manicly before burning out.

The Argonauts ground to a halt. Jason stood looking at the still-smoking ends of the string. The soldiers, jolted out of their complacency by the flash of light and the abrupt end to the music, actually broke into a smattering of applause. Jason had the presence to acknowledge it, throwing his arms into the air in sarcastic triumph before informing them that it was break time.

o   o   o

John, Matt, and Russ sat on some rickety metal folding chairs at the end closest to the stage of one of the long banquet tables. Jason dug through his guitar case for another E-string.

"Hey, we're all 18 now," it occurred to John. Russ, the youngest, had celebrated his birthday in New York. "Let's have some beers."

They had rarely had the opportunity or the inclination to imbibe while playing but this seemed like the perfect time and place to start.

Jason came over with his guitar and a coiled used string. "I don't have another E," he said, sitting down. "This is a B so I'll need to retune when we go back up," he said to Matt.

"Do we have to go back up?" Russ asked plaintively, wiping the sweat from his face and neck. "God, I feel like shit. I feel worse than Tom Seaver must have felt when he pitched the one hit in his Imperfect Game last month."

"I thought you said this was a nice place," Matt said to Jason.

"That's what that agent told me," Jason said, restringing the guitar.

"And God knows," John said, coming back with four waxy paper cups of thin beer, "music agents never lie."

"You'd think I'd be used to being lied to by now," Jason said, winding the used B-string all the way up to the E.

"Do I hear a 'Get thee to a nunnery' speech coming on?" Russ asked.

"Probably," John said, quaffing the beer, which was weak and warm but mighty refreshing at this point. "He's got himself worked up into some paranoid delusion that Manny and Bill Black are sitting in a tree, k-i-s-s-i-n-g."

"Horseshit," Jason said.

"A key word," John admitted. "But you've got to tell more of the story than that."

"What did I miss?" Russ asked, sipping his beer.

"I told you in my letter about seeing Manny up in Jones Park a few weeks ago, didn't I?" Jason asked Russ.

"She rode up with her friend Deb, right?" Russ confirmed. "How lucky are you guys?"

"'If it wasn't for bad luck,'" Matt said gloomily to his beer, quoting "Born Under A Bad Sign," "'I wouldn't have no luck at all.'"

When Matt didn't elaborate, Russ said to Jason, "I thought you talked about a glimmer, a spark."

"An illusion. A hallucination."

"Tell him the whole story," John urged him.

"Okay. It turns out," Jason said, abandoning the futile tuning in favor of the cool beer, "one thing the hotel grounds-crew does every summer is to work the rodeo since the stadium is on the hotel grounds. Rodeo week and monsoon week happened to coincide this year so the first thing we had to do was to slog through the mud to find the drains and open them up. Not that it helped much. By the time we got done, the Lippizaner stallions and I both wore a thick coat of beige mud. The grounds-crew also runs the barrels out for the barrel racing. And guess who came in second in the barrel racing."

"Annie Oakley?" Russ guessed.

"So there I am," Jason went on, "shoveling up horse shit behind the gates when Manny rides back all excited about coming in second. Actually, Queenie may have been even more excited because she lifts her tail and dumps her load while Manny and I are chatting. So, good grounds-crewman that I am, I start shoveling it up and pitching it over the fence. Well, who walks up but Manny's parents. They're congratulating and she's chattering so I just keep shoveling. Queenie, who likes a good joke as much as the next horse, waits till my back is turned to empty her bladder, which of course sloshes down the back of my leg. I'm just trying to figure out what that nice warm glow is when I hear Manny saying to her parents, 'You remember Jason Walker, don't you?'"

"Timing is everything," Russ said.

"When I turned around, I could tell her mom was looking at Queenie's piss stain on my leg but she quickly covered her disgust with that indulgent smile rich people save for ignorant, unwashed, working-class idiots like me. 'So sorry to hear about your brother,' she said. Her father didn't waste that much time on me. 'Are you about ready to go, Mandy?' he asked. 'We ran into the Blacks and they're coming over to the house for a drink. Bill too.'"

"Ouch," Russ said. "I got the impression from your letter that she had written off Bill as temporary insanity."

"The very impression she gave me," Jason said. "Which amounts to yet another shovelful of horseshit donated to the Jason Walker Memorial Manure Bank."

"Come on, Jase," John said, finishing his beer. "It was probably her parents' doing. What choice did she have?"

The table where they sat was on the way to the johns, which the 3.2%-beer drinkers had to visit a lot. It was also on the way to the exit. A group of disgruntled country fans drifted past on their way out but one fresh-scrubbed, crew-cutted G. I. stopped by Russ and said, "Good drumming, man."

Russ thanked him wearily.

"Yeah, I watched you real close," the G. I. went on admiringly, "and I don't think you were ever more than a beat off."

With an effort, John limited his reaction to a snicker and he could see Jason biting his lip. Russ thanked the soldier again and he left.

"Who says this gig was a waste?" Jason said, laughing out loud now that they were gone. "You got yourself a motto. You can have it printed up on business cards: 'Russell T. Jones, Drummer. Never More Than A Beat Off.'"

"Your mama'll be so proud," John said.

"Do two insults somehow add up to a compliment?" Russ wondered.

The black soldier who had defended them earlier hobbled by on his way back from the john. He stopped, chuckling, to say, "Don't let this place get you down, fellas. You all doin' a fine job. You mind if I set a spell?"

"Thank you, sir," John said, pleased to hear something positive. "Please, have a seat. This is Russ, Matt, and Jason, and I'm John."

The man had a round head, a broad face, and a wide smile. His uniform looked neatly pressed but it also looked new. Once he got past the awkward process of sitting and putting aside his crutches, he sat with an air of self-assurance and gravity unlike the belligerence of the other soldiers. His voice had a soft drawl but he spoke precisely. "Nice to meet you all," he said. He shook Jason's hand. "Jason, you say?"

Before Jason could reply, a couple of other soldiers, emboldened by seeing one of their own talking to the band, came over to the table and sat down with them.

"Don't worry cause nobody's clapping," said the first, a tall lean fellow with red hair and freckles. "You guys are okay. Some of these assholes are just bummed because they're shipping out soon."

"Yeah, you guys rock," the other said with a New Jersey accent. "You want we should buy you a beer?"

Jason looked at his watch. "We better be getting back up to play soon."

"How's about when you're done?" New Jersey went on. "You up for some fun?"

"What did you have in mind?" John asked.

"Hedda?" New Jersey asked Freckles with a nudge.

"Hedda," Freckles concurred.

"Hedda?" Jason asked.

New Jersey lowered his voice. "You guys like pussy?"

Even if any of them could deny it, in a place like this, who would?

"What about big tits?"

John raised his hand. "I do."

Matt glowered at him.

"We know where you can get both," Freckles said proudly, "in one easy package."

"She's called Hedda Hagedorn," New Jersey explained. "She lives over in Widefield with her mom but her mom's a lush and she's always out lushin' every night. Hedda ain't too bright—"

"Dumb as a post," Freckles clarified.

"—but she just loves to fuck. All you gotta do is bring her booze and some kinda gift."

"A gift?" Jason asked.

"She likes anything shiny, like tinsel or a sparkly ball or something."

"One guy brought a glass doorknob," Freckles suggested.

"As long as she can hold it in her hands and look at it, you can do anything you like, poke her anywhere you want."

"Like the kitchen?" Jason asked wryly.

"Tell 'em 'bout her tits," Freckles suggested.

"She's got torpedo tits," New Jersey said, holding his empty hands a foot from his chest. "She has to special order her bras from a tentmaker. Three guys have smothered to death letting her be on top."

"Well, while I've got my hands full," John said presumptuously, "what are these other poor saps going to be doing?"

"Not to worry," New Jersey assured him, "Hedda'll take all comers."

"How many comers we got?" John said, looking around at the others, smiling. "Jason?"

"I'm not taking sloppy seconds," Jason said.

"You guys bring protection?" New Jersey wanted to know.

"I don't think there's that much protection in the world," Jason said.

New Jersey shrugged and he and Freckles drifted away.

"We could have at least checked out the torpedo tits," John suggested. "If we all felt her up, we could change the name of the band to the Juggernauts."

This proved too much for Matt. "You're disgusting," he said to John vehemently. "How can you even…?" Without finishing, he got up and went back on stage.

"What's eating him?" Russ asked.

"Beats me," John said. "He must know I'm only joking."

"For what it's worth," Jason said, "he asked me earlier if you had said anything about how your last date with Deb went."

"What does he care?" John wondered. "Deb and I are nothing serious. She finds me amusing but to tell you the truth, I think there's someone else she's more interested in."

"How *did* that wet T-shirt contest come about up in Jones Park, anyway?" Jason asked, looking at Matt running scales on the Wurlitzer.

"What all happened up there that day?" Russ wanted to know.

"Only the Shadow knows what lurks in the minds of men," Jason said portentously. "We better get back to work."

As they stood up, the black soldier who had sat down with them put his hand on Jason's arm. "Your name wouldn't be Jason Walker, would it?" he asked.

"Actually, it would," Jason said, puzzled. They billed themselves just as the Argonauts and so far hadn't had reason to introduce themselves individually to the crowd.

"I thought it might be you!" the man said. "Your brother Steve told me you played in a band but I thought he said the Astronauts, so I wasn't sure."

"You knew Steve?" Jason asked and John could see some of the pain of the last six weeks come back into his face.

"Oh, sure!" he said. "Him and me went to Nam together. My name is Ezekiel Adams but most people just call me Easy."

"Don't you have a brother named Uppan?" John joked.

"No, sir," Easy said with a chuckle. "That'd be my cousin. He likes the Army more than I do."

Jason had been thinking back. "Yeah," he said. "Steve mentioned you in a letter once but he spelled it E. Z."

"However you spell it, it still comes out easy," Easy said with a grin. "Anyway, I just wanted to tell you that your brother was like a brother to me too and I miss him. He was a good man."

"I really wish we could talk about this some more, Easy," Jason said. "But we've got to get back up there and play. Are you going to stay for a while?"

Easy smiled regretfully. "Sorry, boys, but I'm gonna do something the Devil never did."

"What's that?" John asked.

"I'm gonna leave you."

"Can't you stay for just a few songs?" Jason asked.

"Maybe a couple but I've got a curfew," Easy said. "I just wanted to say hey, tell you that you ain't the only one missing your brother."

John could see the bartender, who came as close as anyone to being in charge, getting antsy about the length of their break, checking his watch. "C'mon, we better get going," John said to Jason, pulling on his arm.

While Jason quickly tuned the SG to Matt's Wurlitzer and then tuned it again to itself to make up for the Wurlitzer's idiosyncrasies, John asked Russ how he felt.

"Remember Rizzo in *Midnight Cowboy*?" Russ asked.

"Ratzo? Yeah."

"If I get feeling a whole lot better, I might feel as good as Rizzo."

John laughed. "Come on, it's not like you had anything better to do tonight."

"They're holding that big concert in upstate New York this weekend," Russ said. "I could have changed my airline reservations and stayed with my dad a few extra days. But I couldn't get tickets."

"Oh, yeah, that thing in Woodstock," John said. "They showed it on the news last night. I hate to tell you this but you probably wouldn't have needed tickets anyway."

"Why?"

"I guess they had like 200,000 gate crashers."

Russ's pale face turned sour with disgust.

As soon as Jason had finished tuning, Matt played the opening chords to "Louie, Louie." It had become a signature piece, the closest thing to a sea-faring song in the Argonauts' repertoire. The Wurlitzer actually sounded just right on the intro and John sang the lead with the appropriate unintelligible nasality. They had customized it slightly, changing the "Yeah, yeah, yeah, yeah, yeah, yeah" of the refrain to a unison chorus of "Ar, ar, ar, ar, ar, ar," which had started out as the traditional Argonaut Pirate Growl but which, sung at that tempo and in that key, ended up sounding like a pack of rabid dogs. It was an inside joke; they didn't worry about whether the audience got it, which was just as well this time, since no one paid any attention whatsoever.

They went right into "Good Lovin'," which John sang as well and this went over a little better with the copulationally-challenged draftees.

"What about 'Yer Blues'?" John asked Jason, looking at the next song on the set list.

"Wanna die?" Jason said, quoting the song and recalling the reaction to "Born Under A Bad Sign."

They launched into "The Last Time" instead. John assumed that he wasn't the only one who saw how appropriate that seemed, since this gig would almost without a doubt end the Argonauts once and for all. Irony was far beyond the remaining dregs of the crowd.

"What about 'My Generation'?" Jason asked between songs.

"Your generation couldn't care less at the moment," John observed.

"I'll bet they're cheering the Who up in Woodstock right now," Russ added bitterly.

Jason stared at him a moment without saying anything but then windmilled into the song. But he had barely stuttered through the first verse when Russ quit playing and stood up.

"What are you doing, man?" Jason demanded, turning around.

Russ pointed to the floor with his drumsticks. Water seeped under the bathroom wall behind them, flooding the stage area. Evidently the toilet had clogged some time ago because the water was pale yellow with urine and contained black flecks of snuff and colorful bits of someone's barfed-up pizza.

"Don't touch anything!" Matt shouted to the others when he saw the water. "Russ, yank the cords!"

Russ gingerly pulled the cords from the sockets. "Jesus Christ!" he said, tiptoeing out of the water. "That's about enough of this!"

Jason grabbed his arm as he went by. "Come on, Russ, they'll get this cleaned up. Besides, we're supposed to play till one."

Russ yanked his arm loose and went back to pull his drums out of the filth.

Meanwhile, a loud dispute had broken out between the Georgia boys and the Okies about which fuckhead flushed the toilet. Having succeeded in getting themselves shit-faced on the 3.2% beer, any rationality soon gave way to name-calling, which led to shoving, which escalated to grabbing, which quickly disintegrated into a full-blown fist fight. Though they were all trained fighters, they hadn't trained for fists but for guns and fortunately most of the ones carrying guns had already left. Combined with the fact that most of them were too drunk to walk straight, it soon degenerated into a sloppy brawl, clumps of muscular young bodies tipping over the banquet tables and sending the metal folding chairs skittering across the linoleum.

Easy had grabbed his crutches and scrambled away at the first sign of trouble and he now hobbled over to Jason and the others. "At least you got a rise outta them," he said to Jason with a smile.

"Oh, yeah, we're flushed with success," John said, rolling his bass cabinet out of the water.

A couple of MPs who had peeked in earlier saw the melee in progress and came in blowing whistles and wielding billy clubs. The combatants sullenly dispersed, shouting at friend and foe alike, until a modicum of order was restored. The kegmaster, now that he could be heard, proclaimed, "The Doghouse is now closed! Everybody get the hell outta here!"

Outrage and grumbling followed but the presence of the big MPs persuaded the enlisted men to settle any further grievances and disputes outside.

The Argonauts wasted no time hauling their equipment out of the putrid effluvium. John and Jason got their guitars and amps into Jason's car in short order and John helped Matt carry the Wurlitzer out to the Tank while Russ tore down his drums. Jason, meanwhile, had gone to ask the bartender for their money.

"More bad news," he told the others when he came back. "They don't pay us here. I've got to go to the officer's club."

"What!?" Russ exclaimed. "We put up with all this crap and now we have to wait around for the money?"

"Actually, no," Jason said. "It's going to be a check anyway, not cash. I'll give you guys your share after I go to the bank on Monday."

"You have got to be kidding," Matt said icily.

"Hey, I'd pay you right now out of my pocket if I had the money. Sorry."

"Come on, Russ, let's get out of here," Matt said.

"I'll call you after work on Monday," Jason promised as they walked out.

"We both work after work on Monday," Russ pointed out over his shoulder as they went out the door.

"Well, that went well," John said to Jason when they were gone.

Jason just rolled his eyes.

"Come on, someday you'll look back on this and laugh."

"Someday I'll die too," Jason said. "So maybe I'll die laughing."

Easy, for some reason the only other person besides themselves and the bartender allowed to stay, put in his two-cents'-worth: "You guys went over better than you think."

"How do you figure?" Jason wanted to know.

"Last week," Easy said, "instead of beating up each other, they beat up the band."

"See, Jason?" John said, hoping to lighten the mood. "It's like the old saying I just made up: It's better to be a beat off than to get beat up."

It didn't help. "Oh, yeah, we're living the dream," Jason said. "Let's go. Easy, thanks for sticking around and for the nice words about my brother."

"Because he was your brother," Easy said, clasping Jason's hand thumb-around-thumb, "you're my brother."

"Right on," Jason said.

"I don't suppose I could hit my brother up for a favor?" Easy went on.

"Name it, bro."

"The reason I said I had to leave is that I gotta get back to my barracks before bed check and it's mighty slow going with these stilts."

"Hey, we'd be glad to give you a ride, man."

"I'll make it worth your while."

o   o   o

Dex Walker had given Jason his 1953 Ford station wagon to run into the ground. It was large and dark green with the window posts painted to look like the wood Ford had used just a few years earlier on the classic woodies. Suffering a variety of ailments in the generator, battery, voltage regulator, and solenoid, it had become known as the Wonder Car because they always wondered whether it would start. Luckily, it had a nice low first-gear ratio, making push starts relatively easy when necessary. Since Jason had put the back seat down for the equipment, they all piled into the front seat, John in the middle. Wonders never ceasing, the car started the first time and Jason let it roll a little to let the un-synchromeshed first gear catch up to the motor.

"Nice ride," Easy said.

"When it goes," Jason said.

"I don't suppose you guys blow any weed, do you?"

"Only when we have it," John said. "Lamentably, we have none."

From his uniform pocket Easy extracted a thin, tightly rolled joint. "You do now," he said. "If I could trouble you for a light, we could partake right now."

"Excellent, my man!" Jason said, punching in the cigarette lighter. "Where am I taking you?"

"Take a right," Easy said. "It ain't far. Thank you." He took the lighter and lit the joint, passing it to John.

Having smoked marijuana several times now, John took what he considered to be a standard hit. The smoke, though, seemed to burst in his lungs. He lost most of it in a fit of coughing. "Holy cannabinoly!" he choked out. "That's some killer stuff!"

Jason, forewarned, took a more conservative approach but it still sent his eyebrows up toward his widow's peak.

"What is this?" John asked Easy as he watched him take a delicate hit.

"Thai stick," Easy said with a minimum of breath. "Got it in Nam."

"Phew!" John said. "Lemme try again."

He took the joint from Easy's long fingers. Already he felt the effects of the cannabinol. The cherry on the joint glowed brighter as he inhaled. It reminded him of a campfire, a tiny campfire. Focusing on the minuscule embers he slowly passed it on to Jason. Jason was busy driving. "Man, that's incredible stuff," he said, concentrating on the road. "I shouldn't do much more of that."

"Just a taste," John suggested, holding the joint to Jason's lips.

Jason whistled in a tad and pulled his head away. "You can have the rest of my hit."

"The only thing I've got left to do tonight is to get my stuff out of the car, right?"

"Unless you want to leave it in. Nobody'll mess with it in my driveway."

"Well, then, beam me up, Scotty!" He carefully took another hit and offered it to Easy.

Easy waved it off. "Naw. You guys go ahead. Save it for later if you like. Right again."

John felt good that he'd been right again but couldn't remember what it was he'd been right about, before or now. Jason rotated the steering wheel clockwise using the ivory-colored plastic knob Dex had clamped to the steering wheel. Easy hummed a song and then sang in a soft voice, "I wish it would rain." John looked at the joint barely smoldering way down at the end of his arm. He felt himself lean forward and stub it out in the ashtray. He realized that everything around him had become part of an elaborate, exquisitely drawn cartoon.

"Do you sing?" Jason asked.

"I try a little," Easy said. "But I can't sing like you guys can sing."

John opened his mouth to say that all he did was open his mouth and noise came out, but no noise came out. While his mouth was open he discovered that he could breathe either through his mouth or through his nose, or both, but he couldn't figure out a way to breathe in through his nose and out through his mouth at the same time, or vice versa. It seemed a shame.

"Fat lot of good it did us tonight," Jason said.

John noticed for the first time that Jason hadn't shaved, the blonde stubble hard to see against his tan face. Jason's eyes looked tired and dark and his jaw muscles clenched as he drove.

"Tough crowd," Easy said. "Old enough to drink, old enough to fight and die, too young to vote."

Easy, on the other hand, was impeccably shaven and his curly black hair had been cut very short. He smelled soapy, like he had just bathed. John's right knee bumped the hard cast on Easy's left leg.

"You got a stone leg," John told him.

"You got a stone head," Jason told John.

John's teeth did feel like little rocks and his skull seemed solid enough. For that matter, he had always taken his mind for granite.

"Would you vote for this war?" Jason asked Easy.

"No, I'm pretty sure I wouldn't," Easy said. "But my folks haven't had much practice voting."

"Some people are trying to change that lately," Jason said.

"Some of them are dying," Easy said. "Martin."

"Bobby," Jason said.

"The good die young," Easy said.

For just an instant John could see everything clearly: the white barrack buildings, the scruffy Chinese elms and piñons, the yellow lines on the blacktop. He opened his mouth to express this momentary revelation but a clap of thunder obliterated the few words he'd gathered.

"I miss my brother," Jason said. "More than I thought I could."

John had one sister, several years older. Jason was the closest he had to a brother. The enormity of what it would be like to lose someone like that swept over John. He gazed at the familiar face, trying to memorize every detail in case it disappeared someday.

"They don't come any better," Easy said.

"How well did you know him?" Jason asked.

Fat raindrops splattered against the windshield. In two seconds a heavy downpour enveloped the car. The din sounded like a roll on a heavy snare drum. More lightning scattered the shadows.

"Member that snake?" Easy asked.

Lightning is a snake, all forks and fangs and lidless eyes. A million volts of venom.

"He told you about that?" Jason asked. He flipped on the windshield wipers which, on the Wonder Car, were powered by the compression of the engine. Accelerating or climbing a hill, they crept across the windshield slower than the first day of school. Between gears or downhill, geysers of water erupted onto other drivers' windshields. Under pressure, during a strain, you couldn't see as far as you could spit. But relax, coast, and you could see forever.

"He said you touched it," Easy said.

"It was real," Jason said.

"I know. He believed you. He said he couldn't touch it. But he knew you could."

"Had to," Jason said.

"Here."

Jason flipped up the turn signal arm, lighting on the dash a beautiful emerald-green arrow. But the signal blinked at random, not with the dreary monotony of most turn signals. A wonder car indeed, John realized once again.

They pulled into the gravel parking lot of the barracks and Jason shut off the motor. The rain had ended as abruptly as it had begun and already the crickets had resumed their tireless chant. The Wonder Car ticked quietly as it cooled.

"How bad is Nam?" Jason asked.

"Lotsa snakes," Easy said. "Lotsa surprise endings."

John's right arm still tingled and twitched. He quickly glanced at it, thinking it had somehow turned itself inside out, the muscles raw on the surface, the skin buried below. The mood in the car felt oppressive again.

"Do you have that joint?" he asked Jason.

Jason checked in his pocket and behind his ear. "No," he told John. "Do you?"

John looked between his fingers, then in the ashtray. "Yes," he said, retrieving it and punching in the lighter. When the lighter popped, he jumped, having forgotten to expect it, then he had to repunch it to reheat it, then he relit the joint and passed it to Jason.

Jason stared forward out the windshield, twirling the knob on the steering wheel. "So did you hear what happened to Steve?" he asked, taking a hit off the joint, passing it over to Easy.

Easy had been staring out the side window but turned back to them to accept the joint. "What did they tell you?" he asked, taking a little hit and passing it back to John.

It had burned down to a roach. John carefully sucked another hit; the others passed again. John put it into his waterproof match container with some others. The container smelled of tar and ash and smoldering weeds. The Wonder Car smelled of Dex's cigarettes and the sticky tar-paper floor and gasoline. John smelled of sweat and smoke and fear. He didn't want to eavesdrop, especially on the story he could hear in their voices, but he was caught in the middle.

Jason bit his lip while he thought about it. "We got an official condolence from the company commander. It read like a form letter. Said that P. F. C. Steven A. Walker died in the line of duty on July 4 in Dac To, Republic of Vietnam, blah, blah, blah, God and country and all that. Purple Heart, maybe a Silver Star for gallantry in action."

"Fine," Easy said. "Jus' fine."

"Yeah," Jason said. "But short on details. Mom and Dad—it's enough for them. But I want to know what happened."

"I could tell you," Easy said. "I was there. In fact, I got your address from company records so I could write you about it. But then, I don't know. Maybe I chickened out. I never wrote many letters. And anyway, what's done is done. Let sleepin' dogs lie."

"Easy, I've got enough lying dogs in my life already," Jason said. "I'd just as soon hear the truth for a change. If you've got something to say, say it."

Easy heaved a sigh. "I'd be lying if I said I had nothing to do with it. Fact is, I made a mistake."

John said, "Good thing nothing like that ever happened to us, huh, Jase?"

Jason rocked the steering wheel back and forth. "Go on."

"Well, you know," Easy began, "Steve liked high places. That's why he liked that rock climbing stuff up in Cheyenne Cañon. He liked to get up and get a look around. We even hauled all that climbing gear out in the jungle once and climbed one of those great big trees. And, my lord, he loved them helicopters. Best view in the world from one of them."

"He sent us pictures."

"Yeah, he showed me those. Trouble was, we were working supplies just outside Da Nang, driving forklifts. Don't get much of a view from a forklift. Everybody got real bored with it but your brother, he was really gettin' cabin fever. So one day we got a call to airlift a bunch of boxes of pamphlets from Que Son to Dac To and I jumped at it, figured Steve'd love a chopper ride."

"I imagine," Jason said.

For John, the cartoon had ended. The blue light from the mercury vapor streetlight falling on the dash, the hushed tones of the others, the sense of being in the heart of the beast here on base, gave the whole thing a *film noir* tone. He felt like they were sliding on an icy road: they couldn't stop, couldn't avoid the coming crash, and couldn't speed it up to get it over with.

"See," Easy went on, "I used to be a sergeant. Your brother was like my main man. But I had no authority to let him come along in that helicopter. Got my ass busted for it. That's how come I'm hangin' at the Doghouse steada the O. C. Sent me back here to deroast awhile. But I'm sure glad I got to see you boys play. Steve said you were pretty good but I don't think he knew how good."

"Well, it all went down the tubes tonight," Jason said.

"If only," John said wistfully.

"So anyways," Easy went on, "a friend of mine named Billy Ray is flyin' the Huey and another guy named Eddie comes too. I figured, this ain't no combat mission. All we got is fliers. And the hills we're flyin' over been quiet for a while. So Steve and I torch one up and then I curl up on the boxes and take a nap cause the breeze feels good and it's hard to talk over the blades."

"What's Steve doing?" Jason asked.

"Sittin' by the turret gun soakin' up the view. Well, I start to stir when I hear Billy Ray bring the Huey down to the landing site. But when we were still maybe 50 feet up some VC in the trees with a grenade launcher hits the Huey. From inside that can it sounds like the end of the world. It blows the strut off and turns us ass over elbows. Eddie's the closest one to it and the shrapnel rips him to shreds, blood and stuff flyin' all over everywhere. Billy Ray takes a big chunk of it too, in his arm, but somehow he kept the Huey under control. It flipped me off of them boxes and I hit the metal deck right on the knee, shattered my kneecap."

"What about Steve?" Jason asked.

"He'd been sittin' there the whole time without wearin' a safety harness. I called to him when I broke my knee but he didn't answer. I looked over and he was gone. Musta slipped out the open door."

"Just fell out?"

"I reckon. I wasn't seein' things too clear about then."

"That's weird," Jason said, his forehead resting on the steering wheel. "I dreamed about him the first time I went to sleep after I heard. It was kind of a long day and I fell asleep on the couch. And right after I closed my eyes, I saw him falling away, calling to me, calling to Mom."

"I'm so sorry," Easy said thickly. "So sorry."

"Did you go down for his body?" Jason asked.

"Couldn't," Easy said. "Couldn't land without the strut. Billy Ray just barely got us back to Dac To and we crashed landed there. Killed Billy Ray. I'm the only one made it back."

"Back to Dac To?" Jason asked. "I thought that's where you were."

Easy turned quickly to stare out the window again.

For John everything had become too real. Each moment, each vivid impression, became incised in his awareness. He could feel the shattering concussion of the explosion, smell Eddie's guts, hear the straining whine of the Huey's motor trying to lift them out, sense the helpless, terrifying tumbling as Steve fell, the inevitability of the final crumpling of the fragile body on the muddy ground, so obliterative it shook the soul free.

He also sensed that Easy's story had raised as many questions for Jason as it had answered. Jason wasn't the type to leave any sleeping dogs unroused.

When Easy didn't respond, Jason said, "Steve and I didn't always get along. In fact, when we were little we used to be at each others' throats all the time. Part of it was that he liked to pick on me. Another part of it was that I was always jealous of him. He was always bigger and faster and stronger than I was. He was the one Mom and Dad pinned their hopes on, I was just the back-up plan. Now, I don't want to steal any of his thunder. But what did he do that would warrant that Silver Star?"

"Man, I already said too much," Easy moaned.

"Then saying a little more can't hurt much," Jason said.

"Okay, but I could be in a world of hurt if anybody finds out I told you this. I didn't know about it myself till after. We weren't takin' those pamphlets to Dac To, we were takin' them to a base in Laos."

"Laos? I didn't think we had any bases in Laos."

"Not suppose to. But we do. It's the only way we can try to cut the Ho Chi Minh Trail."

"What are you saying? That Steve's Silver Star is just a way to buy silence? That nobody'll question his death if he was a hero?"

Easy looked at Jason. "Man, I'm sorry. I just shoulda kept my big mouth shut. I surely don't need the DIA on my back. I meant what I said before. Your brother was a fine, fine man. You know what I think you should do? You should just let him keep his medal."

Jason opened his mouth to say something else but changed his mind. After a minute he said. "Easy, I can't thank you enough for talking to me about this."

Easy said, "Hey, wish I had better stuff to say. But I gotta go in now to make bed check. You gonna be okay?"

"Who knows?"

"Just remember, like the man says, it don't pay to take life too serious. It ain't nohow permanent."

"Don't I know it."

"I don't suppose you could help me get out?"

John and Easy slapped palms and then Jason helped him out and got him propped up on his crutches. They walked together a little ways and then turned to one another and hugged, Jason's long curly blonde hair a sharp contrast to Easy's close-cropped head. In the light of the pale new moon the embrace took on an air of statuary.

John slid over into the warm spot where Easy had been.

Jason got back in and turned to him. "Hell of a night, huh?"

John reached over and gripped his shoulder in a gesture of solidarity.

"Easy told me they ship him back to Nam next week when he gets the cast off."

"Wow."

Jason tried to start the Wonder Car but got just a clunk when he turned the key. Sometimes it helped to wait a minute. "How can I tell people the truth about my brother without making him look bad? Without seeming like I'm just jealous?"

The Thai stick had made coherent thought difficult at best but John didn't think he could figure that one out had he been straight. "I don't know," he said.

Jason tried the starter again. Nothing. "And why is the Army, the government, lying to us about this war?"

"I don't know," John said again, wishing he could be more help.

The third time was the charm. The engine started and Jason turned on the headlights and looked around. "Okay," he said, straightening up. "Where the hell am I?"

Finally, something John could help with. "America," he said.

. . . O . . . O . . . O . . .

A few years ago I recorded an album of remakes of songs written in the late 1960s which I titled Only Children. *Since I recorded all the instruments and sang all the parts, I had to spend a year playing with myself. (I used to use that joke on stage.) The title had three meanings: No two songs were written by the same person, so each was an only child; the songwriters, all in their late teens or early twenties, were barely more than children when they crafted songs with such mature themes and lasting relevance; and a few songs that few people would ever hear were the only children I could reasonably expect from spending a year playing with myself.*

I heard Alan Watts speak in Boulder in the late '60s. He told the story of his Confirmation into the Anglican Church. He and the other young teenage boys dreaded what he referred to as the "Very Serious Talk" the school chaplain would have with each boy as part of the preparation for his Chrism. The boys expected the Very Serious Talk to initiate them into the innermost secrets of the Christian church, secrets so holy that speaking of them in public was taboo. The Very Serious Talk, as it turned out, amounted to little more than an admonition to avoid, at all costs, masturbation, leaving Watts little doubt about the most important thing in the Christian religion.

There have been times in my life, though, when I didn't have to play with myself and almost ended up with children. In fact, a band, not surprisingly, provided the only child I truly considered mine, at least for a while.

Back in my days as a drummer, I auditioned for a rock-and-roll band called Tight Squeeze. The young lead singer, the lead guitarist's girlfriend, was a wild woman with a throaty, boisterous voice of incredible range. She lobbied to hire me because "he'll drive the little girls wild." I immediately fell madly in love with her.

Within a week, we all learned that she and her previous boyfriend had conceived a child. Within a month the lead guitarist split up with her and quit the band. The singer, having severed her relationship with the child's father and finding little consolation in her brief fling with the rhythm guitarist, turned to me. I tried, as a friend, to give her good counsel about her options, including giving up the child, but she had resolved to keep it.

By now, I wanted her beyond reason. I don't know that I drove her completely wild but I like to think I got her close enough to walk the rest of the way. I knew my chances of hanging on to a ball of fire like her were slim but I threw caution to the wind.

She moved in with me and I assured her, and truly felt, that the child would be mine as much as anyone's. One spring day her water broke at her mother's house and her mother took her to the hospital. I rushed there myself as soon as I heard to help her through her labor. After about six hours, I dashed across the street for a burger and came back to find that the baby's umbilical cord had wrapped around his neck so they had done a quick Cesarean section. Disappointed that I hadn't been there at the critical time, I nevertheless felt an incredible pride and love when they handed that little bundle to me, the first to hold him.

Music has not only provided me with most of my relationships, it has destroyed them as well. That Ball of Fire and I found the pressures of living on the road with a tiny infant too great so she moved on to the bass player, who evidently was next in line. She and I attempted a reconciliation after that, during which we inadvertently conceived a child of our own. But she suffered an ectopic pregnancy and I lost not only my child but almost its mother as well.

A few months later our love was gone for good. She let me take the little boy on weekends for a while but we both knew that my only tie to the child was love and we both knew from experience that love comes and goes. The night she broke the news to me that I couldn't see him anymore, I went home and cried for half an hour but then had to go to work, my first night with a new band. The show must go on.

I don't know what she told the boy as he grew up about the long-haired drummer in all his baby pictures. I do know that losing him hurt me as much as anything ever has. A few years later, back to playing with myself, I included my feelings for that little boy in a song I wrote called "Heaven and Hell." The last two lines are:

> *Heaven's just the ones you love around you.*
> *Hell is when you have to say good-bye.*

November 11, 1999

A damp drizzly November had settled into Russ's soul. He sat, grim about the mouth, at the small bar in Tweak, his shirt cuffs folded back a couple of times, his elbows on the brushed copper, his chin on his fists.

Oscar the bartender, whose black slacks and white shirt always looked pressed and fresh, came over to him. "Anything I can get you, R. J.?"

Russ looked up. He sometimes forgot he owned a bar; he rarely drank here. He perused the bottles lined up on the shelves. "You know, I am tempted," he told Oscar.

"The only way to get rid of a temptation," Oscar said, "is to yield to it. What'll it be?"

While Russ contemplated his choice, Christine came in, hung up her coat, and put her purse behind the bar. She looked sultry in a black skirt, dark hose, and a tight black turtleneck that accentuated Russ's favorite distractions. She sat on the stool next to his. Working a split shift, she had returned half an hour before she had to hit the floor again at four.

"How are you feeling?" Russ asked her. She had complained of a sore throat earlier.

"I feel like—" she said hoarsely and then broke off in a fit of coughing.

"Say no more," Russ told her, placing his hand comfortingly on her back as she laid her head on her arms. "If it's any consolation, you look great."

She glanced over at him sourly and then put her head back down.

"What you need is a pick-me-up, something soothing, something bracing," Russ said. "Oscar, what did you make me that time I had the flu?"

"Ah, just the thing," Oscar said. "A Sunset."

"That's right. Could you make her one of those and a Manhattan for me? And what was that last CD? Louis Prima?"

Oscar checked the jewel case and nodded.

"Play it again."

Oscar raised his eyebrows but played it again.

As Oscar mixed the drinks, Buzz came up from the kitchen, smelling of sweat and grease. "Hey, Mr. J." he said to Russ, "are we out of capers again?"

Russ thought about it, idly looking at the tattoo on Buzz's forearm that read simply, "Creed." "Did you check the shelves in the gun room?"

"I checked everywhere," Buzz said.

"How can we possibly be out of capers?" Russ demanded irritably, not specifically of Buzz. "What the fu— What the hell is going on around here? We had a whole can of capers just last week. I saw them with my own eyes. How can these things just disappear?"

"Looks like a caper caper, Mr. J.," Buzz said affably. "I guess I'll whip up some hollandaise sauce for that salmon instead. So, Christine, make sure all the servers know."

Christine just groaned.

Oscar set the drinks in front of them. "There now," Oscar said to Christine, touching her arm. "Try it."

She raised her head and looked at the drink. "Oh, I don't know," she said, her voice breaking badly.

"It'll help your throat," Russ promised, "more than what you've been doing which, from the sound of it, has been gargling with razor blades and ground glass."

"I still won't be able to sing tomorrow," she croaked bleakly, rubbing a drop from the cordial glass with her thumb.

"I didn't know you were a singer," Buzz said.

"Oh, I'm in a play at the Grove Street Playhouse this weekend," Christine told him softly. "I've got to sing a couple of songs."

"I didn't know you were an actress," Russ said, impressed.

"I studied at Julliard," Christine said.

"Really? So did my sister," Russ said. He raised his glass. "To the roar of the greasepaint."

They both sipped their drinks.

"Mmm, that is good," Christine admitted, looking at the cordial glass. "What is it again?"

"A Sunset?" Russ asked Oscar.

"Actually, the original name was *Coucher du Soleil*," Oscar explained, "French for 'sunset.' It's something I learned from a wandering minstrel years ago who claimed it worked wonders on a singer's throat. It's a layer of Chambord, the red sun on the bottom there, a thin horizon of Cointreau, topped with a rich, russet cloud of Grand Marnier."

"It is soothing on my throat," Christine said.

"What kind of stuff do you sing?" Buzz asked her.

"Oh, I've done all sorts of things," she said hoarsely. "I used to sing in a band when I was in school."

"I gotta get back to work," Buzz told her, "but maybe we could get together sometime. I'll bring my ax. We can see if there's any overlap."

"If my voice ever comes back," Christine told him as he went back downstairs.

Russ couldn't picture the beautiful Christine with a guy like Buzz but then Russ could write a multi-volume set of books on what he didn't know about women. He would have to devote one whole book just to Sylvia. He certainly couldn't predict how she would react to the news he had received just an hour ago.

A pudgy, round-shouldered young man, wearing a tight vest and black, thick-soled, round-toed shoes approached them, asking, "Do any of you work here?"

"May I help you?" Oscar asked.

"I had a question about one of the paintings in the other room," he said.

Oscar declined his head in Russ's direction and Russ asked, "What did you want to know?"

"I see you have paintings by both Guy Ellis and Sylvia Ellis," the man said, a faint lisp in his voice. "Sylvia Ellis is his daughter?"

"Wife," Russ corrected him, then corrected himself: "Widow, actually."

"Is the $4500 for just that single Sylvia Ellis?"

"The artists set the price," Russ pointed out coolly.

"No, I mean, are there other parts included? Here, let me show you."

He and his partner, a short blonde shy-looking fellow with a wispy mustache, led the way into the gallery portion of Tweak. They stopped in front of an abstract Sylvia had painted a decade before. The bottom third of the canvas was a tangled maze of broken jagged slashes, steel gray, sky blue, blood red. The field above was a steady gradient from azure to indigo, blank and empty but for a single shape, a graceful white curve that seemed in flight.

The pudgy man pointed to the lower right corner above Sylvia's signature. "See? Does that mean one of three, like a triptych?"

"Actually, no," Russ explained. "That's the title of the painting, '103'."

"Ah," the man said, squinting again at the painting. "Huh. Gee, I really like this. Could you give us a minute?"

Russ bowed ever so slightly, more from habit than any feeling of deference. "Take your time. I'll be in the other room."

As Russ sat down next to her again, Christine said, "I'm sure Syl would be happy to sell another painting."

"You'd sure think so," Russ said, sipping from his Manhattan. "Although lately, there's just no telling how she's going to react to things."

Christine, her spirits lifted a bit by the Sunset, looked at him while he stared into his drink. "Is everything okay? You sound pretty gloomy."

"She's been gloomy," he told her, drinking.

"Maybe it's the time of year," Christine offered.

"Today in particular. I actually managed to sleep in this morning and when I finally got up at eleven, she was in the middle of her two minutes of silence."

"That's right," Oscar said. "It's Veteran's Day, isn't it?"

"What does that have to do with it?" Christine asked.

"It's an old tradition," Oscar explained. "Goes back to the Armistice at the end of World War I, which was signed at eleven o'clock on the eleventh day of the eleventh month. Everyone used to observe it with two minutes of silence."

"Ellis, the veteran," Russ said pointedly, "got her in the habit."

Oscar said, "Ah," knowing Russ's ambivalence about Ellis.

"You can't really blame Russ," Christine said to Oscar, "if he's a little sensitive about reminders of her first marriage."

"Hell, I don't begrudge Ellis his couple of minutes of silence," Russ said bitterly. "It's the 45 minutes of silence she gave me afterward that bother me."

"How long has this been going on?" Christine asked him quietly.

"At least since Halloween," Russ told her. "That Egypt Air 990 crash really upset her."

"Well, that's understandable, considering how Ellis died."

"Plus," Russ said, lowering his voice, "she's just starting her period."

"That's always a drag," Christine empathized.

Especially if you're completely convinced, Russ thought to himself, the way he and Sylvia were convinced, that she would be having morning sickness instead of cramps this month.

Of course, he knew better now. But he didn't feel like talking about his own physiological failings with Christine.

The pudgy man came back in from the gallery, his silent partner trailing behind. "Could I ask another question?"

"I think you just did," Russ pointed out, "but help yourself. Questions are free today."

"What is that '103' painting supposed to mean?"

Russ looked at him blankly, not knowing what to say.

Oscar came to his rescue, saying, "Art never expresses anything but itself."

"I know that," the man said shortly. "I mean, are there, like, a hundred and two others or something?"

"I assure you, it's one of a kind," Russ told him, not in the mood for obtuse questions.

The pudgy man, frustrated, looked first at Russ, then at Oscar, then, in a huff, turned on his heel and walked out, his blonde shadow dogging his steps.

Neither of them held the door for Michelle, who breezed in with a flutter of scarf and long blonde hair. Russ hadn't seen her since that night at Les Deux Gamins and was a little surprised to see her now. Tweak wasn't one of her usual haunts.

"Hi, Christine, Oscar," she called cheerfully. "Hey, Russ, have you seen your wife?"

"Not since this morning," he told her, adding, "And I haven't heard from her since last night."

"Shoot," Michelle said, checking her watch. "I've got to run. Will you give her a message if you see her or hear from her? In case I don't make it tonight, will you have her tell Paul that I got the part in that commercial?"

Russ clenched his jaw. First, Paul's umbrella had hung, apparently forgotten, on the coat rack by the front door of the townhome for a couple of weeks. Then last week, oddly, it had disappeared and a couple of days later Paul left Syl a message on the answering machine thanking her. Not particularly suspicious by nature, Russ was having trouble coming up with innocent explanations for Sylvia's sudden interest in this guy.

Nevertheless, to Michelle he said simply, "If I happen to catch up with her I'll give her the message."

"Thanks, Russ," she said, kissing the air near his head. "*Ciao*."

After she left, Christine said, "Is everything okay between you and Syl? You make it sound like you two are barely speaking."

"To tell you the truth," Russ said, lowering his voice to the confidential level the truth requires, "lately Sylvia has acted as distant and preoccupied as she did when we first met. I honestly don't know what's she's doing. Or who she's doing it with."

"Surely you don't think…" But she left it to his imagination to think of what he shouldn't think.

"Nothing would surprise me at this point," Russ said. "She's been getting phone calls from people she hasn't talked to in years. She's had a bunch of stuff to do that she doesn't want to talk about. Paul's name keeps popping up. She's even quit painting. What does that sound like to you?"

"I don't believe it," Christine said, shaking her head. "I don't know her all that well but not Sylvia."

"Anything's possible."

Russ's cell phone chirped in his back pocket. He took it out and opened it up, said hello.

"Russell," his father said. "How are you, son?"

"I'm okay, Dad. How are you?"

"Not too bad today. I walked Tiny Cat all the way down to the lake and back and neither one of us had to stop once."

"Way to go."

"Listen, son. Your mother's been pestering me all day, wondering how your doctor's appointment went but she didn't want to call you because she didn't want you to think she was concerned. Did you get the results?"

"Yes, I did," Russ said quietly. "It looks like it's not going to happen. At least *I* can't make it happen. Sylvia seems to be fine."

"Russell, I can't tell you how sorry I am to hear it. Do you want to talk to your mother?"

"You know something, Dad? This isn't the best time. I'll talk to you both about it later."

"Sorry. Did I catch you at work? How are things there at Tweak? Did you get the books straightened out?"

Louie had a vested interest in Tweak. When Sylvia had finally emerged from Ellis's shadow enough to make a name, and an income, for herself as an artist, she had urged Russ to pursue his dream. Until then he had done most of the heavy lifting when it came to their finances but he had grown increasingly frustrated with the idiotic business practices at the restaurants where he worked. For months he had walked by the empty storefront on Bleeker and Christopher and dreamed aloud about opening his own place there. When she urged him to look into it, he had always fallen back on the excuse that they didn't have the kind of money to open the kind of place he had in mind.

One summer evening, over lemonade on the porch up at the farm, she had mentioned this dream to his parents. He had never brought it up because he knew his parents would work the thing to death but before he could stop her, the cat was out of the bag. Sure enough, Monday morning Louie was on the phone to a friend of his in real estate, talking long term lease on the property. Russ had been right about the money: a prime corner storefront, large by Village standards, renovated, brought up to code, plus an added hood downstairs, all the necessary appliances, and an expensive agreement with the liquor board—the whole package ran well into six figures.

Russ, of course, was aghast when he heard the actual amount, which was four or five times the outrageous amount he had estimated. Louie, on the other hand, was undeterred. He sat Russ down and made him an offer he couldn't refuse: he wouldn't loan him the money; instead, he would *give* him the money, not as a gift but as a living legacy, a portion of Russ's inheritance. Russ balked, knowing full well that free money is as scarce as free love or free time but, after weeks of cajoling from his wife and his mother, he eventually consented and Tweak was born.

But Russ's suspicions had proven correct. Despite his best efforts, Louie couldn't help becoming interested in Tweak's fortunes. And Russ, for his part, couldn't help feeling accountable to him.

"I ran those numbers three times this afternoon," Russ told him. "I just can't get it straight. I'm going to talk to Rolando about it when he comes in."

"Who else works on the books besides you and Rolando?" Louie asked.

"That's it."

"Maybe it's time to get out the ax," Louie said bluntly.

"Come on, Dad," Russ said, weary of his father's melodramatic streak. "I can't go around firing people just because I'm too stupid to balance the books."

"I'll tell you what's stupid," Louie said. "Letting someone take money out of your till is stupid."

"It's my money, Dad," Russ pointed out.

"I know it is, son. It just seems like sometimes you have trouble standing up for what's yours."

"One thing I did find out at the doctor's today," Russ said, feeling testy, "is that, with one exception, there's nothing wrong with my balls."

His father didn't say anything.

"Hey, Dad," Russ said, relenting, "I'm sorry. You caught me at a bad time. I'll call you later, let you know what's going on."

"Sure, son," Louie said dismissively.

"Give my love to Mom."

But his father had already hung up.

"Shit," Russ said, folding up his cell phone and sticking it back in his pocket. Only then did it occur to him that Christine, and possibly Oscar, had heard his end of the conversation. Oscar imperturbably cut lemons at the other end of the small bar; Christine's head lay on her arms again.

Russ drained his Manhattan. Except for one couple on the gallery side, Tweak was empty. With Oscar's back turned, nothing stood in the way of Russ's letting his eyes roam around the beautiful woman on the stool next to his. Nope, nothing wrong with his libido. He drank in the way the tiny blonde hairs on the back of Christine's neck swept up and back. Her perfect breasts, well-defined under the tight black turtleneck and maximized in size and shape by the way she leaned against the bar, seemed the perfect antidote to all the bullshit life had piled on him lately. One small consolation to his condition, it occurred to him, was that he could fuck Christine six ways from Sunday and never get her pregnant. It felt kind of liberating in a way. Yeah, that's how he felt: fucking liberated.

As though his thoughts had grown too loud, Christine's head popped up; she looked at her watch. "I guess I better get started," she said. She glanced at Russ and for just a moment he sensed a trace of fear in her eyes.

That's what you get for blabbing about firing people, he said to himself. To Christine he said, "I wish I could send you home. Maybe you can get Rolando to close up for you."

"Oh, I'll be fine," she rasped, getting up. "Besides, I need the money."

"Where is Rolando, anyway?" he asked, checking his own watch.

"He, uh, said he had an appointment," Christine said. "I'm sure he'll be here soon."

"Maybe I'll stop back in later and talk to him. But I've got to get out of here for a while."

"Don't worry about a thing," she assured him. "Everything will be fine here."

He got up and got his light jacket. "See you, Oscar."

"Have a good evening, Mr. Jones."

Mr. Jones? Russ thought. He never calls me Mr. Jones.

o   o   o

Today was the first really cold day of the fall. The sun, a low-life at this time of year, had finally tired of skulking like a burglar along the rooftops of the Village and now, just after four, had faded into impotence and anonymity in the uniform gray overcast. The city reverted to black and white.

Feeling like Harry Hope venturing from his bar for the first time in years, Russ had no sooner stepped out the front door of Tweak than a guy pushing a cart full of junk jewelry nearly ran him down. "Bejees!" Russ snapped at him. "Can't you see I'm walking here?" A cop, stalled in traffic, looked away. The usual crowd of freaks jostled along the sidewalk. For some reason, today, it irritated Russ. Bleeker seemed bleaker than ever. Only a strong, moral principle prevented him from deliberately stepping into the street and knocking off people's hats.

Unlike Harry Hope, Russ made it all the way across the street, jaywalking right in front of the apathetic cop. He went into the 327 Bleeker Grocery but found his buddy Sid wasn't there, so he bought a roll of chocolate Necco wafers and a copy of the *Sporting News* and left.

The chocolate Neccos were a find but he craved something stronger. He cut cater-cornered through the intersection to the Juice Bar which, in addition to 27 varieties of healthful fruit and vegetable juice drinks and smoothies, also had ice cream. The menu for the 27 drinks included not only the ingredients but also the ailments the drinks supposedly helped to alleviate, like kidney stones, asthma, and poor circulation. The guy behind the counter, whose name was June, asked him if he wanted the usual. Russ had gotten in the habit of ordering number 7: an orange, peach, papaya, banana smoothie supposed to promote "sexual harmony," the closest he could find to something that might increase the odds of conception.

"Not today, June," he said recklessly. To hell with prudence. "Give me a double scoop of banana fudge ice cream in a cone."

"Sprinkles?"

"Sprinkles galore!"

He drifted out onto Bleeker again, devouring the ice cream in large, tooth-jarring mouthfuls. Sylvia had told him yesterday about the function tonight that Michelle mentioned; there was no point in rushing back to Grove Court. So he slouched along, hearing in his head Paul McCartney's voice singing, "Oh, that magic feeling: nowhere to go." Antique stores had gotten old; Kitschen no longer seemed cutting edge; Condomania was pointless.

Shivering from the ice cream cone and the chilly wind, he went across the street to the Broken Spine, a cramped, below-street-level used-book store that nearly always inspired him to read something unanticipated. The desk clerk, a morose, effeminate older man who never wore clothes lighter in color or taste than his espresso, nodded to him and went back to reading his *Voice*.

Russ had come into the Spine just a few weeks ago but that day he had made a beeline for the Sexuality section. No point in looking there now. Maybe Philosophy. What better time to be philosophical?

From force of habit he checked on Ospinsky and Gurdjieff and found none. Maybe something from the Eastern Religion section. Years ago he had dabbled in Buddhism and Zen and the way things looked at the moment, meditating on non-attachment might not be a bad idea.

He decided he wasn't up to something requiring that level of austerity. What about fiction? Maybe he could lose himself in an engrossing story.

But his own story seemed engrossing enough at the moment. He didn't have the patience for some damned novelist's cockeyed notion of reality. Why get all worked up about a bunch of total strangers?

The only book he stopped to look through was a coffee table book of pictures of New York women, photos artistic, glamorous, sensational, disturbing, crude, obscene. He could fuck every one of these women and run no risk of pregnancy. Fucking liberated.

Discouraged, he left without a purchase or a glance from the man behind the counter. He walked back toward Tweak but knew that if he went in, he'd get stuck there for hours. He turned right on Christopher instead, stopping in McNulty's for a pound of Kenyan coffee. Farther down, the Lucille Lortel Theater, which had brass stars set in the sidewalk *a la* Hollywood's Walk of Fame, was running a play called "Y2K."

Any excitement he had felt about the turning of the millennium had long since drowned in a flood of prepackaged sentimentality and tawdry commercialism. The big date, just a month and a half away, appeared likely to bring neither a bang nor a whimper, just a long collective yawn.

For the millennial entertainment at Tweak he had gone with his first hunch and hired Lacey Tremaine, who was booked a second time this weekend. Rolando's glowing revue of her first week had been the only comment he'd received one way or another but he had run out of patience for trying to find someone better.

Walking down Bedford toward Grove Court, he passed the high brick walls and heavily grated windows of Public School 3, with the quote set in concrete: "Childhood shows the man." What did his childhood show him? For thirty years he had dreamed of making it in the Big City. Well, here he was. Had he made it? Or was he still dreaming?

o   o   o

He jiggled his key in the deadbolt until it turned and he let himself into the townhome. He called to Sylvia but got no reply. The place sounded hollow but the heat felt good after his chilly walk. A red light blinked twice on the answering machine.

He pushed the message button and listened to the whiny sound of the tape rewinding while he glanced at the *Sporting News*. The way the Yankees had not just swept but crushed the dreaded Atlanta Braves in the World Series had done little to assuage his disappointment about the ignominious end of the Mets' season. After all, the Yankees had appeared in nearly a third of the World Series. Big deal. The only other team he followed closely was the Denver Broncos, a relic of his formative years in Colorado. But, after triumphant back-to-back Super Bowl victories under John Elway, they had sunk into the cellar of the AFC West Division and Sunday night had to face a rejuvenated, first-place Seattle Seahawks team before a national audience.

The machine clicked. "This is the Daxor Corporation returning Sylvia Ellis's call," a woman's voice said. "Sorry we missed you. In response to your question, we will be open until six o'clock tonight." She left a call-back number.

Yet another indecipherable bit of Sylvia's business. The machine beeped and the second message began to play.

"Sylvia? … Sylvia? … Oh, I hoped I'd catch you before you left," a man's voice said on the answering machine but right then, the phone rang. Irritably hitting the stop button, Russ answered the phone.

After a momentary pause a woman's voice asked, "Could I speak to Russell Jones, please?"

Oh, goody, some sort of solicitation or survey. He fought off the impulse just to hang up and said wearily, "Speaking."

"My name is May Mendoza. John Kaufman gave me your number. I hope you don't mind my calling."

This brightened his mood. "Well, hi, May! No, I don't mind a bit. How are you doing?"

"I'm fine, thanks. In fact, thank you very much. That's mainly why I called, to thank you."

"You're welcome. For what?"

"For telling John about the job at Crestwood."

"Oh, that's right. Did you talk to Lucy Van Deutch?"

"Yes, and I got the job! I started three days ago," May said, the excitement plain in her voice. "Today's my day off and then I work over the weekend too."

"Fantastic!" he said. "How do you like it?"

"Everybody's been really friendly and I don't think I've messed up too bad yet. Lucy's been very understanding, so far at least. Anyway, what a beautiful place! John said that it used to be your home."

"My parents owned it when I was in high school. I only claimed the bedroom in the northwest corner upstairs. I haven't seen the place since they turned it into a restaurant. What's it like?"

"Oh, it's just wonderful! I think I like your old room the best. It's got the hardwood floors, of course, and they've decorated it with antique crocheted curtains and original watercolors."

"Boy, it sure wasn't that nice when I lived there. What are the chances I'll get to see all these improvements? Did you talk to them about New Year's Eve?"

"Uh, yeah, I did," May said. "I gather from what John told me that you held that Piñon Nuts Gathering thirty years ago in the dining room, right?"

"Gee, how strange to hear someone else talk about the Piñon Nuts after all these years," Russ said pensively. "And yes, we did eat in the dining room but we were in the living room when your mom took that picture."

"Well, the dining room isn't used for dining anymore but I think I can arrange things so you guys can get a table in your old bedroom, if that's okay."

"Great! Although I assume you'll be joining us as well."

"Lucy wants me to work through the dinner rush but said I could join you later. So you're really considering this? John made it sound like you'd have a hard time getting away that night."

"Things have changed on this end," Russ said, suddenly conscious of the echo in the quiet townhome. "I have no idea what'll be happening by New Year's. I left a message to that effect on John and Susan's machine a few days ago but he never called me back. Have you spoken to him?"

"He called me Sunday night," May said. "Did he tell you that I went up to visit him again?"

"No, he didn't tell me about that. But then I haven't spoken to him since he told me about your visit last month. What did you two do?"

May paused a long time before responding. "He did something very kind and caring for me and I got him in a lot of trouble."

"What happened?"

"He told you about the letter I found, didn't he?"

"The one Jason wrote your mom?"

"Yeah. Incidentally, John said I write just like Jason. He said that was enough to convince him that Jason was my father."

"He saw you write?" Russ asked. "Wait a minute. You don't hold a pen between your middle and ring fingers, do you?"

"Yes! How did you know?"

"I just remember Jason holding his that way."

"So you agree with John?"

"It sure would be a weird coincidence otherwise."

"Did John tell you about the letter?"

"A little," Russ told her. "He said you thought one part seemed to imply that your mom had tried to terminate her pregnancy. In fact, he said he could see how you reached that conclusion."

"Right," May said. "So I asked him if he could think of a reason why she would want to do that—you know, abort me. One thing he came up with that might have made her consider it was the effect the psychedelic drugs she did back then might have had on her genes. I hadn't done those myself so I wondered if maybe the drugs might have affected her judgment too. John decided to show me that, even though those drugs can make you feel pretty strange, they wouldn't make someone do something like that."

"Show you? How?"

"We did some mushrooms and went for a hike."

"You're kidding! How was it?"

"I had a great time! John did too, I guess. At least till the end."

Russ took the phone over to the couch and sat down. This sounded far more diverting than the *Sporting News*. "Tell me about the end."

"Okay," she said, "but before I forget, do you remember Tom Huston?"

The name sounded familiar but he couldn't place it. "Did he go to Cheyenne?"

"I don't know. John promised to tell me about him but he never did. That's when the trouble started."

"Trouble? What happened?"

"Well, John reserved a motel room for me so I wouldn't have to drive back to the Springs while I was tripping. One of the other rooms caught fire while we were on the hike. The motel people called his house so his wife went to see why John had rented a room. She got there just before we did and when she saw us together she assumed we were... uh..."

When she didn't finish, he asked, "Were you... uh...?"

"No!" May protested. "At least not... I mean, nothing that would... Anyway, we sure didn't do what she assumes we did."

"Assumes?" Russ asked in dread. "Still?"

"He said she just refuses to listen," May said. "She won't take his calls and she won't meet with him. I just feel awful."

"You make it sound like they've separated."

"Not exactly," May said. "He's decided that he really needs to do a lot of research for his article for the paper so he's staying in a motel in Loveland."

"That seems a bit ironic," Russ said. "Separated in Loveland. Are you going to visit him up there?"

"Not you too!" May cried. "We didn't do anything! It's not that way!"

"Sorry," he said. "You made it sound a bit ambiguous before."

"Okay," she said, sounding like she was trying to convince herself as much as him. "When we were on our hike—and, you know, tripping?—I started wondering about what Mom must have been going through when I was conceived. I asked him what sex was like when you're hallucinating and he kind of demonstrated for me that it can be distracting."

"And during this demonstration, your pants were..."

"My pants were on! His pants were on! We were up in the mountains. It snowed! We almost froze to death. Nothing happened. I mean, nothing happened that..." Again she didn't finish.

"'Methinks the lady doth protest too much'," he said.

"God, you're as bad as he is," she said, exasperated. "Always throwing in those quotes. What do you mean?"

"I mean, you sound like you have a guilty conscience."

"Well, I must admit he did..." She paused to consider how to put this. "I suppose you could say he got to second base."

"All right, John!" Russ kidded her.

"Actually, he really didn't get all the way to second base," she amended hastily. "I mean, I had pulled up my shirt and, well, my bra, but he barely touched me and then it started to snow. And we had to go right then. So..."

"So he got thrown out trying to steal second," Russ said.

"Well, sort of," May conceded, "And I can even see how someone might want to argue the call."

"In any case, you two aren't having an affair."

"An affair!? No, we're not having an affair! I mean, John's attractive and I like him a lot but I have no intention of—" She paused. "I mean, I don't want to mess up his life any more than I already have. For that matter, my own life is pretty screwed up right now and I would just as soon not make it any worse."

"John said you were having a rough go of it," Russ said. "Although he also said that your grandmother helped you with your housing situation."

It took her a moment to respond. "Yes, she did," she said finally, with a sniff.

Russ could tell she was upset. "Are you all right?"

"Not really," she admitted, sniffing more.

"What's wrong?"

"Nana's in the hospital," she sobbed.

"Oh, no! What's wrong?"

"She caught the flu a couple of weeks ago and she just couldn't seem to get over it. Her doctor said that sitting in a nice warm bath might make her feel better, might take away the chills. Well, when she was getting out of the tub night before last, she got dizzy and fell and broke her hip."

"That's awful!"

"I usually call her before I go to work and when she didn't answer yesterday I went to her condo to check on her. There she was, still lying in a heap on the bathroom floor, naked and shivering, too weak to talk. I called an ambulance and got her to the hospital. They had to operate on her hip. I went over after my shift last night and sat up by her bed most of the night. She just looks so tiny and frail!"

"Oh, what a shame!" Russ said, hearing her blow her nose. "Didn't your mom have a brother? Is he there in the Springs?"

"My uncle Peter lives in Florida now and he's called several times already," she said, fighting down the sobs. "But he's a dentist and he really can't afford to just cancel all his appointments and come up here for weeks at a time. She might be in the hospital the rest of the year."

"So you're stuck there by yourself," Russ said sympathetically. "At least, more or less. John said you had a daughter. That's some comfort, I suppose. Although it must make it hard to spend a lot of time at the hospital. Do you have someone to take her?"

"Oh, her father's taking her," May said and then broke down completely.

Russ felt helpless. What she needed was a hug but that doesn't work on the phone. He tried to offer what consolation he could. "At least he's helping out."

"You don't understand," she said soggily.

"Well, explain it to me. Maybe I can help."

"Oh, Mr. Jones—"

"How come John's John and I'm Mr. Jones?" he interrupted.

"Okay, Russ then," she said, pulling herself together somewhat. "I'm sorry to lay all this on you. I mean, you barely know me. And you already got me a great job and I'm very grateful. I don't want to force you to listen to my sob story."

"Hey, it might keep my mind off my own troubles. Go ahead. What don't I understand?"

"It's just that, I found out last week that Paco, my ex-husband, and Shirley, his—what is she? his girlfriend, I guess—are moving to Buena Vista."

"Oh," Russ said, letting this sink in. "And what about your little girl?"

"Well, I've had some legal problems lately so he has full custody of Libby. I feel so helpless but there's nothing I can do to stop him."

"I don't remember Colorado that well," he admitted. "How far is Buena Vista?"

"I don't know. Two hours maybe. Too far."

"When are they moving?"

"They already gave notice on their apartment. They have to be out by the end of the year but he may move sooner if he can find a job and a place to live there."

"That doesn't give you much time," he conceded.

"I just don't know what I'll do without my baby," she said bleakly. "I love her so much it hurts."

Better to have loved and lost, thought Russ gloomily. Aloud, he said, "It must be very hard."

"You just don't know," she said. "John said you don't have children yourself but that you're trying. All I can say is, I hope you never have to go through anything like this."

"It looks like I never will." He tried to keep the bitterness out of his voice.

She sniffed. "It sounds like you married a lot wiser than I did."

"Well, that's not exactly what I meant."

"What did you mean?"

"Oh, it's a long sad story."

"You let me cry on your shoulder or in your ear or whatever," she said. "I'd be happy to return the favor. It might get my mind off of my troubles."

It would feel good to talk about it but he didn't want to dump on her. "Well, just suffice it to say that I know Sylvia won't be running off with my child."

She sniffed again. "You don't sound very happy about it."

"Well, we've had a little problem with the pregnancy."

"She didn't miscarry, I hope."

"No, you have to be pregnant in order to miscarry."

"She can't get pregnant?"

"Not by me."

He could tell she didn't know quite what to say. At least he'd managed to get her to stop crying, which was some consolation.

"I'm so sorry," she said at last. "Are you sure? I mean, they have so many ways of fixing that now."

"No, I'm sure," Russ said. He had wanted to talk to somebody about this for a couple of hours now and May seemed like as good a confidant as any. "I went to the doctor last week and they ran some tests. It turns out I couldn't even get a hamster pregnant."

She laughed tentatively. "What does that mean? Why would you want to?"

"It's just one of the tests they run, called the HPA, the Hamster Penetration Assay. They remove eggs from hamsters and do something so that normal human sperm can penetrate them. They also did what's called a hemizonal assay where they slice actual human eggs in half and let my guys try to get into one half and known fertile sperm try to get into the other. In both tests, my guys just stood around gawking while everybody else had all the fun."

"Well, that's too bad," she said. "But isn't there a way of like injecting the sperm into the egg?"

"Yes, there is and we considered that. But they looked at my little dudes with an electron microscope and discovered that they have no mitochondria."

"I don't know what that means."

"Join the club. I guess mitochondria are like batteries that supply energy for cells. Without them, the sperm can't swim."

"Is it like a genetic problem?"

"Not exactly. In fact, from what I gather, they're not sure what causes it."

"How's your wife taking the news?"

"I haven't had a chance to tell Sylvia yet."

"How do you think she'll react?"

"It's hard to tell. Frankly, in the last few weeks things have changed between us. You know, she's quite a bit younger than I am. In fact, she's not much older than you are. When we got married, she made a point of asking me if I wanted to have kids, you know, maybe not right away, but eventually. She comes from a big Italian family from the Bronx, Catholic of course, and all her siblings have produced grandchildren. Sylvia's the oldest so she gets a lot of flack from everybody about it. I think, as far as she's concerned, the whole point to our getting married was to have kids. Otherwise, she would have been content with the infamous 'long-term relationship.' Well, 'eventually' is now. She can hear her biological clock ticking and it turns out mine has a busted mainspring."

"But she wouldn't use your problem as a reason to end your marriage, would she?"

"It feels like it," he admitted, getting up from the couch to walk around while he talked. "At least, it feels like she's losing interest."

"There must be other alternatives. What about adopting? Or maybe—well, I suppose this is none of my business."

"She wants to have her own baby," Russ said. "She's made that very clear. And were you going to suggest artificial insemination?"

"I'm sorry. If this is too personal…"

"No, that's okay. We talked about that too. And I think she gave it some serious consideration. But she finally said, quite firmly, that she wants to have her husband's baby."

"Well, I guess I can't blame her."

"Nor can I. But if she's thinking of moving on, of finding someone who can give her children, I would hope she'd have the courage to tell me to my face. But to tell you the truth, this feels a little bit like the other shoe dropping. I couldn't quite believe I persuaded her to marry me in the first place. I mean, she has a successful career as an artist, she used to model, she's pretty well known in the local art scene. Meanwhile, I can't draw anything but beer and criticism. I guess I've always felt like she was a little out of my league."

"Come on," May said. "Aren't you being a little hard on yourself?"

"You know, I'm no spring chicken anymore. I've been in and out of a number of relationships, each of which seemed like the real deal while I was in it, each of which seemed destined to fail once I got out. Some people refer to it as serial monogamy. It's not like I haven't been down this road before."

"Well, it seems to me," she said, leaping to his defense, "that if she's so shallow that she's willing to throw away everything just because of something like this, maybe it is destined to fail. You can do better."

He had wandered into the studio. The pensive image of Sylvia in Guy Ellis's watercolor, her thick black hair, her deep dark eyes, her sensual body, caught his eye. "You know something?" he asked introspectively. "I don't think I can do better. I could find someone else, maybe even someone more appropriate to my circumstances. You know, someone closer to my age, maybe someone who already has children. But someone better? I don't think so."

"But isn't she being a bit unreasonable?" May asked. "I mean, your problem isn't even your fault, is it?"

"From what the doctor said, it's not even a recent problem. I've probably been driving the Little Engine Who Couldn't my whole life. Boy, when I think back on all the times I worried about birth control, sweated out somebody's late period…"

"See? You're understandably bummed out about this. Maybe you're projecting your pessimism onto her."

"Oh, no, she's definitely changed. I recognize the signs. You must know what I'm talking about. What happened when you broke up with Paco?"

"He came home drunk one night and beat me up. Broke my nose and put me in the hospital. Then he moved in with Shirley."

Russ hadn't seen that coming. "Wow. I'm really sorry. I had no idea. So maybe you don't know what I'm talking about."

"So explain it."

"Oh, she's just gotten really quiet, walks around preoccupied all the time. If I ask her what's wrong, she says she doesn't want to talk about it. She stays out late with friends she hung out with when she was single, doesn't tell me where she's been, comes home at all hours."

"Is she there with you now?" May asked confidentially. "I didn't even think to ask earlier."

"No, she had some kind of an affair with her art buddies."

"That's a good way to put it. Paco used to be vague like that, just tell me he was going out. Then he'd end up spending the night with some cocktail waitress."

"I didn't mean 'affair' in that sense," Russ said. "I think Sylvia's probably more subtle than that. I mean, I can't quite picture her bra hanging over the bar at the Hog and Heifer."

"What's the Hog and Heifer?"

"Oh, just a funky, semi-biker tavern in the meat packing district, which is where a bunch of the galleries moved when SoHo got too expensive and passé, including some of the ones Sylvia deals with. The bar's claim to fame is that women get so drunk there that they take off their bras and donate them. They must have two or three hundred bras hanging over the bar, one of them supposedly coming from Julia Roberts. But that really isn't Syl's style. For one thing, she rarely wears a bra."

"See?" May asked. "You've probably got nothing to worry about."

"Oh, I didn't say that. A lot of the art buddies I mentioned before are men Sylvia met through her first husband."

"So she was married before. She's not out with her ex-husband, is she?"

"Oh, no. He was killed ten years ago."

"Ooo, that must have been rough."

"Yeah. She took it very hard. In a way, I don't blame her. He was a pretty amazing guy, from what little I know about him."

"Amazing how?"

"He was an incredible artist. In fact, maybe you've heard of him. Guy Ellis?"

"No," May said. "But I don't follow that sort of thing much."

"Well, he had quite a reputation here in New York and, to a lesser extent, in Europe as well. Some of his paintings hang in museums."

"I see what you mean. He sounds like a pretty tough act to follow."

Russ thought about it. "Did you see any of President Clinton's impeachment trial last February?"

"No, I was in jail at the time."

"Boy, you have had a rough year," he said.

"There have been a few bright spots lately. You and John, to name a couple. Anyway, what did I miss?"

"Well, the highlight, if there was one, of the whole boondoggle was former Arkansas Senator Dale Bumpers' impassioned defense of what Walt Kelly used to refer to as 'the presidency.' Bumpers told the story of a country preacher extolling the virtues of the Son of God at a revival meeting. Again and again he challenges the congregation there in the tent to testify if they know anyone that approaches Christ's level of perfection. Finally a meek little man in the back of the tent stands up and clears his throat and says, 'Reverend, I know someone like that: my wife's first husband.' That's how I feel every time Sylvia mentions Guy Ellis. From what little I've heard about his personal life, though, he was hardly a saint."

"In any case," May offered encouragingly, "Sylvia can't be out with him tonight."

"That's true," Russ said, watching the red light blinking on his answering machine. "But as you called, I was listening to a message some man left her."

"I should let you go," May said hastily. "Once again, though, I can't tell you how grateful I am to you for the tip about my job. I feel like you and John both have been so nice to me and meanwhile your lives are starting to look as messed up as mine. I hope I haven't brought my bad luck to you."

"Well, my problems don't seem to have anything to do with you. And from what I've heard from John over the years, he and Susan have been a little shaky for a long time. Anyway, ironically, the problems John and I are having might make it easier for us to get together on New Year's Eve. It sounds like there's not much point in staying home with the wives."

"I suppose that's true, although I would gladly skip this reunion entirely if it meant that you two would be able to iron things out with them. I almost hate to ask about Matt. Have you talked to him? Is he a victim of the May Mendoza Curse yet?"

"Actually, I've been so caught up in things around here that I haven't had a chance to call him again. I'll give him a jingle in a few days. But for what it's worth, he and Deb are as happy a couple as you'll ever find so he's bound to be better off than we are."

"I sure hope so."

"Thanks a heap."

"That didn't come out the way I meant, did it? Anyway, you know what I mean. I hope things brighten up for both you and John and if you think it would mean anything to him, say hello to Matt for me."

"I'm sure it will mean a lot. Thanks so much for the call, May."

"Oh, just in case you do make it here, how many will there be? Just you, John, and Matt? Or will Tom Huston be coming too?"

"I don't even remember Tom. But you better put us down for four, just in case. I'll ask Matt about Tom."

"Anyway, I'm sure we'll put on a glorious meal for you guys."

"I'm sure you will. Oh, and give my best to your grandmother and wish her a speedy recovery. Talk to you soon."

"Bye, Russ."

o o o

Okay, so who's this guy calling Sylvia? The image of Paul, his elegant features, that happy-go-lucky smile on his face, loomed large in Russ's mind as he hit the button on the answering machine to play the rest of the message.

The sound of the handset rattling from its cradle was followed by Sylvia's breathless voice saying, "Hello?"

"Oh, Sylvia," the man said, "It's me again. I'm glad I caught you."

"Sorry, I was in the other room getting my coat."

"Right as I was hanging up, I remembered that I have an appointment at 5:15. Is there any chance we could do this at 5:45 instead?"

"Sure," Sylvia said. "No problem. Actually, maybe I'll stop at Macy's first anyway. It occurred to me that it would be nice to dress it up a little and it certainly wouldn't hurt to be discreet. I don't know. I've never done anything like this."

"I must admit," the man said, "I haven't either."

"It just doesn't make sense to hang on to it any longer. The main thing, I suppose," Sylvia said nervously, "is to prevent…um, well, leakage, you know?"

"Not to worry," the man said, chuckling. "I'll see that that doesn't happen."

"Cause I've got to come back down here to the Village on the subway," she said, adding, "although I don't suppose it would be the first time such a thing leaked on the subway." She cracked up thinking about it. "In fact, I'm wearing a blue dress."

The man laughed too. "But I assume that, unlike Monica, you wouldn't keep the stain as a souvenir."

Sylvia sighed. "No, I guess I'm past that now."

"You know where you're going, right?"

"Gee, it's been years since I've been up there. What's the number again?"

"7120."

"That's right. Well, I'll see you at quarter to six then."

"Looking forward to it."

The mechanical voice of the answering machine said, "4:02 p.m."

Russ stared at the machine in disbelief. Obviously, Sylvia had forgotten that the machine would keep recording even after she picked up the phone. But this was outrageous. While Russ was busting his hump trying to keep Tweak afloat, Sylvia's yakking with her lover on the phone about their rendezvous! And not even talking in the intimate terms of new lovers but making crude frat-house jokes like all this was old hat!

Up to now, he had been willing to give her the benefit of the doubt. He could understand, perhaps even empathize with her, if she had begun to get discouraged with their childless marriage. But to flaunt her infidelity like this, to go so far as to trivialize her adulterous affair with bawdy little innuendoes—it made him so angry, it knotted his stomach.

But what to do? His father's words—"sometimes you have trouble standing up for what's yours"—still rang in his ears. He'd be damned if he'd stand idly by while Paul, or whoever this guy was, cheerfully, blatantly, cuckolded him.

He glanced at his watch. Ten after five. If he grabbed a cab right now…

He bolted to the closet for a coat, something heavier than that light jacket. For that matter, if he hoped to observe without being observed, he ought to wear something he didn't wear much. He grabbed a tan London Fog trench coat Ellen had given him when he first moved back east, something he never would have worn in Oregon and rarely wore here. And since there was no telling where this would lead or how long he might have to wait, he brought the *Sporting News* along as well, stuffing it into the pocket of the trench coat.

He jammed his hat on his head, dashed out the door, flew down the stairs, jogged the half block to Hudson, and hailed a cab. "Macy's," he told the driver. "And there's twenty bucks in it for you if you can get me there in twenty minutes."

The cab driver used his horn like a rapier, slicing boldly through the sluggish, clotted rush-hour traffic. As they headed up to West 14th, Russ stared out the window at the gray people rushing along the gray sidewalks, thinking their gray thoughts in the gray twilight.

What struck Russ was not how wrong he'd been about Sylvia but how wrong he'd been to get involved with her. After all, the main thing he'd known about her when they got involved was how much he didn't know about her. He knew she had this mysterious, tragic marriage to Guy Ellis and a long history of involvement with the odd (at best) art community of Greenwich Village but she hadn't wanted to talk about all of that in the wake of Ellis's death. He had been willing to let by-gones be by-gones but now it appeared some of those by-gones hadn't yet gone by.

It's not like people didn't warn him. Ellen, at least until she too fell prey to Sylvia's charm, had urged him to be cautious about getting involved with a "bohemian." Even some of Sylvia's friends, who had encouraged him to offer Sylvia the kind of affection and tenderness that would help her get over Ellis, looked away when he started talking to them about getting involved with her. Russ hadn't been willing to buy into the Perils of the Big City routine at the time, figuring it would do him good to toughen up, to let the City chew him up a little.

Now, as the cab headed up Sixth Avenue, Russ began to loath the gnashing of the City's teeth. The goal, after all, had been to get chewed up a little and spit back out, not chewed up and swallowed, like so many other preterite souls seemed to have been. He tried to focus on the blurred citizens jostling along the crowded walks: slick businessmen weighed down by briefcases, homeless women with junk-piled grocery carts, punked-out boys with nowhere to go, shop girls afraid to meet anyone's eye, elderly natives wondering where their city went, bewildered children tethered like pets to busy parents. How much a part of this city did he want to be? Where did he fit?

But as the cab got closer to Macy's, Russ's thoughts turned more practical. The three-and-seven Broncos had a better chance of making it back to the Super Bowl than Russ had of finding Sylvia in Macy's. But the one section of the store she almost never missed was the perfume counters and, on her way to this *tete-a-tete*, it seemed likely she'd stop there again. So Russ told the driver to drop him near the Broadway entrance to the store, tipping him the $20 anyway, even though it had taken 25 minutes to get there.

He leaned against one of the display windows filled with harvest themes and turned up the collar of his trench coat to ward off the wind that swirled wildly down here at the bottom of the canyon of buildings. He took out the *Sporting News* and opened it, not really interested in reading, just to give himself some cover if and when Sylvia came out. It suddenly occurred to him how absurd this whole thing seemed. He had become Mickey Spillane, the tough gumshoe trailing a sleazy broad who's gotten herself mixed up with the Mob. But it made no sense to back down now. He felt like the pretty nurse who's selling poppies from a tray in "Penny Lane": "And though she feels as if she's in a play, she is anyway."

He didn't have long to wait. After standing there just a couple of minutes, sure enough Sylvia walked out, clutching a plastic bag, her long black hair tied in a colorful silk scarf—one he had given her for their anniversary—her long black pea jacket pulled tightly around her. At this hour, 34th and Broadway was a swirling maelstrom of humanity so the problem wouldn't be her catching sight of him so much as his losing sight of her. He waited until the lights on Broadway changed, then quickly hustled along with the crowd across the street, the bright scarf acting as a beacon. The shoulder-to-shoulder press of pedestrians almost pushed him right into her as she stopped short to cross 34th as well. He walked past her, so close to her that he could smell her Magie Noir, then stopped and turned and watched until the light changed, hustling behind the surge to keep up.

She turned up 34th, oblivious to all around her, concentrating, no doubt, on her imminent romantic interlude. The small voice in Russ's head that kept crying, How can she do this to me? quickly faded beneath the more rational voice saying, Why has it taken this long? Look at her. She's young, beautiful, talented, successful, living in the greatest city on earth, as were countless young, handsome, talented, successful men. But just because Russ could understand it didn't make it right.

The question was, where did they plan to meet? He had barely asked the question before the answer loomed right in front of him: the Empire State Building. Where else? He couldn't believe how obvious it was, how trite. She would play Meg Ryan to his Tom Hanks in *Sleepless In Seattle*, rushing headlong to the Observation Deck and their fated meeting, their impassioned embrace, except that Sylvia and Paul, or whoever, wouldn't have the bother of a little kid tagging along. Russ found the saccharine tackiness of the whole thing revolting.

She went into the 34th Street entrance, Russ having to hustle to make sure he didn't lose sight of her. He smiled and shook his head as he watched her walk to the elevators. It must have been a long time since she'd been there: she'd evidently forgotten that the Observation Deck had a separate elevator system. Smirking slightly, he took out the *Sporting News* again and took up a position on the other side of the elevators where he could watch for her to come back out on her way to the Observation Deck elevators.

But after a couple of minutes it became clear she wouldn't come back out after all. Panic gripped him. Had she spotted him and just used this elevator ruse to throw him off the track? That seemed too much like something out of a James Bond movie. Maybe she was meeting this guy somewhere else. Maybe they had some secret place on the upper floors where they held these trysts. But most of the building is just office space.

Maybe the guy worked here, had an office here. Russ racked his brain for clues. On the recording on the answering machine, she had asked for his number. If Russ could remember the number, he could call the place, ask where they were located. But the guy had given just a four-digit extension. What was it? Seventy-one something. But maybe that wasn't a phone extension. Here at the Empire State Building, it could be a suite number.

He put the newspaper back in his pocket and went to the elevator banks, pushing the button for the bank that went to the 71st floor. When the doors opened, he and several other people got in, pushing various buttons. Russ felt flushed now that he was out of the frigid wind but he couldn't very well take off the trench coat. He needed to have his hands free. For what? he asked himself as the express elevator's sudden lurch upward distorted his sight and further turned his stomach. What was he going to do? Punch this sleezeball's lights out? Grab his woman and drag her home? Well, if nothing else, he'd need his hands just to gesticulate as he read her the riot act. Whatever. He hadn't gotten that far yet.

Thankfully, no one else got off on the 71st floor and the hallway was empty, giving Russ a chance to get his bearings without feeling too foolish. The floor directory didn't list anything likely to serve as a meeting place. He walked to both ends of the hall, looked down the short corridors to the doors to the various offices. One place looked as good as another. He went back to the directory to see if he'd missed something.

Ah, there's something. Daxor Corporation. Wasn't that the name given on the first message on the machine? That couldn't be a coincidence. Suite 7120. That was the number. Russ congratulated himself on his sleuthing abilities as he walked to 7120, the Daxor Corporation.

The woman at the front desk asked if she could help him but he had already spotted Sylvia's scarf in a waiting room behind the desk. "Thanks," he told the receptionist. "I'm just here to have a few words with my wife." He walked into the waiting room, loaded for bear.

The room was on the south side of the building, overlooking the southern tip of Manhattan. Sylvia, still wearing her coat, sat reading a magazine. Russ didn't say anything, just stood and waited for her to look up.

When she finally did, the look of guilty surprise when she recognized him spoke volumes. "Well, hi, honey!" she said, bewildered. "How on earth did you find me here?"

"I guess you're just not as subtle as you think," he said contemptuously.

"What are you talking about?"

"Smart move, wearing the coat," he sneered. "It makes it easier to hide a stain on that pretty blue dress of yours."

"Stain?" she said, looking puzzled. Then the light dawned. "The answering machine!"

"The answering machine," he confirmed.

"Oh, you heard that conversation, didn't you?"

"Indeed I did."

Her features crinkled up and for a moment he thought she was going to cry but then she reluctantly burst out laughing instead.

"You find this amusing?" he asked her icily.

"So you thought…?" but she laughed again.

Just then a man in a white lab coat came into the waiting room. "Sylvia?" he said. "It's good to see you again."

Still chuckling, she stood and shook his hand. "It's good to see you too, Mark," she said. "And Mark, this is my husband, Russell Jones. Russ, Mark Simmons. He works here."

Russ shook Mark's hand firmly, sizing up the fellow. He was a couple of inches taller than Russ, with short curly sandy hair, watery blue eyes, a bad complexion, and tufts of untrimmed nostril hair puffing from his bulbous nose. This was certainly no Paul.

"It's nice to meet you," Russ said genuinely, reassured to find his competition so mediocre. He turned to Sylvia. "Have you lost your mind?" he asked her, baffled by her choice of paramours.

She chuckled yet again, which began to irritate him. "Mark is a lab technician for Idant Laboratories, which is part of the Daxor Corporation."

"So?" Russ asked impatiently.

Mark cleared his throat. "Would you like to talk to your husband alone?"

"Why don't you just stay right where you are, buster," Russ said to him. "What's going on here, Sylvia?"

"Russ, it's a long story. I think you should let me explain."

"You can start by explaining what the hell you're doing here."

She bristled at his tone. "As I said, it's a long story. But you need to calm down. You're making a fool of yourself."

"It's better than letting you make a fool of me," he said, which didn't quite make sense but he was on a roll and couldn't stop himself. "Just tell me what you're doing here."

"All right," she said, suddenly serious. "Idant Laboratories is a semen bank."

Russ's gaze shifted from Sylvia to Mark and back to Sylvia and then, dumbfounded, he turned away. He walked to the window and looked out over the nightscape. Even as upset as he was, and behind a thick sheet of plate glass, he still felt queasy being up this high. Far below, the buildings of midtown seemed minuscule, insignificant. To the south, the cubist forms rose and consolidated until the skyline of downtown and the financial district rose up to blot away the horizon. In the gray twilight the city struck him, as it always did, as a crystal set, a fantasy of light and shadow, the dark concrete and steel insubstantial, the luminous glass awake and alive. The distant waterways and sparkling bridges brought home the realization that this island city is unique, separate, self-contained. His father had always said of New York that everywhere else was just Bridgeport. From this window Russ could see all of lower Manhattan, the center, the nexus, the heart.

And a perfidious heart it was. Russ's love of Sylvia and his love of New York were inextricably intertwined. In winning her, he felt he had won the city. Now he realized what folly that was. He had won nothing.

In a way, he felt disappointed that she wasn't having an affair with this Mark character. That, odious as it would be, at least would represent a tried-and-true, genuine human impulse. The infidelity and deception of that sort of adultery sprang from passion. This calculated, cold-blooded attempt of hers to fob off some store-bought bastard as his own child seemed far more insidious. No wonder she had laughed at him. She had no intention of sullying herself with some stranger. Why should she, if she could dispassionately bear him a mechanical child, Russ none the wiser?

He turned back to her. "You thought you could get away with this? You figured I'd never find out?" He turned to Mark. "What kind of an operation are you running here? Don't you require some sort of consent forms from the husband?"

Mark looked at Sylvia, baffled.

Sylvia, in turn, looked at Russ, trying to fathom what he meant. Then, once again, the light dawned. "Oh, you thought I was going to… Oh, what a mess! Honey, you've jumped from one wrong conclusion to another. It's not what you're thinking at all. Oh God."

Mark looked at his watch.

"Mark, I'm so sorry," she said when she noticed it, looking at her own. "You close at six, don't you?"

"I can't stay here without keeping a bunch of other people here too," Mark said. "Sorry."

Sylvia looked down, trying to figure out what to do. "Listen," she said to Mark at last, "I guess this just isn't going to work today. I have no idea what I'll tell the others. We'll just have to do it another time, that's all. I'm so sorry to have put you to all this trouble."

"No trouble at all," Mark said. "Just give us a call when you get things straightened out. It was nice seeing you again. Nice meeting you, Russell," he added, giving Russ a wide berth on the way out.

"The others?" Russ asked Sylvia after Mark had gone.

"Oh, you must be so confused," she said to him. "And I'm so sorry. But I'm afraid there's just no short answer to this."

"So give me the long answer."

"Well, we can't do it here. They're closing."

"Then we'll go somewhere else."

o   o   o

They left the building through the main lobby and Russ hailed a cab. He held the door for Sylvia and got in behind her. When the driver asked him where to, Russ said, "The Village."

As the cab slowly weaved its way through the snarl of traffic on Fifth Avenue, Russ and Sylvia silently looked out opposite windows. When they stopped for the light on Broadway, Sylvia broke the silence: "I can't believe you followed me there."

"I can't believe you went there," Russ said, not looking at her. "In fact, I'm not sure I can believe you at all."

"At least give me a chance to explain."

"I've got nothing else to do tonight. You can explain till you're blue in the face when we get home."

She thought about that awhile. "Maybe we should go somewhere else to talk about this."

"How come?" he asked snidely, turning to her. "Expecting more messages?"

He saw her repress her anger. "Please?" was all she said.

"Okay, let's stop someplace and have a drink. Where are we? Union Square? What the hell is around Union Square?"

"How about Pete's Tavern?" the cabby suggested, knowing the places people usually wanted to see.

"What the hell," Russ said. "Pete's it is."

O   O   O

More a landmark than a tourist destination, Pete's Tavern, operating since 1864, claimed to be the oldest continuously operating bar in the city, surviving Prohibition by having the patrons enter through a cooler in the flower shop next door. It still retained much of the original decor, including the big square tin ceiling panels, painted burnt umber, the paint chunking off in spots. The tile floor, chipped and cracked, certainly looked authentic, as did the big rosewood bar.

The place was crowded, mostly with middle-aged locals glad to be done with the day. As luck would have it, the second booth from the door opened up just as Russ and Sylvia walked in so they quickly sat down.

"Well?" Russ said impatiently.

"Aren't we going to get a drink?" Sylvia asked, looking again at her watch. "This is going to take a little while."

Russ looked over at the bartender, a mild-looking, middle-aged man with short gray hair and a bland smile. He was leaning on the corner of the bar closest to the door, talking to a chunky, out-going brunette with a big smile. In response to something she was saying, the bartender looked first at Russ and then at the booth by the door. Russ raised his finger to him and he walked out from behind the bar.

"What would you like?" Russ asked Sylvia.

"Oh, let's see," she said. "How about a white wine and a smile?"

"The bartender will have to furnish both of those."

"Believe it or not," Sylvia said defensively, "what I planned to do at Daxor was intended to make things better between us."

"I'll bet."

The bartender passed them by, saying to the older gentleman in the first booth, "Mr. Porter, Rhona would like to buy you a drink. The usual?"

When the man assented, the bartender turned to Russ. "What can I get you?"

"The lady—my wife, that is—will have a white wine and I'll have..." He almost said a Manhattan but somehow that had lost its appeal. "I'll have a bourbon...Old Granddad... make it a double, on the rocks."

"Don't you usually take it with soda?" Sylvia asked him as the bartender walked away.

"Somehow on-the-rocks seemed more appropriate tonight."

"You're blowing this all out of proportion."

"Well, I'm sure you, as an artist, know more about proportion than I do. Why don't you explain it to me?"

She sighed and chewed on her thumbnail. "God, where should I start?"

"How about the beginning?"

"This is mostly about Ell."

That came as no surprise. Everything in her life seemed to relate to him in one way or another. "Fine," Russ said. "You never have told me the whole story about the famous Guy Ellis. Now's as good a time as any, I suppose. How did you meet him, anyway? It was at some sort of party, wasn't it?"

"Remember the art class I took at NYU?"

"Oh, yeah, yeah. That's where you met what's-her-name."

"Nada, right. Well, she got invited to this party in the East Village, one of those 'events' like Andy Warhol used to throw, with lots of artists and celebrities."

"This was right after high school, right? How old were you?"

"I was 18 and Nada was 20. But we couldn't pass up the chance to meet some real artists."

"And the incomparable Guy Ellis was there in all his glory."

"Well, he was there. When I first saw him, I assumed he was a drunk gate-crasher or something. He had on this ratty old camouflage gear and was crawling into the bathroom on his hand and knees to puke. After he finished, the woman he was with led tours of small groups into the bathroom to view the body. He had passed out on the floor, curled up around the toilet. His scruffy beard was soaked with his vomit and his fly was open."

"Obviously you took the tour," Russ concluded as the bartender brought their drinks.

"Someone had shown me some of the paintings Ell brought to the party and they were incredible. I wanted to try to make sense of how a scuzball like that could paint so magnificently."

"What did you find out?"

"That he was pretty quick with that left arm. I was appalled that even the woman he came with wouldn't help him at all so I took a wet washcloth and wiped the vomit from his beard. I thought he had passed out so I knelt down by him and the next thing I knew that left hand of his was rubbing my crotch."

"He lost his right arm in Vietnam, right?" Russ asked, figuring he would never get a better chance to ask these questions. "Did he ever tell you how he lost it?"

"It happened in 1964. He was one of those advisors that Kennedy sent to instruct the South Vietnamese army. He was leading a squadron through some rice paddy, showing them how to check for land mines. Evidently, he missed one. He was on his belly and tripped it with his right elbow. It blew his arm completely off and tore through his ribcage. He told me that, as he lay there with the blood spurting out of what was left of his arm and listening to his breath bubbling out of his side, he assumed he would die at any moment. But, to his amazement, the next thing he knew, a couple of the men in the squadron had crawled out along the path he'd made and grabbed his ankles and dragged him back."

"Good God."

"He eventually came to that same conclusion. But as he recovered in the V.A. hospital he thought his life was over. He wished they had left him in the paddy. He hated people referring to him as a disabled veteran. He also hated what he'd seen in Vietnam: the way the French, and the Catholics, had disrupted the traditional Vietnamese culture, the way Ho Chih Minh was deceiving the people into thinking a communist take-over would mean freedom, the way the Americans just assumed that what they were doing was right. So he spent the next 20 years, he told me once, basically trying to finish the job the land mine started."

"Was he an artist when he went to Vietnam?"

"Oh, he said he used to doodle all the time in school but he never took it seriously. In fact, he was planning to make a career in the Army. But he told me that losing his right arm —he was right-handed—completely changed his life. He discovered elements of his personality he never knew existed. Part of his therapy in the hospital included painting to try to reorient his brain to being left-handed. He said he just used to make a bunch of angry scribbles with the brightest, most virulent colors he could find but he discovered that the other vets responded well to them. When he got out of the hospital, his disability checks paid for most of his living expenses and he found he could sell his 'scribbles' for enough to keep himself drunk or stoned or something most of the time, like at the party."

"So when you two met, it was love at first snatch."

"Don't be crude. Actually, I thought he was revolting. But I was also blown away by his ability as an artist. And at that point I was still young and naive enough to think that only great suffering could create a great artist."

"And now you know better?"

"Now I know that great suffering either makes a person great or it destroys him, or her. What creates a great artist is great effort. And it required an incredible effort for Ell to become an artist. His suffering—he said his right hand felt like it was forever being crushed in a vice—and his efforts to alleviate his suffering, which amounted to trying to keep himself numb all the time, only got in the way of his art. But when he stayed sober long enough to paint—well, you've seen his work."

"He was a master," Russ admitted grudgingly.

"The art class at NYU taught me the technique of an artist," Sylvia said. "I wanted to study the soul of an artist. So I asked the woman Ell had brought to the party if he ever gave lessons. She looked me up and down and said, 'Oh, I'm sure he'll take you on,' and she gave me his number. When I finally worked up the nerve to call him, he was drinking a lot more than he was selling so he took me on—as a student," she added when she saw Russ roll his eyes.

"Uh-huh."

"At that time he had a whole menagerie of models that he painted and hung out with and sometimes slept with."

"A menagerie?"

She sipped her wine, looking at the golden liquid in the glass, smiling. "He had attracted quite an odd assortment of people. I wanted no part of that. For that matter, I was still engaged."

"Oh, right. To Frank, the high school sweetheart."

"Not that I wasn't attracted to Ell," she admitted. "He wasn't bad looking, though he had let himself go. And he had a way of looking into your soul that I found…well, daunting, but exciting too."

"You must have appealed to him as well," Russ pointed out. "Michelle once told me that the people who knew Ellis usually credited you with helping him turn his life around."

She shook her head. "That wasn't exactly my intention. I took the subway to the Village once a week for those lessons and he usually got too drunk to hold the brush. He'd just shout at me that I was doing it all wrong. 'You don't paint with your hands, damn it!' he'd scream. 'You paint with your eyes!' Well, one day I showed up and he had smoked so much opium that he couldn't even move. I got so pissed, I decided just to blow the whole thing off. So I sketched him just the way he was: his long ratty hair and beard, his beer belly sagging in his dirty undershirt, the drool on his chin, the dead look in his half-closed eyes. Oh, I was merciless. I still have the sketch; I'll show it to you sometime if you like. Anyway, I put it on the table and left, figuring it would make him so angry he'd never want to see me again. But he called me up a couple of days later to thank me. He said that none of the other people who used to hang around with him—he told me once they put the "sick" into sycophant—ever had the courage to point out how badly he was fucking up. He insisted that I keep coming for lessons and that he would clean up his act."

"All based on that one sketch?"

"Well, I can't take all the credit. This was in the mid-80s and AIDS was spreading like wildfire through the Village. He had gotten hepatitis from a needle a few years before and the writing was on the wall. But he was true to his word: he cleaned up his act."

"He gave up his 'menagerie'?"

"He quit sleeping with them. He still used them as models."

Russ took a pull from his bourbon. "Were some of them men?"

"You've wanted to ask me that a long time, haven't you?"

"People ask *me* that."

"Well, I honestly don't know the answer. I assume he tried most everything and in the Village he couldn't very well avoid gay temptations. But remember, I came onto the scene late. As far as that goes, I helped put an end to it. I guess for a long time some people used to refer to me behind my back as Yoko."

"Ouch."

"But the change did him a world of good. He began to funnel the energy he used to put into self-destruction into his art instead, and into my lessons too. He started using me as a model, having me pose, drawing or painting me, then explaining to me how he had done what he did."

"So you took over for his whole menagerie?"

Sylvia took his hand and looked earnestly into his eyes. "I know you're jealous—I think maybe you've always been jealous of Ell and it's understandable—and I know at this point my credibility seems shot but it's important that you believe what I'm about to tell you. Ell didn't just quit sleeping with the others. He quit sleeping with *anyone*."

"He became celibate?" Russ asked doubtfully.

"I didn't say that. He found a way, as most men do, of relieving the tension. He used to refer to it as 'working on his masturpiece,' with a 'ur'."

"UR indeed," Russ said.

"What?"

"I mean, you are the one who inspired this?"

"Well, I had a hand in the change he went through. But any inspiration he found came from within himself. After he had quit having sex with others for a while, he told me he realized that his promiscuity stemmed in part from the loss of his right arm. He said that he had always used his right hand to masturbate and when he tried using his left after he lost the right, it felt like a stranger. At first he found it so disconcerting that he preferred to be with actual strangers. In a way, he tried to run away from himself. But when he decided to end the promiscuity, he discovered he liked the way his left hand felt like a stranger. He could seduce himself. He said he felt like the two halves of his brain communicated in a way they had never done before."

Russ looked at his own left hand.

She saw him do it and said, "You're right-handed. Do you ever use your left hand?"

"For that? No, I guess I don't. That would be odd. But on the other hand…"

"Exactly. Anyway, Ell discovered something else. Before too long he got really horny, as you might expect. He thought it would become so distracting that he wouldn't be able to work. But after a while the constant state of arousal added a sensuality to his work that he, and others, found quite appealing. He made up his mind that he would no longer get physically involved with his models, that he needed to maintain the distinction between artist and subject."

"But weren't you one of his models?"

"That's what I'm telling you. He and I didn't have sex."

Russ drained the bourbon and motioned to the bartender for another. "But you did get married."

"Well, that just sort of snuck up on us. When he cleaned up his act, he started cranking out some amazing paintings and drawings. I would show up for my lesson and he had finished half a dozen beautiful pictures. But he put all his energy into creativity and the finished paintings just collected dust in the studio. It seemed like a shame to me for all his work to go to waste so I started bugging him to get out and sell some of them. I finally ended up dragging him to the galleries that occasionally showed his stuff and making him show them the new material. He sold some more things but he hated it. He came up with a thousand excuses not to do it. Finally I got so exasperated with him that I told him I would just take the paintings around whether he went with me or not. By default, I became his representative."

"Weren't some of these paintings of you?"

Her head fell back and she closed her eyes. "God, he made me look so beautiful!" She looked at Russ again. "Well, you've seen those sketches."

He had indeed. As fantastic as Sylvia looked sitting across from him in the booth, the sketches Ellis had done showed her young and lithe, languid and nude, drawn with a passion that beggared description, that went beyond mere sensuality, that approached reverence. Despite his jealousy, Russ thought of Ellis with admiration and gratitude for capturing those images.

"So he did full paintings like that?" he asked her. "And you went around selling them?"

"I didn't sell those. It made me too self-conscious. But yes, he did some gorgeous oils of me."

"Who has them?"

"He sold them to various people. He considered them too erotic for most art shows."

Russ cringed, as he always did, when he thought about nude portraits of his wife hanging over mantelpieces around the city. "But let me get this straight. He did those beautiful nudes of you and yet you two didn't have sex."

"He did those *because* we didn't have sex. I used to tease him and taunt him and it drove him crazy but he put all his energy into painting. It drove me crazy too—that's when I broke up with Frank—so I devoted myself to selling his stuff. He let me keep half, which also motivated me, because by then I could sell a piece for thousands of dollars."

"What about his other models? Did he just drop them?"

"Oh, no, not at all. He kept using them as models. But when he quit making love to them, they just drifted into other relationships. Some of them had been married all along. I was the only one unattached so I could put all my time and energy into representing him. Pretty soon I was doing the books because he had no patience for numbers. And, as you know, I love to cook—I mean, I am Italian—so I started cooking for him too and then cleaning up. Before long, I was spending all my time at Grove Court."

"What did your parents say?"

"They thought I was nuts but then, the first-born is always a little crazy. They liked the fact that I was doing something I loved—Ell really was teaching me to paint, after all—and that I was making money doing it. At first, they, like everyone else, didn't believe Ell and I weren't sexually involved but when they finally accepted it, they started urging me just to stay down in the Village rather than come home late at night on the subway."

"How did Ellis feel about that? Having a fabulous babe stay at his place and not touching her."

"He referred to me for a while as his training wheels. I kept him from losing his balance. But he really did grow fond of me, I think."

"People don't get married because they're 'in fond'."

"Oh, I think he loved me, in his way. I grew on him. But the marriage started out mostly as a practicality. I was handling his money, taking care of the house, living with him. If we were married, it automatically would solve some problems and answer some questions that otherwise felt awkward."

"Were you in love with him?" Russ asked.

She sighed. "Yes. I did my best to deny it, to myself and to everyone else. But I was. I think he knew it before I knew it. And I knew marriage didn't mean much to him. But he knew it meant a lot to me. His attitude was that if getting married would make me happy, great, but he didn't want it to change our relationship. And since he still wanted to use me as a model, that meant we still couldn't have sex."

"And you agreed to that?"

"No, I didn't. For one thing, I knew my parents would never rest until I had children. But you knew that."

Russ nodded bleakly.

"So I insisted that I would continue to model for him and do all the other things I was doing, as long as we could have a regular Catholic wedding and he would seriously consider having children someday. He agreed, as long as I wouldn't pressure him into having sex and kids for a while because he really liked the way things were and didn't want it all to change. I thought about it a long time and finally consented. That was the night he painted 'Pensive,' that watercolor that hangs by the window in the studio."

"Was he raised a Catholic?"

"Oh, yes, very strict. And it actually backfired on me to insist on the church wedding. Neither of us had been married before so we went through the pre-Cana and all that. And he fell in love with the church. He felt an odd sort of kinship with the celibate priests and he liked the reassuring ritual of mass and all the art work. He told me he had never really appreciated the devotional aspect of Catholicism, the emotion it brought out in him. I'm not sure he put the whole faith of his heart and soul into it but he found the big echoing cathedral and the smell of incense and the soft chant of the liturgy inspiring."

"But surely the church must have frowned on your unconsummated marriage."

"Well, yes, but he did even more penance for confessing to the masturbation. He said the priests must have found that a hard thing to keep from getting out of hand. But seriously, he thought the church's insistence on procreation was based not on theological rectitude but on self-interest. The religion that has the most kids ends up with the most followers. He saw that as the basis of most wars and conflicts, from biblical times to now: we need what you have because there are more of us than you. Anything that stands in the way of having lots of children is a threat to the church."

"But you wanted to have children, right?" Russ asked. "Still do, I assume."

"No," she corrected him. "I wanted, and still want, to have a child. Not a bunch of kids. Just a child."

"And at any cost, then as well as now, I assume."

"No, that's not true either. Not then. Not now."

"So you didn't pressure him."

"I don't think I did. Not consciously. And I hope you don't feel like I'm pressuring you. But after Ell and I were married, that question just hung in the air. I mean, without kids, the marriage didn't change much between us. But he knew quite well that everything would change if I got pregnant."

"And you both assumed, I guess, that he could get you pregnant at the drop of a hat."

"That was certainly my assumption. I mean, look at my family. I'm the oldest of six kids, and I'm only 34. I already have 19 nieces and nephews. Frank and I used condoms religiously and he was the only man I'd been with. For all I knew, nobody would even have to drop a hat for me to get pregnant."

"I guess I showed you."

"Russ, I'm sorry…"

"Just keep going. So Ellis just refused to consider having kids?"

"No, he did consider it. But it had become a larger issue by then. Remember, we had already known each other for quite a while and had been intimate in almost every way but sexually. Even that's not true. I knew a lot about what he did by himself and I knew that I had become a large part of his fantasies. But let's face it. Most couples have sex after a few dates and it's just not that big a deal. But Ell had been saving himself, or however you want to put that, for years. To have sex again had become a momentous event, not just a 'Well, let's get this over with.' Going back to plain old heterosexual sex also represented the last thing standing in the way of his whole-hearted participation in Catholicism. Consummating our marriage took on a religious significance, particularly for him. It became as much a consecration as a consummation. It meant a commitment to being engaged in the world which he hadn't felt since he'd come back from Vietnam. So when he finally, reluctantly, agreed, he placed one big condition on it."

"Which was?"

"That, before we had kids, or even sex, I would allow him to go to Europe for at least a year. He had always wanted to get in touch with his artistic, cultural, and religious roots, particularly in France. He loved the Impressionists, he loved the cathedrals. He wanted to immerse himself in it long enough, deep enough, to make sure he was doing the right thing by letting me suck him back into the real world, as he put it."

"How did you feel about that?"

She sipped her wine. "Well, of course, part of me didn't want him to go."

"Were you afraid he would get involved with someone else?"

"It crossed my mind, sure. But I wasn't as worried about that as I was about him just getting lost in the ideal world of his art and not wanting to return to me."

"But you agreed nevertheless."

"With a big condition of my own. I made him consent to let me bear his child whether he came back or not."

"Ah," Russ said, the puzzle fitting together a little. "The semen bank. How did he like the idea?"

"He talked to a priest about it, who told him that the church considered artificial insemination—even if it's homologous, the semen of the husband—as immoral because the only practical way to obtain the sample is to masturbate, which the church considers immoral. Well, since he had been doing that the whole time anyway, he figured, what the hell, maybe two abominations can make a right or something. So before he left at the end of 1987, we went to Daxor and made a deposit. I don't think I ever seriously intended to use it. I think I just wanted to make clear to him that he had something to come home to."

"So, except for the ending, how did the trip go?"

"It was incredible! He did some of his best work over there, including 'Metamorphosis.' I haven't seen some of the paintings from that period since they hang in museums now or are owned by collectors. He sent me photos of some of them, though, and I think he really did find a way to reconcile his past and his future."

"So obviously he decided his future included you."

"He told me that if he had children, he would want to be there as part of their daily lives. He knew that it would be years before he could make it back overseas, if ever, so he wanted to make the most of it. He spent the fall in England and seemed to be having the time of his life. But one night in early December he called to tell me that he had decided to come back even before the year was up."

"You must have been thrilled."

"I was so excited I couldn't eat or sleep or sit still for weeks. He finally called to tell me he was going to fly back on the winter solstice so the promise of the new sun would shine on us, so we could be together, really together, for the holidays. He'd catch a flight out of Heathrow on the 21st, Pan Am 103."

Pan Am 103, containing a bomb planted by Libyan terrorists, blew up over Lockerbie, Scotland, killing all 270 people aboard.

"Didn't I just see something about Flight 103 in the *Times*?" Russ asked her.

"The two men accused of planting the bombs are finally supposed to go on trial early next month."

The bartender brought Mr. Porter in the next booth another drink and asked if they wanted another round as well.

Sylvia looked at her watch and sighed. "Might as well," she said to Russ.

"Two more," he told the bartender, then turned back to Sylvia. "I knew parts of this story but it's nice to have it all retold in order. Thanks. And let me furnish the postscript: You had this perfectly good sample of perfectly good sperm and you figured I'd never know the difference."

"No, you've got it all wrong," she said, bristling again.

"Well, then, why did you hang on to that sample all these years?"

"I don't know," she confessed. "I guess it became sort of a memento. At least at first, I found some solace in knowing that some part of Ell was still alive."

"So why didn't you use it? Why didn't you go ahead and have his child anyway?"

"I thought about it. But it was too painful to dredge up those memories at first. And then I met you. Daxor has a plan where you can pay the fee two years at a time. I just got in the habit of paying the fee rather than having to decide either to use it or lose it."

"Then why didn't you tell me about it?"

"Well, obviously, it was kind of a long story. And I know you don't like to hear about that part of my life. And I don't blame you. In fact, you helped me make up my mind about that semen sample."

"I did?" Russ asked, surprised. "How?"

"Remember that night we made love on my work table in the studio?"

"How could I forget?"

"Well, I got my bill from Idant Labs that day too. At one point you said something about some part of me still hanging on to Ellis. You didn't know how literal that was but you were right. Zena told me just about the same thing when I consulted her that day. She said my spiritual self wasn't allowing my physical self to get pregnant because I still had that alternative. According to Zena, Ell's spirit won't rest until that bit of living tissue is laid to rest and his spirit might wreak all kinds of havoc in the meantime."

"Well, I know the Catholic church used to believe that any portion of a person's body should be given an ordained burial but I can't believe they'd sanction anything to do with this."

"Well, of course you're right. That's not what I had planned at all. For one thing, you know I'm not involved with the church anymore anyway. If the way Ell died was part of God's plan, I just hope He leaves me out of His plans from now on."

"So what did you plan to do?" he asked, drinking his bourbon.

She sipped her wine and thought about it. "People—even you—ask me if Ell was gay, or bisexual. He wasn't that simple. He didn't fit any of the standard categories. I know he used to think about me sexually but I'm sure he thought about plenty of other people that way as well. God only knows who or what was on his mind that day at Daxor. But somehow I felt like it wasn't just up to me to decide what to do with that semen sample. So I contacted some of his former models and lovers. That's why Paul was there at Les Deux Gamins that night."

"I didn't know he was a model," Russ said, not wanting to know if he was a lover too. "Did Michelle model for him too?"

"Oh, yes, when she was still a teenager."

"He was the luckiest man in the world."

"We were lucky too," she reminded him. "He truly was an incredible man and an inspired and inspiring artist."

"I know. You're right. So anyway, what was the consensus?"

"Well, at first some of them offered to buy the sample, either to use it themselves or just as a relic. But I mean, I didn't feel right telling even *you* about it. How could I consent to let someone else have it? So I decided—and eventually they all agreed with me—that it should be laid to rest, once and for all."

"How?"

"We planned to take it out on the Staten Island Ferry and give it kind of a burial at sea. I thought I'd carry it in that shell casing that he used to use—that I still use—as a paintbrush holder."

"Where did that come from anyway?"

"It was something he got in Vietnam, a sawed-off 25-mm cannon shell. He told me it came from a cannon called the Bushmaster. He used to love the way American gun manufacturers came up with names like that, to make sure that even the dumbest soldier would identify his weapon with his penis."

Russ laughed. "So when were you going to do this?"

"Today. Veteran's Day seemed appropriate. I was supposed to meet everyone an hour ago."

"But then I barged in…"

"Do you understand the jokes about the blue dress now?"

"Yeah, I guess. But obviously you didn't get the sample, right?"

"We'll just have to reschedule this thing for another time, I suppose."

"Well, I got a bit of news this afternoon that has some bearing on this. I got the results of the fertility tests back."

"And?"

"And my sperm lack mitochondria."

"I have no idea what that means."

"It means they have no get-up-and-go. I will never be able to get you pregnant. So maybe it's just as well you didn't get rid of that sperm sample."

"Why?"

"What do you mean, why?" Russ said. "You may need it now."

"No, you were right," she told him earnestly. "I have been clinging to that part of my past and I need to lay it to rest. I'm married to you now."

"But what if something happens to me?" he asked her, confused. "What if something happens to us?"

"Like what?" she asked, looking intently into his eyes. "What are you saying?"

They held each others' gaze for a few seconds at most. But Russ knew in his heart that something had changed between them. Perhaps they could go forward from here but they certainly couldn't go back.

"I'm just saying," choosing his words carefully, "that you should keep your options open."

"You really don't trust me, do you? You think I'm the type of woman who would sneak around behind your back."

"Well, this afternoon hasn't been my finest hour either," he admitted. "I did some sneaking around myself. I could understand if you had some second thoughts about me."

Tears welled up in her eyes. "You don't love me anymore."

"Of course I love you," he said. "But I don't want to be responsible for you destroying that semen sample. You may need it someday."

"But I don't need it," she insisted. "I don't need it now. I won't ever need it. Whether you and I have children someday, or whether we never have children at all, it has nothing to do with that semen sample."

"Honey, I'm sorry. You're upset. All I'm saying is that you shouldn't make a rash decision about this. Right now, in the context of our marriage, you feel this way. But maybe if you stand back, give it some time, think about it, you might feel differently. I don't want you to take this drastic a step because of something I said."

"But I already took a drastic step because of something you said."

"What did you do?" he asked, the bourbon slowing his brain. "What did I say?"

"I married you," she said, standing up. "Because you said you would always love me."

"What are you doing?" he asked, watching her pull on her long pea coat.

"I'm standing back," she said. "Like you suggested."

"Do you want me to come?" he asked, feeling paralyzed.

"Would it do any good?" she asked him.

Russ wanted to say something but his anger and resentment over the implied slur of her question choked him.

Taking his silence to mean he had nothing to say, she said, "Don't wait up," turned and walked out.

With a philosophical flourish Russ threw himself upon his bourbon as though it were a sword. What else could go wrong?

...O...O...O...

Love does not make the world go 'round. The earth spins regardless. Love makes the world spiral upward, in a helix.

I got into music for a surprisingly common reason: I'm quite shy and I can't dance. Playing music got me invited to parties and dances, and eventually to bars, where I could at least look at the pretty girls from the stage. Maybe it's hard-wired into my brain but some part of me must keep looking until I've found the prettiest girl. Once in a while—not as often as I'd hoped, damn it —one looks back.

That's how I met the Princess. I was performing for a Christmas party one enchanted evening when suddenly I saw a stranger across the crowded room. Our eyes met and sparks flew, sweet music began to play, and I burst into song—well, actually, I was singing to begin with, but that's the image anyway. She came to the stage to make a request and we began to chat. She possessed great beauty, much that she was born with, some that she had purchased at a cosmetics counter. But I can't create a fantasy with skin-deep beauty alone. Only the mystery of something partially hidden, like the tease of lingerie, can hold my attention, inspire my devotion.

Man is a curious animal. Our large and all-too-often idle brains won't rest until we've explained away each mystery. Isn't that the goal of science? To unlock the mysteries of nature? But poking around under Mother Nature's skirt to ogle her lacy underthings can present hazards, not the least of which is finding that we liked the fantasy more than the explanation. Certainly in the case of the Princess, I discovered things under her fine lingerie—metaphorically speaking— that I didn't want to see.

Hence the cruise to Alaska. One day I tired of sitting in that leaky trailer in Valdez thinking about this latest of my many bad choices in love. So I drove to the other side of the bay to check out the salmon hatchery.

The idea of a hatchery is simple but effective and seems, at least at first blush, benign or even altruistic. Salmon, as most people know, spend most of their lives at sea, returning to their native stream to spawn and die, finding that stream by a very sophisticated sense of smell. So all the fish born in a hatchery return there to spawn, swimming right up the stream toward home, not knowing that the stream has been diverted through what amounts to a fish-killing factory. There they are quickly dispatched, sliced open for their milt and roe, which are unceremoniously dumped into a bucket, and then the fish carcasses are sold for cat food or whatever. Simply by pouring the bucket of milt into the bucket of roe, the eggs are fertilized and the process begins again.

But at least a couple of problems have arisen with this system. For one thing, the hatchery fish, having man's protection through the perilous first stages of life, compete with the wild fish for resources. Another, more insidious problem is that the hatchery fish, with no survival pressure in those early stages, tend to be ill-adapted for life in the wild and in fact seem a bit slow and stupid.

Probably the people who run the hatchery will find ways of making these salmon less inferior. But I think ultimately they'll find that the problem stems from a lack of love. I don't claim to know what criteria salmon use when choosing a mate in those final hours of their lives. But salmon-chanted evening across a crowded stream bed they do choose and that makes all the difference. Just to have returned to that stream bed at all, sometimes traveling hundreds of miles up river to get there, proves a certain kind of worthiness. But the fish tough enough to make it there still must select the worthiest mate. By choosing, they strengthen the species and adapt the helix of their DNA to the spinning world. Perhaps it's just an animal urge but who am I to criticize that?

My Princess is long gone now and perhaps my chance to spawn as well. I can't escape my nature, though. My eyes still latch onto the prettiest girl in the room. There's a young woman where I'm working. She's beautiful, graceful, and probably half my age. I can't seem to take my eyes off of her. There is truly no fool like an old fool. But I'm sure she has her own complicated life, undoubtedly a boyfriend to take care of her, perhaps children of her own already. After all, I'm getting to the age that mothers look like daughters. Soon this pretty girl will be gone and another will come along. There are lots of fish in the sea. All I hope for now is to maintain the fantasy. Without that sense of mystery, the world would grind to a halt.

November 16, 1999

Everything seemed different to Matt. But only one small part of him, no bigger than a walnut, had changed. Little things can mean a lot.

He had driven up this driveway thousands of times. He had never noticed the sound the grass made as it tickled the underside of the Volvo. The garage-door opener had a hitch in its git-along. Surely that wasn't new but he'd never seen it before.

He pulled into the garage and killed the motor and sighed. He wanted just to sit awhile but even that made him uncomfortable. The doctor had referred to the procedure as "fine needle aspiration" but nothing about it had felt fine and only the first syllable of "aspiration" held any relevance at this point.

In any case, sitting felt lousy. Matt opened the car door and, gripping the steering wheel and the window frame, pulled himself slowly from the car. His back reminded him that he'd forgotten to stop on the way home to fill the prescription for hydrocodone Dr. Wu had written him.

In a way Wu's reaction had frightened him the most. Not that it seemed overblown. The guy, about Matt's age, exuded cheerful professionalism and they had established, if not intimacy, at least congeniality over the years. So last week when Wu peeled off the latex glove and went immediately to writing in the chart rather than his usual chatting (he had once joked that rectal exams were the easiest to enter into the computer billing program because they were already digital) Matt thought it odd. Today Wu looked visibly shaken.

In any case it sure hadn't taken long, considering. They weren't expecting Matt back at Novagen this afternoon. He could always find something to do around the house. No point in wasting time.

On the work bench sat the bag of bulbs Deb had bought Sunday at the Japanese Garden sale: daffodil, tulip, hyacinth, crocus. She had limited herself to replacements for the ones that drowned in last winter's 97-day rain jag or that got dug up by raccoons and Matt knew right where they went in the flower bed. He grabbed a trowel and went out to the yard.

Thick, uniform clouds stretched to the horizon like an old gray wool army blanket, keeping the city warm through the winter. Though still barely mid-afternoon, the streetlights on Sunset Road already glinted dimly from the cars of the early commuters hurrying back to home and hearth. Wisps of mist wreathed the shoulder of Squak Mountain; occasionally a shred would disentangle itself and drift like goose-down to the firs below.

Disregarding his new work slacks, Matt knelt in the soft, bark-covered loam of the berm in the lawn. Thrusting the trowel into the damp earth, he wiggled open a slot, plopped down a bulb, and tucked it in. Repeating this three or four times, he shifted his chilly knees to another spot and buried some more. He imagined how the bright, resurrected flowers would look next spring beneath the little variegated dogwood that crowned the berm. Maybe Deb would smile.

Planting those didn't turn out to be enough work to justify his ruined pants. He hung the trowel back up on the pegboard in the garage and got out the trusty plastic leaf rake. In fall, that always needed doing.

Most of the year the ancient big-leaf maple on the southeast corner of the house stood aloof from the petty doings in the yard. In winter the thick mats of mosses and licorice ferns on the sturdy limbs stayed green while everything else slept. In spring the small delicate red flowers waved in the breeze. In summer squirrels gamboled and tumbled through the shady playground. But in fall, the curling, leathery brown leaves, big as placemats, smothered all below. Every day bushels more pirouetted to the ground. Matt herded together the latest arrivals, gathered as many as he could hold between the wide rake and his other arm, and headed for the compost heap behind the little barn, spider webs brushing his face as he went.

Tahoma, the feisty snow-white Arabian colt Deb had bought a couple of years ago after they'd had to put Kalakala down, whickered from his stall. "It's only me," Matt told him through the wall. "She'll be back after a while."

Tahoma whickered again so Matt dumped the leaves on the heap and went into the barn. He peeled off a healthy wedge from the open hay bale and gave it to the head-tossing colt, then he threw a cup of grain into the little trough for good measure. Too young and hungry for proper manners, the colt devoted himself to his snack so Matt went back to the compost heap.

Composted, the big-leaf maple leaves, so substantial when they fell, seemed to vanish from the heap the way cotton candy vanishes in your mouth. He used an old rusting pitchfork to mix the armload of leaves on the top of the heap into the moldering grass clippings and celery tops and withered chrysanthemums. Steam rose from the freshly-turned compost and beetles scrambled back to privacy. The heap looked comfy. Maybe they could do that with Matt, throw him on the compost heap, work him back into the garden. His bone and blood would add phosphorus and iron but his flesh would be too persistent, would attract too much vermin.

He leaned the pitchfork against the wall of the barn and looked around. So little time, so much to do.

One thing he had neglected this hectic year was the creek. The small rivulet, a tributary to May Creek, ran through the edge of their lot, shrinking to a trickle in the dry summer months, swelling to its banks after the heavy winter storms. The McCleary lot, and most of May Valley, had been logged during the timber boom at the beginning of the century. Before the hemlocks and firs could re-establish themselves, the invading Himalayan blackberry vines spotted the lack of shade and rushed into the breach. The berries were big-seeded but tasty and plentiful—Deb made jam every summer. But the canes, sturdy, armed with needle-sharp spikes, and able to grow several inches a day, overwhelmed everything in their path, the way a bad but tempting idea, like reviving disco music or putting Newt Gingrich in charge, takes over.

Nothing short of brush killer, the gardener's equivalent to nuclear annihilation, could stop the blackberries. So successive owners of the house had abandoned the corner of the lot to them, which seemed a shame, since the defenseless little creek, which cavorted over a picturesque waterfall and dabbled in a couple of peaceful pools, easily could be lost beneath a 20-foot tangle of vines. When Matt and Deb bought the house in the mid-1980s, Matt had taken it upon himself to keep the berry vines at bay, at least along that one stretch of creek.

Digging them out by the roots proved impossible, especially among the rocks. Cutting everything short didn't work since the canes thrive on open ground. So Matt got some hand pruners and some sturdy leather gloves and laboriously cut the hundreds of vines as close to the dirt as possible so that other native plants could compete and, hopefully, take over.

He had worked at this for a decade now and the results were beginning to show. Grasses and sword ferns and bleeding-hearts had taken root and held the soil. Buttercups and daisies lined the creek in spring. Western red-cedar and alder and even a small volunteer holly tree had gained a foothold.

But time had gotten away from him this year, with the added pressure of the Y2K problem at Novagen. At a glance he could see the fine-toothed oval leaflets of the blackberries poking up through the grass. Wearily he took the rake back to the garage and traded it for the gloves and nippers.

The work and his light jacket kept him warm and the cool damp air felt good on his face. His back hurt—hell, everything between his navel and his thighs hurt—and he tried one last time to convince himself that it was his age and the cool damp air that caused the ache. But he knew it wasn't so.

The impenetrable cloud-cover stifled the lingering Northwest twilight but he still could spot most of the rapidly hardening shoots that, left unchecked, would erupt into malignant tentacles come spring. Carefully stepping on the rocks whenever possible, he bent to trim one, then another, then a patch of half a dozen that clustered around the borders of one of the large stones of the waterfall. But when he tried to straighten, he realized his back wouldn't let him. He braced his hands on his knees and gritted his teeth but the pain grew too severe. He fell to his knees and remained hunched over, his eyes squinted shut and his lips compressed, until the red waves subsided.

"This is insane," he said aloud to himself. "No one else on earth but me gives a rat's ass whether these God-damned vines take over. You know what? Screw it!" He thrust the hardened steel of the nippers into the stony ground and laboriously pushed himself back to his feet. "Sorry, creek. Can't help you."

Matt limped to the garage and put the nippers back on the pegboard and the gloves on the workbench. He pushed the button to close the garage door and went into the house.

o   o   o

The McCleary house dated back to 1923, when just about everything east of Lake Washington was still fresh secondary-growth forest, when the only businesses here were the mill down on the lake, which Microsoft co-founder Paul Allen had recently purchased to create a business park, and the coal mine, long defunct and now buried under condos and Factoria Mall. Built as a farm house, it had begun as a long narrow clapboard affair with a massive fieldstone fireplace and a bay window in the drawing room that looked out over

May Valley. Additions over the years had expanded it like a Scrabble game: more kitchen space with a skylight to the west, the two-car attached garage behind that, a sunken den opposite, and, five years ago, the McClearys' own three-dimensional quirk, a partial second floor with a roomy master bedroom and bath above modernized laundry facilities and an office for Deb's philanthropy.

Before they had committed to the addition they considered doing what many a Microsoft millionaire had done: spend a few hundred thousand for an old beach-house on the lake in Medina or on Mercer Island, tear it down, and put up something spectacular that would drive assessments up and the neighbors crazy. But Deb had already heard plenty of horror stories from fellow retirees about the tribulations of building from scratch and this old farm house had grown to feel like home to them both, especially to Matt. It did have the little barn for Deb's horse, too, with a mown field in which to ride. Besides, Matt still had to deal with those pesky berry vines.

But even this homey place seemed different now. He looked around at the familiar kitchen with the eye of an evicted tenant, hoping he'd be spared the heavy lifting. For all he knew, Deb would want to move. He wouldn't blame her. Well, what to do first?

He got out his address book and the cordless phone and sat at the old kitchen table. He only sat a moment, though, before his discomfort pushed him back to his feet.

He sighed. Might as well start with the easy things. Deb's aunt had sent a homemade pecan coffee cake last month for her birthday but had let a shard of shell slip into the batter. Matt had cracked one of his bicuspids on it and had an appointment Thursday for a root canal and cap. But as yet the tooth didn't bother him too much. He called his dentist's office, told them something had come up and that he'd call back to reschedule another time. Kind of a cop-out but easy enough.

He also called Dolores Muñoz at Morgan Stanley Dean Witter where, because of the disparity of their incomes, Matt and Deb held separate accounts.

After exchanging pleasantries with Dolores, he explained, "I was wondering something. Deb and I still have the separate accounts, right?"

"Sure," Dolores said. "Would you like your balance?"

"No, that's okay. I know I'm like a flea to her elephant anyway. I just got to thinking, what would happen if one of us should predecease the other?"

"I can double-check," Dolores offered, "but I assume you and Deb are the named beneficiaries on each other's account."

"I think we are too. But before my Dad passed away, he set up his account in joint tenancy with me so that we could avoid any hassles with probate."

"I remember that and your father was wise to do so," Dolores told him. "But in the case of a surviving spouse, both accounts are considered community property anyway, so probate isn't an issue. Why do you ask?"

"Oh, just wondering. I want to make sure all the ducks are in a row."

"It is wise to think of things like that ahead of time," Dolores pointed out. "But, God willing, you shouldn't have to worry about it for some time."

"Yes," Matt agreed. "God willing."

It wouldn't hurt to call Phil Banks, their lawyer. They had known each other since the mid-80s, when Matt had worked for Fish and Wildlife over on the Olympic Peninsula and Phil had represented the Quillayute people in their court case over fishing and timber rights. They had bruised each other a few times in the course of the litigation but each had come to respect the other's integrity and intelligence. Deb found Phil a bit too blunt, thought his lack of tact had contributed to Phil's divorce, but had come to respect his opinion. In fact, it was she who first contacted him.

Phil no longer charged them for phone calls but Matt, leaning against his shiny black Steinway in the living room, came right to the point anyway. "How's that easement situation coming?"

King County had forced them to grant an easement for a proposed widening of May Valley Road and Phil had insisted on, and received, a promise from the planning commission to add an asphalt curb and a larger culvert to prevent storm run-off from flooding their yard.

"It's all wrapped up," Phil assured him. "I talked to Deb about it last week. I assumed she discussed it with you. All your t's are dotted and your i's are crossed."

"She didn't mention that she spoke to you but I'm glad to hear it's straightened out. So once again the title to our little homestead is free and unencumbered, right?"

"Right," Phil said. "And I'm glad to hear Deb's keeping her conversations with me a secret. It means I'm wearing her down."

"She said something about that when she mentioned you last. Although, as I recall, her exact wording was that you were wearing her patience down."

Phil laughed. "Well, I assume you'll do the decent thing when the time comes and not stand in our way."

"When the time comes, I don't think it'll be me you have to worry about. But while I've got you on the phone, let me ask you something else."

"Ask away."

"Remember when we signed those living wills a few years ago?"

"Sure."

"Wasn't there a phrase in there about 'no extraordinary measures'?"

"That's become a standard term, yes."

"I'm not sure I recall exactly what constituted 'extraordinary measures' to keep someone alive."

"In general, it refers to things like ventilation, long-term heart-lung machines, intravenous feeding. The types of measures, for instance, that keep someone's body alive when they're technically brain-dead. Why do you ask?"

"Just curious."

"Are you okay?"

Matt heard the beep of call-waiting. "Nothing worth worrying about," he told Phil. "Listen, I've got another call. I'll talk to you soon."

The other caller was Deb. "Hey, babe," she said cheerily. "How was the doctor's?"

"A pain in the ass," he told her, sitting only briefly on the leather arm of his recliner. "Where are you?" He could tell she was in her Mercedes.

"Oh, God," she moaned. "The radio said that I-90 was the slower floating bridge so I took 520 instead. But some jackass just stalled his car in the left lane so now it's a floating parking lot and I just passed the Arboretum exit. And I still have to stop in Redmond as well. This is going to take forever. I'm sorry."

"Not to worry."

"Are we still on for tonight?"

That question had been in the back of his mind all afternoon but he hadn't formulated a response.

Their sex life had evolved considerably over the years. The first time they made love, in a nook beneath a clump of scrub oak behind her parents' house one balmy summer evening 29 years ago, his anticipation, his dazzlement, and his nervousness had so overwhelmed him that at the moment of climax his nose began to bleed. Deb, wiping the red drops from her face, laughed with relief when she realized she hadn't actually induced a fatal hemorrhage but she never again underestimated his ardor.

The first few months after they married, they made love every night, which gradually moderated from delirious ecstasy to passion to affection. Eventually, though, she depleted his libido to the point that merely toying with the top button of her blouse no longer prompted him to snap to rigid attention. The first few nights they went to sleep without having sex worried them both so much they discussed seeing a counselor to salvage their relationship. But soon both realized that the night off made the night on that much better.

Everyday reality insinuates itself into the most spirited affairs. The pressures of their senior year in college, and then his post-graduate work and her job, soon whittled their sex life down to every third night if they were lucky. By the time they both had careers, they had settled into a routine of making love at church times: Wednesday nights and Sunday mornings.

Deb's 20-hour days at Microsoft took their toll on the relationship but she noticed that, far from losing interest sexually, Matt seemed horny all the time. She discovered that she could sweet-talk him into satisfying her but insist that he postpone his gratification for a night. He discovered the difference between his own satisfaction and dull satiation. Together they discovered that she could have four or five orgasms for every one of his, a ratio they both enjoyed immensely. So she began to husband his orgasms, making sure they took full advantage of each precious one. The degree of self-control required suited his personality well and she cherished his slavish desire to fulfill her needs and pleasures.

They struggled to find the right interval though. If they waited a full week, he got so horny he was tempted to satisfy himself, which they agreed he should save for times when they were apart, or for his mountain-top fertility ritual. But as he got older and as they got busier, the twice-a-week regimen grew burdensome. So several years ago they had come up with a schedule for love-making: Sunday, Thursday, Tuesday, then Sunday again. They even made up a special calendar that hung in the bedroom which they both consulted before planning anything, making allowances for special occasions, separations, and those times of the month when her cramps made thoughts of sex nauseating.

They stuck to their schedule faithfully, gladly. He insisted on waking her on that fifth day (fourth, on Thursdays), and often the morning or two before, if not with penetration, at least with the sort of kissing and licking that brought goose-bumps to the back of her neck and sweat to the base of her spine. He had grown to feel a slight resentment of his own orgasms because they spoiled all the fun for a few days. For her part, she thrived on his devotion and delighted in finding various ways of taunting and teasing him to make his arousal that much more deliciously complete.

Tonight, Tuesday, was the fifth night. It pleased him to hear her talking about it, sounding excited about it, because for the past few months she had seemed as disinterested as she ever had. In fact, this morning, when he had tried to wake her the traditional way, she had insisted that she would prefer just some hugs and kisses. He wasn't sure what had been bothering her but he knew that what he had to tell her wouldn't help matters at all.

But bad news can always wait. "As far as I know," he hedged in reply to her question, "we're still on for tonight."

"Great," she said, "because I've got someone for you."

"Really?" he said, intrigued in spite of himself. She sometimes taunted him by describing some attractive woman she had seen that he couldn't have because, obviously, he was married. Once in a while he would see someone who appealed to him physically and Deb would insist that he take out all his randy notions on her instead, but for some reason that didn't hold the same fascination as when she brought someone new herself.

"You know, I had to go downtown to meet with Dennis Hayes about the demonstrations we're planning for the W. T. O. Anyway, while I was down there, I stopped at Benaroya Hall to pick up those symphony tickets and the girl at the ticket booth—oh, my, she made me look like Granny Clampett."

"Yeah, right."

"I'm serious. She was hot: tall, tan, skinny, boobs out to here — oh, you'll enjoy her."

"Except for the boobs, she sounds like a latté."

"And lattés keep you up, right? Anyway, this bridge is a nightmare. I don't suppose I could talk you into making dinner?"

"What do you want?"

"We've got those salmon steaks."

"The usual way?" Which meant poached in Chardonnay and butter on the barbeque, smoky with alder chips, and served with a lemon-dill sauce he had improvised once.

"I'll give you anything you want," she offered.

"All I ask is time."

She giggled with anticipation. "Take as long as you like. Oh, and could you give Tahoma a little something to tide him over till I get there?"

"Already did."

"You're so sweet. What would I do without you?"

He thought about it. "Maybe you should get across the bridge you're stuck on before you try to cross that one."

"— — supposed to mean?" The call-waiting beep had cut off the first part.

"Sorry, sport, I've got another call. I'm a popular guy today, I guess. We'll talk when you get here."

"See you soon, you big hunka-hunka."

He pushed the button for the other caller. "Hello?"

"Matt? Arnie Farquhar from NyChem. I've got those compliance estimates you wanted."

He recognized the name and he recognized the voice and knew they didn't match, but he couldn't figure out who it was. It couldn't be Arnie Farquhar. But he could think of nothing to say but "Uhhhh…"

"Is there a problem?" the caller asked.

Recognition dawned. "Jeez, Russ, you had me going. And yes, there is a problem."

"Damn, I didn't think you'd be home," Russ said. "I planned to leave a Arnie Farquhar message and my number, see if I could get you as confused as you were last time we spoke. So what's the problem?"

"For one thing, we at Novagen got sick of NyChem dragging its feet on this Y2K thing, so we're using a supplier in Michigan now. And Arnie Farquhar got canned over it."

"Damn, you're good," Russ acknowledged. "I suppose you helped the Seahawks beat the Broncos last night too."

"Did the Hawks win? I've had other things on my mind. But I can tell you how the Broncos can get back on track."

"How's that?"

"Get Elway to quit selling cars and beer and get back to quarterbacking."

"That'd probably work," Russ conceded. "You are the man with the plan. Ever meet up with a problem you can't solve?"

"One just today," Matt conceded, looking out the front window at the drizzly evening.

"What's that?"

It occurred to him that he really hadn't thought through who to tell when. Maybe he owed it to Deb to tell her first. Hedging to Russ, he said, "I just found out about a deadline that's been pushed up."

"A little thing like a deadline's got the great Matt McCleary stumped? I don't believe it.

Didn't you tell me once about some problem-solving scheme you came up with?"

"Oh, yeah, the Five Steps. I hadn't thought of that in a long time."

"What were they again?"

"Let's see. The acronym is ARDAR: Awareness, Resolve, Deliberation, Action, Result. You have to be aware of the problem, decide you want to solve it, figure out a way you think will work, put your plan in action, and check your results."

"I remember that now. I liked it because it has AR in it twice. Remember our discussions about Alternate Reality?"

"Vividly."

"So the ARDAR method works on any problem?"

"Oh, it doesn't necessarily help you solve a problem. That Step Three can be tough. But problems are never really solved without completing all five steps. I thought it had some merit till I realized it's basically just the old scientific method."

"How's that?"

"In science, you become aware of facts that clash with the established theory of how something works. So you have to decide whether it's enough of an inconsistency to warrant tossing out the old theory and coming up with a new hypothesis. If so, you have to design an experiment to test the new hypothesis and then run the experiment. Last, you have to check the results to see if the new hypothesis can replace the old theory."

"All in a day's work for you science dudes, I suppose," Russ said.

"We prefer the term 'Grand Poobahs Of The Cosmos'," Matt declared airily, "and sometimes we get done in half a day."

"I had no idea."

"Actually, some theories resist experimental test for centuries. For that matter, science isn't the only place where those steps get used. I stumbled on it doing ecology work. Nature uses the same steps to create species."

When he didn't elaborate, Russ said, "Well, don't keep me in suspense."

"I didn't know if you'd want to get into this sort of discussion. You must have had another reason for calling."

"It seems like everyone I know, including me, has problems lately. If I can help them find solutions, so much the better. Plus, lately I've been contemplating writing some sort of philosophical treatise. Maybe I can work this in somehow. In fact, it reminds me of an image Sonja Weinstock used to use, where existence can be described as a hierarchy, from physical, to organic, to intellectual, to enlightened."

"Well, I don't know if any insight I might impart would qualify as legitimate philosophy. This ecology rap is more niche-y than Nietzche but you asked for it," Matt said, walking into the john to take an uncomfortable, dribbling leak. "An ecological niche corresponds to a problem which living creatures, with their variable genes, try to solve. A few freaks, like a bird with a stronger bill or a giraffe with a longer neck, can thrive on that new nest site or food source or whatever. The population with that genome grows until it fills the niche. At some point the population maxes out and that combined with the inevitable environmental changes alters the niche that created the new species in the first place. Eventually that particular niche changes so much that the species it helped create becomes extinct."

"You make it sound like extinction is inevitable."

"As far as we know, it is. Even the new self-replicating nanotechnologies, computer viruses, and man-made biological viruses could only exist as long as the host exists. Of course, the time it takes a biological species to reach that point varies immensely. For some it's just a handful of generations. Other species survive for tens of millions of years virtually unchanged."

"So we're talking *yugas* here."

"Small Eastern European cars?" Matt wondered facetiously.

"No, *yugas* are units of time in Indian cosmology."

"That's right, I have some dim recollection of that."

"It fits your five step plan perfectly. First, Brahma sleeps. When he wakes his day lasts something like four billion years, and his day is further broken down into four smaller cycles called *yugas*. The first, the golden age, lasts a couple of million years, dwindling down to the fourth, the *Kali Yuga*, lasting 432,000 years. I have no idea why I can remember that number but not my own phone number. In any case, things deteriorate through the successive *yugas* and, as you may have guessed, we're living in the *Kali Yuga*, which explains why things are so screwed up. The classic Hindu image is of a cow standing on all four legs, then three, then two, then teetering on her last leg in the last *yuga*."

"Interesting. So one of Brahma's days lasts, within a factor of three or four, the length of time since the Big Bang, and this final pathetic *yuga* we're stuck in lasts, within the same factor, about the length of time that genus *Homo* has been more or less *sapiens*."

"Some of those Hindu cats were pretty *sapiens*."

"You know, the Big Bang fits that five step model too."

"Lay on, MacDuff."

"You start with the potential for matter and energy."

"Brahma sleeping."

"Exactly. Then comes the Bang itself, followed by the creation of space, expansion of the universe, and eventually either contraction or a steady state of entropy, depending on the amount of dark matter out there."

"The creation of space? God gets closet organizers?"

"Actually, another way of looking at the expansion of the universe is simply that more space is being created. The amount of stuff stays the same. That's the first Law of Thermodynamics: conservation of matter and energy. It's just that there's more and more space for it to expand into. In fact, there's a whole lot more nothing in the universe than something."

"The Cosmic Void."

"Indeed. In any case, it's as though the universe is inhaling and there's some question about whether there will come an exhalation."

"Interesting that you should bring up breathing which, of course, plays a big role in most Hindu-based religions like Buddhism and Zen."

"Same five-step process, right?" Matt said, trying to take a deep breath and immediately regretting it. "The self exists. That's always the first step. Then comes the need to breathe, inhalation, saturation, then exhalation. Almost anything cyclical in nature follows the same process. Like a Ferris Wheel: first you have to buy your ticket and get on. They start it and it takes you backwards and up and all you see is machinery and other people's legs. Then you go forward and up, with that exhilarating sense of promise about getting to the top. After you peak, the wheel pushes you out into the unknown and you feel yourself falling. Then finally it pulls you back to where you started."

"Otherwise known as the wheel of *samsara*," Russ added. "You've got this all worked out, don't you?"

"Oh, it crops up lots of places. Back in the '80s, when keyboard synthesizers became all the rage, Deb bought me a nice Roland for my birthday one year so I could play electric piano and organ and all sorts of things that the Steinway can't cover. Anyway, the Roland had something called ADSR: attack, delay, sustain, release. All music notes follow those same parameters: the onset of the tone, the time it takes to reach full volume, how long it lasts, and how it terminates."

"I didn't know you still played that much."

"I'm no Glenn Gould but I still fumble my way through some Bach once in a while."

"Are you looking for a gig?"

Matt laughed, which hurt so much he had to lean against the stove until it passed. "Don't make me laugh."

"I'm serious," Russ said. "I went to all the trouble to hire this singer named Lacey Tremaine to play New Year's Eve at Tweak. We shuffle the contracts through the mail, I design some little posters and flyers for her, line up radio spots, the whole nine yards. So what does she do?"

"Let's see, what's the old joke about living with girl singers? They don't know when to come in and when they do, they've forgotten their key."

"I should be so lucky. Lacey just about ended up with the keys to Tweak."

"What happened?"

"From what I've figured out so far, she and my night manager, fat-faced Rolando, got drunk last Friday after I left and they got a wild hare. They took all the money from my till and flew to Barbados."

"So you're out your entertainer, your manager, and your night's receipts, all in one swell foop. That's rough, Russ. I'm sorry."

"Oh, it doesn't end there. Rolando messed up the books like you wouldn't believe. He's been skimming supplies and money from me for months and I guess I just wasn't paying close enough attention to notice. It's going to take me weeks just to straighten it all out and my accountant has already warned me that I may owe a bunch of back taxes now, since Rolando's been juggling the books to cover his skimming."

"Drag."

"Tell me about it. And this afternoon I found out something else I didn't know. I promoted one of my cooks to replace Rolando, a guy named Buzz, which turns out to be appropriate. He's one of those post-Gen-Xers with a shaved head, a goatee, and, I just found out today, a rap sheet from last summer's Woodstock anniversary mess. What happened with that, anyway? I almost went to the first one, you may recall. But, no, I had to come back to the Springs to play that lame gig at Ft. Carson that Jason got us. Remember that?"

"Quite well, yes."

"Anyway, twice as many people showed up for the original Woodstock with arguably worse conditions but very few problems. Thirty years later, the thing ends up in a full-blown riot. What gives?"

"You're asking me? The reasons I heard included price gouging, for tickets as well as for water and food, the extreme heat, and violent song lyrics. But maybe it's just a difference in the generations. What surprised me was hearing someone as conservative as John McLaughlin talking about the good old days of the hippies."

"From what Buzz told me," Russ said, "drugs played a part in it too. That's what he got arrested for, which takes some doing at an event like that. Anyway, he now informs me that most of my staff, including, of course, the now infamous Rolando, work at Tweak mostly to support a drug habit. What am I supposed to do about that? I don't want to come off as one of those straights we ridiculed so mercilessly when we were that age. But I also don't want to see all these kids who work for me throw away their money and their lives. What's your vaunted Five Step Program have to say about that?"

"As I said, it describes the five steps of solving problems, not what the solutions are. Although, I must add that addiction follows the same pattern: awareness of the drug, experimentation, habituation, tolerance, and withdrawal. What sort of drugs are they abusing?"

"Abusing?" Russ said. "Well, as far as that goes, almost everybody at Tweak abuses the big three legal drugs: alcohol, tobacco, and caffeine. Then there's the usual pot and cocaine. Some crack but thankfully not much, from what Buzz said. But he told me even some classics like psychedelic mushrooms and LSD are making a comeback. Buzz's personal favorite, though, is something he called salvia, which he claims is still legal. I don't suppose you know anything about that?"

"I have enough trouble staying up on developments in my own tiny field of expertise. I haven't been part of the drug scene for a long time. John probably knows more about that than I do."

"Interesting you should mention John," Russ said. "Have you heard from him or from May?"

"No, but I didn't expect to. Why? Was one of them going to call me?"

"Actually, May called here last week and we had a long conversation. In fact she wanted me to say hello to you."

"What's she like?"

"In some ways like her mother: troubled, sensitive, a bit flighty. She's had a rough go of it lately, that's for sure. She's got that same wild streak her father had."

"Her father?"

"Jason," Russ said confidently. "She told me that John saw the way she holds a pen. Remember that?"

Matt could picture Jason sitting at the desk next to his in Mr. Graber's physics class at Cheyenne, meticulously working out the calculations on a test, the pen between his middle and ring fingers. "Sure I remember. May holds hers the same way?"

"According to John."

"When did he see her write?"

"That's where the plot thickens. I guess he took it upon himself to turn May on to psychedelics so she would be able to relate to what her parents went through if they did indeed try to have her aborted."

"Unbelievable!" Matt exclaimed.

"So she went up to Estes a couple of weeks ago and they ate some shrooms and went for a hike. I guess that went pretty well, although they did get weathered off. But when they went back to Estes, Susan caught them together and assumed the worst."

"Is that a fair assumption?"

"Not according to May. She said they did a couple of touchy-feely things in the course of the trip but nothing scandalous. Unfortunately, John can't seem to convince Susan of that. So he's moved out, staying somewhere in Loveland."

"Another victim of the most dangerous drug of all."

"Psilocybin?"

"Testosterone."

Russ laughed. "Boy, you got that right. Anyway, I was hoping that one of them had contacted you because like an idiot I didn't get May's number, I don't remember her last name, and I have no idea where John is staying in Loveland."

"Did you call Susan?"

Russ coughed. "I chickened out. Why? Do you want to call her?"

Matt thought about how that conversation would go. "I see what you mean. I haven't spoken to them in years. What were you going to talk to them about? Is it urgent?"

"Well, I thought I'd let them know that it's pretty doubtful I'm going to be able to do this

Gathering on New Year's Eve. Things are just too up in the air here for me to be able to commit to something that far out."

"I'm sorry to hear it," Matt said, though he actually felt ambiguous. He was relieved that he wouldn't have to burden Russ with the reason why he probably wouldn't have been able to make it there himself but he was disappointed that he wouldn't get a chance to see his old friends.

"Incidentally, May asked me if Tom would be joining us."

"Tom?"

"I don't remember his last name. She said John remembered him but their conversation got cut short before he could tell her about him. Do you remember him?"

"I don't remember anybody significant named Tom," Matt said, thinking back. "But I've had other things on my mind, as I'm sure you have. It sounds like you've got your hands full at Tweak."

"To tell you the truth," Russ said soberly, "unless things start looking better, I may sell Tweak to anyone crazy enough to want to buy it. I'm thinking about moving out of this city."

"What?! Heresy!" Matt exclaimed. "You've wanted to live in New York since Hector was a pup. What does Sylvia say about this?"

He could tell from the length of Russ's pause that he'd touched a nerve. Finally Russ said, "I'm not sure Sylvia and I are going to make it."

"Oh, no! Oh, Russ, I'm so sorry to hear it! You know I think the world of you both and I thought for sure you'd found the one. Do you want to talk about it?"

"I've already chewed your ear a long time. Like I said, I thought I'd get your machine and leave you a message. What are you doing home so early anyway?"

"I had an appointment that didn't take as long as I thought it would. And Deb called to tell me she won't be home for a while yet. So tell me about what's come between you and Sylvia."

"In a way, come's come between us. How much do you know about sex?"

"To be fair, I really ought to let Deb answer that," Matt said. "I know I like it so much I plan my life around it."

"Spoken like the old dog that you are. And I assume you have a five-step program that fits."

"Of course. The first step is desire, then arousal, then coitus itself, culminating in the pathetically brief climax that makes common men feel like gods and brings world leaders to their knees."

"Or at least their interns," Russ said, "Ba-doom-boom—tchishhh! But I only counted four steps."

"Oh, yeah, how could I forget? After that comes the afterglow, when Deb rubs my back and I float out across the universe."

"You know, beneath that hard scientific shell, you're really just an old softy."

"Not as soft as I used to be," Matt said, recalling the sensation of Dr. Wu palpating his prostate.

"Anyway, I thought maybe you'd know something about the biology of sex since you've been working on that AIDS kit."

"Yeah, I know a little about it."

"Remember last time we spoke I talked about how I wasn't sure my little salmon had what it took to fight their way upstream? Well, I was right. They don't."

"Did you get yourself tested?"

"Yeah, and what they told me was that my sperm don't have mitochondria but I don't know mitochondria from hypochondria."

"Jeez, Russ, I'm sorry to hear it. For what it's worth, mitochondria are small organelles in the cytoplasm—the goop—inside a cell. They are absolutely essential to cells in converting stored energy to useful energy. Sperm cells are basically little more than a nucleus containing the man's half of the DNA, plus a little tail, a flagellum, that propels it through a nutrient solution in the man's seminal fluids. A whole bunch of mitochondria at the base of the tail provide the power. Without them, your armada is dead in the water."

"So when the guy at the lab looked at one of my sperms through the microscope, he saw a little disclaimer printed on the side: an asterisk followed by the words, 'batteries not included'."

Matt laughed again, his diaphragm tugging on his back ribs painfully. "Yeah, that's the essence of it."

"And I could pass this on if somehow I managed to have kids?"

"Actually, mitochondria are extragenetic, or at least have their own genetic inheritance system apart from the genes of the individual. They're passed from the parents to the offspring through the cytoplasm. In fact, they probably started out, back when Brahma was still stretching and yawning, as independent creatures, bacteria most likely, that were enslaved by eukaryotic cells, cells like ours which have a nucleus. But as far as passing the problem on to your kids, I don't really know the answer to that. It seems likely your sons might inherit the problem. What did the doctor tell you?"

"Pretty much the same thing but I didn't understand it as well as I do now. Thanks. The bottom line is, I'm not going to father children."

"Not without extraordinary measures. How's Sylvia taking this? She had her heart set on having kids, didn't she?"

"Oh, she still wants to have a child. But obviously it won't be mine."

"Well, artificial insemination might not be a bad option for you two."

"Maybe. Why? Are you interested in making a semen donation?"

This gave Matt pause. "I'm not sure mine is any better than yours at this point," he said. "Besides, you'd have to clear something like that with Deb. It's out of my hands."

"Well, speaking of out-of-hand semen, here's a left-handed twist to this whole situation. You remember that Sylvia was married before."

"To that painter, right? Guy Ellis. Killed in the Lockerbie crash, as I recall."

"Well, most of him, anyway. I found out Thursday night that before he went to Europe, he left a sample of his sperm frozen at a semen bank here in the city."

"Ah," Matt said, pondering it. "The iceman cometh."

Russ cracked up. "Thanks, Matt. That's the first laugh I've had in days. And just the other day I was feeling like Harry Hope too. Syl and I saw Kevin Spacey in that Broadway revival of 'Iceman' last spring. Anyway, what do you think?"

"About a revival of the Iceman?"

"Guy Ellis," Russ specified. "Not Eugene O'Neil."

"The sample's still viable, presumably," Matt said. "I mean, Ellis died years ago, right?"

"Sylvia told me later that the lab has kept samples for a couple of decades that still did the trick."

"Can she use this sample legally?"

"From what she told me, it's just considered property since it's not technically living tissue. And since she was his heir she can do with it what she wants."

"Still, ethically, it seems like pretty thin ice, using it without being able to obtain Ellis's consent. How do you feel about it?"

"To say I have mixed feelings would be a gross understatement. My manhood has suffered a swift kick to the scrotum so I'm still reeling a little from that. And I've always struggled with Sylvia's opinion of Ellis, which fell just short of him being able to walk on water. Further, as you probably remember, my first wife had someone else's kids. I grew pretty attached to them and felt like I was doing my part to bring them up right. But when push came to shove, the kids belonged with her and I could just go jump in the lake, which, since I'm *not* able to walk on water, felt pretty cold. I think if Sylvia and I used Ellis's sperm and then our marriage didn't work out for some reason, she would have to divide her loyalties between me and Ellis's baby and I know damn well who'll win that one too."

"I see what you mean. Well, certainly no one could blame you for feeling that way."

"And even if things do work out between us, what does that make me? Just a lazy-spermed old geezer baby-sitting someone else's kid. Hell, Ellis has been dead for eleven years and he's still got a better shot at getting Syl pregnant than I do."

"I doubt if Sylvia sees it that harshly. You're beating yourself up pretty badly over this."

Russ paused to calm down. "That's what May said too. And you're both right, I suppose. But you know, I'm not convinced that using Ellis's semen would be in Sylvia's best interest either. It's bound to resurrect some feelings for Ellis that should have been laid to rest years ago. And, well, she's never thrown it in my face but having kids was a big part of why we got married. I sometimes wonder if she wouldn't be better off starting fresh. And now I think she already may be looking. She hasn't spent much time around here over the weekend. She didn't come home at all Saturday night. Maybe I should just bow out gracefully and let her find someone, hopefully someone still breathing, who can give her a nice, straightforward shot at a normal family."

The phrase "bow out gracefully" struck a chord deep in Matt's psyche; he made a mental note to look into it later. "You know, Russ," he said, "I respect you greatly and what you just said is a noble sentiment. And you and I both know that all relationships eventually end. I mean, even the standard wedding vow acknowledges that in the phrase, 'Till death do us part,' and few marriages last even that long anymore."

"Which I assume represents step five."

"Sure. You meet someone, you're attracted, you date and fall in love, you get married or have some sort of relationship, and then, one way or another, you separate. It's the stuff most stories are made of. First, you have a work, say a novel. You present the characters and their situations, then you complicate their lives until they're a living hell. Everything you set up has to be played out, of course, and then you wrap it up with, hopefully, a satisfying resolution or denouement. It's not a coincidence that Shakespeare's plays come in five acts."

"You know, you've got this down. You ought to write up McCleary's Five Step Plan and send it to me. I'll try to include it in this book I'm working on."

"I don't think I'll have the time."

"In any case, are you saying that Sylvia and I should split up?"

"Not at all," Matt said. "I'm saying that separation is inevitable and you have to take advantage of whatever time you have together. How bad is your situation?"

"Bad. And a good share of it is my fault. I'm sure she must have been as let down as I was to find out I can't father a child. But then I screwed things up royally in the way I found out about that semen sample of Ellis's. Maybe I was suffering an overdose of testosterone but I got it in my head she was cheating on me so, under the impression that I was Sam Spade or something, I followed her to the semen lab and made a world-class fool of myself. I ended up saying some stupid hurtful things that she may never forgive."

"Well, was she going to the semen lab to use the sample?" Matt asked. "I think you'd be justified in being upset about that."

"That was the conclusion I jumped to as well," Russ said dolefully. "Actually, she was going to destroy it."

"Really? Why?"

"She thought it might be interfering with her ability to conceive—a long story involving a clairvoyant. But she also felt like she could never expect me to feel comfortable about her having her dead first husband's baby."

"Would that make you uncomfortable?"

"Hell, yes! Ellis is a tough enough act to follow as it is. But at the same time, I urged her not to destroy it. I mean, I don't want to have that karma, that responsibility, on my conscience. What if something happened to me? Or what if she and I split up?"

"Did you tell her that?"

"Yes. Which obviously didn't help matters. She took it to mean I had lost faith in our marriage."

"Have you?"

"No. I don't know. I don't think so. Oh, this is all so fucked up I don't know what I think anymore. But I'll tell you this: all this stuff is starting to get to me. I meant what I said about selling Tweak. Sometimes I think the best thing to do would be to get out of the City for a while. Sylvia could have a little space to think this stuff through and I could finish that philosophical book I mentioned earlier. Maybe spend the winter up at the farm while my folks are in San Diego."

"Wouldn't it be better to try to resolve your differences face to face?"

"We're not getting anywhere. We don't talk. She thinks I don't trust her and now she doesn't trust me. She thinks I'm having her followed. It seems like every day we spend together just makes things worse. The ghost of Guy Ellis haunts Grove Court more than ever."

"I can understand your jealousy of Ellis but I'm not sure you should be jealous of his sperm. After all, you know now that you're never going to father a child biologically. Any child you love and care about will have some other father."

"That's true."

"I'm pretty sure Sylvia didn't fall in love with the mitochondria in the flagella of your sperm. I remember when you wrote to tell me that you two were getting married, you sounded pretty excited about starting a family with her. And it seems like you two have enjoyed making whoopee ever since. You know, parenting is as much a social task as a genetic one."

"I remember I quoted 'Makin' Whoopee' on the back of the envelope," Russ reminisced. "'He's washing dishes and baby clothes. He's so ambitious, he even sews.'"

"That, I don't recall. I'd have to look it up."

Russ chuckled. "What do you mean?"

"Oh, I'm a saver. I've still got all the letters you've sent me, going all the way back to those first dark days of college."

"I had no idea," Russ marveled. "But knowing you, it makes sense. And of course they're all in alphabetical order too."

"Chronological."

"I don't suppose they include any of those discussions we had about the various realities."

"Beats me. I've just tossed them in a box. I haven't read that stuff since I got it."

"Why did you keep it?"

"I don't know. If memory serves, some of those letters were pretty entertaining. I guess I just figured, well, someday…"

"Well, someday, if you come across something relevant, could you send it to me?"

"I'll fax it."

"Matt, you are an amazing guy. You've given me a lot to think about, as usual. Whenever I need answers to life's tough problems I know I can count on you."

"I don't know about that."

"Come on. You must have a five step program for life itself, don't you?"

"Oh, that I have. But I'm afraid it's mostly about sex."

"Hit me."

"Okay. Life starts, of course, with conception. Then birth shoves you out into the world and your problems begin. Once you hit puberty your problems triple. After that come the reproductive years, which are hopefully productive years as well, even if you don't reproduce. Then the inevitable decline and death."

"You still won't concede a step six?"

"What, an afterlife?"

"Could happen."

"If so, I think it's probably back to step one in some form or another. In any case, I haven't made it through step five yet."

"Have you thought about how you'd want to die?"

"As a matter of fact, I have. But it doesn't look like it's going to happen that way."

"Why? How were you hoping to die?"

What Matt had in mind was "old" but that would raise more questions than it answered and he wasn't even sure it would be true. "Young," he decided to say, playing the middle-aged card instead, easing himself down at last into a chair. "How about you?"

"I want to die peacefully in my sleep, like my grandfather," Russ said. "Not screaming in terror, like the people who were riding with him in the car at the time."

Matt laughed, which hurt so much it brought tears to his eyes. "I told you before, don't make me laugh."

"I'll let you go, Matt," Russ said. "Thanks again for the input. You brought up some things I hadn't thought about."

"Give Sylvia my best."

"I wish. And I wish things weren't so messed up here. It would be great to see you again."

"Maybe another time."

o   o   o

Well, that tied up that loose end. He looked at the clock. Deb still wouldn't be home for a while. He was curious about a couple of things Russ had said but that required going upstairs.

He heaved himself out of the chair and walked across the tile of the kitchen floor to the stairs. Just lifting his own weight tested his endurance. Grabbing the oak hand rail, he pulled himself up, one by one, each carpeted step.

At the top was a landing with the bathroom to the left and the bedroom to the right. He took a left.

He sat down this time, his breathing soft and shallow, waiting for the urine to pry its way past his prostate, tapping his foot on the hard green-stone floor. When it finally came, the sharp twinge straightened his spine. He caught a glimpse of himself in the mirror. How long had he looked like this?

After he flushed he went to the sink and washed his hands and face. Maybe it was just the lights over the big mirror but he looked sallow and his eyes looked sunken. He checked in the little brass shaving/tweezing mirror on the accordion hinge too, with the same result. Well, nothing he could do about it.

He checked the medicine cabinet. Forgetting the hydrocodone hadn't been too bright but he wouldn't have taken that this early in the evening anyway. He settled for a couple of ibuprofen and went into the bedroom.

When Deb had retired five years ago, her Microsoft shares splitting faster than plutonium atoms, and they had decided not to build a new house, they debated getting a boat instead. They fantasized about calling at every port around the Sound, up and down the coast, sailing over the bounding main. But at that point the AIDS epidemic was gathering momentum like a chain reaction. With the promise of the drug cocktails still unfulfilled and early detection the only hope for slowing the momentum, Matt felt guilty about just shoving off and leaving Novagen in the lurch. And while Lyle Lovett made having a pony on a boat sound fanciful, in fact having a boat would take a lot of time away from Deb's still passionate love of horses.

So instead they designed the bedroom addition like a pilot house. A sturdy deck surrounded it on three sides with a teak rail and a short flagpole sticking jauntily out. Wide eaves and canted windows kept the view of the broad valley clear through anything short of a gale. Inside, the brass fixtures and dark green light shades continued the motif, with varnished tongue-in-groove oak beneath the broad windows and an old steamer trunk for a night stand. The windowless wall adjacent to the landing had a gas fireplace with Chihouly glass on the mantle and above it, lit by built-in spots, some of Matt's better photographic efforts, including the sunset reflection he'd captured at Sand Point in October. The house was situated far enough back on the lot and surrounded by such big trees that they had as much privacy as they'd have far out at sea and on those warm winter nights when the wind blew up from the southwest, they would open the windows and let the smell of the ocean fill the room. If you closed your eyes, the breeze shaking the raindrops from the leaves of the big-leaf maple hushed like the distant surf.

Matt went into the deep walk-in closet and looked up on the top shelf at the plastic crates of letters, pulling down the one marked "60s." He set it on the steamer trunk and switched on the gas fireplace to take the chill from the room. He kicked off his shoes, slipped off his damp-kneed pants, and lay on the soft copper-colored satin of the down comforter. Just taking the weight off his back helped and lying down didn't further goad his ass the way sitting had. He closed his eyes for a moment but knew he wouldn't sleep. With a sigh, he scooched over to pull the comforter over his bare legs and he propped himself up on the feather pillows.

Why *had* he kept all those letters over the years? Maybe just for a time like this. He had always assumed that, barring mountain lion attacks while hiking the Olympics, he'd be able to do this in the leisure of his declining years but the decline looked steeper than he anticipated. Oh well.

The early years of the '60s looked pretty thin, mostly cards from aging relatives and far-away older siblings. But the last few months of 1969, his freshman year at the University of Washington, more than made up the difference. Okay, September, let's see. Here's something relevant. The address on College meant this was the letter Russ and Jason wrote together during their brief stint as roommates in Boulder. His mind flooded with nostalgia when he saw the erasable typing paper torn from a tablet and the almost illegible output of the old manual typewriter with its worn ribbon. While Matt had always striven for formality in his correspondence, the rest were a shiftless lot, abandoning capitals and, in Russ's case, even correct spelling as well.

sept 11
matt old twig —
   greetings from the big rock. my roommate — that strapping lad
wise beyond his years, the inimitible (or some such word with
fewer eyes) jason christopher walker — slaves over the hot two-
burner on what? (i'll ask) spareribs and sourkraut. we live in
squalor here at the blue spruce but with luck we'll find
universital reality so colorful as not to notice the drab paint
and weedy grass.

$ $ $ $ $

   okay matt, russ insists i write part of this too.
   aced the first test for my dreaded calculus course today but the
pace we're on bodes ill for making that a habit. mental studs like
you waltz through this plebeian stuff i know, but mere mortals
struggle.
   "the only difference between life and death is that death lasts
a lot longer." can't remember who said this. probably somebody now
dead.
   as is the fabled ho chi minh, as you may have heard. so last
weekend the powers that may be and like-minded freaks like me
coagulated on the steps of the state capitol to try to get thru to
the powers that shouldn't be that now's the time to try something
other than napalm and agent orange to win the hearts and minds of
the vietnamese. the reply came through a bullhorn: this is our
capitol, not yours, so gedafugoutahere. we bid a tear(gas)ful
farewell.
   so there i stood with some other victims trying to counteract
the effects of the gas with the soothing smoke of a certain herb
when what before my wandering eyes should appear but the fabulous
a.t., known since we were boys as "man" but most decidedly a woman
now, and at her side the equally fabulous d.o. of jones park fame,
wearing a micro-mini that ended so far north you may have seen it
from seattle. i hazarded a guess to her that such attire must be
de rigor mortis at regis, to which she sniffed and said regis
sucks and men suck and the world sucks and manny told me later
that john had done the unthinkable (and i hate to think what that
is — she didn't say) but that deb has since forgiven him.
   anyway, the three of us, along with some bolder freaks i've
gotten to know (gary, igloo, little o, etc., otherwise known as
the mind machine) went over to burns park to get high and manny
and i sat and rapped while the others goofed on those weird
sculptures they have there. our minds (manny's and what was left
of mine) connected in ways hitherto unknown to me with persons of
the female persuasion, covering topics as far flung as the glen
canyon dam nation and crosby, stills, and nash, and alternate
forms of reality. needles to say (and it needles me still) i got
just to the point where i could almost summon up the foolhardiness
to propose i call her sometime when everybody else decided they
were bored. little o had a semi-date with a girl he met last time
at tulagi's (this club on the hill in boulder) and we were in his
car so i had to go.
   manny and deb thumbed their noses at us and walked off arm in
arm singing "show me the way to the next whiskey bar" and doing
leg kicks together, which would have been more than enough to make
me crazy, but then they went on to the line about "show me the way
to the next little girl, oh, don't ask why, oh, don't ask why." oh
my god. but see, in my book, whys are wise.

```
    russ points out that this started out as his letter. sorry.
write on, man.
                              J


    i'll write again but for now i've got to study for a german
test. don't melt up there. later.
                                  russ
```

Matt had remembered such a letter existed; he had forgotten its content almost entirely. What constituted "the unthinkable" Jason referred to? Despite John's faults, Deb had found him interesting for a while. What could she have found so egregious? Why had she forgiven him?

Well, in for a penny, in for a pound. He got out the next letter from Russ written September 19 from an address on Marine Street in Boulder. The reason for the new address came from this paragraph:

```
    so far germ. das grabben mein short herrs but philos. is
beautiful— the prof. is faaantAstic— also in the class is a cosmic
and i-catching classmate named prudence at whose svelte side i sit
even as i write. she looms large in my legend.
```

No mention of Jason. Russ later denied any sort of rift but Matt had trouble believing that Russ moved out so quickly just because he found living at Prudence's house preferable to the Blue Spruce.

But what Matt sought was in one of Jason's letters. Maybe this.

```
                              o/4
    clear eye,
    always glad to hear from you, though the missive was not
massive. you begged to be caught up on local events and i'm happy
to report that there's a bit of a gee in the gnus.
    saturday the whole mind machine dropped for the fabulous fall
ball. my brother, i know you are less than hep to better living
through chemistry but i'm here to testify that lysergic acid,
internalized, becomes far more than the sum of its parts, more
than a lonely proton searching out negativity. it burns through
all the rust and corrosion to reveal the bright shiny skeleton of
your soul. it literally opens your eyes and forces you to see
things in a different (and very psychedelic) light. unmerciful.
ineffable. an extreme other version of reality.
    i was completely tripped out. i mean, i peaked more than old zeb
pike ever peaked. they called it orange sunshine. i dropped only a
quarter of a barrel and still i could barely maintain. a group
called conal implosion started the ball and for me each note
sounded too intense to be just the chords of a song. every sound,
every impression seemed infinite in depth and duration. the byrds
played (and you know i know them like the back of my head) and i
couldn't keep track of what song they were singing. after the
moonrise (oh god! the whole crowd applauded — so big and orange it
scared me) somebody named buddy guy came on and got up on a
twenty-foot ladder still playing these killer blues riffs on his
guitar (which had a reeeeeally long coil cord) with a
handkerchief!
    so there i was (though i could hardly tell at the time) minding
my own mind when my shoulder became aware of tappage. i turned and
there stood manny, wearing this unbelievably brilliant sweater and
```

looking like the sweet fudge every good boy deserves. i recall
babbling and drooling like an idiot, though the mind machine
denies it. anyway, man, in the goodness of her heart, plopped
herself down and held my hand thru the rest of the concert, angel
of mercy that she is.

the concert lasted hours that felt like years. when at last
silence prevailed i got my tongue unwrapped from my eye teeth so i
could see what i was saying and i found myself talking to man like
a friend and looking at her like a fool. we talked of my problems
with russ and deb's problems with john, who evidently resents
being compared to you, my foul weather friend.

but then magically deb appeared from the great beyond and told
manny that bill had to get going. manny must have seen my heart
splatter all over my shoes because before i could flinch, she
planted this amazing kiss right on my lips. of course the rest of
the mind machine squawked about discrimination so she ended up
kissing the whole sick crew. i found myself back in the ranks of
the freaks and man and i were just friends again. she said she'd
see me at thanksgiving and asked me to write and i said yeah
write. then she and deb faded like just another hallucination into
the blackness of the night.

gee. now what?

j

Nothing like drugs to make the rocky road of love more stony. Matt had remembered
Jason's line about Deb comparing John to him but at the time he had no clue if Deb had
held him up as a good or a bad example. At that point, he hadn't spoken or written to John
since leaving Colorado, being disgusted with him for having such a casual attitude about
someone as desirable as Deb and disgusted with himself for lacking the temerity to do
anything about it.

The next letter came from Russ, which Matt just skimmed. Earlier Russ had asked
specifically about references to the various categories of realities and in this one he
compared the high from the famous Acapulco Gold to a form of alternate reality. Matt
shook his head in wonder at the prescience of the Piñon Nuts. At that point in the late '60s
academia still debated continental drift. Matt wouldn't hear anything that might provide a
scientific basis for alternate reality until physicists started talking about string theory and
time-reversible subatomic particle interactions in the 1980s. But the only reference in Russ's
letter linked AR to drugs, of doubtful relevance to Russ's writing project.

The next envelope had Jason's return address on College and might be the one Matt
sought. Sure enough, it contained not one but three letters. Might as well start with Jason's.

halloweeneen

matt,

wow. two whole pages out of the quiet one. thanks man. i needed
that.

glad you enjoyed my account of the fall ball. i've sent manny a
couple of weird letters wondering what the hey, so far unrequited.
as you've already noticed, i'm including with this a couple of
letters from john, of which more later.

it sounds like you're tearing the ivy off the walls up there at
you-dub-you. way to go. i continue to struggle. after that first
aced test in calculus, i've dropped from b to c to d. it doesn't
take higher math to project that curve.

my mind is elsewhere, i admit. there's a big war demonstration
nov. 15 in d.c. that i'd love to join so i could protest this
idiocy in vietnam. until people start to stand up and call

bullshit, nothing's ever going to change.

i just feel so helpless. you talked about the roller coaster of life having its ups and downs. that i can handle. you pays your money, you takes your ride. what bugs me is that the roller coaster goes in a circle. it's the same old shit over and over.

i hear you thinking, c'est la merde. nobody gets out of here with clean shoes. but why should i stand for it just because everyone else does? i want to get off this stupid ride. so what if the car hasn't come to a complete stop? if i feel like jumping, that's my business. there's got to be some alternative to going round and round.

i feel like everything's flying apart. sorry i come on so strong sometimes. i guess i must have pissed off russ pretty bad to make him move out after just a few weeks. not that i blame him, i guess. if the tables were turned i might have done the same thing. and i screwed up trying to get the argonauts back together. i beat a dead horse. now you and john don't even talk anymore.

which brings me to those letters of john's. i'm sending you the first one to prove a point. he wrote to me about manny coming up to the fall ball but she came and went by the time i got the letter. if i'd known about it in advance maybe i could have done things differently. i'm not sure what, but something.

the second letter includes the news that john and deb have split. i know you have your differences with john but i think you'd agree that deb is the best thing that's ever happened to him and it seems to me like he's willing to just chalk the whole thing up to experience.

so here's what i'm asking, and if you don't want to do this i'll understand. i thought maybe you could write to deb (just care of regis, denver, i guess) and put in a good word for john. i know she values your opinion— hell, i think she's just as convinced as everyone else that you will rule the universe someday. but i'm not sure this can wait indefinitely. women can change in a heartbeat. it might not hurt my cause with manny either. i think i'm getting tarred with the same brush.

anyway, it's up to you. just trying to do my part to keep things together. which brings me to thanksgiving. i assume we'll all be back in the springs. i have to spend the big day with the folks, our first holiday without steve. but maybe the next day, the 27th, i could get everybody to the house for a post-turkey dinner of some sort, along the lines of the breakfast we put together last summer. i miss you guys. since russ moved in with prudence, i hang around with the mind machine and they're okay but it's not the same. mostly i just hang with uncle willie. that never gets old.

god, this is a dreary fucking letter! i guess i'll put it out of my misery. see you in a few weeks.

jase

    Fishing for that brookie in Deb's shirt that day in Jones Park had long since soared up the charts of Matt's all-time favorite memories by the time he got this letter from Jason. That first drizzly fall in Seattle, Matt found it took every ounce of concentration to think of anything else *but* Deb. Performing some tricky titration in organic chemistry lab, part of his mind still fumbled with those damned hooks on her bikini top.

    He liked to blame John for moving in too quickly on her, not giving him a chance, but he knew better. John had actually done him a favor: even if John and Deb hadn't started dating, Matt knew in his heart of hearts that he would never have been able to work up the nerve to call her. He redirected his loathing from himself to John.

That fall Matt saw pretty girls everywhere in Seattle. He could appreciate their beauty but only in the critical way that a dedicated museum-goer looks at art: something to be appreciated, not possessed. Some part of his mind had locked onto Deb and he couldn't seem to shake it loose.

He sometimes fantasized about writing impassioned letters to her, baring his soul, confessing his love. Okay, the fantasies only lasted about fifteen seconds before the reality check kicked in but for Matt that represented a major loss of control.

And now Jason wanted him to write to Deb extolling John's best qualities. He had laughed out loud when he first read it. The more he thought about it, the more he resented Jason for even asking such a thing. But his impartiality overruled his jealousy. He owed it to Jason to hear him out. He read the first letter John had sent Jason in Boulder, dated September 26, and found this passage:

```
    ran into manny yesterday and she informed me that she and deb
are going to boulder for something called the fall ball, taking
place tomorrow, the fabled 27th. claimed steve miller and the
byrds are on the bill. how come you didn't tell me about it? how
come deb didn't tell me about it? how come you didn't ask manny,
for that matter? of course, by the time you read this we'll both
be s.o.l., won't we? i've got a swim meet anyway, but christ.
    c.c. is filled with a lot of prick teasers, as i'm sure boulder
must be, as i'm sure you've surmised. were it not for my long-held
longing to de-bra debra, i could gladly run amok among the coeds.
alas, no progress on either front. or back. deb and man keep ma
bell fat and sassy, so any false move on my part reverberates
almost on the instant up in denver in the hallowed halls of regis.
what's a fuckhead to do?
```

In the margin of the letter he had written "Nixon Wins. America Loses." On the back, in large rounded outline hand-lettering he'd written "Wood Ewe Bee Leave It? I'm Not Stoned." The whole thing seemed juvenile if somewhat amusing but it did nothing to inspire Matt to write in glowing phrases to Deb about John's character. He particularly resented John's open desire to sneak around behind Deb's back, either to date other girls or to unfasten her bra. But even as Matt nursed his righteous indignation, that other part of his own mind still fished in Deb's shirt.

Reluctantly, he read the other letter John wrote to Jason, which was haphazardly typed on an unbroken, rolled-up length of toilet paper, dated October 22. This passage caught his eye:

```
    sorry to hear of your school woes. so your psych prof proved
she's a psycho. whodathunkit? natheless, keep thine own head
together. there's no point in obsessing on this thing about steve.
what can you do? we are lower than a worm's navel, my bro. next
stop, underground.
    speaking of insane women (what else could justify this elegant
stationary?) and other addictions, i'm trying to kick the deb
o'donnell habit. she's made this easier by calling me a shithead
and refusing to speak to me. made some outrageous claim that i,
like all my ilk (that means you, my ilky friend, among others),
have the attention span of a gnat and...and...what was i saying?
anyway, i've decided to bow out gracefully before she kicks my
sorry ass into next week.
```

There was the phrase "bow out gracefully." Russ had used it on the phone earlier, talking about Sylvia. And, three decades earlier, when Matt saw it in John's letter, he changed his mind and decided to write to Deb after all.

In high school Matt had always felt less comfortable with John than he had with Jason or even with Russ. John, the athlete, the sosh, the ladies' man, represented everything Matt felt his own life lacked. Thus far he had envied John's easy brief liaisons with girls. Now that Deb had come into the picture, though, he began to resent John's cavalier attitude.

But the word "cavalier" could imply a certain nobility as well, a certain gentlemanly code of behavior, and the phrase "bow out gracefully" reminded Matt that better angels dwelt beneath John's sometimes rough exterior. Matt realized that his own jealousy tainted his view of John and that John had qualities that Deb might value but might have overlooked.

So Matt resolved to write her a letter. He broke, in disgust, five pencils writing three drafts until he got the wording right and then had to type it half a dozen times before producing a clear copy. He reintroduced himself to her in case she couldn't recall him immediately, diplomatically leaving aside all reference to trout. He discreetly mentioned that it had come to his attention that she and John had had a disagreement. He said he had known John since childhood and, despite a forgivable, perhaps even engaging, rambunctiousness, he had never known John to act out of selfish or improper motives. He found John witty, intelligent, hard-working, and decent and, taking into account his relative youth and the extraordinary times in which they all lived, someday John undoubtedly would become an outstanding member of the community and, implied if not stated, any woman's notion of a fine catch. He hoped he hadn't intruded and he signed the letter "Respectfully yours, Matthew McCleary."

His stomach in knots, he stamped the envelope and waited until the drizzle stopped to run the letter to the mailbox. As soon as the metal door clanged shut behind it, he felt a huge relief. Unburned bridges are useful only for retreat. Now that he had tacitly taken himself out of the running for Deb, maybe he could get on with his life and end this pointless obsession.

That lasted about two weeks. Then one rainy dark November afternoon (he still recalled it vividly), there, in with his *Scientific American*, his pizza ads, and his phone bill, lay an elegant white envelope from a Denver address.

It rocked him. He had written to Deb with the same star-struck admiration Judy Garland felt while writing, and singing "You Made Me Love You," to Clark Gable. A lowly fan sent off that sort of letter simply as a tribute, never expecting a reply.

He sat staring at the envelope for half an hour. The stationary was white-on-white, reminding him of ski tracks in fresh snow. The handwriting looked precise, confident, artistic. The stamp, anticipating the approaching holidays, depicted a golden angel in a medieval setting. He even caught the faintest hint of her cologne. He hated to tear the delicate paper, to destroy its perfection.

But, feeling like the rest of his life hung in the balance, he opened it anyway.

> Matt (she wrote in her fine hand),
> Fancy hearing from you! I must say, I was most surprised and pleased. And I know I can't match your precision with my chicken scratching but do bear with me. I type only when absolutely necessary. (All too often of late!)
> I can't tell you how much I appreciate your taking the time and effort to write those nice things about John. You truly are a great friend. I admit, I knew most of the fine qualities John possesses before reading your letter but you wrote of them so eloquently that I did reconsider my feelings and I did see him in a different light.
> Unfortunately, John and I are no longer seeing one another. I think the decision was

his as much as mine. We remain friends and I wish him all the best. I hope he feels the same.

By the way, he often spoke of you in the highest terms as well and left me baffled, I confess, while trying to explain some of your philosophical discussions. Perhaps you could enlighten me some time. It sounds more interesting than some of the subjects we're covering here at Regis.

My parents have promised me for months that we'd spend the long Thanksgiving weekend in Hawaii but my mother broke her leg skiing a couple of weeks ago so we'll be staying home after all. One small consolation will be spending time with Mandy again, who lives just three doors down. Do bop in.* Really. Otherwise I shall be most perturbed.

How are you enjoying Washington? With all the rain you get up there, the fishing must be great.

I better hit the books again. Thanks again for the nice letter.

> Love,
> Deb
>
> *even if not to be philosophical!

The news that John had indeed bowed out gracefully, the open invitation for Matt to visit her, the absurd implication that he would even consider "fishing" with anyone but her, and especially the "love" before her name created such a surge of joy and hope in him that tears came to his eyes.

Thirty years later, it still brought tears. Even alone, he felt so self-conscious that he hid his eyes in the crook of his left elbow, his shirt sleeve absorbing each weak drop. He lay that way awhile, the years, the pain, the dread falling away to let the love buoy him up.

o   o   o

He must have dozed off because the next thing he knew, Deb's cool fingers caressed his chin. He woke quickly, keeping his left arm bent so she wouldn't see the wet spots on his sleeve.

"Sorry, I didn't hear you come in," he said to her, sweeping away the cobwebs. "Have you been home long?"

"I just got here," she said, still smelling of damp woods and fresh air and alder smoke from the neighbor's chimney. "What are you up to?" She looked around at the letters strewn across the comforter.

He sat up guiltily, painfully, and began to restack the letters in the plastic crate. "Just rereading that first letter you wrote me," he said truthfully. "For the thousandth time." Only a slight exaggeration.

She rolled her eyes in disbelief but kissed him anyway. "I'm sorry I'm so late, sweetie. Traffic was a bear. My God, it's almost eight! Did I ruin dinner?"

"Oh, jeez! You know, I forgot all about it."

She smiled her wicked little smile. "As far as that goes," she said, slipping her cool hand under the comforter to unbutton his shirt, "we're technically in Playtime now anyway. Want to order a pizza?"

The nights they made love, the nights they marked on the calendar, had come to be known as Playtime, their own private version of alternate reality, with distinct rules and procedures. First and foremost, inhibitions were not allowed, with the concomitant corollary that imperfections, the few, thankfully, that either had, were not an excuse for shyness. Another rule was that Playtime should be as hassle-free as possible. That often meant ordering a pizza from the little carry-out shop a few blocks away, which recently had become a Playtime tradition in its own right when a very cute young lady named Stella started as the delivery driver. She generally arrived at their door in less than twenty minutes, always flustered, always courteous. Deb loved to make Matt give her a ten dollar tip because it made him blush to try to force it on her and it made Stella blush to accept it. And it was great pizza to boot.

So while Deb went to the bathroom, Matt pushed 12 on the speed dial and ordered a medium pepperoni, mushroom, and black olive with extra cheese.

"Was it Stella?" Deb called from the john after he hung up.

"Couldn't tell."

She came back out and dug through her purse for her wallet. "I hope it's not her night off," she said, pulling out three ten-dollar bills.

"Pizza's only like eleven," he pointed out.

"I know," she said. "Let's up the ante. I want to see if you can get her to take that much."

"No way."

"You'll give it or she'll take it?"

"Either."

"Come on, try," she urged him. "You both get so red in the face. There's no way you're going to get a withered old hag like me to blush like that." As she said it she kicked off her high heels into the walk-in closet and began unbuttoning her collarless electric-blue silk blouse.

He shook his head as he watched her. She still looked fantastic. He had never quite gotten used to it. In fact, one of his great pleasures was watching grown men, of all ages, regardless of how important they were or thought they were, turn into tongue-tied, bumbling idiots in her presence. Sure, her golden locks were shot with silver but the silver shone as brightly as the gold. Her active lifestyle and the fact that she hadn't borne children had preserved her figure. The laugh lines in the corners of her eyes simply drew attention to the unfaded brilliant sapphires and the few age creases on her upper lip disappeared when that mischievous smile broke out, which happened frequently and usually spelled trouble for the recipient of the smile, generally Matt.

She smiled now, the corners of her mouth curling lasciviously, as she saw him get out from under the comforter in just his shirt and jockeys. As he set the letter crate back on the top shelf, she pulled around the waistband of her pleated gray wool skirt and unbuttoned it.

"So, really, why were you looking at those old letters?" she asked, hanging up the skirt and blouse.

"Russ called this afternoon, mentioned a couple of things that we wrote to one another back then," he said, massaging with his thumbs the soft skin on her neck and shoulders.

"How's he doing?"

"So-so."

"Trouble at Tweak?"

"Among other things."

"Nothing serious, I hope," she said, looking up at him, concerned.

He kissed her forehead and went back to sit on the bed. "You'll be happy to hear that I can go with you to the Millennium Moonlight Ball on New Year's Eve after all."

"Oh no!" she said, coming into the bedroom and slipping out of her slip. "I mean, I'm glad we can be together but the Piñon Nuts Gathering fell through?"

"Looks like it."

"That's too bad! I know you were really looking forward to it. I was too and I wasn't even going." She put the slip in the hamper, lingering a moment to absorb the news, and then sat next to him on the bed. "What happened? Is Sylvia pregnant?"

"No. That's one of the problems. Russ found out he has immotile sperm."

"That'll do it," she said, pulling the comforter over their legs. Outside, the drizzle had turned to rain but inside, the fire warmed the room both physically and psychologically. "Is this a recent problem?"

"No, his bearings probably have factory defects. And he and Sylvia have already discussed using a sperm donor. Remember her first husband?"

"The one who was killed?"

"Evidently some of his sperm survived cryogenicly."

"But can they use it? I mean ethically?"

"Russ isn't sure he wants to. And I didn't know what to tell him. What do you think?"

She finished unbuttoning his shirt while she thought about it, her hand gliding over his chest and jockeys. "I think that would be asking a lot of Russ."

"Russ thinks so too."

"I guess it depends how badly Sylvia wants kids. I mean, you and I know there are worse things in life than not having kids. She's got her painting; it's not like she doesn't have any sort of creative outlet. And if they decide they do want a family, they could adopt or something. I mean, that little Cuban refugee boy whose mother was killed at sea might be available, if nothing else. It just seems a little odd to use something frozen from someone dead when there are so many living men on this planet who could contribute. All but one, anyway."

"Well, Russ can contribute but his sperm are just spectators."

"I meant you."

His heart sank. He didn't think she knew any more about his own health problems than he had told her, which so far amounted to little. "What do you mean?" he asked cautiously.

She slipped her fingers inside his jockey shorts and gently toyed with him. "I mean I'm saving what you've got for myself."

He did his best to hide his great relief but couldn't hide his growing interest. "Now you're talking."

She reached above his head. The padded headboard contained a stereo, individual reading lights, and several cubby holes, from one of which she pulled a pair of small blunt-tipped scissors. "Would you like to do the honors?"

Considering she had retired a wealthy woman and her personal fortune continued to grow, she had fairly simple, inexpensive tastes. Most of her extravagances went to others in the form of gifts and charities. But she dearly loved to shop for clothes and loved even more to shop for lingerie, indulging herself in the sheerest, the silkiest, the sexiest she could find.

But it soon became obvious that for every addition to her collection, something else had to go. Donating even the finest lingerie is impossible and wearing out even the most delicate items would take several lifetimes. So rather than simply throwing away the lingerie whose time had passed, they established the rule that during Playtime Matt could rend and twist her underwear to his heart's content, which they both found quite stimulating. In fact, she had made it a habit on Playday to put on her least favorite bra and panties in the morning, allowing her mind to drift at various times in the course of the day to the fine silky underthings she wore that wouldn't survive the night.

They found, however, that tearing even the sheerest teddy or the flimsiest panties could prove uncomfortable for her, though she gladly conceded, eventually even welcomed, the occasional scrape or scratch from impulsive passion. For that matter, just getting the things to tear daunted him at times. So Playtime now included using the scissors to cut the sturdiest parts of the fabrics so that when the time came he could quickly and easily strip away the last of her clothes and cavalierly toss them aside.

No rule governed where to cut the garments. One obvious option involved cutting holes that created access to her erogenous zones. Another option involved slicing almost, but not quite, all the way through a bra strap or the elastic strip on panties so that just a tug would sever it. She sometimes would wear these pre-stressed items for quite a while, relishing the feeling that her bra or panties or teddy literally hung by a thread. Once in a while, when she felt especially daring, she would venture out in public wearing pre-stressed lingerie under clothes she knew would conceal it should a strap or seam give way.

Tonight she wore black garterless stockings and lace-trimmed satin underwear the color of pomegranate juice. Matt, the more frugal of the two, still felt slight qualms about destroying such beautiful lingerie. Besides, he loved to watch her do the honors, at which she had become quite adept, knowing just how flimsy a bra strap could get and still support the weight of her breasts.

He kissed her shoulder as he watched her carefully whittle down the satin straps. He longed to bury his face in her soft cleavage but she decided, after slicing almost all the way through each side of her delicate panties, to remove the crotch as well, during which she inadvertently nicked her tender skin with the sharp edge of the scissors. He immediately rushed to the scene of the accident, kissing the imaginary wound, and then licking and nibbling and teasing until her back began to arch.

But before he could bring her to climax, his own back began to ache so badly from kneeling on the bed that he had to stop and lie down next to her.

When she noticed his clenched jaw and closed eyes, she asked, "Are you okay? How's your back?"

"Eehhh," he conceded.

"Are you sure you're up for this?"

He looked at her sarcastically. He was obviously up for this.

"I mean, what did Dr. Wu say?"

He had dreaded that question. All he really wanted was one more night without it, which didn't seem like too much to ask. "Can we talk about it later?" he asked her. "It's just so nice to see you back to your feisty self again. What happened?"

She eased her fingers back into his jockeys, careful not to scratch him with her nails, and began to stroke his erection. "Maybe that girl at Benaroya Hall did it," she said. "I looked at her—gorgeous, skinny, young—and I thought, I used to be all those things. But you know what she told me as she handed me the tickets? She said I had a beautiful aura."

"No doubt about that," he said, though at the moment her more substantial portions looked damned good too.

"Life's too short to waste it living in the past. And who knows what tomorrow will bring? If we don't enjoy ourselves now…"

"I wholeheartedly agree," he said, grabbing the bra at her sternum and twisting it, stretching the enfeebled straps.

"Oh, no, you don't, buster," she said, pulling his hand away. "Not till I get you out of your shorts." She grabbed the scissors again and dived under the covers, the cold hard metal all too close to his erection.

Apart from the Lorena Bobbitt overtones of the situation, Matt, like many men, had always worn his shorts well into the rag stage. This had never been part of the Playtime deal before.

"Don't you dare!" he exclaimed as she put the scissors to the waistband.

"What's right for the goose," she said, a dangerous premise considering her barely-covered ass was pointed right at him.

A few quick snips and he felt one side of the jockeys go limp. "Oh, great," he said, slapping her bottom as she severed the other side as well and pulled the cotton briefs out from under him. "I hope you're satisfied." He felt his entire body stiffen as her tongue slithered along his exposed shaft.

But she stopped even sooner than he had. "Satisfied?" she said contemptuously. "Not even!" She pulled his ruined briefs from under the comforter and held them up like a trophy. "The question is, what to do with these?"

"Run 'em up the flagpole, see if anybody salutes?" he said facetiously.

She got that gleam in her eye.

"No," he said, in disbelief that he had suggested such a thing.

But already it was too late. She sprang from the bed and went to the door that led to the dark deck.

"You'll freeze to death!" he cried.

She walked boldly out into the rain and fumbled with the rope on the little flagpole. By the time she managed to tie the underwear around the rope and run it up to the end, her silvery hair began to sag and her own scant underwear, as well as her very naked skin, glistened.

He shook his head and laughed. She had clearly lost her mind but obviously not her youthful exuberance.

But with a frightened squeal, she dashed back in and slammed the door, turning around and whispering melodramatically, "Stella!" Sure enough, headlights bumped slowly up the long drive.

"Well, I can't go down there," he said, gesturing at his lack of underwear and the tumescence that had returned at the sight of Deb's goose-bumped skin and the rigid nipples in her bra.

"I'm soaking wet!" she rejoined. "Just put on your pants and shirt."

"Oh, for Pete's sake," he acquiesced, getting up and pulling on his trousers. "Well, I'm not giving her a $20 tip. You couldn't see her blush from up here anyway."

"But you have to!" she insisted, walking to the bed and pressing the money into his pants pocket. "You can describe her reaction to me."

The doorbell rang.

"This was your idea," he said. He looked at her shivering in her mutilated underwear. "I know," he said, inspired. "You're coming with me. You can listen."

He went to her and firmly grabbed the hair on the back of her head. Despite her protestations, he pushed her ahead of him out of the bedroom and down the stairs.

Beside the heavy oak front door was a large coat closet with louvered doors that let damp coats dry.

"We can't do this!" she insisted in a whisper as he forced her into the closet. "What if we get caught?"

"Shh!" he said, kissing her and then gently closing the door when she was inside. "Just don't make a sound and she'll never know."

He opened the door and there stood Stella with the bulky pizza warmer. She looked about 20, with straight black hair, eyes the color of bittersweet chocolate, and pouty lips that broke into a hesitant smile when she saw him.

"Hi, Mr. McCleary," she said nervously, opening the warmer. "Here's your pizza."

"Hi, Stella," he said, taking the warm box from her and setting it on a small table next to the door. "How are you?"

"I'm doing great!" she said, but got right down to business. "That'll be $11.35."

He reached into his pocket for the three tens but before taking them out, he said, for Deb's benefit, "Good Lord, you're soaked! You're going to freeze to death standing out in the rain like that."

"Oh, I'm fine, really," Stella said. "It feels good to get out of the shop."

"Well, I think you deserve a little extra for your trouble," he told her, handing her the three tens.

She looked at them and then quickly back at him. "Oh, Mr. McCleary, I really can't accept that. You're usually too generous as it is." She handed back one ten and started to make change.

"At least keep the change," he insisted, and then inspiration struck again. "Oh, and I know what. My wife's got an old bumbershoot. Why don't you take it so you can stay dry on your deliveries?"

She reluctantly agreed so he opened the closet door wide enough to get to the umbrella but not wide enough for Stella to see inside. Deb stood dumbstruck, her eyes terrified but her smile unabated. Matt ran his hand down her silky flesh before he grabbed the umbrella, then he hooked her left bra strap with the handle.

"Oops, it's caught on something," he said to Stella through the louvered door.

He tugged on the strap. It easily broke and the cup fell away from Deb's breast. She opened her mouth in outrage but didn't make a sound.

"There you go," he said to Stella, handing her the umbrella. "Enjoy it with my wife's compliments."

"Well, thank you," Stella said to him, blushing and popping the umbrella open. "You folks are always so nice to me."

"We just wish we could do more."

He watched her walk to the car, turn it around, and head back down the drive.

"She does have a nice tush," he said, closing the front door and opening the closet.

"I can't believe you did that!" Deb said, her arms akimbo, the broken bra strap hanging down. "I loved that umbrella! And you just give it away to the first little cutie who comes along and then you leave me standing here with my bra halfway off."

"Oh, I'm sorry," he said, jerking the other bra strap till it broke as well and pulling the satin down to set free her outstanding breasts. "Are you shivering or quivering?"

"You're so mean to me!" she said, sucking in her lower lip, coming to him to let him enfold her in his arms. "Why do I love you so much?"

"Because you know what's good for you," he said in his best approximation of machismo. "Now go back up there to that bed and get ready to be punished for the naughty girl that you are."

He handed her the pizza, turned her around, and pushed her toward the stairs, then grabbed a bottle of Chianti and followed. She stopped on the bottom step and defiantly stuck out her tush. He grabbed her panties and she struggled forward until they broke, then she skipped up the stairs. He followed, shoving the panties in his pocket and gazing up at her, naked but for the black stockings and the strap of elastic of the bra.

By the time he struggled up to the bathroom, once again took a slow excruciating leak, and went back into the bedroom, she had snuggled between the sheets and pulled the covers up to the bridge of her nose. Mischief filled her eyes as she watched him strip off his pants and shirt.

The pizza box stood open, a couple of bites missing from one piece . She had also picked off some of the pepperoni. He helped himself to a wedge and stood by the bed, naked now himself, contemplating his next move.

"You're shameless, you know," he pointed out to her. "Standing there almost naked just inches away from that unsuspecting young lady."

"You made me!" she protested weakly. "It was just so terrifying, so degrading, so… mmm." She quivered again. "What's gotten into you tonight? I'm usually the one to come up with things like that."

"What you said before made a lot of sense," he said, washing down the pizza with a swig of the Chianti she had poured into a tumbler. "Who knows what tomorrow will bring? Besides, you're flying the heavy-weather pennant out there." He gestured with the pizza at his underwear dripping from the flagpole. "So you just better hang on. It's going to be a bumpy night."

He took another bite then tossed the pizza back into the box and crawled into bed next to her. Whether it was the wine, or the short nap, or just the comfort of having her near and happy, he felt much better than he had earlier. He kissed her on the lips, tenderly at first. Neither could long resist the excitement of the moment, though, and soon their mouths silently confessed to one another the secret pent-up yearnings they'd been feeling the last few weeks.

But despite the warmth of the kiss, she still prudishly held her bra in place with both hands. "What is this?" he demanded, pulling away the bedclothes. "I thought I got rid of that bra."

"Do you like pasties?" she asked.

"Meat pies?" he wondered, looking at her naked, dry, but still goose-bumped torso.

She giggled and shivered. "No, no—although, well, that too, I suppose. I mean pasties, those things strippers wear on their boobs."

He shrugged, bewildered.

"Well, maybe you'll like these," she said. She pulled the bra cups from her breasts to reveal a round slice of pepperoni neatly covering each areola, with improvised tassels made from long strings of mozzarella.

"Oh, I definitely like those," he said, scooching down to lift the cheese with his tongue. He slurped it up and then nipped at the pepperoni. She put her arms above her head and closed her eyes. He finished the cheese and both slices of meat but didn't stop, licking the sauce from her erect nipples and then taking her trembling breasts into his mouth to make sure he hadn't missed anything. She murmured her pleasure and he echoed it.

Her hands fumbled on the headboard, finally finding the cordless phone which she handed to him.

"What's this?" he asked.

"Why don't you tell Stella how much you're enjoying the pizza?" she suggested, pressing 12 on the speed-dial.

His hand had crept down across her belly and his middle finger sought the tiny beacon of her clitoris. The last few years, as her menopause progressed, she often lacked the fluidity of her younger days but tonight it felt like the dam had burst. "Maybe you should tell her yourself," he suggested.

She quickly hung up the phone.

He continued to toy with this gushing reception he'd received. "Is this just the rainwater from before?" he asked, spreading the juices around.

She shook her head.

"Motion lotion?" to which they had been forced to resort on occasion.

She shook her head again.

"Well, maybe we'd just better probe into this situation," he decided, rolling onto her, lingering right at the brink. "Discover the cause of this phenomenon."

She put her arms around his back and pulled him close, closer than close. He kissed her face all over, working his way down to the side of her slender up-turned neck, pretending to bite, growling ferally. She went limp at the sensation but then began to return each of his thrusts with interest.

But before long his back betrayed him again. He slowed, then stopped, pulling the bedclothes away so he could roll them over, still joined.

Once on top, she knelt, her knees popping. She scrutinized his face. "Are you okay, hon?"

He closed his eyes. "Never better," he replied, not completely lying. "I'm just dying to feel one of your big O's. I feel like I owe you an O."

"You don't owe me a thing," she maintained, gradually starting up again, her belly-dancing motions making an art of what easily could be merely physical. "If anything, I owe you about 10,000 orgasms."

"Regardless," he said, luxuriating in her subtle but irresistible manipulations, "I'm not doing all the work tonight." Her severed bra straps tickled his belly.

"Are you sure you want to leave it up to me?" she asked, slowing the pace but increasing the intensity. "I'm liable to work you to death."

He opened his eyes to see the intensity of her expression as she approached the summit. "'A consummation devoutly to be wished'," he said. Trying not to distract her, he unfastened the useless bra and tossed it aside, thirty years of practice making the unhooking easy. He cupped her breasts in his hands to feel the way they shimmied and shook as she grew closer to climax.

As compatible as they were, they each found it easier to achieve orgasm while on top, controlling the pace, guiding the motion. Nevertheless, tonight, when he felt her tense, inside and out, as she approached her climax, he followed right on her heels.

But as she plunged over the precipice and yielded to the ecstasy, the realization overwhelmed him that everything he had ever wanted, everything that had ever mattered to him, was wrapped up in this one exquisite package. He had long ago reconciled himself to the idea that death would sweep away all the forgettable substance of the world. But this beautiful spark, his *raison d'être*… How could he say good-bye to this?

The tension, the constriction, the welling-up of his own orgasm subsided and the tension, the constriction, the welling-up of tears in his throat and in his eyes prevailed. He felt as though the trap-door he'd been standing on all day had dropped open, leaving him tumbling helplessly down the dank well of despair. With a rush as undeniable as orgasm, the tears overtook him and he began to cry.

Still in the throes of her climax, Deb fell onto his chest and put her arms around him, straightening her legs. Instinctively she held him tight and rocked back and forth gently.

Deb had never seen him cry. He had only cried twice since he became a man. The first time, in fact, may have marked the end of his boyhood. Jogging down the trail from Jones Park the morning Jason disappeared, he'd been forced to slow to a walk because the tears, as much from frustration as grief, blurred his vision. The second time had happened just three years ago, a year after his father passed away. He'd gone camping in the Stewart Range, in the eastern Cascades. The night had been cold and damp so he'd built a fire. The next morning he used his raccoon-proof paint tub to rehabilitate the fire ring, spreading the ashes around the forest floor. He stopped at the stream to wash out the tub and somehow the strewing of the ashes brought home to him that his father truly had departed and the childish tears unmanned him.

He hoped that the first few salty tears would get it all out of his system but then convulsive sobs began to rock his frame. Tears ran down into his ears and once again he put his left arm over his eyes.

Deb propped herself up. "Oh, baby, what is it?" she asked him and he could hear tears in her voice as well.

He wanted to tell her that he loved her, that she meant all the world to him, but he couldn't get the words out.

"Did I hurt you?" she asked, taking her weight off of him.

He still couldn't speak so he shook his head no. She rolled off anyway, just in case.

Weeping is a hallmark of humanity and carries with it poignancy and even a certain dignity. He felt himself carried helplessly beyond weeping into bawling, his reddened eyes puffy and saturated, slobber in the corners of his mouth, the sloppy goo that would be coming out his nose were he upright flowing instead down the back of his throat. He was horrified at what she must think of him to see him this way and that just made matters worse, the sobs racking him so hard he had to roll away from her onto his side. To top it all off, the pressure from his diaphragm on his back ribs hurt like hell.

Deb stroked his arm helplessly, then cuddled up behind him, her cheek against his back.

At last the pain made the bawling unbearable and his sobs subsided. He rolled back toward her and lay his head on her shoulder. But he soon realized that the various fluids covering his face would get all over her so he rolled back onto his back, covering his eyes with his arm again.

"Can you talk about it?" she asked gently.

He swallowed and cleared his throat. "I just love you," he croaked, "more than… anything. More than life."

She leaned over and kissed his cheek. "I love you too," she told him. "But you've loved me for over thirty years and it never made you cry before." She dabbed the sheet against his wet cheek. "Can I get you something? A tissue? How about a washcloth?"

He nodded gratefully, hoping he could collect himself while she was in the bathroom. He had hoped to spare her this ugly scene. So much for hope.

When she came back in, he pulled himself upright and she straightened the pillows behind his back. He wiped his face with the washcloth while she got back in bed.

"In one of the letters that I read this afternoon," he said, not looking at her, "Jason wrote me that you and John had had an argument, that he had done 'the unthinkable.' Do you know what he was talking about?"

He could feel her looking at him perplexed. "This is what you want to talk about?" When he just shrugged, she thought about it. "Oh, honey, that's so long ago. I remember we had some arguments, at least I remember one in particular, but I don't remember anything that would qualify as 'unthinkable.'"

"That may have been Manny's word. What was the argument about?"

"I don't know. Who remembers what arguments are about thirty years later? I think I— You remember that John was pretty much a party animal back then, right? As I recall, before I went up to Regis he and I got into it about some of the things he was doing: drinking, smoking, doing drugs, chasing other girls. Well, I confronted him about it, asked why he felt the need to do things like that."

"What did he say?"

"Oh, he gave me some cockamamie excuse that he just couldn't help himself, that he was basically just too weak to do anything about it."

Matt was afraid it was something like that. He carefully folded the washcloth and set it on the steamer trunk beside the bed. When he sat back up, she tried to hug him around the waist, which hurt so much he winced.

She took her hands away but pointedly asked, "So what did Dr. Wu tell you?"

There's no putting it off anymore, he thought. No dignity left to lose. Might as well get it over with. "The second PSA test they ran, the one in July, was a false negative," he said. "The first one was right."

"Are they sure?"

"They ran another this time, plus a prostatic acid phosphate test. Both came back positive. Very positive."

"What does 'very positive' mean?"

"It means I definitely have prostate cancer," he said numbly. "The only question is the severity."

"Oh, God, honey, no!" she cried, putting her arm tenderly around his chest this time to hug him. "No wonder you're upset! Why didn't you tell me sooner?"

"I just found out today."

"I mean earlier, like when I called this afternoon. Or is this one of those Macho Man things?"

"To tell you the truth," he said, looking into her frightened eyes, "I kind of blocked it out myself. I don't think the word 'cancer' has crossed my mind since I left Wu's office."

"Well, what else did you find out?"

"Not that much. Like I said, they have to figure out what kind of cancer it is. I mean, most men, if they live long enough, get prostate cancer. Sometimes it's not even treated right away, they just do what's called 'watchful waiting,' where they keep an eye on it. And then there are a bunch of treatment options as well."

"When are they going to know about yours?"

"Wu took a sample for a biopsy today," he said, changing his position uncomfortably at the memory. "Did what's called a fine needle aspiration. That was the pain in the ass I mentioned on the phone."

"He did it himself?"

"Simple enough procedure. He said he's done lots of assholes and he's never wrecked 'em."

"At least he's able to joke about it. Isn't that a good sign?"

It was his turn to hold her hand in both of his. "You didn't see the look on his face after he palpated my prostate. Honey, he was shook. I've never seen him like that. He said he couldn't believe he didn't feel anything when he did the DRE in July."

"So he and the blood lab both missed it?"

"He was remarkably frank about it. He said you might be able to press a malpractice lawsuit. Not so much against him, since DREs are pretty crude, but against the lab for the false negative. He did offer to cover any expenses the insurance doesn't, which I thought was quite a decent thing."

"What do you mean, *I* might be able to sue?" she asked suspiciously.

It had slipped out. He had his own suspicions about the severity of the cancer, from Wu's reaction, from what he knew of this condition and of science in general, from how he felt. But until anything was confirmed, he had intended to paint the brightest picture possible. This would require some fast footwork now.

"I meant that you may have to handle things like that because I may be undergoing treatments."

"Well, you know money's no object here," she said, her voice taking on the assertive tone she used in business. "You're going to have whatever it takes to get past this. What kind of treatments are we talking about?"

"It depends on the cancer," he said, losing himself in the matter-of-fact language of science, forgetting for the moment that he would be the patient. "There are some promising new immunotherapies. There's good old radiation, including interstitial, where they insert radioactive isotopes right into the prostate itself. And there's always surgery, like a TURP, or even a prostatectomy."

"What's a TURP?"

"Transurethral resection of the prostate. Kind of a roto-rooter thing."

"All of which have side effects," she assumed, to which he nodded. "Including sexual," to which he nodded again, looking down. She took a deep breath. "Well, whatever it takes. How soon will we have to start?"

"It'll depend on the stage of the cancer."

"Months? Years?"

"It's impossible to say. He also mentioned a new drug being developed called endostatin which has actually killed human prostate tumors in mice. They're doing clinical trials at the Dana-Farber Cancer Institute in Boston to determine safe dosages and Wu said he might be able to get me in."

"When would that start?"

"Probably right away," he said. "The first round would be a six-week course."

"So you'd have to go to Boston?"

"If I'm chosen to participate. If I am, Wu said I might be able to come home before the holidays. But maybe it's just as well the Piñon Nuts Gathering fell through."

She stared pensively at the fire. "That really is a shame."

"I got an interesting bit of news from Russ, incidentally. You know May, Amanda's daughter?"

"Of course."

"She called Russ a few days ago. I guess she and John went for a hike in Estes and when they got back, Susan caught them together and assumed the worst."

Deb looked startled. "Are they having an affair?"

"Russ asked May the same thing and she denied it. But it looks like John may be single again." He tried to sound casual about it but could feel her eyes boring into his.

"Wait. Is this somehow related to your asking me about that argument I had with him back in college?"

He shrugged. "I suppose he's changed a lot since those days, that's all."

"So?"

He looked into her beautiful eyes. "So you could do worse."

"What are you saying?" she asked, becoming exasperated.

"Well, I've always known that I wasn't necessarily your first choice. Maybe you should consider other options."

"Have you lost your mind?" she exclaimed, hitting him on the shoulder. "How can you even suggest such a thing? Other options!?" She hit him again.

Matt hadn't expected this reaction. He felt like he was just looking out for her best interests, the way he had always done. "I just hate to put you through all this, honey. I wouldn't blame you a bit."

"I can't believe what I'm hearing!" she said, her eyes flashing, completely angry now. "Oh, I could just..." She put her hands to his throat symbolically.

He closed his eyes. "Oh, baby, please do. God, I don't want to die this way. I always hoped I would just disappear up in the mountains sometime, spare you all this grief."

"So if you disappeared up in the mountains, I wouldn't grieve?" she asked, relaxing her grip on his throat. "That's not what you're afraid of. You're afraid I'll see you weak and vulnerable. You're afraid someone will have to take care of you."

That hit the nail on the head. "You're right. I am weak. Hell, I'm rotten to the core. Why stick around for that? Why watch?"

Her choke-hold became an embrace, her anger, tears. "You don't get it, do you? Maybe I just haven't said it enough, said it right. Matt McCleary, you are strongest man—no, person —I've ever known. I don't know what I would have done without you. You're the best thing that's ever happened to me. You know that aura the girl at Benaroya admired? You put that there."

"Maybe I helped keep it there," he conceded, "but it was there all along."

"You know, I've had as many doubts in my life as anyone, I suppose. But one thing I've never doubted since that day in Jones Park when we first met, is that I am loved. That's the greatest gift life can hold. And if I haven't made you feel that way, then I'm a fool and I'm sorry."

"I was starting to have my doubts these last few months," he admitted. "What's been bothering you?"

She looked away. "I guess I just wasn't prepared for Amanda's death. I just can't believe the last time we talked turned out to be a huge argument."

"You know, Russ and John are convinced that May is Jason's daughter. Russ told me this afternoon that John saw the way she holds a pen."

She looked back at him again, her eyes brimming with tears. "She is Jason's daughter. I know she is. Amanda told me."

"So you knew?" he asked. "Why didn't you tell me?"

"I swore to Mandy that I would never tell anyone, even May. But now, with Mandy gone…"

"That was one of the main things we were going to discuss at the Piñon Nuts Gathering."

"I know. I was planning to tell you."

"When?"

"Before you left. When you needed to know. Some things are awfully difficult to talk about. When were you planning to tell me about your cancer?"

He kissed her. "Tomorrow," he said. "After Playtime."

"Oh, I'm so sorry!" she said, plastering his face with kisses. "We didn't finish, did we? That is, you didn't…"

"But what are we going to do about May?"

"May's a big girl. She can take care of herself now. We'll figure out some way of telling her down the road. I'm more concerned about you. I mean, are you up to any more Playtime tonight? I don't want to hurt you."

"We may have to take it a little easy," he admitted. "But I could sure use some tenderness. We can start dealing with all this other crap tomorrow. For tonight, let's let Playtime be the only thing that matters. Just one more night. Please?"

"Playtime goes on as long as you like," she said, rubbing her warm body against his. "And I already had my fun. I'm all yours now. You can do anything you want."

"In my dreams," he said.

But his dreams were never that good.

...O...O...O...

"Once upon a time" begins many a good story. It implies that the story happened sometime in the indefinite past. The "one" portion of "once" specifies that it happened one particular time, lending credence to the story. It focuses attention on one particular event as well. We don't want to know about those years Cinderella spent picking lentils from the ashes, we want to hear about the Ball, the transformative event.

The problem out here in the real world is to pick the transformative lentils from the ashes of humdrum existence. "Once" conveys that transformative power when used as a conjunction: "Once I write The Great American Novel, I can live on Easy Street." (As long as the rent on Easy Street is only $27, of course.)

Supplementing my meager income as a musician with a variety of temporary, normal jobs has meant that I've done a lot of things once. But those experiences never seem transformative. Each sounds like an unfinished sentence: Once I started my own landscaping business... Once I learned how to drive a dump truck... Once I got a job as a chef... Once I inventoried a million fish hooks...Once I performed the Antelope Dance...

Anyone who has seen me dance—and there aren't many who have—would want me to explain that last one. I didn't get paid for the Antelope Dance. I just had to do it.

I drove up into the Beartooth Mountains near Yellowstone once, intending to car camp for the night. I didn't go under the best circumstances: I had wrenched my knee, my back had gone out in a blaze of spasms, I had lost my voice from singing too much, a post-operative infection from a hernia operation felt like a red-hot poker jammed into my side, and it rained. Even though the only home I had to go home to was a dingy dump of an apartment in a town I didn't know, I decided to forego camping and go home.

The first part of the drive home I enjoyed. My circle route took me over the Chief Joseph Highway and I've felt a kinship with the Nez Perce story for decades. The weather cleared, too, and the evening turned pleasant. But my body yearned for the bed, so I looked forward to getting off the winding mountain road and back onto the highway so that I could make better time.

As the last light lingered on the open plain and I got up to highway speed, I looked around and thought, "Gee, this is classic antelope country. I'm surprised I haven't seen any."

That thought still echoed in my mind when a pronghorn bounded from the tall roadside weeds and into the path of my car. I barely had time to jam on the brakes before I hit it, killing it instantly. The body rolled and tumbled in a cloud of tan hair that the pavement ripped from the skin. It skidded to a stop before I did, ending up in the other lane of the highway.

I pulled to the side of the road, sick at heart. I had always prided myself in not having taken a life in that senseless way. I've hit my share of ground squirrels and birds, I suppose, but a pronghorn is in a different category. For one thing, if it had bounded up over the hood I might have been killed too. Besides, I have a particular fondness for the uncommon pronghorn, the only antelope on the North American continent. I admire their scrappy leanness and bounding grace.

Shaking, I backed up the car and got out. In the headlights I could see the vacant stare in the antelope's black eye and the pool of blood and viscera oozing from the still, graceful form. Heaving a sigh, I grabbed the hoof and pulled the body off the road and down into the weeds for the scavengers. And then I drove on. What else could I do?

But it didn't seem enough. I felt my heart had to express something. So once—just once, thankfully—I performed the Antelope Dance.

As I said before, I'm not much of a dancer. Nor do I have any idea how any native culture would deal with this situation. In modern American culture, we certainly don't mourn road kill. Hallmark doesn't make a "Sorry You Ran Over That Woodchuck" sympathy card. So I improvised.

Squatting on the floor, I imagined myself as a new-born antelope lying in the crunchy grass of the windy prairie. Then I rose up and gathered the earth's abundance, feeling the warm sun on my back and the wind in my little horns, prancing with joy at the nimbleness of my sturdy legs, slaking my thirst at the clear brook, mating, bearing young—making up a little move for each of these things. I danced in a circle and sang a tuneless chant, not a song with words but a song with feeling. It was good and I felt better.

Death is, I suppose, the ultimate example of the transformative event. Since most people die just once, no one has much experience at it. It's almost always improvised and too often graceless. Maybe that's why we like to do it alone or with just a few close friends or family members on hand, in case we mess it up and embarrass ourselves.

November 24, 1999

May slumps uncomfortably in the chair. She thinks she may have dozed off.

Her mother's voice comes from upstairs: "Not now. May's in her room."

"So?" her father says. "Your sweet baby sure ain't no virgin. If she can't get her ass to school, next stop for the little bitch is juvey." At least it sounds like Bill's voice, slurred from drinking.

"Such a bastard!" her mother says.

"You would know," he retorts snottily. "God knows I've had my doubts about her."

"Take your hands off of me!" Shrill, frightened.

"She may not be my daughter but you're still my wife."

May can hear the slap, the heavy thuds as their bodies hit the floor.

"Get off me, you pig!"

"Once more, for old times' sake."

"I'd rather die."

Stalemate.

Silence.

Dread.

Revulsion.

The voice startles her: "May?" It sounds like Paco.

She cringes. Maybe if she just stays quiet, just goes along with it, this won't last long.

"May?"

No, that's not Paco's lilting insinuation. It's husky and low and intimate. That's Marcus's voice. Her heart skips. She touches the wiry black hairs on the ebony skin of his chest. His cologne overpowers her. She melts into his strong arms.

"Mandy?"

Her head had drooped too far and all her muscles jumped, yanking her back to reality. The dream fled as she collected herself. Her hand felt wet where her lips had rested. She wiped it on her jeans and looked around guiltily.

Nana's room was on the west side of Penrose Hospital and out the dark window May could see the first pink alpen-glow of dawn on the snowy slopes of Pikes Peak. She had slept at least a couple of hours sitting with her feet curled beneath her in the sticky vinyl-upholstered armchair next to Nana's bed. One of the nurses must have covered her with the blue blanket. They also had replaced Nana's saline bag on the I.V. tree, emptied the plastic bedpan where her catheter drained, and refilled the water pitcher. Nana's slight frame lay neatly tucked under the sheets and covers. Her silver hair sprawled uncharacteristically disheveled on the pillows and her face looked gaunt and troubled.

"Mandy!" she cried weakly but urgently. "Don't cry, child."

May threw off the blue blanket and sat next to her grandmother on the bed. "Nana, it's me. I'm right here."

Nana grew very still at the sound of her voice but she didn't open her eyes. She became so still, in fact, that May had begun to worry that she had stopped breathing. But then Nana began to sing in a voice thin, high, and childlike:

> Hush, little baby, don't you cry
> Fly like a bird into the evening sky.
> Up into the pretty stars you go
> Leave all your troubles far below.
>
> Sleep, little baby, through the night
> The world looks better in the morning light.
> Listen to the pretty bird that sings
> She lets the angels guide her wings.

"That's pretty, Nana," May said, taking Nana's hand, which felt cold and bony and dry. "What's it called?"

"You rest now, honey," Nana whispered reassuringly. "Everything's going to be all right."

"I slept a little," May told her. "I had a dream about Mom."

"Your mama won't leave you." She gripped May's hand tightly, harder than May thought she could, considering her condition.

May smiled at the irony of Nana's thinking she was May's mother instead of her grandmother. "I won't ever leave you either, Nana. For half my life, you've been my guardian angel. Now it's my turn to take care of you."

"It's going to be fine, honey," Nana said, still without opening her eyes. "That El Paso boy's got you all in a tizzy. But by next week you'll forget all about him."

May was confused. "What El Paso boy?" she asked. Colorado Springs is in El Paso County but she had never heard anyone use that phrase.

Nana's eyes drifted open briefly but May couldn't tell if any recognition dawned before they closed again. "I'm so sorry, honey. Don't listen to me. You can be with anyone you choose."

"I'm with my favorite person right now," May assured her, patting the age-spotted hand.

"Try again. You won't be Pam Anondis."

"Pam who?" May asked.

Nana smiled weakly but before she could reply, the nurse came into the room.

"How are we doing this morning?" she asked softly.

May stood up from the bed and tried to rub the sleep from her eyes. "She's been a regular chatterbox," she said.

The nurse, plump, starchy, and bright, checked the saline drip and its concomitant smaller bags of antibiotic and painkiller. Then she gently extracted Nana's arm from beneath the covers and strapped the blood pressure cuff onto it, the blue veins spidery and flat, the skin mottled with purple and red bruises from the I.V.s. As she pumped the rubber bulb, she asked Nana, "What have you been chatting about?"

Nana just groaned and tried feebly to pull her arm away.

"She sang me a lullaby," May told the nurse.

"I'll bet it wasn't the first time," the nurse said to Nana. When she got no reply, she placed the stethoscope on the crook of Nana's elbow and listened carefully while slowly releasing the pressure from the cuff. She entered the result on a chart and took out a digital thermometer.

"How's she doing?" May asked in an undertone.

The nurse put the thermometer in Nana's ear and quickly read and recorded her temperature. "Have you had breakfast?" she asked May.

"I'm not really a breakfast person," May said.

"How about a cup of coffee? On me."

"Sure." May bent over her grandmother and kissed her forehead. "I'm going out for a minute, Nana. Don't you go anywhere."

Nana didn't respond at all.

The nurse led May to the nurses' station and poured her a cup of coffee. "Does your grandmother have other relatives in town?"

May's heart sank. "My uncle Peter and his wife are flying in from Florida this afternoon. Why?"

The nurse had poured herself a cup as well, into which she stirred a heart-stopping amount of powdered creamer and sugar. "Put it this way," she said, sipping. "I hope the plane isn't delayed."

"Is she really that bad?"

"Oh, her vitals aren't much different than they were three days ago. And I told you then to brace yourself."

"Is there anything else you can do? Is she in much pain?"

"She's already on vancomycin, one of the most powerful antibiotics we have. And if we increase her dosage of morphine it may repress her autonomic functions. It might even stop her heart."

"So there's no hope?"

"Where there's life, there's hope. But after going through this many, many times I've begun to recognize the signs. Her whole body is beginning to shut down. Your grandma may not last through the night. But then again," she added, brighter, "I thought she was gone Sunday and she's still with us. She's certainly a determined lady. Who knows? Maybe she'll fool everybody and outlive the lot of us."

"God, I wish Uncle Peter had booked an earlier flight." The coffee tasted terrible but May craved the warmth it brought. "I feel so helpless. I just don't want to screw anything up."

The nurse put her hand on May's wrist. "Listen. You stayed with her all night. You've been here all week, just about. You're doing everything there is to do and I know you've been a great comfort to her. Some things are just in the hands of God."

May appreciated the effort but had trouble taking her words to heart. She felt sure her mother or Poppa Harvey or almost any other responsible adult would know better what to do in this situation. She could only watch helplessly this wonderful lady, to whom she'd begun to feel quite close in the past few weeks, inexorably slip away. "I think I'll just go back and see if she's awake."

Nana was indeed awake, leaning up on her elbow to try to reach the plastic water cup, the I.V. tube pulled taut and the tree about to tip over.

"Oh, Nana, let me help you!" May cried. She rushed to hand her the cup, Nana easing back onto the pillows with a moan.

May gently put her hand behind Nana's head and held it up so she could drink, some of the water overflowing the weak lips onto the hospital gown. Nana nodded when she'd had enough.

"Thank you, dear," she said as May dabbed the gown with a tissue. "What are you doing here so early? Didn't you have to work last night?"

May inwardly heaved a sigh of relief. She may have forgotten I was here during the night, she thought, but at least she knows who I am. The light shone once again behind Nana's tired eyes.

"I got off early last night so I could come have breakfast with you this morning," May lied. "What'll it be? French toast? Ham and eggs?"

Nana closed her eyes and grimaced, shaking her head.

"At least some of this Jell-O?" May offered.

"No, nothing yet," her grandmother said. "Thank you though."

"How are you feeling?"

Nana's breathing came quick and shallow while she tried to reply. "Not too bad," she said at last.

"How did you sleep?"

"I can't tell." She coughed weakly, ineffectually.

"I think you were dreaming when I got here," May said, feeling awkward about making small talk but not knowing what else to do.

Nana's parched lips cracked into a vague smile. "I think I dreamed about your mother."

I did too, May thought, recalling her own dark dream. "I think you thought I was her," May said, trying to sound light-hearted. "You called me Mandy."

Nana opened her eyes and they swung listlessly to her granddaughter. "What did I say?"

"You said something about an El Paso boy," May said, happy to engage in this much conversation with her. "And somebody named Pam."

Nana nodded gravely. "I remember the El Paso boy," she said. "Your mother met him in Texas one summer."

"Really? What was he like?"

"Mandy never wanted to talk about it much," Nana said slowly. "She never even told me his name. But she came back from there so upset."

"Well, you must have made her feel better about it because you made me feel better and you weren't even talking to me."

"You listen better than she did," Nana pointed out, a trace of the old mustard coming back into her demeanor. "She never cared much for my advice about the company she kept."

"Who was Pam?"

"Pam." She shook her head and stared blankly at the crucifix tucked in its nook on the opposite wall.

"You said her last name too," May recalled. "Nonnidus. Nondalus. Something like that. It was a weird name."

"Pam Nonnidus," Nana repeated, thinking back. Then her eyebrows arched and she broke into a smile and even tried to chuckle. This last, unfortunately, brought up more phlegm than the cough had and May had to grab a tissue and wipe it from her mouth and chin.

"My sweet angel," Nana said gratefully, clearing her throat. "You could always make me smile."

May smiled too. "What did I say?"

"Didn't your mother ever tell you the story of Epaminondas?"

"Oh, is that what you said? Epaminondas?" May said. "I don't think she told me that one. Is it one of those myths?"

Nana shook her head in dismay. "We've lost so much," she said. "Everybody's so worried about offending anybody that all we have is Pablum."

"What's Pablum?" May asked, puzzled.

Nana just shook her head again.

"At least tell me about Epamiwhatsis," she urged her, afraid Nana would slip away again. "Is it in a book? I could look it up in the library."

"I don't think it's in the library anymore. It went the way of Little Black Sambo."

May wanted to ask who Little Black Sambo was but didn't want to further dismay her grandmother. "What was it about?" May asked to her. "Are you up to telling me?"

"May, honey, I don't know," Nana said, slowly shaking her head.

"Please?" May asked politely. "How about if we fortify you with some of this Jell-O first?"

When Nana didn't object, May gingerly helped prop her up on the pillows, Nana groaning at even the slightest movement of her broken hip. When she got her squared away, May spooned out a cube of red Jell-O and held it to Nana's reluctant lips. Nana let it slide into her mouth and she meditatively rolled it around with her tongue.

"The story was called 'Epaminondas And His Auntie'," the old woman said after swallowing.

"Uh-huh," May said, silently rejoicing at this spark of interest she'd created. "What happened to him?"

"He went to his Auntie's house," Nana went on, "and she sent him home with a gift."

"That's nice," May said, giving Nana more Jell-O.

Nana swished the melting Jell-O in her dry mouth. "But by the time he got back home the gift was ruined."

"Oh, no!"

"So his mother saw what had happened and told him what to do the next time to avoid it," Nana said, pausing to breathe. "But each time Epaminondas goes to his Auntie's house the gift is different and what his mother told him to do the last time ruins each new gift."

"I guess I'm confused, Nana," May confessed, unsuccessfully offering more Jell-O. "What does this Epaminondas story have to do with my mom?"

"Before your mom married your dad, she dated a few different boys," Nana told her. "When she came home from Texas heartbroken again she complained to me that she felt like Epaminondas. Figuring out what she did wrong with one boy never seemed to help her avoid making different mistakes with the next boy who came along."

May had cringed to hear Nana refer to Bill as her dad but didn't want to correct her. "Was Jason one of those boys?"

"Yes, I suppose he was," Nana said absently. "Could you help me lie down again, dear? It's just too uncomfortable to sit this way."

May silently assisted her as she gradually worked herself back down.

"Oh, my gosh!" Nana exclaimed as May tucked the covers around her.

May jumped back, afraid she'd hurt her somehow. "What is it?"

"I forgot what you told me about Jason, didn't I, dear?"

Relieved, May said, "That's okay, Nana. John and Russ just said I held a pen like Jason. It doesn't prove much, does it?"

"No, but every bit of daylight you can see between you and Bill helps," Nana said.

"That's true."

"I'm not sure I ever told your mother properly but I've always felt a little bit responsible for pushing your mother into that horrible marriage. I suppose my advice was just as poor as the advice Epaminondas got from his mother."

"But would Jason have been a better father?" May asked. "John told me a little bit about him but not much. What did you think of him?"

Nana closed her eyes again and her pause lasted so long May assumed she'd fallen back asleep. "Jason was smart and likable and good-looking," Nana said at last, her eyes opening again sleepily. "And not afraid of hard work. But he wasn't one to play by the rules. He seemed like a dreamer who would never settle down. I wanted your mother to have the good things in life. I didn't want to see her scrimp and scrape for every dime the way Harve and I did when we first started out."

"I could use someone to take care of me that way," May admitted.

"But I was wrong," Nana said emphatically, tapping May's hand with her own. "Your mother didn't need someone like Bill. In fact, the day she told me they were getting married she said she wished she had some alternative. I guess I just didn't listen."

May could tell she was getting upset, which was the last thing she wanted to do. She decided to change the direction of the conversation. "Anyway, I guess I'm going to find out more about Jason on New Year's Eve."

"Oh?" Nana said, closing her eyes again. "Oh, that's right, your Piñon Nuts party. How is it coming along?"

"I told you I called Russ in New York, right? Well, he definitely sounded interested and he told me that Matt, the one who lives in Seattle, wanted to come as well. I've been trying to get a hold of John for days now but he's never at the motel in Loveland where he's staying. I left a message for him at the paper yesterday but I haven't checked my answering machine yet to see if he called last night."

"You've spent too much time here with me," Nana said. "I know you have other things to do. Peter will be here soon and take over for you."

"He said their plane gets in around 5:00. He and Jan will probably drop their things off at the condo and then come right here so they should be here by six o'clock or so. I'm afraid I'm going to have to leave by mid-afternoon today. It's going to be a big night in the restaurant."

"You don't have to stay all day, dear. You need to get some rest."

"Oh, I'm fine," May said, though her eyes felt like they rubbed in their sockets whenever she moved them. "I've really enjoyed spending all this time with you. I just wish the circumstances were better."

"I'm not very good company, I suppose. But I do enjoy listening."

"You just concentrate on getting yourself better. And you know me. I can babble on endlessly. What would you like to hear about?"

"How are things at the restaurant?" Nana asked, knowing May could always talk about work.

"Not bad," May said. "Tonight's going to be really busy and then tomorrow we're booked solid for six hours. I hope I haven't screwed up any more reservations. I told you about the Schwab fiasco, didn't I?"

Nana wrinkled her brow but didn't say anything.

"Oh, they made reservations for 12 last weekend and somehow I just wrote down the two, so they ended up having to wait for almost an hour before we could free up enough tables. Lucy wasn't very happy with me."

"Lucy Van Deutch is a crank," Nana said.

May was surprised. "I didn't know you knew her."

"We played in a bridge club together years ago."

"Well, she's been pretty nice to me, for the most part. She's even letting me handle the Cogswell party. They book every Christmas and New Year's and everybody says they are great tippers but very finicky. So I'm a little nervous about that."

"You'll do fine," Nana assured her.

"I get along great with everybody else, though," May went on, pleased with the look of peace and contentment that suffused Nana's tired features. "One of the waitresses, Tara, and I are getting to be good friends. She's about my age and has a little boy and a little girl. She's really pretty, long dark hair, deep brown eyes, really tall. And really good with her customers. So is Angie, for that matter. She's older, in her fifties, I suppose, but she's just a scream sometimes, especially when she starts making fun of all the highbrow people that come in there."

"Mm-hmm," Nana murmured.

"I'm getting to know the chefs a little better now too. Eric Van Deutch still works every afternoon on menus and sauces but a guy named Lyle is the official head chef now and God, can he cook! They always let me try the specials so I can tell people what they're like and I run out of ways to tell people how good they are. And then there's Clark, his assistant, who's kind of wacky, and Scott, a quiet older guy who does the salads. Oh, and Marcus," she added, trying to make it sound like an afterthought.

"Mm-hmm," Nana murmured again, more quietly.

May felt a guilty pleasure in talking about Marcus. Her feelings for him had grown so recently, so quickly, that everything associated with him seemed promising and new. The Epaminondas story earlier, in fact, had made her wonder if Marcus was so different from Paco that none of the lessons she had learned from her marriage would apply. Besides, Nana was drifting off again and May was dying to talk about him, even if no one listened.

"Marcus is the broiler chef. He always gets really sweaty from all the heat but somehow his clothes always look crisp and he always smells great. He has a really sexy laugh and he calls me his Mayfly. I've never gotten that close to a Black man before but he makes me want to—" she shivered just thinking about Marcus's sweaty neck "—mmm, just eat him up."

Nana's only comment consisted of a soft puttering from beneath the sheets, after which a whiff of feces filled the room. May pressed the button for the nurse.

"Are you okay?" May asked her grandmother softly.

"Mm-hmm," Nana said again, dreamily.

The nurse bustled in and switched off the call light. "I was just on my way down here.

Uh-oh. I guess we've had a little accident, huh?" She lifted the covers. "Oh, dear. I tell you what," she said to May. "Why don't you take a little walk, get some fresh air, while we clean things up in here?"

"I should check my messages anyway," May said to her, standing. "Is there a pay phone in the lobby?"

"Right by the front door," the nurse said.

o   o   o

The lobby of Penrose Hospital faces Cascade Avenue, where the morning commuters flew by, puffs of steam trailing behind their tailpipes. Puffs of cigarette smoke wreathed the heads of May's fellow habitués as they sucked in that last big drag at curbside before entering the non-smoking zone of the hospital. The promise of dawn remained largely unfulfilled, the sun dampened by thick overcast. Morning-shift workers and early visitors streamed through the lobby. May bought another, hopefully better, cup of coffee from a little stand and went to the pay phones and sat down.

She had never before used the remote message function on the answering machine and in fact had spent ten precious minutes before work yesterday pushing buttons and switching knobs trying to figure out the complicated thing before finding the instruction manual her mother had left underneath. Unsure how this would work, she dialed her number and held her fingers over the one and the zero, ready to prompt the machine to play the messages.

The phone rang twice and then the announcement, in her mother's voice, came on: "Hi! This is Amanda. I wish I could answer your call but at the moment I'm out dispelling the gloom of the season in the warm glow of friends and loved ones. I'd love to talk to you though! Leave a message after the beep and I'll be sure to get back to you. Merry Christmas! Bye!"

May had recorded over Amanda's regular message months ago but this must be some sort of alternate outgoing message May didn't know about that she had switched to in her blundering yesterday. In any case, it felt so good to hear her mom's happy voice that May got a lump in her throat. She rested her forehead against the cold pay phone during the beep and then said, "Oh God, Mom! I'd give anything if you could get back to me right now!"

Not wanting to make a scene in the lobby of the hospital, she hung up the phone and took a moment to collect herself. She had never expected to hear that voice again.

She still hadn't gotten her messages though. Bracing herself this time, she put in another quarter and dialed again. Hating to do it, this time she pushed the prompt buttons right after her mother said, "Hi! This is Amanda."

The machine told her, "You have three new messages," and the tape whined through the rewind.

"Um, this is Lucy Van Deutch," the first caller said uncertainly. "I'm trying to reach May Mendoza. I believe this is the right number. Anyway, May, if you get this, I just wanted to tell you to be sure to get here no later than 4:30 tomorrow. Gloria's daughter has the flu and she may not make it in so we're going to need all the help we can get. I hope I can count on you. Remember: 4:30 tomorrow. Bye."

"7:26 p.m.," the machine informed her.

"Hi, May, it's John. What a great idea to put your mom's Christmas message on! Anyway, sorry it's taken so long to get back to you. You can reach me at a new number," another 970-area-code number that she scrambled to write in her address book with her eye liner. "I won't go in to work until 9:30 or 10:00 in the morning so you're welcome to give me a call before then—collect, if you like. Sorry I missed you." He paused. "Sorry. Rather: I miss you.

Talk to you soon. Bye."

"9:04 p.m."

"Oh God, Mom! I'd give anything if you could get back to me right now!"

"8:43 a.m. End of messages."

She hung up. As odd as it had been to hear her mother's voice unexpectedly, her own sounded even more foreign to her. Not only did she not hear her own voice often, it sounded more desolate and lonely than she could have imagined. She whimpered like a motherless child. You're a big girl now, she scolded herself. You may not have a mother but you have a grandmother and a daughter counting on you to take care of things. So just pull yourself together.

She took a deep breath and picked up the phone, dialing one of those collect-call numbers advertised on TV, then dialing John's, deciphering her hasty scrawl one digit at a time. She gave her name when prompted and heard John's voice accept the charges.

"Hi, May!" he said when the connection was complete. "Long time no hear. How are you?"

"Okay, I guess," she said reflexively. "How are you?"

"Not too bad. I've moved, as you could probably tell by the new number."

"Are you still in Loveland?"

"Far from it," he said bitterly. "No, I've bid a grateful adieu to the Fawn Hollow Apartments."

"Didn't you like it there? The name sounds great."

"Ugh," he said. "Half a dozen cinder-block cubicles painted rusty brown. Cheap sleazy little boxes. Nope. I won't miss Fawn Hollow. I've moved back up to Estes, got a cozy little yellow house on Virginia Drive that I'm renting from a teacher friend of mine, close to downtown but with a great view of Lumpy Ridge."

"It sounds nice."

"It is nice. You ought to come up sometime." Sounding hesitant, he added, "In fact, what are you doing this weekend? If you don't have plans you'd be welcome to stay here." Then he hastened to add, "It's a two-bedroom."

"Thanks, but I've got to work," May said. "Besides, Nana's in the hospital. That's where I am now, in fact."

"Oh, no! I'm so sorry to hear that! What's wrong?"

"Oh, she broke her hip and now she has pneumonia too."

"That's terrible! Is she going to be okay?"

She steeled herself. "No," she said, admitting it out loud for the first time. "Probably not."

"Oh, May, this is awful! Are you by yourself down there?"

"I will be if she dies," May said, fighting down her tears. "My Nana's been my guardian angel. I don't know what I'll do without her."

"I mean, do you have family there with you?"

"My Uncle Peter and his wife are coming in this afternoon."

"Is there anything I can do? Would it help if I came down?"

"I don't think there's much anybody can do," May said.

"Do you need to get back to her?"

"Oh, the nurses are changing her bedclothes and giving her a sponge bath. It's going to take a little while. And Nana and I just had a wonderful conversation so maybe she's begun to turn the corner. In any case, to tell you the truth, I could use a break. It's been a tough week. So you got your own place, huh?"

"Yeah," he said disconsolately.

"So no progress with Susan?"

"She got a lawyer."

"Uh-oh."

"Yeah. We're legally separated now. The only way I can talk to her is through her lawyer and everybody knows how easy it is to effect a reconciliation that way. God, I hate this! I had to submit a written list of my possessions and effects I wanted from the house. She put them all in the garage and left the door open so I could pick them up Saturday while she and the girls went to a movie. She's changed the locks and won't let anybody answer un-caller-i.d.-ed calls."

"Oh, John, I'm so sorry I created so much trouble for you!"

"It's not your fault."

"But if I hadn't…"

"We didn't do anything, remember?" John said, sounding testy. "God, Susan's blown this whole thing so far out of proportion the whole town thinks I'm getting more action than a televangelist. Or the president, for Christ's sake."

"Nobody believed him either," May pointed out.

"Hillary did," he said. "Or at least she pretended to."

"How are your daughters taking it?"

"Susan won't let me talk to them. So far, the resistance has managed to get just one message through the blockade."

"What do you mean?"

"Alice called me down in Loveland on Saturday. She got a hold of one of the prepaid phone cards that Anne has been using to call Wayne at the Juvenile Detention Center in Ft. Collins."

"Wayne's the kid who took the hostages at the school, right? She's still involved with him?"

"Behind our backs, evidently. And to hear Alice tell it, Darth Mater has lured Anne over to the dark side. I guess Anne not only blames me for the problems between me and Susan, she also believes I'm in some way responsible for the mess that Wayne's in."

"What's that got to do with you?"

"In reality, nothing. But to Anne, I'm just part of the establishment that locks up a young man who only threatened to shoot people to make a point."

"What does Alice think about all this?"

"Susan's cover story to the kids is that I'm working on this article down in the valley and it may take as long as a month. You know, Alice is only 11. She doesn't understand any of this stuff. She just wants things back the way they were, with Mommy and Daddy together at home and just one big happy family. She offered to sell every one of her Beanie Babies so we could afford to all live together again."

"Oh God."

"Just about broke my heart. I can't imagine where she got the notion that money can solve every problem in America."

"You mean, other than the commercials for the lottery?"

"And every other money-for-nothing scheme guaranteed to bring peace and joy to the lucky winner."

"You're not having financial problems, are you? You're still working for the newspaper, right?"

"Oh, yeah," he said gloomily. "But the paper's now owned by the *Denver Post* so we're just another wart on the dragon. Tim, my old editor and good friend, got so disgusted with it that he quit and moved to California."

"Are you still working on your article about marijuana?"

"That went out the door with Tim. I'm back to hawking ad space to local business people who are tightening their belts for the long cold winter up here and wondering if they'll be able to hold out till the tourists flock back next June. And, believe it or not, I'm one of the lucky ones at the paper. Several people are sweating their jobs."

"You don't sound too happy."

"No kidding." He paused, then softened. "On the other hand, I'm freer than I've been in many years. If I lose the job, I'll do something else. If Susan thinks she can raise the girls and maintain the house by herself, more power to her."

"I'm starting to feel that way about Paco too," May admitted.

"What's happening on that front?"

"Did I tell you that Paco and Shirley moved back to Buena Vista?"

"No! When did this happen?"

"Last weekend."

"And Libby went with them, I assume."

"There's nothing I could do to stop it. Boy, if it weren't for Nana and my job, I'd be tempted to sell the house and move away."

"Really? Where would you go?"

"I don't know. Jupiter, maybe," she said. "Or some deserted island somewhere."

"By yourself?"

"Unless I could find the right person to be with."

"What's the right person like?" he asked.

"Beats me," she said, but she had to fight down the memory of Marcus's sweaty chest to say it.

"I guess that leaves me out," John said. "Because I would never beat you."

She chuckled. "You'd be hard to beat too," she granted.

"I'm sure Susan could give you some pointers."

"None of that now."

"Listen, I'd better get to work or I'll end up on the bubble myself. Maybe I'll give you a call later, see how Nana's doing. Do you work tonight?"

"Of course. The holidays are huge at the restaurant."

"Oh, jeez, I almost forgot! That's one of the things I wanted to talk to you about. Russ called me over the weekend."

"I talked to him myself a couple of weeks ago."

"He told me you did."

"How's he doing? He sounded pretty down when we spoke."

"Man, he's as down as I've ever heard him. You knew he and his wife were trying to get pregnant?"

"And can't, from what he told me."

"Right. Well, he feels like their marriage is on shaky ground now too."

"Not another one!"

"He's even talking about selling Tweak, his restaurant in the Village. I guess he's actually put it on the market."

"Good heavens."

"So the long and the short of it is that he doesn't see any way he's going to make it back to Colorado on New Year's Eve. He said he talked to Matt up in Seattle and Matt didn't sound that disappointed about canceling it either."

May didn't say anything.

"I hope this isn't a big hassle for you," John said. "I mean, canceling the reservation and all. You shouldn't have any trouble filling the table that night, I wouldn't think."

"No, no trouble," May said distantly.

"Anyway, I've got the whole weekend off with nothing to do, so feel free to call anytime. I'd like to hear how Nana's doing." May heard a couple of clicks on the line. "Could you hang on?" John asked. "I better get this."

The line went dead.

The news that the Piñon Nuts Gathering was off hit May hard. For one thing, Lucy Van Deutch was impressed when May brought in business when she was hired and canceling it seemed worse than not bringing it in at all. It had also been the one small bright spot on her social horizon, the one thing she had to look forward to in what otherwise looked to be a pretty bleak holiday season.

She also knew that getting together with John, Russ, and Matt would probably be the only way she would ever get to know Jason. Just based on the admittedly flimsy evidence she had, she had already come to cherish the notion that Jason was indeed her father. She had begun to view it as her ticket out, the only way she would ever be able to escape the dreary monotony of her life. If they didn't get together and talk about Jason, her entire hope that some alternate outcome existed might prove just another of life's pointless pranks.

Assuming Jason was her father, both her parents would have died in the mountains near Colorado Springs but neither body had been found. Without that physical proof of death, May's imagination had been free to construct unlikely but possible scenarios of one of them miraculously reappearing. She could almost accept her mother's death as final, though hearing her voice on the answering machine had triggered that hopeful part of her mind that, just for a moment, could grasp that straw. But since she knew so few details of Jason's disappearance she could never quite dissuade herself from clinging to the slim hope that somehow Jason would show up New Year's Eve like the other three Piñon Nuts. But if even the ones who definitely were still alive wouldn't show, it seemed absurd to think that Jason, somehow still alive and remembering that old pledge, would miraculously reappear.

The phone clicked back on. "May? Are you still there?" John asked.

"Still here," she said bleakly.

"I'm going to have to run. That was the paper calling. They just got word that the Juvenile Detention Center found Wayne Giles hanging in his cell this morning, apparently a suicide."

"Oh no! That's horrible!"

"Yeah. So I'm going to have to—hell, I don't know what I'm going to do. But I better get started. Good luck down there and keep me posted on your grandmother's condition."

"Good luck, John."

"Thanks. Talk to you soon."

Oh goodie, May thought. Another fat load of stuff to deal with. But by now they must be done with Nana's bed.

When she got back up to the room, Nana was gone. In the bed lay a heap of inert, worn-out flesh and bones. But Nana was gone.

. . . O . . . O . . . O . . .

When I was a drummer, people used to compliment me by saying I "cooked," that I had some "good chops." But cooking proved one of the limiting factors in my career as a musician.

I first came to this realization when I lived in San Francisco with Jessica, a woman I first met in Boulder. She had been part of the Bay Area music scene that helped define the psychedelic sound of the late '60s. Even though that sound had faded, Jessica still had connections in Show Biz I desperately needed.

Unfortunately, Jessica's misguided—or unguided—efforts at Better Living Through Chemistry had taken their toll on her, physically and mentally. In addition to using the usual recreational drugs, she was addicted to Quaaludes and several bouts of hepatitis had left her liver so weak that she could get drunk on a tablespoonful of beer. A cheap date but more erratic than erotic.

She did introduce me to several San Francisco musicians and in fact I jammed with some of the ex-members of the group It's A Beautiful Day. Everyone, myself most of all, came away disappointed and I realized I would have to work much harder if I hoped to earn money playing music.

But when I left San Francisco, it wasn't because of Jessica's drug problems or because of my own inadequacies as a drummer. I left because Jessica never saved leftovers. Sure, I know musicians are supposed to be grasshoppers, living for the moment with never a thought for tomorrow. But I just couldn't hack eating in restaurants or ordering pizza all the time, with the extra going right to the trash. I fled the City By The Bay with visions of Tupperware in my head.

Over the years, I've cooked some great meals for myself—I rarely have anyone else to cook for —and I've found that simple dishes, improvised from ingredients on hand, often turn out the best. I don't own a lot of fancy doodads and gimcracks, relying mostly on a cutting board and one old chef's knife with as much history as edge.

My interest in cooking comes from my mom, I suppose. When I think of her cooking one of her classic holiday meals, I always picture her standing up to eat her grapefruit. At the time, I just assumed that she preferred it that way. Maybe standing made the grapefruit taste better or she simply liked to stretch her legs.

I realize now that those elaborate, delicious meals required enormous preparation and skill and that she simply didn't have time to sit down to eat her grapefruit on Thanksgiving morning. To the people unfolding their napkins, a great meal is a blessing and a joy; to the weary cook, it's just a job.

November 27, 1969

Maybe it was the mushrooms. Maybe it was the wine. Either way, the sauce looked more like soup.

But Russ didn't have time to worry about that. He grabbed the spatula and flipped the next crepe, which had cooked so long on the first side he had to spank it down with the spatula to cook the other side. He glanced over at Jason, who stared numbly into the sauce pan.

"How's that going?" Russ asked him, sloshing the shrooms around in the boiling sauterne.

"A penny a lump," Jason said, dripping some from the wooden spoon, "and I'd be rich."

"Is the burner too high? I smell something burning."

"Oh, shit! The crackers!"

Jason yanked open the oven door, grabbed the cookie sheet, burned his fingers, said "shit" again, plucked a magnetized hot pad from the stove hood, and pulled the cookie sheet from under the broiler. The saltines, supposed to toast like marshmallows, instead had darkened to shades from leather to charcoal.

"We can always have the beans without the crackers," Russ suggested.

Jason checked the green beans. "Not if I don't turn them on," he said in disgust, cranking the knob to medium high. "Watch your crepe," he added to Russ, who had been stirring the white sauce while Jason dealt with the crackers.

The crepe was crisp. "Arrgh!" Russ moaned, dumping it on top of the other dozen of various shapes and degrees of doneness. "You thought we could cook this dinner ourselves?" he wondered aloud, spooning more batter into the pan before realizing he hadn't brushed the pan with butter, meaning it would stick like the earlier ones.

"I thought there'd be four of us cooking," Jason pointed out. He crudely hacked chunks of turkey breast from the carcass left over from the Walkers' Thanksgiving dinner the evening before and dumped the chunks into the lumpy white sauce. "Considering what a good cook Mom is, she owns some terrible knives," he lamented, throwing the knife aside to tear the turkey with his hands instead. "Where are those guys?"

Matt had called 15 minutes before, saying that the Tank, sitting idle for months while he was in Seattle, refused to budge. John had taken his car, the Yellow Fellow, to pick him up, theoretically a ten-minute jaunt. But snow had begun to fall and the Fellow, John had pointed out before he left, didn't have the best tires.

"Speak of the devil," Russ said, seeing the Fellow's headlights coming down the drive. "These mushrooms don't look very saucy," he pointed out to Jason. "Maybe thicken it with some flour?"

"I think we have some defective flour on our hands," Jason said, wiping lumpy white sauce onto the hand towel. "Better not risk it. This stuff's pretty bad as it is. Maybe I'll toss in some of these. At least some of the lumps will taste good." He grabbed a handful of what looked like old shoepeg corn kernels from a small bag on the counter and tossed them into the lumpy white sauce.

"What are those?" Russ asked him.

"Piñon nuts," Jason said, stirring them in.

"As in piñon pine trees?" Russ asked, becoming familiar with local plants.

"Yeah. My mom got them down in Taos last month. They're pretty good." He popped a couple in his mouth and then a couple in Russ's mouth too. "They taste kind of buttery and piney."

Matt and John came in the kitchen door, smelling like fresh air and weed.

"Damn, smells good in here," John said.

"Hey, Matt!" Jason called in greeting but turned to John. "Could you chop some celery?"

"Sounds dicey but I'll try," John said, addressing the ribs and knife on the cutting board. "How about some onions too?"

"I like onions but they don't like me. But you're a smart feller," Jason said, referring to an old Spoonerism. "Want to be a —?"

"No onions," John agreed hastily.

"'Strange thing, gathering of tribes'," Russ sang along with the record on the turntable, *The Notorious Byrd Brothers*. "How are ye, laddy?" he asked Matt.

"Better than nothing," Matt said. "What can I do?"

"Scrape a crepe?" Russ suggested, handing him the spatula. "I'll see if I can rehabilitate some of those crackers." He dumped the burned crackers into a bowl and began breaking off the darkened corners.

John dumped the diced celery into the white sauce and Jason turned down the beans, the steam from which threatened to scald Matt's hand as he tried to finesse the sticky crepe from the pan.

By the time McGuinn had finished his double guitar lead on "Dolphin's Smile," hunger and impatience got the best of them and they decided to dish up. Matt plopped a couple of crepes on a plate, Jason ladled some turkey/piñon nut glop onto them and rolled them up, Russ spooned the runny mushrooms across them, and John added some green beans and crackers. When all four plates were done, they carried them into the dining room.

The Walkers lived in a custom-built but modest home on the side of the hill separating the Broadmoor plateau from the neighborhoods clustered along Cheyenne Creek. The house had been built on the grade of the old trolley line that had connected Broadmoor to Colorado Springs, and it had a panoramic view of the peaceful valley below and the Front Range beyond, with the white dome of Pikes Peak peeking from behind Cameron's Cone.

Russ hadn't spent that much time at the Walker home. In high school they had tended to gravitate to the Jones house on Mesa, where the high ceilings and Ellen's antiques and impeccable style seemed conducive to discussions of what Russ called "interweavalities." The Kaufman home, a Spanish-style stucco box known affectionately as the Pink Palace, was closer to the high school but somehow didn't seem grand enough for the subjects they pondered. They had unanimously ruled out the McCleary house as too formal, too stuffy. You can't argue about which is more a work of art, a photograph or a phonograph record, without at some point putting your feet up on something and saying "Pfah!"

Except for Argonaut rehearsals, Jason spent more time at his friends' houses than at his own. Jason's basement bedroom, which Dex had created out of two-by-fours and paneling, proved too small and dreary for much of anything but sleeping. Jason had covered one wall with memorabilia: fortune-cookie fortunes, a "yield" sign they'd found, pictures of women's legs and rock stars, even a chart Jason kept, totally subjectively, of how his days had gone. Over his twin bed hung his prize possession, a picture of Shakespeare's house—"I sleep under Uncle Willie's place," Jason liked to say. But the adjacent family room held Dex's old mahogany-finished Laughead piano, which Matt found a joy after struggling with the Wurlitzer. They could leave the amps and drums set up and since it was in the basement the neighbors rarely complained.

Upstairs, Nora Walker's influence dominated: the matching maple sideboard and dining room table, the leaf-and-rust shag carpet, the corduroy couch, the eclectic mix of large framed art prints on the walls. Perhaps the best room in the house, though, was the bedroom above the garage, with windows that opened out into the scrub oak trees and a sunny west view of the mountains. But it had belonged to Steve and so far Nora had left it the way Steve had left it.

Friends and family had done their best to make up for Steve's absence this Thanksgiving by showing up in droves at the Walkers' so the leaves still expanded the maple table which a white cloth still covered, spotted here and there with cranberries and gravy. The banquet-sized table left the four friends plenty of room to expand their girth or their hand gestures without fear of bumping a table-mate.

While Russ took the silver from the sideboard and distributed it to each place, John lit the left-over stubs of the candles and Matt arranged the chairs.

Jason flipped on the porch light: when the snow blew in from the northwest, that corner of the living room gave the impression of the prow of a ship. Then he took off the Byrds album and put on something else.

From Charlie Watts's fast drum shuffle, followed by the conga and Mick Jagger's monkey screams, Russ could tell it was *Beggar's Banquet*. "Excellent!" he said.

"What else could I choose for a banquet like this?" Jason said, waving his hand disparagingly over the crepes.

"If I may play the devil's advocate here," Russ said as Jagger sang the opening lines of "Sympathy For The Devil," "shouldn't we have something to toast with?"

"With this dinner? God, yes," Jason agreed. "Let's see." He went into a small closet and hauled out a bulky box of California wine. "Mom got a membership in a wine club last year," he explained. "She'll never miss it." He pulled out the plastic tap and they started filling goblets with the warm Chablis.

"Where is your mom?" Matt asked.

"She went a party with the S. D. C. crowd." System Development Corporation had hired Nora as a receptionist a few years before and she had worked herself up into middle management. "She won't be home till late. And Dad's playing tonight, of course."

They deferred to Russ for the toast, since he had suggested it. He raised the goblet. "*Alle Menschen werden Brüder.*"

"*Gesundheit*," John rejoined as they drank.

"*Danke*," Russ said, the room-temperature Chablis tasting sour and vapid.

"What the — ?" Jason wondered about the toast.

"Schiller," Russ explained. "Beethoven used it in the Ninth."

"Meaning?"

"'All men become brothers'," Russ translated.

"I, for one," Jason said, "am all for that. I've been running low on brothers of late. Thanks, guys, for showing up for this. Dig in, if you dare."

Russ tried a bite of the stuffed crepe. The lumps in the white sauce, if distracting, were manageable — some, presumably the piñon nuts, actually pretty tasty. The celery was crisp, the turkey delicious. The crepe tasted like one of the ones he'd cooked too long, despite being mushed by the soupy mushroom/wine sauce. But the green beans had turned out just right and the crackers, burnt as they were, added an interesting texture and taste.

Jason had watched him without partaking himself. "Well?"

"Not bad," Russ said honestly. "What did you expect?"

"I've got no expectations," Jason said, trying some. "What do you think, Cough Man?"

John, at the far end of the long table, had tackled about a third of the crepe in one dripping forkful. Swallowing, he said, "No expectorations at this end either."

"I'll drink to that," Matt quipped dryly, then turned to Jason. "So I hear you saw the Stones."

"Yep. Moby Gym, Ft. Collins," Jason said. "Their first gig in the States in like three years. God, they were hot. Jagger would jump in the air, come down in full splits, and still be singing. Incredible."

"How long did they play?" Matt asked.

"I'm not sure. I was pretty stoned," Jason said. "Hour and a half, maybe two hours. Lou Reed and B. B. King opened for them. Man, B. B. almost stole the show."

"I heard the Stones are trying to put together some sort of free concert next week, their answer to Woodstock," Russ put in. "They're looking for a place in the Bay Area to hold it."

"Are you going?" Matt asked him.

"Me?" Russ said. "Hardly. I've got to stick around here." Near Prudence, he added to himself and then tried to put that whole subject out of his mind again.

"I'd love to go," Jason said. "Hell, I'd love to go anywhere. Take me to the airport, put me on a plane."

"Yeah, well, you don't have a woman like Russ does," John threw in.

"What's with that?" Jason demanded of Russ. "How come you're the only one here enjoying the caress of gentle fingers, the subtle whiff of perfume?"

Russ took three gulps of the tepid wine. Prudence had cheerfully informed him last week that her monthly visitor was three weeks late. Wednesday afternoon he had left her knitting contentedly and thinking up baby names. So far the subject of matrimony hadn't come up and she was hardly the "bow-legged sow" the Stones were singing about in "Dear Doctor," but he trembled nonetheless.

He hadn't yet discussed this postdicament with anyone, though, and tonight didn't seem like the time to start. Instead, he tried lobbing the question back. "What about you and Manny?" he asked Jason. "I thought you told me you kissed her at the Fall Ball."

Jason blushed and concentrated on his plate while Matt and John made cat-calls but then shook his head. "I don't know what it is with me and Man." He turned to Matt. "I tried to get that across in that letter I sent you. I mean, we had this great weekend but when it came time for the good-byes, I felt like the last in a line of freaks, all of whom she liked, none of whom she loved. We've exchanged a couple of letters since then. Hers are always friendly but nothing more. I don't seem to be able to get any traction. I called her last time I was down here, three weeks ago, and she was too busy with Deb the whole time to do anything with me."

"Speaking of whom," John said, turning to Matt, "Manny told me about that letter you sent Deb at Regis. Thanks, bro. Manny really liked the bit about my 'better angels.' Though 'worser demons' might have been more appropriate, in my case."

"We've all got those," Matt admitted.

"Boy, there's one that gives me a whole lot of trouble, though," John said, adjusting the napkin in his lap. "I wrestle with it most every night but it just seems to get harder all the time."

After the hear-hears stopped and the last strains of "Parachute Woman" faded, Russ asked, "What letter was this?"

"It was Jason's idea, to tell you the truth," Matt said.

"I got the impression from what John told me," Jason explained, "that Deb, and maybe Manny too, considered us just a bunch of empty-headed light-weights."

Russ took umbrage. "I resemble that."

"Me too," John admitted mincingly, "but I'm too much of a pansy to do anything about it."

"So I asked myself," Jason continued, "who's man enough to stick up for us?"

"And let's face it," John said, raising his glass to Matt, "no one's got more balls than the Mac Truck."

"I've got just the two, I'm afraid," Matt demurred. "Not that either one made any difference. I no sooner got Deb's reply than I heard from Jason that she's in a 'deeply committed relationship' with someone else."

"That's what John told me," Jason said.

"That's what Manny told *me*," John said.

Jason shrugged. "Oh well. I figured a letter from Matt would be worth the price of postage, at least. I mean, if it didn't get Deb and John back on course, at least it would give Matt a chance to stick his oar in the water. Unless I miss my guess," he said to Matt, "you've had a thing for Deb since Jones Park."

"Looks like we're in the same boat now, old man," John said, clinking glasses with Matt. "And nobody's sticking nothing in nothing."

"Except Russ," Jason pointed out. "And the drummer looks pretty shattered."

Russ had choked on a chunk of meat and had to wash it down with wine. As willing as the next guy to join in bawdy badinage in the past, the Problem With Prudence now loomed large enough to suck all the cheer from that sport. "So you guys are all just giving up without a fight?" he threw out defensively, to change the subject.

John and Matt pushed the remains of the crepes around their plates and didn't look up.

Jason refilled his goblet from the wine box. "I hate to let Manny slip away," he admitted. "She's always seemed very special to me. To tell you the truth, John, I thought you'd be the one she'd fall for."

"Hell, I'm just the bass player, looking 'nervous about the girls outside'," John said, quoting Jagger. "Besides, there's Bill Black to contend with."

"Neither one of you can out-charm Bill Black?" Russ challenged Jason and John.

"I can't out-spend him," John said.

"Maybe in some other universe," Jason agreed, "where things like that don't matter, we'd stand a chance."

"Some alternate reality?" Russ asked.

"Manny's term," Jason noted.

"My point exactly. What do you want?"

"I don't know," Jason said dispiritedly. "It's hard to have a woman who's a friend. Sometimes I think all I want is what Jagger's singing about: a woman to lie next to me on the floor, working on this jigsaw puzzle."

"Have you called her?" Russ asked.

Jason shuddered. "I had the usual pleasant chat with her mother when I got home Wednesday night."

"Isn't that a treat?" John said. "That old bat scares the bejeezuz out of me."

"Anyway," Jason went on, "she sounded happy to inform me that they were going out of town but that she'd be *sure* to give Mandy the message that I called."

"Uh-huh," John said. "Don't hold your breath."

"Besides, they're probably going somewhere with the Blacks," Jason added gloomily.

Brian Jones's recorder part faded out and the record arm lifted. The room grew quiet enough to hear the faint ticks of the snowflakes against the windows.

Jason sighed and heaved himself up to flip the record. "Anybody want anything? Other than a decent meal."

"This really isn't so bad," John said, sopping up the mushroom sauce with the last scrap of crepe.

"I think we can safely rule out 'chef' from the list of my job prospects," Jason said, sitting back down.

"Considering we didn't have a recipe or as many hands as we thought…" Russ put in.

"Besides," Matt said, "I thought your destiny was to be a singer in a rock-and-roll band."

"What else can a poor boy do?" Jason said, echoing "Street Fighting Man." "What do you guys think? Is the time right for violent revolution?"

"To look at the TV news," John said, "you'd think it had already begun. That ugliness in Chicago last month, protests everywhere. It's just a damn good thing that rally in D. C. stayed peaceful."

"Is that really a good thing?" Jason asked.

"What are you saying? You want people to get hurt?" Russ asked.

"People are already getting hurt," Jason pointed out. "Guys like Steve die every day in Vietnam and for every one of them, we kill five or six Vietnamese."

"According to the Army, anyway," John said doubtfully. "But those figures have probably been cooked more than these crepes."

"You really think they're lying about stuff like that?" Matt asked.

"They've got to keep throwing the hawks a few bones," Jason maintained. "War's big business, remember. People killed, units sold: they look the same on the tally sheet of the military/industrial complex."

"What do your folks think?" Matt asked. "Isn't your dad a life-long Republican? And your mom's part of the military/industrial complex now, isn't she? I thought S. D. C. was helping to program the computers for NORAD."

"I have no idea what they think," Jason said. "I haven't been around that much lately. And when I am here, we don't talk about stuff like that. We keep up appearances, that's all. At least, that's the way it feels. Sometimes I wish we could all just say what's on our minds, get it out in the open."

"How would they react to what you've got to say?" Matt asked.

"Dad's had a pretty short fuse lately and Mom and I... well, she's always said that one fine day she's going to have to play Mama Bear and kick Baby Bear out on his own."

"Where would you go?"

"'Down that road as far as I can go'," Jason quoted "Prodigal Son." "Bring my guitar and try to change things that way."

"That's a scary road," Russ pointed out. "By yourself, no home to go to."

"No older brother to kill the fatted calf, either," Jason said. "Yeah, I am scared. But at least I'd be free to do and say what I want."

"That sounds good to me," John said. "Making money doing something you love. Seeing different places and meeting new people every day."

"That's right, Russ," Matt said mockingly. "Remember all the fabulous babes we met at the beautiful Doghouse that night?"

"You've got to start somewhere," Jason said defensively. "You play some dives at first, then move up to regular places like the Krazy Kat, eventually get into rooms like the Tool up in Boulder."

"Wait a minute," Matt said suspiciously. "Is this some kind of a pitch to get the Argonauts back together?"

"No way," Jason hastened to say. "Jason and the Argonauts died in the Doghouse. I know that. Even if we all got together to play sometime, it wouldn't be as the Argonauts. For one thing, Colorado already has a group called the Astronauts."

"Didn't they just play the moon last week?" John asked, referring to Apollo 12.

"The sky's the limit," Jason said with conviction. "I'll tell you this: if you want a band to fly, it's got to soar."

"And what's this band going to be called?" Russ asked.

"That's a soar spot right there," Jason said. "It takes a great name. Let's see. The Byrds took the bird thing. So take it up a notch. The Hawks, maybe."

"Isn't that what Dylan's back-up band used to call themselves when they backed Ronnie Hawkins?" John asked.

"Okay," Jason said. "Take it a step further then. How about the Eagles? No one's using that, are they?"

"And if the Beatles ever break up," Russ suggested, feeling the wine, "you could hire a couple of them and call yourself the Beagles."

John hunched his shoulders forward like Ed Sullivan. "And now for you youngsters: Jason Walker and the Beagles!"

"I'd have to change my name like my dad," Jason said, smiling. Dex had anglicized "Walken" to Walker.

"Dog Walker and the Beagles!" Russ proposed.

"Groupies flinging their bloomers onto the stage," John fantasized.

"Some strange stray cat and her 15-year-old friend hiding in my closet till I get back to the hotel," Jason said.

"Seriously. What would you do if you ever found yourself in that situation?" Russ asked Jason. "Would you go for it?"

"Damn, it sure sounds tempting," Jason admitted, staring dreamily at the dirty plate before him. "I mean, it's no capital crime. Are you saying you wouldn't?"

"He's already got the fabulous Prudence," John pointed out.

"Hypothetically," Jason specified to Russ. "If there was no Prudence involved."

"Would I?" Russ asked. "In a heartbeat. Will I? Hell, no. Not in a thousand years. I think any one of us who thinks he's going to make it big as a musician is dreaming."

"What do you think, *Frere Jacques*?" Jason asked John. "Are you dreaming?"

"Dreaming? Yes," John admitted. "Will the dream become reality? Probably not."

"So what's the future hold?" Jason asked.

"Realistically? Normality," John said. "You work your 9-to-5, go home to the wife and kiddies, watch TV, go to bed."

"Sounds liberated," Jason said sarcastically.

"So the wife works and I change diapers," John said.

"I can just picture you waiting for her outside the factory, the smelly little bundle in your arms," Jason said.

"And at that point she'll probably be a sight for sore eyes," John replied defensively. "Is that so bad?"

Jason looked at Russ, who shrugged. Matt silently played with the scraps of crepe left on his plate.

"You know what?" Jason concluded, relenting. "That wouldn't be bad at all. In fact, I should be so lucky. Here's to normality." He raised his glass.

"To the hard-working people," Russ said.

"To the salt of the earth," John echoed.

By now, of course, the Stones, too, sang of the salt of the earth and the former Argonauts raised both glass and voice, singing along raucously, inaccurately, joyfully.

o   o   o

The chick singers behind the Stones had just toasted the "two thousand million," the "humble of birth," when Jason's eyes froze on the doorway to the kitchen. The music retreated to just an acoustic guitar for a few bars and in the quiet space Russ heard Nora Walker's voice say, "How gallant!"

Jason glanced guiltily at the half-empty wine goblets and they all reached toward them until realizing the damage already had been done. The revival-meeting ending of "Salt Of The Earth" came on loudly and Jason got up to turn down the stereo. "You're home earlier than you said you'd be," he said to his mother.

When Nora didn't respond right away, Russ turned to look at her expression, wondering just how angry she might be. He could easily imagine her shouting, like the brave queen in "Jig-Saw Puzzle," "What the hell is going on?"

She had worn a tight strapless black-sequined cocktail dress to the party and she looked sharp. None of the other mothers ever looked sharp the way Nora Walker looked sharp. Russ's mother Ellen looked stylish and elegant, Kate Kaufman comely and good-natured, Eugenia McCleary distinguished and formal. But Nora, with her trim figure, engaging smile, and unwavering blue eyes, fascinated and intimidated Russ in a way other mothers didn't and, from what he could tell, Matt and John felt the same. But she also could be, he knew both first-hand and from Jason, arbitrary and cold.

For now, at least, she just leaned against the door-jamb, looking bemused and possibly a bit tipsy.

"We'll clean all this up," Matt ventured politely.

"You're looking lovely tonight, Mrs. Walker," John said, sounding like Eddie Haskell.

"How gallant," Nora repeated, oblivious to their brown-nosing, "to toast hard-working people with wine you had neither permission nor legal right to drink and which I bought with my own hard-earned money—"

"We'll pay you back," Jason interjected.

"—and then not even offer me a glass," Nora finished.

"Please join us!" John said, springing up to pull over another chair while Russ got a fresh goblet from the sideboard and filled it from the tap on the box. John held the chair for her as she sat down between him and Russ. Russ could smell her perfume mingled with cigarette smoke.

"So how was the party?" Jason asked her.

"Noisy and crowded," Nora said. "Too crowded, in fact. Some of us decided to meet at the Bee instead," the Golden Bee being an Old-English-style pub beneath the International Center at the Broadmoor. "I just came home to change. My shoes are killing me and sequins are much more fun to look at than they are to sit on. How was your dinner? What did you make?"

Jason groaned and rolled his eyes. "It was a beggar's banquet."

"It wasn't that bad," Russ said. "We made turkey crepes."

"Yes, I noticed the turkey still sitting out," Nora observed.

"Oops," Jason said and went into the kitchen to cover it and put it back in the refrigerator.

"Did you leave me any turkey?" Nora asked Russ.

"You still have a full breast," Russ said.

As he said it, Nora pulled up the top of the strapless cocktail dress. The inadvertent double entendre made him wince and blush. He quickly glanced at the others. If they stifled smiles, they stifled them well.

Jason broke the awkward pause by asking his mother from the kitchen, "I tried making those green-beans-and-crackers you served yesterday but I didn't know how you browned the saltines."

"I sauté them in a pan. What did you do?"

"I tried broiling them."

"That explains that delightful aroma," she said tartly.

"It really wasn't that bad," Russ said, trying to defend Jason's efforts at least.

"Jason's nuts were really tasty," Matt said and Russ could tell that, as soon as he said it, he felt as chagrined as Russ had after the turkey-breast remark.

"Jason's nuts?" Nora asked archly.

Jason came in from the kitchen, drying his hands on a towel. "Those weren't my nuts," he explained to Matt with a smile. "Those were, and always will be, my mother's nuts." He turned to Nora. "I used some of those piñon nuts you brought back from Taos in the crepes. I hope you don't mind."

"I don't mind," Nora said. "Your father bought them."

"I cooked and ate my father's nuts?" Jason said in mock horror.

"They tasted great," Russ said, trying to deflect the conversation from that course.

"You are what you eat, you know," Matt pointed out.

"I know I'm crazy about them," John said. "So I guess that makes me a piñon nut."

"Me too," said Jason.

"There's the band name we were looking for!" John said, inspired. "The Piñonauts!"

"You're all nuts," Nora concurred with a smile.

"Then I'm a chip off the old nut," Jason said. "Is Dad playing at the Bee this week?"

"No," she said. "Your father's filling in for Tom O'Boyle in the Terrace Lounge. Did he talk to you earlier?"

"He left before I got up," Jason told her. "He had to go into the bank today, didn't he?" Dex worked a day job at a branch bank on the east side of town.

"I thought maybe you two might have talked when he came home to change."

"Russ and I went to the store."

"Huh," Nora mused. "He told me it would only take a couple of hours."

"Well, we were here till about 4:00," Jason said. "Why was he getting off early?"

Nora took another sip of her wine. "Well, I guess I might as well tell you," she said, looking at her son. "He's getting off permanently."

"What do you mean?" Jason asked.

"I mean, he submitted his resignation," she said.

Russ felt uncomfortable at this news and at the abrupt, almost callous way Nora had delivered it. He could tell by the way Matt played with the base of his wine goblet and John with his fork that they were wishing they were somewhere else.

"He resigned? Why?" Jason asked.

"Because they asked him to," Nora said bluntly. "Your father knows everything there is to know about how to keep books on paper. But when Norwest bought the bank, they decided to do all the bookkeeping with computers. And your father knows about dance cards, not punch cards. They offered to make him a loan officer but he turned them down. He said that in the thrilling days of yesteryear he'd been the lone arranger in a band and didn't have any desire to be the loan arranger in a bank."

Jason looked stunned. "Boy, he's worked at the bank as long as I can remember. What's he going to do?"

"Get another job, I suppose," Nora said.

"You mean, besides the music?" Jason asked.

"The music." Nora snorted contemptuously. "We can't keep you in college with what Dex makes at music, buster."

"Maybe I should get a job," Jason offered.

"Doing what?"

Jason smiled wryly. "I could always be a cook."

Russ and the others chuckled.

"You may have to find some sort of job," Nora said soberly. "After all, we haven't seen your grades yet."

Jason didn't say anything, or look up.

"College is tougher sledding than high school, isn't it?" she asked him.

"There have been a lot of distractions," Jason said sullenly.

"What were you planning to major in?" she asked. "Refresh my memory."

"Biology," he replied. "The study of life."

"I thought, with all the time you've spent protesting, that maybe you were considering Poli. Sci."

"There's a lot of life on the streets right now," he said. "Somebody's got to speak out against this war."

"Lots of people are speaking out against this war," Nora said. "I don't think your one small voice is going to make much difference either way. You better make sure the distractions don't get in the way of your education."

"Some things are more important than college," Jason maintained.

"And you, of course, at the ripe old age of 19, already know just what those are."

"It seems to me," Jason said testily, "that if I'm old enough to fight in a war, I'm old enough to have an opinion about it."

"But as a member of this democracy, you have to respect the opinion of the majority."

"I'm not a member of this democracy until I can vote," Jason said. "And I don't think the majority, no matter how substantial, should have the right to make life-or-death decisions for me."

"Well, brace yourself, because that's the way it is."

"Do you want me to end up like Steve?"

It was Nora's turn to sound testy. "There are much worse ways to end up, mister." Russ could see her eyes flash and then grow misty.

"You think that Silver Star makes him a hero?"

Nora drew herself up and pointed her finger at her son. "First of all, I don't put much credence in that story you heard from some drunk in a bar. And secondly, that Silver Star proves, if nothing else, that Steve was man enough to live up to his obligations."

"So I'm not a man because I don't want to fight a war I don't believe in?" Jason cried. "I'm fighting *against* a war. Wars are easier to start than they are to stop."

"And they're easier to lose than they are to win," Nora said. "At least Steve died trying."

"Steve never should have died at all," Jason said. "He never should have been where he was. The United States Army never should have been where it was."

"So you think," Nora said, her eyes still brimming, "based on your two whole months of college and the wealth of worldly experience you've gleaned from working a couple of summer jobs, that you're qualified to tell the generals and the elected officials what to do."

"No, I don't," Jason admitted. "I just don't think they should tell *me* what to do."

"Well, if you don't stay in college, you may have no choice," Nora pointed out. "At least Steve did what he did by choice."

"I've always got a choice," Jason said. "Maybe I'll file for Conscientious Objector status."

"As what? A Christian Scientist?"

"As a Buddhist," Jason claimed, though Russ, and probably Nora too, could tell he was bluffing. "Buddhists find killing any living thing abhorrent."

"Tell that to the turkey," Nora said, and Russ had to chuckle.

"Oh, you wouldn't understand," Jason said in frustration.

"Why? Because I'm a member of the Establishment, as you and your friends have so conveniently labeled my generation?"

"Doesn't S. D. C. have a vested interest in war?" Jason snapped. "At least in the Cold

War?"

"For your information, S. D. C. has many other clients besides the government. Besides, don't you have a vested interest as well? Who do you think is paying for your college education, even for this little banquet you've put together? Puppies ought to be fully weaned before they bark too loud."

"Maybe I'll kill two birds with one stone," Jason said. "I'll become a professional musician. Make my living taking on the Establishment with my songs."

Nora snorted dismissively. "That's not much of a living."

"Dad's done all right with the music business."

"Your father makes—or used to make—his living as a bookkeeper."

"There's more to life than money," Jason said. "Didn't you two meet at one of his jobs?"

"Here's some advice for all you budding young musicians," Nora said, looking around the table. "It's one thing to attract a woman. Hanging onto her is something else entirely."

"He's hung onto you."

Nora closed her eyes and sipped her wine. "As usual," she said to herself with a sigh, "he leaves it up to me."

"What's that?" Jason asked, bristling.

Nora fixed him in her unflinching gaze. "That's right, you're a big boy now, aren't you? Well, then, you ought to know this, although it probably won't come as much of a shock. Your father and I have decided to get a divorce."

Again the room fell quiet. Even the snow had quit falling. Russ looked at Jason, who stared at the ceiling, his jaw muscles twitching. Then, avoiding Nora's eyes, Russ glanced furtively at John and Matt, who sat slouched in their chairs, staring at the tablecloth.

Maybe invisibility works for them, Russ thought, but I can't take this. He got up and stacked the plates and carried them into the kitchen. Setting them into the sink he heard Jason ask, "When?"

Nora was right in saying it came as no great surprise. Russ had felt an undercurrent of marital tension in the Walker home throughout the two years he had known Jason. It was hard to believe, though, that Nora would just spring this news on Jason this way, in front of his friends. But then, what's the right way, when's the right time, for news like that?

The phone rang and Russ decided to answer it for them. "Walker residence."

"Hi, um," a young woman's voice said. "Is Jason there?"

"He's, uh, tied up at the moment. Can I take a message?"

"Would you just tell him Amanda Tyree called?"

"Oh, hi, Manny. This is Russ."

"Hi, Russ. I thought I recognized your voice. I called Kate Kaufman earlier to see what John was up to and she said he was there at Jason's and you guys were putting on some kind of a feast."

"Well, we've finished the feast and moved into the discussion portion of the evening."

"What are you discussing? Anything interesting?"

"Oh, at least interesting. What are you doing?"

"Just trying to convince myself I have a life, even if it's only vicarious," she said gloomily. "Peter and my parents are up in Aspen and Deb is on a date and I'm bored out of my mind."

"At this point, boredom sounds pretty good," Russ said, listening to the somber tone of the conversation in the dining room.

"There's plenty here to go around, if you guys want to come over," Amanda said.

"I'll try to work that suggestion into the conversation. If nothing else, I'll have John or Jason call you after a while."

"Thanks, Russ."

Any other time, Jason probably would be thrilled with the news that Manny had called, even if it had been to talk to John, but tonight all bets were off. In any case, Russ headed back into the fray.

"Those are your choices," Nora was saying. "And I'm sure your fellow Argonauts will be happy to help out as necessary."

"They're not the Argonauts anymore, Mom," Jason said wearily. "The band disbanded."

"So how are you going to make a living at music? You're going to be a one-man band?"

"Maybe," Jason said stubbornly. "Or I'll put together another band. Any suggestions about a name for that? You came up with the Argonauts name, after all."

"You did?" Russ asked her. He had always assumed Jason did.

"Naming him Jason was my idea," Nora qualified. "I wanted to name him something exciting and adventurous. Dexter Jr. certainly wouldn't stir anyone's blood. So I named him after a Greek hero and an Italian explorer: Jason Christopher."

"And the rest is history," Russ said, relieved that some of the tension had dissipated.

"Or mythology," Jason said glumly.

"Did you ever read the myth?" Nora asked him.

"I saw the movie," he offered.

"I remembered the story of Jason and the Argonauts being kind of a fun adventure," Nora said. "But when you were little I looked it up in a mythology book at the library. It didn't have the happy ending I expected."

"Well, lay it on me," Jason said resignedly. "What's a little more bad news tonight?"

"I don't remember it all that well," Nora admitted. "As I recall, Jason's wife found out he had an affair, so she killed their children. He ended up wandering from city to city, 'hated of men,' I think the phrase went."

"Gee, thanks, Mom," Jason said sardonically. "You've made dying young much more appealing."

"Oh, and I was worried you'd over-react," Nora said, equally sardonically. "Well, you're a man now. Your fate is in your own hands. Just keep in mind that your actions, whatever they are, will have consequences. Seemingly trivial things you do today can come back to haunt you later on."

"I don't know about you guys," Jason said, looking at Russ and the others, "but that sure cheered me up. Who were you talking to on the phone?" he asked Russ. "Satan wondering why I'm past-due on that soul I promised him?"

"More Man than devil," Russ said. "As in Manny."

Despite his black mood, this news obviously surprised and cheered Jason. "Really? What did she have to say?"

"She sounded desperate," Russ fibbed. "I guess they're snowed in over there, no food, burning the furniture to melt snow for drinking water, with no relief in sight. This was her last pitiful call for help before her fingers froze too hard to dial the phone."

"We'd better rush right over there," John said.

"Are you talking about Amanda Tyree?" Nora asked.

"Yeah."

"Oh, I'll bet Cynthia Tyree is just tickled to hear you guys calling her daughter 'Manny'."

"I'm not sure Manny's mom has ever been tickled by anything in her whole life," John said.

"Well, she may be tickled to find out that you boys won't be showing up there tonight," Nora said.

"Why not?" Jason asked. "After all, I'm a man now, as you've pointed out."

"You're a man who's been drinking," Nora retorted. "It would be irresponsible of me to let you drive in this condition."

"We'll take my car," John offered.

"You've been drinking as well," Nora said firmly.

"I'll drive them, Mrs. Walker," Matt said. "I only had half a glass of wine."

"That's true," John and Jason both testified.

"I didn't see your car out there," Nora said.

"My car wouldn't start," Matt said and then fibbed, even more smoothly than Russ had: "Your son was kind enough to lend me his car for the night until I can get mine running. I could drive us to Amanda's and bring him back here."

Nora looked at Matt and his half-full goblet. "If it starts to snow again," she said sternly, "I want you back here on the double."

They pushed back their chairs excitedly. "Thanks, Mom," Jason said, "on behalf of all of us nuts."

"Ah-ah-ah!" Nora said, freezing them in their tracks. "Before you nuts go charging out of here, I still see a lot of dirty dishes and pots and pans. Consider your nuts pinioned until you clean this up."

"All right, come on, you guys!" Jason said.

Quicker than the road crew in *Cool Hand Luke*, they whisked the dishes from the table, rinsed the goblets, stuck the plates and silver in the dishwasher, stowed the leftovers, stacked the dirty pots and pans, and wiped the counters.

Jason knocked on his parents' bedroom door.

"I'm changing," Nora said through the door.

"We got most of it," Jason called to her. "I'll do the rest in the morning."

"Be careful."

"You too."

O   O   O

Outside, the snow had stopped falling and the wind, having more energy than purpose, doodled fanciful drifts along the lee of the bare lilac hedge. The piñon smoke from the neighbors' chimney spiced the cold night air while overhead, broken clouds bustled across the diamond sky.

"Shotgun!" John called as Matt got into the driver's seat of the Wonder Car.

"Cool! I haven't ridden in the back seat in years," Jason said, getting in.

Russ got in back on the other side, the plastic car seat slick and brittle from the cold. He looked over at Jason and said, "Sorry about your folks."

Jason shrugged and looked out the window. "It's been a long time coming," he said, and then added to Matt, who spun the Wonder Car's starter, "Give it some gas."

Matt tromped the worn pedal and the car roared to life. He ground the stick into reverse and backed up the driveway, the small snowdrifts soft beneath the tires.

"I didn't hear everything your mom said to you," Russ went on to Jason, "but if there's anything I can do…"

"Yeah," Matt said to Jason, "you know we're here for you." At the top of the Alsace hill, he turned onto Polo Drive, the winding street deserted, only one other set of tire marks in the drifting snow.

"Thanks, guys," Jason said.

"Did your mom say what happened between her and your father?" Russ asked.

"Nothing special," Jason said. "They've been growing apart since I was little. I think they were just staying together 'for the kids' and now, with Steve gone and me up in Boulder, why go on? And who knows? Maybe they'll be happier apart anyway."

"Is she going to stay in the house?" Russ asked.

"S. D. C.'s transferring her out to California."

"Wow. When?"

"She's not sure," Jason said. "Sometime next year. But she and Dad are going to separate right away. And since neither of them can afford to keep the house without the other's help, they're going to have to sell it."

"Too bad!" Russ said. "It's a great house."

"I know. I'm going to miss it. She told me Dad would probably get an apartment here in town where I can stay if I want. If I used her California address as my residence, I'd have to pay out-of-state tuition."

"Drag. But you'll still go out and visit her, right?"

"For a while I'll either be working or in school," Jason said. "But I guess in theory, yeah. I didn't get the feeling from what she said tonight that she's just dying to pay my way out there so I can mooch off of her."

Jason stared out the window as they drove past the old polo grounds, now just an empty field, the defunct stands roofed with Spanish tile. Beyond that stood the imposing Tudor house of Governor John Love, whose daughter had been a schoolmate of theirs at Cheyenne.

"Anyway," Jason went on, breaking the awkward silence as they hit Mesa Avenue near Russ's house, "thanks for bailing me out earlier, you guys. I'm sure you were as anxious as I was to get out of there."

"I can't believe she didn't flip out about the wine," Russ said.

"She had me worried when she mentioned pinioning our nuts, though," John said. "Talk about handcuffs."

Jason chuckled. "She's been this way since she started driving her sexy new Capri. It's got rack-and-pinion steering." He shuddered at the thought.

"That's worse," John agreed. "Who wants their piñon nuts racked?"

"I couldn't believe I said we ate your nuts," Matt said to Jason. "Your mom's pretty cool."

"Yeah, cool," Jason said. "Except when it comes to Steve."

"Boy, you two got going hammer and tongs over that," John said.

"Did I tell you I got a letter from Easy?" Jason asked John.

"Who's that?" Russ asked.

"The guy Mom referred to, the one who told me how Steve died. Well, you met him when we did, that night down at the Doghouse."

"What did he say in his letter?" John asked.

"He's back in Nam, of course. I guess morale is really low over there now. He gave me the name of his commanding officer at the time of Steve's death, in case I wanted to find out more about what happened. I tried to look into it but needless to say, I couldn't get past anybody's secretary. I wrote a letter, too, but no one replied."

"Did you sign your name?" John asked.

"Sure," Jason said, puzzled.

"Bad idea," John said. "Now your name is on somebody's list somewhere."

"Hell, it must be on all sorts of lists," Jason said. "I've been signing every anti-war petition I can find."

"It may come back to haunt you," John told him as they drove past the long white stucco wall of Pauline Chapel.

"I may be a ghost myself by then." He turned to Russ. "So what did Manny say, really?"

"Just that she was bored," Russ said. "Her folks are in Aspen and Deb's on a date."

Matt pulled up the long drive to the Tyree house. Lights shone from the downstairs windows, glinting off the snow, which was a little deeper here next to the mountains. Amanda's bedroom light was on too, above the wooden trellis covered with woodbine that served as a carport and as Matt drove in, Amanda came to the window and waved to them.

"This is quite a house," Matt said, shutting off the Wonder Car.

"Haven't you been here before?" John asked him.

"I've just been by."

"Me too," Russ said.

"Oh, this place is much too grand for the likes of us," Jason said.

They followed Jason through the back patio to the kitchen instead of around the north side to the formal entrance. Amanda threw open the door for them.

"Welcome, hardy travelers!" she greeted them, kissing each on the cheek as he came in, directing them to hang their coats on the pegs behind the door. "So glad you could make it. How were the roads?" she asked Jason.

"I didn't drive," Jason told her. "John and I got too liquored up, according to my mom."

John patted Matt's shoulder. "So we left the driving to ol' Hoss here. He knows the way to carry the sleigh, et cetera, et cetera."

"How are you, Matt?" she asked. "College life doesn't seem to have dulled that lean and hungry look about you."

"Any hunger I had was obliterated by the fine meal we had at Jason's," Matt replied. "And may I add that college seems to agree with you as well."

"Well, thanks!" Amanda said. "What do you say, Russ?"

"I've got to agree with Matt," Russ said sincerely.

She looked great. She wore penny loafers, snug new jeans, and a sweater with a squarish reindeer pattern prancing across the gentle curves of her bust. When she smiled, which was often, a slight overbite of very pretty teeth came over her bottom lip. When she laughed, almost as often, she giggled like a little girl, the color coming up into her face like a blush, which Russ found quite charming.

She grinned at him now, saying, "Aren't you sweet? Thanks for rallying the troops."

"Well, naturally," John said, "when Russ told us of your dire circumstances… Just how bad is it over here?"

"Oh, dire indeed," she beamed. "It's like the Donner party, without the amenities. And here you gentlemen risk life and limb to come to my aid, full of compliments, and I have so little to offer you."

"We're full of something, anyway," John said in an aside to her.

"Just the invitation was more than we deserved," Matt said politely.

"I could make some hot apple cider, if you like," she offered.

"That sounds great," they all agreed.

She got out a gallon bottle of cider and a large pot. "What did you guys make for your dinner?"

"Crap," Jason said.

"It's pronounced 'crepe'," Matt corrected him.

"A rose by any other name…" Jason said bitterly.

"Or a nut," John added.

"We'll do better next time," Russ assured him.

"Is this a regular thing?" Amanda asked, getting out five mugs. "Like a cooking club?"

"See?" John asked. "She thinks we're nuts."

"And she didn't even try the crepes," Matt said.

"If we're nuts, then we're piñon nuts," Jason said.

Amanda giggled as she dropped cinnamon sticks into the mugs. "Piñon nuts?"

"That's right, ma'am, the Piñon Nuts!" John said in his best TV announcer's voice. "Four brave soldiers in an army that travels on its stomach, fighting for Truth, Justice, and the American Way!"

Amanda tinkled a couple of whole cloves into each mug and asked, "Just what form does this crusade take?"

"Eradicating that scourge of today's youth," Jason said, pulling a small lump of aluminum foil from his pocket. "Marijuana!"

"That isn't much marijuana," Russ pointed out.

"Well, actually," Jason said, peeling back the foil to reveal a dark brown sticky lump of hashish, "we've just collected the pollen from the flowers to prevent the Devil's Weed from reproducing. It's a complicated, difficult strategy. But the point is, in order to rid our great land of this dangerous narcotic, to keep it out of the hands of school-children, we should incinerate it as soon as possible." He turned to John. "Do you have that pipe?"

John felt his pockets but came up empty. "I wasn't warned about geeks bearing gifts. I brought nothing." Then, inspired, he asked Amanda, "Where's your bathroom?"

She smiled quizzically and pointed him in the right direction.

"He's lost his mind," Jason explained to all.

"I'm sure it'll turn up in there," Matt said.

"How are Gary and the rest of the Mind Machine?" Amanda asked Jason.

"Far out, I think it's fair to say."

John popped his head back into the kitchen. "Nope, not there. Do you have another bathroom?"

Even more puzzled, Amanda directed him to the master bath upstairs, then took a lemon from the refrigerator and sliced some thin wedges which she put in the mugs.

"Did your mom tell you that I called?" Jason asked Amanda casually.

"No! When?"

"Wednesday, when I got home. She said you were going out of town so I was really surprised when Russ told me you phoned."

"Oh, I was supposed to go to our cabin in Aspen with them this weekend," she said, stirring the cider. "But they invited the Blacks to go too."

Russ and Jason glanced significantly at one another, eyebrows cocked.

"And that's bad because..." Russ prompted her.

"Oh, I like Bill well enough, I suppose," Amanda said, lowering their eyebrows, "but his father can be so crude sometimes."

"Eureka!" John said, coming back into the kitchen, proudly displaying the trophy of his hunt: an empty toilet paper roll.

"What in the world?" Russ asked.

"You'll see," John said. "I'll need some foil, tape, and a pin."

Amanda, intrigued, rummaged through the utility drawer until she found each item. With a knife, John cut a finger-diameter hole near one end of the cardboard tube. He crimped the foil over the hole, denting the shiny metal slightly with his thumb, then taped the foil in place and made a series of pinpricks in the dented bowl.

He held up the finished product. "Behold! The Portable Hashish Reduction/Elimination Device."

"PHRED?" Jason asked.

"You got a better name?" John asked him.

"Just that of a mythical hero who evidently dies a miserable death," Jason said. "Where shall we do this?"

"Let's go out back," Amanda said, heading toward the dining room.

"Coming?" John asked Matt.

"I think I'll pass this time, thanks," Matt said. "Somebody's got to watch the cider."

"I'll give Matt a hand," Russ said.

"Shoot yourselves," John said with a shrug, following Amanda and Jason.

"This is a great place," Russ said after they left, admiring the oak cabinetry, the terrazzo floor, the weathered-brick work-island in the middle with the slotted racks for stemware through which a light shone onto the countertop.

"I can see why Jason feels intimidated," Matt said.

"And confused," Russ said, rubbing the lipstick Amanda had left on his cheek. "She does seem to treat us all equally as friends."

"Jason's got to make some sort of move, then."

"What about you and Deb?" Russ asked. "I hadn't heard you were corresponding with her. Have you got a thing going on? What did happen up in Jones Park, anyway?"

"Oh, she... I mean, we..." Matt sputtered. "Put it this way: I don't know what happened. All I know is that I can't stop thinking about her. And she couldn't care less."

"What's she like, anyway?"

"You've never met her, have you? Oh God, she's beautiful and intelligent and poised—basically, out of my league. Which is a moot point now, anyway, since she seems to be involved with someone else."

Russ clucked like a chicken.

"Easy for you to talk," Matt said. "You've already got a woman so your worries are over. What's your secret to winning that special someone?"

Forgetting to use a condom, Russ thought to himself. Aloud, he said, "Sheer luck. But sometimes you just have to put yourself out there. Let her know how you feel."

"I tell you what," Matt offered. "If I ever see her again, which seems unlikely, I'll be sure to let her know how I feel. But tell me about this thing with Prudence. You're actually living with her?"

"Put it this way. Everything I have in Boulder, other than my typewriter, fits inside a large suitcase. At the moment, the suitcase is sitting on a funky wing-backed chair in Prudence's room in an old house on Marine Street. But I'm not paying rent there, just chipping in on groceries and the other bills."

"Still, you've got a steady thing going."

It may become too steady, Russ thought. "It's not bad," he conceded to Matt.

"I'm surprised you're not more enthusiastic," Matt said. "You know, Jason took it pretty hard that you moved out on him. I always assumed it was the delights of living with Prudence that prompted the move. Are you sure there wasn't a problem between you and Jason?"

Russ wearily rubbed his eyes with his fingers. "Let's see. First of all, Prudence and I are going through a rough patch at the moment so I probably sound less enthusiastic than I truly am. But I have to admit, living with Jason wasn't always a bed of roses. I mean, he's a wonderful guy and will always be my friend, but he's always *on*. He's always working on something, always trying to push things along. It can get pretty intense after a while."

"What's intense?" Jason asked as the other three came back in, the hash smoke pungent in their clothes and obvious in their eyes.

"The circus," Russ said. "How are things outside?"

"Chilly!" Amanda said, checking the cider, which steamed fragrantly. A couple of the reindeer on her sweater had noses more prominent than before.

"You guys need to check out the pool room," John said.

"Let's take the cider in there," Amanda suggested, ladling the steamy liquid into the mugs. She handed each of them a coaster with his mug.

"Boy, this smells fantastic!" Jason said, carefully balancing the mug as he walked.

"I didn't bring swimming trunks," Russ pointed out.

"No diving in this pool," John said. "You'll rack your balls."

"Sounds intense," Matt said, following.

"What circus?" Jason asked.

o   o   o

Harve, Amanda's father, had done up the pool room right. Everything, from the plush beige carpet to the walnut paneling to the gilded plaster moldings on the ceiling, looked deluxe. Bookshelves filled with leather-and-gold-leaf-bound collections covered the south wall below the windows. The north wall held a built-in entertainment center, all Macintosh electronics, as well as a built-in cigar humidor. The east wall, adjacent to the patio, featured a large stained glass window which matched the Tiffany shade over the pool table. The table, with its spotless green baize, carved walnut legs, and leather baskets, stood in the center of the room, with various comfortable-looking leather-upholstered seats scattered about for the spectators.

To the west, French doors led out to a secluded garden. A small patch of lawn was bordered by a brick retaining wall with a couple of brass lamp-posts on each end. From the center of the wall hung a clam-shell basin over which a cherub stood on a pedestal, his hands behind his head, a small painful-looking icicle hanging between his legs, hinting at what he did in the warm months.

"Whatcha think, Brer Fox?" Jason said, sidling up to Russ, who stood agog taking in the pool room.

"I think I've died and gone to heaven," Russ admitted. "Man, this is a room for the ages."

"He's right, Manny," Matt concurred. "This is incredible."

"You know," Jason said, sidling up to Manny, "my parents are thinking of putting me up for adoption."

Amanda giggled again, her hand crumpling her auburn hair which, a little shorter than last summer, fell right back into place. "Then I better go into the nursery and change the sheets in the crib for you."

"Crib sheets?" Jason protested. "I may be immature but I'm no cheater."

"Can we shoot some stick?" John asked, fingering the cues.

"Help yourself," Amanda told him.

"If only it were that easy," he said, hefting and sighting along the shaft of various cues.

"How about some music?" Amanda offered.

"Music?" Jason said. "What's that?"

"What would you like to hear?" Amanda asked.

"Ladies' choice," said Matt.

While John and Jason settled on cues and Matt racked the balls, Amanda put on an LP. Russ quickly recognized the first cut as "Lucky" from *Eli and the Thirteenth Confession*, a favorite album of Prudence's as well.

"Good choice," he told her.

"Who is this?" Jason asked.

"Laura Nyro," Russ told him. "She's pretty cool. Not only writes great material but also sings all the vocal parts on the record."

"What I wouldn't give for a good studio," Jason said. "Who breaks?"

"Wait a minute, gents," Russ interrupted, his sense of propriety taking over. "Have you settled the stakes?"

"I'm broke," John declared.

"Money's gauche," Jason maintained. "Bet what your heart desires."

"How about my head?" John said, contemplating. "On the island of Maui, an isolated valley with a waterfall. Above the stream, hidden in a grove of paluka-luka trees, is a small clearing in which grows some of the tallest, hairiest, stoned-est marriage-you-wanna in the whole red-eyed world. I'll bet my own weight of it on this one game."

"Phew!" Jason said, wiping his brow. "That's a hefty wager, especially compared to my two measly scraps of paper."

"Which are…"

"Backstage passes to that free concert the Stones are putting on in the Bay area. You get to party with the boys before they go on and stand right down in front for their set."

"All right, then, gentlemen," Russ said. "John's burgeoning weight of Maui Wowie against backstage passes to the last great concert of the decade. Let's have a good clean game and, in deference to the lady, no spitting and no belching."

"I still don't know who breaks," Jason said.

"You deserve a break," John told him, magnanimously waving his hand toward the table.

Jason set the cue ball opposite the triangle of racked balls. He curled his finger around the cue, his curly blonde hair brushing against his wrist, his blood-shot blue eyes fidgeting. "Uh-oh, flashback."

"Acid trip?" John asked.

"Physics lab," he explained, still stroking the cue through his fingers. "I mean, once I hit the cue ball, the whole thing goes ballistic, right? Just plain old Newtonian physics."

"Shoot first, ask questions later," John insisted.

"See? Intense," Russ said in an aside to Matt, who nodded knowingly.

Jason broke forcefully, the balls scattering around the table, the 6-ball finding the side pocket. "Little 'uns," he said.

"I want to hear more about physics lab," Amanda said, sitting next to Russ on the love seat, gingerly sipping her hot cider.

"I mean, is that the way the universe works?" Jason said, sinking the 3-ball in a corner. "The break corresponds to the First Kablooie, when God sets the whole she-bang in motion." The 2 fell in a side pocket. "All the subsequent events, even the laws governing the subsequent events, are then pre-determined." The 7 fell too but then he muffed a tricky bank shot.

"I thought you were a free-will man," John said, the 15 skimming along the bumper into the side pocket.

"According to Matt, I have no choice," Jason said, standing again after John missed an easy side shot. "But isn't science based on the assumption that all things are ultimately, theoretically, knowable?"

"Theoretically, maybe," Matt amended. "Practically, no."

"Wouldn't the fact that all things are even theoretically knowable imply that events are predetermined?"

"Just because something is knowable," Amanda put in, "doesn't mean it's predictable, does it? I mean, you can know someone pretty well and still not be able to predict what they'll do."

"I predict," Jason said, lining up a tight shot on the 1-ball against the bumper, "this will fall in that side pocket." He shot and missed. "True knowledge would have predicted that correctly, wouldn't it?"

"Since your skill at pool," Amanda said, "—or lack of it, in this case—is involved, you'd have to have knowledge not only of the laws of physics governing the game but also the laws governing your own behavior, your own limitations."

"You're right," Jason said, watching John sink three in a row. "That type of self-reference complicates things considerably. It's like pointing two mirrors at each other. Let's simplify the question. What about just the physical universe?"

"Thanks for bringing it down to my level," John said, finally missing.

"What do you mean?" Amanda asked Jason.

John had left the 5 for Jason as a gimme and Jason sank the 4 easily as well. "Okay, let's say you rack the balls on this table and leave them there. An earthquake hits, shaking the balls all around. Some fall into pockets right away. Maybe a few hold out a long time but eventually, if the earthquake lasts long enough and the pool table manages to survive, all the balls find their way into the pockets without anyone ever touching them. No skill involved. Predetermined, right?"

"But random," Matt said. "Not necessarily knowable."

"Shoot," John insisted.

Jason missed the banked 8-ball shot. "Doesn't everything appear random until you figure out how it works?" he asked.

"This game does," John said, sinking his last stripe but missing the 8-ball shot.

"That's where fundamental probability takes over," Matt said. "Some events just aren't predictable. It's like radioactive particle decay. The average rate of decay can be determined but the individual event is unpredictable."

Amanda, like the others, clapped when Jason sank the 8-ball but then she turned to Matt. "Didn't Einstein believe that God doesn't play dice with the universe?"

"He didn't rule out pool," John said, handing his cue to Russ.

"So what's riding on this game?" Jason asked his new opponent.

Russ chalked the cue. "Let's see. How about a hand-copied Tang Dynasty manuscript of the Hui Neng Sutra?"

"Yikes!" Jason said. "He sees me and raises me. Hmm. Okay. Front row seats to the Super Bowl, right behind the bench."

"Which bench?"

"NFL, so you sit by the winners."

"Didn't Joe Willie teach you anything last January?" Russ said.

"No. But what were we talking about?" Jason asked, watching Matt rerack the balls.

"Unpredictable events," Matt reminded him.

"Oh, yeah, right, right. Okay. Let's say I'm an atom of some unstable isotope."

John stepped between Jason and Amanda, saying, in a voice like Dudley Doright's, "Look out, Nell! Deadly radioactive jasonium! If necessary, I'll throw my body across yours to shield you!"

Amanda snickered. "From one measly atom? I hardly think so. Keep talking, atom."

Jason watched Russ break without sinking a ball. Jason sank the 12, saying, "Okay, let's say the half-life of jasonium is 70 years. But I, one single atom of jasonium, could disintegrate in 15 seconds or last another billion years, right?"

Russ, sinking a couple of solids, said, "Long live individual reality."

"For any given atom," Matt conceded to Jason, "I suppose that's true."

"So an individual jasonium atom can pretty much do what it pleases when it pleases,"

Jason reasoned, making a difficult double-bank and then missing an easy corner shot.

"That's true on the atomic level," Matt said, "but in our macroscopic world, it's those averages, those probabilities, that count."

Amanda murmured her concurrence. "Those types of quantum events, like the disintegration of an atom, are imperceptible to our senses. At least, that's what my Physics-For-Liberal-Arts-Majors professor at C. C. told us."

"Actually," Matt said, watching Jason miss another easy shot, "I guess, in a very dark room, the unaided human eye can detect a single photon, which is a quantum event."

"Really?" Jason asked, intrigued. "That's amazing."

"Enlightening," Russ added, already down to the 8-ball but blowing a difficult full-table bank.

"How so?" Jason asked him.

"Yeah, Russ," John protested. "No fair hogging all the enlightenment."

"It just reminds me of the Indian sages who meditate in an absolutely dark room for days and then one tiny shaft of sunlight is let in. Enlightenment follows like day follows night." He lined up a fairly straightforward 8-ball shot and sank it but the cue ball fell into a side-pocket first. "Damn."

"Close but no cigar," Jason crowed, pretending to polish his fingernails on his lapel. "Just call me Colorado Slim. Who's my next victim? Manny?"

"I think you should play Matt first," Manny said. "And Russ, you're welcome to a cigar anyway. In fact, all of you, help yourselves. Dad will never miss them. He shouldn't smoke them anyway."

John, Jason, and Matt each picked one from the humidor, John lighting them from his Zippo. Matt took a couple of puffs and then dropped the cigar in his lap. He scrambled to pick it up but burned his fingers when he grabbed the lit end.

"Maybe we're on to something," Jason said, watching Matt fumble. "Maybe if we distract him with pool and cigars, we can bring him down to our intellectual level. Evidently he won't let us dull his faculties with drugs."

Matt, leaving the pesky cigar in an ashtray, chalked his cue, saying, "I made a fool of myself when you got me high up in Jones Park."

"That's not what Deb said," Amanda mentioned nonchalantly. "More cider, anyone?"

She collected the mugs and went to refill them.

"What was that supposed to mean?" Russ asked Matt after she left.

Matt looked puzzled. "I have no idea. I sure felt like a fool."

"Could it be," Jason speculated, "that your probability curves don't predict every possible outcome?"

"Probability!" Matt snorted. "If there was such a thing as an *im*probability curve, this one would go hyperbolic."

"We'll just have to pump Manny for information when she gets back," John teased.

Matt bristled. "Nobody pumps anybody," he insisted.

"There is none so blind…" Jason said.

"Yeah, well, we'll see," Matt said.

"What's at stake this game?" Russ asked.

"So far," Jason said, "I've won a shitload of dope—"

"Thanks, bro," John interjected, meticulously racking the balls once again.

"—and a priceless manuscript which, if I could actually read it, might teach me a thing or two. What can I afford to lose? How about my crown as Love's Greatest Fool?"

"I have my own claim to that title," Matt contended.

"Hey, you interlopers!" John exclaimed. "I was there first!"

"You pikers," Russ said, imagining handing out his own, far cheaper cigars nine months hence. "You have to have a woman to be a fool."

"If he wins," Jason said to the group, "Matt owns the crown undisputed. Okay?"

Matt smiled and shook his head. "Okay, fine. And I'll put up Einstein's brain."

"Is it still around?" Russ asked.

"Yeah, the guy that did the autopsy kept it," Jason said.

"So that's why Matt's so brainy," John said. "He carries a spare."

"Not for long," Jason said.

Matt lined up his break shot. "Why, I've half a mind to…"

"To what?" Amanda asked, coming in with the refilled mugs on a tray.

"To throw away," John said, puffing at the cigar. "And take it from someone who knows: it's not half bad."

Matt hit the 1-ball squarely and the triangle of colored balls burst apart, the 6 and the 13 finding pockets in opposite corners. Having sunk one of each, Matt walked around the table looking for the easiest shot.

"Doesn't that bother you?" Jason asked him.

"What? Sinking two balls at once?" He chose the 15 and sank it easily. "Big 'uns."

"No," Jason said. "The capricious nature of the universe."

Matt's 12 found the corner and wobbled indecisively but wouldn't fall. "I don't know that I'd call it capricious," he said to Jason.

"Maybe lawless, then. What about that totalitarian dictum of physics: everything not forbidden is compulsory?"

"What about it?" Matt asked, sinking the 12 after Jason missed his shot.

"How does it apply to that one lone rebellious jasonium atom? Let's say he's slated to disintegrate after, say, 17 years. He wakes up that morning, looks around, and says, 'You know what? I ain't doing it! Forget it! I'll disintegrate 432,000 years from now instead.' Without a law governing it, who's to stop him?"

"What you're forgetting," Matt said, watching Jason sink three in a row, "is that atoms don't have consciousness. They can't make choices."

"Well, that stinks," Amanda said.

"I'm with her," Jason said after blowing another easy shot. "Somehow a choice gets made. Either the individual atom makes it or some other mysterious agent, unknown to it, unknown to us, makes it. I think I'd rather leave it to the little guy, to the individual, than to some hidden cosmic bureaucracy."

"Atoms aren't individuals," Matt said, missing too.

"Well, obviously they can be divided," Jason conceded. "But what do you think, Russ? Do atoms have individual reality?"

Russ smiled. "It reminds me of Joshu's dog."

Jason stared at him blankly. "You know, considering you're the only one not smoking anything…"

"Joshu," Russ explained, "was a great Zen master. One day a monk came up to him and asked him if a dog has Buddha nature. It has become one of the most famous Zen *koans*, thought problems."

"What did he say?" Amanda asked.

"He said no," Russ told her. "Though what he meant by it has puzzled novices ever since."

"What do you say?" Jason asked, lining up and making two short shots in the corner, sinking first the 14 and then the 9. "About atoms having individual reality, that is. I don't think we want any dogs running around here tonight, whether they have Buddha nature or not."

Russ pondered the question. These discussions were always the perfect grist for his mill. "On one level, I think I agree with Matt. Atoms don't have consciousness, therefore they don't have perceptions, and without either one of those, no true individual reality exists."

"A Daniel come to judgment," Matt said, savoring his cigar, watching Jason sink the 10 easily and then stretch across the table and, using a lot of back-english, finesse the 11 into the side pocket without scratching.

"On the other hand," Russ continued, "there's obviously some sort of choice going on at some level. Maybe that implies some form of alternate reality."

"Alternate reality?" Amanda asked. "I don't remember that one."

"You don't?" Jason asked incredulously. "You're the one who came up with it."

"I did? When?"

"Last summer, in Jones Park, when we had that reality discussion," Jason explained. "I can't believe you don't remember that. I've thought about it a lot ever since."

"You have?" Amanda asked him, her eyes holding his.

"Among other things," Jason said gently but then broke the gaze to ask Matt, "Who's turn is it?"

"Actually, I believe it's mine," Matt said. He lined up and executed a simple bank on the 8-ball, the black sphere rolling across the green field and disappearing into the corner pocket he'd called.

Jason stared in bewilderment at the table. "How did I get so far behind?"

"You sank his last four balls for him," John pointed out.

"Why didn't you tell me?" Jason asked Matt.

"You and I have been close friends for a long time," he said, putting his arm around Jason's shoulders. "I figured you were just doing me a favor."

Jason laughed. "Boy, I really am a great friend, huh? Oh, well. Good hash, anyway. At least I get to sit down here next to the inventor of alternate reality," he said, plopping down next to Amanda.

"No, you don't," she said, getting up. "Now I play Matt. Rack 'em up again, John."

Jason sat in the love seat anyway, chewing his lip, watching Amanda take her own cue from the rack and chalk it. He puffed his cigar, looked at Russ, and shrugged.

"What stakes, fair lady?" Matt asked.

"Ah, let's see. I'll wager the Unicorn in the Garden tapestry," she said, lining up her break shot. "And you, kind sir?"

"Only that which I would offer anyway," Matt said gallantly. "My fealty, my honor, and my pledge to leap to your defense in your hour of need."

"That's right," Jason said. "He won my crown, didn't he?"

"He's no fool," John claimed. "If she wins, he gets to cop a fealty."

"Hush, you guys," Amanda said. "He's given me motivation to win now." She sent the cue ball flying and the balls scattered like chickens. None fell.

Matt, carefully handling his cigar, had missed the break. "Stripes or solids?"

"You're free to choose," she told him.

"Long live alternate reality," Jason said.

"You know, if you're going to attach my name to that term," Amanda said to Jason, sinking a solid after Matt sank one stripe and missed another, "I should know what you mean by it."

"Wow, a pop quiz," Jason said. "And I didn't study. Well, when I said it just then, I guess I was talking about having at least a couple of alternatives. Stripes and solids represent a couple of possible realities."

"But once he chooses one, like stripes in this case, what happens to the alternate reality?"

"Interesting point," Jason said. "I guess it just disappears, like your lap does when you stand up."

That didn't sit right with Russ. "If it's that transient, is it truly a reality?"

"And whatever he chooses isn't an alternate reality anymore," Amanda said, sinking two balls with one shot. "It's just plain old everyday reality."

"That limits alternate reality to whatever doesn't happen, though," Jason said, sounding disappointed. "It would just be the opposite of this reality, whatever that means."

Matt lined up a long cross-table shot. "On the other hand, if alternate reality encompasses all the other possible outcomes, there would have to be an infinite number of alternate realities." He made the shot.

"But to an observer who knows ultimate reality," speculated Russ, "whatever we think of as 'true' reality is just one of those infinite alternate realities. In other words, to that observer, there's nothing *but* alternate realities."

"Maybe so," Jason said, "but where do you have to stand to get that view?"

"That's part of Einstein's insight into relativity," Matt said, putting away a couple of easy shots. "You can't separate the reality from the observer. The frame of reference, the individual reality, as it were, always colors the observation. In that sense, there's no such thing as ultimate reality."

"Really?"

It wasn't a profound question but it had an immediate effect on everyone. Russ looked up and saw that it had been asked by a beautiful young lady standing in the doorway. She wore a very short tartan plaid pleated skirt and a black ribbed turtle-neck sweater. She had shoulder-length blonde hair and the bluest, liveliest eyes Russ had ever seen.

Amanda set down her cue. "Deb! Sorry I didn't come to the door. It's really hard to hear the bell back here."

"I let myself in," Deb said.

"I didn't think you'd make it over tonight," Amanda said, hugging her. "You know everybody, don't you? I know you know John and Jason and I'm sure you remember Matt. Have you met Russ?"

"I don't think so," Deb said, waving. "Hi, Russ."

"Hi, Deb," Russ said.

"Don't let me interrupt your game," Deb said, looking around the room.

"I think it's still your shot, Matt," Amanda said. "The stakes are incredibly high tonight," she explained quietly to Deb.

"Really?" Deb asked again. "What did you bet?"

"That Unicorn in the Garden tapestry."

Deb smiled, intrigued. "What did he bet?"

"How did you put it, Matt?" Amanda asked him.

Matt, who had been lining up a shot for some time now, didn't reply.

"Something about love, honor, and obey, I think," John said helpfully.

Matt finally tried the shot but hit the ball so hard that he not only sank the 15, he also sank the 8 and sent the cue ball bouncing underneath the humidor to boot. Everybody else laughed good-naturedly. Matt blushed and sat down without a word.

"I'm sorry, Matt," Deb said. "I hope our talking didn't throw you off."

Matt smiled crookedly and sought consolation in his hot cider.

"Matt's a machine," John said. "He's been lecturing on relativity while doing cigar tricks and beating us at pool. So how've you been, Deb?"

"Great, John," she said. "Just great. How are you?"

"I used to think I was better than nothing. You've convinced me otherwise."

"Oh, now…" Deb began.

"How was your date?" Amanda broke in. "I'm surprised you're home this early."

"At the time, I thought it was pretty good. You've convinced me otherwise. How do you rate, getting four guys all to yourself like this?"

It was Amanda's turn to blush.

John stepped into the breach once again. "It was a pool emergency. Manny's turned out to be the only decent table we could reach without a dog-sled. You know, any port in a storm."

"It's not much of a storm," Deb said, looking out the window. "Oh, but look! It's starting to snow again!"

Sure enough, the wind had died down and small white flakes drifted lazily past the French doors and added insult to injury by piling up on the cherub's icicle.

"We better get going," Matt said to Jason. "I promised your mom…"

"What!?" Deb cried. "I just got here! Can't you stay for just one more game?"

"It's not coming down very hard," Jason said to Matt, who just shrugged in reply.

"So do I play Matt?" Deb asked.

"Matt sank the 8-ball before its time," Amanda said. "I guess you and I should play. Is that all right with everyone?"

There were no dissenters so John leapt up to rack the balls once again.

Deb picked up the cue Matt had been using. "May I?" she asked him and he nodded, watching her chalk the end.

"You should break," Amanda told her.

"Don't we place our bets first?"

"I suppose," Amanda said. "Okay, let's see…"

"Ooo, I know," Deb said with a mischievous smile. "How about what we played for last summer?"

Amanda peered out into the garden, where the snow fell harder, and then looked back at Deb. "Tonight?" she asked in disbelief, her face flushed. "Oh, that's… that's…"

"What?" Deb taunted her. "Dirty pool?"

Amanda drew herself up at that. "All right, you're on. Break."

Russ had no idea what they had wagered and could tell from the looks on the other guys' faces that they didn't either. But everyone could tell that it amounted to a serious bet, judging by the intensity with which both Amanda and Deb approached the game.

Russ could also tell that none of the guys cared a whit about the score. Each seemed content just to sit and watch the young women play.

Not that long ago—junior high, maybe—Russ had considered the opposite sex some indecipherable, alien species that, except for his mother and sister and a few teachers, had a minimal impact on his life. That had changed at puberty, of course. Still indecipherable and alien all too often, women now represented life's one true goal.

Until a few short weeks ago, that desire seemed destined to go unfulfilled. He had a few girlfriends to his credit and had gained some self-confidence as a lover but he simply couldn't envision himself as half of a regular couple. He had once asked his father about that kind of commitment. Louie told him it was like catching a dragon: you just had to grab it by the tail and hang on, hope it didn't kill you before you got the thing subdued.

So when Prudence came along, available, interested, even insistent, Russ had leapt at the chance, grabbed the dragon's tail. But lately he wondered if perhaps Prudence hadn't pounced on him. Attractive, hip, stylish, and intellectual almost to a fault, she had a way of making her preferences seem like mutual decisions. In fact, she had always claimed to use birth control pills faithfully but she had seemed unconscionably blithe when informing him of the possibility of being pregnant.

Not that getting married to Prudence and starting a family would be such a bad thing. He knew he could do a lot worse. But he also knew he had barely explored all the new and interesting sexual possibilities birth control pills had spawned. He felt like a pinch hitter coming into a game tied in the ninth, hitting a game-winning home run, and then feeling disappointed because the game ended so soon. He still wanted to play ball.

And nothing brought that home more than watching Deb shoot pool. Slight in stature, she often had to lean across the table to make a shot, her short skirt pulled up so high he sometimes caught a fleeting glimpse of her white panties. Or she would lean onto the table, her breast flattened against the wood, her blonde hair trailing across the green baize. He wondered if it might not be worth giving up the bird in the hand just to be able to stare at the one in the bush, especially if it looked like Deb, even if you didn't have a prayer of catching it. He no longer wondered why John and Matt found Deb so appealing.

John, in fact, sat vacantly with his mouth open as he watched them play, his blood-shot eyes avidly following their every move. Matt squirmed uncomfortably in his chair, looking like Odysseus tied to the mast. When Russ glanced at Jason, he found him already looking back. Russ rolled his eyes and Jason smiled and shook his head.

Deb and Amanda, meanwhile, seemed oblivious to the guys, intent on their game, calling every shot, shooting with practiced precision. Russ considered commenting on how quiet it had become but didn't want to break the spell.

So far, Amanda had outshot Deb, sinking all her stripes but the 15. But Deb had left the cue ball right next to the 15 against the bumper and the 15 kissed the 8-ball. Amanda had to sit on the edge of the table to get the angle, holding the cue nearly vertical. Carefully lining up the shot, she made her decisive stroke but the cueball tagged right along with the 8 into the pocket while the 15 rattled to a stop in the other corner.

"Oh, no!" Amanda cried. "No, no, no!"

"Oh, yes," Deb chortled. "It's your turn, sister."

John cleared his throat. "To do what?"

Deb put her arm around Amanda's shoulders. "She has to—"

"—perform some silly little ritual," Amanda interrupted her. "Which I will do after you guys leave."

"Sounds like welching to me," John said. "I think she should pay up now."

"Fine with me," Deb said, grinning at how flustered Amanda looked.

"Oh, like all of you paid off your bets already," Amanda said defensively.

"We really should get going anyway," Matt pointed out. Out the window it looked like a pillow fight had gotten completely out of control, the soft white down gathering on every surface.

"The man's a machine, I tell you," John said.

"If we don't leave pretty soon," Jason said, "we might be stuck here for the night."

John looked at him bewildered. "Your point being?"

"Come on, you guys," Russ said, reluctantly standing. "We should let these ladies settle up. But I think I speak for all when I say, it's been grand. Thanks so much, Man, for having us over."

"No, thank you, guys," Amanda said as they made their way back to the kitchen door.

"Deb, it was nice meeting you," Russ said as they donned their coats.

"My pleasure," Deb said. "And Matt, why haven't you called or dropped by? I told you I would be most perturbed if you didn't."

"Well, I… I mean, you've been…" Matt stammered.

"God, you silver-tongued devil," John said. "What he's trying to say is that he'll call you tomorrow," he told Deb on Matt's behalf.

"Promise?" Deb asked Matt.

"Promise," Matt said and abruptly walked out the door. "Come on, you guys."

"He's driving," Jason said to Amanda, "so we better go. Let's do this again sometime."

"Are you Piñon Nuts planning another get together?" Amanda asked, standing in the doorway as they walked to the car.

"Maybe over the holidays," Jason called back to her. "We'll do it up right. Would you and Deb like to come?"

"Love to." She waved one last time, shut the door, and switched off the outside light.

As Matt started the Wonder Car, John hit him on the arm.

"What?" Matt said, turning on the wipers to clear the windshield.

"What does she have to do, throw a brick through your window?"

"Who?"

"What do you mean, who? Deb, you idiot."

"Oh, give me a break. She went out with her boyfriend earlier tonight. I'm not even sure she's completely over you."

"Me!? I'm yesterday's papers."

Matt put the car in reverse but his foot slipped off the clutch pedal and the car died. He turned the key again but got just a faint clunk.

"Uh-oh," Jason said ominously.

"What?"

"It does this sometimes. Dad told me the solenoid's going out."

"What do I do?"

"Try it again."

After a dozen more clunks despair filled the car like a bad odor. "Now what?" Matt asked. "Could Deb give us a jump?" Deb's Jeep sat right next to the Wonder Car.

"It wouldn't help," Jason said bleakly. "This happened yesterday and Dad got it going just by tapping something with a screwdriver."

"Tapping what?"

"Something under the hood."

"Well, duh!" John said. "What, the pinion nut?"

"Maybe Manny will let me try to call him. He's playing at the Broadmoor not a mile from here. If he can't explain it to me, maybe he could come over. He's bound to be done pretty soon. But, boy, is this lame." He looked in dread at the imposing facade of the home.

"I'll go with you," Russ volunteered.

They rang the bell twice but got no response.

"If they're still in the pool room," Russ said, "they probably can't hear the bell. We didn't earlier when Deb showed up."

Jason knocked too but still nothing. "Now what?"

"Well, we were just here. Let's just go in."

Jason turned the knob and they went into the kitchen but before they could call out, Deb came in from the dining room.

She shot a quick glance toward the pool room and said, "We thought you left."

"My car stalled," Jason said. "Do you think Man would mind if I used her phone?"

Deb seemed to do some quick calculating. "I tell you what," she said, making up her mind. "Jason, you go in and see Mandy. Russ," she said, grabbing her coat, "can I talk to you? Outside?"

Russ followed her out. "What's going on?"

"I don't know if you're aware of it," she told him, putting on her coat, "but Mandy and Jason have a thing for each other."

"Everybody knows that," Russ told her.

"Everybody but them. What they need is a push. Well, I just gave them a push."

"Oh?"

"Most definitely," Deb said, smiling broadly. "But maybe we ought to leave them alone."

"You know," it occurred to Russ as they walked out to the Wonder Car to talk it over with the others, "I know someone else who could use a push."

"I don't know," Deb said, looking at the way the cars were situated. "It's pretty slippery."

"What's happening?" Matt asked, rolling down the window.

"Jason's going to call his dad," Deb said. "So nobody here knows how to get the car running?"

They shook their heads sadly.

"Why don't I drive the rest of you home in the Jeep?" she volunteered. "No point in everybody being stuck here."

John called shotgun again as he got out. Matt reluctantly left the Wonder Car's keys in the ignition before getting out too.

"You rode shotgun on the way here," Russ said pointedly to John. "Why don't you let Matt sit up front?"

"Ah, good idea," John said, holding the door for Matt.

Deb started the Jeep as they got in. "So who do I drop off first?"

"Are you sure one of us shouldn't stay to give Jason a hand?" Matt asked, looking back as they headed down the drive.

"He'll be fine," Deb said, grinning again.

"I live the closest," Russ replied to Deb's question.

"And you're down on Cheyenne Road, right?" Deb asked John as she pulled onto Mesa and drove east.

"Boulevard," John corrected her. "But the Yellow Fellow is still at Jason's."

"Is that on the way to your house?" Deb asked Matt.

"More or less," Matt said.

The Jeep's tires glided silently across the freshly fallen snow. "How's traction?" Russ asked Deb.

"Not bad," she said, watching the road carefully, slowing long before the intersection by Broadmoor Lake. "But I put it in four-wheel drive before I came to Amanda's."

"Didn't you tell me the Fellow's tires are going bald?" Russ asked John. "Maybe you should crash at my place tonight."

"Oh, that's all right, I'll just take it—"

Russ kicked him in the leg. When he looked over, Russ pointed his finger back and forth between Matt and Deb in front. The light dawned and John smiled.

"You know, on second thought, maybe you're right, Russ," he said. "Alsace is pretty steep. It'd be better to try it in daylight, if you don't mind putting me up."

They pulled into the drive at Russ's house and Deb stopped by the back door. A light burned in the kitchen.

"Thanks for the ride, Deb," Russ said. "I'm sure you're in capable hands, Matt."

"You kids be careful now," John insinuated. "I don't want to hear about you two getting lost and winding up stuck in some snowdrift, huddling together for warmth all night."

"Good night, John," Deb said dismissively.

Undeterred, John reached forward and put his hand on Matt's shoulder, saying, "You know what Deb once told me? She doesn't think it's true that no two snowflakes are the same."

"Good night, John," Deb said again.

"It is true, though, you know," Matt said to Deb, looking at the flakes resting briefly on the windshield before the wipers swept them away.

"Oh, come on," Deb doubted. "How could anybody know that for sure? What, is there some little flake inspector who checks them all for duplicates before he lets them fall?"

"It's the radial symmetry all snowflakes have in common that gives us the illusion that they're somehow part of a pattern," Matt said to Deb. "Every flake is actually six pairs of mirror images of one particular permutation of crystallization. But if you look at just one half of one of those pairs, each one is an arbitrary, unique configuration."

"Is that so?" Deb said. "So then each one must have its own individual reality and I thought you said earlier that you didn't believe in individual reality."

"I said there's no such thing as ultimate reality," Matt said.

"Well, you kids have fun," John said, getting out after Russ.

"Nicely done, John," Russ said after the car door closed. The two of them stood looking at the car, where Deb and Matt carried on their conversation awhile before Deb put the Jeep back in gear and slowly drove off.

The porch light came on and Russ's father opened the door. "Are you boys all right?" he asked. "Your mother was worried, Russ."

"Louie," John said to him, watching the Jeep disappear into the falling snow, "I think this is the beginning of a beautiful friendship."

. . . O . . . O . . . O . . .

Cameahwait's sister spots some blue-and-white forget-me-nots growing in a rock outcrop some distance from the trail. She picks some for her hair.

"You better watch it!" Cameahwait shouts at her. "If you're not careful, the Blackfeet will get you!" When she ignores him, he shouts to his father, some distance up the pass, "Dad! Sacagawea's wandering off again!"

With a patient groan, his father comes back down to them. Cameahwait gloats a little as his father takes the blossoms from Sacagawea's hair and carefully places them back on the ground. But his father lectures them both: "In these high places, where even the fearless trees are afraid to grow, time passes very slowly. A moccasin print can last a thousand moons."

Cameahwait woke with a start. Commotion roiled through the camp. He rolled out of the buffalo robe grumpily, his stomach growling. They were down to dried camas root, piñon nuts, and salmon jerky, and everybody was getting a little edgy. If Cameahwait couldn't do something to turn things around, the tribe would look to someone else for leadership. At times like these he missed his father and sister more than ever.

Outside, everyone was abuzz. The women crowded in a circle, passing around new moccasin awls, some amazing flat heavy things that shone more clearly than still water, and vermilion paint, the color of peace, brighter than any he'd seen before.

"Where did you get these things?" he asked.

"Some men who came down from the pass gave them to us," one of the women said. "They shouted at us that they were strangers. They were right. They wore clothes of incredible colors and the weirdest hats you ever saw. They showed us a kind of prayer cloth as red as blood, as white as snow, and as blue as the evening sky, all the red and white in perfect rows and the blue shot with pointy stars."

"Really? This sounds interesting," Cameahwait said, looking up toward the high divide, Lemhi Pass. "Take me to them. What have we got to lose?"

At least, that's the way I envision the events that took place just east of the tiny present-day town of Tendoy, Idaho, on August 12, 1805. Cameahwait brought his small translucent stone pipe with him and smoked with the man who had shouted "Tab-ba-bone!" ("Stranger!") at the women, Captain Meriwether Lewis. The rest is history.

On my trip to Colorado last summer, I camped in the broad valley just south of there, known as Cotes Defile, named for the trapper who discovered it a few years after the Lewis and Clark Expedition. In this case, the word "defile" is misleading in both its meanings. "Defile" denotes a narrow pass or valley but Cotes Defile is a broad park of sagebrush between the jagged snow-

capped peaks of the Lemhi and Bitterroot Ranges. And, far from being defiled by development, the entire valley shows almost no sign of habitation, other than a few fences to keep the scattered range cattle off the road. Except for the highway down the center, the valley has barely changed since 1805.

As far as I know, Cotes Defile owes its pristine state neither to government preservation nor to environmentalist zeal. Rather, the remote location and the lack of resources, other than solitude and beauty, have made it, so far at least, unattractive to exploitation.

I enjoyed Cotes Defile for what isn't there. Maybe it's the legacy of Daniel Boone, who decided to move farther west when he spotted the smoke from his neighbor's chimney. Freedom is a lonely thing. It requires wide open spaces and few people.

November 27, 1999

The wind sighs through the gallows. Something shakes; maybe it's his knees. Hooded, his chin sinking into his chest, his arms useless, John hears the preacher's mumbled rote, muffled by the coarse fabric: "They that are after the flesh do mind the things of the flesh; but they that are after the Spirit the things of the Spirit, for to be carnally minded is death." The hangman fumbles with the trip lever for the trapdoor. But the lever turns out to be John's own throbbing erection. As he falls, he wakes.

His eyes popped open and the first thing he saw was May's filigreed white bra just inches from his eyes.

"Oh, you're awake," she said, struggling to watch the road and steer while reaching into the back seat for something. "Could you hand me my sweater? That blouse was bugging the shit out of me."

Blinking the sleep away, he retrieved the white angora sweater and handed it to her, then held the wheel while she slipped it over her head.

"Thanks," she said, readjusting it. She glanced at his lap. "I'm flattered."

He looked down. He hadn't just dreamed the erection: it bulged in his slacks. "Oh, God, I'm sorry," he said, sitting up. "It's one of the quirks of male physiology. For some reason, REM sleep has that effect. I've had virtually no sleep the last few days. I guess, what with the heater and the rocking of the car, I must have slept harder than I thought I would."

"Evidently," she smirked. "But you could have at least pretended that I inspired it."

"Take off the sweater. It'll come back."

"Yeah, dream on."

"I did dream, actually," he said, the images still strong. "The minister who did Nana's service was in it. Was it just me or did he seem a little harsh?"

"Peter made all the arrangements," May said. "I guess he figured Nana would lean more toward fire and brimstone than sweetness and light. Maybe put the fear of God into me somehow."

"Did it?"

"Yeah, right. Like God gives a rat's ass about me one way or the other."

John peered out the window of the Outback at the few puffy clouds clustered over the mountains. "Just trying to figure out which angle the thunderbolt will take," he said to May.

"You know what I think? A ghost is just a ghost, even if it's holy."

"I don't know," John said. "There's an old Spanish saying: 'I don't believe in God but I fear him'."

John had never felt so justified in that fear. Wayne Giles's suicide and the note he left behind had precipitated one hellacious nightmare and his funeral, scheduled for tomorrow, likely would make things even worse. In fact, the main reason John had gone to Nana's funeral was to get away from Estes, even for just a few hours. You know life sucks when funerals feel like get-aways.

Even his get-away had gone screwy. He had sat patiently through the dreary service, his stomach in knots, his eyes burning, his head lolling in the stuffy room, just to offer May a little consolation and support. He had intended to drive right back up to Estes afterward to try to get some rest. But May had held him tight when they hugged and she whispered a plea that he stay.

After she bid Peter and Jan a stiff farewell, she told John that Dolores, Paco's mother, had called earlier from Buena Vista. Paco and Shirley, after moving back to town just last week, had disappeared, leaving Libby at Dolores's house. May had resolved to go there to pick up her baby right after the funeral but her Fiat's head gasket leaked antifreeze into the oil and she didn't know if it would make the trip. John had gallantly offered to drive her to Buena Vista and back, the one caveat being that she might need to do some of the driving.

The tumultuous events of the last few days occupying their minds, they remained nearly silent all the way up Ute Pass to Green Mountain Falls, where John's eyes grew so heavy he had to ask her to take over. He must have conked out completely because already they were west of Florissant.

He glanced over at May. The circles under her eyes looked darker than ever and her mouth had the set of someone who knows everything she needs to know about anguish except when it will stop. If nothing else, at least he could try to provide her a little diversion. He thought about the Tom Huston story but decided he needed something considerably lighter than that to cheer her up.

"I haven't come by here in a while," he said as they slowed for the little town of Lake George. "Jason and I went to Camp Alexander near here a couple of summers. Bill did too, for that matter."

"Huh." She stared ahead at the road.

"In fact, something happened that second summer that perfectly illustrates the difference between Jason and Bill."

She didn't respond.

Rough crowd, he thought. "Would you like to hear about it?"

"Why not," she said apathetically. "What was this, like a military camp?"

"Boy Scouts," he said. "And we did the usual Boy Scout stuff: swimming, nature hikes, shooting .22s down at the rifle range, earning merit badges. But at night we had nothing to do but sit around the fire, a bunch of adolescent boys camping in the woods, basically unsupervised."

"You didn't have a troop leader or something?"

"Yeah, but he kept a pretty loose grip on the reins. In fact, someone snuck into his tent one night, stole his underwear, and ran it up the flagpole. Anyway, one of the advantages to coming back the second year was that we got to initiate the newcomers the way the older boys had initiated us the first year. And needless to say, Bill—your what? ex-father?—went to camp that second year relishing what he would do to initiate the new kids."

"What kind of initiation was this?"

"The usual degrading sophomoric stuff. The summer before, Jason and I got sent to camp headquarters to get some 'sky hooks.' Got the head guy out of bed. He was not amused. But the worst was tick inspection."

"God, I hate ticks."

"Oh, I don't think anybody ever found any actual ticks. In fact, a few guys may have left camp with nervous ticks because of the tick inspection."

"What did it involve?"

"The poor sap being initiated had to strip down to nothing but socks and run around the campfire a certain number of times. Somehow Jason and I escaped the first year with our ticks intact but it certainly looked humiliating when other guys had to do it. The second year we went, there was this new kid—I think his name was Skip, which didn't help matters—who caught all the flack from the older guys. Bill and the other initiation fanatics made him run around the fire like a hundred times. After about thirty laps he started to cry."

"Why didn't he just quit?"

"You don't understand guys, do you? If a guy wants to be accepted, he's just got to swallow all the bullshit the alpha males feel like dishing out. So Skip wouldn't stop running and he couldn't stop crying. I don't know about all the other guys watching but I know it started to get to me and Jason. Finally, Jason took it upon himself to do something."

"What?"

"He stripped down to just *his* socks and started running around the fire with Skip. I didn't get it at first and neither did Skip. But finally I saw the method in Jason's madness so I stripped down and joined them. Pretty soon half the troop was jogging naked around the campfire. When Skip finally realized how absurd the whole thing was, he got laughing so hard he blew bubbles in his snot."

"Did my dad join in too?"

"No way," John said. "He and the other fanatics got mad and stormed off. That was the last I heard of tick inspection."

"Charming story."

"Maybe you had to be there," John granted. "But if you don't mind my pointing it out, it surprised me to hear you refer to Bill just now as your dad."

"Maybe he is my father after all," May said dispiritedly. "I mean, the only thing tying me to Jason is that bizarre letter."

"And the way you hold a pencil. That's a pretty big coincidence."

"Yeah, but so what? I mean, to tell you the truth, I got my hopes up that Jason was still alive and might show up at the restaurant on New Year's Eve. How stupid is that? Even you guys aren't going to show up. Why should he?"

"May, I'm really sorry the Piñon Nuts Gathering fell through. But just because Matt and Russ and I can't get together doesn't mean Jason wasn't your biological father."

"But as you pointed out when I first came up to Estes to talk to you about it, what does it get me if Jason *was* my father? Here are my choices in fatherly role models: a jerky car dealer who ignored me till I grew tits, or a fire-dancing hippie who tried to have me killed before I was born. Some choice. It doesn't much matter, does it?"

"Believe it or not, sometimes you sound just like Jason," John pointed out. "I can't blame you for feeling bitter about the whole thing. Even if Jason didn't die up in Jones Park that night, he certainly hasn't been heard from in 30 years. I sure wouldn't hang around Crestwood New Year's Eve hoping he'll show."

"I don't plan to. I don't work there anymore anyway."

"What? No! What happened?"

"Well, Wednesday, after Nana died, I got so hung up dealing with Peter and Jan and making funeral arrangements, I totally spaced out calling Lucy at the restaurant. When I called in on Thanksgiving, Tara told me Lucy had taken me off the schedule."

"Oh, what a drag! What are you going to do?"

"I'm just screwed," May said. "I guess I can always go back to the Waffle House. I've got to do something. I've got a house payment coming up."

"I thought Nana gave you the house."

"She did. And she talked me into taking out a home equity loan to consolidate all my other bills. So they're all paid but now my loan payments are higher than my rent was. I thought about just selling the house but, especially now that I've got Libby again, I've got to live somewhere. And nowhere's free."

"Maybe this is a tacky question but what about Nana's estate? Didn't she leave you anything?"

May laughed bitterly. "Oh, that was a slap in the face, too. You know, Peter was Nana's executioner."

"Executor."

"Whatever. Anyway, Nana revised her will last spring when I was in jail and she and Peter agreed that Mom should keep the house and Peter would take everything else, like whatever they got for the condo and the rest of her estate."

"That doesn't seem very fair. Weren't Harve and Cynthia pretty well off?"

"Poppa's illness cost them a lot of money. Nana didn't have much other than my house and the condo and a few investments. Anyway, Peter and Nana also agreed that if Nana gave me anything, my creditors would end up taking it all and they wanted to make sure Libby was taken care of. So they set up a $40,000 trust fund in Libby's name that she can have when she turns 21. But I can't touch it, except for medical emergencies or Libby's college expenses. So I'm stuck with being a wage slave until the loan's paid off. Meanwhile, my daughter's rich."

"If I were you, I'd call Lucy Van Deutch, apologize, and see if she won't give you your job back. In fact, while you're at it," he added, "put in a good word for me too."

"That's right," May said. "You never finished telling me about the situation up in Estes. You didn't lose your job, did you?"

"I don't think so. Not yet, at least. You didn't read anything otherwise in the newspaper, did you?"

"I haven't seen any news at all the last couple of days."

"Ah, so you're the last person to get a good long peek at the Kaufmans' dirty laundry. How much have you heard?"

"Just what you told me: that your daughter's boyfriend hung himself at the Juvenile Detention Center."

"That's right, they hadn't found Wayne's note at that point."

"He left a note?"

"The usual scribbled diatribe against school and jocks and the government and life in general. Jocks in particular. To Wayne, the fact that the Columbine High School football team went to the state championship proved that the jocks in the world would always squash the little guys. Pressure everywhere. It's all too much, he writes. Then he quotes what he calls a Pearl Jam song: "Sail me on a silver sun where I know that I'm free," which is actually a remake of an old Beatles tune that Jason and I used to do. He finishes with this: 'OK, AK. See you on the silver sun. Alternate effects as you enter.'"

"What does that mean?"

"The silver sun? Who knows? I've heard lots of speculation: that the silver sun is what you see on a heroin rush, that it's the spaceship that hides in the comet's tail, that it's the bright light you see as you're dying, that it's the little dome of solder on a circuit board that connects the integrated circuits to the power source."

"What about the 'alternate effects' business?"

"A friend of mine who's a computer buff came up with one theory: ALT FX SU Enter are the keys you hit to exit Windows 95. Kind of a digital swan song. But it didn't take long for one of the snoopy TV reporters to ferret out that the initials A. K. might stand for Anne

Kaufman."

"Uh-oh."

"And a half. So there I am on Thanksgiving, eating my frozen turkey TV dinner, and there's my daughter on *Inside Edition*, tearfully explaining that yes, she was in love with Wayne Giles, but no, she had nothing to do with either the hostage situation or his suicide."

"How did he manage to hang himself, anyway? Detention centers are usually pretty good about preventing that sort of thing."

"He ripped the power cord from a TV. Not only killed himself, he pissed off his fellow inmates to boot."

"Anne must feel horrible about getting caught up in all this. But from what you told me Wednesday, she did seem pretty involved with him."

"Frankly, I'm not sure what to believe from Anne at this point. Once you get caught in your first lie, your credibility sinks fast. Oh, and there's more. After Anne gets so upset in this TV interview that she can't talk, they interview Susan instead."

"Uh-oh again."

"As you might expect, Susan has spent this whole month trashing me to anyone in Estes who will take the time to listen. All of a sudden she finds herself with a prime-time national audience."

"Oh no!"

"The Gospel according to Saint Susan: poor little Anne was just fine until her middle-aged fool of a father started having an affair with some slut half his age, with whom he is now shacking up, for all Susan knows."

"That's ridiculous!" May sputtered.

"Her doctor has bumped her up to the 20 milligram Prozac for a while. So the TV piece ends with a dismal shot of Fawn Hollow, the perky, insinuating reporter confiding to the camera that 'John Kaufman, Anne Kaufman's father, lived for a few weeks in these rundown apartments in a town called, ironically enough, Loveland. At present, his whereabouts are unknown.'"

"What!?"

"My reaction exactly. So yesterday morning I called the TV station to assure them that I am alive and kicking, having moved back up to Estes. There's a mistake. All afternoon my house was under siege. Reporters and camera crews taping updates, mobile satellite units parked on the lawn, helicopters thumping overhead. I couldn't believe it. I felt like Punxsutawney Phil the groundhog on February 2nd. Every time I'd poke my nose out the door they were all over me."

"Asking what?"

"About you, for one thing, the beautiful *femme fatale* who lured a weak man away from his wife and kids. About the responsibilities of a father. One guy asked something that's laughable and disturbing at the same time: did I set up Wayne Giles with the guns and the marijuana just to create a story for the Denver *Post*'s new outlet in Estes Park, the *Trail Gazette*, which doubled its subscribers as a result of the story?"

"You must be kidding!"

"I wish I were. Now nobody talks to me at the office. I don't know if they're going to squeeze me out or not. At this point, I don't really care. I just wish Anne hadn't been sucked into this whole mess. Wayne Giles was right about one thing: it's all too much. Growing up has gotten to be so complicated. I don't remember it being like that. Do you?"

"How old is Anne?"

"She'll be 16 in April."

"Maybe you're asking the wrong person."

"Why? What happened to you at that age?"

"You really want to know?" she dared him.

"Why not? What have we got to lose?"

"Okay, you asked for it. When I was 15 my father tried to sexually assault me."

"God, May! I'm so sorry! Not that I'm terribly surprised, actually, from what I recall about Bill."

"Well, as far as that goes, at least he only tried to molest me. Jason tried to have me killed."

"You know, you can't really—"

"Anyway," she interrupted him, "I was pretty scared because I saw how he treated Mom. So I stayed for a while with this girl Maleeka I knew, who was already 16 and had her license and could use her mom's old Volkswagen. She's the one who introduced me to Paco."

"I didn't realize you'd known him that long."

"God, half my life," she said, as though that distasteful thought had just come to her. "Anyway, Paco was in his 20s and he liked to party like it was—well, like it was this year, 1999, I guess. So Maleeka took me over to his house. I remember he had a whole bottle of Jagermeister and some excellent weed and we all got really trashed. Well, Maleeka wanted to spend the night and of course *he* was all for that but I wasn't so sure. At first I felt like that was what I left home to get *away* from. But Paco didn't seem at all like my father, at least at the time, and anyway, what choice did I have? Maleeka wanted to stay and the only other place I could go was home. Besides, I was pretty trashed by that time, so I just gave in. And I must admit, Paco lived up to it."

"What!?" John exclaimed, impressed. "He slept with both of you?"

"He didn't sleep much, but yeah. I didn't have anything to compare it to but I had a good time."

"That was your first time? A *menage a trois*?" He looked at her with a new appreciation.

"You've got to start somewhere," she shrugged. "Anyway, so when Maleeka left in the morning, I just sort of stayed."

"He must have been really good."

"Like I said, how was I to know? But he owned a nice house on the top of the hill on Brookside and a beautiful electric-blue Corvette and he promised that if I stayed he'd get me anything I wanted."

"What was he doing for a living?"

"He fixed cars at one of the lots down in Motor City. Of course I didn't know it at first but I found out later that he made most of his money selling crack, which had just made it to the Springs then and there was a huge demand."

"What did you do when you found out?"

"By then I'd been living with him for a while and I got really mad at him for not telling me. I even threw an ashtray at his head. But he swore up and down that he was just going to do this for a couple of years to make enough money so he wouldn't have to work anymore and we could afford to move somewhere nice, like Hawaii."

"And you bought that?"

"He promised he'd marry me."

"Uh-huh."

She looked over at him. "Oh, he was serious. He got somebody to doctor a birth certificate so it said I was 18 and we got blood tests and went to the courthouse and did it."

"What did you tell your mom and Bill?"

"Nothing. Whenever I called my mom she got on my case for skipping school all the time and I had no desire whatsoever to talk to my father."

"So you and Paco lived happily ever after."

"For about a week. Then he came down with the flu and some guy called him from up in the canyon and wanted to know if he could get a full ounce of crack."

"Were you and Paco doing crack too?"

"I tried it a few times but I didn't like it. And Paco, for all his faults, was enough of a businessman to know that dipping into his stash would eat up all his profits so he stayed away from it. Anyway, he was too sick to take this ounce to this guy so he asked if I would do it for him, something he had never asked before. So I figured I'd do it this once because it did mean a lot of money. Plus, I'd had a couple of beers and Paco had never offered to let me drive his Vette before."

"Oh, your mom told me about this, I think. You got in a car accident, right?"

"Yeah. I was coming down 8th Street and I admit I was going pretty fast because the Vette just seemed to want to. Anyway, when I came up to where those apartments are before you get to Cheyenne Boulevard, some lady pulled right out in front of me."

May fell silent, looking at the empty road ahead of her as though a car might pull out in front of them at any second, even though they had already reached the long uphill grade to Wilkerson Pass and there were few side roads.

"So what happened?" John prompted her at last. "You hit her, right? Was anybody hurt?"

"I swerved but I still hit the back end of her car and bounced off and slammed into a tree. The lady in the other car wasn't wearing a seat belt so the impact snapped her neck and then her head broke the window."

"What about you?"

"I broke some ribs and my collarbone. But the lady fell into a coma and died a week later."

John didn't say anything. Maybe it was sympathy fatigue: after you've felt badly for someone's misfortunes for the nth time, you run out of conciliatory phrases. Maybe it began to sink in to him that he really didn't know May all that well.

"So are you shocked?" May asked.

"Not shocked," he said. "Your mom told me about some of this. I guess I didn't pay enough attention when she told me about your problems. There must have been legal consequences."

"Let's see. They charged me with involuntary manslaughter, reckless endangerment, driving without a license, driving under the influence, possession of a controlled substance, and possession of a stolen vehicle."

"Car theft?"

"Paco got the Vette in a trade for some crack and didn't have the title."

"Did they arrest him too?"

"Okay, don't laugh," she cautioned him, "but at the time I really thought I was in love with Paco. When I woke up in the hospital, the only thing I could think about was to try keep him from getting in trouble too. I didn't tell anybody—*anybody*—that I was married or where I got the crack or the car. So when I got out of the hospital, they took me straight to jail. They told me they'd cut me a deal on the possession charges if I would just tell them who had given me that stuff. Since I wouldn't tell them, they kept me in jail."

"I had no idea," John said. "Your mom never mentioned all of that."

"Like I said, she was never one to brag."

"Did you talk to a lawyer?"

"I had a public defender."

"Bill wouldn't spring for a regular lawyer?"

"Considering how much interest he'd shown in my body," she said bitterly, "he sure turned his back in a hurry when I needed help."

"So he just leaves you twisting in the wind. What about Paco?"

"I made Paco promise not to come and see me or anything because they would find out about him. What I didn't know, of course, was that Maleeka moved in with him like a week after I went to jail."

John silently shook his head. How do you respond to a story like that?

"You don't hang with many jailbirds, do you?" she asked, almost taunting him. "Pretty exciting, huh?"

"Jason did some jail time too, you know," he said, figuring she might find some solace in it.

She seemed surprised. "Really? What for?"

"The first time—"

"More than once?"

"The first time," he went on, nodding, "he got hauled in during the campus protests up in Boulder. The second time was my fault."

"What happened?"

He took a deep breath and let it out slowly. "It happened just a few weeks after the first time. I guess this was in the spring of 1970. He knew a guy that lived up on the Old Stage Road who had a small plane. This guy used to fly down to Mexico once a month or so to buy some weed and he'd fly it back in pillow cases. Drug interdiction has come a long way since then. Anyway, he sold it for ten bucks an ounce so when Jason told me about it, I asked him to pick up an ounce for me as well."

"God! Ten bucks an ounce!"

"Those days are gone, huh? Anyway, I remember it was a beautiful evening in the spring, the air sweet and still, and the whole world seemed at peace, which, considering what was going on back then, seemed especially welcome. Jason called me from your mom's house and asked if I could meet him because his car had gone belly up. I was just finishing dinner with my parents and I had to run up to the zoo to see if I had a job there for the summer so we agreed to meet at Pauline Chapel."

"Up by the Broadmoor? I know where that is."

"As I drove up, I saw him sitting on the lawn out in front. Right then, a police car drove by and I saw Jason give him the peace sign," holding up two fingers to demonstrate. "The cop stopped and asked him something. Not knowing what was going on, I parked in the lot by the cog railway station across the street. Well, when the cop got out of the car, Jason ran. I don't know if he had seen me or not but he ran the other way, either not realizing I was there or trying to keep me out of trouble. Anyway, he lost one of his moccasins so he didn't get too far before the cop caught him. He still had the two ounces of dope on him and since he'd just been busted a few weeks before, they held him."

"What did you do?"

"What could I do? And his parents had split up. His mother didn't have any sympathy toward him at all and by that time she already had moved out to California. His father remarried but his second wife turned out to be one of those hypochondriacs who can always find something wrong enough to warrant some sort of surgery that she can talk about to her friends for years to come. She had no insurance so whatever savings his father had disappeared in a heartbeat. The judge set an outrageous bail, way more than his father could pay. I helped his father find Jason a lawyer but he couldn't afford much for that either so he wasn't a very good attorney. And without a good lawyer, you're screwed."

"Don't I know it."

"When the judge found out Jason had been busted up in Boulder just a few weeks before, he gave him ninety days down at the minimum security prison in Cañon City. I went down there to visit him once. It didn't seem that bad to me. They had a farm so he got to work with plants. But he hated incarceration."

"I hate to be cooped up too," she said, the Outback slowing as they hit the last rise before the summit of Wilkerson Pass.

"I hear that," he said. "Why don't you pull over at the summit? I need to take a leak."

O   O   O

At this time of year the restrooms were locked so John trucked up the trail a little ways and looked around before unzipping and letting fly on some undeserving aspen trunk.

Wilkerson Pass pales in comparison to some of Colorado's legendary passes and in fact "saddle" might be more appropriate, particularly in good weather, than "pass." The weekend before, a major snowstorm had pelted the state but already most of it had melted or sublimated and today the sun shone brightly, having nothing to dodge celestially but a few harmless mare's-tails. To the east lay the rolling wooded foothills they had just traversed, culminating in the looming massif of Pikes Peak in the distance. To the west lay the wide flat plain of South Park.

The word "park" denotes a level open intermountain area but the areas called parks in Colorado vary widely. Jones Park covers just a few aspen-covered acres. Estes Park is large and open enough to contain Lake Estes and the small town and still have room for an elk herd.

South Park, by contrast, is a huge expanse of grassy rangeland running all the way to the distant icy summits of the Park Range and the Buffalo Peaks. The long lonely highway that crosses it runs in a straight line as far as the eye can see, broken only by a single curve around a solitary butte in the center. Far from the woodsy community of roly-poly foul-mouthed cartoon characters depicted in the popular television show, South Park is a barren grid of ranch land inhabited by a few unamusing cattle, burros, and horses.

Nevertheless, this park held a special place in John's memory, it occurred to him as he zipped up his fly. Over the last few decades he had made love to no less than five different women within the broad confines of South Park.

The memory coaxed a smile from him as he walked back to the car. May leaned against the fender, smoking a cigarette and reading a large wooden historical marker, her long auburn hair tossed by the breeze.

"Did you read this?" she asked as he settled in next to her, playfully bumping his hip against hers.

"I think that's new," he said, reading:

Pikes Peak

In the last dark days of November, 1806, Zebulon Pike and his weary band of 15 soldiers spotted what appeared, from the barren plains of eastern Colorado, to be a large, stationary cloud. After approaching this mysterious cloud for several days, they decided it must be a snowy mountain peak. Hungry and poorly equipped for winter weather, Pike nevertheless resolved to climb the peak that now carries his name. On November 27, frost-bitten and exhausted, the expedition abandoned the attempt and continued their journey westward through South Park, searching for the Red River, the southern boundary of the Louisiana Purchase.

"Isn't today the 27th?" May asked John.

"Yeah," he said, marveling once again at the hardiness, or foolhardiness, of those first explorers. "Can you imagine trying to climb that at this time of year?" he asked, pointing at the peak. "Our hike to Haiyaha was a month ago and we got weathered off."

"I can't imagine anybody wanting to mess with that any time of the year," May said.

"Betcha the weather wasn't this nice in 1806, either," he added, looking at the way timberline on the northwest face had been forced lower by the brunt of the winter storms.

May silently took a last deep drag from the cigarette and tossed it away, staring stonily at the mountain.

John couldn't explain her animosity until he remembered that that northwest face had claimed her mother's life. Considering how much May had lost in the course of the year, he knew no words would suffice to convey his sympathy. He put his arm around her shoulders.

As though just waiting for his touch, tears overflowed her eyes. She began to cry and he enfolded her with both arms, feeling the gentle pulses of her sobs, pressing his lips to the top of her head.

"God, I hate this place!" she said when she recovered enough to speak, wiping her nose on the handkerchief he pulled from his back pocket. "Let's not stop in Buena Vista. Let's just keep going."

"How far?" he asked, holding her shoulders and looking at her downcast eyes.

"I just want to go to some desert island somewhere, leave all this bullshit behind."

"Well, the Subaru's got four-wheel drive but it still might be tricky to drive to an actual island," he pointed out. "Besides, this place isn't so bad. You're just low at the moment."

She looked around at the sere dormant landscape. "What's good about it?"

"Oh, you must have seen it in the summer! At least a dozen different wildflowers bloom along that last stretch we drove. In fact, I'll bet you didn't know this: the old Colorado Midland Railroad used to run near here. On summer weekends a special train used to bring people up from the Springs just so they could get out and pick wildflowers."

"Didn't that deflower the place?"

John chuckled. "I can't think of a better place for deflowering. Here, I'll drive awhile."

She handed him the keys and got in on the passenger's side. When she noticed he still chuckled as he started the car, she asked, "What's so funny?"

"Oh, I was just thinking about something that happened here in South Park," he said, still grinning at the memory.

"What?" she insisted, envious of his good humor.

He looked over at her as he waited for a truck on the highway before pulling out. "You really want to know?" he dared her.

"Why not?" she said. "What have we got to lose?"

"All right," he said, forced to agree with her logic. "I've made love to five women in South Park."

"At the same time?" she asked, clearly impressed.

"Oh, God, no!" he exclaimed hastily. "One at a time, over many years. In fact the first would have been nearly thirty years ago."

"Was it my mom?"

"No," he said, a little surprised she'd ask. "I told you on our hike that your mom and I never did that."

"Sometimes men lie," she said simply.

"Actually," he went on, "it was a girl named Prudence. I met her through Russ. In fact, we met that New Year's Eve, when your mom took the Piñon Nuts picture. When Prudence and Russ split up, she and I had a little fling of our own. We got an apartment the following summer. That's when we made love up here."

"Where?" she asked, looking around.

"That's the subtle beauty of South Park," he explained. "True, there's no place to hide, to get much privacy. But there's also no one to hide from. Prudence and I pulled over right up here, on the back road to Tarryall."

"How was it? Did you do it in the car?"

"Prudence wasn't the back-seat type. She expected Catherine and Heathcliff or something, I suppose. We brought a blanket and a bottle of wine and a book of poetry. Poetry got her hot."

"You read her poetry?" she asked in wonder. "I never got that from Paco. His favorite poem started 'Here I sit so broken-hearted'."

"Ah, yes, a classic," John said. "Prudence, though, fancied herself an intellectual. She had me read Keats:

> A thing of beauty is a joy forever:
> Its loveliness increases; it will never
> Pass into nothingness; but still will keep
> A bower quiet for us, and a sleep
> Full of sweet dreams, and health, and quiet breathing.

"That's pretty," she said wistfully as they drove past the dirt road. "Did it work?"

"It worked on Prudence," he said, wondering if it had worked on May.

Worked on May? Was he trying to start something here? It occurred to him that South Park represented a special zone. The first couple of times he had gotten lucky here seemed just that: luck, coincidence. But after that he had made a conscious distinction about the place: if he found himself riding through South Park, single, with a single woman, then, as far as he was concerned, love-making was pre-approved. No debate required.

But the five women he had made love to—cut the crap: had sex with—long ago in South Park had been women he had known at most a few months and in one case, just a few hours. They essentially amounted to strangers. The only connection he felt to them was desire.

Did May fit that category? He glanced over at her. Her small breasts jiggled slightly in her sweater with every bump in the road. Her black skirt rode up above her knees and her legs looked sleek and strong under the nylon of her hose. She had worn cologne, something inexpensive, Charlie or Jontue maybe, but alluring nonetheless. Tempting.

He still hadn't had sex since Labor Day. Back in the original South Park Sex days, he would long since have become horny as hell. Now that he had reached middle age, sex seemed more a temptation, a fantasy, than a drive. But, by God, after the pressure of the last few days, that kind of release, of relief, might be just what the doctor ordered.

Was it possible? He thought he had detected a few sparks along the way. May, as far as he knew, was single and uninvolved. And Susan seemed determined to go through with the divorce. True, May was Amanda's daughter, so hardly a stranger, but Amanda was gone. Maybe Bill had fathered her after all; John certainly didn't owe Bill anything. And the only connections May seemed to have to Jason were the way she wrote and the fact that they had both done time.

"You never did tell me what happened with your jail sentence," he said to her.

She had been staring out the window, lost in thought. Without turning, she said sadly, "My guardian angel rescued me."

"What does that mean?"

"Since I had already run away from home, the judge wasn't about to release me without bail, and since my parents seemed content to let me rot in jail, I figured I was in for the long haul. My public defender pretty well convinced me that I should just cop a plea and hope for a merciful judge. But then, about a week before my trial, some other lawyer contacted my P. D. with new information."

"Who hired this other lawyer?"

"I guess Nana did. My mom and dad both denied it and it sure wasn't Paco."

"Why?"

"Because Paco got caught. This new lawyer found out that Paco and I were married and that he was the one who had given me the crack. The police busted him with a bunch of the stuff so they dropped the drug charges against me, figuring I was just his innocent dupe."

"What about the manslaughter charge?"

"My P. D. told me that this new lawyer hired a guy to inspect the woman's car, which was totaled. He found out the automatic transmission was frozen in second gear, which meant that she must have run the stop sign when I hit her. So they dropped that charge too."

"Wow, Nana found a good lawyer," John said. "What was his name?"

"I have no idea. My P. D. told me that some kind of legal ethics prevented her from disclosing his name. But he sure pulled my ass out of the fire. I still ended up with a DUI and couldn't get my license until I was 18 but I got out of jail."

"What about Paco? Did he get off too?"

"Oh, hell, no. That lawyer did nothing for him. And since Paco already had a record—something else I didn't know—they threw the book at him. He got seven years."

"So what did you do? Couldn't you get the marriage annulled or something?"

"I was in love with him, remember?" May said plaintively. "And I was still young and naive. I thought it was cool that my old man was in stir. I could play the devoted wife and wait patiently till he got out. Besides, if the marriage was annulled, I would have to move back to my parents' house and I knew what that would be like. Did you see my father at the mortuary today?"

"I saw him but didn't talk to him."

"When he hugged me after the service, he squeezed my ass."

"Ai-yi-yi."

"See what I mean? Well, it turned out that when they sent Paco to the Correctional Facility in Buena Vista, Dolores, his mom, decided to move there too so she could be near her *niñito perdido*. Before she moved, she asked me if I wanted to live there with her."

"Nothing like prison to bring people closer."

"It made sense at the time," she said defensively. "I could see Paco during visiting hours a couple of times a week. I could get a job, be out on my own. I actually really enjoyed it for a while. I felt so free!"

Freedom's such a relative thing, John thought. From Wilkerson Pass, South Park looks like the limitless Old West, nothing but empty space and open range where the deer and the antelope play. Actually, he had seen a few head of bison back by the Tarryall road but they, like most everything in the New West, belonged to someone and lived inside a fence. True, the bison seemed more a part of the natural scene than the cattle did. The cattle grazed the high cold prairie inside the fenced enclosures so short that the ungrazed easement for the road looked like paradise. In the areas with the bison John could barely tell the difference.

But the cattle and the bison could certainly tell they lived inside a fence. Back in the mid-1970s, a calf had gotten separated from its mother in one of the brief but howling spring snowstorms. The calf had made its way to a corner of the fence-lines near the road and died. John had assumed either the rancher or the coyotes would haul away the carcass but it never happened. Over the years he looked for it every time he drove past. That first year it had looked like a dead calf. Then it became a brown-and-tan lump of old carpet. Finally he could see nothing but a handful of scattered bones. Now, nothing at all. The way of all flesh. Perhaps Amanda's body had begun that same process somewhere on the northwest face of Pikes Peak.

"Which one was that?" May asked him.

"Huh?"

"Sorry. I assumed you were thinking about one of those women you boinked."

He looked to the south, along the road to Eleven Mile Reservoir. "I did make love to one along here, actually," he said, glad to switch subjects. "She was wild."

"In what way?"

"Ferally, I suppose. She loved nothing more than to strip down to nothing but her shoes and roam around outside. She loved the sun on her skin and the wind in her hair."

"And she did this right out here?"

"It was early evening on a weeknight in the spring and we didn't see three cars in all of South Park and none on the reservoir road. We drove a ways and she practically begged me to stop and let her out. She stripped down, walked across the cattle guard out into that sagebrush, and just wandered around for the longest time."

"What did you do?"

"I already told you what I did," he said. "I boinked her, to use your term."

"I mean, besides that."

"What else is there?"

She rolled her eyes. "Men."

"Evidently, I'm not half the man your ex-husband is, judging from your first time with him. I only boinked those women one at a time. So I assume Paco was worth waiting for."

"Paco's such an idiot," she said in disgust.

"What? Life in Buena Vista wasn't everything you dreamed it would be?"

"Shit."

"You said you got a job. What did you do?"

"I schlepped greasy hamburgers out to people too lazy to haul their asses inside the Sonic Drive-In. They'd leave me all their nickels and pennies. By the end of the night, my pants would be falling down from all the weight. I'd count it up and have, like, three dollars and change."

"What's Dolores like?"

"She's a Mexican mama. She drinks too much, smokes too much, swears too much, cries too much, eats too much, belches too much. But she's kind of sweet in her own way. I actually enjoyed living with her more than I did with Paco."

"So you stayed there the whole seven years?"

"I shouldn't have had to. Like I said, Paco's an idiot. After four years his case came up for review with the parole board. Two weeks before the review, one of the guards took a pack of cigarettes from him so Paco decked him."

"Slugged a guard?"

"Broke his jaw. Big surprise: no parole."

"So in effect, Paco sentenced you to three more years in Buena Vista."

"That's the way it felt to me. I couldn't take it."

"So what did you do?"

"Something just as idiotic."

"Like?"

"Did you ever hear of the band Streaming Pustules?"

He laughed. "Can't say I did. Let me guess: they did a lot of Olivia Newton-John covers, right?"

"Yeah, right. This was the early '90s, when that grunge scene in Seattle took over, Nirvana and Pearl Jam and all that. The Pustules thought they were somewhere between the Sex Pistols and the Screaming Trees. Anyway, they happened to come into the Sonic one night."

"Was this a local band?"

"Oh, no, they were based in L. A."

"What in the world were they doing in the Sonic in Buena Vista?"

"They had just finished in Taos and were on their way to Aspen. Anyway, they all flirted shamelessly with me and told me that if I would go with them, they'd put me on their next CD cover."

"And you, of course, didn't—"

"I did and I was! The CD was called 'Alive and Kicking'."

"Oh, I remember seeing that now."

"Remember the bare-assed chick on the hood of the car?"

"No, but if you'll pull up your skirt…"

To his surprise, she did, showing him her left cheek tightly wrapped in pantyhose.

"Oh, I remember you now!" he said as she pulled the skirt back down. "Seriously, that was you?"

"Seriously. I ended up traveling with them for like two years."

"Were you involved with somebody in the group? I mean, you were still technically married, weren't you?"

"It was weird. They all had girlfriends or wives and nobody hit on me. I became the mascot or something. We'd party together and all that but nobody ever referred to me as 'so-and-so's woman.' I was just May."

"So you were faithful to Paco the whole time?"

"I didn't say that," she said, smiling. "I became quite the party girl. I just didn't sleep with anyone in the band."

"This was in L. A.?"

"Actually, after we finished the tour they were on, they decided to move to Seattle to be closer to the grunge scene. We got this old walk-up in Belltown and threw some hellacious parties. People like Kurt and Courtney and Eddie Vedder would drop by. You know who I'm talking about, right?"

"Young whippersnapper!" he said, shaking both his fist and his voice like an old man. "Why, in my day I could do the Charleston and the Big Apple…" trailing off with an imitation of denture gumming.

She laughed. "I'm sorry. I keep forgetting I'm talking to the Man Who Fucked Five Women In South Park."

"One right up here," he pointed out. "And, coincidentally, a singer. I dated her for almost a year. She used to love role playing. We came through here on our way to her family reunion."

"What do you mean, role playing?"

"Oh, just goofy little sex games. If anything, she was better at it than I was. Driving through all this nothing, we came up with the idea that I should drop her off and circle back. She would pretend to be a hitchhiker and I would pick her up." Lowering and sleazing his voice: "Hi, there, little girl. Where you headed?" Innocent falsetto: "I'm on my way to my grandmother's house." With an evil chuckle: "Well, climb on in."

"Oh, my, Mr. Wolf," May said, playing along, "what big teeth you have!"

"The better to—say, you're pretty good at this," he said in his regular voice, smiling at her.

"Well, don't make me stop at your teeth!" she protested, with a meaningful glance at the lap of his trousers.

He knew she was joking and he had no illusions about being endowed with anything other than standard equipment. But if he had been waiting for a sign, this looked like a freaking billboard. The Outback cruised at 60; his mind raced ahead at 120, trying to figure out where, when, how. The Outback was relatively new; the part of his mind that knew how to finagle a quickie from a young woman had been up on blocks for years. But despite some rusted joints and antiquated equipment, he still recalled the first line of the owner's manual: keep talking.

"Your stay in Seattle sounds like a kick," he said, immediately kicking himself for not alluding to her blatant come-on.

"It was a kick that kicked back," she said.

"What do you mean?"

"Remember when we first talked about drugs up in Estes and I told you that I had done grass and coke but not psychedelics?"

"You weren't entirely truthful," he concluded.

"Well, sort of. I never did any psychedelics but in Seattle I got into smack and meth for a while."

"Oh, jeez, May," he said, genuinely dismayed. "That's a drag."

"You're telling me."

"Were you hooked?"

"I don't know. There's a couple of months that I really don't remember, to tell you the truth."

"You didn't get HIV, I hope."

"I wouldn't be talking to you now if I had," she said soberly. "But I did get hepatitis from a fix."

"Bummer. Which hep?"

"Luckily, type A. But it still put me in the hospital. I thought I was going to die."

"I had no idea," he said, shaking his head.

"Nobody did. My parents, who weren't speaking to me, assumed I was still in Buena Vista and Dolores assumed I had moved back to the Springs."

"How old were you at this point?"

"I turned 21 in the hospital."

John stared at the long straight road ahead but didn't say anything.

"So, does that make you feel any better?" she asked.

"About what?"

"About your problems with Anne. I assume your daughter's smart enough to avoid the kind of shit that I've been through."

He snorted bitterly. "You know, the human body has enough blood to run the brain or the gonads but not both."

Once again she said, "Uh-oh."

"Anne has chlamydia."

May thought about that. "So she and Wayne…"

"…were doing more than petting, right," he said. "And he evidently had done more than petting with someone else, who also had done more than petting with someone else."

"Well, if it's any consolation, at least chlamydia is easy to treat."

"She's already taking antibiotics for that. But treating the emotional scars is a lot trickier. Wayne bamboozled Anne into thinking that she was the only one."

"Men can be such pigs."

"Hey," he said. "Love makes fools of us all."

"Is that what you told her?"

"I didn't tell her anything. Her mother won't let her talk to me, remember? Of course, she found a way to call Wayne long distance in prison but call her father? No way. That's what hurts. I really thought she and I could talk about things like that."

"What would you have told her? Would you have told her she couldn't sleep with him?"

He mulled that over. "I don't know. 'Couldn't'? Probably not. Maybe 'shouldn't.' I never thought much of Wayne but forbidding a teenager something can easily backfire. Regardless, when I talked to her about sex, I told her that, when the right boy and the right time came along, the only smart thing would be to use a condom."

They had reached the tiny town of Hartsel, nothing more than a few buildings clustered along the sinuous South Platte River. He pulled up to the Badger Basin Country Store and stopped the car. The store had gas pumps but the place looked closed for some reason.

"What's happening?" May asked.

"I need to get gas," he said.

"How badly?" she asked, leaning over to look at the gauge.

"Soon," he said. "The gauge isn't very accurate."

In reality, he had no reason to doubt the gauge, although it was in fact solidly in the red caution zone. But the mention of condoms reminded him that, though he hadn't had occasion to need such protection since before the girls were born, such an occasion seemed to present itself now. In addition to communicating her willingness, May, with her talk of hepatitis and needle use, convinced him that she could prove a risky sex partner for several reasons. Someplace in Buena Vista certainly would carry condoms but by then it would be too late, both because they would have other things to do there and because it was far out of the South Park Sex Zone.

"Can we make it to Buena Vista?" she asked him.

"I'm really not sure," he said, not lying too much. "Maybe we ought to try Fairplay instead." Mentally, he crossed his fingers. Fairplay should have a place to get gas and condoms, still in South Park but it wasn't much closer than Buena Vista. He hoped she wouldn't remember that.

"How far is Fairplay?"

Yes! he thought. "Oh, not far," he said as casually as he could. "We can just come down 285 to Antero Junction. Are we in a huge hurry?"

"Not really. Libby sounded fine on the phone and Dolores isn't expecting me any particular time."

He smiled as he started the car.

"Is this one of your spots?" she asked him.

"What? Right here in downtown Hartsel?"

"You've just got that same smile on your face."

He had stopped here once, in front of an old hotel that had burned down decades before, but with Susan, after they were married. Anne, still a toddler, had fallen asleep in the back and Susan had dozed off in the passenger seat. He had stopped here in Hartsel to tuck a blanket around Anne who, at that age, seemed more active asleep than awake. Well aware of the South Park Sex Zone, John got back in the car and gently stroked Susan's breasts, hoping to rouse her aroused. When she opened her eyes, though, she looked at him like he'd lost his mind. Without further ado, he had started the car and driven off. Alice, born a couple of years later, represented months of concerted effort to give Anne a playmate, not some frivolous sexual adventure.

He didn't feel like sharing that vignette with May, however. Besides, since he and Susan hadn't had sex, it didn't really qualify as part of the South Park Saga. Instead, as he turned right onto Colorado 9 to Fairplay, he said to May, "No, I never got lucky in Hartsel. But I did in Garo."

"Before you tell me about that," she said, "would you mind if I smoked?"

"Smoked what?"

"A cigarette, I guess. Is there a choice?"

He reached into the glove box and took out the tin with the dope pipe. "I don't know that it's choice but it's pretty good. It's that same stuff—no, that's right, you didn't smoke any that day, did you?"

"I didn't need to," she said, holding the wheel for him as he crumbled some marijuana into the bowl of the pipe. "Those mushrooms were awesome."

"I'm glad you enjoyed it," he said, handing her the pipe and lighter. "I hope you enjoy this."

They silently had three hits apiece. The scenery changed on this stretch, closer to the mountains. The rich bottom land along Four Mile Creek supported a few prosperous ranches. Farther along, the red rock along the low ridges, for which the state is named, accentuated the dark green of the Colorado blue spruces and Douglas firs, while the sunny slopes supported mostly ponderosas. The road, too, had more contours along here, demanding slightly more attention of the driver. A few hits of marijuana never really impaired John's ability to drive. Indeed, he often drove slower and more carefully stoned than straight, concentrating less on the goal and more on the journey. But the dope made him more prone to distractions, things like May fiddling with her bra.

"Is there a problem?" he asked her.

"Would you mind if I took this off?" she asked, unsnapping the hooks from the back. "I thought it was my blouse bugging me earlier but I think it was this new bra."

"Take off anything you like," he offered generously.

She pulled up her left arm into the sleeve of the sweater to slip the bra strap past her hand, then reached into the right sleeve to pull out the limp bra, a la *Flashdance*. "It's this damn tag," she said, ripping the offending fabric from the elastic back of the bra. "In fact, could you scratch my back?"

She turned her back to him. Watching the road, he used the fingers of his right hand to scratch the center of her back through the soft sweater, feeling her muscles flex as her back arched ecstatically.

"Oh, God, thank you!" she said. "Much better."

"You're easy to please," he pointed out, both hands back on the wheel.

"In the right hands," she said with a Gioconda smile. "But you were going to tell me about getting lucky in Garo, weren't you?"

He chuckled at the memory. "I don't know that luck had much to do with it," he reminisced. "I think she enjoyed making love to me more than anyone else I've ever been with."

"Why?" she asked, intrigued.

"Oh, it didn't have much to do with my prowess as a lover," he admitted. "She just had the hots for me. I met her right after I graduated college. I wasn't looking for any sort of long-term commitment but that didn't seem to bother her at all. She had a serious weight problem but a really pretty face. And she laughed at all my jokes which I, like a lot of men, find irresistible."

"Ha, ha, ha!" May laughed sarcastically. "Good one, John!"

"Yeah, yeah. Not to worry. I'm having enough trouble resisting you as it is."

"Resistance is futile," she said, Borg-like.

"Are you going to assimilate me into the collective?" he asked, continuing the *Star Trek* theme, adding, "I hope, I hope."

"First I need to drain your memory banks," she said mechanically, then in her normal voice, "So you brought this over-weight woman to Garo, Colorado…"

"Well, Garo wasn't exactly the destination." Garo made Hartsel look like a midtown Manhattan. "I was living in a cheap apartment at the time and my neighbors threatened to get me evicted if I didn't keep this woman quiet."

"Her hysterical laughter at your jokes woke the neighbors?"

"No, her screams. She had a much lower threshold than I do so she would have half a dozen screaming, writhing, back-slashing orgasms for every one of mine. Back then I had an old Volkswagen bus so I loaded her and the camp gear into it and brought her up here. We ended up camping up by Whale Peak but she couldn't wait that long. So I pulled off right along here on one of these little side roads and let her scream her head off."

"Oh, John!" May mocked him breathlessly, "You magnificent stallion!"

"Don't knock it till you've tried it."

"Promises, promises."

That did it. He put his right hand on the back of her neck, pulled her to him and, with one eye on the road, emphatically kissed her.

John literally couldn't remember the last time he had kissed a woman passionately. There had been a lot of social cheek-pecks, countless perfunctory wifely reminders of their marriage, periodic gentle skinned-knee anesthesia, nightly slobbery smootches from sleepy girls, even the occasional affectionate buss when he managed to exceed Susan's expectations. But good old lip-mashing, tongue-touching, heavy-breathing osculation? Maybe sometime back in the '80s. It felt great.

When finally they broke apart, May sat back with her eyes closed, running her tongue across her lips. She heaved a sigh. "Well."

"And let that be a lesson to you," he said sternly.

"What did I do to deserve such treatment?"

"You don't think you've been taunting and flaunting?"

"Of course I've been taunting and flaunting," she admitted. "I thought you'd never notice."

"Really?"

"Okay, John," she argued, "tell me this: how many people think we've already had sex?"

"How many people watch *Inside Edition*? Millions?"

"If you pulled off the road and made mad passionate love to me right now, who, besides the two of us, would ever know?"

"Just your guardian angel."

She turned away to look out the window again.

"May, I'm sorry."

"Do you want to do this or not?"

He thought about it. "Let's see. I'm married to a woman who, for a long time now, has been more my business partner than my wife, who already assumes I've been unfaithful, and to whom I may not be married much longer. I've got way too much pressure in my job. I've got an attractive young woman throwing herself at me. My reputation is shot. You know what? I think I may be presidential material."

She laughed. "So?"

"It sounds good to me. What about you?"

"John, to put it bluntly, I haven't had sex since before I went to jail. For nearly a year."

"Let's do it."

O   O   O

Most of Colorado's old mining towns are gone. Just a few miles from Fairplay, the town of Buckskin Joe sparkled brightly for a few years and then flickered out. But in its heyday, it was home to such characters as Joe Higginbottom, the buckskin-clad miner who gave the town its name; Silverheels, the dance-hall girl named for the shoes a miner made her, who nursed the men of the town through small pox until she caught it herself; and Horace "Haw" Tabor, who ran a store in Buckskin Joe for years until he struck it rich in Leadville, eventually leaving his long-suffering wife Augusta for a young beauty named Baby Doe and a seat in the United States Senate.

Just the other side of Hoosier Pass, Breckenridge's historic buildings have been restored and remodeled as upscale shops or lost in the shadows of the condos and hotels serving the world-class ski area.

Fairplay has managed to avoid either fate, scratching out a living from tourists paying to see South Park City, a replica of an old mining town, and from the passing throng, like John and May, stopping briefly for gas or a meal or a cheap room for the night. At the base of Mt. Silverheels, the town rises along a steep gulch through which tumbles the headwaters of the South Platte River. The riverbed itself lies crumpled and barren, victim of a machine that could float on the river, scoop up the entire bed, extract the gold dust, and spit out the rounded river rock in mounds that stretch for miles, naked but for a few pioneering foxtail pines.

John pulled the Outback up to the pumps and got out to fill the tank, thinking, "Condoms in Fairplay. Sounds about right. If you're going to play, play fair."

As he unscrewed the gas cap and thrust the nozzle into the tank, May got out too. "I'm going to visit the little girls' room," she said. "I don't suppose you'd buy me a cup of coffee?"

"Of course! Anything else you'd like?"

She looked around and then kissed him. "Nothing I could get here."

He watched her walk away. Maybe he was about to do the dumbest thing in his life but from this angle, it sure looked worth it. The Outback's tank was fairly large and almost dry. Impatiently tapping his foot, he grabbed the nozzle and pulled the trigger open all the way. The fuel gushed out noisily.

Finally the trigger clicked off and John untangled the hose and hung it back up. From the corner of his eye, he saw May walk out of the restroom, smoking a cigarette. Without glancing in his direction, she walked to the road and crossed, stopping on the other side to look down the highway, pulling the wind-blown strands of auburn hair from her mouth, nervously tapping the ash from her cigarette.

John stood baffled until it came to him what she was doing. He loped into the store, paid for the gas, got the coffee, and loped back out to the car, spilling the coffee. A car slowed by May but she waved it off.

John started the Outback and turned out onto the highway. As he came abreast of May, sure enough, she stuck out her thumb, her short black skirt fluttering around her knees in the chilly breeze.

He leaned over, rolled down the window, and said, "Hey, there, little girl. Where you headed?"

She leaned on the window sill and looked him straight in the eye. "As far as you can take me."

He did Phil Harris as Foghorn Leghorn: "Well, get on—I say, get on in, little missy."

She tossed away her cigarette and got in. She had renewed her cologne which, along with the fresh mountain air, seemed to radiate from her soft sweater. She hadn't put the bra back on, and her nipples, contracted from the cool air, stood out plainly. She had taken off her pantyhose as well, her bare calves goose-bumped and pale.

"Thanks, mister," she said, leaning against the door to look at him, sipping the coffee he handed her. "I might have waited there for hours. What in the world can I do to repay you?" she asked innocently, blinking her sea-green eyes.

"I'll think of something," he said with a chuckle.

"I hope it's not something really hard," she breathed, "cause I just don't know what I'd do."

"Oh, it'll be hard enough."

She laughed and broke character. "How did I do?"

"Real well. In fact," readjusting his shorts, "fucking great."

"As good as your singer friend?"

"If anything, better," he was forced to admit, sipping his own coffee.

"Good enough to be one of your South Park Girls?"

"Easily. In fact, to tell you the truth, my singer friend wasn't the one who came up with the hitchhiker thing."

"Well, you dirty old man. Where did you get such an idea?"

"From another South Park Girl, one I haven't told you about yet."

"There's another? I thought we already covered all five. There was the poetry chick, the wild woman, your singer, the fat girl—I guess that is just four."

"In a way, I saved the best for last, although she was actually one of the first. It was the summer after I lived with Prudence. I took my bus up here camping one weekend and saw this girl hitchhiking out there in South Park."

"What was she? Crazy? Stupid?"

"She was cute. This was back in the early '70s. Hitchhiking was a more respectable mode of transportation back then. She was, in fact, hitching across the country for the summer. And since I was neither crazy nor stupid, I picked her up. We ended up camping up by Alma. Above there, actually, way back on a dirt road by an old gold mine and mill. Most of the mill was torn apart but some of the rooms in the foreman's house still had old peeling wallpaper and pieces of glass still in the windows. It was really a beautiful night. We sat out and watched the sunset and got high and then went into the house and made love right in the middle of the floor."

"How was it?"

"Pretty good, until a marmot came in for the night. Scared the crap out of all three of us."

"Did you fall in love with her?"

"Yes," he said, thinking fondly of her easy laugh, her tangled braids. "Did I ever see her again? No."

"Why not?"

"I was just one of the stops along her way. I took her back to Alma the next day and she caught a ride with someone else, heading west."

"Why didn't you try to keep in touch with her?"

"I've only asked myself that question a hundred thousand times. Maybe it was too easy.

You find one gold nugget in a stream, you figure there must be more. I guess I figured that if I found one beautiful hitchhiker in South Park, there were bound to be more, dozens, hundreds maybe. God, what a shithead I was."

"How many more did you find?"

"Well, let's see. Counting that girl singer and now you, I guess two."

"So where are you going to take me, anyway?"

"I had planned to go up the Four Mile Creek road but I must have missed the turn. Maybe we'll try the road up to Weston Pass, which should be right up here.'"

Sure enough, in a couple of minutes John found and turned onto the Weston Pass road, at the base of the north slope of Jones Hill and the Buffalo Peaks. In all of South Park, they had passed only a couple of dozen cars. Here, in the lingering patches of week-old snow on the washboarded dirt, John could make out just one previous set of tire tracks.

"Are we going over the pass?" May asked.

"No way. It's a pretty rough jeep road even in summer. But we can go up a ways and have the place to ourselves."

"Have you been to the top?"

"I hiked up there once. What a view to the west! You look across that lush valley by Leadville right at Mt. Elbert and Mt. Massive, the tallest peak and the biggest peak in Colorado."

A willow-lined stream bordered with shelves of thin ice flowed through a culvert beneath the road.

"Did you see the sign by that creek?" May asked.

"No. I was looking at you."

"That was High Creek."

"That's definitely a sign." He pulled the dope tin from the glove box again and relit the pipe, passing it to her.

"So really," she said, letting out her hit, "do you think we'll see anyone up here?"

"Highly unlikely."

"So then it wouldn't matter if I did this." She pulled the sweater over her head and off, tossing it in the back.

John faced one of those decisions that can tear a man apart. On the one hand, if he drove slowly, the car bumped up and down on the washboard gravel; slowly enough and he could afford to take his eyes off the road and concentrate on the way May's breasts jiggled and shimmied and bounced. On the other hand, if he drove fast, the car flew over the washboard too fast to do more than vibrate the breasts but he would get somewhere to park that much sooner. After some serious debate and a number of glances to assess the situation, he opted for the second choice. May watched this whole process with the look of someone who is confident she is in control.

The open sagebrush eventually gave way to patches of aspen and conifers. He turned onto a smaller road and pulled into the first turn-off surrounded by trees. He looked around. They had the place completely to themselves.

"How's this?" he asked her.

"How's this?" she asked in return, leaning over to kiss him.

Their lips wrangled and wrestled and fought for dominance. He ran his fingertips across her ribs, her arm, her breasts, the afternoon sun warming her skin. He put his hand on her thigh and slowly slid it up beneath her skirt. His fingers gently sought her sweet spot and found it warm and wet and ready. It felt perfect.

One more thing needed to be said, something about their separate lives and his many obligations. He disentangled his lips from hers and cleared his throat. "You know, maybe I should explain…"

She put her finger to his lips. "This doesn't have to be complicated."

"But I…"

She pressed her finger harder. "Let me try to simplify it," she said. "Let's just forget about all that Jason stuff. Neither one of us knows what's going to happen tomorrow or next week. So no matter what happens here today, there's a really good chance you and I will never see each other again, right?"

"True," he admitted reluctantly.

"Now, do you want to spend this time talking?"

"No," he said decisively.

"Where do you want to do it? Want to chase me through the woods like a wild animal?"

"Hell, you could probably out-run me." He chuckled as he lifted the latch to pop the tailgate. "The situation reminds me of an old joke. It seems Billy and Janey are at the drive-in movie theater. They watch the movie awhile and then they start to neck. Pretty soon they're kissing like this." Putting his hands on either side of her neck, he kissed her again, strong forceful kisses that left no doubt of his intentions. "And so Billy says, 'Hey, Janey, you want to get into the back seat?'"

"Yes," May answered.

John kissed her again and said, "Well, unlike you, Janey's a little shy. She just giggles and says, 'Oh, no!'"

"Janey's a moron," May said as they both got out of the car.

"So they keep necking," John said as he pulled open the tailgate. "And pretty soon Billy's doing this." He stood behind May, leaned down, and clasped the nape of her neck between his teeth, at the same time taking both of her breasts into his hands. This time, no namby-pamby spider-doing-push-ups. His hands explored every texture and contour of her small, excited breasts. "Once again, Billy asks, 'Hey, Janey, you want to get into the back seat?' And again, Janey says, 'Oh, no!'"

"Janey doesn't deserve to live."

John pulled out the old emergency blanket he kept in the car and laid it across the bed of the Outback, the back seat already down. May got in and stretched out on the blanket. John lay next to her and once again slid his hand up her thigh.

"Eventually Billy's doing this," he said, rubbing his fingers across her slippery clitoris. May closed her eyes and murmured her approval. "And he asks one more time, 'Come on, Janey, are you sure you don't want to get into the back seat?'"

"My God," May moaned as her body tensed. "What's the matter with her? Why not?"

"Billy's question exactly: 'Why not, Janey?' And Janey says, 'Because, Billy, I want to stay here, in the front seat, with you!'"

May didn't laugh and John didn't care. Her fingers fumbled with the zipper on his trousers and finally managed to pull it down. He unfastened his belt buckle and the waistband of the pants. Her fingers insinuated themselves into his briefs and gently fondled his growing erection, her wrist bending to pull away the waistband.

The time had come. He kissed her. "First, we really should do this," he said, pulling himself toward the front and reaching between the seats. His hand fumbled around futilely, his mind completely absorbed in the way her hand manipulated him.

"Are you looking for the pipe?" she asked.

"Uh, no," he said, momentarily paralyzed as he felt her tongue lick the bead of honeydew from the end of his erection.

"Do you mind if I do this while I wait?" she asked, taking him gently into her mouth and rubbing her tongue along his shaft.

His hand flew across the front seats with growing desperation as the realization slowly dawned: Sixteen gallons of unleaded. Two cups of coffee. No condoms. Talk about the dumbest thing he'd ever done. Oh Lord. Now what?

May's warm mouth let him go and she asked, a little impatiently, "What are you looking for?"

"I, uh…" This required fast thinking, which, between the dope and the testosterone, wasn't easy. "You know, what you were just doing felt unbelievably good. I don't suppose I could talk you into…"

"Into what?" she asked, swiping her tongue along his shaft again.

"Into…just…keeping…going?" he said tentatively.

"What am I, your intern?" she joked.

He said, in a soft simpering Arkansas drawl, "Now, you know, I never promised you a rose garden."

"Trust me, Mr. President," she insisted, tugging on his shoulder to pull him next to her again. "I promise I'll never speak to Linda Tripp as long as I live."

Except for her black skirt bunched around her waist, she lay naked on the old blanket. All he had to do was roll onto her. Oral sex couldn't hold a candle to that. But without a condom… He decided to try once more. "You know, if you did that for me, I would be happy to return the favor in any way I can."

"Come on," she pleaded. "I want to feel you inside me." She tried to pull him onto her. When she felt him resist, her eyes popped open warily. "Or do you just want to be able to tell the First Lady you didn't have sexual relations with me?"

"How many people bought that excuse?"

"So you're saying oral sex *is* sex?" she asked. "Tell me this. Of those five South Park Girls, how many did you just have oral sex with?"

"Okay, before you impeach me," he said, "let me come clean with you. Part of the reason I went to Fairplay was to get condoms which I" slapping his forehead with the heel of his hand "completely spaced out. I don't suppose you have one."

"That's what this is about?" she asked.

"I'm just thinking of your protection."

"My protection."

"I don't want to do what your father did."

"You're not molesting me," she pointed out. "This isn't incest. This is completely consensual."

"No, I mean I don't want to make the same mistake Jason did: get a woman pregnant and then disappear from her life."

"For one thing," she said stiffly, "I've taken birth control pills since the last time Paco raped me, which was, incidentally, when Libby was conceived. For another thing, if I *am* Jason's daughter—which I seriously doubt—then that would make me the result of that 'mistake'."

"I didn't mean…" he said.

"Listen," she said, pulling her black skirt back down, "do you want to do this or not?"

"Oh, God, May, I want to do this so badly," he moaned, looking at her young slender body. "And I *am* doing this so badly."

"Wait a minute," May said suspiciously. "You're not worried about *my* protection. That was a lie. You're worried about *your* protection."

"May…"

"When was the last time you slept with someone other than your wife?"

"Not since I met her."

"So you're worried about sticking your" disdainfully picking up his rapidly shrinking erection "nice hermetically sealed penis into some who-knows-where-she's-been slut, aren't you?"

"That's not it at all," he protested weakly. "Although it *is* better to be safe than—"

"Sorry?" she asked incredulously. "Oh, this whole thing is pretty fucking sorry. Did you insist on a condom with all your other South Park Girls?"

He mentally tried on different answers: "I was young and stupid." "Those were different times." "Condoms weren't as—"

"No," she answered for him. "No, you fucked *them* naked but you're not willing to fuck *me* naked. Either that, or you made up all that crap about the South Park Girls just to impress me, just to get into my pants." She sat up and grabbed her sweater. "Well, you know what? Either way, *fuck* you!" She slid out of the car and disappeared into the woods.

o   o   o

Except for one brief rise after Antero Junction, Trout Creek Pass is essentially downhill all the way from South Park to the warm dry valley of the Arkansas River. Downhill all the way suited John's mood perfectly.

Rather than offend May any further by pursuing her through the woods, John had sat in the Outback alternately flagellating himself for being such an uncouth shithead and thinking of all the different things he might have said that would have resulted in his getting laid.

May had finally returned after about half an hour, when the sun slipped behind the Buffalo Peaks. Dry-eyed and sullen, she got in the car without a word. Without a word he started the car and drove back to the highway. Without a word they had driven since, past the scattered ranches, past the wind-blown islands of slender spruce and fir, past the looming shaggy-sided hump of East Buffalo Peak. Despite the clear sky, he knew his brief Indian summer had come to a crashing halt.

This trip had turned out to be the exact opposite of what the doctor ordered. If anything, May now seemed to hold John in lower regard than Susan did. Rather than finding a little relief, he had actually managed to nudge the stress level just a little higher. And he still had to drive May into Buena Vista and then take her and Libby back to the Springs.

In a desperate attempt to break the ice between them, which had grown surprisingly thick considering it was still a mild late-fall day, he pointed to a tall lichen-covered natural wall of rock along the way. "That's a volcanic formation called a dike. It forms during an eruption when a fissure opens up in the earth and fills with magma. After the magma cools, the surrounding rock eventually washes away and leaves that distinctive-looking rock wall. The Spanish Peaks, down in southern Colorado by Walsenburg, are volcanic and have a series of dikes radiating out from the cones, so big I saw them from a jet once. Jason turned me on to them one time when we went camping down at the Great Sand Dunes."

"So Jason was into dikes, huh?" May sneered. "Did he insist on using a condom with them?"

John groaned. "May, I'm so sorry about what happened earlier. But for what it's worth, I'm probably twice as much a fuckhead as Jason."

"You know something, John? I'm getting sick of talking about Jason. He may have influenced your life but, other than whatever happened at the very beginning, he hasn't influenced mine. Let's just drop the whole thing, okay?"

Now there's some ice thick enough to support a Zamboni, John thought. He concentrated on negotiating the tight curves of the two-lane road instead, past the reflective terraces of beaver ponds along Trout Creek. As ubiquitous as beaver had become in

Colorado again, he rarely caught sight of one. And it might be a long time before he saw another, outside South Park anyway.

At the bottom of the pass the wide Arkansas Valley opened up. Tall bare cottonwoods lined the rushing blue-green river; a pygmy forest of piñon and juniper clung to the rounded rock outcrops on either side. To the west and north rose the fourteen-thousand-foot Collegiate Peaks: Mt. Princeton, Mt. Yale, Mt. Columbia, Mt. Harvard. Ivy-leaguers all, the chill lofty summits, the backbone of America, rose like ivory towers in the fading twilight.

As he turned north on Highway 24 for the last couple of miles into Buena Vista, John made another feeble attempt to lighten the mood in the car. Looking over at the bright gray buildings and lime green roofs, the glittering barbed wire and bars, of the Buena Vista Correctional Complex, he said to May, "Isn't that Paco's alma mater?"

"I don't know what Alma has to do with it," she said, looking askance at him, "but yes, that's where he did his time."

Hugely relieved just to hear a civil tone from her, he asked, "Did he end up serving out his whole sentence?"

"They released him on parole about six months before his sentence was up."

"Were you here when they let him out?"

"Yeah."

"How did you end up back here, anyway? Last I heard, you were in the hospital in Seattle."

"Incidentally, for your information," she said haughtily, "I completely recovered from the hepatitis and I've been tested and found disease-free at least once a year ever since."

"God, May, I'm so sorry. I really wasn't trying to imply…"

"Forget it. I guess I don't blame you. It is hard to trust anybody anymore."

"Anyway, I'm glad to hear you recovered completely."

"Well, I was in the hospital for two months. I came down with pneumonia too."

"Jeez. Two months. I hope you were insured."

"No, I wasn't," she said, turning to look out the window.

"How did you end up paying for it then?"

"I didn't. My guardian angel stepped in again."

"Nana? Did you call her?"

"Oh, no, I was too sick."

"How in the world did she know where you were?"

"I have no idea. All I know is that, once again, after I had been there for a few weeks, they changed my doctors and my medication and everything. She may have saved my life. You know, it's easy to slip through the cracks in a place like Harborview."

"That's the hospital?"

"Yeah. It's just above downtown in Seattle, up on Capitol Hill. It's where they bring all the skid row winos and O. D.'s and shooting victims and AIDS patients. Hell, I was one of the O. D.'s. But I woke up one morning in a private room and had flowers and new doctors and everything."

"Did you ever talk to Nana about it?"

"I was always too scared to talk to her. I figured she'd just give me one of those looks of hers like I was a worthless piece of shit to put her through all that trouble. I did try to thank her the day she died but I don't think she heard me." She shook her head bleakly. "God, I can't believe that was just three days ago."

John slowed as they pulled into Buena Vista and he asked her where Dolores lived. She gave him directions to a sleepy side street and a small boxy frame house painted pink. John parked in front and May got out and went to the front door and knocked. After a couple of minutes passed with no response, she came back to the car.

"She must have gone out," she said to John.

"What do you want to do?"

"I guess we ought to wait."

"Here?" he asked. "Are you hungry? Maybe we should grab a bite somewhere."

"Do you remember seeing Casa de Sol on the way in? We could go there."

Casa de Sol looked like an old log cabin expanded for commercial use, with the restaurant's emblem, a brick red sun surrounded by a tawny aurora, in the center of the tan stucco wall by the parking area. Inside, the floor was slightly below ground level, with open ceiling beams so low John felt he had to stoop.

A willowy waitress with thin curled blonde hair framing her pretty face grabbed a couple of menus as she approached. When she recognized May, however, she squealed with delight. "Oh, my God! May? I don't believe it! How *are* you?"

She and May hugged warmly and then May said staunchly, "I'm doing okay. I wondered if you were still working here."

The waitress rolled her eyes. "Like I have a lot of choices," she said as she led them to a table. "Are you coming back to work?" she asked, then added to John, with a broad smile, "May was the best server we ever had here. Other than me, that is."

"John, this is Linda," May said. "She and I were best buds when I worked here." She turned to Linda. "John's a friend of my mom's. He gave me a ride up here from the Springs to pick up Libby."

"Did Dolores tell you what happened?" Linda asked.

"Just that Paco and Shirley had disappeared."

"Oh, we have to talk," Linda said eagerly. "But I've got to get some orders out. What can I get you? Would you like something to drink first?"

"I'd like a Corona—make it two," she added when she saw John nod. "And I already know what I want: a chicken sopapilla."

"How about you, John?" Linda asked.

He glanced quickly at the menu. "I'll try a chicken enchilada."

When Linda left to place their order, May noticed John watching her walk away. "She's pretty, isn't she?"

He looked at May with a poker face, smelling a trap.

"Just think," she went on. "Now that we're in town, you could get some condoms. I'll put in a good word for you with her if you like."

"I know you think I'm a slimeball…"

She patted his arm and smiled. "John, I'm just giving you shit. All is forgiven. Maybe I should try calling Dolores, at least leave a message on her machine to let her know we're in town."

He watched her walk over to the pay phone. He helped himself to some chips and salsa that Linda had brought with the Coronas. From the sound system came a Latin instrumental version of "Perfidia."

He wondered if he was guilty of perfidy. At what point in his relationship with May had he betrayed the faith of his marriage vows? That day at the *Trail Gazette*, when he noticed she wasn't wearing a bra? Perhaps a germ of sexual attraction had sprouted on their hike to Lake Haiyaha but he had come back from the mountains feeling like he had resisted temptation. Susan, obviously, disagreed. But in a way, the fact that he had eaten the mushrooms, ammunition so far still hidden from Susan, constituted more of a betrayal than doing a few spider-doing-push-ups on May's breast.

What had happened a few hours earlier, though, seemed far more perfidious. Without a doubt, he had lusted for May with every fiber of his being and he knew that he had deliberately steered the conversation to that end. The result had been little more than what they did on their hike but he certainly had the intention of having sex with her. On the other hand, hadn't Susan made faith irrelevant by seeking a divorce? For that matter, hadn't Anne betrayed *his* trust by getting involved with Wayne Giles? he thought, watching one of the bus-girls who was about Anne's age.

He washed down another salsa-dripping chip with the Corona, looking over at May, who still talked on the phone. As long as he was beating himself up: Hadn't he broken faith with May as well? He certainly led her to believe they were going to have sex. How could he forget to buy a condom? A Freudian would say there are no accidents. Had some subconscious reluctance sabotaged him?

Why insist on a condom at all? Was it just a programmed response to all the Safe Sex ads? Certainly May had a past but he had a past as well. If he couldn't feel comfortable having unprotected sex with her, how could he ever trust anyone else? After all, part of the problem with May was that she seemed too much like family.

It's all too much, he sighed. Maybe no one's pure enough to warrant absolute faith. People are more like the salsa, a hodgepodge of earthy, spicy bits of strengths and contradictions and conceits. You can't expect the heady clarity of the Corona.

May hung up the phone and came back to the table. "We must have just missed her," she said, squeezing a wedge of lime into her beer bottle. "She's making Libby some dinner."

"Did she say any more about Paco and Shirley?"

"Just that they didn't leave town together. And I'll bet I know why."

Linda came back carrying their dinners on a tray. Using a cloth to serve them, she said, "Be careful. These platters are really hot. So, did you talk to Dolores?" she asked May.

May nodded as she sipped her beer. "She told me they didn't leave together. So does that *bitch* still work here?"

Linda pulled up a chair. "You got it, honey. She worked here till last week. Your ex-bastard came in to see her the night he and Shirley got to town."

"Figures," May said, explaining to John, "Even while he and I were still married, Paco had the *cojones* to nail one of the other servers here, a little slut named Felina."

"Felina?" John asked, swallowing a bite of the enchilada as the sound system shifted to "Malaguena." "What am I, in a Marty Robbins song?"

May shrugged and turned back to Linda. "So what happened?"

"You knew Felina got married," Linda said.

"What!? To who?"

"Remember Felix, the guy who always claimed he had Gulf War Syndrome?"

"I thought he couldn't…"

"Evidently he can't. But you should see his new Jaguar. Anyway, I guess he found out about Paco and spread the word that if he ever found him, he'd cut off his balls and hang them from his rear-view mirror like fuzzy dice."

"I've got some rusty scissors he can borrow," May offered. "So is Felina still here?"

"I thought Dolores would have told you," Linda said. "She and Paco split together."

"You're kidding! God, she's stupider than me. Where did they go?"

"Felina's sister told me they were shacking up with her aunt in New Mexico."

"Where? Raton? That's about Paco's speed."

"Truth or Consequences."

"Oh, jeez," May said. "He's in for it now."

"Couldn't happen to a nicer guy." Linda turned to John. "So, have you met Libby before?"

"Never have," John said, scraping the last of the dark red enchilada sauce and sour cream from his plate.

Linda got up, nudging May with her hip. "Way to go," she said with a smile.

"Who? John?" May said. "Not a chance. He thinks I'm a whore."

"I never said—" John sputtered, but before he could finish, Linda walked away laughing.

"Did I say 'whore'?" May said to him, smiling too. "I meant bitch."

"You know what I think you are? Really?"

She pretended to cringe but said, "Okay. What have we got to lose?"

"I think," he said, taking her hand, "—honestly—that you're a woman who just dribbled sauce on her sweater."

A blob of tomato-y sauce clung to her left, still-unbra-ed breast. "Damn!" she said, rubbing it with her napkin.

"May I help?" he offered.

"No thanks," she said snidely. "I guess I'd just better get used to doing this myself."

"Anyway," he chuckled, "it sounds like a little fur has flown between you and Felina already."

"Felina has the morals of a stray cat," May said. "We used to call her 'Pussy' behind her back. But she sure knows what she likes and she's going to get tired of Paco in about two weeks. Right?" she asked Linda, who had returned with their check.

"I can't believe Felina let him talk her into this in the first place," Linda said.

"So Paco got involved with her while you were married?" John asked May as Linda took John's credit card to settle the bill.

May snorted contemptuously. "He was bopping her while I worked here. He used to pick me up, bring me home, tuck me into bed, and then sneak back over here, pick *her* up, bring her home, and tuck them both into bed. He managed to do this for years before I found out."

"What did you do?" John asked as Linda returned with the receipt.

"That's when I got my second DUI," May said, slipping her light jacket over the stain on her sweater. "She lived in a trailer up near Americus back then and they caught me doing 80 to try to catch them in the act."

John popped a peppermint in his mouth while May and Linda said good-bye, with assurances on both sides that they would keep in touch. Outside, the sky was dark and the air was cold but the moon was bright and past full, waning fast.

As they got into the car, John said, "So, your second DUI."

"That was a couple of years ago," May explained as they pulled away. "That's when we decided to move back to the Springs."

"To keep him away from Felina," John assumed.

"And to keep *me* away from the Buena Vista cops," May said. "Of course, we hadn't been back in town for three weeks before I found out about Shirley."

"This was before you had Libby?" John asked incredulously.

"This was while I was pregnant. I told you, Libby's the result of a rape. He and I were at each other's throats at that point."

"Did you ever consider," he asked delicately, "terminating the pregnancy?"

After a pause, she said, "Yeah, I thought about it. And yes, I know what you're saying. You think I'm a hypocrite to criticize my mom for considering an abortion if I had considered it myself. But you don't know what I was going through."

"And you don't know what she was going through."

"And I guess we'll never know, will we?"

"Are you going to tell Libby you considered it?"

292

"Jeez, you sound just like Nana. I have no idea what I'm going to say to her. That's just a bear I've got to cross."

"Well put."

"It's not always easy to talk to your kids, is it?"

"Or to your parents, for that matter. How come Nana didn't come to your rescue on the DUIs?"

"She did, actually. I got out of the first two with just fines. The third landed me back in jail."

"What were you doing?"

"Like I said, Paco and I were at each other's throats. I met a couple of girlfriends down at Giuseppe's Depot and I guess I drank too much Cuervo. They clocked me doing 60 on South Tejon."

"Why didn't you just leave the bastard? It sounds like you were miserable."

"How happy are you and Susan?"

"*Touché*," he admitted. "Getting out is never easy."

"Getting out of jail was easier than I thought it would be, though," she said. "I was supposed to do six months starting in February but then one day last May they just turned me loose. Evidently, some lawyer had talked to the judge."

"I didn't know Nana that well," John said, "but she never struck me as the Guardian Angel type."

"Me neither. Now that she's gone I'm beginning to realize that nobody else ever cared enough to do that for me," May said as they pulled up to Dolores's house. "Mom sure didn't. She and I fought all the time after I moved back home."

"Why did you move back in with her, anyway? You forgave Paco every other time."

"When they let me out of jail early, I came home without calling Paco to surprise him. He had been writing me these long letters, talking about how much he missed me and that he would never fool around again. When I got home he was screwing Shirley while Libby was crying in the other room."

"Welcome home."

The porch light came on. "I'd better go get my daughter. Could you put the back seat up? I assume Paco left Libby's car seat."

When he got the seat squared away John went up the walk and joined May to see if she needed help. Dolores, squat and wrinkled but cheerful, looked him up and down as May introduced them. Deciding she liked him, she handed him the car seat to put in the car. By the time he had the seat threaded properly through the seat belts—the system had changed since Alice had outgrown her seat—May had finished her good-byes and stood waiting by the car door, dandling Libby on her hip, a fat diaper bag draped from her shoulder.

Dolores had swathed the baby in so many warm wraps that she looked like the Michelin Man. Having survived the treacherous trip from the porch to the car, Libby now had to be stripped of the outer two layers in order to fit into the car seat. She accepted all the fuss and bother equitably and didn't even fuss much when her leg caught on the seat belt as they got her strapped in.

"Wave bye-bye," May told her as they pulled away and Libby waved good-naturedly all around to be sure she didn't miss anyone.

"I'm probably opening myself to more snide remarks," John said as he drove back to the highway, "but may I say that she's really pretty? And if you're not Jason's daughter, where'd she get that curly blonde hair?"

Libby's hair was the color of freshly pulled molasses taffy, her complexion was dark and warm, and her eyes twinkled with intelligence and mischief. She also displayed a coy shyness, which inspired John to try to charm her by playing peek-a-boo while they waited for the traffic light to change. It took him half a dozen tries and a couple of ridiculously silly faces but he succeeded: she broke into a broad grin.

May couldn't take her eyes off of her. "God, I missed you!" she told her. "You're such a big girl now! Yes, you are!"

Libby responded with some unintelligible prattling.

"And so articulate," John pointed out.

"Okay, so she's still working on the word thing. But boy, is she a walker! Just prop her up on something and she's gone."

A walker, huh? John thought, but kept it to himself. "Any particular place you ladies would like to go?" John asked them.

"Take us home," May said firmly.

"Is that okay with you?" John asked Libby.

"Dada?" Libby said.

"Yikes!" John cried.

May laughed. "No, honey, that's not Dada. Dada went bye-bye."

"Bye-bye!" Libby chirped, waving enthusiastically.

"This is John, honey. He's the one who likes condoms."

"Connon!" Libby echoed.

John cringed. "I'm not sure that should be one of her first words."

"I'm going to teach her to pack her own," May insisted. "Men just can't be trusted to take care of things like that."

"So," John said more soberly as they drove to the edge of town. "Do you think you'll be able to keep her?"

"If I get a job."

"I really think you should call Lucy Van Deutch."

"Maybe I will. I really did like that job."

"Were you there long enough to make any friends?"

"A few. One of the guys in the kitchen, a guy named Scott, the salad chef, reminds me a little bit of you."

"I'm surprised they'd hire somebody that old and stupid."

"But he's charming, in his own way."

"Have you got a thing for this guy?"

"Are you kidding? Guys that old are always so busy lugging baggage around that they can't do anything else. But Marcus, on the other hand…"

"Who's Marcus?" he asked, trying to rein in his jealousy.

"He's the guy who does the steaks. He's always sweaty from the broiler and he's got this tight little tush and…mmm. But I don't know if he's into white chicks."

"So he's a person of color?"

"Very much. And of smell too. He's got this amazingly fresh scent even when he's been working. Unlike someone in this car."

"It wasn't me, I swear," John said.

May leaned over the seat to touch Libby's diaper. "Oh, dear. Dolores gave you onions for dinner, didn't she?" She sat back and said to John, "I know it's really soon but would you mind pulling over so I could change her?"

"Gladly," John said, wrinkling his nose at the odor.

May turned back to Libby. "We're going to get you out of that old stinky diaper and put on a nice fresh one, okay?"

He pulled into a turnout for another historical marker and stopped the car. "Want to hear something weird?" he asked May.

May, caught up in finding a fresh diaper and getting Libby back out of the car seat, didn't reply.

Maybe it's not worth it anyway, he thought. He had a dim recollection that Jason too had digestive problems with onions. But so what? Jason's story, even the Tom Huston portion that John had hoped to talk to her about on the way back to the Springs, seemed to lose relevance by the minute.

The news about Marcus hit John pretty hard. He'd been worried about taking advantage of her when, in reality, had they made love, she might have thought about Marcus the whole time. How's that for an ego boost?

His mind full of such dismal thoughts and his nose full of Libby's diaper, he dourly read the historical marker just to kill the time, the waning moon providing just enough light:

Christmas, 1806

After crossing Trout Creek Pass, Zebulon Pike and his party, still limping from frostbite after their failed attempt to climb Pikes Peak, came once again to the Arkansas River with food perilously low. On Christmas Eve, two hunting parties shot a buffalo. Christmas Day was spent at Squaw Creek, feasting on buffalo and repairing equipment. Early in 1807 Pike crossed into the San Luis Valley to the south toward the Great Sand Dunes and built a log stockade. Taken prisoner by the Spanish in La Jara, his expedition failed to reach its goal, the southern boundary of the Louisiana Purchase.

And with all of that, John thought, Zeb Pike probably had a merrier Christmas and a happier New Year than John could reasonably expect.

. . . O . . . O . . . O . . .

I almost wish I could take off this New Year's Eve. I've worked every New Year's Eve for the last—well, as long as I can remember. I've played in 20 different towns in 25 years. Some have been fun, most forgettable. The worst, for some reason, seem to be the decade transitions.

On New Year's Eve, 1979, I was that drummer trying to keep the band Tight Squeeze together. The lead singer, that Ball of Fire, had broken up with me a few weeks before and had taken up with the bass player. The two of them had just announced their plan to fire me and take over the band. But the show must go on and somehow the band managed to survive the job I'd booked us in Scott City, Kansas. Back at the motel, though, the singer and the bass player went to one room, the other band members and I to another. I spent the first hours of the 1980's feeling the rhythmic thump of the headboard against the adjoining wall.

By New Year's Eve, 1989, I was living in Seattle with the Princess. We had, in fact, first made love exactly a year before in the little town in Wyoming where we met but already I could read the writing on the wall about our relationship.

I played that New Year's Eve at a little club in Poulsbo on the Kitsap Peninsula and invited her to join me. Wanting to be the perfect date to usher in the 1990s, she took a bunch of diet pills and starved herself for days in order to fit into the black velvet dress she'd bought a couple of sizes too small. When the free Champagne began to flow at midnight, too much of it flowed into her. After trying to pick up every guy in the place while I could only play and watch, she got violently sick on the long drive home, at one point begging me to pull over and then spilling both her purse and her guts along the side of the road.

So, for a variety of reasons, I think some trepidation is warranted about this coming New Year's Eve, the turn not only of the decade but also of the century and millennium. But now I am as far out of love as I've been since that little blonde girl with the blue eyes and freckles drew that red line—I still believe it—on my green eraser in grade school. And unless some catastrophe kills off most of the male population, I won't do more than work with that young lady who so captures my imagination. So this New Year's Eve, I don't expect much turmoil from my love life at least.

December 31, 1969

Amanda hated her mirror. Actually, the mirror was fine: concave to magnify and surrounded by small light bulbs to light her face evenly. She hated her face. She tried smiling: her teeth looked white and even but her overbite had earned her the nickname "Bucky" in grade school. Her eyebrows seemed to grow rampant, threatening to cover her eyes if she ever slackened her relentless tweezing. Despite her nightly scrubbings with Sea Breeze and her torturous avoidance of chocolate, pimples still erupted beneath the foundation of her make-up. All that paled in comparison, though, to her nose which, magnified by the mirror, reminded her of a picture she'd once seen of a workman using a jackhammer to carve a nostril in George Washington's granite honker on Mount Rushmore.

She grudgingly tolerated her eyes. Green and clear, even she could spot intelligence, kindness, and humor in them. But she found herself wishing she could stare into some deep blue eyes instead.

She reminded herself to be more specific in her wishes: she got a pair of very blue eyes, but they belonged to Debra, who tapped on her door before coming in. Amanda waved her fingers and went back to stroking the mascara along her eyelashes.

"Hi, Amy," Deb said, sitting on the bed. "About ready?"

Friends and family had called Amanda "Amy" until junior high, when she found herself in a class with four other girls named Amy. Few people besides Deb used it anymore and Deb only when they were alone.

"Which do you think?" Amanda asked her, holding up two eye-shadows, one a steely blue that complemented the highlights in her skirt and sweater, the other brown with flecks of gold that brought out the green in her eyes.

"Is that what you're wearing?" Deb asked.

Amanda stood and looked at herself in the full-length mirror on the inside of the open closet door. "Yeah. Why?" she asked, smoothing the skirt.

"No reason," Deb said, with just a hint of disdain in her tone. "It's just a little… ordinary."

Deb opened her coat. Underneath, she wore a sapphire-blue silk dress that matched her eyes. Fully six inches shorter than Amanda's skirt, it showed a lot of cleavage and was supported by the thinnest of spaghetti straps. She smiled when she saw Amanda's jealousy.

Amanda rolled her eyes. "But you can pull off a dress like that."

"In a heartbeat," Deb bragged. "Come on, girl. Do you want to end the Sixties looking like the one who went to a Catholic girls' school? Don't you still have my leather mini?" She rummaged through the closet until she found the tiny black skirt. She handed it to Amanda and started looking for a blouse.

"Mom'd kill me," Amanda said but she took off her skirt and slip and pulled on the leather mini.

Deb handed her a white blouse with French cuffs, saying, "She won't kill you. The worst she can do is tell you to change back."

Amanda appraised the new outfit in the mirror as she buttoned the blouse. Deb was right, of course. This made a bold statement. And tonight, she yearned like she had never yearned before to make a bold statement. From her jewelry box she dug some gold cufflinks set with pearls and worked them into the cuffs. Deb handed her some calf-high black leather boots that matched the skirt, boots Deb had insisted Amanda buy even though the skirt technically belonged to Deb. The two girls were close enough in size to have fairly interchangeable wardrobes.

"Isn't that better?" Deb asked.

Amanda had neither the figure nor the confidence that Deb had to carry off this sort of racy look but she grudgingly admitted to herself that, given the right circumstances, that certain someone might find her appealing. She had strong suspicions, though, that no outfit could top what he'd seen her wearing last time. As she pulled on the boots, she said, "I doubt I'll make it out the door this way but it's worth a shot, I suppose."

"Who's coming to this thing?" Deb asked.

"I called John but it's all very hush-hush. All I know for sure is what it says here." She handed Deb the folded parchment paper containing the hand-printed invitation.

Deb took it but the colorful postcard beneath it caught her eye. "What's that?"

Amanda handed her the card as well. "It's from Bill," she said.

"Where's he?"

"Acapulco. His parents took him down there for the holidays."

"Looks great."

Amanda watched with some satisfaction the envy on Deb's face as she looked at the swaying palms and colorful costumes on the card.

"How long will they be down there?" Deb asked.

"They're coming back Sunday."

"Well, while the cat's away…"

"I am not a mouse," Amanda contended. "Bill doesn't own me."

"You got that right," Deb said. "Besides, no one ever talks about what the cat does while he's away."

"I should be so lucky."

"What does that mean?" Deb asked, intrigued.

"Oh, I don't know," Amanda said, putting on her lipstick. "I mean, everybody just takes it for granted that Bill and I will end up together. And it's probably the right thing to do. But sometimes I just wish I could…"

"Dump him?" Deb finished. "Why don't you?"

"Oh, God. My parents would have a conniption. But, see, if he were to find someone else…"

"Really?" Deb said, sounding intrigued, looking at the card again before handing it back. "Then that would free you up to be with the man of your choice. Or the nut, as the case may be."

"I should be so lucky."

"Maybe tonight's the night," Deb said, looking at the invitation.

On the front was a crude drawing: a hangman's noose of hemp rope, except that the noose at the bottom looked (more or less) like a man's scrotum, wiry hairs protruding from it. Where the testicles would normally hang was written, in John's distinctive outline lettering, "Well Hung."

"I assume John drew the cover art," Deb said.

"Who else?" Amanda said.

Opening the invitation, Deb deciphered the text:

You Are Cordially Invited To
A Gathering of
The Piñon Nuts
— Don't Forget —
The End Is NYE
New Year's Eve, 1969
Celebrate the End of the Decade and
The Beginning of the Decadence
The Jones Digs, Sixish
Resplendent, S'il Vous Plait

"That's how mine read, too," Deb said. "I was hoping they had included more information in yours. What did they do, train a chimpanzee to print these? The tops of the

T's are wavier than the tilde over the N in piñon."

Amanda took back the invitation and looked fondly at Jason's awkward, backward-slanting, nearly illegible scrawl. "It's not that bad," she said, her mind effortlessly picturing Jason's pen clutched between his middle and ring fingers. "I kind of like it this way. It's more personal than something printed or typed."

"So are we the only girls?"

"You wish," Amanda said. "I think that game of pool we played with them spoiled you."

"And I think what happened afterwards spoiled any surprise you might be planning for Jason tonight."

"That was dirty pool!" Amanda said, feeling herself blush.

"But how are you going to top it tonight?"

Amanda looked at herself in the full-length mirror again, almost convinced that she actually looked sexy, but claimed, "I have no intention…"

Deb brushed off her protest. "Come on, let's go."

"Are you bringing a purse?"

"Just this," showing her the tiny clutch studded with rhinestones. "Why?"

"I should have some Kotex with me," digging through the bottom drawer of her dresser for a handbag elegant but large enough.

"Still?"

"You know me. I always save that last blob for a couple of days."

"Bummer," Deb empathized. "But he won't mind."

"Would you stop?"

They went downstairs, strategically stopping at the coat closet so Amanda too could put on her long coat before turning to face her mother, who sat on the couch by the lit Christmas tree, putting check marks on the Christmas card list next to the names of the people who had replied this year.

"Bye, Mom!" Amanda sang cheerfully, hopefully, opening the door.

"Mandy," Cynthia said sternly, stopping them in their tracks.

"Yes?" Amanda said, closing the door.

"Did you finish painting the bathroom?" she asked, still looking through the cards.

Harve Tyree had recently bought a little bungalow in Cheyenne Cañon that they planned to rent out. The prospective tenants, in fact, planned to start moving in over the weekend so all the Tyrees were spending their free time getting the place ready.

"I painted everything but that part above the tub where Dad's going to put the tile," Amanda told her. "That oil paint is impossible to get off my fingernails. I had to file them almost all the way off."

"Did you leave the window open in there the way I asked you?"

"Yes, Mother," impatiently.

"The weather report calls for snow. So while you're out, I want you to swing by there and close the window. It should have aired out by now."

"Yes, Mother."

"Now, about this party tonight," Cynthia said, looking up at her daughter for the first time. "Who else will be there?"

"I honestly don't know, Mother."

"But Russell Jones is hosting it at his parents' house, right? And they're going to be there?"

"You don't think those four boys could cook an entire meal by themselves, do you?" Amanda said, fibbing. The one selling point John had pitched to her was that Ellen and Gina, Russ's little sister, would be visiting Louie in California for the holidays.

"How were you planning to get there?" Cynthia asked.

"I thought we'd take my Karman Ghia," Deb volunteered.

"I want you to take the station wagon," Cynthia said firmly, digging through her purse for the keys. "It has snow tires."

"But, Mom…!"

"My Karman has snow tires too."

Cynthia's expression silenced them. "Frankly, Debra, I trust my daughter more than I trust you."

Deb opened her mouth in outrage but didn't say anything.

"I want you home by midnight," Cynthia went on, tossing Amanda the keys.

"Midnight!" Amanda cried. "But we're going to watch the fireworks on the Peak!"

"You can't see the Peak from the Jones's," Cynthia pointed out.

"We can drive over to Skyway."

"Is there going to be any alcohol at this party?"

"No!" both girls insisted.

"Twelve-thirty."

"Quarter to one."

"Let me see what you're wearing," Cynthia insisted.

Amanda reluctantly opened her coat. Her mother's jaw dropped.

"Everybody dresses like this nowadays, Mrs. Tyree," Deb claimed.

"Let me see yours," Cynthia told her.

Deb showed her the short silk dress.

Cynthia closed her eyes and clenched her jaw. Heaving a sigh, she looked at her daughter. "Amanda, I know you have a good head on your shoulders. I know I can trust you. But so help me, God, if you get yourself in some kind of trouble, you will get neither help nor sympathy from me, you hear?"

"I'll be fine, Mother. Can we go? We're already late."

Cynthia silently nodded.

"Thanks! See you!"

"Happy New Year, Mrs. Tyree!"

"Quarter to one."

o   o   o

"I can't believe she didn't make me change!" Amanda crowed as she drove the Tyrees' yellow Pontiac station wagon down Mesa Avenue toward the "Jones Digs."

"Your mother can be really harsh sometimes," Deb said. "You know, if you ever got in trouble somehow, I'd be there for you."

Amanda snorted contemptuously. "You're usually the reason I'm in trouble in the first place."

"Like when?"

"Like Thanksgiving."

The bet she and Deb had made on the pool game they played in front of the guys the month before actually had its roots in the previous summer.

It had been unseasonably warm in late August, with the temperature climbing into triple digits. Cynthia and Harve had flown with Peter out to the Bay Area to get him settled in at Stanford; Amanda had decided to stay with Deb for a few days. They had a gymkhana meet in the afternoon that left them wilted and sweaty, which they intended to alleviate with a dip in the O'Donnell's pool. But Deb's visiting cousins, a couple of obnoxious brats Deb referred to as the Destructo Boys, evidently under the impression that the pool could be flushed like a toilet, had spoiled that idea, so Deb and Amanda went to the Tyrees' to escape.

Unfortunately, Harve, assuming Amanda would be at Deb's the whole time, had switched off the air conditioning. The girls settled in the pool room, still wearing just their swimsuits to beat the heat. The only hint of coolness came from the little cherub tinkling into the clam-shell basin out in the garden.

The girls, alone and feisty, began to make crude remarks about the cherub's tiny waterworks, resulting in a bet on a pool game that the loser had to go out and kiss the little stone peter. Deb raised the stakes by suggesting that the loser perform this titillating task *sans* suit. Amanda balked at first but they did have the place to themselves and no one could see into the garden from the road. And Amanda, otherwise relatively cautious and conservative, hated to let Deb best her in a dare.

What Amanda lacked in temerity she made up for in pool skills. Deb lost the game. She gamely stripped down to the buff and sashayed out to the cherub, falling to her knees and taking the entire stone member into her mouth until the cool water spurted all across her torso.

So when, in November in front of the guys, Deb suggested they play for the same stakes despite the frigid temperature and falling snow, Amanda couldn't, in the interest of fair play, very well refuse her a chance to get even. Amanda knew, when she sank the 8-ball before the 15, that she had lost fair and square, that the only dirty pool involved would consist of having to strip down and kiss the icicle that the cherub now sported in his groin.

She also knew the Wonder Car's reputation for not starting so she watched from the window until the car started and began to pull out. But then Deb insisted she make good on the bet, her only concession being that Amanda could wear her shoes through the snow. Reluctantly, but also excited both by the chilly challenge and by all the interest the guys had shown in her, she stood in the door of the pool room, slipped off her shoes, pulled off her reindeer sweater and bra and then her jeans and panties, put the shoes back on, and dashed out into the snowy garden.

She learned later, though, that the door no sooner closed behind her than Deb heard Jason and Russ call from the other room. Deb, of course, ended up leaving with Russ and the others, sending Jason into the pool room to ask Amanda if he could use her phone.

It still made Amanda squirm to think about what Jason must have thought, seeing her kneeling naked in the snow to perform some sort of fallacious fellatio on the frozen fountain. Deb had switched on the floodlight to make sure Amanda lived up to her bargain so when Amanda turned to come back in, she couldn't see inside at all. Needless to say, she was completely mortified to see Jason's back as he discreetly fled when she got into the pool room. Any cold she may have felt outside vanished in a flash as she hurriedly dressed, her entire goose-bumped, snowflake-dampened body flushed with the only full-body blush she had ever experienced.

She found him by the back door in the kitchen, fidgeting and having as much trouble meeting her gaze as she had meeting his. He coughed and said, looking at his shoes, "Ah, there you are."

"I thought you left," she said, trying, like Jason, to see if they could get past this by pretending nothing happened.

"Well, the Wonder Car stalled out in your driveway. I was wondering if I could use your phone to call my dad."

"Of course," she said. As he went to the phone she asked him, "So, how long have you been here?"

"Uhh…" He struggled to find the right words and then to meet her eyes with his. "Well, to tell you the truth, at the moment it feels like I've been here all my life."

"Oh, God, Jason, I'm so embarrassed! Where's Deb?"

"She left to take the others home."

"I'm going to kill her!" She clenched both her lips and her fists.

"Well, now, I'm not sure what she did constitutes a capital crime," he said judiciously. "But I do have one favor to ask before you carry out such a rash act."

"What?" she asked petulantly.

"At least let me thank her for giving me one of the happiest memories of my short life."

The next thing Amanda knew she was in his arms and they were kissing, she sobbing for reasons not entirely clear to her, he kissing the tears away as fast as they fell, trying to make it seem as though they had never existed.

Finally, she collected herself enough to let him look up the number of the Broadmoor Hotel in the phone book so he could call his father. His heart didn't seem in the task, though.

"I gotta tell you," he said, staring at the page of numbers, "I never felt so grateful to that old bucket of bolts for stalling out."

It planted a tiny seed of doubt in her. "Are you sure it won't start?" she asked him. "Or did you and Deb somehow…"

"Oh, Man, I swear!" he vowed, crossing his heart. "Here, I'll prove it."

She put on her jacket and followed him out to where the Wonder Car still sat in the driveway. He got in, turned the ignition switch, and the car started right up. He looked as mortified as she must have looked earlier.

"I don't know…" he began, rolling down the window.

"Uh-huh," she said sarcastically.

He slammed his forehead onto the steering wheel so hard she instinctively reached out to make him stop. "I don't believe this!" he moaned. "Matt must have tried this twenty times!"

"Will it run okay now?" she asked him.

"Oh, yeah, it'll run fine. It's just that I…" His voice slowed as he realized the import of what he was saying. "I better not…shut it off…again."

She leaned on the sill of the car window. "Too bad."

He moaned again. "Truer words were never spoken."

"Cause you wouldn't believe what I have to do when Deb gets back."

He swallowed hard as he looked at her, his eyes the picture of frustrated yearning. "What?"

She relented. "I'm just teasing," she said, kissing him again. "Deb's going home and I'm going to bed. So, are you going to tell everyone what happened?"

"Not if there's the slightest chance on earth that someday I might see something like that again," he pledged, sounding quite sincere.

"Oh, I suppose there's always that slight chance," she said, setting the hook in his gaping mouth with just a smile.

"What about tomorrow?"

"Call me." She turned and walked away, feeling his eyes watching her every step. Never before had she felt so alluring, so irresistible.

But the next day, while she and Deb sat in Deb's room to plan her strategy, Jason called and left a message which Amanda's mother conveniently "forgot" until Sunday night, when Jason already had driven back up to Boulder. Amanda wrote him a nice warm letter; his reply, though warm as well, consisted mostly of news of his parents' separation, his mother's plans to move to California, and his father's admission to him that he had begun seeing another woman.

Her parents insisted Amanda go skiing with them in Aspen on Christmas break. When she got home the evening of the 30th, she found the invitation to the Piñon Nuts Gathering waiting in the mail. She hadn't seen Jason since that fateful November night. She didn't quite know what to expect but the prospect of seeing him again intrigued her more than anything ever had.

Her long-standing relationship with Bill fell far short of intriguing. Like Amanda, he seemed to accept its inevitability with alacrity but nothing more. On their dates they conversed the way married couples do, in first and third person, because there was never any news about how they felt about one another. He seemed content with the good-night kiss at her door. She discounted or ignored the insinuations about his past affairs she heard on occasion. She assumed her lack of appeal accounted for his lack of passion; she tried to accept with equanimity her role as The Kind Of Girl You Marry. Stability, either financial or romantic, and especially both, encourages conservatism. Seeking something better doesn't happen until the stability is stripped away. Deb's little prank over Thanksgiving had stripped away, among other things, Amanda's complacency.

Deb, meanwhile, took umbrage at Amanda's implication. "Who did I get you in trouble with over Thanksgiving?" she wanted to know.

Amanda had trouble putting her finger on just who that might be but she said, "You know what I mean."

"When have you ever had a better time than that?"

She had no ready answer to that either but she said, "Let's just not push it tonight, okay? You heard what my mom said." She pulled into the driveway at Russ's house.

"You mean about shutting the bathroom window at that other house?" Deb asked.

"Shit!" Amanda said. "Oh, well, we're already here now and it's still not snowing. I'll do it later."

o   o   o

A large pine-cone wreath trimmed with a large bow of gold-edged red velvet surrounded the brass plaque on the front door, on which was scrolled simply the name Jones. Deb pressed the bell.

As John opened the door for them he shouted into another room, "You rolled boxcars, not snake eyes, Jase. Your ass is going to jail, it is not passing Go, it is not collecting two hundred dollars."

"Thank God!" Jason yelled back.

"Hello, ladies!" John said to Amanda and Deb, with a debonair sweep of his arm to usher them in. "So glad you made it. May I take your coats?"

While he hung first Deb's and then Amanda's coat on an antique wood coat rack that had a mirror in the center of the hooks, Amanda looked around this house that she'd heard about but never seen. Black and white tiles covered the floor of the foyer, a shiny black baby grand piano reflected the large crystal chandelier, and a heavy walnut balustrade curved up the wide flight of stairs to the upper floor.

John, wearing jeans and a black vest over a brightly patterned shirt, had handed Amanda a lit joint as he took her coat. She took a drag and handed it to Deb. John, his back to them and his hand held out, still beckoned with his fingers.

"That's all the coats we have," Amanda pointed out to him.

"Damn!" he said. "You parted with them so willingly I thought maybe you'd just keep going with the rest of your clothes." He turned to face them. "Although, with outfits that enticing," ogling their very short hemlines, "I suppose we could let you keep them until after

303

dinner anyway. Well, come in, come in. Let me show you around. This, of course, is the living room."

High ceilings and tall windows made the living room seem spacious. Furnished with Ellen's floral-embroidered oak antiques, it looked cozy and warm; the brick fireplace crackling with a cheery fire ensured that the warmth was real. Above the mantle hung a reproduction of a dark Rembrandt; other reproductions, sailing ships and wintry landscapes, decorated the walls. The Jones's Christmas tree, a small white fir trimmed with silver ornaments and a long hand-made string of popcorn and cranberries, stood in the corner. Between the overstuffed couch and the fireplace sat a marble-topped table with a Monopoly board set up on it, the game obviously well underway. On the floor by the table sat one of Amanda's classmates from Colorado College, though she didn't recall her name.

"You know Barb Cummings, don't you?" John asked Amanda as he handed Barb the joint.

"I remember seeing you in Beidelman's biology that first block," Amanda said. "But I don't think we've met. I'm Amanda Tyree." She looked with a little envy at Barb's casual-looking wide-flare bell-bottom jeans, soft white blouse, and brocaded vest, wondering again if she'd been wise to listen to Deb's counsel on dress. But she liked Barb's All-American fresh looks and warm brown eyes.

"And this is Debra O'Donnell," John went on.

"Sorry if I don't get up," Barb said, smiling. "I seem to have been elected to keep the Monopoly game going for everyone. It's your turn, John."

John leaned down and rolled the dice. Barb moved his piece, the race car, ahead to Chance. John took the top card and discovered he'd won ten dollars in a beauty contest.

"Like there was any doubt," he noted, adjusting his loud tie in *faux* vanity. "Continuing the tour," he went on to Amanda and Deb, "in here is the solarium, complete with elevator which will carry you effortlessly upstairs should you find yourself too intoxicated later to make it up there under your own power."

"In your dreams," Deb said.

The solarium had a love seat and brass umbrella stand, lots of small-paned windows in which hung variegated philodendrons and a blooming Christmas cactus and, at the far end, the accordion-metal door of the elevator.

"Prudence," Barb called. "You landed on Ventnor. Do you want to buy it?"

"Do I own any of the others?" Prudence called back.

"No."

"No."

"Okay, group, let's go," John said, herding Amanda and Deb back through the living room and foyer like a grade school field trip. "This is Prudence Faricy," he introduced as they got to the dining room.

Prudence looked up from arranging the forks at the table settings around the big oval table. The table glittered with silver and china and candles. "Oh, good, you made it," she said. "You must be Deb and you must be Amanda. Russ has told me a lot about both of you except how beautiful you are."

Amanda had a deep distrust of the easy compliment so she found herself instantly on guard with Prudence. She had wide-set, pale blue eyes, high cheekbones, freckles, a bushel of wavy brown hair, and a practiced smile. She wore a black pants-suit, a maroon blouse, and a long brightly-colored scarf that required Prudence's constant attention to keep it from trailing in the food or getting caught on things.

Amanda, feeling a little high and tongue-tied from her second hit of dope, didn't reply to Prudence.

Deb, though, had the ability, which Amanda envied, to slip into the niceties of the social graces on demand. "What a beautiful scarf!" she said, holding the nub of the joint out to Prudence.

Prudence waved it off with a smile that struck Amanda as condescending. "I guess the hostess ought to keep her wits about her," she said. "Isn't that right, honey?" she asked Russ, who had brought in a bowl of cranberry relish which he set on the table.

"How could anything dull your wit, dear?" he asked her with a straight face. "Deb, Man, happy New Year."

"Thanks for inviting us, Russ," Amanda said. "Everything looks wonderful and something smells divine."

"Prude helped me with the decorations," Russ pointed out, "but the galley slaves account for the smells, good and bad."

"Jason, you didn't roll doubles," Barb called from the living room.

"Good!" Jason called back from the galley. "Jail's probably the safest place for me."

"May we?" Amanda asked Russ, peeking into the kitchen.

"At your own risk," Russ said.

The kitchen, like the other rooms on this floor, had a high ceiling and the first thing that caught Amanda's eye was the tall window on the east wall and the fanlight above it, the separate panes clear but beveled at the edges. Steam clouded the cold dark window, softening the reflection of the small, red cellophane wreath and electric candle that hung there. On the sill sat a large long-haired black cat, dispassionately watching the proceedings. At the breakfast table by the window, Jason, dressed in a paisley shirt with a broad collar and tight bell bottoms, bent over the main course while Matt, more conservative in a white shirt and plain tie, stood at the stove stirring the gravy in the roasting pan. Matt looked up as they entered and Amanda could tell that the sight of Deb in her short dress caught him off guard. He dropped the spoon into the boiling gravy and burned his fingers fishing it out.

"I'm going to need a little help here," Jason said to Matt, unaware Amanda and Deb had come in.

"What can I do?" Amanda offered.

Jason looked up at the sound of her voice, his hands still wrestling the slippery legs of the roasted bird. He started to look back at his task but did a double take, this time letting his eyes feast on Amanda's black leather boots and skirt and her white blouse. The month that they had been apart vanished and she could see the yearning return to his eyes. She had made her statement loud and clear. Silently thanking Deb for talking her into changing her clothes, she went to him and asked again what she could do.

When he finally found his tongue, he said, "Uh, if you'll just hold those legs apart—I mean, these legs," handing her the legs of the bird, "I'll take out the stuffing."

She held the legs apart and smiled at him as he used a tablespoon to scoop the stuffing from the cavity and put it into a bowl. He too looked good, his curly blonde hair falling almost to his shoulders, his long dark sideburns streaked with sweat in the warm kitchen. "It's nice to see you," she said to him quietly.

"Not as nice as it is to see you," he insisted. "You look incredible."

Matt, having said a simple hello to Deb, set about furiously stirring the gravy that had threatened to turn lumpy—stirring so hard, in fact, that a couple of drops splashed from the pan onto Deb's silk dress just below her navel. "Oh, no! Oh, Deb, I'm so sorry!" he cried. "Quick! What gets out gravy?"

"Panic usually works," Jason said, tossing him a dish towel.

Deb, more amused than upset, looked down at Matt wiping the gravy spots. "As much fun as that trout was," she said to him, "I think I like this better."

He suddenly realized what an intimate act his rubbing threatened to become. He humbly handed her the towel, apologized profusely once again, and went back to stirring the gravy, more gently this time.

Amanda and Jason turned back from the tragedy of the silk dress to find the black cat creeping across the table toward the roasted bird. "Othello!" Jason yelped, picking up the cat and handing it to Russ, who had come back into the kitchen. Russ took Othello from him and shooed the big black cat out the door, saying, "Out, damned spot!"

"Ditto," Deb said, vainly rubbing the towel across the gravy stains. "But wasn't that *Macbeth?*"

"He's not particular," Russ said. "He'll answer to any Shakespearean character's name as long as there's food involved. So are we about ready?"

"Let's do it!" Jason said, handing Amanda the bowl of stuffing and carrying the big platter with the bird into the dining room himself. Deb carried a casserole with candied yams and set it on a trivet on the table, Matt following with the gravy boat. Russ brought the mashed potatoes and a steaming bowl of glazed baby carrots sprinkled with dill weed.

In the living room, John, Barb, and Prudence all squealed at some development in the Monopoly game.

"Less din, more dinner!" Russ called to them, starting a scratchy version of a Mozart piano concerto on the turntable set up in the dining room.

They all got up and came into the dining room, Barb saying, "Jason, you rolled doubles to get out of jail—and it was double fives! You landed on Free Parking."

"I'll buy it," Jason said, standing at the end of the table where the bird sat.

"You can't buy Free Parking," Barb reminded him. "In fact, there was like a thousand dollars in there that you won."

"I don't care," Jason said. "I know a good thing when I see it." He said the last looking again at Amanda, who felt herself blush, convinced by Jason's earlier double-take that this was no easy compliment.

Prudence had set hand-written place cards on the plates, alternating the guys and the girls, with Russ at one end and Jason at the other, John between Prudence and Barb and Matt between Amanda and Deb, facing one another across the big oval table. The wine glasses had been filled with sparkling cider and Russ raised his glass.

"To the end of the Sixties!" he offered.

"Long may they wave!" John added.

"Hear, hear!" the others chimed in, clinking glasses all around.

"Are you going to say grace?" Prudence asked Russ as everyone sat down and unfolded their napkins.

"Jason bought most of the food and did most of the cooking," Russ pointed out. "Maybe he should do it."

Jason put his napkin in his lap and giggled. "The only thing that comes to mind is something my dad came up with but I'm not sure it's really appropriate." Everyone urged him on, though, so he said, "Okay, here goes."

> I'm sorry for this meal, oh Lord, and please ignore the guests;
> Their manners are atrocious and the food is not the best.
> All I ask of you, dear Lord, is that when the meal is through
> There's still that same big distance between little old me and you.

Everyone chuckled as they began passing the various bowls and platters, except for Prudence and Russ, who seemed less than amused, and Matt, who sat stiffly erect next to

Deb, taking great pains to see that nothing else spilled on her.

"How's your father doing?" Amanda asked Jason as the others broke into small talk.

"Not bad," he said, handing her the cranberry relish. "He's got a little garden-level apartment on North Nevada, up by the college. I was there this afternoon. He helped me put a new solenoid in the Wonder Car."

"I parked right behind it. It's running okay, then?"

"So well I brought John and Barb here in it," he said. "You'll be pleased to know I won't be barging in on you anymore."

"You're welcome any time," she assured him, adding, "I'm not usually…well, you know."

"Then what fun is barging in?"

"Wow, what a big chicken!" Barb said. Both Amanda and Jason looked up, perhaps a bit defensively, until they realized she referred to the main course.

"Actually, it's a capon," Jason explained, standing to carve it.

"What's a capon?" Barb asked.

"Superman's shoulders," John said.

"It's a rooster without a pecker," Jason offered.

"It's got a pecker," John said. "But its nuts have been pinioned."

"It's a castrated cock," Matt explained to Barb.

"A cock-a-diddle-don't," John quipped.

"And I'm supposed to put that in my mouth?" Barb asked.

"It looks delicious," Deb said. "Everything just looks perfect."

"No more dope for her," John muttered.

"She's right," Amanda insisted. "You guys did a great job of putting all this together."

"Like I said," Russ put in, "Jason did most of it."

"Where'd you learn to cook a capon?" Prudence asked him.

"I learned about capons from my Uncle Willie," he said, carving thick slices of white meat from the breast. "But I learned how to prepare it from my mother. You can make your own Freudian inferences about that."

"Well, you did great," Amanda commended him.

"I had to make up for that last Piñon Nut Gathering at my house. That wasn't fit for man nor beast. Besides, I had to get the grease from working on the Wonder Car out from under my fingernails."

A few people paused mid-bite.

"But seriously," he went on, "I wanted to try, at least, to finish the Sixties right. And spending tonight with all of you is a giant step in that direction."

"Well, if you ask me," Prudence said, passing him her plate for some white meat, "good riddance to the Sixties."

"Really?" Jason asked her. "How come?"

"Are you kidding? War, assassinations, riots, protests—what's to like?"

"But it's kept things interesting," John said, passing his plate too.

"There's an old Chinese curse," Russ said. "'May you live in interesting times'."

"So what's the most interesting thing to come out of the Sixties?" Jason asked the group at large.

"The moon landing," Matt said.

"The miniskirt," Deb offered, receiving some huzzahs from the guys.

"The civil rights movement," Barb said.

"Love," John said.

"I hardly think," Prudence said loftily, "that we invented love this decade."

"Maybe we didn't invent it," John conceded, "but we perfected it. We're taking it out of the dark corners and spreading it around the world. We're setting it free."

"You're high," Barb said, nudging him.

"Can I change my answer?" John asked. "Maybe drugs are the most interesting thing of the decade."

"Which drug?" Matt asked.

"LSD," John said.

"Panama Red," Jason nominated.

"Cannabis has been around longer than ten years," Matt pointed out.

"Longer than consciousness," John said. "But we made it popular. The big tobacco firms have already bought rights to the names Panama Red and Acapulco Gold. It'll be legal in a couple of years."

"What about the Pill?" Barb offered. "That's an interesting drug."

"It's sure had more effect on society than the psychedelic drugs," Deb said.

"Where do you think John's free love comes from?" Russ asked.

"I wasn't just talking about sexual love," John said. "I meant the love that people are using to combat war and hatred and despair."

"But is it making a difference?" Prudence asked. "We still have plenty of war and hatred and despair."

"Once in a while the light shines through," Russ said. "Look at Woodstock."

"Yes, but look at what happened at Altamont a few weeks ago," Prudence countered.

"Nevertheless," Jason said, "I think the music is the most interesting thing to come out of the Sixties. Compare the songs that were popular ten years ago to what's on the radio now. I don't think any other decade has seen such an incredible change in the way popular music sounds."

"How do you account for that?" Matt asked him.

"For one thing, the recordings themselves are better, stereo instead of mono. It's like the difference between something flat and something three-dimensional. Also, the musicians have taken control of the recording process. Like what's happened at Motown: the brothers are in charge and they're producing some fantastic stuff."

"Then what's the best group of the decade?" Matt asked.

"The Beatles," Russ said without a second thought.

"The Stones are right behind them," John said.

"Yeah, but the Stones can't last," Jason said. "One of the originals has already died and the way Mick and Keith are going, they won't last long either. The Beatles have a more positive outlook. They're going to be around a long time."

"What about Yoko?" Prudence asked.

"Yoko-schmoko," John said. "Those guys are too smart to let a little thing like a woman come between them."

Seeing the sharp glance Barb gave him, Amanda said to John, "Take a big bite of those mashed potatoes and think about what you just said."

He too had caught the flash of Barb's glare. "Times like these, I'm gluttonous for the glutenous," he said, complying.

"Potatoes don't actually contain glutens," Matt interjected.

"Let it be," Deb told him.

"Women have come a long way in the last ten years," Barb said, sounding defensive. "The genie's out of the bottle and she won't go back in."

"Which one's Jeannie?" John said in an aside to Prudence, who laughed.

"Hey, cooking dinner for us is just the first step," Barb went on. "Pretty soon you'll be washing the dishes for us, doing the cleaning for us, working for us, voting for us."

"So if things go wrong," John said, "it won't necessarily be a man's fault for a change?"

"Maybe," Barb conceded, "but when things go right, people won't just assume that a man deserves the credit. And more things would go right if women were in charge. How many mothers would send their sons off to fight in some absurd war?"

"I can think of one," Jason said quietly.

John, undeterred, raised his glass. "Gentlemen? To the new boss, same as the old boss! The fair sex!"

Russ, Matt, and Jason joined him in the toast.

"So, ladies," Russ said, "what does the future hold, now that you'll be running things?"

"Less sports on television," Prudence said. Russ looked at her aghast.

"People will be elected based on their qualifications instead how much money and power they have," Barb stated. "Decisions will be made in public instead of some smoke-filled room full of men."

"Hopefully, men will be more open and honest about their feelings," Amanda said. "They won't hide behind that stiff upper lip."

"Which means," Deb added, "they will finally admit, once and for all, that they are slaves to love, put on this planet to cater to our every whim."

The women raised their glasses and the men meekly but wisely followed suit.

"More capon, ladies?" Jason asked.

"I'm as stuffed as it was," Deb said, pushing her plate away, which Prudence did too.

"What do you think, sisters?" Barb said. "Our slaves have served us well this evening. Should we let them speak?"

"What have we got to lose?" asked Amanda. "What do you guys think the future holds?"

"All my life," Jason said, "the Seventies have seemed far off and futuristic. I always had the impression everything would be sleek and modern, even the music."

"But what will the music be about?" Amanda asked him.

"I don't know but I assume it'll build on what's happened this decade. I really can't see us going back to mindless boy-girl love songs now."

"Well, Mr. Love," Barb said to John, "What do you think of that?"

"I think," John said pensively, "that the love horse will be unhitched from the marriage carriage. People will feel more free to be with the partner they choose."

"And who's going to take care of the kids?" Prudence asked him.

"We've got to have some first," John said, putting his arm around her, Prudence giggling. "You don't mind, do you, old man?" he asked Russ.

"Give it your best shot," Russ said with what looked to Amanda like equal parts of relief and resignation. "Although I'm warning you, she doesn't always have them when she says she's going to have them."

"Now, honey," Prudence said, patting his arm, "don't be a sourpuss. What do you see in the crystal ball?"

"I'm just hoping the human race will somehow achieve a higher plane of existence."

"Ah, yes," Jason said. "The human race: lost by all contestants. But we haven't heard from Mr. Wizard. What do you think, Matt?"

"Computers will rule the world," Matt said with assurance.

"You mean they don't already?" John asked.

"You just wait. I read in a *Scientific American* article that the defense department is hooking together a whole bunch of computers to create a gigantic network."

"Isn't that the HAL 9000 series?" Jason asked.

"HAL was just one computer," Matt pointed out.

"One bad-ass computer," John added.

"So how well did Clarke and Kubrik predict the future in *2001*?" Jason asked Matt. "Will we be launching our manned mission to Jupiter by then for our rendezvous with destiny?"

"Considering man hadn't orbited the earth at the beginning of the decade and now we've walked twice on the moon, it's not out of the question."

"But what kind of destiny did Dave the astronaut meet in the movie?" Amanda asked. "What did those psychedelic images depict?"

"Maybe what Russ was talking about," Prudence said. "A higher plane of human existence."

"Certainly an altered state," Amanda said.

"What do you think, Russ?" Jason asked. "Would you call that some sort of catharsis?"

"Or something," Russ said. "Certainly a dramatic transformation. Different cultures have given different names to those moments of revelation: *satori*, *samadhi*, enlightenment, epiphany."

"Call it what you will," John said, "But having seen the movie in an altered state myself, I'm here to testify that Dave achieved some higher plane."

"Maybe it was more sideways than higher," Russ said. "Like a parallel universe."

"Or an alternate reality," Jason said, "a term, incidentally, invented by a woman, who happens to be sitting to my right."

He put his hand on hers when he said it and Amanda felt a warm glow flow up her arm toward her heart. When he left it there, it made the statement to all, for the first time, that they were more than just dinner partners. When Deb noticed it, she winked, which made Amanda smile.

"But what good does it do Dave to go through that experience if he can't bring it back to earth?" Prudence argued.

"But he *does* come back to earth," Deb said. "At the end, as that unborn baby."

"What was that supposed to represent, anyway?" Barb asked. "The Second Coming or something?"

"I thought that was J. C.'s department," Matt said, looking at Jason.

"Jesus, by the turn of the millennium, Jase'll be pushing 50," John pointed out. "A second coming?"

"Once a king, always a king," Jason said, smiling, "but once a night is enough."

"Too bad, Man," John said, and everyone laughed as she blushed.

"But if Arthur C. Clarke meant the turn of the millennium," Prudence said, "why didn't they set the movie in the year 2000?"

"Because the new millennium doesn't start until 2001," Matt said. "The Romans, who came up with the calendar, didn't have zeroes. So this millennium ends at MM and the next begins at MMI."

"Am – am I hearing right?" John said. "We have to wait that whole extra year for the Day of Judgment?"

"I didn't get the feeling," Deb said, "that the reborn Dave was coming back to judge the earth. I thought he was just bringing back the knowledge that had been imparted to him."

"That's a problem with parallel universes and alternate realities," Matt said to her. "Getting there is no problem, theoretically. But bringing back information about what's there violates the First Law of Thermodynamics that rules our universe, the conservation of matter-slash-energy. Information is a form of energy."

"Not when *you* give it," Deb said.

"He's right, though," Jason averred. "Alternate realities may exist only in hindsight: shoulda-s, coulda-s, and woulda-s. We can't extend ourselves into the future or some other alternate time-line and then pop back to the present to make use of what we learned."

"But we can foresee alternate courses of action," Russ said. "Everyone, acting on the basis of his or her own individual reality, jumps from one choice point to the next as the future unfolds."

"And some of those choice points," John said, "determine the fate of the world, like JFK's assassination, or landing on the moon. Say Oswald's hand shakes, or the next Apollo mission—isn't lucky 13 next?—develops even a minor glitch on the way to the moon—events like that alter the course of history."

"Maybe an alternate reality that we perceive as a positive turn of events is more—what? resonant?—with this reality," Jason said. "It's like walking down a path through a thick forest and coming to a fork that you couldn't see even a few steps back. It may lead to a spectacular new vista, a brand-new possibility you didn't know existed."

He looked right at Amanda as he said it and she wondered if he had the view from the pool room in mind.

"But if you wander off the trail just anywhere," he went on, "you're likely to veer into a tangled reality that has little in common with the path you're on. You end up lost in the undergrowth."

"So you're saying there's more than one alternate reality?" Amanda asked, feeling the simple phrase she had invented taking on a life of its own.

"There may be an infinite number of alternate realities," Matt said. "What we think of as this reality is just one of the possibilities."

"Then what makes it seem like this reality?" Amanda asked.

Everyone thought about it a moment.

"The absence of death," Russ ventured at last.

"What!?" Jason said, and a couple of the others echoed it.

"Think about it," Russ said. "From the individual's standpoint, this reality continues until you die. As soon as you die, you're in some other reality."

"But we've all known people who have died," Jason said, looking down. "Like my brother."

Amanda squeezed his hand but he didn't look up from his empty plate.

"We all know people who no longer exist in this reality," Russ said. "That doesn't mean they don't exist in some alternate reality. What everyone in this reality shares is continuity. The sun will come up tomorrow."

"And in those other realities," Prudence asked him, "people don't die?"

"I didn't say that," Russ said. "Maybe we're all fundamentally cowards, dying a thousand different deaths in a thousand different realities. The question is: Does a reality exist where the individual doesn't die?"

"The Bible says there is," Deb said.

"That's just a book," Jason said glumly.

"That doesn't mean it isn't true," Deb maintained.

"'Things that you're li'ble to read in the Bible'," Jason sang, quoting Gershwin, "'ain't necessarily so.' A lot of it reads like fiction."

"Just because something may not be literally true," Deb countered, "doesn't make it a lie."

"The difference between a lie and fiction is merely intent," John said. "Fiction is intended, hopefully, to edify and enlighten but a lie is intended to give the liar an unfair advantage, to keep someone else in the dark."

"In any case," Russ said, "Matt's point about bringing back information from an alternate reality was well taken. Any experience of alternate reality would require some sort of bridge to bring us there and back, whether it's an artistic medium like fiction or a metaphysical metamorphosis."

"What do you think, Man?" Jason asked her. "You invented the concept, after all."

Amanda thought about it. "What about dreams?" she asked. "Don't dreams fit most of the conditions everyone's talking about? A dream begins with one of those choice points, when the dreamer falls asleep. The little death. Then while you're dreaming, it still feels like you're you, but all the rest of the rules have changed. And when that alternate reality ends, you wake up and, unless you try very hard, you don't retain any information from that other reality. You don't remember any details of what happened."

"But it's possible to be aware of dreaming while dreaming," Russ said. "Maybe the consciousness that thinks it's awake comes closest to a non-alternate reality. Even the flimsy bridge of a sleeping mind is not required. One experiences it merely by being present."

"Dreaming seems so deterministic," Jason said. "The events feel uncontrollable. Awake, we at least have the illusion that we have a choice in what happens."

"Your dreams don't sound too pleasant," Amanda said to him.

"'I could be bounded in a nutshell'," he quoted Hamlet, "'and count myself a king of infinite space, were it not that I have bad dreams.'"

The way he said it convinced Amanda, and apparently the others as well, that he spoke from recent experience: his face suddenly looked haggard, his mood introspective. No one said anything for a moment.

"Do you want to talk about it?" Amanda asked him.

"Dreamland is one alternate reality I've experienced," he said, "and it's a lonely place." He looked up and smiled half-heartedly. "But come on. Who wants to hear someone else's dreams?"

"If talking about it would help, go ahead," Russ said, speaking for everyone.

"It's just the usual demons and shit, at least till the end," he said.

"Go on," Amanda urged him.

He took a deep breath and shook his head. "Last night, I suffered the fierce vexation of a dream. It woke me up. I was fighting in a war, part of an army under attack. The enemy was beyond the horizon, a thousand miles away. Big shiny silver missiles screamed across the sky. We ran for cover as fast as we could but couldn't get far from ground zero. Explosions everywhere. Injured and scared out of my wits, I got up and started running away with some old men, all of them crippled or crazy."

"Nice to think you dream about us," John said.

"We finally made it to some sort of shelter," Jason went on, "a bombed-out building or something. Digging through the rubble for something to eat, I came upon a small clay statue of Jesus—I think it was Jesus—painted with amazing detail in soft life-like colors. Someone else found a painting, a frightening picture of King Kong, or maybe the Cyclops. As happens in dreams, the picture suddenly transformed into a real monster. I tried to run away but it caught up with me. It picked me up and began to torture me, trying to rip me limb from limb. Excruciating pain. But this monster wasn't as big as King Kong, it was something I could actually tackle, so in my desperation I attacked it."

"By yourself?" Amanda asked him.

"Everyone else disappeared somehow. Anyway, through some miracle I managed to win the fight. I picked up the monster and flung it around and beat its brains out on the ground. I was in such pain I couldn't see anything but red. After I killed the thing I staggered to a faucet where I lay down and put my hands in the warm water. Washing the blood from my face and hands, I began to cry."

"That's understandable," Amanda said, touching his shoulder.

"But it wasn't the pain or the fight that made me cry," Jason said. "I cried the way children cry, because I knew someone would comfort me if I did. But no one ever came. I remember sobbing, 'I don't want to kill! Please don't make me kill!' I woke up and I really was crying. I can't remember the last time I woke up crying. Not since I was a kid. It really made me realize how alone I am."

"Where are you staying, anyway?" Amanda asked him.

"Dad's been seeing someone so I'm still staying at the house," Jason said. "Unless they sell it before the semester starts. Mom already moved most of her stuff out to California. The place seems mighty empty now."

"Why don't you crash here tonight?" Russ suggested.

"Oh, it's not that," Jason said. "I'm a big boy now. It just seems like you've all got somebody now. I'm the odd man out."

"Look around you, bro," John told him. "We're all here for you."

"Tonight, yeah," he acknowledged, "and like I said earlier, I really appreciate it. But you don't need a weatherman to know which way the wind blows. How many more Gatherings will we have?"

"What are you saying?" Matt asked him. "That we're just going to forget about you? Blow you off?"

"Talk proves nothing," John said. "Wasn't it Mark Twain that said that a hen who has merely laid an egg cackles as if she laid an asteroid?"

Prudence laughed. "That's excellent!" she told John. "Where did you read that?"

"It was in *Pudd'nhead Wilson*," John told her.

"I just read that last year and I don't remember that quote," she said.

"It's in a special edition of epigraphs from *Pudd'nhead Wilson's Calendar* and *Following The Equator* I checked out from the library at the college. It's really cool."

"I'd love to see it sometime," she said smoothly.

"Anyway," Matt said, "if Jason thinks we're just flapping our gums, maybe we should put it in writing."

"Whose writing?" Jason asked. "Cause those invitations I did looked horrible."

"Mandy writes beautifully," Deb volunteered.

Even in grade school Amanda had won awards for her penmanship so she couldn't very well deny it without false modesty. "Somebody will have to tell me what to write," she declared.

"I've still got some of that parchment paper," Russ said, going upstairs for that and a pen.

"So is this something you guys do all the time?" Barb asked.

"I think this will be the first official Piñon Nuts document," John said.

"We better put it in legalese then," Matt pointed out. "And who's signing this?"

"I think it should be the four guys only," Amanda said. "You guys are the original members, after all."

Russ came back with the paper and a fountain pen. He handed them to Amanda and cleared her plate from the table. She pushed back the tablecloth and set the parchment paper on the oak. "Okay," she said, "where do we start?"

"How about 'We the Undersigned'?" Matt suggested.

Aligning the paper on its long edge, Amanda centered the three words along the top of the page.

"The original members of the Piñon Nuts," Matt dictated.

"How about 'original and permanent'?" Russ suggested.

"Yeah, that's good," Matt said, watching Amanda center "The Piñon Nuts" on a separate line. He went on: "Hereby pledge to assemble again on this very spot."

"Wait a minute," Prudence said. "This thing isn't going to be more than hen-cackling if you don't specify the penalties for failing to appear."

Amanda had already centered "Hereby Pledge" on a line; she waited for a ruling on the rest.

"What's the penalty if one of us doesn't show up?" Matt asked. "We take away his membership?"

"Too mild," John declared. "We take away his *member* and never speak to the ball-less bastard again."

"I can't write that," Amanda said.

"How about this?" John said. "'On pain of dismemberment and excommunication.'"

"Worse," Matt said.

"What's worse than dismemberment and excommunication?" John wanted to know.

"Ridicule," Jason said.

"Okay," Matt said. "How's this? 'On pain of dismemberment, excommunication, ridicule, and worse.'"

Amanda had to scrunch up her letters a little to fit all that on one line.

"Okay, so what are we pledging?" Jason asked.

"To get back together for another Gathering," Russ said.

"Where?" John asked.

"Let's do it here again," Matt said. "If that's okay with you, Russ."

"Fine with me," Russ said, watching Amanda write "To Assemble Again On This Very Spot." "So is this going to be next New Year's Eve?"

"I'm not sure we need to sign a pledge for that," John said. "There's a pretty good chance we'll get together again a year from now. How about at the end of the next decade?"

"Why not go all the way?" Russ suggested. "The end of the century and the millennium?"

"So New Year's Eve 2000?" Matt asked.

"You and five other guys with slide rules will be celebrating the end of the millennium that night," John said derisively. "Every other sane person will be celebrating the dawn of the new millennium thirty years from tonight, 1999."

"Sorry, Matt," Jason said. "I'm with John on this."

Matt shrugged.

"So how about this?" Amanda said. "'…on this very spot thirty years hence, the dawn of the new millennium.'"

"Come hell or high water," John added as he watched her carefully print it out, tacking on even this last suggestion.

Amanda picked up the finished product and blew on it to dry the ink. She handed it to Jason. "How's that?"

"It looks mighty official."

"Are you going to sign it?"

"I will if the rest of you will."

The others each assured him they had every intention of honoring the pledge. Amanda handed him the pen and he scratched his flamboyant signature across the parchment. One by one, the other three added their signatures as well.

Prudence looked on amused. "I wish I had a picture of them signing this historic treaty."

"That's it!" Russ said, getting up. "We should take a picture!" He went upstairs again.

"You know what else we should have?" John said, taking a box of small Swisher Sweets from his shirt pocket. "Cigars!"

Matt passed, claiming he couldn't be trusted, but Jason took one and John lit both of them from his Zippo.

Russ came back with a Polaroid camera. Declining a cigar he said, "Now, where should we do this? The table's too cluttered. Let's go in the living room. You want to take it, Manny?"

Russ and Matt slipped into their sport jackets as they moved into the living room.

"You're the photographer, Matt," Jason said. "Where should we take the official Piñon Nuts portrait?"

"How about by the couch here, with the fireplace in the background?" Matt suggested, standing in the center of the back of the couch.

"How does this work?" Amanda asked, finding the viewfinder and trigger, practicing lining up the shot.

"You're the tallest, Matt," Jason said, pulling up a chair and sitting in it backwards facing him, "so you should stay there. Then maybe Russ on one side and me and John on the other. What do you think, Manny?" he said, turning part-way toward her.

"So I just press the button?" she asked Russ, her finger fumbling around while she looked through the viewfinder. Her finger not only found the button, it pushed it. With a flash and a whir, the picture popped out of the camera.

"Hey!" John said. "Don't we even get to say cheese?"

"Sorry, guys," Amanda said. "My finger slipped. Okay, Jason, stand up next to the others. Yeah, that's pretty good. Now, say cheese!" She pressed the button again but nothing happened. "What's wrong?" she asked Russ.

He came over and looked at the camera. "Beats me. I know nothing about things mechanical. Matt?"

Matt came over and looked at it. "I'm no expert on this type of camera but my guess is that the reason it won't take another picture is that it's out of film."

"It's my mom's camera," Russ said. "She may have more film for it but I have no idea where it is. How did the picture you took come out?"

Amanda looked at the ghostly images solidifying on the print. "Well, you guys look okay but you can't even see Jason's face."

"Maybe that's just as well," Jason said. "The camera might really be broken now if you could."

"We'll just have to take another one before we go back to school," Russ said. "When are you going back to Seattle, Matt?"

"Sunday."

"Well, we'll see each other before then," Russ said. "So who's going to be the holder of these historic documents, anyway?"

"It should be someone neutral," John said. "Someone who'll get on our case if we don't live up to this."

They elected Amanda by acclamation.

"Listen, guys," Barb said, "I hate to be a party pooper but I've got to get back to the dorm."

"Oh, no!" Prudence said. "How come?"

"Oh, my grandmother died last month and I had to go back to Michigan for the funeral. So over the break I'm making up some of the work I missed. Sorry."

Amanda felt her heart sink. Since Jason drove John and Barb to Russ's, he would have to drive them back. She looked at Jason and he just shrugged helplessly.

"At least you'll be able to see the fireworks from there," Deb pointed out, sounding a little envious.

"Fireworks?" Prudence asked.

"Oh, yeah," John told her. "Every year the AdaMan Club climbs Pikes Peak and sets off

315

a bunch of fireworks at midnight. This end of town is one of the few places where you can't see them."

"But you can see them from the College?" Prudence asked.

"If it doesn't snow," John told her.

"Can we go?" she asked Russ.

"I've got to stay and clean up," he said patiently. "But if you want to go, go ahead."

"While you're deciding," Jason said, putting on his jacket, "I'll go out and warm up the Wonder Car."

Everyone else went back into the dining room to clear the table. Amanda joined in dispiritedly, trying not to let her disappointment show. She had managed to make her statement to Jason—his double-take was unforgettable—but, even though she didn't know exactly what else she wished would happen between them, she certainly had hoped for more than this.

"So what are we going to do?" Deb asked her while everyone else was in the kitchen.

Amanda sighed. "I guess we should stay and help with the clean-up."

"I know what we *should* do. What I asked was, what are we *going* to do?"

Amanda frowned at her.

"Oh, come on," Deb pleaded. "I think we should go somewhere and watch the fireworks. It's what we told your mom we'd do, after all."

Jason walked back in from outside, muttering, "Goddamn piece of shit!"

"What's wrong?" Amanda asked him.

"I'm sorry. My stupid car won't start again. The battery must be going now. It growled at me a few times and then just coughed and gave up the ghost."

"That's too bad," Amanda said, secretly rejoicing. "Well, since I'm parked behind you, maybe I should give you guys a lift."

"Amanda," Deb said shortly, "may I speak with you?"

"I'll go tell the others," Jason said.

Deb pulled Amanda into the solarium. "What about staying to help clean up?" she demanded.

"You heard him. His car won't start."

"But I don't want to stay here!"

"Matt will probably stay and help clean up too," Amanda said. "He's got an incredible crush on you, you know."

Deb rolled her eyes. "God, do I know it! It's painfully obvious. Don't you know what a drag it is to have someone just fawn all over you?"

"No, Deb, I don't."

It brought Deb up short. "Oh, I'm sorry, Amy. I'm being selfish, huh? Man, but you got Jason's attention with that outfit, didn't you? Aren't you glad I talked you into changing?"

"Yes, I am," Amanda told her. "And I'd let Jason take them back to the college in my car but Mom would kill me if she found out I let someone else drive."

Deb took both her hands in her own. "No, Amy, you should go. I'll be fine playing housewife. But they've got to give me an apron. It's going to be hard enough to get out the gravy stains."

"Thanks, Deb," Amanda said sincerely. "I owe you. And I'll be back to take you home."

"If I don't get Matt to take me home first. He'd be thrilled. There must be half a dozen laws of physics he hasn't told me about yet."

"Oh, give him a chance tonight. He's an incredibly nice guy. He's just shy."

"Oh, all right, I'll do Matt instead of fireworks," Deb relented. "It is just one night. It's not like I've got to spend the rest of my life with him."

o   o   o

By the time they exited I-25 at Uintah Street, thick flannel clouds had covered the sky, the darkness moderated by the reflection of the city lights.

"Well, kids," Jason said, "I don't know about the fireworks."

"Do they cancel them if the weather's bad?" Prudence asked.

"Oh, they set them off," John said. "You just can't see them."

"Maybe the radio will tell us something," Amanda said, switching it on.

KRDO had a national news feed, talking about a couple of South Vietnamese newspapers being shut down for criticizing the government.

"That's the kind of freedom our boys are fighting for," said Jason, riding shotgun. "Switch it."

KYSN was playing "Wooden Ships:" "Wooden ships on the water, very free and easy/Easy, the way you know it's supposed to be."

"Have you heard this song, Jason?" John asked from the back seat, sitting between Prudence and Barb.

"Yeah," he admitted glumly.

"Don't you like it?" Amanda asked him.

"He's still ticked off at David Crosby for quitting the Byrds to join Crosby, Stills, and Nash," John said. "But you have to admit, Jase, it's a good song."

"Sailing off to some deserted island always sounds good to me," Jason admitted.

"Is that what it's about?" asked Amanda, who had heard the song a couple of times but hadn't paid close attention to the lyrics.

"It's about the world after they drop the Big One," John said.

"It did seem a bit ironic talking about the turn of millennium earlier," Jason said. "Does anybody really think we're going to make it that far?"

"It is like sleeping on a waterbed filled with nitroglycerin," John said. "Especially living this close to NORAD. We're one of the first ten sites the Soviets will attack in a nuclear war."

"You may be the lucky ones," Prudence pointed out. "Jason and Russ and I, if we're up in Boulder, may end up surviving the initial attack, which might be worse. I'm with you, Jason. I think I'd rather sail off to some island somewhere."

"And if the war doesn't break out pretty soon," Jason said, "we may *have* to sail to get there. The latest estimate I heard was that we'll use up the last of our oil reserves sometime in the mid-1990s. The next war may be fought with briefcases."

By now they had pulled up in front of Loomis Hall, Barb's dorm, a blocky red brick building that clashed a little with the older sandstone architecture of most of the rest of the Colorado College campus.

"Thanks for the ride, Amanda," Barb said, the first words she'd spoken since they got in the car.

"It was nice meeting you, Barb," Amanda told her, which the others echoed.

"I hope you all have a nice time on your island," Barb said.

As she and John walked to the door and spoke briefly, Jason said, "The name Barb suits her. That last remark was kind of pointed, wasn't it?"

Amanda thought so too but didn't say anything. Throughout the evening, John had paid more attention to Prudence than to Barb.

"How serious are you about sailing off to an island?" Prudence asked Jason.

"Give me a compass bearing and untie the rope," Jason said. "Why?"

"Well, there's a guy named Leon living in our house on Marine Street who's talking about putting together an expedition to an island."

"Seriously?"

"Oh, he's quite serious," Prudence said. "He may need to leave the States for a while pretty soon."

"Oh?"

"He's a member of S. D. S."

"Students for a Democratic Society?" Amanda asked. "They're involved in all the campus protests, aren't they?"

"More power to him," Jason said. "I'm a student and I'm all for a democratic society. I heard Nixon on the news earlier saying that the U. S. shouldn't get involved in the campus disorders. I got news for you, Dick: the disorders are coming soon to a theater near you."

"Leon and some of his friends think the time has come to go beyond sit-ins and marches," Prudence told them. "If Nixon and Congress won't put an end to this illegal war in Vietnam, maybe it's time we took things into our own hands. Leon's joined the Weathermen. I thought maybe you were familiar with them, Jason, when you quoted that Bob Dylan line earlier."

"Ah, yes," Jason said. "I know about the Weathermen. I'm not sure I'm ready to go that far yet but I must admit, something's got to be done to stop the killing. In any case, I'd like to hear more about the island business."

While he said it, John had gotten back into the back seat. He asked what they were talking about.

"We've decided we're all going to sail off to a desert island," Jason told him.

"In our yellow submarine," Amanda added facetiously as she started the big yellow Pontiac and drove back to Cascade Avenue. "Are we going back to Russ's house first?"

"You know, as long as we're here on campus," John said, "if you could swing by Arthur House, I could show Prudence that Mark Twain book. Would you mind?"

"Not a bit," Amanda said, turning right on Uintah.

"It's too bad Barb couldn't stay out," Prudence said, which sounded disingenuous to Amanda.

"So how well do you know Barb?" Jason asked John. "I don't think I've heard you mention her before."

"Oh, she and I have gone out a few times," John said off-handedly. "I didn't want to be the only one at the Gathering without a date."

Amanda turned right on Nevada and stopped in front of Arthur House, a red and pink sandstone Edwardian mansion once owned by the son of President Chester A. Arthur, now a men's dorm for Colorado College.

"What a beautiful place!" Prudence declared. "Where's your room?"

"It's a garret up on the third floor in the back," John said. "So is everybody coming in to see the book?"

"You showed it to me this afternoon," Jason said. "The cover is amazing. If you want to see it, Man…"

"I've never been one to judge a book by its cover," Amanda said. "You go ahead."

"Maybe I'll stay and keep her company," Jason said.

"Back in a flash," John said as he and Prudence got out.

Amanda stared out the windshield after they left, her knees feeling chilly in the short skirt. She felt a little confused about some of the things she had just learned. She decided to broach a relatively easy one first.

"John and Prudence seem pretty chummy," she said to Jason.

"Indeed," he said, staring straight ahead as well.

"Is that a problem for Russ?"

"Possibly so."

"Doesn't it concern you?"

"Does it bother me? Yes, a little, although Russ has told me lately that he's not sure Prudence is right for him so they may not survive as a couple anyway. I'm not sure it's any of my concern though. I don't know about you, Man, but it seems to me that relationships are getting more complicated with each passing day. I don't have a clue what's going on most of the time."

"I know what you mean," she admitted.

"For instance," he said, turning to her, "didn't you tell John that Deb was in a serious relationship?"

Amanda felt a pang of guilt about that but she wanted to be as honest as possible so she said simply, "Yes."

"So who is, or was, this guy? She never mentions him."

"Well…" she said, taking a deep breath. "He was sort of…fictional."

"Fictional," Jason repeated, looking at her steadily. "You mean, because there are so few flesh-and-blood guys around, you felt the need to make one up."

"Deb thought it would be easier to discourage John if he thought she was involved with someone else."

"Why did she want to discourage John?" he asked, looking up at the top floor of Arthur House. "I always thought he was a pretty cool guy."

"Oh, he is," Amanda agreed. "And he's one of my best friends. He's just not ready to settle down."

"Is Deb ready to settle down?" he asked. "Because—and maybe you don't know this—Matt has a thing for her, even though he never admits it."

"Really?" she said, disingenuous herself.

"But Deb said some things at dinner that sounded, well, less than enthusiastic about Matt."

"Oh, Deb has a lot of respect for Matt," Amanda assured him. "But you must admit, sometimes he is a little…dry."

He chuckled. "Yeah, you don't get a lot of folderol from Matt. I always considered that part of his charm."

"Oh, I do too," she assured him. "But I think Deb's looking for someone a little more, um, dynamic."

He nodded thoughtfully. "I'll tell him to turn up the voltage and switch to a 50-amp fuse."

"Don't you dare!" she said. "That's just between you and me, okay? Cause if Deb found out…"

"I'm just kidding, Man," he reassured her, patting her arm. "I'll hold it in the strictest confidence. I would never do anything to get in the way of our friendship."

Maybe that answered the trickiest of her questions. Barb may have been John's date but Amanda evidently wasn't necessarily Jason's. "I really value your friendship too," she said, smiling but feeling a little disappointed. She started the car again and turned up the fan. "It's getting a little chilly. How long do you think they'll be?"

"Why don't you ask John?"

John strolled out of Arthur House to the car. Amanda rolled down the window as he approached.

"Sorry to keep you guys waiting," he said. "You know, I just remembered that I was going to take the Yellow Fellow to the Pink Palace tonight anyway so maybe I'll just drive Prudence back to Russ's after a while. You guys are going to stay out to watch the fireworks, aren't you?" He looked beseechingly at Jason.

Jason looked out the windshield, where tiny square pellets of snow had begun to collect. "I don't think we're going to see much of the fireworks through the snow. What do you think, Man?"

Amanda looked at the snow and suddenly remembered the open window at the bungalow. "There is an errand I need to run, if you don't mind."

"Hey, I'm just along for the ride," Jason said.

"Oh, thanks, you two!" John said. "I knew I could count on you."

"Enjoy," Jason told him with a grin.

John gave him the thumbs-up and dashed back inside.

O   O   O

In the last hour of the 1960s, the Pontiac negotiated the narrow streets, tight curves, and steep grades of Cheyenne Cañon to the little bungalow on Ridge Road. Clusters of snowflakes as thick and white as popcorn mobbed the air, falling so fast it looked like the earth rose to meet them.

On the porch Jason stomped the sticky snow from his shoes while Amanda held the screen door with her foot. Her chilly fingers struggled to line up the key in the new lock her father had installed. Turning the deadbolt at last, she reached inside and turned on the porch light and the overhead light in the living room. The radio, plugged into a switched socket, came on too, playing Jimi Hendrix's version of "All Along The Watchtower."

"Great song. Great album," Jason said, looking around at the canvas drop-cloths scattered about the floors, taking in the bay window. "This place is pretty cool."

"It's real cool," Amanda said, turning down the radio. "Do you want me to turn up the heat?"

"I thought you just had to close the window."

"Well, it wouldn't hurt to drive off the chill so the paint will dry," Amanda said, walking into the bathroom and pulling the window closed. "But I imagine you're anxious to get back over to Russ's before midnight," she called to him.

"So we can help with the dishes? Hardly."

"Would you like to go somewhere else?" she asked, coming back into the living room. "Where?"

"I have no idea."

"Nor do I. I kind of like it here, actually."

Amanda turned up the thermostat and the ancient furnace fan clattered into action, the vents soon belching warm air that smelled of burnt dust. "I'm afraid I don't have much to offer you. There aren't even any chairs but I suppose we could roll up a drop cloth and sit on that. Oh, I know! Dad's got some beer in the fridge. Want one?"

"If you think he wouldn't mind."

"I'll tell him you helped scrape the windows and that was your payment," going into the kitchen and taking a couple of cans of Coors from the stale-smelling refrigerator. Back in the living room, she handed one to him and sat beside him on the drop cloth he had rolled up.

"Do you have a church key?" he asked.

"Uh-oh. Dad keeps the opener on his key ring. What'll we do?"

"How about a screwdriver?"

She fetched a paint-spattered one from the bedroom. He set it on the top of the can and pounded it with the heel of his hand until it punctured the top, the beer spurting out. By the time he had made a vent hole and a couple more holes in the other can, his hands dripped beer. He wiped them on a different tarp and sat back down next to her. They tipped the tops of the cans together and wished each other a happy New Year. Amanda didn't particularly like beer but tonight it tasted wonderful.

The Hendrix tune faded out and the DJ on KYSN, doing an informal retrospective of the decade, threw on what he referred to as a Golden Oldie, which at that time meant anything more than three years old. The song was the Beach Boys' "Wouldn't It Be Nice?"

The song had come out when Amanda was 15 and in the throes of a major crush on a boy named Brad Landis who sat next to her in English. Brad had dreamy, slanting eyes like Paul McCartney's and wore English Leather cologne. After school Amanda would sit at her desk in her room and doodle "Mandy Landis" and "Mrs. Bradley Landis" in her notebook, thinking, "Wouldn't it be nice if we could have our own little house and live in the kind of world where we belong?" Those daydreams seemed far away now.

"This is nice," Jason said, and for a moment Amanda wondered if he had somehow read her thoughts. "So your folks are going to rent this place out?"

"They've already got tenants lined up. That's why we're working so hard to get it ready."

"How much is the rent?" he asked, looking around again.

"I don't know. Too much, probably, for something so small."

"It doesn't seem so bad."

"Really?" she said with a shudder. "I can't imagine living in a house like this."

"Well, you're used to a much bigger place."

"It's not that. I don't know. Maybe it's just because it's empty."

"Yeah," he said, sipping the beer. "Just like home."

"Jason," she said, putting her hand on his shoulder, "I can't tell you how sorry I am about your parents. They're both such nice people but I guess sometimes it just doesn't work out. It must be really hard for you, especially during the holidays."

"Hendrix has another song on *Electric Ladyland* called "Burning of the Midnight Lamp'," he said. "At the end he says, 'Loneliness is such a…drag'."

"You know, any time you need to talk, you can call me."

"I know," he said, looking at his can of beer. "And I appreciate it. But you've got other things going on in your life."

"I'll always make time for you."

"You know what I mean."

She thought she probably did but asked "What?" anyway.

"I mean, you're involved with Bill and all. I don't imagine he's too keen on having your loser guy-friends calling you up all the time."

"For one thing, mister," she said, bristling, "you are not a loser. And for another thing, why does everyone always assume that just because Bill and I go out together sometimes that I'm going to end up staying with him the rest of my life?"

He looked at her and shrugged. "It's the way of the world."

"What does that mean?"

"Well, you both come from families that live in big Broadmoor houses and all."

"So do you."

He snorted. "The Walker Estate barely bordered on Broadmoor and we aren't going to own it much longer. There's not even much 'we' left. Anyway, you know what I mean. Bill's got connections. He's got a future."

"You have an incredible future in store for you!" she insisted. "You're one of the most intelligent, creative people I know."

"I'll try writing that on the deposit slip next time I go to the bank," he said. "The teller will get a kick out of it."

"Oh, you're going to do so many fantastic things! You could be a musician or a scientist or a writer or almost anything you set your mind to."

"Well, I'm going to have to be really good at whatever I do to deserve a woman like you."

"What kind of woman do you think I am?" she wondered.

"You're at least as intelligent and creative as I am," he said, looking away. "Plus your daddy's rich. Plus you're just so beautiful."

That caught her completely off guard. She scanned his face without saying anything, waiting to see if he would crack a smile, to see if he was just teasing. When finally he brought his eyes back up to meet hers, she could see that, far from teasing, he had just confessed to something and feared the consequences.

One of the axioms of Amanda's life had been that regardless of whatever else she might possess, the man who married her would do so in spite of her looks. When her mother told her she looked pretty, Amanda always heard "considering" in her voice. When Bill told her she looked great, she admired his good manners. She had just assumed that Jason, whom she always considered one of the best-looking boys in school, never thought of her as more than a friend because he found her so plain. In fact, she thought the Piñon Nuts called her Man or Manny because they thought of her as one of the guys.

"How can you be drunk on half a can of three-two beer?" she asked him.

"Are you kidding?" he cried. "Even when we were kids I always loved your smile. It's always so warm and open and honest. When you giggle and play with your hair, it makes me wish I could make you giggle again. You know how a person's eyes are the window to the soul? Well, most people have the curtains drawn and you can't tell who they really are, or they haven't washed the windows in ages and it affects their outlook. But when I look in your eyes, I always feel like I can see all the way inside. And then there's what happened over Thanksgiving, which I will be thankful for all my life." He closed his eyes and put his head back and smiled. "That image of you in the garden, in the falling snow—I'll bet I've replayed that 10,000 times in my head." He opened his eyes again and looked her up and down. "And tonight you show up in *that*. Hell, I'm surprised you trust me enough to be here alone with me."

She had listened to all of that in disbelief and now could only smile crookedly as tears filled her eyes.

"Do you think it's midnight yet?" he asked. "Cause I was really hoping to kiss you at midnight."

She cleared her throat. "Close enough."

This was not their first kiss. Their first kiss, which Amanda just assumed he had long since forgotten, happened at a party when they were in junior high. They had done it as part of some stupid party game and both pretended to be cool afterward but she obviously had never forgotten it. Their second kiss happened at the Fall Ball in Boulder and the circumstances and his state of mind made her question his sincerity. She wondered if their third kiss, after he saw her naked in the garden, grew out of consolation as much as passion. She had, after all, cried.

Tears flowed down her cheeks now, for that matter, but she couldn't doubt his passion this time. His strong arms forcefully pulled her body to his but his lips embraced hers so tenderly at first that she almost opened her eyes to make sure they really touched. Soon he grew more confident and the kiss more urgent. She felt herself melting into him, felt the distinction between the two of them blur and fade until they became one.

Sitting side by side, however, meant they had to crane their necks and since neither seemed inclined to stop kissing, she readily acquiesced when he suggested they get more comfortable by unrolling the drop cloth and lying on it. When he lay beside her, he reached his arm across her body, inadvertently or otherwise brushing her bra. She sighed and shivered at the contact, feeling as though the spark that aroused her nipples sent a charge all the way to her innermost being. Emboldened by her response, his hand slid carefully, gently, down from her shoulder until it covered and caressed her breast.

Second in line of her supposed deficiencies, after her face, were her breasts. She considered them small and plain, especially compared to Deb's, for instance, which, even to Amanda, seemed outstanding, an opinion most guys seemed to share, judging by their furtive glances. So she felt gratified and a bit surprised at the depth of Jason's reaction to touching her: his breathing grew fast and heavy and his kisses more insistent. When his fingers fumbled their way past the top buttons of her blouse and slid beneath the stiff lace of her bra, he actually moaned aloud. As she had at her house over Thanksgiving, she felt a rush of pleasure to know he found her alluring and sexy. She even felt regret when he gradually pulled his fingers back out.

But when his hand slid down her side, across the leather miniskirt, and onto the nylon covering her thigh, she realized that a moment of truth rapidly approached. She wasn't absolutely sure she wanted his hand finding its way up her miniskirt but if it did, she *was* absolutely sure she didn't want it to find the sanitary napkin stuck to the panties she wore beneath her pantyhose. She shifted uncomfortably as his hand stroked the inside of her thigh.

He immediately withdrew it and backed off, saying, "Hey, I'm sorry. I guess I got carried away."

"It's not that," she said. "I just have to go to the bathroom."

The bathroom felt cold and damp from the window having been open. After she closed the door and switched on the light, she slid up the waistband of the miniskirt and pulled down the pantyhose. She checked in her panties to see how the Kotex looked; to her relief, it remained unmarked. She pulled the pad from her underwear and then realized that she had nowhere to put it. There was no wastebasket, she couldn't flush it, and she had left her purse in the car, thinking they'd only be in the house a few minutes. While she stood there with her pantyhose and panties bunched around her knees, she caught sight of herself in the bathroom mirror.

She looked a bit frazzled—her hair mussed, her lipstick smeared, her cheeks flushed—but she saw, for the first time, not a girl, nor even a young lady, but a woman. No matter what happened next, there was no turning back now. The miniskirt had made a statement which Jason had heard loud and clear. Was she prepared to back up that statement with action? Or was it just what Prudence had referred to as "hen-cackling"?

She found herself at one of those choice points they had spoken of earlier. What better way to spend the turn of the decade? Who better to spend it with than Jason? Why get rid of the Kotex if she wasn't prepared to share that part of her body with him?

With a curt nod to the woman in the mirror, she made up her mind. While she had never done anything quite like this, she knew that the pantyhose would prove awkward at best. But if she took off the pantyhose, she'd have to find a place for both that and the Kotex, a place where there was no chance she'd forget them, because her father would have a heart attack if he found them there. Nevertheless, she put down the toilet lid, sat on it, unzipped and slid off her boots, and then pulled off the pantyhose. Then it occurred to her that she could stash both the hose and the Kotex in the boots if she didn't put the boots back on until they were ready to leave. Doubtless, a daring move, but she had always considered her legs her best physical feature. She wedged the pantyhose into the left boot and then, throwing caution to the wind, wrapped the Kotex in her panties and put them into the right boot. Remember, Man, she reminded herself, he's already seen you wearing nothing but shoes.

Nervous, excited, and chilly, she padded barefoot back into the living room. She found Jason had turned off the light and the radio, the only light provided by the porch light streaming through the curtainless front windows. He also had pulled another drop-cloth onto the first and he sat with his back against the wall, staring awkwardly out the window at the snow piling up on the branches of the piñon tree.

As he heard her come in, he said, "Listen, Man, if you're not comfortable…" Then he caught sight of her, his eyes drinking in her bare legs. Columbus must have had a similar look on his face when he first laid eyes on the sandy beach of the Bahamas: not what he expected, more than he hoped for, and a sight for sore eyes. "Oh, Man!" he gasped.

"May I?" she asked, sitting next to him, holding her legs together discreetly while he pulled the paint-blotched drop cloth over them. In no time their lips were locked again in a passionate embrace. This time his fingers patiently unbuttoned each of the buttons on her blouse and then groped behind her back to unhook her bra. When at last his hand cupped and cradled her small breast for the first time, it almost seemed to paralyze him. He grew very still, barely breathing at all, as though he thought somehow any sudden movement on his part might spook her, might break the spell and she would disappear. She reassured him with kisses and he began to explore her body tenderly but sensuously.

This time she didn't flinch when his cool hand stroked her soft warm thigh. Gradually, an inch at a time, it worked its way up until his finger touched her vulva, sending a familiar thrill through her entire body. While he very gingerly felt her contours, she took the liberty to find out some more about his. Her hand, thus far content to hold his wide back, found its way around his side and down below his belt. She thought about unzipping his fly but discovered a much larger bulge there than she had anticipated and a wet spot up by the coin pocket of his jeans. She decided instead to try to unbuckle his belt.

Reluctantly taking his hands from her to help with the unbuckling and unzipping, he asked, "Are you sure?"

She answered with murmurs and kisses. He undid the belt and fly and pulled down the jeans and jockeys. As much out of curiosity as desire, her hand took hold of him. It felt larger and harder than she expected and it seemed to quiver slightly. He moaned at her touch. While she debated the feasibility of her being able to accommodate that where she knew it intended to go, he distracted her with a question.

"You're not a virgin, are you?"

She had no simple answer to what seemed like a simple question. She had broken her hymen on Queenie's saddlehorn in a riding mishap four years earlier, so in that respect she was no longer a virgin. She and Deb, who had lost her own virginity the more traditional way nearly three years ago, had talked extensively about sex, and Deb had gone so far as to show Amanda some of the ins and outs of her body and how to achieve a certain level of satisfaction on her own, so she wasn't a complete stranger to the pleasures involved.

But Amanda had never had sex with a man. One night after a kegger out at Star Ranch, Bill had crudely tried to grope her and she had slapped his face, as much for his style as for the act itself. She had never been closer than that.

She also knew that Jason asked the question because he wasn't sure he wanted the responsibility of taking her virginity from her. For her part she could think of no one she'd rather give it to, no matter what happened between them afterward. As attractive as he was, and lead singer for a popular local band, he must have had enough experience at this to guide her through it. After all, she knew of at least three girls he'd been seriously involved with in high school and who knew what he'd done up in Boulder?

His question might also be his oblique way of asking if she was using some form of birth control. She wasn't, but she knew enough about her cycles to know that she probably wouldn't ovulate for at least ten days.

So the simplest answer to his simple question about her virginity was "No, I'm not."

Right then someone a few houses away set off some firecrackers and some muffled shouts filtered through the snow. "Well, happy New Year," Jason said, rolling onto her.

The course of true love never did run smooth. First, her leather miniskirt proved difficult to pull up, especially with him lying on top of her. Once they got past that, he spent more time than she expected groping for the proper opening, finally having to rely on her to guide him with her hand. Then, maybe because she felt nervous, or hadn't completely finished her period, or just wasn't very good at this, her doubts about the feasibility of his being able to fit inside her seemed realized when he could barely stick his head inside her foyer, as it were.

But his urgency and her determination eventually won out. Far from feeling ecstatically wonderful the way she had expected, though, or even pleasant, it felt painful, intrusive, and awkward. She closed her eyes and braced herself as he seemed to force his way farther and farther into her. As each thrust became stronger and quicker she felt more trapped and panicky. As much as she wanted to see this through, and as much as she wanted to please him, she finally decided that she just couldn't take it any longer. She opened her eyes to beg him to quit.

The look on his face stopped her. His eyes were closed, his brow furrowed, his neck and back arched. He seemed to be on the brink of a profound, life-changing metamorphosis. Shuddering, gasping for air, he moaned, and then bellowed: "Oh. Oh! Oh, Man! Oh, God!"

When the climax came, everything got easier. She thrust her hips up to his to help him through it, awed at the immensity of what he seemed to be experiencing. The relatively mild pleasures she had felt in the past paled in comparison.

When his orgasm had run its course, he showered her face with kisses, tears in his eyes. He carefully lowered himself onto her, still supporting most of his weight on his elbows, and she wrapped her arms around his back and held him tight.

"Did I hurt you?" he whispered.

The discomfort she felt before seemed to melt away. She shook her head.

"Oh, thank you, thank you, thank you," he whispered.

She almost told him she loved him. But that seemed trite. It seemed like that might oblige him to say the same whether he felt it or not. Instead, she said, "I will remember this always."

"Oh, Man, that was incredible!" he said hoarsely.

They lay like that for a few minutes until his arms began to quiver. He rolled off of her and pulled up his jockeys and jeans. When he went to put his arm around her, though, he glanced at his fingers and did a double take. Holding his hand up into the porch light, he saw, and she saw too, that his fingers were streaked with blood.

"Oh, Man, I did hurt you, didn't I?" he exclaimed, horrified.

She sat up and looked between her legs. A tiny pool of his semen, tinged with red, had dripped from her onto the drop cloth below. For just a moment she too wondered if he truly had been too large and she had sustained some minor injury. Then she realized that this was just the last blob of menstrual blood her body often retained.

"I'm fine," she reassured him, embarrassed, pulling the drop cloth back over them. "It's nothing to worry about."

"Look at me," he insisted, and she complied. "You lied to me, didn't you? You actually were a virgin, weren't you?"

Far too mortified to admit the truth, she said, "Yes, I lied," trying to figure out if that too was a lie.

"Oh, God, why didn't you tell me?"

"It doesn't really matter, does it?"

"Well, if nothing else," he said grimly, "what about the stain?"

"Once it dries," she reassured him, "it'll be just another blotch on the canvas."

He put his head back on his arm, staring at the ceiling, as though searching for a way to shoulder one more burden. She lay on her side next to him, wishing she could ease his load, thinking, When you cross that threshold into sex, the truth is hard to come by.

...O...O...O...

Show Biz always has a trick or two up her sleeve. One time a job I didn't play put me on a path up a mountain to talk about life and death with a wise man from India.

In the fiery late summer of 1988, a job cancellation in Twin Falls, Idaho, left me with a week off between Pocatello and Sun Valley. I thought about driving up to West Yellowstone and volunteering for the army of firefighters desperately trying to keep the devastating forest fires from consuming the historic buildings of the park. But singing 12 nights out of 13, four and a half hours a night, left me with a sore throat and I really needed to do well at the Sun Valley gig, so breathing pine smoke for a week was out. The first day of my week off was the day they closed all the trails on the east side of the Tetons and closed the whole of Yellowstone. With nothing else to do, I decided to see what the west side of the Tetons looked like.

The smoke from the forest fires burning throughout the Northwest gave the peaks a sepia tone and made, as I wrote in my journal entry from September 11, "the fullness of Venus blush." The first night, I hiked in to the Green Lakes to camp, alone as usual, knowing that, between the fires, the drought, and the remote location on a weeknight, I probably would have the place to myself.

I had one of the oddest experiences of my life there. As I sat on a log by the glassy lake, meditating on the stillness of the evening, I heard, far above me, a strange, almost metallic sound, like something whistling as it tumbled through space: whoeep! whooeeep! whoooeeep! In the absolute silence of the place, the sound took on a sinister quality, especially since it seemed to be coming toward me. I looked around but couldn't seem to locate the source. As it grew louder and closer, I began to feel frightened. I've felt frightened many a time in the mountains, but I generally know the reason for my fear: wolves pawing my tent in the Yukon, lightning in the Rockies, grizzlies in Glacier. This sound was unlike anything I'd ever heard and seemed to be coming right at me out of, literally, the clear blue sky. The cold clammy hand of the unknown threat gripped me and as the whoeeeps! got closer, I ducked and held my arms above my head in terror. Missing me by just a few feet, whatever it was fell into the lake.

Then, of course, I had a classic revelation when a mallard bobbed to the surface. I'd heard the sound of it backpedaling its wings to decelerate. Now I know why they call them ducks.

The next morning it snowed a couple of inches, the first precipitation in weeks and the only possible end to the fires. I decided to hike up Table Mountain, just west of the Grand Tetons, to see the peaks from across instead of from below, the way they're seen from the east. The hike got off to a spooky start when I came across the dead, bloated, but still intact body of a sheep lying across the trail, its open eye frozen and opaque, its white wool matching the snow. Undaunted, I stepped across and tried to catch up with the only other hiker on the trail, a small dark man who never *stopped to catch his breath. He passed me somewhere around the sheep but by the time the top of the mountain came into view, he had become a tiny speck against the horizon. Being a fair hiker myself, I wanted to take a closer look at this prodigy. As I struggled up the steep trail, I could hear the whapping of helicopter blades flying in and out of the valley to the south. By the time I reached the relatively flat top of the mountain, I could tell some sort of emergency had brought in a rescue team.*

I found the master hiker at the eastern edge of the flat top of Table Mountain. He sat with his legs dangling over a cliff that fell away thousands of feet to the valley below and rose just as steeply on the other side to the 13,770-foot summit of Grand Teton Peak. The master turned out to be a disappointed climber whose plan to climb the peak in front of us had gone up in smoke. A native of India, he worked in New Jersey programming computers and had found the dead sheep as disconcerting as I had. We talked about the helicopter too: evidently a camper, caught in the snow in summer gear, had become hypothermic and wandered away from his tent.

Here's what I wrote in my journal: "Sitting right across from the Tetons. The gentleman from India has climbed in the Himalayas and agrees that this is an incredible view. It's clearer today and the mountains, dusted with snow, appear almost bigger than life. Everywhere, the rugged granite canyons are steep and angular and fringed with trees. The peaks, sheer cliffs nearly everywhere, are breathtakingly huge.

"All my life I've wanted to talk to a wise Indian at the top of a mountain, ask him the proverbial, 'What's it all for? Why did Bodhidharma come from the West?' But I didn't. Maybe not having the question is better than having the answer."

The next morning search-and-rescue found the camper dead about a mile from his tent, half naked from some hypothermic hallucination of safety. More snow fell after that and Yellowstone reopened. I came from the west to watch the snow put out the fires.

December 1, 1999

…nothing…

No light. No sound. Blank. Bland.

Then, slowly, it creeps back in. First the ache, the god-awful grinding that accompanies every toss and every turn. Then the throb, the heart's-blood coursing to those brand new, expanding monuments to wildness and freedom. Then gradually, groggily, the sense of self, the awareness of being the host of the pain and malignancy. Finally, reluctantly, inevitably, the encroachment of the consciousness, reborn replete with "Gotta pee" and "Oh, yeah, still here" and "The appointment's at noon."

Matt's eyes fluttered open but the pain medication made it difficult to focus them. His suite here at the Back Bay Sheraton in Boston, just a few minutes from the Longwood Medical Center, was indeed dark and almost silent. He did have to pee but now he always felt like he had to pee.

Surprisingly though, none of the medications he took had interfered with his morning hard-on. He lifted the sheet and looked at it. "Fucker," he scolded it. "Where were you yesterday?"

He had been in Boston a week now. Since his treatments at the Dana-Farber Institute took no more than a few hours each day, he found himself with time on his hands. He felt too crummy to go outside but he hated the thought that he might have to spend the rest of his life indoors. Sometimes the pain medication made him so woozy and groggy that he could do nothing but lie still and listen to Bach or Mozart in his headphones. Over the weekend he and Deb had tried seeing a few of the sights—Faneuil Hall, the Old North Church—before she had to go back to Seattle Sunday night, but he couldn't stay out long. He had brought along some paperwork, some old letters to work on, and, for this first visit to Boston, an old classic he hadn't read since college, *Walden*.

He had forgotten how much *Walden* had meant to him. Thoreau's matter-of-fact but eloquent style, his attention to detail, his love of walking, nature, solitude, independence and, now, even his relatively early death, all resonated with Matt. So yesterday, since he had only an hour at the Institute in the morning, he summoned up his strength and courage and drove the rental car out to Walden Pond. As he went through Concord, where the first shot of discord in the War of Independence was fired, it occurred to him that this drive probably would prove the last shot of his own independence.

He had just read Thoreau's chapter about the pond in winter, had chuckled over the joke the iceman had pulled, offering to let Thoreau be on the bottom end of the two-man pit saw while they cut the ice into blocks. Matt had actually harbored hope that the pond would be frozen, maybe not thick enough yet to support an ice wagon but thick enough to let Matt wander out on the ice, maybe find a thin spot, become the bottom man on the saw. The authorities would probably conclude that he had become disoriented because of the pain medication. Like George Bailey in *It's A Wonderful Life*, his sudden demise in the icy water would benefit his wife—maybe even kick in some double indemnity clause for accidental death—instead of subjecting her, and Matt, to the expensive folderol of a slow painful death from prostate cancer.

But so far the autumn had proven considerably milder than the predicted La Niña conditions; the pond had only a few traces of ice around the shore. A stiff breeze sailed through the straight white pines and bare hickory trees, ruffling the pond, tugging at Matt's jacket, making his eyes water. Still, he had the place pretty much to himself and, walking from bench to bench along the path, he managed to make it as far as the stone cairn people had left in the dim outline of a root cellar, the only evidence that remained of Thoreau's cabin.

Sitting there alone, his thoughts turned to another walker who had preceded him in death. Jason would have liked this place. Like Matt, it would have reminded him of the cabin in Jones Park. Not for the first time, Matt found himself envying Jason's sudden exit from this vale of tears.

He wondered, as he often had, what had happened after Jason left the Jones Park cabin for the last time, already shivering, soaked to the skin. He pictured him losing his bearings, wandering around in the dark, the flashes of lightning providing only momentary clues. Between the six inches of hail on the ground and Jason's already precarious physical and mental condition, hypothermia would have set in within minutes. Maybe he had had time to use the knife, the only thing missing from his pack. Or maybe he staggered around in a daze for quite a while before curling up on the ground and falling asleep. Perhaps one of the lightning bolts that had fallen about their heads for hours had cut his suffering mercifully short. Maybe he had even stumbled over that black bear in the dark, the angry bellow ringing in his ears until the heavy paw made the darkness complete. In any case, he had blazed a trail into that night and now it was up to Matt to follow the best he could into that undiscovered country.

But what about the rub: to sleep, perchance to dream? Two weeks ago, Russ had postulated a sixth step in Matt's five-step ARDAR system about life, a step beyond death. But Matt had grave doubts about a hereafter thereafter. His pain medication had already given him a taste of what to expect: No dreams. Not even sleep, at least not in the sense of that moonlit hay ride from which one awakens dewy and refreshed. Just...nothing...

Not that the body didn't provide an aspect of renewal. The First Law of Thermodynamics, the Conservation of Matter/Energy, dictated, after all, that the physical elements remain in play. The body is recycled, reborn in some other form. Hopefully not as pessimistic as Hamlet's postulate that "Imperious Caesar, dead, and turn'd to clay,/ Might stop a hole to keep the wind away." Rather a reentry into the organic cycle, transformed beyond recognition but still part of the biosphere. In that sense, Matt had always felt small bits of Jason all around him, in the fields and the forests, at the seashore and on the tallest peaks. Jason, as was often his wont, was just scouting the trail up ahead.

"Don't set specific goals," Jason had told him on one of their bushwhacking hikes. "If your goal is just to hike as far as you can and see things you've never seen before, you never come home disappointed."

Matt certainly couldn't feel disappointed about his 48 years of bushwhacking, though he had often missed Jason's companionship. For that matter, Jason's misfortunes had brought the most fortunate thing, by far, to Matt's life: Deb. He had met Deb, after all, on a hike to console Jason for the loss of his brother. And Jason's disappearance had brought Matt and Deb together once and for all.

He had brought to Walden the picture of Deb wearing nothing but the ribbed tank top and the paisley silk boxer shorts. He pulled it from his jacket pocket, took it from the plastic bag, and looked at the image on the flimsy paper, fluttering in the breeze, gleaming in the cloud-strangled shafts of sun. While she had made it clear to him that she certainly would cherish every bit of sexual energy he could muster, she also fully understood his need to perform, probably for the last time, his fertility ritual in some wild setting. Originally he had hoped to drive up into the Berkshires but just getting to Walden had pushed him to the limit. He felt perfectly content with Walden, though, as the repository of his last ceremonial spoonful of genetic material. And between the blustery weather, the time of year, and the day of the week, he wouldn't have any trouble finding the necessary privacy.

But, whether due to his disease, his medication, his age, the cold weather, or maybe the feeling of guilt about what he now had trouble seeing as anything other than a selfish act, he couldn't get himself aroused.

Until now, back at the Sheraton. And any mystique the act might have held yesterday at Walden disappeared here and now. He would be just some middle-aged man beating off in a hotel room. Anyway, the hard-on became a soft-off before he woke up enough to do anything about it.

Trying to flex his lower back as little as possible, he carefully rolled out of bed, shaved, showered, and ate his continental breakfast with Thoreau and, for a change of pace, Debussy. Outside his window a light drizzle glazed the sidewalks and glistened from the spars on Old Ironside. Inside, the usual accouterments of a hotel room—the big beds, the imitation art, the bland furniture, the unused TV—reminded him how much he missed his own room. For the first time in his life, he felt homesick. When he had choked down all the breakfast he could stand, he picked up the phone and called Deb. He hadn't spoken to her yesterday at all, though she may have called while he was at the Institute or out at Walden. To his disappointment, he got the answering machine so he left a message that he had slept pretty well (though he never really slept well anymore) and that he loved her. She was probably out riding Tahoma this morning.

Heaving a sigh, he gathered the breakfast dishes onto the tray and set it outside the door. Sitting down in the armchair, he picked up the folder full of legal documents and wearily began going through them. Everything seemed in order. He had always wanted to make sure

Deb was provided for but, financially at least, nothing he could do would make one iota of difference.

He came across the $10,000 term-life insurance policy that Carmen Muñoz had reminded him about when they spoke a couple of weeks ago. (Just two weeks? Hard to believe.) Morgan Stanley Dean Witter had contracted with some insurance company to provide the policy as a perk to their better clients, the idea being that the insurer would give five years free hoping that the client would automatically renew at the end of the term. The five years ended in May. He had his doubts he would make it as far as May.

May Mendoza came to mind. He wondered how she was doing. Russ had never called back but Matt assumed that the Piñon Nuts Gathering, a long shot to begin with, wouldn't happen. Too bad. Meeting Amanda's daughter, getting together with everyone and talking about old times, had been one of the few bright spots on his horizon.

He had an idea. The life insurance policy, like the rest of his estate, named Deb as beneficiary, but Deb's Microsoft stock could go up or down $10,000 in a day depending on the color of Bill Gates's tie. But from what Matt understood about May's situation, it could make a huge difference to her. He decided to call Carmen Muñoz and make May the beneficiary. He looked at his watch. Seattle is three hours earlier, so it would be just after 7:00 there, but West Coast stock brokers usually worked early hours to correspond to the hours of the New York Stock Exchange. He dialed the toll-free number.

"Oh, hi, Matt!" Carmen said after he identified himself. "It's good to hear from you again. Where are you?"

"I'm in Boston, as a matter of fact," Matt said, a little puzzled.

"I thought you must be out of town, calling so early and on the toll-free line," she said, sounding espresso-perky. "Boston's a beautiful town, isn't it? My college roommate was a Christian Scientist from Boston and I visited her there once. She took me through the Mother Church and a bunch of the other historic places. Are you there for business or pleasure?"

"I used to have a friend who was raised a Christian Scientist," Matt said, thinking of Jason. "And I'm here for neither business nor pleasure. In fact, I'm here for something antithetical to a Christian Scientist."

"What's that?"

"I'm participating in a medical study at the Dana-Farber Institute."

"Oh, dear," Carmen said. "Nothing serious, I hope."

"I'm afraid it is," Matt admitted, figuring some people really ought to know and he might as well start with the person handling his life insurance. "I've got prostate cancer."

"Oh, Matt, I'm so sorry to hear it!" Carmen said. "My father had prostate cancer when he died."

"Is that what he died of?"

"Actually, no. He had Alzheimer's as well and putting him through treatment for the cancer just didn't seem worthwhile at that stage. But I hear they're developing some promising new drugs."

"That's what I'm here for," Matt said. "Dana-Farber is testing a new approach to treating cancers called antiangiogenesis."

"How does it work?"

"Well, instead of treating the cancer directly," Matt explained. "the antiangiogenesis agent, a drug called endostatin, prevents the body from creating new blood vessels. Without a blood supply, cancers can't grow. The results in the studies they've done on mice have been very positive, with some mice actually remaining cancer-free even after stopping the drug."

"That's wonderful!"

"It's great news if you're a mouse with cancer," Matt said. "I'm actually among just the second cohort of five human test subjects, so it's too early to judge results in humans."

"But can you tell if it's working?"

"Actually, this stage of testing is just to determine whether the drug is toxic so I don't anticipate seeing any dramatic change in the cancer other than perhaps a slower rate of growth. I've only been here a week so I haven't seen any definitive lab results yet. The good news, at least as far as the drug trial goes, is that I haven't yet suffered any particular side effects."

"Are they going to have to remove your prostate?" Carmen asked, sounding considerably more sober.

"Unfortunately, we didn't catch my cancer until it metastasized so it's already spread into my lymph nodes, pelvis, and back." Sometimes he surprised even himself at how dispassionate he could sound about his own condition. "I have what's called type D2 cancer, which means that the cancer not only has spread beyond the prostate, the cancer cells themselves are poorly differentiated and spreading rapidly. Surgery is no longer an option for me. That's part of the reason I was selected for the study. They needed at least a few cancer patients in advanced stages of the disease who hadn't tried other therapies that might skew the results."

He could tell by the length of her pause that he had ruined Carmen's morning. "Matt, that's just terrible! I'm so sorry. Do you have any other treatment options?"

Matt closed his eyes and rubbed the bridge of his nose. "Oh, a couple. Without treatment I can expect to live a few months; with treatment maybe a few years. I'm kind of stuck in this drug trial though. I can't get a strong enough dose to fight the disease but I also can't try any other treatment option. After this first four-week dose, I'll have to reassess my options."

"Is Deb there with you?" Carmen asked.

"She flew out with me and stayed over the Thanksgiving weekend but had to go home Sunday night to help Earthjustice organize some sort of protest to the World Trade Organization Conference that's taking place in Seattle this week. She'll be coming back here at the end of the week."

"Have you talked to her?"

"I couldn't get a hold of her yesterday and I just left a message for her this morning. I guess she's probably out riding."

"Well, they did a bang-up job on the protests, as you probably saw on TV."

"I don't watch much TV. What happened?"

"I'm sure she knows more about it than I do so I'll let her tell you. Anyway, Matt, I feel just awful about your condition," Carmen said, her voice already taking on the somber, sympathetic tones people use when they talk to the dying. "Is there anything I can do for you?"

"That's the reason I called," Matt said, beginning to regret telling her as much as he had. He already felt irritable and sympathy grated on his ear. "Remember that term life insurance policy you reminded me about when we last spoke? I think I'm going to change the beneficiary from Deb, who doesn't really need the money, to an old family friend, who really does."

"Let me just pull up your account," Carmen said, sounding more businesslike. The sound of her fingernails tapping on her computer keyboard came over the phone. "Okay, here it is. Now, what's the name of your family friend?"

He gave her May's name and said he'd get back to her with the address.

When she finished, Carmen said, "Matt, I really admire you for how you're handling this and if there's anything else I can do for you—anything at all—don't hesitate to call."

"Thanks, Carmen."

He hadn't thought in terms of having done anything admirable. He had taken the necessary steps in a logical fashion. He did feel good about participating in this endostatin study but he would have felt good about contributing to science in any way. He hated inconveniencing everyone he came in contact with. He hated the stigma attached to dying. People acted as though he were somehow different because of it. But we all die.

Most of all he hated putting Deb through this. It somehow didn't suit his image of her to see her so solicitous, so serious, so weary. In his mind she would always be the vivacious, mischievous sprite of long ago.

o   o   o

Before she left, Deb had stressed time and again that Matt should do anything he felt like doing. He put away the legal documents folder and picked up the manila envelope marked "Letters—1970." These might help while away the time until she called. He also wanted to see if any of Russ's or Jason's letters contained anything that Russ might find relevant today. Part of him longed to hear Jason's voice again, too.

On the top of the heap was an envelope from Deb, her white-on-white stationary, postmarked January 10, 1970. Receiving it hadn't electrified him the way her first letter had but it came as no small surprise nonetheless. He had come away from that original New Year's Eve Piñon Nuts Gathering with the distinct impression that she found him as dull as the dishwater in which he and Russ had immersed themselves most of the evening while she, at his insistence, watched from a safe distance to prevent his marring her dress any further. When midnight rolled around without a sign of Jason, Amanda, John, or Prudence, Matt had offered to take Deb home. As she had when she took him home from Amanda's over Thanksgiving, she listened politely while he droned on about some scientific nonsense. But as soon as the car came to a halt and his nervousness about being alone with her made his mouth go dry, she bolted. He went back to Seattle assuming that he would never hear from her again.

The letter, to his disappointment but not surprise, turned out to be just Deb's bow to the social graces:

> Dear Matt,
> Thanks so much for the lovely time on New Year's Eve and for the ride home afterward. Listening to you guys talk is like sitting in one of my classes here at Regis. Good luck in school there in Washington.
>
> Love,
> Deb

Hoping against hope to keep her interested, he had crafted a reply that drew on each shred of information in her note, using self-deprecating humor to try to convey to her some sense of his feeling of inadequacy.

The next letter in the pile came from Russ.

```
                                    jan 28
m.m.—
    two incredible prodigies born on this date — you and wolfgang
amadeus mozart. maybe he could play rings around you on the keys
but you — at last report — are still alive. way to go.
    i seem to be a worse romantic every day, not that anyone wants
to be on the receiving end of that romance. as you may have heard,
prudence and i have gone our separate ways but salting the wounds
is the fact that we still live under the same roof.
    i must tell you — "it doesn't really matter" and "oh well, what
the hell" have blossomed within. as you know, such thoughts have
lingered since you and jason and i were walking to school that
fateful day last year and we all said "hmmm… walk around the
world." but at that time i still had inhibitions.
    well, the inhibitions are melting. what am i hanging around for?
last semester, my house-mate leon's little scheme for sailing to
some deserted isle sounded like peter pan. now it seems like an
actual alternate reality. when prudence and i bagged it, i felt as
though someone was telling me something. jason, when he's not lost
in the machinations at mind machine headquarters, is on board too.
maybe even overboard. leon isn't exactly his cup of tea but jason
is dying to get a move on.
    leon has thought especially of the tuamotu archipelago east of
tahiti, between 75 and 2000 relatively uninhabited islands with
temperate climate belonging to the french. who would ever know
should we float up on sailing ships? fifteen, maybe twenty people
for two ships seems maximum. unless people with money fly to
tahiti (which seems ridiculous) or work their way over on the
famous tramp steamer. bring things to grow, build with, start on,
whatever.
    i am counting greatly on your wanting to come. we need a cool
head among us. don't say no until you have talked to me and jason
and others or i'll be soooo mad.
                                    Russ
```

Matt smiled as he refolded the letter and put it back in the envelope. He had forgotten about the desert island scheme. But it marked the first time he felt a little worried about Jason. Not so much the "machinations of the Mind Machine" because Matt had seen Jason stoned and knew his feet would be on the ground even if his head reached the clouds. But taking Leon's hare-brained plan seriously didn't sound like Jason at all.

In any case, Russ made only one trivial reference to alternate reality. Matt got out the next letter, Deb's reply to his self-deprecating analysis of her thank-you note:

February 13

Dear Indefatigable One—

You are perceptive—you managed to read something into every one of my 44 words. Mon Dieu! I hadn't planned on that. Maybe it's a good omen. (Unlike the date I'm writing this, Friday the 13th.) You certainly pay attention.

I wasn't being sarcastic. I did have a lovely time on New Year's Eve, believe it or not. Vraiment, it was Q. C.—a rare experience these days. And no, I didn't "leap from the car like it was about to explode." I truly am impressed at how much knowledge you have at your fingertips and I don't consider you and the other Piñon Nuts as boring as my classes here at Regis. If it seemed like I rushed off, it was because I have a curfew. I didn't want to end up like Mandy, whose mother, as you know, grounded her for a month just because she came in twenty minutes late that night.

Mandy and Bill—in case you haven't heard—are no longer seeing one another. I think Mandy's looking for more of a walker (like you-know-who) than a driver like Bill. I'm not sure what Bill's looking for. He's actually going to be in Denver tomorrow for some car convention so maybe he'll tell me then.

Anyway, I better hit the books again. I <u>know</u> you don't rely on luck in school but sometimes I need more than my pretty head to get by. Thanks again for your letter and I'll try to be more careful about what I say from now on.

Love (and no, I'm not sure just what that means)

Deb

Matt had learned later that "Q. C." meant "quite cool." He had wondered at the time, and he wondered again now, how Deb knew Bill planned to be in Denver and that they would talk. As far as Matt knew, Deb knew Bill only through Amanda and never heard her refer, before or since, to doing anything with Bill alone. He wrote a letter in which he wondered about it but thought better of it and tore it up, writing instead a reply that dealt only with things between the two of them.

The next letter, based on the Arapahoe address, came from Jason:

```
                    feb 22
    clear eye —
    boom shakalakalaka boom shakalakala! How beest thou, brother?
greetings and salivations from mind machine HEADquarters (we ask
no quarter, we give none) on the road of the arapahoes at the foot
of the flatirons. not really at the foot, more like where the cane
would rest if the flatirons used a cane.
    thanks for the letter. what kind of physics lab you got there at
you-dub-you? if you guys are working on that high energy particle
crap, watch out for the old pi meson in the face.
    sorry it's been so long since i wrote and i do so now with a
heavy heart. i come to bury the wonder car, not to praise it.
after you and i towed it back to the old house, it never once
coughed and sputtered again. when the house sold, dad had the w.c.
towed to the dump, an ignoble end to a noble steed. i only hope
and pray my own end will prove more glorious.
    unfortunately, if i live out the myth of the captain of the
argo, it shan't be so. remember when my mom brought up that myth
at the gathering of nuts at my house? (now known as "someone
else's house.") i ran across a copy of robert graves's mythology
in norlin library the other day so i looked it up. the
mythological jason incurs the wrath of the gods by fooling around
behind medea's back and does indeed wander homeless from city to
city, hated of men, the way mom recalled. medea eventually has
jason's children but ends up killing them. and do the gods come
down on her for this? no. in the afterlife she roams the elysian
fields hand in hand with some other heavy hitter like achilles. as
an old man jason comes back home and sits down next to his old
ship, the argo, thinking back on the good times and bad. he's just
made up his mind to hang himself from the prow of the ship when
suddenly it keels over and kills him. the ancients saw the image
of the argo's stern (remember, the prow killed him) as one of the
constellations.
    but see, i have cleverly eluded fate. the wonder car now roams
the elysian junk yard and i only am escaped alone to tell thee, or
some such thing. besides, who wants to look up to the stars and
```

see the image of a beat-up 1953 ford station wagon?

the question is: who's my medea? manny? true, she managed to draw me out the way the walrus drew out the oysters. i had the time of my life with her on new year's, found out some things about her that i didn't know were true, which, as it turns out, are no longer true. so i spend six weeks with her head on my head, only to get a letter from her this week consisting mainly of her sob story about bill deserting her on valentine's day. i guess compared to the moby dick of love she and bill have, man and i were just a fluke.

i don't remember if i told you about that guy named easy that john and i met at the doghouse but i got word he was killed in vietnam last week. this has got to stop.

on a lighter note, gary and some of the other mind machiners have been planning a spring break trip to sunny california in gary's mustang. they said that if i want to go, they'll take me to see my mom in santa maria. sounds like a long strange trip but i'm up for it.

i don't know if mom's up for it though. between the mind machine and the protests and everything, i'm having a lot of trouble getting my head around school. so mom was less than thrilled when i had to hit her up for rent money a couple of weeks ago. mind machine headquarters is a condemned old frame house and my room in the attic is unheated and has a four foot ceiling for about half of it, and my rent is still a hundred clams a month. a couple of days ago we got a hundred-mile-an-hour chinook and i thought the whole house would blow off its foundations and land on a witch somewhere.

glad to hear you got letters from deb. from what i gather from man's letter, she and deb aren't as close as they used to be. is this what the seventies are going to be about? everything falling apart? even this thing with russ and leon and the whole sick crew on marine street begins to smack of the absurd. it's a little like the rumor flying around about the beatles coming in helicopters to take people to this private island in pepperland where the streets are paved with gold records and fountains burble with lsd. (pounds, shillings, pence?) but god, i want to do something different. things have to be different pretty soon, don't they?

russ did turn me on to a primo lecture by alan watts at mackey auditorium. hard to believe someone that old could be so in tune with what's happening in the world today. i guess timothy leary is scheduled for mackey in april. i may have to be there for that.

well, i'm out of paper so nuff said.

J

Funny, Matt thought, what different impressions Deb and Jason had about Amanda breaking up with Bill. Deb seemed to think Amanda wanted to be with Jason; Jason seemed to think that Amanda wanted to be with Bill. Everyone seemed to be working at cross purposes.

He moved on to Deb's letter postmarked March 15:

Dear Matt,

All right, Joe Skeptic, what's this noise about "the forgotten man"? Objection! Please explain this most unjust accusation. Of <u>course</u> your letter came! I really <u>have</u> wanted to write but I've had a lot to deal with lately.

Why didn't you send that honest first draft of your letter? I'd like to see it. Why do you label it unsatisfactory? I'd say the one you sent was much more so. What did it accomplish?

"Enlighten you as concerns your position…" Hmmm… Well, you have stated your position as "the clumsy-fingered, dim-witted, incoherent, and yet indefatigable…" I beg to differ.

What is your position? My opinion of you after the last time was rather angry that you were in the Springs for so long and I didn't even see you until New Year's. Being with the Piñon Nuts makes me feel very much on the outside, as I'm sure you've noticed.

I'll try to be honest. I have no logical explanation for my actions, or lack of same. Sometimes, I really struggle to give an honest reaction to people or situations. Mandy thinks I'm mad at her but it's not her at all, it's me.

Of course, I'd <u>love</u> to see you over spring break. Unfortunately, I'm going down to Texas that week for a horse show. Sorry! But please keep in touch.

Love,
Deb

Obviously, whatever Matt had written to her had ticked her off. Evidently she hadn't taken his self-deprecating humor the way he had intended it. He remembered carefully crafting a reply to this letter in which he tried to balance honesty with some good-natured ribbing to try to break the ice he felt forming between them.

Matt stretched his back carefully and checked his watch. He still had plenty of time before he had to get to Dana-Farber. It seemed odd that Deb hadn't called him yet but it gave him time for a few more letters.

The next came from Russ and bore a New York postmark of March 27. In it, he wrote:

```
    leon's best-laid plan for the south pacific seems unfit for mice
or men. i'm getting that fighting inevitability feeling — not that
i'm telling you anything you don't already know, you damned
harbinger of gray dawns. i have obviously added a new layer, a
good strong one, of hatred for my fucking-around nature but it
would kill me to punish myself as much as i now deserve. shit.
(but in a nice quiet post-caring tone.)
    before i left boulder i ran into jason. he looked like shit.
he's losing weight and has dark wings under his eyes. goings-on at
the mind machine headquarters are less than conducive to health
and hygiene. maybe you should write him a stern epistle to mend
his sorry ways…
```

Matt had taken Russ's advice to heart and written Jason a letter urging him to take care of himself. Fat lot of good that had done.

He picked up the next letter with dread. He remembered this one. It was the "Dear John" Deb had never written to John.

April Fool's Day

Dear Matt—

It was nice to hear from you. To tell you the truth, my trip to Texas was horrible. But that's all over now so let's just move on.

Your new honesty scares me! I have come to the conclusion that you are right about my insincerity. I have arrived at the further conclusion that the apparent incongruity in my nature is due not to my feelings (which are usually sincere) but to my actions (which usually aren't). Lately I've <u>had</u> to do too many things I really didn't <u>want</u> to do.

Sometimes I think of you the same way I think of Mandy, as a really good friend. She has forgiven me much. Perhaps, in time, you'll do the same.

But our time is almost up. Please don't hate me. I hate myself enough for both of us. Take care of yourself.

> Yours,
> Deb

Matt had no idea what some of that letter referred to but the bottom line had seemed clear enough: Deb thought of him as a friend and nothing more. He decided once again to bow out gracefully and never wrote a reply. He still didn't know why Deb hated herself back then.

He remembered the next letter too, Jason's last.

```
        the eighteenth of april of seventy —
        barely a man is now — oh, screw it.
        nothing rhymes with seventy.
    matte (or do you prefer your photos glossy?) —
    the rumors of my death have been slightly exaggerated. i
appreciate your concern, bro, but russ is blowing smoke. i'm as
fit and tightly strung as a fiddle.
    not that there's nothing wrong with me. obviously there's
something wrong. people don't seem to like me much anymore. russ
moved out in favor of prudence and we know how well that ended up.
my parents don't dig me. i rarely hear from you or john. if that
doesn't mean there's something wrong, then there's something wrong
(or something). it looks like i'll have to mold an alternate
reality for myself, rather than following someone else's lead.
maybe a one-man life-style is madness but it's all i've got.
    wow, some heavy shit going down in this reality, though. those
apollo 13ers got home on just a reverse thruster and a prayer,
didn't they? luckily, superstition has no bearing on my life,
knock wood.
    too bad the beatles weren't so lucky. after all that bizarre
talk of paul mccartney being dead, it turns out that he's just
gone. oh, well, it happens to the best of bands, as we know.
    did russ write you about leon? turns out he and his weatherman
friends had planned to make good on one of the bomb threats people
have been calling in to the university. hoist by his own petard. a
pipe bomb blew up in his face. he may lose an eye and he's
certainly booked a stay at the gray-bar hotel for a while.
everybody associated with that marine street house is jittery,
including me.
    i'm glad to see the war protests gaining momentum though. even
tricky dick is starting to talk about the protesters himself
instead of sicking his pet bulldog agnew on us. i heard about
plans for a huge rally in washington where the vietnam veterans
can return their bogus medals. i wish i could make it there
myself. dad gave me steve's silver star, which i would love to add
to the heap. much as i miss steve, that medal just galls me
whenever i think about it.
    but enough of that. it's one of those classic spring days and
i'm sitting on the sway-backed front porch of the mind machine
headquarters while the birds bud out and the trees chirp, writing
to my old friend. the rest of the nefarious mind machine have
invaded bob's shack, now known as magnolia thunderpussy. anyway,
how are you, old friend?
    sorry to hear you've given up on the famous deb. i haven't heard
```

from manny in a while so i assume she's moved on to bigger and better things in her life. i hope it's not that giant step back to bill, but it's her life. i guess maybe plebeians such as we aren't destined to ride off into the sunset with the purty gals.

i'm here to testify, though, that there are some very tempting women right here in hipsville and the warm spring days have brought them out in droves, bra-less and swinging freely. if only i could catch an eye. i mean, isn't free love the order of the day? lately i've had it turned around. i'm love free.

not so with dear old pater, however. dad used the fresh divorce decree to blot the ink on the marriage certificate. i have a brand new mommy named phyllis who loves me about as much as my brand old mommy did.

who i did see in california, by the way. she took one look at the length of our hair and the breadth of our smiles and welcomed us to leave in the morning, which we did. disneyland on mescaline: it's a small, small, freakish world.

speaking of small worlds, next wednesday here in boulder we're celebrating something called earth day. i don't know what they're doing up there in seattle but down here we're putting on a concert and protest to try to get the powers that be to quit poisoning and blowing up this cosmic sphere. it's all we have, after all. we have nothing to sphere but this sphere itself.

john's done with swimming for the season and between blocks at c.c. so he's coming up here for this earth day bash and we're going to visit one of the more popular local fraternities, droppa kappa acid. he said something about window pane. the last few trips i've taken with the mind machine haven't gone so well (the way i put it to gary was that i keep painting myself into a corner and nailing the door shut) but maybe with john i'll feel more at home.

i don't feel at home much of anywhere anymore. i don't know what i'll do over the summer. mom and i would drive each other nuts and dad's got the new wife and all. i guess i'll stay up here with the mind machine. or maybe hitchhike somewhere, hit the road awhile. who knows?

so you're going to hang in seattle for most of the summer, huh? good gig at the photo lab. i always said you oughta be in pictures but we'll just have to see what develops. anyway, if you come back to the springs, maybe our paths will cross, maybe take a hike somewhere. until we meet again, happy trails.

J

The only hike they took, of course, was the ill-fated trip to Jones Park. In this letter, Matt could see the dark clouds gathering over Jason's head but at the time he figured, as did everyone else, that Jason had just hit a rough patch and would get past it. Matt certainly couldn't have known what lay ahead at that point, at what a disaster that first Earth Day would prove for Jason. And even if he had known, what could he do from that far away?

o   o   o

The phone rang. Matt stuffed the letters back into the manila envelope and grunted out of the chair.

From years of habit at Novagen, he said, "Matt McCleary" into the phone.

"Debra McCleary," Deb said, mocking his no-nonsense tone.

"Oh, hi, hon," he said, easing himself back into the chair with a groan.

"How are you feeling, sweetie?" she asked gently.

"Eehhh."

"You said in your message you slept pretty well."

"I said it, so it must be true. How about yourself?"

"I didn't sleep well at all," she said, sounding exhausted. "But how's the endostatin treating you?"

"No ill effects so far but I didn't expect any on such a low dose."

"Can you tell if it's working?"

"Well, I don't feel any better but I don't feel any worse. Maybe that's a good sign."

"You've got to be patient, you know. It's not an overnight cure."

"At the dose I'm taking, it's not a cure at all," he reminded her.

"But it'll give us some more time to find something that'll work. We will find something, you know."

"At this stage," he told her realistically, "the fixes might be as bad as the problem."

"We're going to do whatever it takes," she told him firmly.

"Yes, dear," he agreed, but changed the subject. "I talked to Carmen Muñoz this morning. She made it sound like your little demonstration turned out to be a rousing success."

"You haven't turned on the TV, have you?"

"It makes me nauseated," he said, which was true. But his condition also made him feel disconnected from the world so he didn't much care about the latest war or the football scores. "Why?"

"There was a full-blown riot here."

"What!?" he exclaimed, sitting up despite the pain.

"It's all over the news. CNN has given it huge coverage."

"Are you okay?"

"Well, more or less. It's been a rough couple of days."

"I tried calling you last night as well as this morning," Matt said, starting to feel guilty about not knowing about this. "You weren't at this demonstration the whole time, were you?"

"In a way, yes," Deb said. "I've spent the last two nights in jail."

"Oh my God! What happened?" His alarm made his joints ache.

"Well, a bunch of us met at Steinbrueck Park—"

"—down by the Market, right?"

"Yeah. Anyway, we met there first thing in the morning, hoping we could disrupt the opening ceremonies of the WTO by staging a Boston W 'Tea' O Party."

"No actual tea involved though, right?"

"People in Seattle waste caffeine? Not a chance. But we wanted to disrupt business-as-usual to show that we wouldn't stand idly by while this undemocratic trade organization makes secret deals that subvert all our hard-won environmental legislation. And we did manage to force them to postpone the opening ceremonies."

"Are you kidding? How many people turned out for this?"

"Matt, it was incredible," Deb said, sounding awed despite her fatigue. "I haven't seen anything like this since the war protests of the '60s. In fact, Tom Hayden was here. What a flashback! Saying that there's a power to the streets that takes over when all other attempts at democracy have failed. I half expected Jane Fonda to show up, shouting 'Right on!' and shaking her fist in the air. Dennis Hayes was here as well. Remember him?"

"Sure. He helped organize the first Earth Day. I was just thinking about that."

"When he spoke to us about putting these demonstrations together he said that some events are too complex to predict," she told him. "When he said it, I thought only a few of us hard-core nuts would pay any attention to a WTO conference. But this turned out to be one of those unpredictable events. I heard estimates of 35,000 people on the streets of downtown Seattle."

"I don't believe it!"

"I wouldn't either if I hadn't been there myself. We completely shut down the whole downtown."

"This sounds pretty serious. Was anybody hurt?"

"Oh, Paul Schell and Norm Stamper screwed this whole thing up so badly! After promoting this thing as a great boost for Seattle, Schell wasn't at all prepared for this kind of chaos, even though similar demonstrations have taken place at other WTO meetings in Europe. And then when it became obvious that the police had lost control of the situation, Stamper calls out the Storm Troopers."

"Storm Troopers?" Matt asked, flabbergasted.

"I had no idea the Seattle police had that kind of riot gear. These guys looked like something out of *Star Wars*, with the black helmets and visors and armor over most of their bodies. They even brought in an armored vehicle."

"Did it work? Did they stop the demonstration?"

"Are you kidding? You know as well as I that violence begets violence. I mean, most of us—the huge majority—were just plain old law-abiding citizens. But a few of the younger people claimed to be anarchists and they acted like it."

"How?"

"Oh, stupid property damage stuff: smashed windows, spray-painted walls, that sort of thing. But that, of course, forced the police to view the whole crowd as a potentially violent mob. Matt, they fired tear gas at us! Right here in laid-back Seattle!"

"Oh, no! You didn't get sprayed, did you?"

"I only got a little bit when the wind shifted. Some people had chained themselves to pipes and things and they couldn't move. They had tears streaming down their faces. And the police used something else that I hadn't heard of before. It's called a stinger. It's a shell that explodes, sending a bunch of rubber pellets flying through the crowd. They hurt like hell."

Matt felt the hair on the back of his head stand up. "You got hit?"

"Well, I was running away, like most people, so I just caught them on my backside."

"Oh, Deb! You're not hurt, are you?"

"You know, I haven't taken off my clothes since. Let me look at myself in the mirror." He could hear her unzip her pants. "Oh, my! I've got some souvenirs. Remember that night we made love out on Rialto Beach and you pushed me—"

"I did not push you!" he declared defensively. "You know darn well my foot slipped."

"You remember it the way you want, I'll remember it the way I want. Anyway, remember those bruises all those round stones left on my keister? Well, there aren't as many this time but they're a little more...vivid. I wish you could see them."

Matt shifted in his chair, aroused at the image. "I do too. I mean, I wish I could be there to take care of you."

"Would you kiss the bruises and make them better again?" she teased.

"I would do whatever it takes," he said firmly. "Anyway, so how did you end up in jail?"

"The police just started rounding people up and taking them away. It didn't seem to matter what you happened to be doing. I heard they arrested one of the journalists and even one of the WTO delegates. They put us on buses and took us to jail, stuck us in a holding cell."

"Did you call Phil Banks?"

"Actually, we decided, as part of the protest, not to give our real names to the police so they would be forced to hold us. If they try to prosecute everybody they arrested and give each one a jury trial, this will clog up the courts for months. So we came up with false names. Guess what mine was."

"I can't imagine."

"The Marquess," she said proudly.

Once in a while, during Playtime, he would inadvertently nick her with the scissors while cutting a bra strap or leave a bruise like at Rialto Beach. She then would flaunt the mark at him until it disappeared, referring to herself as the Marquess.

"You didn't," he said, knowing full well she did.

"I figured I'd have some marks from those rubber pellets."

"So you've been in jail this whole time?"

"I was going to stay longer," she said, "but this morning I heard the City Attorney is going to cut some kind of a deal so they're going to release almost everybody on their own recognizance. Besides, Phil got wind of where I was and he got me released."

"You must be completely exhausted," Matt said, frustrated that he could do nothing to help, a little jealous that Phil Banks could do so much.

"I've done my share in paying back Starbucks for their broken windows. But to tell you the truth, I haven't felt this exhilarated in years. We couldn't stop the conference but they won't get anything done."

"Carmen sure was a master of understatement," he said. "When she said a bang-up job, I had no idea she meant something like this."

"Why were you talking to Carmen?" Deb asked suspiciously. "I thought we agreed that you weren't going to worry about financial matters until you get better."

"Remember that free term-life insurance policy we got a few years ago?"

"No."

"It's just $10,000. But I thought, if it's okay with you, that I would change it to make May Mendoza the beneficiary. Kind of a gesture, you know, to make up for not getting together on New Year's Eve."

Deb paused and when she spoke her voice sounded thick. "Matt McCleary, you never cease to amaze me. What a wonderful, thoughtful gesture! I'm sure someday that will make a huge difference to May. Oh, if I were there right now, I'd… I'd…"

"You'd what?"

"I'd do whatever it takes to prove to you how much I love you," she said resolutely.

He had not the slightest doubt she meant it and knew she had an amazing repertoire of proofs. "So are you going to come back east tomorrow as planned? Or do you need to stay in Seattle until the legal issues are resolved?"

"Oh, Phil can look after all of that. You couldn't keep me away any longer. I can't wait to hold you again."

"You'll have to be a little gentle with me," he cautioned her.

"Well, you can do what you want with me," she assured him. "After all, I'm already the Marquess. Although," she added, "you might not be interested in that. Did you go up to the Berkshires for your fertility ritual yesterday?"

"I only made it as far as Walden," he confessed. "And I couldn't do anything."

"Are you feeling that bad?"

"Well, yeah," he admitted. "But mostly I guess I would rather save it for you."

"God, you old smoothie!" she said affectionately. "You always know just what to say to put my knickers in a knot."

He chuckled. "I never heard that expression before. Is that a good thing?"

"I'll show you after I get you alone tomorrow."

"You know, I'm not the man I used to be," he told her. "But if anything, I love you more than ever. You're about the only thing that keeps me going."

"Well, you're going to keep going if I have anything to say about it," she said firmly. "Oh, and before I forget, I wanted to tell you that Russ left a message for you on the answering machine. He called just before I got here."

"Did he say what he wanted?"

"He just asked you to call him back if you got the chance. He sounded pretty down."

"I'll have to give him a ring sometime."

"Why don't you call him now?"

"I don't know, hon," he said. "I told Carmen about the cancer and this drug trial and after that she talked to me like I was already dead. I hate making people feel that awkward."

"So don't tell him. He won't know where you're calling from. It might do you both a world of good to talk."

"Yeah, maybe you're right. Thanks, hon. I can't wait till you get here."

"Well, now you'll just have to, so nyehh! I'm sticking out my tongue in case you can't tell."

"Listen, you better watch—" But he could tell she had already hung up.

O   O   O

He smiled as he thought about her, then heaved a sigh and pulled himself upright in his chair. He took his address book from his briefcase and found Russ's number.

Russ said hello gloomily.

"Arnie Farquhar, please."

"Oh, hi, Matt," Russ said dully.

"Hey, cheer up, old man!" Matt kidded him, trying to sound light-hearted. "What's the good word?"

"I guess I'm fresh out of good words at the moment."

Matt could tell Russ was really upset. "What's wrong?"

"My dad passed away during the night."

That settled like a brick on Matt's heart. "Oh, jeez, Russ, I'm so sorry. Was this sudden?"

"Well, yes and no. He had emphysema, as you know, so his last few years have been pretty rough. He had started a whole new exercise regimen, though, and seemed to be feeling much better. But Mom said that during the night he just gasped for air a couple of times and was gone."

"How's she taking it?"

"Oh, no matter how much warning there is, I don't think anybody's ever really prepared. When you've been together most of your lives the way they have, it rips a great big hole in your life to lose your partner."

Matt couldn't help thinking about the gaping hole Deb faced but fought back those thoughts so he could deal with Russ. "How are you doing?"

"You know, I lost my grandparents when I was a little kid. This is the first time death has come right into my immediate family this way. Right now, I just feel numb."

"You and Louie were pretty close, weren't you?"

"Too close sometimes. We had trouble doing anything without stepping on each other's toes. But when you get used to pushing against somebody that way, you damn near fall on your face when they leave."

"When did you talk to him last?"

"That's part of what makes this so tough. Remember a couple of weeks ago—well, just before you and I spoke last, when I found out about my immotile sperm problem. Anyway, he and I got into a discussion of things at Tweak and in the heat of the moment I made a rather crude remark to him and he ended up hanging up the phone. I kept meaning to call him back, or maybe even go up to the farm in person to apologize, but with this mess with Sylvia, I just never got around to it. So the last conversation I had with my father was an argument."

"He probably forgot all about it."

"You don't know my dad the way I do—did."

Matt decided to change the subject. "How's Sylvia doing?"

"I think she got along with Dad better than I did most of the time. She seems pretty upset but then she's seemed upset for weeks now."

"So you two are still having problems?"

"God, Matt, why does love always have to be so complicated? I want to do whatever it takes to make *her* happy. She wants to do whatever it takes to make *me* happy. But neither one of us knows just exactly what it's going to take to make us happy. So neither one of us is happy or has the first clue what it's going to take to make the *other* happy. You know, a month ago, she wanted to have a kid in the worst way. Well, I think we've found the worst way."

"So you haven't resolved the issue of her first husband's sperm sample, I take it."

"I wish you would take it. We not only can't resolve that issue, we can't even talk about it. All she does on those rare occasions when she's here is to paint, which is good in a way, but we don't talk. I spend most of my waking moments trying to sort out the mangled mess Rolando made of the books at Tweak so I can get this thing on the market, so Syl and I don't talk. And now, with Dad gone, I'm going to have to go up to the farm and help Mom sort things out and make all the arrangements. Death seems as complicated as love at this point, with a lot of the same emotions."

"Except with death," Matt pointed out, "one of the parties already knows the outcome."

"It's getting to be obvious what the outcome of this thing with Sylvia will be. I mean, we're both realistic about it. As you and I discussed, all relationships end sooner or later. Syl and I have already slipped into that phase where you don't say anything too honestly for fear of 'ruining the friendship'."

"Sounds like you two are already looking past the marriage."

"I hate the phrase 'just friends', don't you?" Russ asked. "As though friendship doesn't require work and caring and compromise. The only advantage to being 'just friends' with someone is that, theoretically at least, you don't have to work on resolving your differences. You accept the limitations and adjust your feelings accordingly."

"It's better than nothing," Matt said.

"Better than nothing," Russ echoed gloomily. "Yeah, I suppose. Anyway, I better get up to the farm."

"Is Sylvia going with you?"

"No, she's still working on a new piece for her New Year's Eve opening in Dia."

"Sorry we won't be getting together that night."

"Yeah, it's too bad," Russ said. "Some part of me wanted to believe that Jason might actually show up after all these years. Maybe this is just my new-found realism talking but I'm starting to think you're right. Jason probably did die up in Jones Park that night like you've always said and I've just been clinging to that one faint ray of hope. It's time I start accepting the cold hard truth about things and quit relying on faith. Besides, even if I could get everything squared away at Tweak by New Year's, I really, as a *friend*, should go to Sylvia's opening that night. Sorry."

"Maybe it'll do you and Sylvia good to spend some time apart."

"Yeah, I thought of that. I'll probably stay up there a week. Mom and Dad had already packed to go to San Diego so I'll have to help Mom unpack and everything. I haven't told her about the trouble between me and Sylvia and I just can't now."

"What a mess, Russ. I'm sorry."

"The only bright spot lately has been that I've found someone who might be interested in taking Tweak off my hands. At this point I just want to get the hell out of the city. Maybe get some work done on that book."

"I did look through the rest of those old letters," Matt told him. "I don't think you could use much of it."

"Thanks for looking anyway, Matt. I can't believe you saved those for so long. Maybe that's the advantage to writing letters: they last. But I appreciate the call, too. Give my love to Deb."

"I will, and probably add some of my own to it. Again, I'm so sorry to hear about your dad. Give my best to your mom."

"Take it easy, Matt."

"I have no choice any more."

...O...O...O...

The first musical instrument I played was the clarinet, which lasted a couple of months until my mom came to see my grade school concert and noticed my fingers flying but no sound coming out.

So the folks asked me what instrument I really wanted to try and I immediately said drums. They cringed but bought me some Spitfire 7A sticks and gave me a Quaker Oats container to use them on.

I've come a long way since then but I still drum my fingers or tap my toes even when no one else can hear music. It drives people crazy. The best combination, one that undoubtedly dates to the beginning of time, is just palms on lower thighs. Some rhythms, some cadences, work there and nowhere else. A snare drum or a hand drum just won't do. Maybe it's because you close the circuit, you become drummer and drum. I don't know and, like most drummers, I don't care. If this idle drumming of my fingers drives you crazy, kindly accept this Bit of Crumb (this one's for you, Ed): "Get a bucket. Fill it with water. Set it on a chair. Dip your head in it three times and bring it out twice."

April 22, 1970

John stands straight, closes his eyes, tries to block out the reverberations. Wearing just trunks, he shakes his arms and legs to loosen up, the high board springy underfoot. He takes a deep breath. He leaps. The board sags under him, then propels him into space. He doesn't just sail, he flies, so high in fact that his back scrapes the ceiling, showers of branching, golden sparks cascading behind him. He looks down. Where he expected to see a pool, he sees instead a field of flowers with faces like cartoon animals: purple elephants, crimson horses, tawny lions, blue and white iguanas. The flowers sing to him in tinny harmony, Disney-ish, but he can't make out the words. He slowly drifts past them, his body brushing the ground and bursting into a myriad of iridescent drops and bubbles that cling to the flowers. The emcee, wiping splatters of John from his forehead, calls, "Wipers!"

John woke up tripping on Flagstaff Mountain above Boulder. The Yellow Fellow, parked with the convertible top down, surrounded him like a womb. To the east, through the dew-fogged windshield, the sky had begun to pale, a giant robin's egg lying on its side with a hint of the coming yolk at the horizon. It dawned on him that the word "wipers" hadn't come from the dream. His eyes swept in discreet increments up from the steering wheel toward the seat next to him, each increment a reality unto itself, a fleeting tableau too complex to comprehend, too intriguing to ignore, too beautiful to describe.

The last of the realities his eyes beheld was Jason, stock still, facing the sunrise, his unblinking gaze and gaping mouth testament to the wonders unfolding within and before him. The tangled fleece of his hair packed his head in golden excelsior. The dilated pupils of his sky-blue eyes revealed dark unplumbed depths. Cotyledons of week-old beard sprang from his face, nourished by the dew and fertilized by the thin coat of acid sweat. Ever so slowly, without altering his gaze, his mouth once again formed the word "wipers."

John's head lolled as his eyes drifted back to the wheel of the Fellow. His arms, exhausted from yesterday's swim meet, felt like lead as they rose. His left hand grasped the black wheel, his right turned the key in the ignition and started turning knobs until it found the one for the wipers.

The sudden mechanical motion of the wiper arms, the chatter of the rubber blades across the damp glass, scared the hell out of both of them. John quickly turned the knob back. The wipers died as suddenly as they had sprung to life. After a moment's silence, the "we're thru, through, throouuugh" of a mourning dove melted into the chilly air.

"Almost," Jason said, fixing his weary eyes on the horizon again.

John looked around and, in a terrifying moment of intense vertigo, realized how high they were. Around him, the lichen-crawling sandstone and bristly ponderosas and yuccas caught the dawn-light from the east, but below, the broad square of Chatauqua Park, the tree-smothered houses of the town, and the red-tiled roofs of the C. U. campus still lingered in deep shade. Below the horizon the fields of winter wheat looked black next to the glow of the sky. Above the horizon a raft of clouds faded from crimson to flame. John put both hands on the wheel to steady himself. He wanted to say, "This is intense." What came out sounded like "Unnghh."

"It's coming!" Jason croaked. Above them the treetops began to blush.

Right on the knife-edge between dark and light, some farmer's minuscule irrigation pipes suddenly burst into brilliant flame. "It's here!" John whispered in awe.

"It's greater than God," Jason testified as the navel of the sun's pregnant belly crept above the earth.

John groaned. There was more to that but he couldn't get his brain to wrap around it. "It's too early," John moaned. "Don't fuck with me."

"More evil than the Devil."

It was a riddle but at this point what the riddle was was a riddle too. John put his forehead on the steering wheel but couldn't keep his eyes closed. He opened his mouth to say something but the menacing whisper of a pick on a tremoloed Les Paul stopped him. Suspenseful chords, full steps apart, going down. I know this, John thought, shying away. But the tom-tom beats on three and four riveted him. The guiro came in, snaky and sharp, then the bass, rock solid on the same note through all three chords. The falsetto voices sliding down then back up a half step sent chills up his neck. Then flams on the snare on three and four again made escape impossible. Jagger, frowning, pointing, bellowed about the storm threatening his very life today.

Baffled about how this happened, John turned to Jason who, as it turned out, already looked back, just as bewildered. At least we seem to be hallucinating the same things, John thought. He found some comfort in it but the intensity of the music and the searing of the sunrise cowed him. He shivered as the first warm rays lifted the dew. The tide of sunlight surged down the slope before them, burning like a red coal carpet, heading for the sleeping town.

This Window Pane forces faith down your throat, John realized. Every moment is different, self-sufficient, resplendent. So intense, in fact, that you can't tell if there's going to be another moment afterward. You just have to let go and trust that the next moment will arrive in due time. The sun may *not* come up tomorrow but it's sure as hell coming up *now*.

Jason pulled his knees to his chest, squinting away the piercing rays. "I'm scared, man," he whispered.

"Me too," John said, even more frightened by the look on Jason's face.

"I don't know if I can do this," furrows deepening in his brow.

"We're doing this."

"If you eat it, you'll die."

"Fuck you."

Merry Clayton, big, black, taking no prisoners, belted out about rape and murder being just a shot away. Then she sang it to them again, her voice stabbing them, accusing them, knowing exactly who they were and what they wanted. Twisting the knife, she sang it one more time, this time her voice breaking on the word "murder," Jagger murmuring his approval in the background.

Jason looked bleakly up at the yellowing raft of clouds. "I can't do this."

John put his hand on Jason's shoulder, the jean jacket warm to the touch. "It's okay, man. We're gonna be fine."

"It's all too much."

"We're doing it together."

Jagger, relenting, crooned about love being just a kiss away, Clayton echoing him. And the kissing away became a refrain, repeated over and over, kissing love away over and over.

Then, without warning, a rift appeared in the space-time continuum. The two voices kept kissing one another away, a pop separating each iteration, the phrase ragged and torn. Then, as abruptly as it had begun, the music ended.

"Stop messing with my head," Jason pleaded, his hands on his temples.

"Me!?" John protested. "You're messing with *my* head!"

Another sonic dimension opened and a deep mellow voice said, "Sorry, kids. I didn't mean to mess with your heads so early."

John and Jason looked at one another in alarm, both ready to flee but unsure from what.

"Man, I should know better," the voice went on, sounding befuddled. It took a deep breath through pursed lips and fumbled around with something. "If I've told myself once, I've told myself…well, actually, if I've told myself once, I don't recall it at the moment. Anyway, I gotta remember to do this *before* I'm on the air." It took another deep breath.

"Radio," John and Jason realized simultaneously.

"I must have turned it on when I turned on the wipers," John said, welcoming the shred of rationality.

"KBLR's daylight only," Jason said.

"I don't believe it," the DJ said. "A seed popped out and landed right on 'Gimme Shelter.' Well, so much for that. This is, uh, KBLR, 1440 AM and it's 5:44, also a. m. My name is…oh, what difference does it make? After that opening, you'll probably be listening to someone else this time tomorrow. Oh well. Maybe I'll try FM next. Hang on." Another deep breath.

"A *seed* popped out?" Jason asked.

John shrugged.

"Anyway," the DJ went on, "for anybody insane enough to be awake already, we're staring into the bloodshot eyes of another day. You're on the Rock in Boulder. Hope you're planning something special for this first ever Earth Day, a day to celebrate this sweet swinging sphere we all share. But, please, let's not get so carried away in our revelations that we forget that all those other bipeds moping about are our brothers and sisters. Some folks got carried away up on the Hill last night and got carried away. So be cool, chillun. It's a day for gettin' together. Which many will be doing at the rally today honoring this brave new world. In case you haven't heard, the rally and concert have been moved from Mackey Auditorium to the Quad in front of Norlin Library to accommodate all you fabulous furry freak brothers. Zephyr, of course, will be playing, among many others, plus the possibility of some very special guests as well. Heads up for that. I may be there myself. Hell, I probably won't have to get up early tomorrow. Shit, I can't say 'hell' on the air, can I? Oh, man, this is too early. Tell you what. I'm gonna go back to what I was doing and you go back to what you were doing, which was listening to the Stones."

A muted trumpet, a quiet trombone, and a descending baritone horn played a goofy sounding Dixieland riff, followed by silence. Charlie's flam put an end to it, and then Mick rather drolly sang about something that had happened to him yesterday.

Those words had no sooner been sung than something unspeakably weird happened. A couple of quiet clicks on the metal of the open window sill next to John drew his attention away from the radio. He found himself face to face with a slender heap of flowing blonde hair and a pair of soulful brown mermaid's eyes. The next thing he knew, looping, leaping heaps of blonde hair swirled through the Yellow Fellow, flowing around both of them, engulfing them in heavy, complicated, odd-smelling, and occasionally painful tornadoes. John yelped. Jason shouted, "Jesus!"

A woman's voice called out "Baghlan! Qandahar! Kabul!"

John spun around and discovered a woman right behind the car looking at him. She had the same blonde hair and dark mermaid eyes as the dogs that the tornadoes turned out to be. She wore a homemade sweater made of knitted squares linked in a checkerboard of shimmering colors, flamingo-pink stretch pants, and tennis shoes. She patted her pink thighs and the dogs leapt from the car and mobbed her instead.

"Sorry," the woman said to John. "They go a little crazy first thing in the morning. You know how it is."

John nodded dumbly.

Jason said, "Nice dogs, lady."

"Come on, boys," she said and walked on down the road, twirlie and girlie.

John turned to Jason. "You think she means us?"

"Are we boys?" Jason asked, watching her walk away.

"Woo!" John howled as the woman disappeared. "Not for long."

"Rich people need it, you know."

"Please don't. Maybe we should head out," John suggested.

"My head can't go out any farther," Jason told him.

John pushed the ignition button of the Yellow Fellow and the motor roared to life. "But you have to help," he told Jason as he slowly pulled away from the cul de sac.

"Watch out for the chokecherries," Jason said as the yellow fender scraped the bushes.

"Is that what those are?" John said, easing out onto the pavement. "My mom makes chokecherry jam, you know."

"I know," Jason said. "Remember my slogan? Mama Kaufman's" deliberately coughing "puts the 'choke' into chokecherry jam." He looked brightly to John for a response.

"Poor," John said, focusing on the yellow line in the middle of the road, which seemed to float above the pavement, as did the shiny black strip down the middle of the lanes where the oil pans of people's cars had dripped. "Mighty poor."

"Poor people have it," Jason said.

"Not yet," John said, negotiating a downhill curve on Baseline Road. Something moving on the pavement caught John's eye and alarmed him. "What's that?"

"Ahead?" Jason asked.

"Is it mine?" John asked, peering forward, aiming the car toward the center of the dynamic streaming universe.

The object in the road turned into a magpie, white with black rainbows, the tail ruddering it toward some sumacs.

"We're flying," Jason said, hanging his arm out the window.

"This is incredible," John admitted.

"How fast are we going?"

"Help me steer while I look." Jason steadied the wheel while John peered at the speedometer. "Ten," he said. "No, twelve."

"What's your hurry?"

O   O   O

The rest of the drive back to Mind Machine Headquarters at the west end of Arapahoe Avenue, what with the honking of the early-rising tailgaters, the calculus required to determine whether it was safe to pull through an intersection, and the intensity of the pink Hopa crabapple trees and royal-purple irises along the way, seemed to take several harrowing, hilarious hours but probably lasted just a few minutes. John, relieved to have arrived, to have the initial rush of acid behind him, shut off the Yellow Fellow.

He had come up from Colorado Springs last night after his swim meet and he and Jason had left for Flagstaff in the dark this morning so John hadn't yet seen the Headquarters in daylight. Built near the turn of the century, the old frame house's white paint flaked and peeled and its front porch sagged, tilting the ragged couch that sat there. Dormers pierced the peaked roof and the crumbling brick chimney looked ready to fall at the first warm chinook. The lawn was yellow and faded but for the bright green rings the dogs had fertilized; a pride of dandelions, some already fluffy globes, lurked in the tall grass.

"Be it ever so humble," John said to Jason.

"Like I said, poor people have it."

"Oh, God," John said wearily.

"It's greater than God," Jason said.

"And more evil than the Devil," John remembered.

He had crashed on the slightly less funky couch in the living room and they hadn't gotten to sleep until 1:00 or 2:00, and then they got up at 5:00 to watch the sunrise. At some point last night, Jason had handed him, in addition to an antler pipe stuffed with an eighth of an ounce of marijuana, a riddle that John not only couldn't solve, he couldn't even remember in his previous, present, and, probably for several more hours, future state of mind.

They walked over and sat on the warped graying boards of the porch. Now that John didn't have to drive he could let his mind and eyes wander, a vast improvement. His eyes hurt from having seen so much already. He leaned down and picked up an old tennis ball, the graying fabric crusty with dried dog slobber. He bounced it against the uneven wood of the porch a couple of times.

"You know what's amazing?" Jason asked.

"Everything?" John guessed.

"And how it all fits together," Jason said. "Like that fellow walking up the street there. He could be our brother, couldn't he?"

John looked and saw Russ walking up the street, wearing tan chinos and a creamy white Indian shirt, his red hair wild and vivid in the early morning sun. He carried a sack slung over his shoulder. John threw the tennis ball at him and said his name.

Looking up, Russ somehow caught the ball without knowing it was coming or flinching at its arrival. Raising an eyebrow, he tossed it back to John. "Gentlemen," he said, stopping.

"Where you headed, brother?" John asked him.

"Across the universe."

"I know a short cut," Jason said.

Russ walked to the porch and sat next to him. "I thought you, being a walker, wouldn't mind taking the long way."

"When there's time," Jason said.

"There's always time," Russ pointed out.

"Indeed," John said.

"And word," Jason said.

"What's in the bag?" John asked Russ.

"Just the necessities of any wandering mendicant," he replied. "I thought I'd head up into the canyon and meditate this fine morning. My first class isn't until 1:00. What about you guys?"

Jason sighed. "I'm about to abandon all hope in school."

"And I'm between blocks," John told Russ, then asked, curious, "Just what *are* the necessities of a wandering mendicant?"

Russ pulled from the bag a rolled-up cylinder of straw matting and some small paper bags. "A *tatami*, raisins, piñon nuts, water, and some herbal tea I just bought."

"What's a *tatami*?" John asked.

"It's a Japanese mat made from rice straw," Russ said. "I sit on it when I meditate."

"'Sitting on a mat about to pray'!" John realized, recalling the line from the Stones song they'd heard earlier.

"You, sir," Jason told Russ, "are in tune with the universe."

"Wow," John said, amazed at the image of the universe's intonation. "Where do you have to stand to hear the tuning note?"

"The center?" Jason guessed.

"Ah," said Russ, nodding. "But the center of the universe is everywhere and the circumference nowhere."

"So Copernicus was wrong," Jason said. "The earth *is* the center of the universe. It's just not the *only* center."

"It's all in the eye of the beholder," Russ said, looking into Jason's eye. "Which looks pretty dilated."

"We dropped for the sunrise up on Flagstaff."

"Dropped what?"

"Window Pane," John said. "LSD. I have more, if you like."

"Today, I think not," Russ said, repacking his sack.

"Thank God great and good men like you are willing to patch up the holes we fuckheads kick in the universe," Jason said. "Can we offer you something in return? How about some hot water for the tea?"

Russ raised both eyebrows this time. "Perfect."

They traipsed single file through the living room to the kitchen, the house still quiet this early, the Mind Machine all traditionally late sleepers. John and Russ sat at the wobbly kitchen table while Jason filled the tea kettle with water and put it on to boil. He got out three battered mugs of different designs and set them on the table.

"How was sunrise?" Russ asked them, seeming both a- and bemused at their state of mind.

"Fantorrible," Jason said.

"And dogs too," John added.

"Did you get breakfast?" Russ asked them.

They both looked queasy at the thought. LSD didn't upset John's stomach the way mescaline did but it still made the very thought of food unbearable.

"But go right ahead," Jason offered to Russ. "Let me know if I can offer you anything."

"I'm fasting until after I meditate," Russ said, opening one of the paper bags and putting a thick pinch of tea into each cup.

"Meditate this," John said, inspired. "Jase, tell him that damned riddle."

The tea kettle sputtered and creaked while Jason rethought the phrasing. "Okay, are you ready?"

> What is greater than God
> More evil than the Devil
> Poor people have it
> Rich people need it
> And if you eat it, you'll die?

"Give us a hint," John said.

"It also makes up most of the universe," Jason said, which didn't help as much as John had hoped.

While Russ sat pondering, a door behind him opened and from some other part of the house came a slender young waif of a woman wearing nothing but white panties, her hair covering her eyes but not the pair of small bruises on her neck. Without a word or a look in their direction, she padded to the bathroom adjoining the kitchen. Trails of her small breasts flitted through John's mind. He looked at Jason to see if once again they were having simultaneous hallucinations.

Jason looked surprised too but said, "She's Bit. Little O's…"

"Oh," John said. Her name jived, considering the hickeys. Whatever you called her, she was certainly bit.

"Who is?" Russ asked.

"That mostly naked babe that just walked behind you," John told him.

Russ looked at him skeptically. "Uh-huh."

The tea water boiled. Jason got up and poured some into each cup, the fragrant steam floating up and tickling John's nose. He looked into the water and saw that small beige flowers had begun to bloom at the bottom of his cup.

Russ sat serenely with his palms on his thighs, his back straight, and his eyes closed. Bit walked out of the bathroom and went out through the door at Russ's back. John opened his mouth to say something about it but decided it would be futile.

"Anything?" Jason asked Russ.

Russ opened his eyes and looked calmly at Jason. "Anything?"

"About the riddle."

Russ closed his eyes again and said, "No, nothing."

"That's what I've come up with too," John said, feeling less a fool. He started to say, "I wish Matt was here," when Jason interrupted.

"Damn! You guys are good!" he exclaimed.

That reaction left John completely lost but he reminded himself that he was tripping after all and not everything would make sense. He took a sip of the tea, which tasted weak but fragrant, not sweet like roses but mature and heady.

"What kind of tea is this?" he asked Russ, who sipped some as well.

"Linden flower."

"That's what it is!" Jason said. "I knew I recognized that smell. Linden flowers always remind me of the turning point of the summer. When the lindens bloom, the downslope begins."

"Linden flower?" John asked in false incredulity. "We're already tripping our brains out on LSD and you give us L. F. T.?"

Jason laughed and shook his head. "You two are the bendin' end! It's too bad Matt isn't here. We could improvise a Piñon Nut Gathering."

"But Russ, like clever Odysseus, is never at a loss," John said, folding back the edge of Russ's sack. "He brought a proxy mat along just in case."

"Well, then we have a quorum," Jason said, raising his teacup. "To the Piñon Nuts!"

"Flower power," John said, tapping the cup and sipping some tea.

"Why don't you hang with us today?" Jason asked Russ. "We promise you won't have to baby-sit us the whole time."

"I need to find some peace and quiet to meditate," Russ said. "You guys are headed the other way."

"We've always been like that, haven't we?" Jason asked him. "Running around the same track in opposite directions."

"But we'll meet up with one another periodically," Russ pointed out, pushing back his chair and picking up his sack once more.

"Say hello to the Void for me," Jason told him.

O   O   O

After Russ left, the Mind Machine slowly clattered into gear. Mike, a grinning jack-o'-lantern with mad eyes, rolled noisily from his mattress upstairs and stumbled down the stairs, flipped on the TV (KWGN reran "My Mother, The Car"), and went into the kitchen to toast some pop tarts and start coffee. He and Jason traded inanities until Drugan—wavy blonde hair, athletic build under a tie-died T-shirt, and a feather sticking up from his head-band Indian-style—puttered up on an old beat-up Vespa, brought in a tool kit, and started taking apart the trap under the kitchen sink to try to find the missing section of his pipe. The ruckus roused rumpled, bleary-eyed Little O who, wearing a blue stocking cap and a parka to ward off the morning chill, came from the back room to get orange juice and cigarettes from the fridge for Bit. The clomp of heavy feet across the ceiling and down the stairs heralded the arrival of Igloo, stocky, swarthy, wearing a ratty bathrobe and heavy wool socks; he slouched on the couch and immediately fell back to sleep. A knock on the flimsy screen-door caused Mike to shout, "Moe! Lester!" Lester, skinny, unshaven, and barefoot, had the studied focus to his eyes of someone with lots of practice choosing between grasping the roach or the hallucination. Moe, short, jolly, energetic, with a pumpkin head and bulging beer belly, plopped a plastic bag of white pills on the coffee table in the living room and declared that anyone willing to count out hundred-lots could keep three per. Gary came out of the front bedroom—tall, clear-eyed, and well-groomed in a short-sleeved shirt and blue jeans, looking far too straight and normal—and proceeded to ream out and reload the antler pipe. The screen-door slammed and in walked Apple Annie, a chunky woman with wild hair, sagging breasts, and a raspy voice (with a "fuck" in every phrase); she wore a stained and wrinkled square-dancing dress and carried a sleeping bag under her arm, complaining about the morning's heavy dew. Drugan, having found the missing piece of his pipe, started it in competition with the antler pipe. Bit, dressed now in shorts and a tube top, followed shyly in Little O's wake. Her name, it turned out, came from "Bit O' Honey," her father's pet name for her. She looked around and then lit several sticks of incense (champa, lotus) to try to counteract the various smells emanating from all the guys in the room. John had taken Moe up on his offer, carefully separating five white barrels at a time into little teams and dropping 20 teams into a baggie, taking three for himself from the pile and putting them in a separate baggie, the LSD coating his fingers and working into his bloodstream. Gary turned down the sound on the TV and put on an album. The room filled with the Sunday morning sounds of John Paul Jones's Hammond B-3 at the start of the second side of Led Zeppelin's first album. Mike, cleaning a big bag of dope, tossed one of the seeds into Igloo's open robe, which several people turned into a contest, Igloo's undershirt soon peppered with round seeds but his sleeping brain blissfully unaware. John discovered that he was no longer assembling groups of five but just staring at the same five white barrels and watching the hallucinated numerals scroll across his vision. He also discovered, with Drugan's help, that he was bogarting Drugan's pipe, which Drugan replaced with an issue of *Zap Comix* John hadn't yet seen. Soon the hullabaloo around him and Robert Plant's screaming about a communication breakdown faded to the pounding of surf as his mind wandered down the bizarre, brutal, blind back alleys of R. Crumb *et al.*, absorbing a bizarre tale of pervert *vs.* dyke pirates, a bearded Flakey Foont emulating Mr. Natural, and some odd abstract panels of Mickey Mouse cartoonery ambiguous in every kind of orientation until first the sneaking suspicion and then the frightening certainty crept over him that somehow the comic book that had so intrigued him for some time now was in fact upside down and backward. He looked around to see if everyone was laughing at him but everyone seemed as oblivious to him as he had been to them. He leafed to what he thought was the end of the comic, the drawings still upside down, the stories regressing toward their beginnings. The back cover, righted, became the front cover of yet another edition of *Zap Comix* he hadn't yet seen, labeled No. 3. He started reading from that direction, only to find that about halfway through, the cartoons began to take on a familiar, if upside down, feel. Before he knew it, he found himself leafing through the stories in the first comic, only upside down and backwards. Disoriented, he asked of no one in particular, "Who wrote this?"

"No one," Mike answered.

John looked up at him. Mike had taken a hit and couldn't say more. Gary, standing tall and amused, patiently explained: "It's a cartoon. It was drawn, not written."

"Who drew it then?" John asked.

"You did," Drugan said. "It was your turn. Sorry. Luck of the draw."

"No," John said, getting more confused. "Isn't someone supposed to read over something like this and make sure this sort of thing doesn't happen?"

"Someone did," Bit assured him.

"Who?"

"Ed."

"Ed?"

"Sure. You know. You're reading along in some book and you come upon a little number raised above the line, and the same little number is at the bottom of the page with a note that says something like, 'Johnson, Sinclair, *et al*, refute this' or 'The Battle of Hastings, 1066,' and then there's a dash and it's signed by Ed. He's the one who edits all the books."

"So you're saying…" John said, hesitant to try.

"That's right," Bit told him, smiling benignly.

"Try," Gary encouraged him.

John tried: "Ed edited it." [1]

---

[1] This joke, we've discovered, doesn't appear in some of the early, non-existent "Alternate Reality" versions of this book. The author wanted it deleted but frankly, he no longer has any say in the matter and we thought it was kind of a funny bit. Sorry for the intrusion.

— Ed.

"Funny, Bit," Little O told her.

John tried it again: "Ed edited it." It wasn't easy. It rolled trippingly on the tongue but he couldn't seem to say it in such a way that it had any rational meaning, just a nonsensical, if enjoyable, rhythm. He started repeating it as a sort of marching cadence, looking around to see if Jason would join in. But Jason had disappeared.

John stood up and then sat right back down. He must have taken a toke or two because a cloud of silliness had fogged the startling clarity of the acid. The lack of food and sleep made him light-headed. He realized that in this smoke-filled roiling room full of freaks he knew not a soul. More carefully this time, he got up and asked if anyone had seen Jason.

"The J-man? Might be up in his room."

"He might be on the seventh moon of Jupiter, too."

"Naw. He went to the shitter and the hogs ate him."

John carefully stepped over the people and things cluttering the living room floor and climbed the steep narrow stairs to Jason's room. The landing at the top, just a couple of feet wider than the mattress shoved against the wall, belonged to Mike. A doorway led to Jason's room and beyond that at a right angle another doorway led to Igloo's, where the chirping of birds came through a broken window. A sheet of cheap Indian fabric thumb-tacked to the low ceiling defined Jason's space, which accommodated just a mattress on the floor like Mike's and a few boxes overflowing with books and clothes. Not finding Jason, John went back downstairs. He peeked in Gary's room, the walls painted black, aluminum foil over the window, black light posters on the walls, and constellations of day-glo paint dots on the ceiling. He checked the front porch and found only Little O and Bit on the lawn playing touch football without a ball. John picked his way carefully back through the living room to the kitchen, checked the john, then wandered through the door Little O and Bit had come through earlier. They slept, as it turned out, in the old root cellar of the house, sunken below ground level, damp and chilly, with fieldstone walls and wood shelves still lined with empty canning jars. Jason wasn't there either but John could hear a guitar.

Going out the back door, he found Jason sitting with his back against the wall of the house, strumming and singing the refrain from "Across The Universe:" "Nothin's gonna change my world, nothin's gonna change my world." He had taken off the jean jacket in the warm morning sun and now wore just a T-shirt with the word "Balls" printed in large letters across the chest, thin sailor's bell-bottoms studded with silver stars, and moccasins.

"Yo, bro," John said, relieved to find him. "How's it going?"

Still playing the chords, Jason said, "I mean it, Johnnie—Nothin's gonna change my world—I can't seem to get out of this—Nothin's gonna change my world."

John damped the strings with his hand and Jason gratefully stopped. He set Steve's old beat-up guitar aside and said, "Thanks, man. I couldn't figure out a way to quit doing that."

"Why didn't you just stop?"

"Easy for you to say," Jason pointed out, "You know the solution. Did you ever hear about Columbus and the egg?"

"Do tell."

"Some guest at a dinner party once pointed out to Columbus that if he hadn't discovered the New World, someone else would have."

"'It was wonderful to find America'," John quoted *Pudd'nhead Wilson*, "'but it would have been more wonderful to miss it.'"

"Right. So Columbus challenged someone to make a hard-boiled egg stand on a table without anything like salt to support it. When they gave up, Columbus took the egg, flattened the shell on the wide end a little and made it stand that way."

"Proving…"

"Proving, I guess, that nobody's as hard-boiled as the man who's been there and back."

"Speaking of being there, when does the Earth Day thing start?" John asked.

"When we get there. Are we taking the Fellow?"

"Why not?"

"You smoked, didn't you?"

"I guess."

"I can tell. A veil has come down. Can you drive?"

"Not alone."

As soon as word got out that John was driving his convertible to campus, everyone in the living room, most of them tripping, all of them high, volunteered to let him take them too. By the time John pulled out of the driveway, people were stacked two and three deep in the seats with a couple of guys lying belly-down on the trunk, holding onto the back seats to keep from falling off. There wasn't much danger: the Yellow Fellow's 20-year-old automatic transmission struggled to pull the extra weight. They did okay on the gentle down-grade of Arapahoe but then stopped for a stoplight with the prospect of a right turn up a slope to get to the Hill.

John waited for the light to change, then thought that maybe it *had* changed, but he also recognized the possibility that he had just started hallucinating in a different color. Peering at it, he decided to ask for a second opinion. "Which one's lit?"

"I am," somebody said.

"Me too," came a second.

"The lights, I mean," John clarified.

"One of them is green," another offered.

"But which one?"

"The red one."

"Are you sure that's red?" came another voice. "It looks yellow to me."

"The middle one's always yellow."

"I think the middle one looks kind of lavender with little black dealies."

"Ooo, yeah, I see what you mean."

"The top one just changed."

"To what?"

"The bottom one."

"Yeah, but what color?"

"Color shouldn't matter. Just the content of your character."

"What if you're yellow?"

"Better red than dead."

"I feel green."

"But what about the lights?"

"Who cares how the lights feel?"

John, exasperated, said, "Okay, folks, let's have a show of hands."

They all stuck their hands in his face.

"What difference does it make what color our hands are?"

"Maybe they're trying to catch us red-handed."

"Okay," John sighed. "How many of you think the light is green?"

"Close enough," they all agreed, so he made the turn.

As it turned out, the Yellow Fellow only made it half a block up the hill before grinding to a halt so all the freaks but John and Jason piled out and pushed. The Fellow, so much lighter, flew up the grade. Everyone waved them a cheery good-bye. But John got only a couple of blocks closer to campus when he realized that parking spaces were few and far between. He circled around and finally found one on Pleasant but by the time he had maneuvered the bulky Chevy into the narrow space, the rest of the Mind Machine had caught up with them, thanking him for the ride and patting the Yellow Fellow's warm hood.

Leaving the top down, John and Jason walked behind the Mind Machine along Pleasant Street, the old concrete of the sidewalks tilted by the roots of the tall silver maples. The sun had burned away the haze and the morning warmed rapidly. Against the half-pillared porches of the old Victorian homes, most of the daffodils had withered but the tulips offered their glowing cups to the sun and the bees. Robins, disturbed from their worming by the rambunctious gaggle of freaks, glided up into the lilac bushes, where deep purple buds clustered like grapes against the fresh new leaves. Children gamboled and hooted, oblivious to all around them. Pleasant indeed.

John watched as Little O put his arm around Bit's waist as they walked. "Nice to see a bit of Bit this morning," he mentioned to Jason.

Jason looked at him. "Mary Jane's whispering in your ear, isn't she?"

"Oh, I don't have to get high to appreciate that," John pointed out. "I never saw a tit I didn't like. Besides, you looked too."

"They are bitty, aren't they?" Jason observed.

"But a bird in the hand."

"True."

"How are you doing, women-wise?"

Jason snorted. "Wise, I'm not."

"But women?"

"I've had to."

"We've all had to sooner or later."

"No, I mean I've had *two*," Jason specified.

John looked at Jason in wonder and admiration. "At once?"

"Hah! Gimme a break."

"But you're juggling them."

"No, I mean I've been with two women now."

"Total?"

Jason glanced at him as they turned right onto 13th Street to go to the Hill. "I'm deprived, you're depraved. What's new?"

John had always assumed that Jason did at least as well as John when it came to women. Rather than press the issue, he said, "So tell me about this latest conquest."

"Well, the last few weeks I've brought my guitar to campus to try to scare up some pocket money. Last Friday this chick comes along and sits down next to me and starts singing along. She turned out to be pretty good, actually, and an interesting person, having been a Haight-Ashbury hippie for three years until she came here to go to school."

"Why Colorado?"

"Her mother was Mexican and her father Irish and they never got along. Jessica—at least that's what she's been calling herself lately—was raised by her grandmother, who lives in Alamosa, so Jessica qualifies as a resident and a minority. Anyway, she liked my music and I liked her singing and we kind of hit it off. She's got a place up on 10th so we ended up having dinner here at the Sink, listening to 'Layla' on the jukebox."

They crossed Pennsylvania and stopped in front of the Sink, a small, brick, corner storefront smelling of burgers and stale beer. A burly football player, wearing a C. U. Buffaloes T-shirt, manned the door.

"What's the Sink like?" John asked Jason.

"Excellent burgers, cold beer. Picnic tables with initials carved on top of initials. Once in a while they have a band in the deepest part of the catacombs."

"Do you want to go in? Have a beer?"

"I don't have my I. D."

They walked up and asked the burly bouncer, who looked at them and, without a word, ever so slightly shook his head.

"So anyway," John said as they ambled on up 13th, "tell me about this Jessica."

"I don't know that she's exactly my type but when that sad piano part at the end of 'Layla' came on, I got feeling so lonesome I figured what the hell. We had a few beers and then hitched a ride out to the Mind Machine Headquarters. She's different, I'll say that. We started playing and I showed her some stuff and she showed me some stuff and pretty soon it was morning."

"You dog!" John said. "Way to go! Could this be the start of something big?"

"She's a kick in the ass," Jason admitted. "But she's living with a guy. She said they aren't involved but she doesn't have to pay rent."

"Ah. So much for that."

Jason shrugged, speaking volumes.

"Maybe this isn't my business," John said, "but what about Manny? I thought I detected some sparks on New Year's."

"Oh, there were sparks," Jason said. "But sparks die out in a hurry. I don't know. Maybe Man and I travel to the beat of a different drum."

"Linda Ronstadt and the Stone Ponies, right?"

"Not anymore," Jason said. "Ronstadt played right here at Tulagi's a few weeks ago with some other back-up band. Jessica said a couple of the guys in the band sang like birds. Better than birds, in fact. Eagles."

"Eagles are terrible singers," John noted, looking up at the tin-plate ceiling on the marquee, the name Tulagi's spelled out in lights on the flagstone facade of the building.

"Still, the Eagles would be a better name than Dog Walker and the Beagles, which you guys were trying to pawn off on me over Thanksgiving."

"Anyway, what's the problem with Manny?"

"For one thing, she wasn't entirely straight with me."

"Who wants a straight woman?"

"You know what I mean. And just when I thought we had grokked one another, she writes me this letter a couple of months ago pissing and moaning about Bill Black and how he 'let her down.' I just feel like I'm not getting anywhere with her."

"That's not the impression I got," John told him. "When I told her I was coming up here today, she made a big point of asking how you were and wanting me to tell you hi and all that. Maybe you're making inroads you're not even aware of."

"Oh, yeah, women can't stay away—far enough, that is."

"Come on, man. It's spring—"

"—when a young man's love turns to fancy."

They had crossed College Avenue and stood by the Flatirons Theater waiting for the light to change. Across the intersection diagonally, the small restaurant on the corner had plywood covering a couple of the windows.

"Did you guys get a storm up here?" John asked Jason.

"Not that I know of," Jason said as they crossed 13th. "Let's go in here. There's an excellent record store."

College Corner, a small block of shops under one roof, had two levels and John and Jason went downstairs. The record store, called Ear Wax, was cramped and dark, with black-light posters of Jimi Hendrix, Steve Miller, and the Grateful Dead on the walls and the cartoonish, eerie music of the Moon Trip on Lothar and the Hand People's album flowing from the stereo. Walking down the street in the sun, John had almost forgotten he was tripping. It came back with a rush in here and when they caught one another ooo-ing and ahh-ing over trippy album covers, they decided they'd better find some more normal surroundings.

They headed next door to Doozy Duds, a coin-operated laundry. Jason gravitated to the front-loading washers, where other people's jeans and towels and underwear sloshed around in the suds. John looked around at the other patrons, most sitting and reading or folding laundry. John's eye landed on one guy, older, with sharp features and a long gray ponytail, talking to a couple of younger guys, one as tall and lean as Ichabod Crane, the other as chubby and squishy as Poppin' Fresh, the Pillsbury Dough Boy.

John sidled over to Jason. "See that older guy over there?" he asked quietly.

Jason looked as discreetly as he could. "Yeah?"

"That's Timothy Leary."

Jason looked again, discretion forgotten. "Get outta town. You're hallucinating."

"I know a hallucination when I don't see one," John said. "That's Timothy Leary. I saw him on the news the other night."

Jason looked once more. "Maybe you're right. It does look like him. And I did hear he was going to speak in Boulder sometime this month."

"I'm going to go over and talk to him."

"And say what?" Jason wanted to know, following.

"I have no idea," John said. "But when am I going to get another chance?"

Leary's penetrating eyes gazed at the floor as he listened intently to what Ichabod was saying. He had the self-assured air of the other college professors John knew. "I thought this thing was supposed to be in Mackey Auditorium," he said to Ichabod as John and Jason approached.

"Well, we're having this big Earth Day rally on the Quad…" Poppin' Fresh told him obsequiously.

"Oh, what the hell," Leary said, shrugging. "It doesn't really matter."

John and Jason looked at one another, recognizing the phrase. The others quit talking and Leary looked at John.

"It's you, isn't it?" John said, immediately feeling like a dweeb.

"And it's you too," Leary pointed out to him.

"What are you doing here?" John asked.

"Laundry," Leary replied, getting a little impatient.

"Well, thanks for being here," John said.

"And thank you for being wherever you are," Leary said, smiling as he recognized the acid vibe emanating from John.

Inspiration struck. "Do you need some acid?" John offered, digging into the pocket of his jeans for the baggie of white barrels he'd gotten from counting Moe's stash.

"Sweet mother of pearl!" Leary hissed, glancing around circumspectly and pushing John's hand back into his pocket before he got out the baggie. "I'm quite self-sufficient, thanks. Why don't you boys run along?"

"Sorry," Jason said to Leary, pulling on John's arm. "Keep up the good work."

Jason hustled him back out onto College Avenue, the wash of bright colors the sunshine brought and the little exchange he had just had with Leary leaving John feeling a little dazed. They headed east toward the campus.

"I've got hand it to you, man," Jason said. "Trying to turn Timothy Leary on to some acid. That's either the coolest or the dumbest thing I ever saw."

"Coals to Newcastle, I know," John said. "But it's the thought that counts."

"What happened here?" Jason asked, stopping, looking across the street at the windows of the University Book Store, cracked or covered with plywood.

"That must have been a hell of a storm," John said.

"Who was it?" Jason said, thinking. "Oh, the DJ this morning was talking about people getting carried away on the Hill last night. I wonder if this was what he was talking about."

"It'd have to be a regular riot to do something like that."

"Not too regular, I hope," Jason said as they headed across Broadway toward campus.

O   O   O

"I am a stranger to this realital university," John told him, looking around at the two- and three-story flagstone-fronted buildings of the University of Colorado.

"Let's take the long way then," Jason said, veering right.

They walked past a building marked "Education" and through a stone gateway to the south side of horseshoe-shaped Hellems. Scaffolding cluttered a flat stage area facing the flagstone benches of a small amphitheater bounded by the walls of the buildings.

"Theater of the absurd?" John asked.

"It's the Rippon. Shakespeare spends summers here."

"When it comes to the absurd," John observed, "better a Rippon than a rip-off."

The scaffolding crew seemed to have broken for lunch and there were few other people around. "Where is everybody?"

"'All the spirits are melted into thin air'," Jason said.

"From?"

"*The Tempest*," Jason said. "One of Uncle Willie's last and, in my opinion, one of his best. Tomorrow's his birthday, you know."

John walked to the edge of the stage, jumped down, and sat out on one of the stone benches. "Remember that all-nighter up in Cheyenne Cañon?" he asked Jason.

"Who could forget?"

"So lay some Uncle Willie on me."

"Oh, what's the rest of that?" Jason said, wandering around the stage. "Something about the great globe dissolving—that's it:

> "And, like this insubstantial pageant faded,
> Leaves not a rack behind. We are such stuff
> As dreams are made on, and our little life
> Is rounded with a sleep."

John clapped, Jason bowed, passers-by stared. Like the other spirits, John and Jason melted into thin air.

"This is the fabled U. M. C.," Jason pointed out as they entered a small square. A large fountain in the center spouted 13 jets of water.

"Umk?" John asked.

"University Memorial Center. Upstairs is the Glenn Miller ballroom—"

"Glenn Miller?"

"An alum of this fine school—and downstairs is the Alferd G. Packer Grill, named for the only man in the U. S. ever convicted of calibanism."

"Cannabalism?"

"Like I meant. So when he had friends for dinner… Say, you hungry?"

"Not any more. So where's the Quad?"

"Past these linden trees."

"As in L. F. T.?"

"You are what you drink."

The next two buildings they passed reeked of thousands of undergrad chem-lab experiments gone awry. Beyond the second, Ekeley, they came to the Quad, half as wide but twice as long as a city block, essentially an open grassy mall with large leafy trees on either side. Some of the older buildings around the Quad reflected other architectural styles like brick walls and pitched slate roofs but all the newer buildings conformed to the motif of flagstone facades and Spanish tile roofs. Norlin Library, at the east end of the Quad, followed that same pattern, with the addition of half a dozen tall square stone columns at the entrance.

People already had begun to collect on the lawn in front of the library, sitting in small groups, studying, chatting, a few tossing frisbees. Three Black guys had set up their congas on the library steps and the liquid rhythms flowed out across the square. From a truck parked nearby came amplifiers, speaker cabinets, cables, and the other equipment a band requires, hauled by roadies and musicians alike up the steps of the library and placed under the colonnade. A couple of campus police cars were parked on the walk as well, the uniformed officers talking to the organizers of the rally, two of whom John recognized as Ichabod Crane and Poppin' Fresh.

"Where should we sit?" Jason asked.

"Might as well get close," John said.

They sat on the south edge of the Quad, next to a small concrete sluice through which ran a quick shallow stream of water, used to irrigate the huge lawn. They sat cross-legged, drumming their hands on their thighs to the conga rhythms.

John had met Jason when both were drummers in grade school. Music, and drumming in particular, formed the basis of their friendship and though they shared many other things, John never felt more in the groove of the cosmic jam than he did right now with the give and take of their improvised rhythms weaving in and out of the background of the congas.

John put his head back, feeling the sun on his face, the bright red light that penetrated his eyelids broken by the LSD into never-ending streams of patterns and shapes. They had swallowed the Window Pane at 5:00 this morning, so now, six or seven hours later, John had passed the peak and begun to mellow.

When he opened his eyes and blinked his vision clear, he found Jason, predictably, watching the activities in the stage area at the entrance to the library even while he maintained the rhythms with his hands. "Well, I'll be damned," he said to himself.

"Then what hope is there for me?" John asked him, playing a three-against-two figure to Jason.

"Remember Jessica?"

"Your hippie chick?"

"I don't know that she's mine," Jason said, ceasing his drumming. "Anyway, she told me a bunch of stuff about herself that I took with big gobs of salt."

"Like what?"

"Oh, the whole Haight-Ashbury thing. She claimed she had an affair with the lead guitar player for Jefferson Airplane."

"No shit?"

"So she said. She also claimed to have slept with the lead singer of Zephyr, the band that's setting up."

John looked to the stage, where bewildered library-goers edged around the drums and hopped over cables. A few of the people on stage wore bright shiny clothes and were probably the performers but John couldn't tell one from another. "Which one's the lead singer?"

"See the skinny chick with the wild shock of curly brown hair?"

"Uh-huh." When Jason didn't say more, John looked at him. "You mean she and Jessica...?"

"That's what Jessica said."

"I see what you mean about the salt."

"I don't know now. See the chick next to her with the wire-rim glasses and the tie-dyed tank top?"

"Are you serious? That's Jessica?"

"So she says."

"But she's not part of the band, right?"

"Not that I know of but she is up there in any case."

"Well, you dog! So Zephyr's a local band? Any good?"

"I've heard them a couple of times. Yeah, they're not bad. They carry that big old B-3 with them and the drummer has some nice licks. Candy, the lead singer, tends to screech a little but she can really belt out a blues song."

John looked at his friend with a new appreciation. John considered himself sexually adventuresome but as far as he knew, the women he had been with had previously only been with other men. Candy and Jessica both seemed on the slight and scrawny side for John's taste but he found the thought of the two women making love intriguing, partly because it was taboo, but also because of the obvious status of these two women. Jason may be a dog, he thought, but he's running with the better bitches.

"So aren't you going to go up and say hello to her?" he asked Jason.

"I don't know," Jason said, shaking his head. "They're obviously busy up there. Besides, she's probably forgotten all about me by now."

"Inroads, man, inroads," nudging him with his elbow. "Who knows where it could lead?"

"Come on," Jason said, discouraged. "Her life is complicated and mine's a mess."

"So what have you got to lose?"

He shoved Jason's shoulder so hard Jason fell over. But he got to his feet and looked up at the stage. "Maybe you're right," he said. "It doesn't really matter, does it?"

"What's the worst that can happen?"

"Wish me luck."

"I wish you well, brother."

"See you."

He watched Jason shuffle up the sidewalk and over to the library steps by the congas, trying to look casual. Jessica called him up the steps and introduced him to Candy and they stood chatting for a few minutes while the technicians turned on the P. A. system and started testing it. John leaned back with his elbows on the grass, proud of himself for helping Jason overcome his shy nature.

The flat stream of water flowing down the little sluice beside him drew John's attention. By now the sun felt quite warm and he trailed his fingers in the cool water to let it carry away not only the excess heat but also the stress of school and swimming. After he'd watched the water flow awhile, he began to feel like the world flowed past the other way.

As he watched, a tiny boat made of paper came zipping down the sluice. He instinctively pulled it out and unfolded it, expecting it to be someone's lunch receipt or something.

To his amazement, the paper was blank but for a couple of penciled words. To his greater amazement, the words were "Hi, John."

"Just when you think the trip is over," he said to himself, wondering again at the baffling ways of the universe. He looked upstream for the source of the note.

Many more people, on their lunch break probably, had sat on the Quad behind him. Sitting much farther back but next to the sluice sat Prudence, who waved to him. He got up and went back to her.

He hadn't seen her since New Year's Eve but he had seen almost everything there was to see that night. He had barely pulled *Pudd'nhead Wilson* from the shelf before her hands were all over him, her lips nibbling his neck. He had some scruples about getting involved with a woman who lived with one of his best friends but she assured him quickly and emphatically that she and Russ wouldn't last three more weeks. John took her at her word—which proved true after all—and took her, a couple of times in quick succession, in fact. They had parted cordially but had only communicated with one another a couple of times since. This was an unexpected bonus.

"Hey, Prude," he said when he got back to where she sat.

"Hi, John," she said, standing and giving him a long, sensual hug. She wore a light cotton shift with bright Peter Max flowers, a turquoise belt, and sandals. She smelled like flowers— carnations, maybe?

"You smell as good as you look," he said softly in her ear as they hugged. "What is that?"

"Hi, John," she told him.

He looked at her to see if she too was part of the universal conspiracy to blow his mind.

"Seriously," she said. "Not 'Hi, John'," waving, "High John," putting her hand over her head.

"Very much, thank you," he admitted, completely confused.

"It's an essential oil from a root called High John the Conqueror Root. I found it at an herbalist's here in Boulder. He said they talk about it in old blues songs. It's supposed to bring luck in gambling."

"What about in love?" he asked, relishing the way her torso had conformed to his.

"Is there a difference?"

"It depends on whether you're wagering your money or your jewels, I suppose," he said as they sat down. "How've you been?"

"Missing you," she told him.

"We saw Russ this morning," he mentioned, broaching that subject.

"I thought I heard him get up early," she said nonchalantly.

"I heard you two split. I hope it wasn't because of New Year's Eve."

"Heavens, no! It was about to fall apart anyway. So where are you staying?"

"I'm crashing on the couch at Mind Machine Headquarters. Unless I get a better offer."

"I'd love to invite you but it might prove just too awkward. I don't suppose there's room on the couch for two?"

"Depends what position they're in."

"I know a few we didn't get a chance to try. But where's Jason?"

"He's up on stage talking to someone he knows."

"Oh, yeah, I see him."

John hadn't looked on stage in a while and it startled him to see Jason standing near one of the microphones with a guitar strapped over his shoulder, evidently helping with the sound check by strumming chords, D to G, against the background of the congas. Jessica, though, leaned over and urged him on, to sing something probably. He stepped up to the mike and sang the opening words of "Change Is Now" from *Notorious Byrd Brothers*.

"Is he tripping too?" Prudence asked.

John thought they'd been pretty subtle. "How did you know?"

"Your eyes, for one thing," Prudence told him. "And the way you were playing in the water earlier, like you'd never seen such a thing before."

"I never got water mail before."

Jason, at Jessica's insistence, went on to the second verse of the song.

"I can't believe he's doing this," John said, thunderstruck.

"This song?" Prudence asked.

"This is a Byrds song so that's not that weird. But just getting up there and playing. I can't imagine being able to play tripping."

"You're playing and tripping," Prudence pointed out.

John had begun drumming on his thighs again. "That's just my nature."

"He sounds pretty good, tripping or not," Prudence said.

"Maybe it's like those spiders," John said.

"Spiders?" Prudence asked.

"They did this experiment where they gave spiders different kinds of drugs to see the effect on the webs they spun. Some were predictable: speed made them spin the whole web right at the center, downers put them to sleep before they finished. But the surprise was LSD. Normally, spiders spin a pretty good web but with a few flaws. On acid, they spun perfect webs."

"Maybe it just reveals their true nature."

Even from this far away, John could tell Jason had closed his eyes and lost himself in the rhythms of the music. Some of the people near the stage had taken up the challenge to "dance to the day when fear is gone," standing up and letting the music possess their bodies, cavorting, writhing, boogying with eyes closed and ears wide open. Jason opened his eyes, saw them, and, evidently out of words, kept the chords and rhythm going.

"Since you're tripping, I guess there's no point in asking you if you want to get high," Prudence said to John.

"There's always a point," he said, drumming along on his legs. "But I don't have any reefer."

Prudence reached into her purse and pulled out a small baggy with some marijuana in it.

"Or a pipe," John said, hoping the result would be as good.

Prudence took out a small brass kazoo which she handed to John. The wax paper had been removed from the sound hole and replaced with a screen. Prudence put a pinch of weed into the bowl of the kazoo and handed it to John. He pulled out his Zippo and lit it, telling her as he handed it back, "I do have some acid, if you're interested."

Her eyes lit up. "What kind?"

"Some white barrels. I don't know how strong it is."

"I'll split one with you."

John carefully reached into the baggy in his pocket and pulled out a tab of acid. He broke it in two and handed her half, swallowing his half with a long swig from the bottle of 7-Up she offered him.

A murmur and some scattered applause rippled through the crowd as someone stood atop one of the speaker columns and slapped a homemade drawing of a flower onto the facing above the library's colonnade. The Cicero quote engraved there—"Who knows only his own generation remains always a child"—now had a flower before the "child."

By this time, a roadie was making the final adjustments to the drum set, another testing the bass amp, so Jason and the conga players, reluctant to desert the dancers, cut their volume to a vamp. Ichabod Crane, sensing the lull, stepped up to the microphone.

"Happy Earth Day, Boulder!" he shouted and John recognized his voice as that of the DJ they'd heard on Flagstaff Mountain this morning.

The crowd yelled back.

"You folks have an excellent show in store for you this afternoon. Zephyr will be out in just a couple of minutes and later on we'll have the Sons of Champlin, plus some very special guests, including this guy—" he leaned over and asked Jason his name, chuckled, and said "—Dog Walker. I'd just like to thank everyone who helped put this special day together, especially Dennis Hayes, who came up with the idea of celebrating this great globe we call home." He glanced up at the hand-drawn flower on the facade. "I might add: flower power is great but after we've been raping Mother Earth for a couple of centuries, we may have to do more than just send her flowers."

Jason, still standing nearby, leaned into the microphone and said, "We could start by getting America out of this fucking war in Vietnam!"

The crowd roared its agreement.

Ichabod looked to the side of the stage where his fellow organizers stood and threw up his hands. "What do you want to do?" he asked them, his voice caught by the microphone.

"Rock and roll!" somebody in the crowd bellowed, and immediately got dozens of seconds.

Jason, seizing the moment, played some double stops on the guitar and looked to the roadie on the drums, who recognized the intro to Creedance's "Fortunate Son" and started playing along, the bass player picking it up easily as well. Before they got to the second verse, though, a loud thump came through the P. A. system and the amplifiers went dead, only the drums and conga playing on, the tempo and volume pushed up by the song. The crowd let out a disappointed moan. Jason looked around the stage but seemed to find nothing but confusion.

"What happened?" Prudence asked John, her hand on his shoulder.

"Oh, somebody probably just tripped over the power chord," John said, sitting cross-legged still, the beat of the congas still impelling his hands on his thighs.

"Doesn't that hurt?" she asked him, watching his hands flail away.

"Naw," he said, the dope they'd smoked making it easy, almost imperative, to get lost in the rhythms.

"Show me then," she said, lying on her side in front of him, facing away, with her butt tucked between his knees. "Let me feel your nature."

He transferred the rhythms to her hip and upper thighs, his hands enjoying the smoother texture of her cotton dress and the softer resilience of her body. He closed his eyes and, for a few fleeting moments that seemed to last a lifetime, imagined himself in paradise.

She broke the spell when she shifted, rolling onto her back. He opened his eyes. She smiled so he just kept going, the rhythms gliding down her thighs and across her belly. She hadn't worn a bra; her breasts and pubic mound stood out in plain relief through the thin fabric of her dress. She obviously enjoyed the way he used her body. He looked at her wavy brown hair fanned across the grass, at her torso reclining seductively on the ground, at the confident come-on in her pale blue eyes, and he realized her nature. She had become one with the Earth. You can't rape the Earth, it occurred to him. She's always willing. If you're not happy with the fruits of what you sow, don't blame her. Blame yourself.

He felt his cock stir in his jeans. He imagined it swelling, growing hard, plowing into her. With what result? Bliss? Love? Commitment? Children? Even as his hands played the flesh of her belly, he pictured it swelling, growing, and becoming ripe.

Instantly he saw her with new eyes. The freckles on her face became the speckles on an over-ripe pear. The seduction in her eyes as she vamped him betrayed her own desires, her own self-interest. This is not perfection, it occurred to him. This is just another flawed human like himself. Take away the drive of sex and the common ground slipped away. He barely knew this person.

But the pressure in his crotch undeniably remained. In fact, even with the hot sun, it sent shivers up his neck and across his face. With a jolt he realized that, no matter how much he may *want* to have sex, he *needed* to pee. And soon.

He stood up quickly. The dope and the half tab of acid had taken hold already and he felt light-headed and then his vision slowly tunneled and faded away. He felt himself swaying and then Prudence's hands holding his upper arms.

"Are you okay?" she asked him.

His vision gradually came back and he saw the concern on her face at this sudden change in him. "Uh, yeah," he told her, regaining his balance. "But I really need to take a whiz. Where can I go?"

She looked around the Quad. "There's a john for every building."

"But what's the building for me? Is there a head that a head like mine could find easily?"

"Try Mackey," she said, pointing north. "Are you going to come back to me?"

John looked at the stage. "I should try to find Jason. He doesn't know where I am."

"Can you see him?" Prudence asked, looking too.

"No. Wow. What's going on up there?"

The conga players had kept going but on the stage some sort of dispute seemed to be taking place between the rally organizers, the musicians, and some guys wearing suits accompanied by the campus cops. Several Boulder Police cars, their lights flashing, had joined the campus police cars and a contingent of burly uniformed cops stood on either side of the library facing the crowd.

"You see that guy standing to the right of the library with the cops?" Prudence asked him, clutching his arm. "The guy with the white bandage over his eye?"

"Yeah."

"That's Leon, the guy who lived in our house on Marine Street until the pipe-bomb he was working on blew up in his face."

"What's he doing here? And why is he with the cops?"

"I have no idea," Prudence said, gathering up her purse. "But I'm going to get out of here. You and Jason might want to do the same. Call me, okay?"

He kissed her and she hustled away. He really wanted to find Jason now but he still had to pee, so he headed toward Mackey.

o   o   o

Along the sidewalk traversing the Quad, a Renaissance Fair had blossomed. German shepherds wearing bandanna collars caught frisbees tossed by long-haired freaks wearing just jeans that sagged from their hips. A homely young woman wearing a simple drab jumper and no make-up had displayed for sale an array of hand-made candles on a blanket while her baby girl rolled around on the lawn. Neo-mountain men wearing beaded and fringed buckskin and moccasins chatted with Ag students about the chances for a late frost. Madras-shirted frat boys kept their arms tucked around their sorority dates lest some tempting alternate reality give the girls ideas. Camouflaged, fatigued vets smoked and drank and cursed and ogled the hippie girls. Varsity athletes hung with their teammates, looking at all the decadence with disdain and envy. Sociology students took notes as they observed the rainbowed throng. By the time John made it to the north edge of the Quad, he felt like he'd seen one each of what humanity had to offer and that his species was, if a little odd, essentially good.

Up on the stage, a whole crowd of people still milled about and John couldn't spot Jason among them from this distance. A bullhorn crackled to life and some of the hubbub died down anticipating some official announcement.

"Hey, kids," came Ichabod's mellow voice, tinny and distorted by the bullhorn. "We just thought you ought to know that the reason there's no music is that the police have cut the power to the library."

The crowd rippled with boos and catcalls.

"Evidently we're allowed to do and say anything we like up here as long as it has no bearing whatsoever on your actual lives."

The crowd hooted derisively. One of the rally organizers, his sleeves rolled up, fought his way through the jumble on stage and grabbed the bullhorn from Ichabod.

"This is bullshit!" he shouted and the crowd cheered. "They can stop the music but they can't stop the truth! Isn't one of the principles of American democracy, that our brothers are fighting and dying for, the right to free speech?"

"Yeah!" the crowd yelled unanimously.

"What are you afraid of?" he shouted at the police. "Power to the people! Power to the people!" The crowd gladly took up the chant until it echoed from the buildings around the Quad.

John had paused to listen, hoping to catch sight of Jason again. It would take quite an effort to work his way up to the stage through the swelling mob and there was no guarantee Jason was still up there. And John still had to pee, more by the moment. He turned back to Mackey.

Mackey looked more like a church than an auditorium, with octagonal turrets, woodbine twining up the flagstone, and golden, Gothic, stained glass windows. The voice of a soprano warming up floated down from the second-floor rehearsal rooms. As John approached the heavy oak doors, chimes like the ones at the Will Rogers Shrine in Colorado Springs slowly tolled the noon hour.

Inside, the art deco light fixtures, blonde oak woodwork, and old-fashioned ticket offices with square frosted windows made it seem less ecclesiastical. The inner doors to the auditorium were locked but John spotted a sign for the restrooms.

Prudence had recommended well. This was no ordinary men's room. The high ceilings and walls tiled in bright earth colors made this resonant space a sanctuary, a refuge of peace and civilization far from the madding crowd, where a man might sit and ponder the meaning of life from his very own throne. John hadn't eaten since he stopped at Uncle Joe's Bar-B-Que Plantation on Arapahoe last night on the way to Jason's so any weird shit that happened would more likely be mental than physical but it might feel good to sit down for a while.

Unfortunately, in the first stall he tried the toilet was plugged and about to overflow, shreds of toilet paper and what looked like a large Baby Ruth bar floating around in the stagnant water. While John stood looking at the undeniable result of the human condition, a small cartoon dialogue balloon opened up just beyond the rim of the toilet and inside it appeared the words, in comic book lettering, "*High John!*"

Enough of that. He walked instead to the line of stately urinals along the wall, the ceramic altars old and crazed but stalwart and true. John unzipped, pulled out his schlong, and rested his arm on the wall and his head on his arm as he waited.

He had waited long enough now that he couldn't just let 'er rip. The ache of the pressure probed like the snout of a mongoose around the inside of his bladder, looking for the gopher hole that would lead it to the cobra. Finding the path, the mongoose forced its wriggly body through the narrow conduit, starting shivers in John's thighs that tightened his scrotum, flew up his back, and cracked his spine like a whip before the vibrations escaped through the top of his head. The cobra, passive thus far, reared its head and spat, the yellow venom gushing out into the ancient receptacle.

Once he got going, there was no stopping it. Suddenly all the waters from the Appalachians to the Rockies flooded Old Man River (or maybe his wife, Mrs. Sip-*pee!*) and overflowed the Big Easy. In fact, it flowed so freely, so profusely, that John began to wonder if perhaps his body had somehow lost the distinction between inside and outside. Maybe once the piss was exhausted, his internal organs and even his bones would somehow dissolve and flow out too, leaving nothing but his shriveled skin lying there on the cold tile floor like a busted balloon. Maybe all the matter in his body would flow downward and all his spirit fly up and the two would become irreconcilably parted. But eventually the tide turned and the pressure abated until the stream faded to a trickle. Yanking his cock a couple of times just to expel the last drops, he tucked himself back into his pants and went to the sink to wash his hands.

As the water splashed over his hands and into the sink, John looked up. He felt himself being sucked into a vortex but already it was too late to save himself. There before him he saw one of the most intriguing, terrifying objects known to the brand-new sport of acid tripping: a mirror.

Mirrors had caught him before. On past trips he had even tried to warn fellow trippers of the hazards of reflection but couldn't find words to express the danger. The freak in the mirror was the ultimate intimate stranger. He seemed to be seeing all the familiar landmarks of his face—his bristly short hair and shadow of beard, his fleshy lips, his protruding nose with its field of pores—for the first time. This guy looks weary and weird, some part of him said to some other part of him.

The real trap, though, was the eyes. Something about the black, dilated pupils and the implied challenge they offered by staring back at him so unwaveringly riveted his gaze and wouldn't let go. Somewhere deep inside that limitless void resided the tenuous spark of his soul, always, no matter how hard he searched, just beyond his sight, his grasp, his ken. Before long he found it hard to distinguish between the real and the reflection. He knew if one disappeared, both disappeared. But what would happen to John if the reflection walked away first?

While reflecting thus, his ears perked up and his scalp contracted at the sound of footsteps. In walked a small Latino with a limp and a tweed-finished saxophone case. John self-consciously tore himself from the mirror and finished washing his hands.

"Hey, bro," the man said, unzipping at the urinal.

"Howzit goin'?" John asked, drying his hands.

"Some bad shit going down here, huh?"

John had no idea if the man referred to the plugged toilet (which, technically, wasn't going down at all), the stronger-than-expected LSD John had taken, the infinite regress of the man in the mirror, or the rising clamor coming from the Quad. He decided on the neutral answer of "You can say that again," heading out the door before the man could take him up on it.

John felt like a new man as he pushed open the heavy oak doors of Mackey and walked back into the bright sun. With the pressure inside him alleviated, he felt cocky.

His eyes and ears told him two different tales. His ears could hear the increasing rancor in the voice shouting into the bullhorn, though from here he couldn't make out the words. His eyes, however, feasted on the back view of a vision of loveliness: a blouse so bright and loud it seemed to shimmer, tight faded jeans, cowboy boots, and cascades of tousled blonde hair. The slavering beast inside him reacted in a heartbeat: great ass, excellent tits, provocative body language. Fascinated, he walked toward where she stood at the intersection of the sidewalks on the Quad.

As John got closer to her, the words coming through the bullhorn became intelligible. A woman's voice was saying, "…candlelight vigil around the fountain at the U. M. C. tomorrow night at eight o'clock. Remember, we can't stop the war in Vietnam by starting one here."

The rancorous bullhorn man, who turned out to be Poppin' Fresh, took back the bullhorn and said, "Yeah, yeah, yeah. I think we should hear from the guy who started this whole thing. Is he still here? The dog guy?"

Everyone on the Quad was standing and John, stopping just behind the beautiful woman, craned his neck to look over the heads in front of them. The crowd on stage, which seemed to have grown as much as the crowd in the Quad, parted to let Jason come to the front.

"This is incredible!" John said to no one in particular, though the slavering beast in him hoped it might start a conversation with the beautiful woman about how he had helped shove his friend into the spotlight.

Jason took the bullhorn and pointed it to the crowd. "Hey, I'm just an average dog like the rest of you," he said, his voice crackling and distorted. "But my brother was killed in the war last summer and he didn't die in Vietnam. He died in Laos. Nixon and his buddies in the Pentagon are lying to us about this war and all I can say is we better dick Nixon before he dicks us!"

The crowd roared.

Jason handed the bullhorn back to Poppin' Fresh, who had been talking to one of the suits on stage. Poppin' Fresh's tone had sweetened a little. "Okay, everybody, listen up! Evidently, Regent Joe Coors is tied up at the bank counting the money we gave him last weekend for beer but Dean Smythe, assistant to the president, would like to have a word with you." Handing the dean the bullhorn, he and Ichabod Crane began to herd people from the stage.

"Thanks, Andy," Dean Smythe said. "Hello, everybody. On behalf of the Administration, I just want to apologize for the rocky start here. But after the events up on the Hill last night, we just want to make sure things don't get out of hand today. As you know, this concert was originally scheduled for Mackey Auditorium but we gave the organizers permission to set things up out here so more of you could attend. But let me just stress this: we don't want to see any of you get hurt and we don't want to see the University damaged or disrupted. So if we can just tone down the rhetoric this afternoon, we'll go ahead and turn the power back on and get Sever—"

"Zephyr," Ichabod corrected him.

"—Zephyr out here to play some music."

Another loud thump came through the P. A. speakers and the crowd cheered. Zephyr, who had been ready to go for some time now, launched into a Joplinesque version of "Ball and Chain." Jason skipped down the steps to the dancers in front of the stage, who applauded wildly and slapped him on the back.

"All right, Jason!" John shouted.

The beautiful woman in front of him whirled around and turned magically into Deb O'Donnell.

"Wo, Deb!" John said, amazed. "What are you doing here?"

"Looking for you," she said.

Deb's beauty didn't surprise him anymore, though it always gave him pause. But something had changed about her. Her eyes looked hard and nervous. "You found me," he told her, "lost in the cosmos as usual. Take my hand. Lead me back."

"Can it, Jack," she said, sounding irritable. "Why is Jason up there giving speeches?"

"I talked him into it," John boasted. "So what brings you up here? Are you by yourself?"

"No, Manny's here with me," Deb said. "The things you told her about Jason got her worried. She talked me into coming up here and surprising you guys and she figured that if you were tripping she might as well be tripping too. I'm just along for the ride."

"You seem bummed," he pointed out.

She turned her face away. "I'm just…not feeling well, that's all. It's not your problem."

John looked around. "So where's Manny?"

"She went up there to look for Jason," she said, looking toward the stage, where Candy's voice lashed the roiling mass of bodies dancing in front of her.

John had sensed danger but it took looking at Candy to make it clear to him: Jessica. Jason. Mandy. No good could come of this. "We've got to find her," he told Deb.

"Then let's go," she said, leading the way.

They walked down the sidewalk on the north edge of the Quad, getting halfway to the stage with smooth sailing, but then the crowd thickened so much that the two of them had trouble staying together. Deb had to stop twice and come back to pull John from some sensory-input trap like a guy blowing giant soap bubbles or a patchouli-scented girl dancing topless.

Zephyr, anxious from the long wait and all the tension, beat out the blues with a vengeance and the closer Deb and John got to the stage, the harder it was to shove and squeeze their way through the crowd. The second half-tab of acid had acted like booster rockets for John and the kaleidoscope of freakdom through which they wormed their way baffled and intimidated him. Finally, at the edge of the semi-circle of people standing to watch the band and the dancers, John spotted Amanda, dressed in white pants, a green crushed-velvet top, and wearing a black choker around her neck. She stood mesmerized by the dancing.

When they got close enough, John could see what hypnotized Amanda: Jessica stood dancing by herself, her hair flailing about wildly, her tie-dyed tank top plainly revealing her small breasts, her hips gyrating aggressively, her full attention on the object of her dance. Between her spread legs, Jason lay on the grass on his back, propped up on his elbows, his eyes following every nuance of Jessica's body, the metal buttons on the fly of his thin sailor's bells bulging.

Deb got there a couple of steps in front of John. She stood next to Amanda and put her hand on her shoulder. "Amy…" she said just loudly enough to be heard over the music.

Amanda turned to her, her eyes bright and shocked. "I wanted to come up here to make sure Jason was okay—"

Jason's head whirled around at the sound of her voice.

"—but he seems to be doing just fine," Amanda concluded contemptuously, her lips quivering.

"Oh, my God!" Jason cried. "Man!" He tried to roll over to get up but his legs and Jessica's intertwined and Jessica tumbled over on top of him.

"He seems to have his hands full," Amanda said to Deb. "Let's get out of here."

"Manny—" John began. He started to tell her that it wasn't what she thought, but in fact it was. He tried to take her arm instead but Deb forced her body between them.

"Men are pigs!" she said to Amanda but loud enough for all to hear. "Fucking animals! Let's go!"

They broke out into the more open semi-circle of dancers and shoved and wove their way south along the walk in front of the library. Jason finally managed to free himself from Jessica and stood up. He looked at John for directions. John pointed south. Jason ran after them.

Jessica had gotten up too and she straightened her wire-rim glasses, shouting at John over Candy's wailing, "What's happening?"

John stood there buffaloed. The acid barreled around inside his head, scattering coherent thoughts like bowling pins, turning each moment into a garish frame from a psychedelic cartoon. All he could manage to say to Jessica was "Don't know."

"Jason!" Jessica called after him.

John too broke out into the whirling mass of dancers, trying desperately to keep his bearings, fighting his way toward his friend in slow motion.

The crowd thinned at the line of sight to the band. At last John got a view ahead. Police stood in nervous groups between Ekeley and the library. From this angle John could see that ambulances and a paddy wagon had been parked in the small grassy plot between the buildings, and cops in riot gear stood listening to instructions. He caught just a glimpse of Deb and Amanda running past the police, the cops calling and reaching out but not stopping them. The guy with the bandage over his eye, whom Prudence had called Leon, pointed at Jason as he ran toward them. The plain-clothes cops standing next to Leon shouted something to the commander of the riot cops, who grabbed Jason as he ran past. Jason tried to pull away, ducking and writhing, but a couple of the other cops grabbed his arms. Even over the music, John could hear Jason scream at them to let him go. At the sound, Deb and Amanda stopped and turned around. With one last desperate heave, Jason tried to throw off the police but one of them grabbed his long blonde hair, yanked up his head, and with his nightstick clubbed the back of Jason's head. The force of the blow jerked Jason's head forward and his body sagged into the arms of the cops. John froze in horror as he saw scarlet streaks blossom in Jason's hair. The cops dragged the limp body to the back of the paddy wagon and hoisted him into it like a sack of potatoes. Slamming the door, they readjusted their riot gear and turned back to face John.

PART III

. . . O . . . O . . . O . . .

I did my most profitable work, both as a musician and as a collector of stories, up in Alaska. Dick, from Dirty Dick's Saloon in Glenallen, had a wealth of colorful tales about life on the Last Frontier.

My favorite involved a friend of his named Harvey, who specialized in heavy equipment and practical jokes. For example, just for a prank, Harvey used a large mobile crane to set a buddy's car 50 feet off the ground in a gigantic Sitka spruce.

Anyway, Harvey had some buddies in a retirement home in Sitka who were looking forward to an upcoming local parade. Harvey, a man's man, decided to give the old guys a treat so he arranged for one of the floats to look like a big cake. When the float passed the home, out of the cake popped a couple of naked women. It thrilled the guys at the home but pissed off the authorities, who promptly ran Harvey out of town.

Harvey, angered by this blatant ingratitude toward what he considered a thoughtful gesture to his fellow man, plotted his revenge. He used his helicopter to lift a mess of old tires into the crater of nearby Mt. Edgecumbe, a dormant volcano. Sneaking back into Sitka, he told the townsfolk, in convincing detail, of having climbed onto the volcano and feeling temblors and hearing rumbling. Then he flew back up to the crater and set fire to the tires, creating a huge plume of black smoke so threatening that the entire town had to be evacuated. Sitka learned not to fuck with Harvey.

In my teens, I assumed that, should I suffer the misfortune of living to the ripe old age of 50, sex would no longer fill my thoughts night and day. Now, as the Big Five-Oh looms large, I realize how foolish I was. Sex—or in my case lately, like that of the guys in the retirement home, the thought of sex—still makes life worth living.

Some people (mostly women) speak disparagingly of the effects of testosterone, attributing to that single hormone all the ills of the world: belligerence, infidelity, territoriality, obstinacy, and all the other tomfoolery men are prone—or erect—to do. But men know that testosterone is the key to an incredible secret world, where women are endlessly fascinating just because they're women, where the outcome of a ball game matters, and where a man can do anything as long as he has enough "balls." Balls can make a man yield to Satan and talk to God. Balls give a man his orientation. No balls, no bearings. I, for one, am still proud and pleased whenever I find the old compass needle pointing due north.

December 22, 1999

The woman's voice, soft and gentle, said, "Sir?" She lightly touched Matt's shoulder.

Matt groaned and opened his eyes, looking around groggily. The woman wore the navy-blue suit of a flight attendant. They must have landed in Seattle.

"I'm sorry to disturb you, sir, but all the other passengers have left the plane. May I help you?"

Matt shook his head to try to clear his mind. The pain-killers lent an air of unreality to everything that happened. "No, I can manage," he told the flight attendant, an attractive young lady who had pampered Matt and everyone else in the L-1011's first-class section of United's 8:15 flight from Boston. He stood up and carefully unfolded his back but didn't stretch, even though he wanted to. The pain in his lower back and pelvis made every bend and torsion excruciating. The attendant helped him pull his carry-on bag from the overhead and sling it across his shoulder. He wobbled unsteadily from even that little weight.

"I have a lay-over here in Seattle," the attendant told him, "so I'm leaving the aircraft now as well. Would you like to take my arm?"

He didn't want to but he wasn't sure he could walk up the tunnel under his own steam without bumping into things. He grabbed her elbow firmly but gently and together they walked up the easy slope to the terminal.

Deb, wearing jeans, a white angora sweater, and a long tan suede coat, stood watching the door, looking tired and anxious. She broke into a wide grin when she saw him. She rushed to peck him on the cheek and to slide the carry-on bag from his shoulder.

"I was afraid of this," she said. "I leave you alone for a few days and you find someone new."

The flight attendant laughed and relinquished her role of steadying Matt to Deb. "He's all yours," she assured Deb before walking away.

"Here I was, worrying about you," Deb said to Matt as they slowly walked through SeaTac, "and you come off the plane arm-in-arm with a beautiful young woman. I shouldn't be surprised, I suppose. You're still as handsome as ever."

Matt snorted, thinking about how his reflection had looked in the lavatory of the airplane: gaunt, tired, sallow, sunken-eyed. "Nice try," he told Deb. "Hell, I look so bad horses faint and women rear."

She chuckled as she held his arm. "Is walking okay? Because we could get one of those carts."

"It feels good to move around," he told her. "But it helps to have someone to lean on."

"Well, you can lean on me," she said as they walked past the metal detectors and out toward the ticket counters.

"Don't we need to go down to baggage claim?" he asked.

"I'm having it delivered," she told him. "I don't want to spend your first night home standing around that stupid metal carousel."

"Where did you park?"

"Right out here," she told him, leading him through the doors on the departure level and out to her royal-blue Mercedes idling at the curb.

The skycap opened the passenger door of the car and Deb waited patiently as Matt refolded his back and pulled in his feet, panting from the exertion but comforted by the smell of her perfume on the leather seats. She came around the car and sat behind the wheel, waving to the skycap as she pulled away and merged with the traffic. Matt closed his eyes and clenched his teeth, bracing himself for the bumps in the pavement.

"How was your flight?" Deb asked as she pulled off the exit to 518 and accelerated down the hill.

"Except for the layover in L. A., I slept through most of it," he told her. "Have you been waiting long?"

"It could have been worse," she said, driving under I-5 and onto I-405. "Between the fog and the heightened security because of our bomb scare, a lot of flights were delayed or canceled."

Matt looked around at the hazy fog. "What time is it?"

"Almost three-thirty," she said.

"I heard about that Algerian guy trying to smuggle bomb materials into Port Angeles."

"They arraigned him downtown today," she said, checking her rear-view mirrors, trying to get out of the line of cars waiting to get onto the Valley Freeway and get into the diamond lane. "But this whole town is jumpy. Norm Stamper has already resigned as police chief and Paul Schell may not be mayor much longer."

"That's right," he said, remembering why she had come home Sunday. "How did your court date go?"

"Except for Phil Banks insisting on getting pictures of my ass, it was a breeze."

"Excuse me?"

"Oh, he wanted to have proof of my injuries in case we want to sue the city," she explained.

"Uh-huh." Phil's kidding about stealing Deb from him rankled more of late.

"Oh, I have the pictures and the negatives," she assured him. "And Phil even gave me a present for you. I'll show you later."

"So, how is your ass?" he asked. Despite his discomfort and fatigue, he still felt energized to see her again.

"My bruises are pretty much gone, dammit," she pouted. "But the night is young."

The diagnosis of his cancer had forced them to scrap their whole schedule of love-making. But they traditionally declared solstice night an official Playtime night as part of his fertility ritual, a symbol of the sun's return.

"The night is much younger than I am," he pointed out. "We're going to have to be gentle."

"*I'm* going to have to be gentle," she corrected him. "You can do whatever you like."

"It may take me all night long to do what I used to do all night long," he quoted his father.

She smiled lasciviously. "And it's the longest night of the year."

"True," he said, looking at the gathering dusk as they exited onto Sunset Drive. Already the thick, uniform overcast had deepened to a steely blue, the lights of the city washing into the evening sky as though airbrushed. "But there's supposed to be a hell of a moon."

"Why's that?" she asked, stopping for a red light.

"Oh, it's a once-in-a-lifetime moon," he told her. "The moon is full at perigee and the earth is at perihelion so it's significantly brighter than usual, the brightest moon since President Andrew Johnson was impeached after the Civil War."

"Really?" she said, scanning the overcast for any lunar trace. "You think we'll be able to see it at all?"

"This haze might last all night."

"It has been pretty cold here but we do have a few renegade cherry blossoms jumping the gun as usual."

"No kidding," he said, surprisingly heartened to hear it. Those delicate, futile blossoms in the dead of winter always made the lean season just a little more bearable.

They rode in silence the rest of the way to May Valley, each lost in thought. But when they pulled into the drive to their house, Deb said, "I need to stop and feed Tahoma, if you don't mind. But you don't need to get out."

"I wouldn't mind stretching my legs. Hey, the house looks great!"

She had strung Christmas lights along the railing around their bedroom upstairs and through the bay window he could see the tree, decorated and glowing brightly in the living room. While Deb went into the little barn and talked intimately with her white colt, Matt plodded around the large yard. The leaves had been raked and the roses mulched, meaning Deb had hired a service to tend the grounds. They had always been able to afford something like that but they both enjoyed gardening enough to make it unnecessary, until now. He walked up by the little stream. Even in the fading light he could tell that the blackberry shoots that he had given up on a month ago had been carefully trimmed to the ground. A crooked smile suffused his face. He was glad she had found someone to take over for him, but a little jealous too.

"Are you okay?" she asked, putting her arm around his waist.

He looked down into her eyes and kissed her on the forehead, sparing his back. "It's good to be home."

o   o   o

"Dinner's ready anytime," she told him when they got into the house. "Why don't you sit down while I poke the fire?"

He eased himself into a chair at the kitchen table and looked around while she threw a couple of chunks of alder wood into the fieldstone fireplace. The place looked great inside as well. She had strung small white lights on the small fir Christmas tree and decorated it with ribbons tied to the ends of the branches and with some silvered plastic icicles he had inherited from his grandparents. A variegated poinsettia, its pot centered in a wreath also lit with small white lights, sat on a doily on the Steinway, the lights reflected in the shiny black finish of the piano. A dark green cloth covered the kitchen table; five red bayberry candles sticking out of a mound of red-berried holly formed the centerpiece. The decorations amounted to far more than they usually did.

"Are you expecting someone?" he asked Deb as she came back into the kitchen.

"Just you," she said, kissing the top of his head. "Are you hungry?"

"Not really," he admitted, though dinner smelled good. "I hope you didn't go to too much trouble. My appetite isn't what is used to be."

"I was afraid of that," Deb said, taking something from a drawer. "Maybe this will help." She handed him a hand-rolled joint.

He took it curiously, not having seen one in more years than he could remember. "Where in the world did you get this?" he asked her.

"That's the present from Phil Banks I told you about."

"Then where did Phil get it?"

"I've learned over the years not to ask too many questions of Phil," she said. "So what do you think?"

"Oh, honey, I don't know," he said, looking at it dubiously.

"I'll share it with you," she offered. "It might improve our appetites."

"I really need to talk to you about some things."

"After dinner," she said, lighting the candles and holding the lit lighter for him.

He gave in. He hadn't smoked marijuana since college but this seemed like as good a time as any to try it again. He held it to his lips and she lit it for him. The old familiar smell and feel filled his lungs and he smiled as he handed it to her. She took a drag too and handed it back.

"So did you and Phil get stoned quite a bit while I was gone?" he asked.

From a pot on the stove she ladled some soup into bowls as their first course. "The last time I got high was with you," she pointed out, setting the bowl in front of him. The soup was one of his favorites, oyster stew, a simple blend of oysters, milk, and butter, garnished with scallions. It always felt comforting to him, though tonight he wondered if the oysters might not constitute some sort of message as well.

He took another toke and handed the joint to her again. The stew really did smell delicious and if that was because of the cannabis, so much the better. Feeling goofy and unreal, he spooned up one of the oysters and ate it, the rich warmth chewy but delectable.

"Maybe it's the dope talking," he said, "but this stew tastes great. I guess a good lawyer would have good weed. What happened at your arraignment, anyway?"

"Phil got all the charges dropped. I figured he would. He said we have a good shot at a lawsuit but I'm not sure I want to pursue it."

"I'm sure he'd enjoy working with you," Matt pointed out, his teeth grinding on some grit in another oyster.

She scrutinized his face. "Matt McCleary, if I didn't know better, I'd think you were jealous."

He pushed the stew away and shrugged, thinking that Phil's name had a way of popping up lately.

Deb stubbed out the joint in the saucer of her bowl. "You've had enough of this. You'd have to be high to think I'd be interested in Phil Banks. But come to think of it, ever since Phil and Cindy split up, you've been worried, haven't you?"

"No, just…lately."

"Why lately?" she asked, then the answer seemed to dawn on her. "Is it what Russ and Sylvia are going through?"

That sounded better than his explanation. "Boy, if it could happen to them…" he improvised.

"But you're not Russ and I'm not Sylvia. Didn't you like the stew?" she added, picking up their bowls and setting them into the sink.

"It was delish, but I suspect there's more dinner on the way."

"Have you talked to Russ lately?" she asked, setting down the next course: spring greens, red bell peppers, sliced mushrooms and tomatoes, all drizzled with a vinaigrette she made using the juice of the dreaded Himalayan blackberries.

"I called him after the game on Sunday to let him gloat."

"So we lost?" she asked. "I was in transit, so I didn't get to hear and I've been too busy around here to read the paper."

"We lost a heartbreaker," Matt said. "The Broncos were up 30-20 at the two-minute warning but John Kitna moved the Hawks so well they tied the score and sent it to overtime. The Seahawks won the toss but on the first snap, John Kitna fumbled and the Broncos ran it in for the winning touchdown. It's hard to believe that the Hawks, who just a few weeks ago had a record of eight-and-two and were solidly in first place, probably won't even make the play-offs. Mike Holmgren must be livid. He's probably booking a flight back to Green Bay right now."

"Did Russ talk about what's happening with Sylvia?" asked Deb, whose interest in sports lasted at most two minutes.

"Russ said he has a buyer lined up for Tweak so he's going to move up to the farm this weekend to be with his mom for Christmas and then stay up there to write for a while."

"So he and Sylvia are splitting up then?" she asked, clearing the salad dishes and going to the stove to dish up the main course.

"He said they're going to make a stab at normalcy over the holidays, for Ellen's sake if nothing else. But he sounded as pessimistic as I've ever heard him. Doesn't it seem like, at our age, we should be past those kinds of relationship issues?"

"You'd think so. Has Russ talked to John at all?"

"I guess John called him the weekend before."

"How's he doing?"

"Susan's filed for divorce and John's got his own place in Estes now. This looks great, hon."

She had made one of his all-time favorite dishes, chicken and dumplings. She didn't cook often but when she did, she cooked well.

"I hope you like it," she said.

He lifted up and kissed her hand. "My mom used to have a trivet on her wall that said, 'Kissin' don't last. Good cookin' do.'"

She smiled crookedly. "So you're tired of my kisses?"

He snorted. "That'll be the day."

"So did Russ or John happen to hear from May?" she asked, staring at the tablecloth while he dug into the chicken and dumplings.

"That's right. I forgot to tell you. Cynthia Tyree passed away."

"Oh, no!" Deb said, seeming more shaken than Matt anticipated. "When?"

"Around Thanksgiving, I guess."

Deb put the heels of her hands over her eyes. "I didn't even send a card. Oh, God! May must be devastated."

"I guess John went down to the Springs for the funeral and spent some time with May afterward."

"Really?" She seemed inordinately surprised and curious.

"You're still wondering if they're having an affair, aren't you?"

"Well, you know John."

"When it comes to that, not as well as you know him. But Russ said that John came away feeling that the only thing he and May agreed upon for sure was that May isn't Jason's daughter after all."

She looked up at him, startled. "How did they reach that conclusion?"

"I guess Russ, John, and May all agree that there just isn't enough evidence to justify spending any more time or energy looking into it."

"But they're wrong!" Deb insisted.

"So I gathered from what you told me. But after all, it doesn't really matter that much, does it? As far as that goes, if May leaves things as they are, she just might stand to inherit something from Bill when he kicks the bucket. If she claims Jason as her father, she gets squat."

Deb sat shaking her head dismally. "Oh, what a mess! I can't believe things are turning out this way."

"It's not like it's your fault," he reassured her.

She shot him a glance but then looked back down, shaking her head again, muttering, "Oh, God."

"If you're that concerned about her, why not give her a call?" he suggested. "She's at her mom's number, isn't she?"

"Oh, I don't know," she said doubtfully. "The only time I've ever spoken to her was when she'd answer the phone for Mandy. I don't know what I'd say."

"Then maybe you should try to get a hold of John. I'm sure he'd love to hear from you."

She scowled at him. "We don't even have his number, do we? Besides, when was the last time *you* called John?"

He took a bite of dumpling and thought about it. "Hmm. I have no idea. I'll bet it's been twenty years. Before we moved into this house. But John would probably enjoy talking to you more than to me."

She rolled her eyes. "I don't believe it. Why on earth are you trying to get me interested in John?"

It was Matt's turn to look at the tablecloth. "I know you and John were once pretty close, that's all. And John, for all his foibles, is really a decent guy. There are a lot worse men out there."

"You mean like Phil Banks?" she asked pointedly.

He shrugged.

She took his hand in both of hers. "Oh, you big dope. Don't you get it, even after all this time? You're the only man in the world I care about. You just jolly well better get used to it."

"I'm not going to be around forever. That's something *you're* going to have to accept."

For a few moments neither spoke, both looking at the tablecloth, idly pushing crumbs around, not eating. Finally Deb sighed and stood up.

"Did you get enough to eat?" she asked quietly.

"Honey, I'm so sorry to ruin this wonderful meal you put together," he told her as she cleared the table. "It really was delicious and the only dope talking now is me. But we really do need to discuss some tough choices we have to make. Maybe if we talk about them now, it'll free us up to do other things afterward."

"Coffee?" she asked.

"I probably shouldn't. But please help yourself. I'd love to smell some at least."

"Why don't you go in and sit by the fire?" she said, her hands on his shoulders. "I'll be there in a minute."

She helped steady his arm as he got up. The marijuana had left him feeling a little light-headed but he managed to walk to the sofa slowly and stiffly as she started the coffee. The fire took the chill from his legs and the soothing motion of the flames gave his eyes something to do while his mind went over how he would approach this discussion. He had known this day would come for at least a month and still didn't know just what he would say.

Deb came in from the kitchen and sat beside him, pulling her knees onto the couch and putting her hands on his shoulder. "How're you doing? Do you need to take any medications?"

"I'll take some hydrocodone later. For now, I'm okay."

"Maybe some chamomile tea?"

"I'm fine."

"How can I take care of you if you don't need anything?" she teased softly.

"Oh, I need something," he said, putting his arm around her shoulders. "I need understanding and patience from you."

"I'll do my best," she assured him, adding, more soberly, "More than that. I value your judgment even more than my own. I know you've given a lot of thought to this and you wouldn't decide on anything unless you truly thought it best. Whatever you decide, I'll abide by it."

"I know you will," he said, pulling her close. "As you know all too well, I have loved you from the moment I first saw you. And you have never, *ever*, let me down."

"I don't know," she said, staring into the fire. "If I had insisted you keep your appointments with Doctor Wu…"

"I knew exactly what I was supposed to do and I didn't do it. Any fault in this situation is my own, not yours, not Wu's."

"Have you talked to him lately?"

"Oh, yes. I have an appointment for Monday, in fact, but we'll have to discuss that. Incidentally, he's going to China."

"What? Doctor Wu is?"

"He feels that he might have detected my cancer at a much earlier stage if he hadn't felt constrained by the H. M. O. to keep costs down. And actually my situation is just one of many he's run into. He said he feels like he can do a lot more good for a lot more people in China than here. He plans to stay at least a year, at a huge cut in salary, needless to say. Although he once again renewed his offer to pay for any of our costs the insurance doesn't cover."

"That's a wonderful gesture," she said. "He's a good man. But we won't need any financial help. Is he still going to be your primary physician, at least until he leaves?"

Matt nodded. "I'm supposed to meet with him and an oncologist and a urologist on Monday."

"May I join you?"

"Of course you can. But you and I need to discuss our options before then."

"Can I get my coffee first?"

"Please do."

He watched her walk to the kitchen, get out the cup and saucer, and pour the coffee. Every move, every gesture, seemed precious to him. He had missed her more in the last three days than he ever thought he could miss anyone. His body, of course, aching and tired, had longed for the comforting presence of hers. As the severity of his condition had become more apparent and his options fewer, though, he had yearned to confide in her and to listen to her counsel. But he suspected already that they might disagree about the proper course and, even though it was his own fate at stake, that he might actually be better suited to make a decision based on reason and not let emotional considerations hold sway.

She carried the coffee in from the kitchen, letting him have a long satisfying whiff before setting it on the coffee table. Settling in beside him once again, she asked, "So, were you able to get any results at all about the endostatin study?"

"No, but I didn't expect to. A high-profile drug study like that could end up with skewed results if the participants or even the doctors and care-givers knew any preliminary data."

"What about that last batch of tests they ran on you? What did they find?"

"About what I expected. If the endostatin had any effect at all, it was trivial compared to the progression of my cancer. The dose was just too small. The good news is, I still haven't experienced any side effects."

"And you're sure you couldn't get a bigger dose? I mean, the later cohorts of participants are getting one."

"No, remember? I had to sign that waiver that if I entered this first phase of the study, I could continue the endostatin at that same level only. With such a small sample, every subject counts enormously and changing the dosage for one would render the data for that subject useless."

"So, basically, this whole endostatin study was a waste of time. We lost a month."

"Oh, no, Deb, you're wrong!" he declared, holding her hand. "I'm proud to have participated in it. Who knows? In just a few years, endostatin or something similar might be saving thousands of lives a year because of the research they're conducting."

"I only care about saving one," she said obstinately, sipping her coffee.

"It would have been a long shot for me in any case. Antiangiogenesis drugs like that will probably prove more effective in preventing the spread of cancer and mine has already spread quite a bit."

"Oh."

"The tests they ran confirmed it. The CT scan found that my lymph nodes are enlarged, and the bone scan seems to indicate that the cancer has metastasized and invaded my pelvis and lower spine. And I got an eight on the Gleason grading system, meaning the cells are poorly differentiated and more malignant."

"So even a radical prostatectomy…"

He shook his head. "Wouldn't do any good. They might do a TURP, that roto-rooter thing, to let me pee easier but more than that would be stupid at this point."

"Do they have any indication why this is happening?"

"Well, as you know, many if not most men will get prostate cancer if they live long enough. It's just more virulent in some men than in others. It looks like there's a genetic predisposition to it but how that relates to severity is anybody's guess at this point. And there are some environmental factors that may, if not cause prostate cancer, at least exacerbate it. Dietary fat is one. Another may be rubber. I used to handle a lot of rubber tubing back in my lab days."

"But there must be treatments."

"Well, there are, but I can't opt for any other treatment and still participate in the endostatin study. Chemo *per se* doesn't seem too effective but extended field radiation, where they irradiate the whole pelvic region, works for some. The rate mine is spreading may remove that option for me, though. There are also some biotherapies that seem promising. In fact, for a while at Novagen we worked with a couple of other biotech companies, trying to develop something called adoptive cellular therapy, utilizing things called lymphokine-activated killer cells and interferon-activated macrophages to stimulate the body to fight the cancer as though it were a disease."

"It is a disease, isn't it?"

"Well, it's not caused by an external agent, like a bacterium or a virus. In fact, you could look at it as part of Mother Nature's recycling plan, one more method of planned obsolescence to eliminate the older, non-productive individuals and make room for younger generations."

"Well, I wouldn't put you in the non-productive class."

"Genetically, productive means reproductive."

"Anyway, what do you think represents your best treatment option?"

"Well, frankly, any of them would be pointless without another form of therapy I didn't mention yet."

"Which is…"

"Hormone therapy." He paused, reluctant to go on.

She looked at him, her eyes soft and sympathetic. "Well?"

"Well, in cancer like mine, by far the highest risk factor is my own testosterone. All the little individual cancers popping up in me are related to that original prostate cancer and they all thrive on testosterone. Eliminate that and a lot of the symptoms, and perhaps even some of the cancers, go away, at least for a while."

"But how do you eliminate testosterone?"

He swallowed. "Well, obviously, the classic method is an orchiectomy." He could tell by her expression that she wasn't familiar with the term. "Otherwise known as castration."

She winced. "Oh, baby!" she cried, clutching his arm.

"They can do somewhat the same thing chemically now," he told her. "In fact, testosterone is produced by other organs like the adrenals as well so they often combine an orchiectomy with androgen-inhibitors like estrogen or a drug called leuprolide. Either way, the goal is to eliminate every trace of testosterone from the body, with the predictable side effects: loss of sex drive, impotence, sometimes hot flashes. Some men even grow breasts, although that can be inhibited with radiation."

"But does it work?"

"It slows the cancer, yes."

"Even cancer like yours?"

"Especially cancer like mine."

"For how long?"

"Without hormone therapy, I might last six months. With it, maybe three years. Maybe more, depending on the effectiveness of the other therapies."

"When would this have to be done?"

"The sooner, the better. It's not a complicated procedure. Wu set it up so it could be done Monday even. He thought it might be best to schedule something before the end of the year, in case the Y2K bug hits us harder than we're expecting."

Deb's lips were set and quivering, her eyes misty. "Oh, honey! I'm so sorry." She laid her head gently on his shoulder.

"I'm sorry too," he said, stroking her hair as he looked into the fire. "I know you didn't sign up for this."

"I signed up for the duration," she insisted, pulling herself together, sipping more coffee. "Can I come with you on Monday?"

Now came the hard part. "You're welcome to. I'd love to have you with me, as I always do. But I'm telling you right now: I've decided against the hormone therapy."

She set down her coffee in a jangle of china and turned sharply to him. "But didn't you say—?"

"I know. And I'm sorry. But, as you said, I've given this a lot of thought and I just don't think I want to go that route. The cure's as bad as the disease."

"It is kind of a Catch-22," she conceded.

"Keep my manhood and live a few months. Lose my manhood and live a few years. Hell of a choice. Did you hear that Joseph Heller died last week?"

"Yes, I did, and I know how much that book meant to you. I'm sorry. But you can't just give up."

"I have to give up something either way. I'd rather face my fate as a man. Honey, I just wasn't cut out for the new millennium. My body has been programmed to do this since I was conceived. It's only natural."

"There's nothing natural about cancer," she maintained bitterly.

"Sure there is. All the different cells of my body—skin cells, liver cells, whatever—have the same genetic code. They only perform different functions because of a complicated system of suppression exerted by all the other cells of my body. My cancer cells have simply broken free of that suppression system. And now my testosterone is going around sowing its wild oats through my body."

"Honey, I know how much you respect the natural world. I do too. But what's at stake is your life!"

"*My* life, yes," he said soberly. "To live out the best I can."

"But you can't just walk out on me!"

"I'm going to leave you either way," he reminded her. "I've thought a lot about this. Maybe five years from now that endostatin would give me a shot at a life. But I don't have five years. Right now, all the treatments we have only manage to prolong my death. I don't want to put you through that. You deserve better. You deserve a man—a *whole* man."

"Wait a minute," she said. "How much of this is about sex?"

Matt stared into the fire.

"You don't want this hormone therapy because we won't be able to have sex anymore. Right?"

"Well…"

"Oh, Matt, honey!" she cried, clutching his arm. "It's not worth dying for! *I'm* not worth dying for!"

"No, you're wrong!" he told her vehemently, feeling a lump in his throat. "You *are* worth dying for! Loving you is all I've been living for! You're the only thing that's ever really mattered to me!"

"But, darling…"

Matt put his finger to her lips. "Please? I know this isn't easy. But try to understand."

"But…"

"Please?"

She heaved a sigh, blinking. "Okay. I'll try."

He sighed too. This had actually gone better than he had hoped. "So what do you say? Shall we go to bed? It's Playtime, after all."

She smiled wanly. "Whatever you like."

o   o   o

Matt declined her help getting up the stairs so she put away the leftovers and set the dishes in the dishwasher while he went up to the bathroom to take his usual slow painful leak. When he finished, he went to the medicine chest and took a hydrocodone, looking in the mirror, wishing he could do something to make himself look a little more appealing. Nothing came to mind, so he went into the bedroom and took off all his clothes but his jockeys and slipped between the sheets. The bed at the Back Bay Sheraton in Boston hadn't bothered him but his own bed felt infinitely more comforting. On the steamer trunk, Deb had set a bud vase with a spray of cherry blossoms.

Deb came upstairs and quietly stood at her dressing table, taking off her earrings. Her face, reflected in the mirror, looked somber but composed.

"You weren't kidding about the cherry blossoms," Matt told her. "They look great."

"Well, I cannot tell a lie," she said, turning to him and smiling, a smile dazzling enough to make up for any insincerity. "I forced them."

"Oh, you mean you soaked them in hot water for a while to make them bloom? Oh, well, that's fine. They still cheer up the place," he told her, adding, "Last week was also the two hundredth anniversary of George Washington's death."

"So I heard."

"I always thought it a pity he didn't live to see the new century. I should be around long enough to usher in the new millennium at least, God willing."

"Do you think you'll be up to going to the Millennium Moonlight Ball with me?" she asked, sitting on the edge of the bed.

"I don't know. I'd love to, but we'll have to see how I'm feeling."

"I understand. I brought this up just in case," she added, holding out the joint, about three-quarters left.

"Why not?" he said. "What have we got to lose?" He watched her relight it and take a hit. "Can you see the moon yet?" he asked, taking the joint.

"I'll check," she said, walking to the door. "I can't tell." She went out onto the deck and looked up at the sky, the smoke of her hit mingling with the cold hazy fog that the city lights turned pastel colors.

Matt took a hit, admiring, as always, her beautiful figure. He wondered if their discussion earlier had ruined any chance of losing themselves in Playtime.

As if reading his mind, she unfastened her jeans and wriggled out of them, wearing just a lacy white thong underneath. Facing away, she bent over and waggled her ass right at him.

When the cold forced her back inside, he asked, "So, could you see the moon?"

"No," she grinned, taking the joint and another hit. "Could you?"

"Mmm, mmm, mmm," he said. "Now that's what I call a beautiful moon."

"Want to see some more?"

"I'll take anything you've got."

Grabbing the bottom of her white angora sweater, she peeled it up and over her head, tossing it aside. Beneath, she wore a white lace teddy that he remembered as one of her favorites. She stood by the bed, saying, "What can I do for you?"

He took her hand and then noticed that red scratches covered her forearm—both her forearms, in fact. "What's all this?" he asked her. "Did you get a cat?"

She pulled her hand away. "No. It was those damned blackberry vines."

Matt was stunned. "*You* cleared those vines by the stream?" She had never before done anything like that. In fact, he didn't even think she knew about that little project of his. "I just assumed you hired someone to do that."

"I know how important things like that are to you."

"But…" He couldn't believe this. He kissed the scratches on her arms. "You didn't have to do that. That's just a silly little bit of my left-over idealism, weeding out man's mistakes to let the natural world shine through and all that."

She knelt by the bed and looked him in the eye. "Those things you do are not silly. They're good. You're the only person I know who cares about things like that and runs his life accordingly. That's why I love you so much."

"Enough to go to bed with me?" he asked, holding both her hands.

"I thought you'd never ask," she gasped, leaping into bed next to him and snuggling her chilly body against his warmer one.

"Should we light the fire up here?" he asked.

"I want you to warm me up," she declared, taking his hand and rubbing it across her torso.

He found himself aroused with almost Pavlovian immediacy. The feel of the soft skin of her belly, of her contracted nipples under the teddy and bra, of the mound of her pubic bone beneath her panties—it never failed. Soon the snuggling took on a rhythmic churning as he thrust his bulging jockeys against her hip. She turned to him with a sniff and a *faux* pout.

"What's wrong?" he asked.

"Remember that gorgeous flight attendant you walked out with?"

"Mm-hmm," he murmured, kissing her shoulder.

"When you made love to her—"

"I never!"

Undeterred: "When you made love to her, did you take off all her clothes?"

Playing along, he said, "She took them off for me."

"But I'm so ugly, you'd just as soon leave mine on."

He fingered her teddy. "If these weren't your favorite undies…"

She pointed to the strap, which she had trimmed with scissors to just a few threads.

"Are you sure?" he asked, tugging on the nearly-severed strap.

"What am I saving them for?"

One simple jerk and the strap broke. He pulled off the white lace, exposing the bra underneath, noticing that she had trimmed its straps, too. "Did you just do this?"

She shook her head, putting her hand into his underwear and fondling his growing erection.

"You mean you came to the airport…?"

She nodded. "I'm a very bad girl. You know that. And bad girls don't deserve to wear such pretty things."

He tugged on one of the bra straps but it didn't break. He pulled harder; it still held.

"Maybe if you held the whole cup," she suggested.

He slipped his hand under the bra, his knuckles pressed into her warm breast. He gave the fabric a solid jerk and still it held. "I don't want to hurt you."

She sniffed contemptuously. "I'm not made of spun sugar. Go ahead."

This time he yanked hard and finally the strap broke, her breast shimmering free. The other strap proved as reluctant and breaking it left a red mark on the skin of her shoulder.

"Now, see?" he said. "Look what you made me do."

She fingered the mark and grinned. "So you gave me a souvenir. So what? Compared to what the Seattle Police did with their rubber bullets—ooo, yeah!" She rolled over and stuck out her butt. "You saw those bruises. I refuse to let some anonymous cop have all the fun."

Matt felt a little taken aback. As kinky as he and Deb got, she rarely had this sort of attitude. He patted her bum.

"Panties first," she insisted.

The lace thong, made of much lighter material than the bra straps, gave way easily and he pulled it from under her. He gave her waiting tush a slap.

"Did that leave a mark?" she asked.

He looked carefully at her creamy white cheeks. "No."

"Well?"

He slapped her again, harder this time. She giggled. He spanked her freely. She giggled some more, egging him on.

He wasn't sure he wanted to do more. For one thing, his hand hurt. "I can see my finger marks," he told her, looking at her derriere.

"Yeah, but those will disappear in five minutes," she said, rolling back over and looking at him defiantly.

"What's gotten into you?"

"Nothing yet," she said lasciviously, spreading her legs. He slid out of his shorts but before he could roll onto her, she said, "Oh, no, you don't. I want to be as naked as that flight attendant."

Her bra cups, now that the straps were broken, hung limp, but the elastic portion still hugged her chest. He started to unfasten the front clasp.

"Not that way," she insisted, putting her arms over her head.

Without unfastening it, he slid the springy lace up across her breasts and past her arms. Fondling her bare breasts quickened his breath and hardened his cock.

Still she grinned, mischievous, determined. "See? I won't break. Take off your kid gloves."

He sucked her nipple into his mouth and nibbled on it, his right hand sliding down to her crotch. She quivered as his fingers found their way into her vulva. He released the nipple and began to slide down the bed.

"Where are you going?" she demanded.

"I thought I might give you—"

"Listen," she said, pulling him back up. "This isn't about my pleasure. This is about your pleasure. I want you to do whatever *you* want to do. Anything you've ever wanted to do."

He couldn't quite tell what prompted her to act this way but this didn't seem like the time to question it. Without a doubt, her offer appealed to him. He racked his brain for some unfulfilled longing, some kinky thrill, lingering in the back of his mind. But she had long since gone above and beyond his wildest desires. "You *know* what I want to do," he said, rubbing his erection across her thigh.

"Well, you go right ahead. What position?"

He thought about it, lying on his side beside her. For foreplay, he liked being on the bottom, which left both his hands free. But he wasn't sure he had that much stamina tonight. For his own climax, he preferred the top but his back and pelvis wouldn't allow that. "Maybe just like this," he said, pulling up her right leg and sliding his hips toward her until he lined up tab M onto slot D. This position took the strain off his back and left his right hand free to roam about her exquisite body.

She gasped as he slid into her, her eyes closing, her hand clutching his to her breast. Once inside her, he felt safe and warm, even whole, as though something missing had been restored. He pulled her close and gloried in the way she returned his thrusts. A warm tide of comfort and home and love swept away his pain and anguish. Any reserve, any hesitation, either of them felt vanished as the native rhythms of their bodies took over, propelling them together toward the gates of paradise.

With a sudden rush he felt the dam burst. She sensed it too and forced his hand ever harder into her tender breast, covering his hand with hers, her nails scraping, digging into the pale flesh. With a cry born of pain and passion, he let all his pent-up desires flow unimpeded into her.

Afterward, panting, kissing her neck, he felt her body gently quivering. He hugged her closer. The quivers turned to shakes. He pulled away to look at her face but she turned away. "What is it? What's wrong?" he asked.

"Nothing. I'm fine."

But he could tell she was crying. He had rarely seen her cry. Over the years, she had had little reason to cry, for one thing. But she also had a disposition that made her fight when frustrated and stiffen when grieving. He hadn't expected this.

"Did I hurt you?" he asked.

She shook her head no but began to sob.

"Oh, Deb, honey, come on. Talk to me."

"I just don't think I can do it," she sobbed.

"Do what, babe?" he asked, turning her shoulders toward him so he could see her face.

"I just don't think I can let you go," she cried, burying her face in his chest.

"Oh, babe, I wish with all my heart that I didn't have to put you through this. But that's all the more reason to be done with it sooner rather than later."

"No, you're wrong," she blurted. "Damn it, you're wrong! I love you—I *need* you—more than you know."

"It'll be tough, I know. But you're strong. You'll get through this."

"No! Don't you see? I'm not strong! I'm weak. Oh, God, I'm so weak!"

"What are you talking about? You're incredible."

"Oh, if you only knew! Oh, Matt, I'm a horrible person!"

"What makes you say that? You're a wonderful person."

"No, I'm weak, horrible, selfish, meddling, lying—oh, I just can't do this. I know I told you that I'd abide by your decision but I just don't think I can. I just want to die, to die with you. Can't I do that? What do they call that in India, when a woman immolates herself on her husband's funeral pyre? Suttee? That's what I want to do."

"Is that why you wanted me to hurt you earlier?"

"It's only fair!" she cried. "You're willing to die just so you can make love to me a few more times. What's a little scrape or bruise compared to that?"

He hadn't foreseen this. "But I don't want to hurt you," he insisted. "All I've ever wanted is to make you feel good."

"So why do you want to quit?" she demanded.

"Well, it's not like I *want* to quit," he said. "For that matter, if I forego the orchiectomy, I can at least give you pleasure for a few more months maybe."

She rolled over to face him, reaching down and touching his still-sticky, now-limp penis. "So you think this is the only way you can give me pleasure."

"In bed? Oh, I know I can do other things," he conceded. "Things that you apparently enjoy. But ultimately…"

She rolled her eyes. "Oh, if you only knew how much those other things mean to me."

"You're just saying that."

She bristled. "I could prove it."

"How?"

She thought about it. "Well, why not? I've bared my body to you. Why not bare my soul as well?"

"This sounds like it might take a while. I need to get up."

"Oh, I'm sorry! Are you all right?"

"I just need to… Well, the other day as I struggled for the umpteenth time toward the john, I thought of a little millennium humor. Ready? The King may be coming—" He paused, for effect, and to straighten his back.

She smiled, sniffing her tears.

"—but the Emperor is pissing."

She laughed, and he felt better.

o   o   o

By the time Matt got out of the bathroom, Deb had turned on the gas fireplace, got herself a glass of wine, and donned a silk kimono. It reassured him to see her a little more collected. He climbed back into the bed next to her, kissing her.

"I don't think I've ever seen you bare your soul before," he pointed out.

She sipped her wine. "That's because I never have. And let me just say up front how sorry I am. Please don't hate me! I really never meant to hurt you."

"I know you wouldn't and I could never hate you."

"You don't know what I'm going to say," she said. "Oh, God, where to start?"

"The beginning usually works pretty well."

She took a deep breath. "Well, in some ways this is all Jason's fault."

That got his attention. "Good Lord! This goes back a ways, doesn't it?"

"Remember that New Year's Eve party at Russ's house?"

"Where I splashed gravy on your beautiful blue dress? Who could forget?"

"Did you ever know what happened with Jason and Amanda that night?"

"Not really. They didn't come back until after I took you home."

"Well, they made love that night. That was Mandy's first time."

"I had no idea. That wasn't when May was conceived, was it?"

"No, it wasn't. Anyway, Mandy told me something that night that screwed up everything."

"Oh?"

"You know, at that point she and Jason had a thing—"

"—that we all knew about and they didn't."

"Right. Well, before we came to Russ's that night, Mandy told me that if she had a reason to drop Bill—like if she found out he was seeing someone else—that she would be free to be with Jason. So I made a stupid decision. I called Bill."

"Ah!" he said. "You know, when I went over those old letters in Boston, I found some reference to you knowing something about Bill—oh, that he was going to be in Denver."

"Yes," she said, her eyes distant. "Valentine's Day. He took me out to dinner."

"Really? I had no idea." He had never liked Bill any more than anyone else had and he shuddered to think of Deb going out with him. But since she and Matt hadn't yet gelled at that point, he had no right to criticize. "How was it?"

"Oh, Matt, it was horrible!" she burst out. "After dinner, he asked if I wanted to go for a ride—he had that beautiful T-bird—and we ended up on Lookout Mountain. The next thing I knew, he was all over me! He ripped my dress and threatened to just leave me up there if I didn't let him… let him…"

Matt felt the hair on the back of his neck rise. "Oh no! Oh, Deb! Oh, Jesus! He raped you?"

She nodded bleakly. "I never told anybody. I felt like it was my fault. I mean, you know the way I used to dress back then and I was the one who called him, after all."

"That didn't give him the right." Matt's hackles were up. "That bastard."

"God, I felt so… so filthy. Like I couldn't get his smell off of me."

"How did Manny tolerate that guy?"

"He never did anything like that to her. At least, before they were married."

"So you never told her about this?"

"I told her I went out with him. I had to. She had to know. And it worked, as far as that goes. She dumped him. But I didn't tell her all of it, at least not right away. I couldn't tell anybody. I hated men. I hated myself. Well, that's when I wrote those horrible, snotty letters to you."

"They weren't that bad," he reassured her, stroking her kimonoed arm.

"You quit writing back," she pointed out.

"To tell you the truth," he confessed, "I've always assumed you started seeing John again. I just figured I'd bow out gracefully. In any case, I'm so sorry Bill did that to you. It must have been traumatic."

"It was more than traumatic," she said, her eyes welling with tears. "He got me pregnant."

This rattled him to the core. He stared at her, dumb struck.

"Oh, darling," she cried. "I'm so sorry to have to tell you all this! You must think I'm just despicable."

"Bill got you pregnant?" he said in disbelief. "What did you do?"

"What could I do? I was going to a Catholic college. I couldn't tell my parents. They would have killed me. I couldn't confide in Mandy. I didn't want to have anything to do with Bill. I cried for a week. Finally, one of the other girls at the dorm told me she knew how I could get an abortion."

"Legally?"

Deb sniffed. "I couldn't get a legal abortion in Colorado back then. This girl, though, knew a doctor who would do it. In Mexico."

"Oh no!"

"What choice did I have? I couldn't keep the baby. I hated even the thought of having Bill's baby. At the time, an abortion seemed like the right thing to do. So on spring break, I did it."

"Where in Mexico?"

"Juarez. I was told to be in a doorway on the corner—God, I still remember it: Laredo and 16th of September—by the Canada shoe store. A green and white Cadillac picked me up and took me to an abandoned house. There were just a few sticks of furniture in the waiting room and a gurney with a bright light overhead in what passed for the operating room. They gave me a general anesthetic, maybe ether. I remember feeling sick from it."

Matt felt a little sick just hearing about it. He kissed her hand.

"I remember waking up before the procedure was finished. I asked about whether it was a boy or a girl, which of course is impossible to tell at that stage. When they finished, they took me to another room where there were some twin beds. A couple of other girls were there too. We all cried. I lay there for an hour or so and then decided to leave. They just turned me loose in Juarez. I finally got a cab—not really a cab, just a guy with a sign on his car. He couldn't drive across the border so he dropped me off and I had to walk across the bridge and the few blocks to the motel."

"By yourself?" Matt asked, his head dizzy and his stomach in knots at hearing this dreadful story about his own sweet Deb.

"Oh, I didn't want anyone to know!" she exclaimed. "It just seemed like some awful nightmare. I used to have this vision: I could see this big empty space in the distance that would come closer and closer. When it got close enough it sucked out some essential part of me and then receded into the distance. This happened in my dreams, when I was awake, all the time."

"Oh, Deb, why didn't you call me or something?"

"I didn't know you that well then—certainly not well enough to talk about something like that. I couldn't even talk to Mandy about it, much the less a man. For a while I didn't think I'd ever be able to be with a man again. I didn't feel like I could get intimate with anyone without telling him about the abortion but I couldn't face the prospect of talking about it, especially to someone respectable like you."

"I would have understood."

"I don't think I could have tolerated that either. I didn't want understanding or pity or anything. I just wanted to forget about it, to put it all behind me. But of course that didn't work either, because about a week later I got an infection."

"From the abortion procedure?"

"Medical standards are much lower in Mexico. Oh, I got so sick! I had this disgusting discharge and a terrible fever but I didn't dare see a doctor because he'd know right away what I'd done. Eventually, my roommate at Regis took me to a clinic in Denver and got me some antibiotics. It got rid of the infection but by then a bunch of scar tissue had formed, which blocked my fallopian tubes."

"Oh," Matt said dully. "So you never had to have your tubes tied."

"Matt, sweetie, I'm so sorry! I never should have lied to you. But back then, when we were first married, I really wanted you to love me and I was afraid that if I told you the truth…"

He wanted to tell her again that he would have understood but back then, the truth might have created a huge rift between them. "In any case," he said, "it comes out the same, whether your tubes were tied or blocked by scar tissue."

"So you honestly never wanted to have children? I always felt guilty that I somehow talked you into that because I knew I couldn't."

"That's how I really felt back then and I have no regrets now. I'm just glad you weren't scarred any more than that."

"I was emotionally scarred," she said. "Like I said, I hated men for a while. I hated everybody. I even fought with Mandy and we hardly *ever* fought. She finally came to realize that, in going out with Bill, I had just carried out her wish, and she forgave me. But she didn't forgive Bill. And getting rid of him did enable her to give in to her feelings for Jason. She really thought Jason was completely different from Bill."

"He was."

"Well, when Mandy and I went up to Boulder on Earth Day to see him, she caught him with another woman."

"I never knew that."

"You were up in Seattle. You missed a lot that spring. Anyway, I'll never forget that look on Mandy's face when she saw that woman and Jason together. It seemed like her innocence turned to ashes before my eyes. So I told her we should just leave, which we did, but Jason ran after us. That's when they arrested him."

"Is that what happened? I never did hear that whole story."

"He wasn't doing anything but running after us but the police were so jumpy I guess they just reacted. When they stopped him, Jason shouted out to us, shouted Mandy's name, so we turned around. The cop had grabbed Jason's long hair and he hit him over the back of the head like he was trying to crack a coconut. I thought he killed him. Mandy did too. She screamed and started to run to him but I pulled her away. They would have arrested us too if we'd gone back and that wouldn't have helped Jason at all. John ended up in the same helpless position. We could only watch them cart him away."

"How long was he in jail?"

"Just a couple of days, I found out later. I guess he and the others who were arrested that day and the day before did what we did a couple of weeks ago: gave phony names and insisted on court trials. Rather than clog up the system with a bunch of trivial civil-disobedience cases, they ended up just turning everybody loose. But Mandy and I didn't know that. Jason never called. Mandy was a basket case. First she'd be worried sick that he was dead or in jail but then she'd turn around and hate his guts for being with that other woman. And of course I was in no position to defend men at that point."

"At least you had each other."

Deb took a gulp of her wine. "Yes, we certainly did. Oh, God, I've never told another living soul about this. Do you hate me?"

"Of course I don't hate you!" He kissed her hand again. "It's just such a shame you had to go through all that. And mostly by yourself, from the sound of it."

"Not entirely." She looked at him. "Try to keep an open mind. Please?"

"Of course."

"Well, a couple of weeks later—Mother's Day, in fact—Mandy's parents went out to California to visit Peter so Mandy went out to dinner with me and my mom and dad. It was a beautiful day, warm and sunny, so Mandy and I swam in our pool afterward and then I took her home. I happened to have some pot, so she and I sat on her bed and got high. We pissed and moaned about men in general and Bill in particular. Oh, and she made us some Sea Breezes. So we got pretty loose. Anyway, at some point I included Jason on the list of scum-sucking, heartless assholes and she slapped me."

"Mandy slapped you!? I don't believe it!"

"I didn't either. I just stared at her with my mouth open and tears in my eyes. All of a sudden she realized what she'd done and she cried out and took me into her arms, apologizing and showering me with kisses. The next thing I knew I was kissing her too."

"Really!"

"Oh, Matt, I wish I could tell you how it felt! Mandy and I had been such close friends for so long. We had always shared the most intimate details of our lives with one another. I was always a little more, um…adventuresome than she when it came to sex and so I would tell her about things I discovered—well, I've told you about some of those things as well. Anyway, we didn't have to ask any questions of one another. There was no ice to break. For the first time in months I felt safe and happy."

"What are you saying? You and Man made love?"

"Are you shocked?"

"No. Interested," he said. "Really. Interested."

"Oh, Matt, it felt incredible!"

"What did? What did she do?"

"Nothing that you haven't done. I mean, as you know, it's not what you do, it's who does it and how it's done."

"But did you…?"

"Did she bring me to climax? Oh, my, yes! It wasn't the same as when you and I make love. I wouldn't trade what you and I have done for the world. But…well, put it this way. When a man makes love to a woman, a virgin anyway, it's referred to as deflowering. But what Amy and I did that day felt like *re*flowering."

"Amy?"

Deb blushed. "I can't believe I said that! I used to call her Amy when we were in grade school. But after she officially became Mandy (or Manny, as you guys used to call her) I only called her Amy when we were alone."

"Anyway, you reciprocated with her, I assume."

"Of course! Oh, honey, that day was just so special! You know, when you scootch down under the covers in the morning and wake me up with your tongue, I often close my eyes and—after all these years—imagine that I'm with Amy again."

Matt stared out the window at the cold pale haze.

"You're upset, aren't you?" she asked, running her hand through his chest hair.

"No, I'm not," he said. "Just trying to digest all this. I mean, I can hardly be shocked. You've never been squeamish about other women."

"Well, it's not like I'm interested in having sex with other women, except in our little alternate reality of Playtime. Mandy's the only one I ever did anything with in real life."

"Was that the only time?"

She nodded.

"Why did you stop?"

She sipped some wine. "I didn't tell you what happened afterward. Oh, Matt, she looked so sweet! She fell asleep. I lay there stroking her hair for a while, listening to her breathe. But as I thought about what we had done, I realized it was too nice."

"Too nice?"

"Maybe my Catholic upbringing prompted it. Anything that feels really good must be a sin, you know? And then I remembered that I had promised my mother that I would go to evening Mass. So I slipped out without waking Mandy and went home to change. I stopped back at her house on the way to the Chapel to see how she was, to see if she wanted to go with me. But when I went into the bedroom, there beside Mandy was Jason."

"Oh, so that's when May…"

"Right."

"Hmm. Awkward moment."

Deb's unfocused eyes gazed back across the decades. "I didn't know how to react. At first I felt like an intruder. Then, just for an instant, I felt betrayed. But then I looked at them: Mandy's face as flushed and beautiful as a rose, Jason beaming with happy wonder, as though he had just unraveled one of the secrets of the universe. They belonged together. I couldn't stand in the way of that."

"So what did you do?"

"I decided—to use your phrase—to bow out gracefully. I told Mandy I'd call her later and turned to go. But she called me back. She pointed out that all three of us knew everything there was to know, that no one had any secrets. Which was true. Jason knew what Mandy and I had done and I knew what she and Jason had done. So Mandy called a truce."

"A truce?"

"A moment of peace in the war between the sexes. She called me over and made me sit on the bed. She held my hand in one hand and Jason's in the other. She made us both promise that we would never tell anyone about what happened that evening. And until now, I never have."

Matt's heart swelled with admiration and love. "You see why I trust you? You're such an incredible woman."

"You're forgetting what happened after that. Jason called John to tell him he had picked up an ounce of dope for him. He needed a ride to Pauline Chapel, which is where I was going anyway, so we both agreed we should let Amy stay in bed. I know it sounds pretty silly at the cynical end of this century but for just a few moments, peace and love reigned in that little part of the world. I fell in love with Mandy that day and I'm not sure I ever really got over it. But I realized—happily—that Jason loved her more. Oh, you should have seen them saying good-bye! Jason hoped John would give him a ride back but even if he had to walk, he could have returned in twenty minutes. Still, you'd think he was going to the moon for all the hugs and kisses they lavished on each other. Finally, when I told him I had to leave, he left her with—what else?—Shakespeare:

> "Sleep dwell upon thine eyes, peace in thy breast!
> Would I were sleep and peace, so sweet to rest!"

"He loved his Uncle Willie," Matt said.

"But he didn't love me," Deb said. "You know, Jason and I got along okay but I never felt close to him. And he seemed so uncomfortable on the ride to the Chapel." She took another sip of wine. "Love doesn't come in triangles."

"You're right. When more than two people are involved, it's more like vectors, with two distant points each exerting conflicting forces on a central point."

She smiled and touched his cheek. "You're so cute. I love the way you gather the problems of life into a single, tidy bundle. Anyway, Jason's problems sure multiplied that day. Oh God, if I had just skipped Mass!"

"He got busted outside the Chapel, right?"

She nodded. "And I didn't even stay for Confession."

"How come?"

She chewed her fingernail. "I knew in my heart that I would never be able to reconcile how I felt about Mandy with a Catholic God. In fact, I never went to Confession again. For that matter, part of the reason I never told you about any of this was how awkward Jason seemed about the whole thing. I figured maybe a man just couldn't understand how I felt, how much that moment meant to me."

"I'm not sure I do," Matt confessed, "but I'm trying. Your moment didn't last long, though, did it?"

"Nope," she said bitterly. "By the first of June, Jason was in prison in Cañon City and Mandy knew she was pregnant. She and I couldn't even talk about what had happened between us. I mean, what were we supposed to do? Thirty years ago we couldn't just declare ourselves lesbian lovers and get a place together. The thought of the ridicule and grief people would give us terrified us both. The baby brought the real world crashing down on our heads. But at the same time, I felt a bond with the baby too, since I had actually been there *before* its conception."

"But Manny must have freaked when she found herself pregnant and the baby's father in jail."

"She freaked, all right. She called up Bill—I didn't know about this until afterward—and practically threw herself at him. Bill, the bastard, didn't look a gift horse in the mouth. He fucked her at the first opportunity."

"Why on earth—? Oh, I see. She gave the baby an alternate father."

"Right. When I found out, I told her she'd lost her mind. But when she asked me for better ideas, I didn't know what to say. And then Jason wrote her these passionate letters from prison, talking about how he was going to find a way to get out of there and come for her, take her away so they could start a life together."

"Did he know she was pregnant?"

"She didn't tell him that until she told him that she was planning to marry Bill. But Jason knew that the baby was his. His letters became frantic, insisting he could find a way out of his mess, begging her not to marry Bill. But finally Mandy became desperate. She couldn't hide her condition much longer. That's when I told her about my abortion."

"About Bill raping you?"

"Oh, God, no! I think that would have killed her. I told her I got careless and slept with some guy I knew at Regis. I hated to put her through what I had done but I hated more the thought of her marrying Bill. So we set up an abortion with the same doctor in Juarez at the beginning of August."

The pieces fell into place for Matt. "Oh, okay. That's why you were in El Paso when Jason disappeared up in Jones Park."

"Then you called the next morning just as we were about to walk out the door to go across the river. You gave Mandy the message you said Jason begged you to relay: simply that he 'didn't want her to do it.' She said you broke down and cried when you had to tell her that he had disappeared during the night."

"Oh Lord. No wonder Jason seemed so desperate for me to deliver that message. The story he told me was that Man was thinking of transferring to UTEP."

"That's what we told everyone, including our parents. Oh, honey, you sounded so upset when you called!"

"I *was* upset, maybe more upset than I've ever been in my life. I couldn't believe I had let Jason just slip away like that. Jeez, Mandy must have been devastated."

"She and I couldn't quit bawling. Finally, we both agreed that somehow she ought to find a way to keep the baby, that the world just couldn't bear to lose Jason and his only child on the same day."

"I'm glad I called when I did."

"So am I, honey," she said, gently hugging him. "My heart went out to you. I knew how much you cared for Jason, how torn up you must be, but still you put our needs before your own. I fell in love with you then and there and I've loved you ever since. I knew that I could never find a better man than you. And I never have."

"If I'd been a better man, maybe Jason wouldn't have died that night," Matt said bitterly. "May might have grown up with a real father. She and Mandy sure didn't get much help from Bill."

"I know," Deb said. She took a deep breath. "You know, as long as I'm baring things tonight, there is one other aspect to this story you probably should know."

"As long as Bill doesn't come into the picture again, why not?"

"Well, it's because Bill wasn't in the picture that I did what I did."

"Which was…"

"Well, I kind of took it upon myself to keep an eye on May. I was worried. While Bill and Mandy were married, I couldn't do much but watch them tear each other to shreds. And that horrible marriage must have taken its toll on May. But I figured, between them, they'd at least take care of her. But May just kept getting in more trouble. One day when May was 15, Mandy called me in tears, telling me that May was in jail."

"Wow. Jail. I didn't know about that. For what?"

"Driving under the influence, possession, vehicular homicide."

"Oh, Lord."

"Mandy had become so frustrated with May's attitude that she wanted to just leave her in jail. And of course, Bill wouldn't lift a finger to help her. So I decided to take matters into my own hands."

"Oh?"

"This happened while you and Phil Banks were negotiating that Quillayute settlement and even though you didn't care much for him as a person, you really seemed to respect his abilities as a lawyer."

"Still do."

"I had just started at Microsoft and I finally had a pretty decent income. So I called Phil and asked if he could do anything to help May."

"Really? He never mentioned that."

"Honey, I know you're getting tired of me saying this, but I'm sorry. I went behind your back. I made it clear to Phil that he worked strictly for me on this and made him swear that he would never tell you about it. I knew that I couldn't tell you about any of this without telling you all of it. Maybe it was wrong but it seemed like the best thing to do at the time."

Matt clenched his teeth. If she hadn't already given him half a dozen massive jolts, this would have laid him out. As it was, he could do nothing but shake his head in disbelief. For thirty years he thought they had shared their most intimate lives and now it turned out that she had another, complicated, serious life about which he knew nothing. He felt betrayed by her methods—no denying it—but her motives still seemed above reproach. He could hardly blame her. But the fact that Phil Banks once again entered the picture made him queasy.

"So did Phil do the job?" he asked, trying not to sound sarcastic.

"Actually, yes," she told him. "He got May out of jail and got that low-life she was secretly married to, Paco—who was really the guilty party—convicted. Phil's a good lawyer. He has the morals of sewer rat but he's a damn good lawyer. I assure you, we had—have always had—a strictly professional relationship and I paid him an exorbitant amount of money for his services."

"You did?"

"That's why all those hours I put in at Microsoft didn't seem to pay off for a long time. Remember when you told me I should just look for some better company to work for if Bill Gates and Paul Allen couldn't pay me more?"

He chuckled. "That's right. That's when I suggested that you try to get a job at that Beta-format VCR company."

"Anyway, I not only didn't tell you about helping May, I didn't tell Mandy or Bill, or even May, because all those same questions would come up. Mandy would never have accepted charity like that anyway. After she and Bill split up, she wanted nothing to do with money. For that matter, May moved to Buena Vista to be near Paco while he was in jail. Mandy didn't seem to want much to do with her daughter at that point either."

"Did May get straightened out?"

"Actually, no, but this time I didn't find out about it from Mandy. Phil called me one day to tell me that the girl I had hired him to help had shown up half-dead with hepatitis and pneumonia at Harborview."

"Here in Seattle?"

"She evidently had become involved with some rock band and had gotten into intravenous drug use. And you know how it is at a hospital like that. A patient with a lawyer like Phil Banks gets a lot better care than some addict off the streets. And of course, by then, I was making enough money at Microsoft that I could afford to upgrade her care without putting that much of a dent in my income."

"So you still didn't tell Amanda?"

"She would have hated me for it. Her attitude was that May got herself into those problems, she ought to get herself out."

"Did she?"

"She got out of the hospital. But then, like a fool, she went right back to that asshole she married."

"And they, of course, lived happily ever after."

She snorted. "Last year, after May had his kid, Paco beat her up, put her in the hospital, and started shacking up with some floozy. So one night last January May got drunk and ended up in jail with a DUI."

"Sounds like a job for the Caped Crusader."

She returned his sarcasm with a smile. "Smarty pants. Actually, I didn't find out about it until last May. What was I supposed to do? Just let her rot behind bars?"

"Her mother seemed to think that was the best course."

"Actually, no. Mandy didn't exactly approve of May's behavior but she didn't think she deserved to be behind bars for it, or that Paco should have custody of their little girl. And, actually, Phil found out that a previous DUI should no longer have shown up on her record so he got her sentence reduced to time served."

"And you never told Manny about any of this."

"Actually, I did." Her bottom lip began to quiver again. "Oh, Matt, I am such a horrible person!"

"You still haven't given me any proof of that."

"Last August, I called Mandy to see how May and Libby were doing and just to talk. I caught her on a bad day: some household project had brought back a bunch of memories, the baby was fussy, and May, who really was trying to pull her life together, had grouched at her. Mandy said something about wishing May would just disappear from her life again and I told her she should try to be a little more patient. She snapped at me, saying something about how I had never had to be responsible for a child. Without thinking about it, I just blurted out, 'Who do you think bailed May out of her problems all these years?' And I told her about all the things Phil Banks had done on May's behalf."

"What did she say?"

A tear slid down Deb's cheek. "She didn't say anything. She hung up on me. I felt so awful! I tried calling her back but she didn't answer. Either she didn't want to talk to me or she had already gone out to the glider port."

"Oh, no! So that was the day she was killed."

Tears streamed from her eyes. "I never got a chance to explain, to apologize! She was my best friend, Matt. And the last time we spoke, we argued. Oh, God, every time I think about it, I just want to die."

"I understand now why her death hit you so hard."

She turned to him. "So don't you see? I just can't bear to lose you too! You're more than just my husband, my lover, my friend. You're the only link I have left to that secret world, to Playtime. I can't find my way back there with anyone else."

Matt didn't know what to say. Obviously she had not just invented some ploy to sway his decision about the orchiectomy. Still— "If I have the operation, I won't be able to satisfy you."

"Oh, baby, you satisfy me in more ways than I can count! In fact—" She touched his limp penis again. "It'll be a while before this gets hard again, won't it?"

He shrugged.

"But you could give me an orgasm right now, couldn't you?"

"Oh, Deb, that's right!" he exclaimed. "I completely forgot! I didn't satisfy you earlier, did I? I'd be happy to—"

She kissed his lips to quiet him. "See how you are? You can restore the bloom to my rose any time you like, can't you? Oh, honey, there's a whole new world of love that we could explore. We can call our own truce. We can get past the tension between a man and a woman and love each other just as people. Inside me are petals of tenderness and affection that have never fully unfolded. You can bring me to life."

"But won't you miss me as a man?"

"Of course! I'd be lying if I said otherwise. But I would miss you far more as a person, as a friend, as a playmate. Please. Won't you reconsider?"

He sighed. He never could deny her. "Okay. I'll reconsider."

"Oh, thank you!" She showered his face with kisses. "Honey, I love you more than words can say."

"We better get some sleep," he told her, pulling her body close, switching off the light. "Unless you want me to… I mean, I still owe you an orgasm."

"Darling, you don't owe me a thing. In fact, I owe you about ten thousand orgasms, so just put it on account. What I worry about is finding some way of pleasing you."

"You don't have to…"

"I *want* to! From now on, I'm going to spend so much time with you, you'll end up wishing I'd just leave you alone."

"Never happen. But what about all your projects, your charities?"

"I don't know. I guess I'll just have to find someone to help me. You and I are going to be too busy enjoying ourselves. And just so you know, money's no object. Whatever you need, whatever you want, you just ask and if it's in my power, it's yours."

"Okay, I've got my first request."

"Anything."

He wiped the tears from her cheek. "A smile?"

She smiled and his heart melted once again. He pulled her close and kissed her and then they rolled over to sleep like spoons, her body molding to his perfectly. In just a few minutes her breathing became regular and her warm body relaxed. For a while he lay thinking. Then in the flickering firelight he watched one of the forced cherry petals fall from the branch and float silently to the steamer trunk below. With that, he fell into a peaceful doze.

...O...O...O...

Love never has a happy ending. We're only happy when love never ends, when the beautiful maiden and her Prince Charming live happily ever after.

So how can I, a balding, middle-aged man, lonely and unloved, write a happy ending? So far in my life, love has always died, taking a part of me with it each time.

One of the worst endings was one of the first and I still feel like a big chunk of me died back then. It tore me up so badly, in fact, that so far I've avoided writing about it. But if what I'm writing is to have any validity whatsoever, I guess I better deal with it.

When I went to college in Boulder, I fell in love with a friend. I've met most of the women in my life through my music but she loved me just for me. Perhaps that's why it hurt so much when I realized she and I couldn't be together. We didn't even have a torrid physical relationship. We only made love twice. But we had so much in common and I had so many deep insights and happy moments in the short time that we were together that the unavoidable end blind-sided even cynical me. I barely ate for a couple of weeks after that, walking like a wraith along the back roads, wanting not just to thrust my knife deep into my aching heart but to twist it until the offending flesh was gone. But I didn't. Some silly part of me still clings to the ridiculous hope that someday, soon before it's too late, she and I could find ourselves together again.

So why go on? Why fall in love again after that? Beats me. And I mean, it beats me bloody and senseless. But fall in love again I did, even though I've never been able to afford a really good woman.

I fell in love with a waitress at a place I played. I loved her so desperately that I willingly gave up most of what I had in order to keep her. That, of course, doomed the affair. When most of my possessions and dignity departed, so did she, with a cook wanted in three states for murder. There's an ego boost. Nevertheless, I pined for her and begged her to see me again, to talk it over with me, to tell me the truth. She said, "I don't want to see you hurt." I took that to mean she felt compassion. Wrong. She felt squeamish. But she told me the truth. I hurt, so she didn't want to see me.

Then I fell in love with a sweet young thing—too young, in fact, even younger than the young lady who so fascinates me at work. This girl seemed completely devoted to me for years. She helped me start my solo act and, in fact, has helped me play with myself ever since. But reality always sets in: she fell in love with a rock band and within days had virtually forgotten about me.

My longest, latest, and perhaps last love lingers still. Knowing I was too poor and too honest to hold onto a woman like the Princess, I found a woman as poor and, I thought, as honest as I was. I encouraged her to dig herself out of debt and helped her with her troubled kids. She showed a genuine interest in me and all my impractical dreams. Together, we shared life's sorrows and joys, found a lot of common interests, and made love like there was no tomorrow. She complained only that my road work kept us apart. So, after several years, when I felt sure that we would last, I decided to stay at home even if that meant getting a normal job and I asked her to marry me. I made it clear to her that I intended to share all I had with her and that I would care for her kids as my own. She visited me on one of my road trips and when she left I felt so devastated that I broke down and cried at the airport. It scared the hell out of her. When I got home, I discovered she had found someone new. We stayed friends and she continued to wear the modest ring I gave her. But the last time I saw her, not long ago, she had taken off the ring.

I don't see a way to cobble a happy ending out of any of that. And now I find that the fascinating young lady at work has fallen for one of my coworkers while I watched from the sidelines. I never considered her a realistic possibility anyway but I sure cherished the fantasy that somehow we could be friends at least.

So once again I return to that blithe spirit who has stood by me through it all: my muse. Even her interest in me begins to falter, though. I intended to write a song to include in this but I've never finished it. After all, even if I did finish it, who would listen? Most people only want to hear songs they've heard a thousand times before.

Anyway, it's called "The Last Man Standing," a slow waltz about the game of musical chairs. I planned to write the first verse from my perspective on stage; from there it looks like everyone's taken, everyone's got a partner. In the second verse, I wanted to talk about all the other musicians I used to know who have long since moved on to normal jobs and better lives. But all I ever wrote was the chorus, which went like this:

> *I see the whole room dancing*
> *When the song begins to play,*
> *But I'm the last man standing*
> *As the music fades away.*

December 24, 1999

Russ looked around the Grove Court townhome to make sure he didn't forget anything. No, he could forget nothing. He looked around to make sure he hadn't left anything behind. But of course he left behind more than he could bear to lose. So he looked around once more just for old times' sake.

He knew he would miss this place. In the years he had spent here, he felt like he had arrived. Now, all too soon, he had to depart.

He started to pick up his suitcase and leather overnight bag but then remembered something he really wanted to do once more. He went into the studio and looked at "Pensive," the Guy Ellis watercolor of Sylvia that hung by the window above her work table. He had many great memories of her but he knew he could never better Ellis's subtle, artistic viewpoint. He sighed and touched the frame with one of his knuckle kisses.

On the work table, already framed, lay her current project, a new oil painting she planned to premiere at her New Year's Eve opening in Dia. For the past couple of weeks Russ and Sylvia had maintained an uneasy truce, avoiding intrusions into one another's space as much as possible, so Russ hadn't yet seen this.

Modest in size and scope, it depicted a detail of the cityscape: the base of an old brick wall with a round drain set in the concrete of the walk below. The wind and water had carried some detritus into the frame: a popsicle stick, a condom wrapper, last fall's leaves, cigarette butts, and a tattered bird's nest with bits of shell and blobs of white droppings still clinging to it. One of the small seeds the bird had brought back to the nest had fallen into the woven grass and twigs. Nourished by the droppings and watered by the spring rain, the seed had sprouted, the first oblong leaves shriveled, the more complicated secondary leaves reaching for the sun. A bit melancholy, perhaps, but an appropriate theme of renewal for the new millennium. Carefully, tenderly, he gave the wood frame a knuckle kiss as well.

Russ still had a few larger items he would have to come back to Grove Court for: his leather chair, some kitchen things. But he might never be here alone again.

He would have plenty of time alone at the farm. Ellen planned to go out to San Diego after the first of the year after all and Russ would have the place to himself to work on his book of philosophy. To get himself psyched he had found at the Broken Spine a used copy of Jean Paul Satre's *Being and Nothingness*, a book he had never read. This seemed like a great time to catch up on his reading. *Aut libri aut liberi*: "Either books or children."

He took a deep breath, gritted his teeth, shouldered his bag, lifted his case, and left.

O   O   O

Russ got to Tweak before the dinner crowd did. He set his suitcase and bag under the bar and sat on one of the stools.

The trauma of being uprooted often brings a sense of newness to familiar surroundings, kind of a permanent state of *jamais vu*, when ordinary, everyday objects appear strange and unfamiliar. Russ felt that way looking around Tweak. He had created Tweak in his image and likeness and being the introspective sort he saw every problem as a reflection of his own inadequacies. Now that he had resolved to give it up, he saw his restaurant with new eyes. For all its faults, this failed dream still mattered to him, still appealed to him. He probably would have liked this place more as a customer than he did as the owner. Some soft jazz, mostly an electric guitar and a woman's voice, filled the empty spaces in the scattered, quiet conversations. The servers, in their slow moments, had strung lights around the windows. Oscar had even allowed a tiny artificial Christmas tree on the end of the bar.

Oscar asked Russ if he wanted a drink. He thought about it and decided to have a Manhattan.

Christine came to the bar and ordered a couple of martinis. Her tight red sweater caught Russ's eye but failed to lift his melancholy spirits. "Did you get dinner?" she asked him as Oscar set down the Manhattan.

"Not yet," Russ said. "I guess I'll just stop somewhere on the way up to the farm."

"Buzz put together an excellent holiday sandwich," Christine said. "Why don't you try one?"

"Why not? I may never get to eat here for free again."

"I can't believe you're leaving," Christine said softly, touching his arm before entering his order into the computer.

"To everything there is a season," Russ said philosophically.

"But are you sure you can't find a way to work things out with Sylvia? I mean, this whole business with Ellis's sperm sample just seems so...trivial."

Christine and Russ had grown closer the last few weeks, Russ confiding in her about the problems in his marriage. Once in a while—not often—he could look past Christine's beauty and see her just as a friend.

"The sperm sample won't even be a trivial problem much longer," he explained. "Sylvia's decided to dispose of it."

"When? Do you know?"

"They had planned to do it on the anniversary of Ellis's death, the 21st, until Syl got a reading from Zena, whose powers of clairvoyance saw doing something like that so close to the solstice as a bad omen. Plus, she pointed out that too many people would have trouble finding the time to get together the week before Christmas. So they moved it to next week instead. Zena sensed that the 27th would be propitious."

"Maybe you and Sylvia will be better off in the long run without it," Christine speculated. "You could always call David Crosby."

Russ chuckled. Crosby had recently been revealed to be the sperm donor for the singer Melissa Ethridge's child. But his amusement faded fast.

"I think destroying Ell's sample just shifts Syl's emotional baggage about Ellis onto me," he said as Buzz came up from the kitchen and set the sandwich in front of him. "She will no longer have the option of using it so she doesn't have to worry about it. But I'll have it on my conscience that, for my sake, she destroyed the last living vestige of Guy Ellis. If I ask her to get rid of it, it sounds like petty jealousy. I mean, we're talking about the helpless sperm of a disabled veteran who died a dozen years ago. Not much of a rival. But if I try to persuade her to hang onto it in case she needs it in the future, I sound like I'm planning to leave."

"Are you?"

"I wasn't before. But now? I don't know. The whole sperm sample episode, and the way I found out about it, exposed some deep faults in our marriage. Sylvia and I come from such different backgrounds. Maybe she'd be better off with some nice young stud from Little Italy who could give her a yardful of kids."

"But what about you?"

"I'm so burned out I can't see straight," Russ said, swallowing a bite of the sandwich: turkey, cranberry sauce, and cream cheese on a Kaiser roll—quite good. "I need some down time. Besides, I'd like to contribute to future generations in my own way. Without all the distractions of the city, maybe I can get some writing done."

"Anybody can be good in the country," Oscar pointed out as Christine left to check on her tables. Oscar's concession to the season consisted of a red plaid cummerbund over his usual impeccable white shirt and black slacks.

It occurred to Russ that he knew little about Oscar other than his quiet efficiency and clever aphorisms. "What about you?" he asked the older man. "Do you have any kids?"

"Nope," Oscar said, wiping the brass bar.

"Regrets?"

"Here's the way I see it," he said with a wry smile. "Children begin by loving their parents. After a time they judge them. Rarely, if ever, do they forgive them."

"You don't have much to be forgiven for anyway, do you?"

Oscar just kept smiling as he buffed the shiny brass taps.

"What about contributing to future generations and all that?" Russ asked.

"When you have no children of your own, everyone else's children are equally yours," Oscar said. "And there are certainly plenty of struggling and unwanted kids to go around."

"That's true," Russ admitted. Most of his employees were young enough to be his kids.

Oscar went to change CDs.

"What was that last one?" Russ asked him. "I liked it."

"Thank you," Christine said, carrying some empty plates over and setting them in the bus tub.

"Was that you singing?" Russ asked, impressed.

"Just some stuff Buzz and I put together last week."

Buzz had come back up from the kitchen to get a bottle of wine. "Whadja think, boss?" he asked Russ.

"Excellent sandwich," he said, taking another bite. "And the music is even better. That's you on the guitar?"

"I studied guitar for eight years, mostly classical and jazz."

"But what about…?" Russ asked, waving his hand to indicate Buzz's goatee and tattoos.

"I can hang with rock too," he said. "And that's where the money is. Christine and I just did this CD for fun. I've got a little four-track digital recorder and a CD burner on my computer."

"You're kidding!" Russ said. "Are you two looking for gigs?"

"Gigs?" Christine asked. "Who wants to hear live music when they can just pop in a CD?"

Russ suddenly felt guilty. "Want to play here New Year's Eve?" he offered.

"That'd be great!" Buzz said. "Too bad you're selling the place before then."

"Oh, yeah," Russ said gloomily. "Say, my Realtor told me that the guy who wants to buy the place might come in. Mr. Douglas, I think. Was he here?"

Buzz and Christine both glanced at Oscar.

"Mr. Douglas did indeed pay us a visit," Oscar said.

"What's he like?"

When Oscar paused, Christine spoke up. "He talked about a lot of changes."

"He's gonna fuck the place up," Buzz said unequivocally.

Russ knew the change might prove unpopular but he hadn't expected this vehemence from Buzz. "What did he say?"

"He wants to yuppify the place, call it 'Christopher's'," Buzz said. "He wants to polish the floors and paint the brickwork and put acoustic tile on the ceiling."

"He didn't like the artwork either," Christine remembered. "He said it made the place look too much like a gallery."

"It is a gallery!" Russ exclaimed.

"Not for long," she said. "He talked about having an old photo of the Village blown up to wallpaper size for the other room."

The turkey sandwich turned to ashes in Russ's mouth. He figured a new owner would institute changes but he had hoped to avoid hearing about it until he was far enough away not to care. "Do you think this guy's serious?" he asked Oscar.

"Oh, very," Oscar assured him.

"Do you know him?"

"Alfred and I go back many years," he said. "In fact, we lived together through much of the '60s."

Russ had never known that Oscar was gay but he had known so many gays in the Village that it didn't really cross his mind to wonder anymore. It certainly had no effect on his feelings. "He'd really do all that?"

"Put it this way," Oscar said. "Alfred used to make me wear a special waterproof suit to scrub the grout in the shower with a toothbrush."

"He wants to change the menu to nothing but nouveau cuisine," Buzz sneered. "How fresh is that? A big empty plate with fancy radishes and a piece of meat so small the animal probably wouldn't miss it."

Russ pushed away his plate and downed the rest of his Manhattan. He had to squint from the glare of his brightly burning bridges. Changes like that kept the "new" in New York but Russ didn't have to like it. To the others, he said optimistically, "It won't be that bad. You'll wear this Alfred Douglas down faster than you wore me down." But he couldn't bear the thought of this aging gay man's inability to appreciate Christine to the fullest. He sighed and stood up.

"Well, you take care," Christine told him, giving him a hug that carved a deep groove in his psyche.

Oscar handed him his suitcase and bag, saying, "You made work a joy."

"As did all of you," Russ said, shouldering his bag again. "I'm sure I'll be back, at least briefly, in a week or two. Meantime, have yourselves a merry Christmas."

"You too," Christine said.

As he walked out the door, Russ could hear Buzz say, "God bless us every one!"

O   O   O

While Russ and Sylvia hadn't agreed on much of late, they did agree to try to avoid spoiling everyone else's holiday with news of their separation. Sylvia had left earlier to spend some time with her parents in Riverdale up in the Bronx. Russ would take the subway there and they would drive her father's car up to the farm, Sylvia driving back to the city Sunday morning with Ellen to take her to the airport.

He walked past the sex shops on Christopher, his suitcase banging against his leg. It made him feel like a little kid lost in the Big City. As he waited for the light on Seventh Avenue, he looked south to the broadcasting towers atop the monolithic World Trade Center buildings rising in the night sky, beacons not of hope and freedom, like the Statue of Liberty, but of blind, raw, merciless power. The City had won. Russ just couldn't hack it. He fled like a frightened rabbit down the subway entrance and waited on the platform for the 9-train.

Even here at Sheridan Square the uptown subway car was crowded. He slid the suitcase under the orange-and-amber plastic seat and held his leather bag on his lap, assuming the pose of passive neutrality that kept a protective zone of apathy around every rider. The conductor mumbled something unintelligible into the P. A. system, the electronic doorbell rang in distorted discord, and the train lurched ahead, the standing riders swaying back and gripping the stainless steel railings. The only words in the car had been scratched by vandals into the windows and steel panels, as unintelligible as the conductor's. The train no sooner reached its clattering full velocity than it slowed again for the 14th Street stop and another wad of glum humanity forced itself into the finest cracks.

John Rocker, the hyperactive closer for the Atlanta Braves, had guaranteed himself a lifetime supply of junk thrown from the stands at Shea with some impolitic remarks in *Sports Illustrated*, calling New York "the most hectic, nerve-wracking city" and "depressing." He went on to say, "I'm not a big fan of foreigners. You can walk an entire block in Times Square and not hear anybody speak English." Hell, Russ had thought reading it, you can walk a *mile* in New York and not hear any English. Rocker had lamented, "Asians and Koreans and Vietnamese and Indians and Russians and Spanish people everywhere you go. How the hell did they get into this country?"

Russ, like every other New Yorker, wanted to ask Rocker, "How the hell did *you* get into this country?" All New Yorkers are immigrants. If the city were filled with nothing but John Rockers, it would be the dullest, most insane place on earth. Instead of the monotonous, neutral beige of too many other American cities, New York offered a lively pastiche of hues that blended and clashed and kept things interesting.

But that didn't mean New Yorkers had any desire to be chummy. At Times Square the car took on about twelve more people than could fit in the space comfortably, people packed so tight that no one could possibly fall. One of them, unfortunately, turned out to be a pasty-faced alcoholic wearing a Santa hat and overflowing with premature Christmas cheer. Ignoring the glares of the disgusted people around him, he began to sing carols as he swayed: "Ga res chee merra gennlemen leh nussy udis may!" He leered around mid-sway. "Come awwhh! Everbody!" He tried swinging his arms to lead the choir but they would have none of it. A well-dressed black woman elbowed him and a fat Indonesian-looking courier silently pushed him upright. Undeterred, the man sang, "Silber bell, silber bell, iss Chrissmuss tymina city." He looked at the mini-skirted Puerto Rican shop girls in front of him and said, "An now you sing: Row, row, rowyer boat gennly downa str — hic! Ump! Parn me." His chin sank to his chest a moment and Russ thought maybe he'd remembered that life is but a dream. Russ had underestimated the Christmas spirit, however: "Allus com, allus bry," he resumed, mid-carol. "Round young virgin tenderin' mile. Whazzamatta? Everbody disremember what daze is?" Russ had the distinct impression that some people got off to wait for a later train just to get away from the guy.

By the time they got to Washington Heights, the car had emptied out enough to let the guy roam up and down the aisle, trying to enlist the help of some black kids, an old Jewish couple, an Arab mother with frightened children, a bored-looking businessman, a young couple whose faces glittered with various metal knobs and rings, and a woman who appeared to have Down's syndrome, all to no avail. Finally, at Dyckman, he stumbled down to Russ's end of the car and sang, "Havver sell a murry liddle Chrissmuss, mayor harby lie."

Russ broke down and sang the next part: "From now on our troubles will be out of sight."

The man stopped and stared at him, stunned to get any help at all. "Yousir," he declared, leaning close enough to Russ to curl his eyebrows with his breath, "are a gennlemunnanah scholar."

"And you're drunk as a skunk," Russ pointed out as they crossed the Harlem River.

"Mebbe," the drunk admitted, leaning down to talk to Russ's face, "budeye don' smells bad."

"Bet me," Russ told him as the man got off at 231st Street.

"Anna murry fuggin Chrismuss tayoooo, azzole!" the man shouted as the doors hushed closed.

Russ rode all the way to the 242nd Street stop, the end of the line for the 1- and the 9-trains, his car virtually empty. "Must be my stop," Russ said to himself as he picked up his case and bag. "The end of the line. Looks like there won't be any more of these Joneses to keep up with once I'm gone." He walked out onto the lonely platform and down to the street, the stairs nothing but a metal grate, the height giving him the willies.

Sylvia's parents lived just a couple of blocks away, in an old six-story apartment building with brick facing and a stucco back. Clothes lines hung out the back windows. Russ could hear laughter and singing from Characters Bar as he passed but the auto repair shop where Sylvia's father Tony worked stood silent. As much as Russ dreaded having to tell Tony that he and Sylvia were splitting up, he dreaded more having to face the whole family now, pretending nothing was wrong.

At the entrance he rang and they buzzed him in. The elevator clunked to a stop at their floor and he went to the door and knocked.

Sylvia's mother, Cleo, answered. "Russ!" she cried, hugging him to her ample bosom. "So nice to see you! Come in, come in! Everybody, Russ is here!"

Not only were all six of Sylvia's siblings and all 19 of her nieces and nephews packed into the small living room, some of them had brought friends, to whom Russ had to be introduced even though most of the time he couldn't even remember the name of the person introducing him. Not only were all the seats on the chairs and sofa taken, people stood and sat and crawled on every square inch of carpet as well. Ages ran from mid-80s for Tony's parents, who sat bewildered by all the action, to three months for the youngest, who gurgled contentedly as she was passed around the room like a hot potato. The huge majority of those present were under 30, many still kids, some, judging by the way they draped themselves over one another, working on more kids, everyone talking to everyone else simultaneously and as loudly as possible. The only person who didn't give Russ a wave and a smile was Sylvia.

He first caught sight of her as she sat chatting with her sister, her dark eyes dancing as she listened to the latest gossip. For just a moment he saw the old Sylvia: lively, fun, uninhibited. But as soon as their eyes met, the veil came down again and the pallor and gloom returned to her face. She nodded to him and got up, making her excuses for having to leave so soon.

"Hey, Russ!" Tony hailed him, clapping him on both shoulders. "How da heck are ya? Ya wanna beer, maybe a little wine?"

"Thanks, Tony, but I probably shouldn't," Russ said, pulling his face into something like a smile. "I've got a long drive ahead of me."

"Oh, right, right," Tony said, digging into his pants pocket and handing Russ the keys to his old Camaro.

"I really appreciate your letting us use your car," Russ told him.

"Come on!" Tony bellowed. "We're family, ain't we? Sides, where'm I goin' dis weekend? Ha?"

"So soon?" Cleo lamented as she saw Sylvia pulling on her coat and picking up her overnight bag. "Can't you just stay for lasagna? Maybe canoli?"

"Russ's mother is expecting us, mama," Sylvia said, hugging her mother. "I'll call you when I get back on Sunday."

"Hey, Russ," Tony said jocularly, "remember da time you brung us to da farm an' we saw dem goats…" He waggled his thick eyebrows and nudged Russ's ribs with his elbow.

"Tony!" Cleo hissed, slapping him on the arm.

"Oh, yeah, right, right," Tony said, looking chastised.

"You kids have a good time," Cleo said, kissing them both on the cheek, "and I hope Santa brings you everything your hearts desire."

Russ and Sylvia walked silently down to the street and put their bags in the back seat of Tony's Camaro. The car started right up and Russ turned around and drove toward Broadway.

"So," Russ said to Sylvia as they sped up on the thoroughfare, "didn't you tell your folks about my—what? problem? failing?"

"I told them," Sylvia said tersely. "News like that takes a while to sink in to my dad, that's all."

Russ stared at the stream of red tail lights ahead of them. Boy, he thought to himself, if Tony has trouble with that, how's he going to handle our divorce? Aloud, he said, "Some Christmas, huh?"

"You know what occurred to me?" she asked without looking at him. "In a way I'm still a virgin. I've never had a man's viable sperm in me. Frank used condoms, Ell never made love to me, and your sperm… well, you know."

"Yeah, I know."

They didn't speak again until they got to the farm.

o   o   o

The farm sat atop a ridge, two towering sugar maples, three or four times taller than the house, framing the front. Built in the 1840s, the house had two stories with a window into the attic above. It was painted white, the shutters and window frames blue, and curly gingerbread clustered at the tops of the supports for the large, roofed front porch. To the side was the garage and next to that a small barn where the goats Tony mentioned and a few ducks sheltered for the winter. Originally a dairy farm, it had, like Louie, retired gradually, with a few animals still living out their remaining years in peace on the spacious grounds.

Inside, Ellen's antiques seemed right at home. Her marble-topped table sat in front of the fireplace in the sitting room, as it had in the Mesa house. In the parlor Louie's piano still waited for him to bang out a few old standards, all in E-flat. A spacious, workable kitchen and a dining room with a west-facing bay window rounded out the ground floor. Upstairs, the master bedroom and Ellen's sewing room looked out onto the porch roof, and a couple of other guest rooms faced the small pond to the north. Russ and Sylvia usually slept in the larger of the guest rooms, next to the bathroom. It had only a couple of twin beds but they had never minded cuddling in one on the cold winter nights.

The weather was actually more clement than Russ had expected: the clear skies kept the temperature in the 20s but, far from the city lights, the stars looked very bright and the light dusting of snow made it feel like Christmas without having to shovel anything. Russ pulled the Camaro onto the gravel drive and shut it off. He had hoped that Sylvia's silence meant she had slept the whole way but he knew better.

"Let's go in and say hi to Mom," he told her. "I'll bring in the big stuff when I put the car in the garage."

Ellen greeted them at the door. For the most part, the years had been kind to her, dulling neither her wits nor her grace, but Louie's death had cast a pall across her broad smile. She welcomed them in and gave them each a hug.

"You look wonderful," Sylvia told her.

"Oh, honey, I know you're lying but I don't care. It's just so good to see you. How was your drive?"

"Uneventful," Russ said. "How are you feeling, Mom?"

"Oh, sweetie, I don't know," she said. "I'm pooped, for one thing, from having to repack everything for my trip to San Diego. I just can't imagine what this will be like without your father."

They set down the overnight bags and went into the parlor, Sylvia sitting by Ellen on the sofa, Russ standing with his back to the fireplace.

"But the change of scene will do you good," Sylvia told her mother-in-law. "And all that sunny weather—I wish I could go too."

"Why don't you both come along?" Ellen suggested.

Russ couldn't tell how serious she was. "I wish we could, Mother," he said, "but you know…"

"Oh, I know," Ellen said. "You both have such a lot to do, so many interesting projects to work on. Incidentally, Rusty, I put away all my sewing things so if you want to use the sewing room to work on your book, feel free."

"Thanks, Mom," Russ said.

Ellen saw Sylvia staring into the fire. "Are you all right, dear?" she asked.

Sylvia shook it off. "Oh, I'm fine. Just thinking about everything I have to do."

"Well, you both must be tired," Ellen said. "I know I am. Maybe we should call it an early night and talk more in the morning after we open our presents."

Presents, Russ thought, mentally slapping his head. He hadn't gotten Sylvia anything and from the look on her face, she hadn't gotten him anything either. Christmas seemed uninspiring this year. They would just tell Ellen that they were exchanging gifts when they got back home.

"I better get the rest of the things out of the car," he said.

"Well, if you see Big Cat, tell her to come in," Ellen said. "She isn't a kitten anymore."

"I will."

Outside, the night felt very still and silent. He got back in the car and pulled it into the garage. When he got out, he turned on the light on the ceiling so he could see what he was doing. As he got out the bags, he glanced over to the old tractor tire with the blanket spread across it, where Big Cat usually slept in the warmer seasons.

His heart fell to his feet. Big Cat lay on the blanket but he could tell at a glance that she was dead. He walked over to her. The vermin she had so avidly chased, exacting their revenge on her stiffened body, scurried away. Tears welled up into his eyes as he stood there looking at the rumpled, rigid carcass. "Oh, God, no!" he cried out. "Oh, not tonight!"

But death is ever rigid and unyielding. Feeling like he had swallowed a cherry stone, he picked up the suitcases and went back into the house.

He found one shred of mercy there: Ellen had already gone to bed. Sylvia still sat in front of the fire, watching the glowing embers as though searching for something she had lost. He really wanted to talk about Big Cat but he was afraid she wouldn't understand. Besides, why spoil her Christmas? Big Cat would still be dead tomorrow.

"I guess I'll take these upstairs," he choked out to her. "Do you want to come up?"

She heaved herself up from the sofa and picked up the overnight bags. They went up to their usual guest room but this time she set the overnight bags by separate beds. They sat on opposite sides of the beds and silently began to unpack the things they needed for the night.

"You know," she said quietly after a while, "I could sleep in the other room if you like."

"It doesn't matter," he said. He thought that would be all but then he blurted out, "It just fucking doesn't matter."

She came over and sat beside him. "I'm sorry, Russ. This will be over soon."

He looked at her. "It's not that," he said, looking away. "It's just…everything. I found Big Cat."

"Where was she?"

"In the garage. She's dead, Syl."

She put her arm around his shoulders. "Oh, that's awful! I'm so sorry! I know she meant all the world to you."

"Oh, Syl, you have no idea," he moaned. "Remember how Big Cat used to climb up the rose trellis and sit on the window ledge of the sewing room? How she used to sit there for hours staring out across the valley, just thinking? Syl, she was going to inspire me to write my book! Oh, God, with her gone too, I don't know what I'm going to do." He put his head in his hands and stared bleakly at the floor, his eyes burning.

She sat silently beside him awhile. Finally, she asked, "Didn't I leave a set of oil paints in the attic?"

Russ blinked away his tears and turned to her. This just about tore it. All he hoped for was a little sympathy but all she could think about was her damn art supplies. "Oh, Jesus, I don't know," he told her.

"I hate to ask you but could you go up and check?"

"Now?"

"Please?"

"Can't it wait until morning?"

"I have an idea that I'd really like to work on tonight. I'm sorry."

Russ, like most men, felt more comfortable with anger than tears. With a disgusted sigh, he stood up and walked out.

The attic had just one bare bulb and a hundred years of junk to look through. At last he found her paints, sitting on top of an old console radio.

"Here," he said when he got back to the bedroom, shoving the box at her. "Anything else?"

She opened the box and looked inside. "This should work. I don't want to keep you up. Would you mind if I worked in the sewing room?"

"Do whatever you like," he said bitterly.

"Thank you," she said, touching his hand. "Why don't you get some sleep?" She gathered up the box and her bag and went into the other room.

Big Cat's death got under Russ's skin as nothing else had in a long time. His ongoing break-up with Sylvia had resulted in anger and frustration but until it was over, he couldn't grieve about it. Even at the beginning of the month, when his father died, he had cried a few perfunctory tears but hadn't really broken down.

He got ready for bed feeling like a zombie, like his entire world had crumbled out from under him: he had lost the restaurant, his marriage was on the rocks, he found out he couldn't conceive a child, and his father had died—all in just six weeks. Somehow, he had managed to stay strong through it all, to keep a stiff upper lip. Now, lying alone in his cold single bed, tears began to stream from his eyes. Over a cat.

Hope, that thing with feathers, seemed to be fluttering out of his grasp. He felt stupid for even trying to hold onto it. What a fool he'd been over the years! The one downy mote of hope he'd clung to the longest began to seem like the most foolish: that Jason somehow still survived. What had that hope accomplished? It had done no one, including Jason, any good whatsoever. All Russ had succeeded in doing was putting off the grief. Well, the time had come to accept it: Jason wasn't coming back, any more than his father or Big Cat were coming back. For the first time since he was very small, Russ covered his face with a pillow and cried himself to sleep.

...O...O...O...

Gigging, though often routine and dull, never came within a mile of being a normal job. And nothing beats writing for leading you down the most peculiar rabbit holes.

A quarter of a century ago, I started to write a novel. Unfortunately, by the time I got the planning and research done, events had made its raison d'etre *irrelevant. I doubt that I'll ever put the time and effort into writing a book again.*

Earlier today, just for laughs, I got out the manuscript of that old novel. Looking through it, I came across my research for a story I intended to include that just proves, I suppose, that there's no such thing as a normal job.

During World War II, a chemist named Albert Hofmann was working at Sandoz Laboratories in Basil, Switzerland, researching organic compounds called indoles, specifically those found in ergot, a mold that grows on rye grain. For centuries moldy rye bread had been associated with a strange, sometimes fatal, condition called St. Anthony's Fire, which causes hallucinations and even gangrene in the extremities. St. Anthony's Fire may have caused some of the peculiar visions reported in the Salem witch trials in Massachusetts.

One spring day in 1943, Hofmann was purifying isomers of an indole compound called lysergic acid. He obtained a few milligrams of what he labeled "lysergisaure diethylamide" but inadvertently spilled a tiny amount (just a quarter of a milligram) onto his fingers. He began feeling odd and decided to call it a day, riding his bike the four miles to his house. By the time he got home, he was experiencing a variety of bizarre sensations and vivid hallucinations. The indole compound he had produced, the 25th in a series of analogous compounds synthesized by Sandoz, eventually became known by its initials, LSD-25.

I wonder how Hofmann answered his wife when she greeted him with the usual "How was your day, dear?"

May 10, 1970

Amanda wants to fly. Just a couple of squeezes from her thighs sends Queenie into a trot, Amanda posting in the saddle, the leather slapping against her bottom, the wind streaming through her hair, the piñon trees on either side a blur. As Queenie breaks into a canter, Amanda laughs and closes her eyes in ecstasy, the rhythm of the ride carrying her to a higher plane.

She doesn't see the edge of the bluff until it's too late. Queenie's front hooves paw the air and for an instant Amanda thinks they're going to fall into the deep arroyo. But a warm zephyr floats up and buoys them, actually begins to lift them, and now the ride smoothes out. Queenie's hooves, with nothing against which to strike, prance through the air without a sound. Amanda strokes her large undulating wings, dove-white and soft. She wraps her arms around Queenie's neck and looks around the countryside far below. She has never felt so free.

Queenie's hoof strikes something—*tonk!*—and it startles Amanda but not enough to end this fantastic ride. Another sound—*tink!*—and Amanda feels herself slipping from Queenie's back. Reluctantly, she watches the winged horse break into a gallop and disappear into a towering white cloud. Floating, not falling, Amanda waits.

The third sound—*tunk!*—pulled her away from the dream and back into the warm peaceful Sunday afternoon. For a few moments, she lay there under the sheet luxuriating in the gentle breeze coming through the open window, wafting the scent of flowers to her. Maybe it wasn't flowers. Maybe it was Deb's perfume.

What she and Deb had just done seemed more like a dream than the dream had. But love is always a dream.

She wouldn't say she loved Deb more than she had this morning. But she certainly loved her differently. They had been intimate friends most of their lives so her feelings for Deb already ran pretty deep. Their intimacy had always extended to sharing the finest details of their bodies. But what they had just done went far beyond anything Amanda had ever done, or even dreamed.

Amanda already knew something of sexual satisfaction, especially since New Year's Eve. Breaking up with Bill and, more recently, finding out about Jason's infidelity had led her to seek self-satisfaction more often with less guilt. But never by herself, and certainly not on New Year's Eve with Jason, had she achieved the soaring climax that Deb had found hidden deep within her. She felt like she now understood what all the shouting was about, why lovers gladly risked everything for a single night together.

But with Deb, what did she risk? The tiff they had about Deb going out with Bill on Valentine's Day had, if anything, strengthened their friendship, brought them closer together. She certainly wouldn't want anyone to find out about what they'd done this afternoon but she couldn't imagine Deb betraying that confidence. And what they had done felt so gentle, so loving, so inexhaustible, that the possibilities seemed endless, the future secure.

Men, on the other hand, seemed to offer nothing but a few brief moments of bliss—more often theirs than hers—followed by betrayal and heartache. Deb certainly had more experience with men than Amanda did and, especially lately, seemed disgusted with the whole lot, Bill in particular. She had definitely opened Amanda's eyes to Bill's true nature. So it had surprised Amanda almost as much as Deb to find herself defending Jason after what they had witnessed at the Earth Day concert in Boulder. She still couldn't believe she had slapped Deb. But somehow Jason seemed different....

Movement at the window caught her eye. She looked closer. Lilacs, mostly white with a few purples mixed in, waved by the window. Highly unlikely, considering Amanda's bedroom was on the second floor and the Tyrees didn't own a lilac bush. But as she watched, the lilacs continued to wave like some floral flag of truce. Startled, she sat up in bed, pulling the sheet around her. She wondered if she should be frightened but what sort of evil intruder brings flowers? A hand appeared, someone's right hand, holding the lilac stems. Carefully balancing the succulent bouquet on the window sill, the right hand grasped the inner edge of the sill and then a left hand joined it. Slowly, looking like the head-and-fingers image in an old "Kilroy was here" drawing, a head came into view, first wild curly blonde hair and then Jason's playful blue eyes, peeking cautiously into the room.

Amanda couldn't help but smile.

"Ah, you're awake," Jason said, pulling himself up until he rested on his elbows on the sill. "I brought you flowers."

Seeing him again left Amanda speechless. Tears welled into her eyes.

"I rang the bell," he went on, "but I guess you didn't hear. Deb drove off just as I was walking up so I figured you were home. I tried throwing pebbles at your window but I guess you didn't hear that either. So I climbed onto your woodbine trellis just to make sure you were all right. I hope you don't mind."

She wanted to rush to him, to pull him into the room and hug him and kiss him. But, if nothing else, she wore nothing but the sheet. She still didn't know what to say.

"Well, you seem to be all right," he continued uncertainly, "so I guess I'll just be shoving off then." He glanced down to the pavement.

"Don't you dare!" she cried. "You'll break both your legs!"

He smiled. "So you're speaking to me at least. And don't want my legs broken, at least not both at once."

"Get in here before you fall!"

"If you insist."

He pulled himself up and over the windowsill and tumbled onto the floor, wearing a tie-dyed T-shirt, jeans, and his old moccasins, one of which had fallen off. Kneeling, he gathered up the lilacs and then walked, still on his knees, to the bed. Humbly offering her the flowers, he said, "Man, I am so sorry about what happened up in Boulder. I have no excuse. All I can ask is, please, forgive me?"

"Oh, Jason!" Still holding the sheet with one hand, she wrapped her arm around his neck and pulled him close, kissing the top of his head. "I've been so worried about you! I thought you were dead or in jail or—or—I don't know what." She ran her hand across his head until he winced. "Oh, I'm sorry! Did I hurt you?"

He straightened, rubbing the back of his head. "I've still got a pretty good knot back there. Luckily, I don't use my occipital lobe that much."

"When I saw that cop swing that nightstick, I thought he killed you."

"All I saw was stars. Woke up in the Boulder County Jail feeling like a train wreck."

"They didn't take you to the hospital?"

"Naw. There's no nightstick tougher than my noggin and no jail strong enough to hold Jason Walker."

"How did you get out?"

He grinned sheepishly. "Aw, they let us all out on our own recognizance and the only name I gave them was Dog. So now I'm less worried about the police than about the dog catcher."

"Why didn't you let me know you were okay?" she demanded.

He dropped his head. "I thought maybe you hated me."

"I did hate you," she admitted.

"Maybe," he said, looking back up. "But you also loved me."

It was her turn to look away. "What are you talking about?"

"I saw it in your eyes," he said. "Before you ran away. Only love can hurt somebody that much."

"You *did* hurt me! Who was that woman dancing for you?"

"Her name is Jessica. She's just someone I met in Boulder, a singer."

"Are you in love with her?"

"No."

"Is she in love with you?"

He snorted. "No."

"Did you…?"

He chewed his lip as he thought about his response. "We spent one night together, about a week before the concert," he confessed, adding hastily, "But the only reason I did anything with her is because I thought you and Bill were still together."

"Well, we're not. Not anymore."

"Really?" he asked, searching her eyes, his own eyes bright, the pupils dilated.

"Really," she assured him.

"Oh, Man, that's great! Oh, that's incredible!" Gathering up the lilacs, he stood up and started dancing around the room, tossing the full, fragrant clusters of blossoms one by one around the bed. "So does that mean I can do this?" He knelt again and kissed her.

She closed her eyes and kissed him back, her lips hungrily clutching his.

He broke away again, obviously too excited to sit still. "Oh, Man, this is perfect! This is fantastic!"

"What is?" she asked, catching some of his enthusiasm.

"Everything!" he said, sweeping his arms. "The whole world! This beautiful day!" He touched her cheek. "This beautiful woman."

She blushed and turned away. "You must be high."

"Man, I'm more than high."

She looked at his eyes again. "You're tripping, aren't you?"

"Like I've never tripped before," he confessed. "Lester, one of the Mind Machine's suppliers, got a hold of some Sandoz acid. Oh, Man, it's incredible! Pharmaceutical quality. Tan gelatin capsules with printing on them and everything. No speed or impurities. Much healthier."

"When did you take it?"

"This morning up in Boulder. I hitched a ride down here with one of Gary's friends who dropped me at the Circle Drive exit of I-25. From there I walked all the way up to the Old Stage Road to pick up some dope for me and John."

"Did you smoke some of it?"

"No, pot clouds my clarity when I'm tripping. Why? Do you want some?" He dug into his pants pocket for the baggie of cannabis.

"Actually, I smoked some earlier," she said but didn't mention Deb.

He took his hand from his pocket, stood very tall, and said in a sing-song voice, "I'm higher than you are! I'm higher than you are!"

She laughed.

He went on, a little more soberly, "It's not just the acid, though. Man, this is such an amazing time to be alive! The whole world is changing and we're the ones who are changing it. I've been on the natch the last couple of weeks and I felt just as high. Man, we're winning the war."

"In Vietnam?" she asked, surprised. She hadn't heard anything like that on the news.

"No, the war against the war," he said, pacing around. "Man, the truth is finally starting to come out. Nixon lied about not sending arms to the Cambodian government right up to the day he sent 20,000 troops across the border. It's only a matter of time until people find out about all the illegal, immoral things the U. S. is doing in Southeast Asia, like the secret base in Laos where Steve was killed. And people are finally starting to say enough is enough. Man, do you realize how many schools and universities are closed or on strike? I mean hundreds. That guy from *Death Valley Days* that California hired to act the part of governor had to shut down 27 schools just in that one state. And tens of thousands, maybe hundreds of thousands, of people are going to Washington to pound on the front door of the White

House and say the word Americans have the most trouble saying: Enough! Yesterday, Nixon took time out from referring to us as bums and actually took the time to listen to what we have to say."

"After the shootings at Kent State this week, he'd better."

"Can you believe that happened in America? National Guard troops firing on unarmed college kids? Killing four of them? I guess night before last Nixon showed up at the Lincoln Memorial in the middle of the night, rambling on to the demonstrators there about World War II and football and surfing. I heard he flipped off a guy through the window of his limo. Nixon's days are numbered."

"But how can we get rid of him?"

"If nothing else, we'll vote the bastard out in a couple of years. The Democrats are sure to nominate someone who'll speak out against the war, someone who doesn't have blood all over his hands, and he'll win in a landslide. Unless Tricky Dick figures out some way to rig the election. And God help him if the American people find out about *that*. They'll throw the bum out on his ass."

"I can't believe how worked up you are about this," Amanda said, happy to see him so enthusiastic.

"I've felt like a lone voice crying in the wilderness until now. Finally I'm starting to hear other voices. I've been working on the student strike committee up in Boulder. What we're trying to do is get the University to allow the striking students the option of taking a pass/fail instead of a letter grade so we can work on this without flunking all of our courses."

"That's great."

"It's incredible for me," he admitted. "I've pretty well fucked up this school year, what with one thing and another. But if I can finish the year with passing grades, I can start fresh next year and do this right. Make Mom happy."

"Did you call her today?"

"I sent her a card so she called me this morning while I was tripping. We had an amazing rap! She still doesn't agree with my position on this stuff but at least she's beginning to see that it's a valid position, that I'm not just some kook. I think if I can get my shit together in the next few months, she'll keep helping me with my college expenses. Where are your folks, anyway?"

"Out in California with Peter. They were just going to visit but Stanford's shutting down too, so they're going to help him move his stuff back here."

Jason looked around and smiled. "So we're free to do what we want."

"What do you want to do?" Amanda asked, pulling the sheet a little closer.

"You know what I want to do, Manny?" he asked, sitting beside her on the bed and putting his hand on her knee. "I want to head out to the new frontier."

"Where's that?" she asked with a little trepidation.

"It's right here, actually. It's not a place. It's a state of mind, a quality of spirit."

"Oh. I thought you meant you wanted to settle the West or something."

"I do want to settle the West. I want Americans to put away their guns and live together peacefully. I think the West could learn a lot about peace from the East and we sure can't learn it bombing them back to the Stone Age. But more than that. I want to live on the new frontier of self-awareness. I want to explore that alternate reality, to use your term. Man, just today I've learned more about myself and the world around me than I learned all last year."

"Like what?"

He struggled to put his thoughts into words. "I guess just that people, deep down inside, never really grow out of being children, beautiful children who want nothing more than to be free to play at whatever they like. The Establishment wants people to believe they're the true Americans. Bullshit! *We're* the true Americans, Man. *We're* what this country's all about. The quest for freedom is the quintessential American dream. We've got a chance, right now, to make that dream come true."

"It sounds like a dream, all right," Amanda said skeptically.

"Maybe you're right. Maybe I am just high. But I think we have a chance—if we all work together and try really hard—to make this world a better place. We can do more than put a man on the moon. We can turn the tide of war so that we're dismantling all those nuclear weapons instead of building them. Just by our good example, not with our tanks and guns, we can show the world that freedom beats communism any day of the week. We can wake up to the fact that there's not a First World, a Second World, and a Third World. There's just one world. We have to take care of this beautiful planet because there's nowhere else to go. We can't do what we did in the last century, exploiting the earth's resources like there's no tomorrow. Man, there's a tomorrow. I haven't felt this way in a long time but I really believe there's a tomorrow."

"It sounds like you've got it all worked out."

"There's just one thing missing," he told her, taking her hand. "I don't want to go to that new frontier alone, end up some bitter old man playing solitaire and thinking about what might have been." He swallowed. "Man, I'm going to have to make this up as I go along. I know I'm starting from scratch. I know I've got next to nothing and you deserve so much more than I could ever offer. But if you and I could be together through this long strange trip of life, I'd be the happiest person on the planet."

Amanda's heart leapt into her throat. "Oh, Jason, what are you saying? I mean, are you asking…?"

"What?" he asked when she didn't go on. "To get married?" He didn't look as freaked as she feared. "Oh, Man, I'm asking more than that. I mean, we can sign a piece of paper if you want but my parents proved to me that a piece of paper doesn't guarantee much. I'm asking you to be my love, my one and only love all my life, and still be my friend the way we've always been friends. Or am I just dreaming?"

"Oh, Jason," she cried, throwing her arms around him, the sheet falling away, "if you're dreaming then I must be having the same dream!"

The kiss they shared seemed to last forever and still seemed to end too soon. But when he backed off to look at her beaming face, he noticed everything she wasn't wearing under the sheet.

"Now I know I'm dreaming," he said with a grin.

Amanda blushed but didn't pull the sheet back up. "Dream on."

He kissed her more passionately this time, easing her back down onto the bed, running his hand across her warm skin, across her bare breasts. He pulled his legs up and lay beside her on the bed. Between kisses, he asked, "Remember New Year's Eve?"

"Mm-hmm," she said, nibbling on his earlobe.

"When I asked if you were a virgin?"

"Mm-hmm," she said again, afraid to say more.

"That was actually your first time, right?"

"Mm-hmm," she confessed, it seeming like the truer answer.

"It was my first time too."

She backed away to look at him, to see if he was kidding. "Really?"

"Really. I know it's not easy to talk about this but I've got to tell you that the reason I spent the night with Jessica was to find out if sex would always be like New Year's Eve was. And I'm here to testify: I will never be able to love anyone the way I love you right now."

"And I will never love anyone the way I love you," Amanda said honestly, knowing that whatever she and Deb might share in the future, it wouldn't compare to this. "I didn't need to be with anyone else to know that."

"Well, I'm sorry," he said, kissing her. "It will never happen again. But you know… There was another reason I asked you if you were a virgin that night."

"To see if I was on the Pill?" she guessed.

"Well?"

She shook her head.

"Now?"

She shook her head again.

He looked crestfallen for a moment but then his resolve returned. "You know what? I don't care. I think moments like this come along only once in a lifetime. We did this once before and nothing happened. And if we create a new life today, then so be it." He unbuttoned his fly. "You're stuck with me now anyway. If we start a family, then we'll have a family. If it's a boy that turns out like me, then heaven help him. But if it's a girl that turns out like you, the world will fall at her feet. And in the meantime, I'll become a real person."

"You are a real person."

"You know what I mean. I'm never going to make much of a living playing music. I'll get a normal job. What do you say?"

She didn't say anything. The rising tide of his *joie de vivre* lifted everything in its path, carrying Amanda with it. She too felt like a new world was unfolding before their eyes and that not seizing this moment might mean passing up her one true chance at happiness.

Meanwhile, his hand, roaming around and down, had found the answer to his question another way: her vulva was still quite slippery from what she and Deb had done earlier. "Ah," he said, exploring. "Well. Hmm. Let's see. What could this mean?"

"It means there's no time like the present," she found herself saying.

Amanda had the fondest memories of what she and Jason had done on New Year's Eve but the sex itself had proven nerve-wracking and painful enough that she felt a certain dread about going through that again. This time, however, he took things slower and more gently, easing himself into her more gradually and giving her time to catch up. Deb's tongue, for that matter, had smoothed the way to an extent.

This time Amanda felt transported. As delightful as making love with Deb had been, this felt exhilarating and complete and a bit dangerous. His urge took complete control of the situation and though he hardly seemed insensitive to her pleasure, his single-minded concentration, his complete absorption, made this more than authentic. It became indisputable, undeniable, irreversible. Amanda didn't want to back out anyway but Jason seemed to carry her forward, to show her another new frontier that went beyond even what had seemed so new and intriguing just an hour before.

This time, when his back arched and his voice cried out in wordless wonder, she entered that alternate reality right along with him.

Afterward, he lay there on her so still and so silent he seemed to have fallen under a spell. He barely breathed. Only when at last she had to shift his weight did he come back to her.

"Oh, Man," he whispered, awestruck. "I can't believe what just happened! I felt like I floated up out of my body and could look all around from a great height. I could see beyond the material world, as though somehow I could picture all the different levels of existence and experience. Each different level was within a circle, like a Venn diagram. Some of the circles—like philosophy and religion, for example—overlapped a lot and others—like math and art—hardly at all. It reminded me of Odysseus' rings."

"Odysseus' rings?"

"Remember when Odysseus challenges all of Penelope's suitors to an archery contest? He sets up twelve ax handles in a line and shoots an arrow through the rings on the ends of the handles. For just one brief moment, as I floated, I got to where the rings all lined up so that I could see all the way to the end of the one tiny corridor they all had in common. Oh, Man, it all makes sense! It all fits together!"

When he didn't go on, she asked, "Well, what did you see?"

He grinned and shrugged. "I don't know."

She laughed at the absurdity of it all and pushed him off of her so hard that he rolled off the bed onto the floor. At first she was afraid she might have hurt him but he sat up laughing too.

"I'm sorry," he said, rebuttoning his fly. "It really happened but I don't know how to put into words what I saw. But anyway, if you're going to be like this after we make love, maybe I'll just go back to that other woman."

"Don't you dare!" she said, pulling him close again and kissing him.

"Why not?" he said with a twinkle in his eye. "It's a whole new world, remember? I mean, I wouldn't be upset if I found out *you* made love to another woman."

It gave her such a pang that she had to turn away.

"What's wrong with you?" he asked, tugging on her knee. "I'm just pulling your leg."

He tried to turn her head so he could see her face but she couldn't bear to face him.

"Oh, my God, Man!" he whispered as the light dawned. "This is unbelievable! I know why you were so slippery when we started. Deb was just driving away when I got here, right? You and she were…"

No sooner did those words come out of his mouth than a woman's voice said, "Amy?"

They both looked up. There in the doorway stood Deb, dressed in her Sunday best.

...O...O...O...

I read A Catcher In The Rye *when I was Holden Caulfield's age. Cynical and alienated myself, I readily identified with the book. I particularly liked the concept of the title: a body catching, rather than kissing, a body, comin' through the rye. As a child, "getting caught" generally meant some authority figure, like a parent or teacher, putting the kibosh on some enjoyable activity, like sledding in my Sunday suit or kissing Dumb Diane in the music practice rooms. But when you don't "get caught" a few times, you realize that no one's holding the net for you anymore; that if you fall, you hit the street.*

I've spent many a Christmas on the road. Most of the time, the only person in town whose last name I know is me and at that season I'm not always on the best terms with myself. Once in a while, some well-meaning bartender or patron will invite me to the house for the holiday and sometimes I go and try to enjoy myself, though many Christmas traditions are only appreciated by those who know the tradition. The last few years I've opted to spend the day by myself, not so much in a "Bah! Humbug!" sort of way as just sparing myself and others the clash in perceptions of what the day is supposed to mean. But I always appreciate the gesture, that they want to "catch" me lest I fall through the cracks. It's easy to relegate humanitarianism to sending off a few tax-deductible pennies a day to help some Third World child and overlook the lonely soul next door or in the next cubicle.

Maybe this year I'll try to be the catcher. That young lady at work is about to fall and could use a helping hand. Of course, she'll probably resent "getting caught," as most young people do, but if I don't do it, who will? Besides, this town has become pretty much like any other: I hardly know a soul. What have I got to lose?

December 25, 1999

Russ is lost. The still morning air chills him to the bone, makes him feel apprehensive. The paling sky doesn't dim the solitary star. He stands with his back to the wall. Before him lies a small field of amber grain, bounded a stone's throw away by another wall, long and black, as tall as he is. As he tries to orient himself, the sun rises above the wall, blinding him. He puts up his right hand to shield his eyes but he can't stay here.

The wall at his back ends a few paces to either side. He turns to the right and goes around the corner. The view to the south looks the same: amber grain, long black wall. The only difference is that a few leafy green weeds have sprouted and overtopped the grain. He keeps going.

He turns to the right again, around the next corner. Amber grain, long black wall. The weeds have grown taller. The shadow of the wall to his back, which seems to be part of a large, roughly cubicle utilitarian structure, falls across the field, stretching to the far wall and beyond. Russ feels even colder here so he moves on.

Around the next corner he finds something different in the far wall: a notch of some sort, the wall lowering to just over thigh-high. Beyond the wall, for the first time, he can make out the horizon, not only far away but far below as well. He has to get down from here. He turns to the structure behind him and finds a door. To one side he finds a button. He pushes the button and hears machinery clatter into motion.

As he waits, listening to the elevator slowly grinding up to him, he gets a sinking feeling that he's made a huge mistake. He can hear voices echoing up the elevator shaft. They're not coming to save him. They're coming to *get* him. A wave of terror sweeps over him. He has just moments before the door will open. He has just one chance to get away.

He starts running through the amber grain toward the notch in the wall, hearing the elevator clunk to a halt behind him. As he approaches the notch, he can see more of what's below him. It's a city. He slows. It's Manhattan. He's on the roof of the World Trade Center, looking north up the island. He can't escape this way. The striations on the walls of this monolith are vertical, not a toe-hold in sight. If he should fall, he knows with a dead certainty that no one waits below to catch him.

He looks behind him. Atop the elevator shaft sits the broadcast tower, immense, pointing to a heaven beyond his reach, grounded to the earth far below. The door begins to open. He has to act now.

Cautiously, one step at a time, he eases toward the notch, each step revealing more of New York: the Empire State Building, the Chrysler Building, the Woolworth Building. He begins to tremble as he nears the edge, hoping somehow to find a step, a rope, anything. He can feel his palms sweat, his sphincters tighten, his body begin to sway. Fighting his vertigo, he eases himself close enough to peek over the low wall to the street far below. Suddenly from beyond the edge a man's right arm thrusts up toward him, the hand reaching for him, trying to grab hold, trying to pull on him, pull him toward the abyss…

Russ woke up in a cold sweat. The bed sheets were soaked and wound around him. He tried to fight his way free but ended up falling from the side of the small twin bed to the cold hard floor. Aching, dazed, he wiped the sweat from his face onto the sheet and struggled to his feet. Through the window he could see the sky beginning to pale with the coming dawn of Christmas. He couldn't go back to bed after that dream. He glanced at the other bed. Sylvia hadn't even pulled the spread from the pillows. She must have spent the night in the sewing room after all. Real life didn't strike him as much of an improvement over the dream. He had to get out of here.

Shivering, he fumbled his way into his clothes. He tiptoed down the creaking stairs so he wouldn't disturb the others and went to the kitchen at the rear of the old farmhouse, slipping his feet into his boots, pulling on his coat. Quietly opening the back door, he stepped out into the frigid morning.

His boots crunched the thick hoarfrost coating the grass. He gulped a few lungfuls of the clear icy air but couldn't seem to shake the terrifying image of that hand reaching toward him. He had never had such a vivid, ominous dream. As horrible as he felt, he knew he had to keep the image alive to find out what it meant, the way finding the source of pain identifies the injury. He felt like he had fractured his mind. It reminded him of an old Rolling Stones song, "Sway," which referred to a day that broke up your mind.

"Easy for you to say, Mick," Russ said aloud as he crunched his way over the slight rise that separated the farmhouse from the pond. "What's left after you destroy that notion? How do I break out of the circle of time?"

Russ felt awful. His sinuses were clogged, his eyes burned, his stomach felt queasy. He tried sucking the mucous from his nose down his throat, then hawked the loogie into the bushes. It didn't seem to help. Maybe he was coming down with a cold. He turned up his collar and pulled on his heavy winter gloves as he walked.

The artificial pond covered about an acre. Louie had dammed a small stream a decade earlier to create it but it already looked as though it had been there forever. It lay in a small swale so the shadows hung slightly thicker over it. The oak and maple trees, so brilliant in fall foliage just a couple of months ago, stood bare, gray, and silent in the predawn light. A patch of ground fog lingered above the thin ice that had formed over most of the pond's surface. A small island in the middle, from which grew one small leafless tree and a few shrubs, had patches of open water around it that steamed in the subfreezing air.

Russ walked to the far side of the pond. A floating platform his father had built for swimming and fishing had been pulled part-way up the bank for the winter. Russ stepped onto the slanting, frosty wood, only to have his foot slide right out from under him. For just an instant he felt like maybe the arm in the dream had been his father's, pulling him toward the pond he had created, trying to reunite father and son. Yelping in terror, Russ fell on his ass but his other foot, not yet on the platform, kept him from sliding onto the thin ice of the pond.

"Jesus!" he cried, sore from the fall but glad to be dry. He clutched the edge of the platform until he felt secure again. If he had fallen in, he might have drowned or frozen to death before Ellen or Sylvia would think to look for him. "Then again," he said aloud, "I guess death would be one way to break the circle."

But Russ was enough of a Buddhist to know that even death wouldn't mean an end to the circle of life. It would just guarantee a rebirth as some even more miserable, godforsaken creature. You don't hope to conquer death, you try to live well enough in this life not to be reborn and have to go through it all again.

But he sure as hell didn't have much proof of reincarnation or an afterlife. The people he knew who had died seemed to stay pretty thoroughly dead. For that matter, people with periods after their names seemed to have dominated his life lately: Louie. Jason. Guy Ellis. Now even Big Cat.

He blinked away the seeds of tears, which made his nose run. He took out his handkerchief and wiped his nose, then cleared his throat and hawked another loogie onto the ice.

It occurred to him that this gunk in his sinuses came from crying himself to sleep last night, not from a cold. Either way, it still ran down his throat. Catarrh, they used to call it. The word sounded like a term Big Cat's philosophy cronies would use to describe the Cosmic Hairball, purring out that last syllable, as they sat under the sacred catalpa tree by the cataract.

In any case, sometimes the tears just have to be flung out, purged from the body. It defined catharsis. Aristotle, Russ remembered from his philosophical studies, used the Greek word *katharsis*, purification, to indicate emotional purification through the medium of art, like the purging of pity or terror by viewing a tragedy. Psychiatrists appropriated the term to mean bringing one's fears and problems out into the open in an attempt to relieve them.

"Isn't that what I came here for?" Russ asked himself. "To seek catharsis? To raise the shades and let the light shine into the darkest corners? To seek some alternate reality? Well, have at it, then. What am I afraid of?"

That answer came easily enough: he feared that arm coming at him from the far side of that abyss. Whoever came up in the elevator, though scary, didn't get him, after all. Obviously, his unconscious mind had conjured up those voices. He easily could list half a dozen people from New York alone who seemed to want to push him to the brink. But whose arm had tried to grab him from beyond that wall?

Maybe because he'd been thinking about reincarnation earlier, a story told by the Buddha came to mind.

A man is walking through a field one day when he hears a tiger running at him from behind. Terrified, the man begins to run headlong through the field, so fast, in fact, that he ends up tumbling over the edge of a cliff, saving himself at the last possible second by grabbing a hanging vine. Just as he breathes the slightest sigh of relief, the tiger's mate comes out of the jungle below him, circling around and waiting for him to fall. The man looks up and sees the first tiger slavering at the top of the cliff. As if that weren't enough, a couple of mice come along and start gnawing the vine. Certain that he has just a few moments left, the man spots a berry plant with a single ripe berry growing on it. With his free hand, he plucks the berry and eats it. He had never tasted anything so sweet!

The Buddha told the story to point out that until you understand how fragile and fleeting life is, you can't appreciate how sweet it is. Russ had dangled from that vine enough times in his life to know that. But how did that story connect to his dream?

As he contemplated it, the sun began to rise, the first rays touching the mist rising from the pond and filtering through the tree and shrubs on the small island. Where a moment before he had seen nothing but the amorphous veils of fog, there suddenly shone a glorious sunburst. The shadows of the tree and shrubs streaming through the glowing mist only added depth to the brilliant, fiery corona.

Maybe that's what enlightenment looks like, he thought, raising his right arm to shield his eyes. But what does it feel like? His dream had begun peacefully enough at sunrise, after all. The terror started when that hand reached up to him from beyond the wall.

Then it happened. The answer came to him in a flash brighter than the sunrise. Maybe the hand wasn't trying to pull him down. Maybe it was trying to get him to catch hold, to pull it back up, to keep that person from falling!

Perhaps the feel of the sun on his face contributed but Russ got chills. He couldn't explain it but he felt as certain as the sun's coming up that some profound change had occurred in his life, that some part of him that so far had slept had suddenly awakened. He realized that by ending the dream where he had, he hadn't saved himself, he'd merely chickened out. He had lacked the will to hold his ground and lend a hand to someone who needed help more than he.

It was a profound revelation. He wanted to do what Blaise Pascal, the French mathematician and philosopher, did after his epiphany in 1654: write down on a piece of paper the essence of this insight and sew it into his clothes so it would always be near. But he couldn't quite put into words the depth of his feeling. He felt like the Magi must have felt when they followed that bright star to a humble stable and beheld the Christ child. He felt like a new man.

Now that he was awake, he could make a stand, lend a hand. But whose arm reached up to him?

His father immediately came to mind. Louie had certainly crossed the great divide. But how could Russ save him, pull him back in any sense? Well, for one thing, he could honor his father's last wish and show enough balls to stand up for his own. Tweak wasn't just Russ's dream, after all. Louie's dream in helping him start Tweak was that Russ would succeed in New York. If Russ hung onto the restaurant, he could keep his father's influence alive. And he could save Oscar, Christine, and Buzz from the anal-retentive Alfred Douglas in the bargain.

Jason came to mind as well. Jason had described to Russ in frightful detail the nightmares he suffered after his brother's death in Vietnam: Steve falling from the helicopter, reaching up to Jason as he fell, his hand just beyond his grasp. Now, if Russ and the others didn't get together and talk about Jason—for their own sakes as much as for May—maybe he too would slip away, fall from living memory.

For that matter, perhaps it was Ellis who reached up to him in his dream. It was a man's right arm, after all, the arm that Ellis lost in Vietnam. But Russ instantly felt his defensive barriers kick in. Why should he help his soon-to-be ex-wife's long-dead husband?

He knew he was jealous, not just of Sylvia's first husband but also of the artist, the man. How many times had someone come into Tweak, seen one of Ellis's paintings, and said to Russ, "Don't you wish you could paint like that?" Russ would come up with some polite response but to himself he always said, "God, I'd give *my* right arm to paint like that!" Russ knew himself to have many excellent qualities. He was intelligent, perceptive, sensitive, even creative. But he could never match Ellis's artistic ability, nor Sylvia's, and his envy too often overpowered his appreciation.

But what is art? Art isn't an object. It's an act, a manifestation of will. It's neither the paint nor the canvas, neither the ink nor the paper, it's the act of applying the one to the other. Art can change the world. It's karma in the best, truest sense. It's yang, active, out there. If a man fails to act, if "the native hue of resolution is sicklied o'er with the pale cast of thought," the result is tragedy. Ask Hamlet.

Russ found the germ of an idea. Something about the connection between art and artificial. He didn't have the whole thing worked out yet but creation is something that happens before all the facts are in. Any work sufficiently complex to be interesting is too complex for anyone, even the artist, to comprehend in its entirety before its creation. No artist, no matter how many sketches she does, can know beforehand how the finished painting will look. Jagger and Richard can't know when they write the words and melody to a song how the full production will sound. Even the most skilled, meticulous novelist can't know, before he writes the first line, every twist and turn the plot will take. Somehow, you just have to start and have faith that you can solve the problems as they arise.

In any case, he had shivered on the frosty float long enough to become acutely aware of his very full bladder. He carefully stood up and walked back to the house, the wheels of his mind spinning a mile a minute. He had to talk to Sylvia about this.

By the time he got back inside, kicked off his boots, and took a leak, his germ of an idea had grown considerably, his excitement growing right along with it. He took the stairs two at a time and went into the sewing room.

Judging from the paints and brushes and colorful rags scattered about, Sylvia had found the sewing room as conducive to painting as Russ hoped he would find it for writing. Something about the view out that window, with the cat sitting on the sill and the huge maple trees and the farms and hardwood forest stretching into the hazy distance, lent itself to cogitation and introspection. But Russ could see nothing of Sylvia or what she had painted.

He went back into the bedroom and found her asleep in the second twin bed. She looked so sweet and still he decided to sit on the floor next to the bed and watch her awhile rather than wake her right away. While sleep negates artifice, it isn't really artless, and it's often easy to tell the sleeper's state of mind by how she's sleeping. Sylvia seemed to be sleeping well and peacefully, a sharp contrast from the furtive distrust he had seen in her eyes lately while she was awake. He carefully pulled a strand of her jet-black hair from the corner of her mouth and then ever-so-lightly touched her cheek.

Not seeming startled, her eyes drifted open and saw him there. She smiled and he had forgotten what joy her smiles brought him. "I came in and you were gone," she said drowsily. "Where were you?"

"Fasting in the wilderness," he told her. "I bring glad tidings."

"Really?" she said, blinking and stretching. "Did you see what I painted?"

"No, but that can wait," he said, dying to share his experience with her. "I've come to a great realization."

"You look like you have," she said, perusing his face, which he could tell radiated joy.

"I know you don't have much of an opinion of me anymore," he said, "but I really wish you'd hear me out on this because I think it's important."

She put her fingers to his lips. "I'm probably more interested in hearing this than your mother is. Let's go into the sewing room."

He went into the sewing room and sat facing the door, waiting for her to perform her ablutions and put on a robe. She came in bundled in slippers and robe, glanced out the window, and then pulled up a chair across from him. "So talk to me."

He came right to the point. "You're still planning to hold your burial-at-sea ceremony for Ellis's sperm sample Monday night, aren't you?"

She nodded warily.

He looked around at her work space and spotted the cannon shell casing that she, and Ellis before her, used as a brush holder. He picked it up. "You're going to carry the sample in this, right?"

"I guess."

"Well, I don't think this is the proper vessel to hold that sperm."

"Oh? What do you think I should use then?"

"I think you should use your womb."

She looked at him askance. "What in the world are you talking about?"

"I think you should have Ellis's baby."

"Oh, Russ," she sighed. "That's not what it takes. You don't have to do this."

"It's not what you think. This isn't some last-ditch effort to keep our marriage from falling apart. What's done is done. I know that."

"Then what difference would it make?"

"Does art make a difference?"

She looked taken aback, then puzzled. "Of course I think it makes a difference. But I'm an artist."

"Well, I think it makes a difference too and I'm not an artist, at least not the way you and Ellis are artists. But I can do something artful that just might make a big difference in the world: persuade you to have Ellis's baby."

"That's not so much art as artificial."

"Well, the insemination would have to be artificial but my reasons for trying to persuade you are real."

"Go ahead," she said tentatively.

"Listen. I know how disappointed we both were when we found out that you and I couldn't make a baby. We probably took out our disappointment on one other. But you know what? Big deal. So my sperm can't get you pregnant. Hell, any fucking monkey can make a baby. That's not art, that's biology."

"Well, I'm not sure artificial insemination is an art either."

"Insemination, artificial or natural, requires a tool. Every man uses a tool, whether it's his penis or a glass tube. Art requires a tool too, like a paintbrush or a guitar. Obviously, artificial insemination isn't always an art, any more than the simple fact that someone, or some monkey, puts pen to paper makes that art. It takes an act of will and the right materials to produce art. I know that you and Ellis could create a beautiful baby."

"But you don't want to be any part of it," she assumed.

"I'm *already* part of it. If I can't persuade you to keep Ellis's sample—to *use* Ellis's sample—then nothing is created. Since he can no longer act, Ellis's artistic heritage is lost forever. When it comes to sex, a man has to act. His sperm have to swim, seek out the passive egg. Well, I can't get my sperm to swim but I still might be able to get you pregnant."

"Part of the reason I didn't want to do this is because I thought *you* didn't want to do this."

"I *didn't* want to do this," he admitted. "But I've changed my mind." He reconsidered that phrase. "No, that makes it sound as if I had conscious control over the change. Put it this way: my mind is changed. Now I want to put this out there into the world. I want to make the only artistic statement I can. I mean, neither Ellis nor I working alone seems to be able to produce an heir, but between us…"

"But neither one of you can stick around to help change the diapers."

"I wouldn't mind doing that," Russ said, looking down at the floor. "But I know your feelings for me have changed. I see it in your eyes. And I don't blame you. I did some stupid things. I should have trusted you more. I shouldn't have let my insecurities get the best of me."

"I did some stupid things too," she said, taking his hands and squeezing them until he looked up again. "I should have told you about all this years ago. Believe me, I never thought that sperm sample would be any more than a keepsake. I certainly never thought it would become a problem between us. It wouldn't have become one if I had just gotten rid of it before or if you… well, you know."

"Yeah. I know."

"But what I'm trying to tell you is that my feelings for you *haven't* changed. I tried to do what you suggested. I tried standing back. I went back to the life I used to live in the Village and hung out with the people I knew when Ellis was alive. That's not me anymore. I miss you. All your quirky idiosyncrasies that some people find maddening make every day magic for me. I never know what to expect from you. Like now."

"But I'm no Guy Ellis."

"And he wasn't what you are. He made me think and work and wait. You make me happy. That's why I love you."

"You do?" he asked, stunned. "I sure couldn't tell lately."

"I've been afraid to show you. I don't want to get hurt again. I mean, you seem to have your heart set on coming up here to the farm to write the same way Ellis had his heart set on his trip to France. And I'm sure whatever you write will be as interesting and artistic as anything Ellis ever did."

"I don't know about that," he said, shaking his head. "With Big Cat gone I feel like someone pulled the rug out from under me."

She smiled and patted his hand. "You still haven't seen what I painted, have you?"

He looked at the sewing table, which held all her art supplies but no painting. "Where is it?"

"In here," she assured him.

He looked around. The room seemed full of the usual stuff: Ellen's sewing machine and all her baskets and boxes full of supplies, the old sofa with cat-frayed upholstery, the stitched, framed homilies on the walls, the same view out the window.

Then, for just an instant, Russ experienced an alternate reality. He saw Big Cat sitting outside on the window sill where she had sat so many times, where he had seen her sitting when he glanced in here earlier. He momentarily thought he must have dreamed he found her dead on the tractor tire in the garage last night. But no, that was all too real.

Then he saw what he had missed this whole time. Sylvia had painted Big Cat's likeness on the glass of the window, capturing her calico fur with the finest of brush strokes, down to the cow-lick where her back leaned against the windowpane and the curl of the tip of her tail wrapped around her front paws. She gazed with her usual mystic serenity across the broad valley. Sylvia must have stayed up most of the night to have created such a startling, realistic, affectionate portrait.

Russ turned back to her with tears in his eyes. No words could express his feelings.

"Do you like it?" she asked him. "I thought it might help you with your writing."

He held his arms out to her. She got up and sat in his lap. They put their arms around one another and rocked back and forth, Russ burying his face in her thick fragrant black hair. When he finally could choke out some words, he said, "That's the finest gift anyone has ever given me. I love it." He kissed her. "It's just too bad I won't get a chance to see it more often."

She backed away to look at him, crestfallen. "Why not?"

"I'll be too busy in the City," he said firmly, "changing diapers, keeping Tweak on its feet, loving you. We won't need to wait until you're ovulating to make love anymore, you know."

Tears filled her eyes too. "Are you serious?"

"Well, we may have to take it kind of easy once your first husband knocks you up but after the baby comes, you're mine, kiddo."

"But about Tweak?"

"I can't sell Tweak to that prig. It would be a crime against humanity. I'll just have to take out a loan, maybe hire an accountant to straighten out the books. Besides, I may have found an act for New Year's Eve after all."

"But what about your philosophy book?"

"I've got too much life to live to write a book about how to live your life. Maybe when I'm older and the kid is in college I'll get around to it. Now, if I could just find a place to crash in the City…"

She had been smothering his face with kisses. "You know," she whispered in his ear, "I know someone who's looking for a roommate."

"Anybody I know?"

"You know her better than you think."

"There is just one more thing, though," he said, a bit more seriously. "I want to try to put together a Gathering of the Piñon Nuts after all."

She looked at him. "You think that's possible? New Year's Eve is only six days from now."

"It is written: Nothing shall be impossible. God created heaven and earth in six days. I have faith. Somehow, we've got to do this. I think John and Matt and I should gather once more to remember Jason. We owe him, and May, that much. Do you mind?"

"I think it's a wonderful idea. You know I've got to stay here for my opening in Dia, right?"

"Well, we'll just have to try to spend every night of the next millennium together. You know what? I think I'm going to call Matt right now."

Sylvia looked at the clock. "It's 5:30 in the morning in Seattle, honey."

"Okay, so we'll make love, have breakfast, open all the silly presents Mom got us, and then call him."

O   O   O

"How's that, master?" Deb asked.

"Just about perfect," Matt had to admit.

One of the many pleasant surprises Deb had waiting for him when he got back from Boston was a covered Jacuzzi she'd had installed on an extension of the deck around their bedroom, the jets of which hit the sore spots on the small of his back with gentle precision. Naked, he eased all the way down into the warm bubbly water. "Aren't you going to join me?"

Deb stood attentively in the icy air. She already wore her third set of lingerie of the day and they had just finished breakfast. She had slept in a stretchy lace body suit that she insisted he cut to shreds with the scissors before she'd even get out of bed. She had donned a sheer black nightie with white ruffled hem, collar, and shirt cuffs, her best approximation of a maid's uniform, to fix breakfast. For breakfast she had chosen a Playtime classic: popovers slathered with lots of butter and drizzled with tupelo and orange blossom honey, plus Dom Perignon mimosas, substituting honey tangerine for orange juice. She had brought it all up on a silver tray, insisting he use her "uniform" as his napkin, making him tug on it until the pre-cut straps gave way, then lounging naked on the bed beside him sipping her mimosa while he ate. Before helping him out to the Jacuzzi, she had slipped into a full-length smoky-blue satin nightgown underneath which she wore nothing but a couple of strategically placed self-adhesive gift bows.

"Would you like to unwrap your Christmas present before allowing me in there with you, master?" she asked, her arms already goose-bumped in the chill foggy air.

The very thin straps of the nightgown required very little persuasion to part and the satin crumpled in a heap at her feet. When he beckoned to her, she stepped gingerly into the Jacuzzi, straddling his legs and standing with her arms behind her back. Matt feasted his eyes on the glittering gold bows she had stuck like pasties to her magnificent breasts.

"Aren't the bows customarily on the outside of the gift wrap?" he asked her.

"Yes, master. I'm sorry," she said, hanging her head in shame. "I suppose you'll want to punish me now."

He gently tugged on the left one to test the strength of the adhesive. "I don't want to hurt you."

She leaned down and whispered in his ear, "I had to use some double-stick tape just to get them to stick at all." She stood back up and put her hands behind her back again.

He pulled off first one and then the other, leaving her bare nipples puckered in the cold air.

"Now, that didn't hurt a bit, did it?" she asked, leaning over so he could kiss them.

"It didn't hurt *me*," he said.

"That's all that matters, master," she said humbly. "Do what you must to me."

He nibbled her firm flesh. "But I want this to last all weekend."

She supported her breast to give him a better angle. "But this weekend is the last, master," she reminded him. "You might as well use it up."

Their talk Wednesday night, especially her confession of her very brief affair with Amanda, had persuaded him to go through with the orchiectomy on Monday. He hated the thought that his emasculation would result only in a more gradual but still painful decline and merely postponed the inevitable but he had never had the mettle to deny Deb anything. Thursday had been pretty rough, both of them angry and hurt about how mercilessly his cancer had snatched away his future, both of them grieving for the voluntary, necessary loss of his physical manhood.

By Christmas Eve, though, they realized that they had to take advantage of Christmas and Boxing Day because, come Monday, Playtime would never be the same. So they had invented a weekend trip to Sun Mountain Lodge in Winthrop, notifying family and friends who might call them on the holiday of their plans. Then, like the carnival before an endless lent, they settled in for one last weekend of making love like there was no tomorrow.

As much as he enjoyed her goosebumps, he soon pulled her into the warm water next to him. She stretched out languorously beside him, her soft hands gliding over his body, caressing him, rubbing him, stroking him.

"I've never felt so spoiled in all my life," he told her, feeling guilty.

"Good!" she declared. "This time I want you to be completely satisfied."

He pulled himself up to reach for his mimosa. "When have I ever seemed dissatisfied?"

She gently prevented him from getting up further. "Well, I must not be a very good slave if you don't trust me to do even the simplest tasks for you." She stood up, the water streaming from her naked body, and bent over the edge of the Jacuzzi to get the mimosa. He spanked her playfully. "Now that's more like it," she said, handing him the drink.

He noticed a small red mark on her forearm. "Did I nick you with the scissors?"

She looked down at it. "No, I burned it taking the popovers out of the oven." She looked back up at him. "Would you quit worrying about things like that? I'm just your sex slave, remember?"

"But I don't want to see you hurt," he said, touching the burn softly.

"Why not?" she asked. "Haven't I hurt you?"

He couldn't deny that some of what she told him when he got home from Boston— aborting Bill Black's baby, hiring Phil Banks behind his back—had made him swallow pretty hard. But, "It's no big deal," he told her. "It certainly doesn't mean you have to be my sex slave."

"I don't *have* to be, I *want* to be," she said. "I was raised a Catholic, remember? I've been carrying around some of those secrets I told you the other night for 30 years. I'd never confessed any of it before. I've hauled around that huge load of guilt the whole time. Now I need some form of expiation. God, if I could have traded those 30 years of guilt for just one good hard spanking, I would have jumped at the chance. So if you'll just abuse me a little for the next couple of days, maybe it will ease my burden. Besides, it turns you on, doesn't it?"

"You already know the answer to that."

"That's what this is all about, turning you on. You know, I won't be able to turn you on the same way after Monday. We may be able to find other ways of satisfying one another, maybe even have some semblance of regular sex. But this weekend will be my last chance to make you spring to attention the way you do. Until tomorrow night, that's all that matters."

"But what about your satisfaction?"

"I'll bet I've had three or four times as much sexual satisfaction as you have over the years. If you find you still want to, I'm sure you'll be able to satisfy me for years to come. For now, this Playtime, the only thing you should think about is doing whatever you've most wanted to do. I know you would never do anything that would truly hurt me. I trust you with my life. That's why you're the master and I'm the slave. Now, what can I do for you?"

He certainly found her *carte blanche* attitude arousing. She smiled to see him looking her up and down, appraising her.

"That's more like it," she said. "When you think of sex, what's the first thing that comes to mind?"

He had so many fantastic memories. But if he had to choose one… "Remember that picture I take camping with me? You're wearing that tank top and the paisley boxers?"

She started to get up. "I still have those boxers. Shall I get them?"

"Sit down," he commanded her, and she meekly sat. "Remember what happened after that?"

She closed her eyes and quivered. "Oh, now you're talking. You tied my hands, right? And then tied the end of the rope to that plant hook on the ceiling. I hung there like a pinioned bird. Plucked, too, for that matter. I think I was wearing this same outfit, wasn't I?"

"I don't know. Stand up and let me look."

She stood naked on the bench of the Jacuzzi with her feet on either side of him. Throwing her head back and closing her eyes, she extended her arms up to an imaginary hook above, wisps of steam rising from her slender body. He fondled her with his left hand and fondled himself with his right. How many times had he imagined himself right here?

"Wasn't I pretending to be a call girl that night?" she asked without looking down.

Right then the phone rang. Matt groaned.

"Shall I get it?" she asked.

"Nah, let the answering machine pick it up. Today you're not even a call girl, you're just an ordinary hooker."

She giggled.

"As I recall," he went on, "you were a bedroom hooker that night. But we have other hooks, don't we? What about the one for the Christmas cactus hanging in the bay window in the living room?"

He got her attention with that. She glanced down nervously.

"Objections?" he asked.

"I'll do anything you tell me to do, master."

"And then if I wanted a call girl," he went on, "I could always call Stella and order a pizza. I wonder if she'd mention to me that I had a naked woman hanging in the front window like a piece of meat?"

By now, she had become so squirmy she had to sit down in the Jacuzzi again. She kissed his face and neck wildly. "We may never be able to order a pizza again," she said, "but it might be worth it. See? Now I feel like a sex slave."

"And I feel like the ruler of all I survey," he said, sliding further down into the bubbling water. "Come here, slave," he said, pulling her onto him. "Amuse me."

She knelt on the bench and impaled herself on his sword, her tissues squeaky from the water. He clutched her breasts and rocked her up and down until his back hurt too much to go on.

When he stopped she opened her eyes. "Are you okay?"

"Just a little sore," he said, grimacing.

She slid off of him. "Do you need some more medication? How's the Percoset working?"

"Not too bad. Wu was right, it really takes the edge off."

"What about something else? Can I refresh the mimosa? I've got another joint, too."

"Phil Banks took care of you quite nicely, didn't he? How many do you have?"

"I don't know. Half a dozen or so. I'm sure I could get some more from him if you needed it."

"Oh, so you're just trying to finagle another 'consultation,' huh? Haven't had your fill of Phil." Her mouth dropped open in protest but he silenced her with a stern look. "What do we do with a naughty slave?"

She lowered her eyes, trying not to smile. "Punish her."

"Then maybe you should just assume the position."

She crawled halfway out of the Jacuzzi and leaned on her elbows, her knees on the bench, her creamy white derriere a ready target. He slapped her wet cheek hard enough to leave a hand print. She squealed but turned the other cheek.

"That's enough for now," he told her.

"No fair!" she cried. "Now the other one's jealous! Spank it too!"

"You better lower your voice, slave," he told her, lowering his. "It may be foggy but the neighbors are just through the trees there. We wouldn't want them to hear the din of inequity from our den of iniquity, now would we?" He spanked her other cheek anyway and she yelped into the crumpled fabric of her nightgown.

She raised herself and tried to look at her backside. "Did you leave a mark?"

"I can see the outline of my fingers."

She rolled her eyes. "That'll be gone in ten minutes. All the other slaves will think my master's a wuss. Maybe I'll go get another joint, see if we can't get you into the spirit of this."

"Turn off the ringer on the phone while you're in there. You're my call girl exclusively now."

She got out of the Jacuzzi and gathered up the nightgown. He watched her blushing ass jiggle as she scampered along the deck. The Jacuzzi was high enough to enable him to see through the bedroom windows. When she got to the flagpole she draped the nightgown across the lingerie they'd tattered earlier, the pennants of her penance. She had not only decided to clear out all her lingerie in order to start fresh, she had also told him that for every piece he stripped from her this weekend, she intended to donate a thousand dollars to the American Cancer Society or the organization of his choice.

He had to admit, she was winning him over. A part of him still felt that they both might regret this decision to have the orchiectomy, or the hormonal equivalent, but any doubts he had about how much he meant to her were rapidly dissipating. He had always thought her too independent, too successful, too attractive, to really need him. Now that he saw some of her hidden flaws and insecurities, he understood that she had built the foundation of her success on the bedrock of his integrity. He felt more needed and loved than ever and very grateful to have discovered it while there was still time to appreciate it. He could almost buy that she was having as much fun this weekend as he, though that hardly seemed possible. He took a deep breath of the sweet clean northwoods air. It felt good to be home.

She came out of the bedroom and sashayed along the deck, now wearing the paisley boxers and one of his old T-shirts, the ribbed collar torn. A lit joint hung jauntily from her lips.

Handing him the joint, she asked, "Would you like to strip me now or have a wet T-shirt contest?"

He took a hit. "Wet."

She got back in, dunked herself, and stood back up. The shirt clung to her chest enticingly, revealing a purple lace half-bra underneath. She took the joint and had another hit while he grabbed the thin cotton of the old shirt and ripped it apart. Handing back the joint, she wriggled out of the shirt and thrust her chest out to him, her breasts bulging in the skimpy, tight bra.

He put out the joint in the ashtray and then grabbed her bra straps and tugged but the straps held.

"Remember, master, it's all for charity," she mentioned casually. "I didn't cut the straps as far this time. I wouldn't mind a few souvenirs."

He jerked the straps harder. Her breasts bulged further but the elastic fabric still held.

"Okay, let me make you an offer you can't refuse," she said.

"What's that?" he asked, still holding the flimsy cups of the bra.

"I've already offered my body to you this weekend, no holds barred. But let's face it: on Monday you'll begin to see me for the withered old hag I really am."

He guffawed.

"Anyway," she went on, "to show you how serious I am about the souvenirs, I'll give *ten* thousand dollars to the American Cancer Society for every mark you make that I can still see Monday morning."

"Oh, dirty pool!"

"If you won't do it for yourself, do it for all the other men out there."

Her right bra strap broke with the next yank but the left took three more tries before it finally snapped. She jumped and clutched her shoulder, then sat down next to him.

"Oh, God, I did that too hard, didn't I?" he said, distressed. "Let me see."

She took away her hand and looked at her shoulder. The fabric had left a slight abrasion across her collarbone. "You are such a kind, generous, unselfish man!" she told him, kissing him.

"You're out of your mind," he told her, kissing her bruised shoulder.

"But not close to being out of money," she said. "Microsoft is going to win that lawsuit." She turned around. Up from the waistband of the boxers protruded the end of a plastic ruler. When he extracted it, she told him over her shoulder, "When I was in grade school the nuns used to whack my behind so hard I'd have a welt for a week. They used to refer to atoning for a sin as 'satisfaction'." She pulled down the boxers, under which was nothing but his already fading hand prints and the purple thong that matched the torn bra. "You can't keep up with some feeble old nuns?"

He wielded the ruler, fighting off his scruples. She bent over the side of the Jacuzzi again.

"You'd better not cry out again," he warned her. "I don't want to get angry calls from the neighbors."

"I turned off the phone."

"Who called? Did you check?"

"Arnie somebody. He went yakking on about some system he had that wasn't Y2K compliant yet. It might have been a wrong number."

"Why in the world would somebody call me on Christmas morning about some computer glitch?" Matt puzzled. "Did he say what system it was?"

"Ardor maybe? And then he went 'Ar-dee-ar-ar-ar!'"

"Did you get his number?"

"Was I supposed to?"

"Get it."

"Now? But..."

The ruler stung her butt. "Now, slave."

She hastily pulled up the soggy boxers and scrambled from the hot tub. By the time he had figured out how he would handle this, she came back out wearing a white silk blouse over the paisley boxers and carrying the cell phone. He sat up as she stepped back into the water to warm the damp boxers, holding the phone up out of the water.

"Where's the number?" he asked.

She glanced down at her blouse. "Under there."

He couldn't tear the silk but the buttons popped right off. The number was written upside down with a felt-tip pen on her left breast.

"Can you read it?" she asked.

"It doesn't matter. You're going to call."

"What!?"

"Are you my slave or not?" He glowered until she nodded. "I want you to pretend to be my secretary. Ask for Arnie Farquhar. When he comes on the line, ask him what the problem is."

Reluctantly, she looked at her bare breast and dialed the number. He slipped his fingers into the leg of the boxers and past the thong to play with her while she asked for Farquhar and waited.

"I can't believe you're making me do this," she told Matt nervously, then went back to the phone. "Mr. Farquhar? This is Matt McCleary's secretary. We got your call this morning and Mr. McCleary wanted me to ask you to explain the problem."

He had a hard time keeping a straight face while she listened intently to what Farquhar was saying. He pulled down her billowing boxers and kissed her pink ass.

"Could you hold one moment?" she told Farquhar and then covered the mouthpiece. "He sounds goofy. The gist of it is that the algorithms aren't syncopated right, whatever the hell that means."

"Not syncopated right?" Matt bellowed, feigning outrage. "I syncopated those myself! Well, you tell him he can just kiss my lily-white ass!"

Her eyes grew very wide. "I'm not telling him that!" she hissed, handing him the phone. "You talk to him."

He took the phone from her and said, "Hey, Russ, how's it going?"

Deb punched him on the shoulder and then took a couple of gulps from the mimosa.

"Your secretary sounds hot, McCleary," Russ said. "I may have to hire her away from you."

"You couldn't afford her, Farquhar. Sure, she works for slave wages here but she knows I'll treat her right."

Russ laughed. "Matt, you're a better man than I. How's your Christmas?"

"Fantastic," Matt had to admit, looking at Deb peel off the silk blouse. "How's yours?"

"Enlightening."

"Really? In what way?"

"In more ways than I can express. But let me cut to the chase. I think we should have that Gathering of the Piñon Nuts on New Year's Eve. Can you make it?"

"I thought *you* couldn't make it. What happened?"

"Many things, all good. But we can discuss that in the next six days. What do you say?"

Matt thought about it. Sitting here in the Jacuzzi he felt pretty good but a trip to Colorado might prove tricky. "Actually, Russ, I've been under the weather lately."

"Nothing serious, I hope."

"Well, frankly, yes. I've found out I have—" He balked at telling the truth. "—walking pneumonia."

"That's a drag! It must be from doing all that walking on your hikes. But you sound pretty good."

"It comes and goes. Have you talked to John?"

"I called you first since you and I have to go the farthest. Obviously, there's no point in doing this unless we can all make it."

"What about May?"

"I don't have her number. Listen, I know this is a long shot but I have faith that this will come together. Here's what you should do. Call John, give him my number, and he can call May and give *her* my number. If one of you can't make it, he or she will have to call me and explain. Got it?"

"Do you think May could still get us into Crestwood that night?"

"I have no idea," Russ said. "If not, I suppose we could do it somewhere else, like the Broadmoor. That's where I was working that fateful night, after all."

"That's right. But let's try Crestwood first. I don't even have John's number, though."

"I do. Ready?"

"Wait a second. Let me get something to write with."

Deb grabbed her silk blouse and pulled the felt tip pen from the pocket, then offered her breast as a notepad.

Matt grinned and said to Russ, "Okay, go ahead."

"I'll give you his old number in Carriage Hills and his new one on Virginia."

Matt scribbled the two numbers on Deb's white skin. "I can't promise anything, Russ."

"This is going to happen," Russ said. "I can feel it."

"Well, someone will call you back after a while."

"Okay. See you."

"Bye."

"What did he want?" Deb asked after he hung up.

"He wants me to go to Colorado Springs on New Year's after all."

Concern filled her eyes. "Oh, honey, I don't know."

"Let's go inside and talk about it."

She helped him up from the Jacuzzi and handed him the phone, the mimosa, and the ashtray with the joint in it so she could hang her pennants over the flagpole. He got into bed and stared out at the fog while she went to the bathroom. By the time she went into the closet and put on a baby blue, baby doll nightie, he'd made up his mind.

"I'm going to do this," he told her as she slipped into bed with him.

"Will you be recovered enough from the operation by then?" she asked.

"The operation will just have to wait until the next millennium. If I go to this thing, I'm going with my manhood intact."

"Oh, Matt! Is that wise?"

"I'll bet when the Three Wise Men left to follow that star, their wives asked them the same thing. But like them, I just feel like this is the right thing to do."

"But what about the cancer?"

"The cancer will get worse," he admitted. "But only for a week or ten days. Deb, I really want to do this."

She set her jaw. "Then I'm going with you."

"What about the Millennium Moonlight Ball?"

"They won't cancel it just because I don't show up. And I was there when that Piñon Nuts pledge was signed, you know. I didn't sign it but I was a witness."

"Oh, I get it. You don't think I can handle this trip by myself."

"I never said that."

"You want to be around so you can do all the hard stuff for me."

"Well, you might need a little help with some things."

"All right then, you can start right now."

She sat up. "What do you want me to do?"

"Call May."

She shrank back down. "Oh, Matt, I don't know."

"You're going to have to talk to her when we get there. And sooner or later you're going to have to come clean with her about bailing her out of trouble over the years."

"But…"

"Oh, so it turns out you're *not* my slave."

"That's dirty pool!"

"I learned from the master."

She chewed her thumbnail and stared out the window. "I suppose you're right," she admitted finally. "I am going to have to call her sometime. But, Matt, what am I going to say?"

"You're going to ask her if there's any way she can get dinner reservations at Crestwood for at least five people on New Year's Eve."

She took a deep breath and let it out. "All right, give me the phone. I'm really nervous about this so don't mess with me, okay?" Her face assumed the sober expression she used for talking to business people as she looked at the buttons on the phone. "I haven't used this speed dial button since last August." She pushed the combination. "I still can't believe Amanda won't answer."

She waited as the phone on the other end rang four times. Then, as she listened, her business countenance shattered and her lips began to tremble. Within seconds tears coursed down her cheeks. She hung up the phone and began to cry.

"Oh, honey, what is it?" he asked, taking her hand.

"Amanda *did* answer," she sobbed. "I got the message she put on her machine last Christmas. Oh, Matt, I miss her so much!"

He stretched out on the bed, put his arms around her, and pulled her close. He gently rocked back and forth while she cried. When at last her sobs turned to sniffles, he said, "I'm sorry, hon. I never should have made you do that."

"How were you to know?" she said, reaching for a tissue.

"Why would that message still be on there?"

"I guess May must have just left it on the machine. Oh, God, it felt so good to hear Amy's voice again!"

"Listen, maybe this is just too much for you. Maybe you ought to stay here in Seattle and I'll go to the Gathering by myself."

"I'll be fine," she said, blowing her nose.

"Can I get you anything? You want some tea?"

"No, thanks. Besides, I'm the slave, remember?"

"Listen, you don't have to do that anymore," he said, squeezing her. "I understand. Besides, if I postpone the orchiectomy, we'll have another week at least for Playtime."

"Hey, wait a minute," she said, looking at him. "Are you trying to weasel out of this Playtime?"

"I just thought…"

"You think you're going to do anything to me this weekend that I wouldn't love you to do again next week?" She sat up defiantly. "Or are you just trying to give me the slip so you can romance some new flight attendant?"

"Give me a break. You just don't have to be my sex slave if you don't want to."

"Listen, mister," she said, poking him in the chest with her finger. "You are never going to find a better sex slave than I am and don't you forget it. Now, what do you want me to do?"

He mulled it over, looking at her. He had managed to arouse her again. "Okay," he said, handing her the phone again. "Call John."

She took the phone but told him, "You know, whenever I run into your other slaves, we always talk about how mean you are."

"You won't do it?" he asked, reaching for the phone.

"I didn't say that," she said, not giving it up.

"You're willing to call Phil Banks and hit him up for dope but you won't call a guy you dated a few times 30 years ago."

"Oh, all right," she said, looking beneath the baby doll nightie at her breast. "Which number should I call?"

"Let's see." The thin straps broke easily, the nightie sliding down. "His new place is the one on Virginia Drive. Oh, if he could only see you now." He played with her numbered breasts as she dialed. "Yes, Virginia, there is a Santa Claus."

She listened awhile. "Damn!" She hung up. "I got his machine too."

"I guess you'll just have to try the other number."

"Isn't that Susan's number? I thought they weren't even speaking to one another."

"It's Christmas. Maybe he's there with the kids."

"But I don't want to stir up a hornet's nest."

He pulled her down on the bed and worked the torn nightie over her head, leaving her naked once again. "What's the matter? Is my slave afraid of a few little stings?" He nibbled on her nipples. "Remember, it's all for charity."

"Promise you'll show me no mercy the rest of the weekend?" she asked as he gingerly rolled on top of her.

"Promise."

o   o   o

John and Susan had owned the house in the Carriage Hills subdivision of Estes Park for ten years. Every Christmas had looked about the same as this one: the living room buried knee-deep in wrapping paper, gifts and toys scattered about helter-skelter, various electronic devices emitting discordant sounds. Colorado has more white Easters than Christmases, so outside the sun shone bright and warm, melting any snow not in shadow. In the shadows the snow bore the wandering hoof prints of the elk herd, in town for the winter.

It all looked different to John, though. Out of context. He waded through the wrapping paper and flopped down in his old easy chair. This chair was a good example. He had napped in it a thousand times, the upholstery home to pieces of toys, crumpled coupons, and sundry bits of food; it displayed poop stains from a succession of gerbils, guinea pigs, parakeets, puppies, and one very frightened chipmunk, as well as blotches of throw-up from the girls themselves when they were small. But now he only thought of one thing when he saw the chair: Susan had sat in it for her interview on *Inside Edition*.

The split-level house certainly looked bigger than his little rental on Virginia Drive but he had never noticed how many walls there were here. The various electronic devices blared out their tireless cacophony to one another and the inhabitants seemed content to let the machines do the talking. Alice lay on the floor of the living room playing with her new Pokemon cards while the video of *Pocahontas* played on the TV. Anne's new CDs of Matchbox 20 and Sugar Ray boomed from her room. Martha Stewart lectured Susan on antique doorknobs while Susan steamed the old wallpaper from the walls of the master bedroom closet. Earlier, when they got back from church, Susan had turned on the stereo in the living room which added the soft strains of "I'll Be Home For Christmas" to the mix. Theoretically, John *was* home for Christmas. But he didn't feel like it.

One more voice joined the electronic chorus: the phone rang. Alice, not quite old enough yet to consider the phone her life line, didn't budge. John didn't consider it his place to answer it anymore.

"Anne, could you get that?" Susan called from the master bedroom.

Anne didn't respond.

"Oh, for pity's sake!" Susan kvetched. She answered the phone.

In a minute she came down the stairs, her church clothes already traded for old baggy sweats and her frosted hair gathered under a scarf. She walked to John and thrust the cordless phone at him. "It's for you," she spat. "I think it's May." She embellished the "May" with a bunch of sarcastic floral curlicues. She turned on her heels and went back upstairs.

John sighed. He had a whole new appreciation for the sentiment that "Christmas comes but once a year." He said hello into the phone, realized Susan had pushed the hold button, pushed it himself, and said hello again.

"John?"

"Yes."

"Hi. It's Deb McCleary, from Seattle."

He sat bolt upright in the chair. If he had had false teeth, they would have fallen out. "Good heavens! Hi, Deb! What a treat to hear from you!"

"It's good to hear your voice again too. How long has it been?"

"I think I called to make sure you guys hadn't been wiped out by Mt. St. Helens. When was that? 1980?"

"Something like that. How've you been? How's your Christmas going?"

"About the same as usual. This time of year, the women around here all fall in love with some fat old guy in a red suit so I'm just under foot."

"I love you, Daddy," Alice said without looking up.

It surprised John. He didn't think she was listening. "I love you too, Pumpkin."

"I'm not a pumpkin, Daddy."

"I love you too, Rutabaga."

Alice giggled.

"I heard you've had some problems on the home front," Deb said. "But it sounds like things aren't too bad."

"Well, as you heard, Alice loves me. Anne, on the other hand, gives me the same sorts of looks Eric and Lyle Menendez probably gave their parents."

"Matt said she'd been in some kind of trouble."

"Some kind of trouble indeed. Evidently you don't watch the tabloid TV shows."

"Is she okay?"

"She will be," John said, "if she ever gets back her sense of humor."

"I hope I'm not catching you at a bad time. Was that Susan who answered the phone?"

"Oh, yes. She's, uh… steaming at the moment."

"Oh?"

"Taking off some old wallpaper. She was fuming earlier. Changed all the potpourri. But how are you guys doing? How's the old man?"

"Getting older by the minute. Would you like to talk to him?"

"Sure."

"*Joyeaux Noël, Jacque!*" Matt said, his voice a little weaker than John recalled. "How's life treating you?"

"Like a diaper. Hey, what a nice Christmas surprise to get to talk to your lovely wife!"

"Oh, Deb was quite excited about calling you. In fact, she ripped off all her clothes."

John could hear Deb say, "I never!"

"Don't try to deny it, you little hussy," Matt went on, "or I'll get out my belt." To John he said, "Why do you think it's been so long since I've called you? I just can't trust her."

"Oh, yeah, women have just been falling all over me lately," John said glumly.

"So I suppose you've got some fabulous babe lined up for next Friday night."

"Hah!" John snorted. "Why? What's next Friday? Oh, New Year's Eve."

"Russ called me a little while ago, saying he thinks we should put on this Piñon Nut Gathering at Crestwood after all."

"Will miracles never cease? I thought you and Russ were way too busy to do something like that."

"He wasn't too specific but he sounded like things have really turned around on his end.

And things aren't so hectic for me as I thought either. The Y2K bug seems like it's going to be not so much a bang as a whimper. Plus, I've had walking pneumonia so I've taken a sabbatical from work."

"Sorry to hear about that. How bad is it?"

Matt paused. "Well, walking pneumonia won't kill me. But Deb also wanted me to tell you that she's coming too. In fact, she's just dying to show you the outfit she's wearing."

"Say no more," John said. "Sign me up. What do I have to do?"

"We tried calling May at home but couldn't get her. I don't suppose you'd know how to get in touch with her."

"I haven't talked to her since her grandmother's funeral. At that point she had quit her job at Crestwood."

"So we no longer have an in there."

"I told her she should try to get her job back but I'm not sure she even tried."

"Maybe you could call there and try to make reservations anyway. Russ mentioned the Broadmoor as a back-up site."

"That wouldn't be as cosmic but I suppose it would work."

"Do you want to try to get a hold of May or should we keep trying?"

"I will. I should see how she's doing anyway."

"Great! Let me give you the number at the farm where Russ is staying this weekend so one of you can call to confirm or cancel. Where did you write that number, Deb? Oh, there it is. Could you hold that up a little so I can see it better? Oh, yeah, that's great."

John copied the number onto a scrap of wrapping paper using one of Alice's crayons. "I'll try her after a while. If she's up for this, I'll have her call Russ back. We're going to have to act pretty quickly on this if you and he are going to get plane reservations."

"Hey, I'm really looking forward to seeing you guys again and I'll try to get Deb to put some clothes on before then."

"Not on my account! We'll talk soon."

"See you."

Well, a little ray of sunshine to pierce the gloom, John thought as he took the phone back upstairs to the master bedroom. He replaced it in its cradle and said to Susan, "Maybe I'll take off."

Susan didn't turn around. "How is she?" she asked icily, ripping a long strip of paper from the wall.

John chuckled. "That wasn't May. It was Deb and Matt McCleary calling from Seattle."

"Oh." Susan put the steamer against the wall again. "What did they want?"

"To wish us a merry Christmas, for one thing. And to ask if I wanted to get together with them down in the Springs for New Year's Eve."

"Are you going to do it?"

"I don't know yet. We've got to set up a bunch of stuff. Russ would be coming too. We'd be putting on a Piñon Nut Gathering."

"A what?"

John had never told her about the Piñon Nuts. By the time he and Susan met, the Piñon Nuts seemed old hat and the two of them had spoken more in the last two minutes than they had since Susan caught him with May after the Lake Haiyaha hike.

"It's kind of a dinner club we had back at the beginning of college," he explained.

"Are you going to bring May?"

He stared at Susan's back. She had already managed to stick bamboo slivers under most of his fingernails. Why should one more bother him?

While he stood mulling over his reply, Anne's music blared louder from her room as she opened the door. She came into the master bedroom carrying her Christmas stocking.

"Very funny, Dad," she said bitterly, handing him a small cardboard package. "I just found those."

"You might need them sometime," he told her.

"What are they?" Susan asked, turning around.

"Condoms," Anne said.

"John!" Susan cried. "What the… What's wrong with you?"

"Hey, if she's going to act like an adult, she better start acting like a responsible adult."

"Well, for your information," Anne declared bitterly, "I am through with boys forever. When I finish high school, I'm going to get out of this stupid town and join Greenpeace."

"They've got an all-girl Greenpeace now?" John asked.

"Oh, you wouldn't understand," Anne said and stormed off in a huff.

"How dare you!" Susan shouted at him. "How dare you bring your sleazy lifestyle into this house on Christmas!"

"Jesus, Susan!" he shouted back. "Wake up! I've never done anything to encourage Anne to have sex. What she did with Wayne Giles, she did behind *my* back as much as yours. She's growing up, whether you like it or not. If she's going to be involved with boys, I'd just as soon she didn't catch any more diseases, wouldn't you?"

"Why don't you just take those things with you when you leave. You're the only one who's likely to need them."

He turned to go but changed his mind. This might be his only chance to get in a few licks of his own. "You know, I didn't answer your question before. As a matter of fact, May will be there but I won't be taking her. She's the reason we're getting together for this."

Susan had gone back to steaming and didn't reply.

"The reason she came up here to Estes in the first place," John went on, undaunted, "was to tell me that she found some evidence that she's actually Jason Walker's daughter."

"Not that any of this is my concern," Susan said to the wall, "but who's Jason Walker?"

"My old high school buddy. I've told you about him. He disappeared in 1970. So Matt and Russ and I want to get together with her to tell her what he was like. Unlike Alice and Anne, May never had a chance to know her real father."

She whirled around and pointed the steamer at him. "That's why the two of you needed a motel room? To talk about her father?"

"I got her a motel room so she wouldn't have to drive all the way back to the Springs after our hike."

"You reserved the motel room two days before she came up to Estes."

"Okay, the truth is that she came up to tell me about Jason a couple of weeks before that. She and I planned to take that hike. But I did it to help her understand what her parents were going through when she was conceived."

"So you admit you lied?"

"I lied about that, yes."

"Did you sleep with her?"

Right then, the phone rang. They both glared at it and it didn't ring again.

John knew he didn't have a simple answer to Susan's question. One of the litanies of the House Prosecutors in President Clinton's impeachment was that "Sex is sex." Even the President's allies criticized him for splitting hairs, parsing the questions, evading the truth. But the truth is that sex *isn't* sex. It's not all or nothing. But Susan was in no mood to debate what the meaning of "is" is.

"No," he answered, technically telling the truth at least. "I didn't sleep with her."

"Uh-huh," she sneered.

"But I wanted to, I'll tell you that."

"Then why didn't you?"

"Because she didn't want to sleep with me. You know why?"

"No. Why?"

"Because I'm old and corny and a married man. She had her eye on a young black guy she was working with."

"Too bad," she said sarcastically.

"Not really. There are other things I care about more."

"Like what?"

"Like my wife and kids, my home, my job, my standing in the community."

"But you were willing to give those things up."

"No, *you* were the one who was ready to throw it all away without a word."

"What's the point in talking? You'd already found some pretty young thing."

"I found an old friend's daughter. And the only reason I was attracted to her at all is because I thought I'd lost you."

"What are you talking about? We split up because I caught you with her."

"When was the last time you really wanted to make love to me?"

"Well…" she said. "I mean… Well, you could have…" But she didn't specify.

"Let me tell you a story," he said. "An old married couple is out driving one day and they pass a couple of young lovers cuddling with one another in the front seat as they drove along in their car. The wife turns to her husband and says, 'How come we never sit close like that anymore?' He turns to her and says, "*I* ain't moved.' I'm not the one who lost interest, Susan."

Susan didn't laugh at the joke but she didn't turn away either. While they stood looking at one another, Anne knocked on the doorjamb and came in. "Mom, can I go to a movie?"

Susan switched off the steamer. "With who?"

"Danny Wright. We're going to see *The Sixth Sense*."

"Danny?" John asked. "Kind of a funny name for a girl."

Anne rolled her eyes and smiled.

Susan nodded wearily and said, "I want to eat around 6:00 so be home by 5:00."

"Thanks, Mom," Anne said. She started to leave but came back and gave John a kiss on the cheek. "Merry Christmas, Dad. Thanks for the CDs." Then she vanished.

"Hearts heal quickly at that age, don't they?" John asked Susan.

"I'm making a turkey for dinner," she said. "Would you like to stay?"

"Really?" John asked, surprised.

"The girls wanted me to ask you."

"Well, thanks, but I probably should go home and try to get a hold of May. If we stand any chance at all of putting this thing together, we're going to have to hustle."

"Why don't you call her from here?" she offered.

He looked at her, even more surprised, but she busied herself with the steamer. "Sure," he said unsurely. "If you wouldn't mind."

"You don't have your tools with you, by any chance?"

"In the car. Why?"

"You know the new sprayer faucet in the kitchen sink? Last week I accidentally dropped it down the garbage disposal while it was running."

"I think I still have the old faucet out in the garage. Want me to put it back on?"

"I would really appreciate it."

O   O   O

May, trying to fold napkins to look like swans, had just created another ugly duckling when the phone rang. Wearily she got up and went to the hostess station to answer it. "Merry Christmas from Crestwood. How may I help you?"

"Could I speak to Lucy Van Deutch please?" said the woman on the phone.

"I'm sorry, Mrs. Van Deutch won't be in today. Could I take a message?"

"This is Sandra Cogswell and I just wanted to register a complaint about our meal last night."

May could feel her stress level rise instantly. She knew all about this complaint. "I could have Mrs. Van Deutch—"

Sandra Cogswell wouldn't be denied. "We have never had such poor service at Crestwood in the ten years that we've been coming there. The hostess seated us right by the elevator so every time the doors opened we felt like we were in the kitchen."

"I'm sorry, ma'am, but we had some parties who stayed longer than expected."

"Oh, you were the hostess, weren't you? Well, let me tell you, your attitude leaves a lot to be desired. When that busboy poured water in my husband's lap, you acted like it was a joke. Plus, we waited patiently for our table for over an hour and it still took nearly another hour to get our meals, which by then were cold. And when my husband got home last night he went over his credit card receipt and discovered you had not given us our meals for half price the way we were promised."

"Actually, Mrs. Cogswell, I believe you'll find I did give you one free meal. But you still had to pay full price for beverages which, as I recall, was most of your tab."

"Are you calling me a lush? Or a liar?"

"I'm just—"

"You know, I've got a good mind to cancel our reservations for New Year's Eve. What would you say to that?"

May tried to think of something to mollify her but somehow just couldn't get her lips to pucker one more time to kiss Sandra Cogswell's plump snooty ass. "May I recommend the Waffle House?" May said politely. "Reservations aren't required and they don't have an elevator at all."

"Why, I never!" Sandra Cogswell sputtered and then hung up.

In resignation, May turned to Friday's page in the reservations book and crossed off the Cogswell party.

Angie, Crestwood's senior server and one of May's favorites, laughed as she folded swans. "Are you getting a kick-back from the Waffle House for those referrals?"

"They wouldn't even give me my last paycheck," May told her. "And when Lucy finds out what just happened, she'll probably send me back to the Waffle House to wait on that snotty bitch." She whirled around to make sure no one had heard her say that but the restaurant had hit the late afternoon lull and no one was about. "God, I'm losing it. Could you watch the door while I go have a smoke?"

"Consider it my Christmas present."

May walked through the swinging door into the kitchen, grabbed a cigarette and her coat, and went out the back door. The day had turned out clear and mild with the late afternoon temperature reaching almost 60 degrees so she didn't even have to zip up her coat. She leaned against the wall and lit the cigarette, feeling the nicotine instantly calm her jangled nerves.

Scott, the salad chef, sat on the back stoop, evidently on a break too. "How's it going?" he asked her.

May groaned. "God, I hate Christmas!"

"Too many unrealistic expectations," he said.

"Don't you hate working on holidays like this?" she asked him.

"I don't have kids so it doesn't really matter that much to me," he said. "I've worked so many now I've lost track. Do you have family waiting for you at home?"

"My daughter's staying with her father," she told him.

"How old is she?"

"She'll be two the first of June," May said, distracted by Marcus's silver Thunderbird coming up the drive. It pulled into the space next to her beat-up Fiat, still thumping with the repetitive bass line of a Run/DMC song even after the motor fell silent. May dropped her cigarette and stepped on it to put it out and then walked to the car.

As she approached, Marcus got out, wearing a gray sport coat that clung to his powerful shoulders, a canary-yellow satin shirt buttoned all the way to the top, and pleated slacks. He looked to May like Denzel Washington, with the same slender nose, narrow face, and warm smile. His dark eyes lit up when he saw her. He said, "Hey."

"Hey, you," she said to him, putting her hands on the lapels of his jacket. As always, he smelled great, his aftershave funky and alluring, his clothes fresh and clean.

"How's the Mayfly today?" he asked her, putting his finger under her chin to tilt her head back so he could kiss her.

They had only kissed a few times and it still thrilled May down to her toes. "I'm much better now," she told him afterward.

"Gotcha little somethin'," he said.

May could feel herself flush. "You didn't have to do that. I didn't…"

"You just gave me what I wanted," he told her. "Check my pocket."

She started to reach into the pocket of his trousers but he quickly glanced over at Scott and pulled her hand away. "Coat pocket, babe. Maybe we get to that other pocket tomorrow."

She giggled and reached into his coat pocket, pulling out a small unwrapped box. Opening it, she found a pair of earrings shaped like fishing lures. "Oh, Marcus, I love them!" she cried, throwing her arms around his neck and kissing him again.

"They reminded me of my little Mayfly," he said. "You still up for dinner tomorrow?"

"Of course!" she said, admiring her earrings again.

"Well, I best get changed. Scott's got the eagle eye on us."

"Hey, Marcus," Scott said. "How're you doing?"

"I'll walk in with you," May said to Marcus, putting the earrings in the pocket of her coat.

Scott stood to let them by but said, "Before you go in, May, can I talk to you for a minute?"

May kissed Marcus's hand before letting it go. She turned to Scott. "What's up?"

Scott stood quietly until Marcus had gone inside and the door closed behind him. "You know, it's none of my business…"

May instantly bristled. "Every single time someone has said that to me," she interrupted, "they've been right."

He threw up his hands submissively. "Whatever."

She felt a little guilty. She didn't know Scott all that well but he'd always seemed like a nice enough guy, quiet and good-natured. He did have an "eagle eye," as Marcus had put it; she often noticed him looking her direction.

But she might as well hear him out. "I'm sorry," she said to him. "I've just had a rough time lately. What were you going to say?"

"Well, I notice you and Marcus have gotten pretty close. I just wondered how well you know the guy, that's all."

So that's it, she thought. "Don't worry," she told him. "I know he's still married. He told me all about it."

Scott looked a little relieved. "Ah, good."

"He and his wife are going to separate after the first of the year. He'd do it now but they don't want to upset the kids over the holidays."

"Uh-huh," Scott said, looking at the ground.

"Why?"

"Do you remember Tara? She quit a couple of weeks after you started."

"Sure. And I know all about the little fling she had with Marcus."

"She was waiting until after Thanksgiving."

"Yeah, well," May said, feeling less sure of herself, "so I won."

"You know how Marcus lets the music play a minute after he stops the car? You know what he's doing?"

"He told me he always says a little prayer before work."

Scott raised his eyebrows. "Maybe. But he's also taking off his wedding ring."

May thought about it and couldn't decide one way or the other how true that seemed. "What are you telling me this for?" she asked Scott, resenting this cloud of mud he'd stirred up in the one clear pool of her life.

"I just thought you ought to know before you got too involved."

She looked at him. He looked okay, middle-aged with a fringe of short curly gray hair around the sides of his head, bald on top, and blue eyes that looked intelligent enough. But May could never tell with guys like this. "Is it because Marcus is Black?" she asked him.

Scott looked genuinely taken aback. "Hey, no. Not at all. I like Marcus a lot. I like his wife and kids too. He just likes to roam whenever he can."

"You know what?" she asked defensively. "I don't know if that's true or not but I'd rather hear about it from Marcus, okay? What is it with guys your age? It seems like you're all butting into my life lately."

Once again, he threw up his hands. "Hey. I'll butt out. Sorry to intrude."

He turned around and went back into the kitchen and she walked in right behind him. He had a scar on the back of his head and May had a sudden impulse to whack him there again.

The kitchen had grown noisier with the approach of the dinner hour. Marcus had changed into his white coat and toque. He looked up as she hung up her coat and he winked at her. She smiled back but Scott had planted the seeds of doubt. She looked at Scott too but he had turned his back to get something from the salad cooler next to the window with the fanlight.

Why the hell did he have to butt in? she asked herself as she went back to the hostess station. Marcus was the one ray of hope in her bleak existence and now she couldn't even be sure of that. Some Christmas.

The phone rang. She picked it up and gave the Christmas greeting again.

"Hi, I'd like to make reservations," a man said.

"Of course. What night would you like?"

"Well, I was *hoping* to get in on New Year's Eve but I know it's short notice."

"How many in your party, sir?"

"There will be four—no, five, come to think of it. Is there any chance?"

"We just had a cancellation, sir. It would be upstairs and the late seating. How does that sound?"

"Perfect!" he said.

"What's the name?"

"Kaufman."

Before May could write it down, she recognized the voice. "John?" she asked.

"Why, yes."

"Hi, John! It's May."

"That's why your voice sounded so familiar. Hi, May! How are you? So you got your job back after all."

"Yeah, Lucy understood about Nana's funeral and all. Actually, I'm still the newest employee here so I still have to watch my step. In fact, I lost one of our regular customers earlier so I'm glad you called. You took their reservations. Lucy can't very well complain about that. Are you coming in with your family?"

"No," John said. "Are you ready for this? Russ and Matt and I are trying to put together the Piñon Nut Gathering after all."

"You're kidding!"

"Nope. So I assume you're working that night."

"Yes. Not that I want to."

"Why? Got a hot date?"

"No, he has to work too."

"Is this Marcus? The guy you told me about up in Buena Vista?"

"Yeah."

"How's that going?"

"Not bad until tonight."

"Problems?"

"Oh, one of the other guys that works here just told me something that makes me wonder. Jeez. Couldn't I have just one thing in my life go right?"

"Maybe the guy was just trying to look after you."

"Maybe," May said sullenly.

"Maybe he's got his eye on you himself."

"I doubt it. He's quite a bit older than I am."

"So?" John asked, and then chuckled. "As far as that goes, you know what Santa brought me for Christmas? Condoms."

May laughed. "It's a little late now, John. We're not in South Park anymore. So you and Susan are still on the outs?"

"Actually, I went to church with her and the girls this morning. Got a lot of craned necks from the congregation. But Susan and I actually talked for a change. I think I may have straightened her out about what happened between you and me."

"You didn't tell her what happened in South Park, did you?"

"I still can't figure out what *did* happen in South Park. But for what it's worth, I told her we didn't have sex."

"We didn't!"

"Okay. I just wanted to make sure we both felt the same about that. Anyway, things are looking a little brighter on the home front. Anne's getting over that whole ugly mess with Wayne Giles finally. I'm even staying for Christmas dinner tonight. What about you? How's Libby?"

May groaned. "Remember how Paco ran off to New Mexico with that slut from Buena Vista?"

"Ah, yes. Felina, as I recall."

"Well, like I figured, she dumped him a couple of weeks ago when she found out that he was calling Shirley from her phone. So he came crawling back here to the Springs with his tail between his legs and cajoled Shirley into taking him back. And just to piss me off, he talked the judge into giving him full custody of Libby again. He claimed the whole New Mexico trip was strictly business. So Libby's back with him."

"But you've got your act together a whole lot better than you used to."

"I've only been working here a little over a month and I know Lucy has her doubts about me. I also had to have the head gasket done on my Fiat so I'm back in debt again too. I'd really have to improve my situation a lot to change the judge's mind. Listen, some people just walked in, so I better go. I'll put you down for five people at the nine o'clock seating on New Year's Eve. Why five, anyway? Is Susan coming?"

John laughed. "Hardly. Actually, Matt's wife Deb will be coming. You'll like her. She's a Microsoft millionaire and just one of the nicest people you'll ever meet."

"So who's the fifth? Sylvia?"

"No, my dear. You. You're still a big part of why we want to do this. It's basically your party."

May really hadn't given much thought to the whole Jason thing since she saw John last but it gave her a warm feeling to think these guys still cared enough about her and her mother and Jason to come all that way on such a big night. "Thanks, John," she said, proudly writing her own name down in the reservation book. "Tell the others I'm really looking forward to meeting them."

"You can tell Russ yourself," John told her. "I want you to call him back, collect if you have to, and tell him the Gathering is on. Here's the number."

She wrote it down but said, "Should I call him tonight? It's pretty late there."

"Wake the bastard up!" John declared. "This whole thing was his idea to start with. Oh, and ask him about Tom Huston. Tell him Huston wasn't a friend of ours, he was a friend of King Richard's."

"Who's King Richard?"

"Russ heard him speak at the Broadmoor once. He'll know what I'm talking about. Anyway, thanks, May. I've got to finish some plumbing and eat a bird. I may talk to you sooner but we'll see you New Year's Eve."

...O...O...O...

Why did I return to Colorado? Maybe it was a gut check, a return to the scene of the crime. But Colorado Springs, where I grew up, has grown up too and moved on. There's nothing to keep me here. No friends, no relations, not even notoriety. I remember pulling into town last summer, that big dumb smile on my face: Hey, folks, I'm back! Yawn. I got out the phone book and looked up every name I could remember. Nothing. I just assumed I would run into people I knew. Wrong. How big a fool am I, gleefully rubbing my hands together, planning to spring this elaborate surprise—Yes, back, after all these years! Who cares? I feel like I'm disappearing, fading into the background.

At what point do I concede defeat, admit that the reason for coming here has vanished? Whatever shallow roots I once had withered long ago. This town has become just like all the other places I've worked for a few weeks or months while I was out on the road. For that matter, am I just out on the road now? Is this "normal" job just another gig, another limited engagement? Should I head back up to the Northwest? At least I've got some music connections up there.

Gathering the Piñon Nuts again after 30 years was unlikely at best. I can't even get my own nuts together. But if nothing else, I thought I might make a new start, make some new friends. All I've made so far is a fool of myself trying to give a heads-up to that young woman at work. I can only imagine what she thinks of me. Why do I still cling to the ridiculous fantasy that a beautiful young woman, at least twenty years younger than I, would want to be friends with some pathetic geezer? We have almost nothing in common. What she does is none of my business, as she so aptly pointed out. My interest in her was totally inappropriate. Friendship is out of the question.

So I remain the odd man out. Some fantasies are best left fantasies. Why can't I leave well enough alone? There's no point in waking up from a perfectly good dream. All the transformative events of my life are over and done with. There's no fancy Ball in my future. My destiny is to spend my waning days picking lentils from the ashes.

And speaking of futility, what about these stupid memoirs? What a colossal waste of time, rehashing ancient memories, going over them at night and trying to win. Who will ever read this "Dear Diary" stuff? Even I haven't read my journal in years. I used to believe that if I could just get my troubles down in black and white, I could tinker with them until I found a way to fix the problem.

The last time I worked on my journal consistently and in depth was 20 years ago, back when I lost that Ball of Fire and her little boy. I lost much more than that at the time. She hired a couple of the guys from my band out from under me, so I lost my place to live and my job too and I'd gone into debt to buy her an engagement ring. When I got a call to work as a drummer in a country band playing on the road, I couldn't say no.

The band reeked. The leader and lead singer, whose nickname was Duck, had for a gimmick the ability to sing any of several hundred old country songs while quacking like a duck—that is, when he hadn't drunk enough rum and Dr. Pepper to send him into diabetic shock. I bunked with the 300-pound steel-guitar player who had to bathe his gums in hydrogen peroxide every night to keep his teeth from falling out. I had a lot of time to spend on my journal.

When we got to Rapid City, South Dakota, Duck decided to fire me and the rhythm guitar player, Tim, because we had the audacity to cover for Duck when he couldn't make it to the stage. As we finished out the week, I did a lot of writing. At one point Tim asked me, "So, are you working on your book again?"

Book? I thought to myself. I assumed no one else but me would ever read any of it, which so far has been the case. Nevertheless, here's what I wrote before abandoning the journal for four or five years: "Considering this journal as a work that might survive me, what have I dealt with? Petty, tacky, relatively unimportant matters, the daily thoughts and works of an all-too-common man who can't rise above the everyday nonsense and deal more in depth with things that really matter." What matters? Nothing. Ba-doom-boom—tchishhh.

I wrote that journal entry nearly 20 years ago and now I find myself back in that same old rut, still trying to tinker my way out of my problems. I pace like a caged beast, restless as ever. My feet are killing me.

I've frittered away so much time on these dorky little road stories that I no longer have time to deal with the transformative event that sent me out on the road in the first place, the one part of my life that actually might interest someone. That event still constitutes the far horizon in my past, as the coming end of the millennium constitutes the horizon up ahead. But how could I tie that huge sloppy mess into one tidy bundle, the way I have with so many other transformative events? Maybe I shouldn't have killed that innocent kid. Maybe I should have stuck around and faced the music.

But the music was "Hail To The Chief." It's hard, even after all this time, not to blame that Quaker SOB for cutting me off from everything I had and everyone I loved. But that bastard is dead and buried. Let lying dogs sleep.

One possession that's almost as close to my heart as my old chef's knife is my antique wind-up mantle clock. When it was given to me, it had a hitch in its git-along. I sat down and took a close look at it and found that the seat of the primary gear had worn out of round. My usual cheap-ass solution: stretch an old piece of florist's wire across a couple of bolts on the brass back plate to suspend the gear. The clock has run that way for years.

For a few brief, terrifying moments in my life I have felt certain that my time had come, that the seat of my primary gear had worn out of round. Somehow I've always managed to patch things back together with scotch tape and bailing wire, to keep living on borrowed time. But maybe, like the clock, this borrowed life of mine is just an old piece of junk worthless to all but me, taking up space and marking off the empty days tick by tick. Maybe I'd be better off tossing it. Maybe it's not worth fixing anymore. Maybe the show doesn't have to go on.

August 8, 1970

Russ wheeled the clattering, overloaded bus cart from the third floor landing in the stairwell into the Broadmoor's service elevator and pushed the "M" button. So far, this summer had been a drag. His father had stayed in town all summer, working on a project at Alexander Film, and he and Russ had been at loggerheads most of the time. Just to keep them from each others' throats, Ellen had insisted Russ once again work as a busboy at the hotel. Until tonight, that meant a dreary stream of nondescript, work-filled days with little money and no social life to show for it.

But tonight, Russ thought as the elevator doors opened onto the mezzanine at the top of the lobby's marble spiral staircase, made up for every dull moment of the last two months. As he wheeled the cart past the open doors that led onto the portico, he paused to gaze into the warm summer evening. He already knew he would remember this night for the rest of his life.

He was so excited about what he had heard that he barely noticed when one of his fellow employees, at least judging by the black pants and white shirt, greeted him from a chair by the one of the chess boards in the long game room along the front of the mezzanine level. Russ gave him just a perfunctory "Hi" as he pushed the cart past.

The fellow said, "So Jimmy Cox had it right."

Russ didn't understand the remark and it intrigued him enough to stop and turn back to the guy. "Jimmy Cox?"

"Yeah. Nobody knows you when you're down and out."

Russ could hardly be blamed for not recognizing Jason at once. His long blonde curls had been replaced by a wiry buzz-cut and his face and neck looked sunburned and sore. His dirty white shirt looked frayed and it hung loosely from his shoulders, his pants, at least three sizes too big, were cinched up by a khaki belt, and he wore beat-up, dusty Army boots. He looked more haggard and gaunt than Russ had ever seen him and the lively sparkle of his blue eyes had given way to a dull desolate stare.

"Jason?" Russ asked in disbelief. "Is that you?"

"What's left of me."

Russ went over and clasped his shoulders. "Oh, man, it's good to see you! But what are you doing here? I thought you were still doing time in Cañon City."

"I got out," Jason said tersely. "Long story."

"Are you okay?"

"No."

Russ could tell Jason wasn't exaggerating. He looked around to see if anyone was watching but the evening's excitement had shifted to Broadmoor South, at least for now. Still, Russ had never seen such a busy day in the dining room and he couldn't very well just stop and chat. Jason looked a wreck but if his ill-fitting clothes had fooled Russ, they might fool the rest of the staff. "I've got to take this stuff down to the kitchen," he told him. "Why don't you come with me?"

Jason shrugged and with an effort pulled himself to his feet. Russ pushed the cart through the dining room, glancing back to make sure Jason still plodded wearily along behind him.

Mr. Calderone, the kitchen manager, hailed them as they went through the swinging doors into the bustling kitchen. "Jones, who's that with you?"

"This is my friend Jason. He works on the grounds crew," Russ fibbed. "He's just headed down to the cafeteria."

Mr. Calderone looked Jason up and down suspiciously. "Who's your boss, Jason?" he quizzed him.

"Uh, Mr. Switzer," Jason told him.

Mr. Calderone nodded. "Okay. Can't be too careful today," he told Russ. "I don't need the Secret Service all over us." He went over to talk to the chefs.

As Russ pushed the bus cart over to the dishwashing cubicle, Jason asked him quietly, "Secret Service?"

"Didn't you know?" Russ said in an undertone. "The President is in town. He's speaking to the Governors' Conference in the International Center tonight."

"Ah," Jason said. "I wondered why I saw so many cops. Wow, King Richard the Turd in the flesh, huh? Is he staying here?"

"No, he's flying on to California tonight. But you wouldn't believe what I heard a while ago," Russ said, loading the bus tubs from the cart into Lucky Lowe's cubicle. "In fact— Hey, Lucky, how's your garbage?"

Dirty dishes teetered in tall stacks on the stainless steel counters around Lucky. The grizzled old vet, madly spraying racks of plates before shoving them into the dishwasher, groaned. "It's getting mighty heavy."

"Want me to take it down to the loading dock for you?" Russ offered.

"Thanks, kid," Lucky said, pausing to wipe his sweaty face on his sleeve. "I gotta get some ice up here sometime too."

"How about if Jason and I run down there for you?"

Lucky sighed as he looked at the mountain of work around him. "Know what? I need a break. I'll come with you guys. If they run outta stuff, they can just open up some boxes of new."

He and Russ lifted the overflowing garbage can onto the heavy wooden cart and put a stack of nested, empty ice buckets next to it. The three of them got into the service elevator and pushed the button for the loading dock.

"So Nixon's right here in the hotel?" Jason asked Russ.

"He's over in Broadmoor South now," Russ told him. "They're giving a state dinner in the Penrose Room before the Conference. But earlier they set up a hospitality suite upstairs on the third floor. I just bussed those dishes. God, Jase, I've got to tell you about what I heard but first tell me how you got out of prison."

"Prison?" Lucky said, looking askance at Jason. "What were you in for?"

"Flashing a peace sign at a cop," Jason said as the elevator stopped and Russ pulled open the doors.

"Didn't think that was an actual crime," Lucky said as they maneuvered the cart out toward the loading dock.

"It is if you've got a couple of ounces of marijuana in your pocket," Russ said. He sympathized with Jason and didn't think he deserved imprisonment but his reckless behavior sometimes seemed to court trouble.

"You one of those hippies?" Lucky asked, looking Jason up and down. "Cause you don't look like one of those hippies."

"My rainbow died," Jason explained, helping Russ heft the garbage can off the cart and into line with all the other garbage waiting to be hauled away. Jason noticed the handle of a knife sticking out of the can. "What's this?" he asked, pulling it out.

"They're chucking it," Lucky told him. "See the notch?"

The notch was at the base of the blade. "It still looks pretty good to me. Can I keep it?"

Lucky shrugged. "Makes no never mind to me. Just don't go 'round stabbing people with it."

"I'm a hippie, remember?" Jason said, tucking the knife into the waistband of his pants behind his back. "Make love, not war, and all that. Besides, this thing could come in handy for peeling taters on K. P."

"K. P. sounds more like the Army," Lucky pointed out.

"Those seem to be the choices: prison or the Army."

"Well, the Army sounds bad enough," Russ said as they loaded an empty garbage can onto the cart, "but you made prison sound awful in your letter."

"It is awful."

"How come you only wrote me that one letter, anyway?" Russ asked.

"You didn't even reply to that one."

"I haven't had much time this summer," Russ said, feeling guilty. "But you always said you could be happy with just an empty room, a pencil and paper, and some time to think. Given that much time you could have written a lot more than a letter or two, like short stories or a book. Look at O. Henry."

"No, it's too damned noisy in the cell block," Jason said as they headed down the long dark tunnel to the ice room. "I can't concentrate. I could only get some real writing done if I committed some sort of serious crime, got myself convicted as a mad assassin or something so I could spend time in solitary confinement, get a little peace and quiet. But just my luck, I got kicked out of jail."

"What are you talking about?" Russ asked.

"Wednesday morning the guard came in and kicked me awake, told me I was in the Army. Next thing I knew, I was on a bus to Fort Benning, Georgia."

"How did that happen?"

"The best I can figure is that the University got wind of my felony, took a look at my G. P. A.—those pass/fails I took that second semester didn't help—and kicked me out. So much for my student deferment. When the judge heard that my bust was the only thing making me ineligible for the draft, he dropped the felony charge and commuted the rest of my sentence. Bingo, I'm in the Army."

"They can't do that!" Russ protested.

"Of course they can. Otherwise, all you'd have to do to escape the draft is steal a carton of cigarettes. A lot of guys would rather spend a few months sitting on their ass in jail than getting it shot off in Vietnam."

"So you're AWOL?" Lucky asked.

"I guess."

"How did you get away?" Russ asked him.

"The bus stopped in Clinton, Oklahoma, for lunch a couple of days ago. I went to the john, saw an open window, and booked. Traded my fatigues for somebody's laundry hanging on a line. That guy was considerably more substantial than I am," he added, hitching up his pants as they waded through the puddle in the tunnel.

"So how did you get here?"

"Hitchhiked. Walked a lot of it."

Russ shook his head in disbelief. "What do you think, Lucky?" he asked. "Are Army prisons better than civilian ones?"

"I did a couple stints in the brig during the war," Lucky said. "It ain't never fun."

"Jeez, Jase," Russ said. "It seems like you're getting yourself in deeper all the time."

"That doesn't matter. I just had to get back up here."

"How come?"

Jason paused. "I had to try to talk Manny out of doing something stupid."

"Oh, yeah," Russ said. "John told me she was talking about marrying Bill. I don't know, Jase. It seems like you're fighting the inevitable on that one. She and Bill have had their disagreements but maybe it was just meant to be. What did she say?"

"I couldn't get a hold of her," Jason said bleakly. "I tried calling her but her mom told me she already left for Texas."

"Texas? What's she doing down there?"

"She's, uh… thinking about transferring to the University of Texas, El Paso."

"Good Lord. From C. C.? What in the world for?"

"I told you it was stupid. Oh, Christ, Russ," he said, his voice cracking. "God, I've just fucked everything up. Manny's been like this light bulb at the end of the tunnel. She's what I've been aiming for."

"Sorry, Jase. It must be tough."

"It hurts too much to laugh and I'm too big to cry."

They pulled the cart into the ice room and unloaded the empty buckets, knocking out the heavy mesh bottoms before stacking them onto the other empties, Russ having to reach over his head to set them on top of the columns.

As they loaded three buckets of cubed and three buckets of chipped onto the cart, Russ said, "You know, you may have to accept the fact that it's just not going to happen with Manny. But it's not a matter of life and death, for heaven's sake. There are lots of other women in the world."

"Not like Manny," Jason said with conviction. "She's my *bon ami*. She held my hope for the future. With her in my life I felt like I might find a place to fit. Now, I don't know. Let's face it, there are a lot more Prudences than Mannys in this world."

"Who's Prudence?" Lucky asked as they headed back into the tunnel. He had listened without comment to their conversation so far, grateful perhaps for the chance to catch his breath.

"She's my ex-girlfriend," Russ told him, then asked Jason, "You heard about her and John, right?"

"When John came down to see me in Cañon City, he said they were going to get a place together this summer. Sorry, man."

"No big deal. Yeah, they're living above the Egg House a couple of blocks from the college. John's life-guarding."

"Is Matt in town?" Jason asked. "I checked the drugstore but he wasn't there."

"He is in town but just for a couple of weeks. He got a job in Seattle this summer. His parents moved again and got a smaller place."

"So you're the only one of us lucky enough to serve the President."

"Okay, I've got to tell you what happened upstairs," Russ said, unable to contain himself any longer. "I told you they set up a hospitality suite on the third floor, right? One room was for a little informal press conference and the adjoining room was just for the presidential party to kick back in for a while before the dinner. Nixon brought along Henry Kissinger and John Mitchell. Anyway, after the news conference, they closed the doors to the other room and Mr. Calderone sent me in to clean up the stuff from the reception. I gotta tell you, it was pretty cool. I mean, I could still smell the aftershave of the President of the United States! The only thing between me and them was a door and the Secret Service guys."

"So you didn't get to see him at all," Jason said.

"No, but listen to this. I had to go to the bathroom, right? Somebody left the window open in there and as I'm taking a leak, I hear another window open. There's those little roof affairs over the mezzanine on the third floor so I could hear really well. And what I hear is a guy with a really deep voice and thick German accent say, 'Sorry. Is that better?'"

"Kissinger?"

"Had to be, because then a guy says, 'Thanks, Henry. It's stuffy enough in here without the cigar.' I could tell it was Nixon by his mush-mouthed tone."

"Are you serious?"

"And then I hear John Mitchell say, 'Anyway, Dick, what are we going to do with Tom Huston?' and Kissinger says to Nixon, 'Did you talk to Hoover?'"

"As in J. Edgar?" Jason asked as they splashed through the puddle again.

"Listen to this: Nixon says, 'I told you about what that old biddy said to me when I brought up the subject of retirement, didn't I?' and the other two just groaned. Nixon told them anyway: 'That S. O. B. had the gall to point out that I was still a young man.'"

"The President said that?" Jason said, laughing.

"Called the head of the F. B. I. an S. O. B.?" Lucky asked incredulously.

"Yep," Russ said. "Then he went on to complain that Hoover had put a bunch of footnotes all over some plan this Huston guy came up with. 'Destroyed our deniability,' Nixon said. 'Threatened to take it public. The bastard just doesn't want anybody taking precedence over his precious F. B. I. Huston's right: at some point Hoover's going to have to be told who's president.'"

"That's spooky. What's over the F. B. I.?" Jason wondered.

"Beats me," Russ said. "Anyway, Mitchell pointed out that the risk of disclosure was greater than the possible benefit. He reminded them not to forget the first rule of governance: cover your ass. They couldn't afford to get caught with their hands in the cookie jar."

"The Attorney General said that?" Jason said. "Wow. What did Nixon say?"

"He said they'd have to deal with Tom Huston the way they did with the Huston Plan, namely, keep him quiet. At that point, I heard the Secret Service guys come into the room I was in to see what I was doing so I flushed and left."

"That's incredible, Russ!" Jason said as they wheeled the heavy cart into the elevator. "So who's Tom Huston?"

"I have no idea but I wouldn't want to be in his shoes."

"What are you going to do?"

Russ thought about it as the elevator took them to the kitchen. "I guess I'll just finish my shift."

"I mean, about what you heard?"

"I don't know. Nothing, I suppose. I mean, what can I do? Walk up to the President in the middle of the Governor's Conference: 'Oh, by the way, I was eavesdropping earlier and I heard you say…' Get real, Jason. I don't want to get mixed up in something like that."

"Maybe you're right," Jason said as they pulled the cart into the kitchen. "It just seems like somebody ought to know about stuff like that."

"What are you going to do?" Russ asked him.

"Nothing, I suppose."

"No, I mean tonight."

"Nothing, I suppose," Jason repeated wearily.

"Where are you going to stay?"

"You know, my dad's divorced again."

"Yeah, John told me."

"Well, he's broke too and my grandfather has been sick. Dad went back to Chicago to look after him and take care of my grandmother. He figured I'd be in prison or the Army so I wouldn't need a place to stay. Why should he hang around here?"

"So, do you need a place to crash?"

"Are you sure you want an outlaw in your home?"

"Stay at my place tonight," Russ insisted. "We'll talk this whole thing through. Maybe we'll even ask my dad. He might be able to give you some good advice."

"Whatever," Jason said. "All I know is I've got to crash for a while. I haven't slept since Kansas."

"Have you eaten anything?" When he just shrugged, Russ handed him a half a loaf of the French bread they baked at the hotel each day. "Take that and find someplace to catch a few z's. I get off at ten so meet me by the wine bottles at a little after."

Jason bit off a chunk of bread and nodded. "Thanks, man." He turned and wandered back through the kitchen door toward the game room again.

"Watch that knife!" Lucky called to him.

"Yeah, don't stab yourself!" Russ called too.

"Sounds like your friend's in some hot water," Lucky said to Russ after Jason went out the door.

"Nothing we can't fish him out of."

o   o   o

Around 9:00, word spread through the kitchen that Nixon had changed his plans slightly. A motorcade waiting for him at the entrance to Broadmoor South had attracted a small crowd of local citizens and conference members, with enough protesters present to make the Secret Service uncomfortable. So Nixon had decided, the evening being quite pleasant after an unusually heavy afternoon thundershower, to forego the motorcade and walk from Broadmoor South along the lake, letting John Mitchell and Henry Kissinger run flak by riding over in the limousine. Entering the main hotel at the mezzanine, the President would go down the escalator, leave the main lobby by the front entrance, and walk the half block to the International Center to give his speech to Governor John Love and the other 1800 people attending the conference. The last minute change of plan made it difficult for the Secret Service to cover the route properly, Mr. Calderone pointed out, but it foiled any demonstrations planned for the original motorcade.

Russ, along with several other kitchen employees, begged Mr. Calderone to let them take a short break so they could go out in front of the hotel to see the President pass. The evening rush having pretty well died down, Mr. Calderone let them go, with the proviso that everyone was to comport himself in a way befitting the dignity of both the President and the Broadmoor. With the others, Russ hustled out of the kitchen and went downstairs.

As he rode the escalator down, Russ thought about the fact that the President of the United States would ride the same escalator in just a few minutes. He wished he knew where Jason had gone. He undoubtedly would like to have seen Nixon pass too.

Russ had lived in the area and worked at the Broadmoor long enough to become complacent about the place but the old hotel had certainly taken on a new luster in the last few hours. Some of the familiar sights—the hallway to the restrooms lined with glass cases containing old classic wine and liquor bottles, the Tavern with its classic decor that hinted of Western themes, its soft music from a dance band, the original Toulouse-Lautrec posters on the walls—seemed more world class now, less provincial. And the red carpet at the entrance took on added significance when trod by the most powerful man in the Free World.

The evening had indeed turned out fine, the earlier downpour having settled the dust, the stars glittering in the night sky, and the dry clear air scented by the hanging flowerpots and blooming linden trees around the entrance to the hotel. A few officers from the Broadmoor Police and the El Paso County Sheriff's Department directed Russ and the others to a spot near the small covered gateway at the north end of the valet parking area. Russ recognized among the cops the officer who had caught them at the rock climbing area the summer before. As he stood with the rest of the buzzing crowd waiting for the President to appear, Russ felt spellbound by his surroundings.

The Broadmoor Hotel was built in 1918 by Spencer Penrose, the black sheep son of a distinguished Philadelphia surgeon. Penrose and his partner Charlie Tutt struck it rich in the gold mines of Cripple Creek and expanded their wealth in copper and other mining interests. The hotel was Penrose's pet project and he had created a masterpiece, designed by the New York architectural firm that designed the Ritz-Carlton and Grand Central Station. The pinkish stucco, tile-roofed building rises in several columns to different heights, dominated by a central column topped by a bell tower on the ceiling of which gold stars had been painted on an azure sky. Italian artisans decorated the trim with hand-painted fruit and had created colorful gargoyles and cornucopia on the balustrade above the portico. The portico is supported by arched columns that frame the entrance and has its own low balustrade, below which on the facade is written, in raised gilt letters lit by a spotlight, THE BROADMOOR, the small "A" a trademark of the hotel.

It was designed to impress and impress it did. To Russ it represented the epitome of wealth, elegance, and power. Standing here, waiting to see the President of the United States, Russ's problems, and even Jason's, seemed shabby and insignificant.

The onlookers began craning their necks and a few clapped as a group of black-suited Secret Service men issued from the main entrance and then some cheers rang out as the President walked out onto the red carpet. Shaking a few hands, grinning that distinctive Nixon grin, the President waved to the small gathering as he and his bodyguards walked out from beneath the portico.

Russ found himself clapping too, though he was struck by how short Nixon looked. Dressed in a black suit with a blue and red tie, he seemed stockier and plainer than Russ had imagined. He didn't strike Russ as someone he would even notice on the street, were it not for all the trappings of fame and power. The whole group stopped for a photo opportunity in front of the fountain.

Then above the clapping and cheering, a voice rang out from above, saying, "Congratulations, Dick!"

Russ looked up to the roof of the portico. There, above the raised "A" in the center of the balustrade, stood Jason, his hands resting on the concrete, his face catching the light from the spotlight.

Nixon heard it too and, still smiling, he looked up at Jason and waved. The Secret Service nervously tightened up around the President but he waved them back. "Thank you, son," he called genially to Jason and began to turn away.

"You're standing right where I stood when I found out you got my brother killed," Jason shouted down at him.

Nixon said something to one of the Secret Service men, who spoke into his radio. Nixon, turning back to Jason with his smile restored, said, "Listen, son, if you have a grievance—"

"If?" Jason cried. "You're giving me 'ifs'? Listen, you S. O. B. We know about your dirty tricks. We know about the Huston Plan. You're the traitor here! Off with his head!" He punctuated the last line with a wave of his hand, followed shortly by the clatter of steel onto the concrete behind him.

Nixon blanched when he heard the name Huston and a couple of the Secret Service men leapt toward the entrance to the hotel.

Jason bent and then reappeared, holding up the chef's knife that had fallen from his pants. "Not to worry," he called out, holding it up. "I couldn't possibly hit something as small as your heart from here."

But already pandemonium had broken out. A woman screamed, "He's got a knife!" and suddenly people began shoving and pushing to get away. The police and Secret Service surrounded the presidential entourage and hustled them off to the International Center. Russ caught one last glimpse of Jason as he bolted toward the glass doors of the hotel and then he disappeared from Russ's view for the last time.

<h1 style="text-align:center">...O...O...O...</h1>

Writing is a hermit's sport. My appearance matters as little as my disappearance. The wee hours too often find me treading that same worn path on the floor, totally absorbed, oblivious.

Reduced to black and white, my life takes on a cartoon quality. I feel like the short-lived, middle-aged Uncle Max in Calvin and Hobbes, *who, when asked by Calvin's mom if he ever had an imaginary friend, replied, "Sometimes I think* all *my friends have been imaginary."*

And speaking of imaginary friends, tonight's the night. I can't believe I managed to sucker myself into thinking any vestige of that former life, of my former self, still exists. I suppose, if I'm not too busy, I could take a quick look around the place just for old times' sake but I've got to face facts. The Piñon Nuts have long since scattered and taken root on distant shores. All the best to them wherever they are.

Maybe I will move back to Seattle. I'll wait to give notice until next week. Eric's got enough on his mind tonight, dealing with the results of my trying to "help out." No one will shed a tear to see me go, least of all my young lady "friend."

But I got what I came here for. I found the answer to my question. That boy from long ago is dead. To stay here is pointless. It's time to move on.

Well, there's the alarm. Time to wake up, if only I'd been sleeping. Time to let go of the dream and get back to real life. But hey, I gave it the old college try. I put myself out there one last time. From now on, if I can be found at all, it will be at some normal job or maybe, on my days off, wandering through the fields and the forests.

So anyway, any last requests before I go? "Auld Lang Syne"? Don't be absurd. By myself?

<h1 style="text-align:center">December 31, 1999</h1>

For May, the last few hours of the millennium bore a striking resemblance to the rest of the millennium she'd come to know and loath.

As soon as she got to Crestwood, even before she took off her coat, Angie informed her that Marcus had phoned in earlier to tell Lucy that his wife had threatened to leave him if he ever set foot in Crestwood again. So, with no notice, he quit. Earlier in the week, May had discovered the truth of Scott's warning and broken off her relationship with Marcus. But his new-found commitment to his wife not only rubbed a little more salt in May's wound, it left Crestwood in the lurch on its busiest night ever.

Then about 7:00, at the height of the early seating rush, May's neighbor Barbara had called to tell her that Paco and Shirley had stopped by the bungalow, hoping to leave Libby, squalling from an ear infection, with May so the Gruesome Twosome could go out for New

Year's Eve. Already drunk, they had created such a scene that Barbara went out to complain about the ruckus and without further ado, Paco handed Libby and the diaper bag to Barbara and drove off. Barbara, who had small kids of her own and a new boyfriend, had reluctantly promised May she would watch Libby until May got home but May knew she would owe Barbara big time for this.

When the rush of the early seating and the slow kitchen Marcus's absence had caused overwhelmed Angie and the other servers, May, finding a lull at the cash register, volunteered to help. Anxiously checking the door to see if the party that had just walked in might be the Piñon Nuts, May had dropped a plate of endive-and-radicchio salad in the lap of an older gentleman, whose thick glasses didn't prevent him from noticing that the raspberry vinaigrette didn't come close to matching his tan slacks. She politely agreed with the man when he called her "ham-handed" but dreaded having to bring the news about the ruined salad to Scott, who worked faster than one of the old plate-spinning acts on Ed Sullivan as he tried to keep up with the salad chores while also covering for Marcus at the broiler.

When she walked through the swinging doors into the kitchen, she saw Scott standing at the salad chef's work station in front of the large window under the fanlight. Sweat already soaked his toque and ran from the short grizzled curly hair at his temples as he garnished some salads with straw mushrooms.

"Scott—" she began.

He held up his hand. "Lyle," he called to the head chef, "could you turn that big oven up to 450? I want to brown those ducks when I first put them in. Sorry, May. What can I do for you?"

"I dumped a radicchio salad in somebody's lap," she explained apologetically.

"I'll do another in a minute," he said, placing the finished salads on a tray. "Could you take these out to Angie?"

"Sure," she said, shouldering the tray. "Oh, and can I talk to you a minute when you're free?"

Scott looked up at her and smiled. "I'm always free. But I've got to turn some tenderloins."

"Let me take these out to Angie then."

When she returned with the empty tray he asked her "What's up?" as he assembled a replacement radicchio salad.

"I just wanted to apologize to you," she told him, putting some warm rolls in napkin-lined baskets and covering them over.

"It's only one more salad," he said.

"I mean for snapping at you on Christmas when you told me about Marcus."

"Sorry to intrude in your personal life," he said, rather stiffly.

"No, I'm grateful," she insisted. "You were right and I'm glad I found out when I did. Thanks for caring enough to say something."

"But I'm sure you're not looking for a father," he said, handing her the finished salad.

She smiled at the irony. "Actually, I've had some father issues lately," she pointed out.

Angie stuck her head through the door. "May, your party's here."

"Great!" she said. "Thanks for the salad, Scott." She went out and handed the salad to Angie, asking her, "Could you take this to that gentlemen with the stain on his pants?"

"So another man's pants fall prey to your irresistible charms," John said to her.

She chuckled. "Yeah, right," she told him, kissing him on the cheek. "So you made it! Thanks for coming. You look great!"

He wore a navy blue suit with a faintly pink dress shirt and a bright blue tie. He had cut his hair shorter but his beard had filled in, the gray streaks at the corners of his mouth looking distinguished.

He put his arm around her shoulders and said, "Don't get me started. May, this is Russell Jones, former occupant of this fine abode."

"Russ, it's wonderful to finally meet you," she said, extending her hand.

"And you, my dear," he said, gallantly kissing the back of her hand.

She liked Russ instantly. He wore a black suit with a bright red vest that bulged over his paunch and a spiffy black bow tie and he carried a black leather satchel. His blue eyes twinkled merrily and his nearly-bald pate made him look wise.

"Where are the others?" she asked.

"They'll be in momentarily," John said. "I told you when we spoke day before yesterday that Matt said he'd had walking pneumonia. I better warn you, he's not feeling too well. Oh, here they are. Matt, Deb, this is May."

Deb held Matt's elbow as they came through the door but it looked as though she supported him more than she escorted him. Matt, dressed formally in a dark suit and burgundy tie, was tall and very thin. His eyes looked dark and sunken and his posture seemed erect only with considerable effort. Deb, though, dazzled May with her silvered blonde hair, the elegant designer dress and jacket she wore beneath her expensive coat, and her exquisite perfume. In fact, May felt a little intimidated by her.

But as May took Deb's coat to the cloak room, she heard Deb say to her husband, "Gee, I thought Mandy was just being self-deprecating when she told me her daughter had turned out prettier than she. You keep your hands to yourself tonight, buster."

When May turned back to them, she saw Matt smiling wanly. "I promise I'll keep my hands off May," he told Deb, "but I can't promise to keep them to myself." He pulled her close and squeezed her arm.

May fought off a blush. "Would you like to look around?" she asked everyone. "The place must have changed since you were here last."

"It's lovely," Deb said, gazing at the bow-decorated crystal chandelier and the polished marble floor in the foyer.

"I like the evergreen roping and twinkle lights on the balustrade," John said.

"And the piano is right where Dad kept his," Russ pointed out.

"I was sorry to hear about your father," May said to Russ. "He must have been a wonderful man to have chosen such a beautiful home."

"I shall not look upon his like again," Russ said.

"Nice quote," John said. "A little Uncle Willie in Jason's honor, huh?"

"Yep," Russ said, adding as he looked past the cash register, "Well, this is the scene of the crime. Thirty years ago tonight we signed the Piñon Nuts pledge on the oval oak table that used to sit right in front of that window."

The old dining room had been divided into a cloak room, the hostess station with its cash register, and the counter area where the wait staff assembled dinners, beverages, and salads and put them on trays. Through the swinging doors came the clatter of the bustling kitchen.

"It sure brings back memories," Matt said.

"But I assume we won't be eating in here this time," Deb added.

"I planned to seat you upstairs in Russ's old bedroom, if that's okay," May told them. "You got here a little earlier than we were expecting, though, so your table won't be ready for a few minutes. Would you mind waiting in the lounge?"

She led them into the former living room, where the major change had been the addition of a small service bar along an interior wall, above which a TV with the sound turned down showed ABC's Peter Jennings in the midst of his 24-hour marathon Millennium broadcast. The fireplace crackled, though, and candles on the coffee tables enhanced its soft light.

Deb and Matt sat on the long couch in front of the fireplace next to some other early arrivals for the late seating. John stood nearby but Russ lingered a moment in the foyer, where he dropped a bill into the brandy snifter on the piano and spoke quietly in the ear of the young woman playing classical music.

"What did you request?" John asked Russ when he came in.

"The same thing I played on the record player 30 years ago," Russ told him. "Mozart's Piano Concerto Number 21. She knows the andante movement."

"May I bring you something from the bar?" May asked them.

Russ decided on a Manhattan, John a Glenlivet, Deb a Chardonnay, and Matt a mineral water. While May waited at the bar for the drinks, Lucy Van Deutch, a short plump silver-haired matron, came in from the solarium.

"Angie said your party arrived," she said to May.

"These are their drinks," May said, picking up the small tray. "Would you like to say hello to them?"

"Of course!" Lucy said as they walked over to the others. "Russell, it's so good to see you again!"

"Hello, Lucy," Russ said, hugging her as May distributed the drinks. "I had some qualms about seeing the old place in its new identity but I have to admit, you've done a wonderful job. Everything looks great."

"Thanks, Russ. Your mother wrote me of your father's passing in her Christmas card. I'm so sorry."

"Thanks. How's Eric?"

"Overworked but happy," Lucy said. "May tells me that some of you came all the way from Seattle to be here tonight."

"We just got in three hours ago," Deb told her.

"Seattle's had more than its share of the news lately," Lucy said. "I heard they had to cancel some of the New Year's Eve activities."

"They had to erect a chain link fence around the base of the Space Needle to keep people away from the traditional celebration site," Deb told her. "The mayor decided it just wasn't worth the risk. The Algerian man they arrested in Port Angeles three weeks ago had enough explosives in his car to blow up a building. We also canceled the Millennium Moonlight Ball, which is part of the reason I was able to come to the Springs with my husband."

"Well, we're glad you made it," Lucy said. "May tells me you're gathering to remember an old friend. I hope your dinner tonight at Crestwood will serve his memory well."

"I'm sure it will," Russ told her. "In fact, we unanimously decided to have the duck with wild rice special May told me about to commemorate the capon Jason cooked that night."

"Capon is an unusual dish for a young man to choose," Lucy said. "He must have been a pretty good cook."

"He was that and more," John said.

"We could have used him here tonight," Lucy said. "Did May tell you that our broiler chef quit earlier?"

"Was that Marcus?" John asked May and the glance they exchanged spoke volumes. When she just nodded, he said, "I'm sorry."

"Marcus let us all down," Lucy said. "But May never has."

"What about when my grandmother died?" May mentioned, still feeling guilty.

"That was perfectly understandable, dear," Lucy assured her. "Your grandmother wasn't much of a bridge player but she was a wonderful woman and you had every right to take some personal time for her funeral. In fact," Lucy announced to the group at large, "we've been so pleased with May's abilities we've decided to let her be your server tonight. If she can avoid spilling your salads in your laps, she may become a permanent member of our wait staff."

This news thrilled May. "Wow. Thank you!"

"You deserve it," Lucy told her. "But for tonight you also need to continue as hostess and I see some people waiting to be seated. Anyway," she said to the others, "thanks for joining us this evening and I hope you enjoy your New Year's Eve."

May turned to Russ after Lucy walked away. "How can I ever thank you for turning me on to this job?"

"You could bring us another round of drinks after you seat those people," he suggested.

For the next half hour May flew around Crestwood like a whirlwind, filling water glasses, running credit cards, greeting late arrivals, finding coats for departing guests, but all the while her mind flew even faster, thinking of all the problems she could solve on a server's wages, nearly double her wages as a hostess.

She also felt proud and privileged to be part of the Piñon Nuts. These friends of Jason's had seemed almost mythical before, in the sense that she hadn't quite been able to picture them as real people until she met them. Russ, Deb, and especially Matt looked older than she had imagined them but they seemed sophisticated, thoughtful, and very interesting. She wondered anew what sort of man Jason must have been to keep such good friends for so long.

The old May Mendoza reality came flooding back, however, when she went into the kitchen for some lemon wedges and found Lyle and Scott standing over a large oven-pan full of charred ducks.

"I forgot to turn the oven down from 450, didn't I?" Scott asked.

"It sure looks like it," Lyle said.

"Now what?" Scott asked him.

Lyle just shrugged and went to drain another large pan of fettucine noodles.

"Those aren't my ducks, are they?" May asked, her heart sinking.

Scott used his knife to peel back some of the crisp black skin. Underneath the meat looked dry and dark as well. "These aren't anybody's ducks, I'm afraid," he told her. "Unless you want to tell them it's *canard a flambe*."

"What am I going to do?" she asked, hating to disappoint the others on such a special night.

"Lyle's got some more fettucine with lobster and truffle sauce, I think," Scott offered. "Or here, let me take a look." He squatted to look through the refrigerated meat drawer.

Fighting off her growing depression, May picked up his knife, which had a notch at the base of the blade long since smoothed over by years of sharpening. "Don't we have better knives than this?" she asked him when he stood back up.

"Oh, that's one I've had for years," he said, taking it from her and fingering the imperfection. "It came this way. In any case, I suppose I could throw together some tenderloins of beef *au poivre* or something, if you like."

Disappointed, she thanked him and went back into the lounge, where John and the others chatted about the announcement earlier in the day of Boris Yeltsin's resignation.

"The face of Mother Russia certainly has changed in the past decade," Russ pointed out.

"So, what's the word, May?" Russ asked.

"Well, your table is ready. Would you rather use the stairs or the elevator?"

"The elevator might be best," Deb said, helping Matt stand.

May led them past the other diners in the long solarium, the windows crowded with hanging poinsettias and blooming Christmas cactuses. They crowded into the elevator and May pushed the button for the second floor.

"You've upgraded the elevator, I see," Russ said as the car slowly carried them up. "I kind of miss the old accordion doors."

"It opens to the kitchen now too, though," May told him. "It also goes downstairs to the dishwasher and storeroom and office. The solid doors keep some of the noise away from the people in the solarium."

"This elevator inspired my father to turn this house into a restaurant, you know."

"I didn't know," May said as the lift stopped.

Upstairs, May led them past the former bedrooms, each with its own character and large enough for just a dozen people or so. At the northwest corner of the upper floor they came to Russ's old room, with its crocheted curtains and original watercolors depicting various Victorian homes around the area. May led them to the table by the north window, the red tablecloth and oil lamp complementing the gleaming china and flatware and the snowy napkin swans.

As they pulled out their chairs and sat down, May broke the bad news to them. "I'm afraid our salad chef, who has been trying to keep up with the salads and run the broiler too, had a little mishap with the Roast Duckling with Sauce Bigarade tonight. I'm really sorry. I know you were counting on it. We do have, though, in addition to our regular menu, a very good fettucine with lobster and truffle sauce—I had some earlier and it was yummy—and Scott, the salad chef, offered to make beef tenderloin *a… a…* something I don't remember. I could ask. Would you like a few minutes to think about it?"

They all deferred to Deb, who quickly decided on the fettucine.

"You know," Russ said, "Jason didn't bat a thousand on his meals either. I think I'll take my chances on Scott's tenderloin *a* something or other."

John and Matt concurred and May jotted down everyone's preferences on soup, salad dressing, and potato choice.

"And we'll need some wine as well," Russ said, perusing the wine list.

"I'll send up the sommelier and then get your salads," May told them.

She went downstairs, wrote up the order and put it in, and then relieved Lucy at the cash register for a couple of minutes. When Lucy returned May went into the kitchen, where Scott told her the tenderloins would have a whiskey and peppercorn sauce and reminded her to keep the vinaigrette out of the laps of the customers. By the time she got upstairs with the salads, the sommelier had brought the Piñon Nuts a bottle of Chateau Neuf Du Pape Vieux Telegraph for the tenderloins and one of Chassagne Montrachet for the fettucine, leaving an extra glass for May.

They insisted she stay long enough to join them for a toast. They raised their glasses but for a moment no one spoke.

"What would Jason say?" Deb asked Matt.

He smiled. "I remember at that one breakfast Gathering we had—which was before the Piñon Nuts name was even coined—Jason toasted the end of the world and I proposed the beginning of the next."

"Sounds appropriate enough for tonight as well," Russ said. "The end of the world!"

"And the beginning of the next," Deb added, looking at Matt. They all clinked their glasses and drank.

"I have some news to impart," Russ said as they sat back down. "But I want to wait. This is not an official Gathering until May can join us as the representative of her mother, the official secretary of the Piñon Nuts. And her father," he added. "Assuming Jason's her father, that is."

"Have you heard from Bill?" John asked May.

"Just last week," May told him. "He called on Christmas to tell me he needed some minor surgery to cauterize a hemorrhoid."

"Some things never change," John said with a grin. "I always thought he was a flaming asshole."

It got a good laugh from all but Matt nudged Deb with his elbow until she cleared her throat.

"I have some news as well," she said. "In fact, this is part of the reason I wanted to be here tonight. As you know, May, your mother and I were good friends. Perhaps not as close in the last few years as before but at the time you were born we were very close indeed. And I can tell you, beyond the shadow of a doubt, that Jason, not Bill, was your biological father."

"Really?" May said and Russ and John echoed it. "She told you?"

"You were conceived on Mother's Day in 1970, the day Jason was arrested for possession of marijuana."

"So it's true," May said, hardly believing it even though she'd thought about it for a month and a half.

"Oh, by the way," Deb went on, "I watched you write our order. You're right, John. She does hold her pen the same way Jason did."

Matt and Russ agreed.

"I told you," John said to May with a smile.

"Well, I have a million questions I want to ask," May said, feeling a little dazed, "but I guess I better get back to work and let you eat your salads. Oh, the tenderloins will have a whiskey and peppercorn sauce. I hope that's okay."

"That sounds fine," Russ said. "Now get your work done so you can join us."

The rest of May's shift went by in a blur. Between handling the cash register and serving upstairs, she barely had time to catch her breath. Lucy corrected a couple of missteps but in a way that assured May that her promotion to server might not take long. The guys in the kitchen quit treating her like a hoity-toity hostess and started giving her the same grief they gave the other new waitresses, which made May feel accepted.

Later, as the last smiling face representing Crestwood, she accepted with aplomb the many raves about the evening, along with a few complaints, mostly about the lack of ducks, as she handed people their coats and wished them a Happy New Year. The fact that no other major mishaps marred the evening seemed to confirm the thought that lingered behind her every action: she was Jason's daughter and that somehow made a difference. Maybe the distinction would have little practical effect on her life but it sure changed her attitude about herself.

Because of the substitution of tenderloin for duck, the Piñon Nuts ended up getting served almost last, which they accepted amiably, assuring May that they were just killing time until she got off anyway. When finally she made it upstairs to clear away their plates, she asked how it was.

"Absolutely superb!" Russ declared, sitting back and patting his happy paunch. The others concurred, using words like "fabulous" and "unforgettable."

Even Matt, who had remained pretty quiet through the meal, spoke up. "I trust you'll relay our highest compliments to Scott, or whatever the chef's name was."

"I will be happy to," May assured him. "May I bring you dessert? We have a Black Forest Torte that is to die for. Or how about coffee, or an aperitif?"

Only Russ and John had enough of a sweet tooth for dessert but all ordered an after-dinner drink. When May brought the order down to the bar, Lucy told her that she would handle the few remaining hostess chores if May wanted to punch out and join her friends. So excited she fairly floated, May hurried back to the kitchen and punched her card in the time-clock by the door.

"All done?" Scott asked, scrubbing down the broiler grill.

"Just off the clock," she told him. "I'm going up to talk to my friends. Incidentally, they all raved about their dinners. The guys said the whiskey and peppercorn sauce for the tenderloins was out of this world."

"I'm glad they enjoyed it," he said.

"How about you? Do you have plans for the rest of the night?" May asked him as she went to the cooler for Russ's torte and John's ice cream pie: a light meringue shell filled with French vanilla ice cream and fresh strawberries, topped with whipped cream.

"Me?" Scott asked. "No, nothing in particular. Lyle's been here since this morning so I told him I'd close up for him. I'll be here for hours."

"Do you have family to go home to?" she asked him.

He paused to think about it. "I guess I was hoping I'd hear from my brothers but it doesn't look like that's going to happen. Maybe I'll just go home and write."

"Oh, you're a writer," May said, dolloping whipped cream. "What are you working on?"

"Just some memoirs."

"What are they about?"

"Not much, really. Just little blurbs about my travels and observations about life in general. I don't know that they'd interest anyone but me."

"Maybe you should write a book," she suggested. "The Great American Novel."

He dismissed it with a laugh. "I can't imagine writing an entire book. I'm sure it would be unbelievably complicated and take unbelievably long, especially working a job like this. Besides, I have trouble coming up with enough to fill a few paragraphs. Where on earth would I find a story good enough to keep readers interested for hundreds of pages?"

"Oh, I'll bet you could come up with something. Improvise, like you did with the dinners."

"Well, thanks anyway," he said, turning to her. "Thanks for talking to me tonight. You made the night a lot easier. Actually, if you don't mind my saying so, you remind me of someone I knew a long time ago."

She looked at him. His smile seemed benign but that last statement had all the earmarks of a come-on, and not a very good one. His earlier remark about always being free had had a funny ring to it as well. Well, she sure wasn't interested in another relationship at this point and even if she were, something about him didn't appeal to her that way. He seemed like a nice guy but quiet and something of a loner. She picked up the dessert plates with one hand and her purse with the other and backed out the swinging door.

"It's been fun working with you, too, Scott," she said neutrally. "Happy New Year!"

"You too!"

o   o   o

By the time May got back upstairs with the desserts, the Piñon Nuts had the room to themselves. Russ and John stood when she came in and they all applauded.

Russ raised his snifter of Armagnac. "To May and Lucy and Scott and all the fine employees of Crestwood who truly made this a night to remember!"

Deb poured May a glass of wine and handed it to her. "You've done a wonderful job tonight. Both your parents would have been proud of you."

"Speaking of proud parents," Russ said, raising his snifter again, "I have that announcement to make, now that this is an official Piñon Nuts Gathering. Sylvia and I, with a little help from her late husband, are pregnant!"

That news required another round of applause and drinks, another toast (to "the next generation of great artists"), and Churchill cigars for all, though all agreed to save them for another time and place.

"And there's more," Russ went on. "My lovely wife Sylvia, who gladly would have attended tonight if she didn't have an important opening at a new gallery in West Chelsea, sent along something she did just for us." He picked up his black leather satchel and took from it an artist's sketch pad. Before opening the pad, he said, "Remember that breakfast Nut Gathering? The pictures my mom took? Mom found the one of Jason and gave it to Sylvia, and this is what she did."

The only picture May had seen of Jason was the one from the safe deposit box, taken New Year's Eve, in which his back was turned, his face partially obscured by his blonde curls. Sylvia's watercolor, exquisitely executed, was a small but engaging portrait of Jason, his hair fairly short, his eyes lively, and his smile genuine. Everyone ooo-ed and ahh-ed but May couldn't take her eyes from it. Jason seemed so young and yet the face seemed somehow familiar, as though she had always known it, or had seen it just recently.

"Sylvia thought you should have it," Russ said to May.

She looked up. "Oh, I couldn't!"

"Actually, you're right," Russ said. "You can't. At least not yet. Sylvia only started it a few days ago and she wants to finish some of the background and have it properly framed for you. So I need to bring it back with me. But we'll mail it to you, okay?" He closed the sketch pad and put it back in his leather satchel, setting the satchel out of the way on the now-empty table behind him.

"Oh, I'll treasure it!" she vowed. "I just wish Mom could have seen it."

"I do too," Deb said.

"So you forgive Jason?" John asked May.

May thought about it. "We all make mistakes," she said, "especially when we're young. So what did happen, anyway? Does anybody know if Mom really tried to abort me?" she asked, instinctively turning, as did the others, to Deb.

Deb reached across the table and took May's hand. "I'm afraid so," she said solemnly. "And I have to confess that I helped."

"Whose idea was it?" May asked her. "Mom's or yours? Or Jason's?"

"It was mostly your mom's idea but I knew how she could do it," Deb said. "Jason certainly had no part in the decision. In fact, he did everything in his power to prevent it. He actually *did* prevent it after he disappeared. Had he not done what he did, you might not exist, and I might have overlooked the one man who truly loved me." She let go of May's hand and took Matt's in both of hers.

"As far as that goes," Russ said, "Jason may have lost his life trying to save yours. I told you the other night about how he went AWOL from the Army and hitchhiked back here."

"Oh, yeah," she said. "That's when he threatened President Nixon, right?"

"He wasn't much of a threat," John said. "And I doubt if he would have done even that much had he not been so distraught over all the other problems in his life, first and foremost his concern for your mom, and for you."

"But Russ," May said, "you didn't tell me what happened after that."

"That's because I don't know that much about it," Russ said. "I never saw or heard from Jason again after he ran back into the hotel that night. John and Matt saw him the next day but we were all so paranoid back then, we never got together to discuss it after he disappeared. That's part of why we're here tonight. So what happened, guys?"

"Would you like to tell her?" John asked Matt.

Matt, sipping his Courvoisier, looked tired but content. "No, you go ahead."

"Well, jump in when I make mistakes," John insisted. "Anyway, what Jason told us was that after he scarfed down the French bread Russ gave him, he went out and curled up on the portico above the entrance to the hotel and fell asleep."

"Didn't the Secret Service check the portico before the President came through?" Russ asked.

"The portico has little extensions to either side next to the building. Jason said he curled up on one side where a desk or something blocked the view out the window. The best Jason could figure was that the Secret Service must have been in a hurry because of the last-minute change of Nixon's route and just glanced out to make sure no one was actually standing on the portico. After Nixon exited the building, they must have pulled the agents from the mezzanine level.

"Anyway, as soon as Jason saw the panic created by his encounter with the President, he knew his ass would be grass if they caught him. But when he got inside, he had the presence of mind not to run or draw attention to himself. He walked back into the kitchen to try to find Russ."

"But I was outside, watching Nixon," Russ remembered.

"So Jason asked the dishwasher—"

"Lucky."

"That's right, Lucky. He asked Lucky if he needed help emptying his garbage."

"Lucky never turned down help with that," Russ put in.

"I guess on the way down to the ice room to pick up ice, Jason explained his situation to Lucky and Lucky decided to help him."

Russ broke in: "Lucky was there when I told Jason about overhearing Nixon and the others. I think he was almost as disgusted by what I overheard as we were."

"Tell us about the ice buckets," John said to Russ.

"The ice buckets at the Broadmoor?" he asked, puzzled, and John nodded. "Well, okay. We had these ice buckets that were maybe three feet in diameter, with handles on the sides and a removable grate for a bottom so the ice would drain. Why?"

"When they got to the ice room," John continued, "Jason and Lucky figured out that if Jason stood up straight, Lucky could kick out the grates and stack the empty ice buckets around him in such a way that it would seem impossible for a person to be standing there. Evidently it worked. Lucky went back up with the ice by himself. Jason said that after a while he heard the Secret Service come down with Lucky to look through the ice room but they didn't look inside the stack."

"How long was he in there?" May asked.

"He stood there straight up and stock still all night, he said," John told her. "Finally, around dawn, frozen and so stiff he could barely walk, he sneaked out to the loading dock, climbed up on a garbage truck and rode out on top of it."

"It's a good thing he did, too," Russ said. "The Secret Service talked to me for two hours about Jason after he disappeared but I had no idea what happened to him either. For three days after that, there was a black sedan parked across the street from this house. And somebody at the hotel told me he also saw guys in suits watching all the entrances to the hotel for at least a couple of days."

"But like John mentioned," May said, "he wasn't much of a threat, was he?"

"Well, the Secret Service," Matt put in, "especially in Nixon's day, took any threat to the president very seriously. Plus, Jason was in some real trouble. He was AWOL from the Army and had been busted a couple of times a few months before."

"I'll tell you what kept the black suits at the B-moor, though," John said, turning to Russ. "Jason brought up the name of Tom Huston to Nixon, didn't he?"

"Yeah," Russ said. "I told May about that the other night."

"Jason also mentioned Tom Huston in his letter to my mom," May said. "Who was he?"

"In 1970, I doubt if many people knew the name," John said. "I only came across it during the Watergate hearings. Do you remember that, Russ?"

"I was in Oregon in the School by then. We didn't pay much attention to that stuff."

"When May showed me the letter, it took me a couple of weeks to place the name," John said. "After I did, I decided, just for laughs, to find out some more about him. So when I was in Fort Collins researching my ill-fated article about marijuana, I went through some old books about Nixon and Watergate. Tom Charles Huston was a former national chairman of Young Americans for Freedom and a radical right-wing speech writer for Nixon. Pat Buchanan wrote some of Nixon's drivel back then too and Huston made Buchanan look like a bleeding-heart liberal. Anyway, Huston was just 29 in the summer of 1970 when he hatched a scheme to create a secret interagency committee combining the Central Intelligence Agency, the Federal Bureau of Investigation, the Defense Intelligence Agency, and the National Security Agency, with none other than Tom Huston in charge of the committee."

"Are you serious?" Russ asked incredulously.

"Dead," John said. "One of the books quoted Huston as saying, 'Repression is the inevitable result of disorder. When forced to choose between order and freedom, people will choose order.'"

"Well, that's scary," May said.

"Anyway, two weeks before Nixon made his August trip to Colorado, he signed on to— no, actually, he verbally *approved*, not wanting anything in writing—this Huston Plan that Nixon knew would authorize government officials to perform a variety of unconstitutional and criminal acts like wire-tapping and tampering with the mail. This was, incidentally, right around the time Nixon started taping all the conversations in the Oval Office."

"So they actually formed this committee?" Russ asked.

"As a matter of fact, no," John told him. "And Nixon inadvertently told you why. When J. Edgar Hoover heard that his precious FBI might fall into a subservient role to Tom Huston's committee, he raised holy hell. He purposely created a footnoted copy of the plan with all his objections to the illegalities it proposed, taking away Nixon's deniability. Hoover also had dossiers on most public officials and let the White House know that he could expose some pretty seamy stuff if they tried to cross him. Attorney General John Mitchell objected to the Huston Plan as well, thinking it too risky. Six days after it was proposed, the Huston Plan was quietly withdrawn."

"What happened to Tom Huston?" Russ asked.

"He was quietly withdrawn as well. A couple of weeks later he was no longer on the speech writing team for the President."

"Good Lord!" Russ said. "So when Jason mentioned the Huston Plan to Nixon—"

"Nixon must have just about shit. He was paranoid anyway and hearing some yokel talking about making the Huston Plan public must have flipped him out. That's why the Secret Service tried so hard to catch Jason and that's why they kept the whole incident so quiet. The *Gazette Telegraph* reported it something like this: 'Pressing crowds of local citizens, news representatives, and hotel guests created security concerns.' A couple of days later, the short item about Jason's disappearance didn't mention the incident at the Broadmoor at all. The last thing Nixon wanted was a bunch of awkward questions about Tom Huston."

"I had no idea Tom Huston was such a big deal," Russ said.

"Neither did Jason," John pointed out. "He just took a shot and accidentally hit a bull's-eye. But he had every right to be scared. Considering his situation, the Army or even the state pen might have been better than falling into the clutches of the CIA or the FBI."

"But he got away," May said.

"At least temporarily," John said, sipping his Chambourd. "The next morning, bright and early, birds chirping their heads off, the phone woke me up. This was the summer I lived with Prudence," he told May. "Anyway, it was Jason. He told me he just wanted to say good-bye and begged me to do him a favor: would I please, please, *please*, try to get a hold of Manny for him. 'And tell her what?' I asked him. He thought about it. 'Just tell her not to do it,' he said at last. I had never heard him so upset so I asked him what was wrong. Eventually, the whole ugly business with Nixon came out. He told me he rode the garbage truck quite a ways until it started to head up to the dump in Old Colorado City. He jumped off near Cheyenne Mountain High School and used the phone by the gym to call me. He had to call collect because he didn't even have a dime for the pay phone. I asked him what he planned to do and he said it didn't matter what happened to him as long as he didn't drag anybody else into his mess. And then he started to cry."

"Really?" Matt said. "I don't think I ever saw him cry."

"I only heard him but it convinced me that we had to do something. I offered to pick him up but he said he better not show his face in town for a while. I couldn't argue with that so I told him to meet me somewhere out of town. He didn't go for it at first but eventually I persuaded him to wait by the second bridge on the Seven Bridges Trail up in North Cheyenne Cañon."

"Then you called me," Matt said.

"Right. I filled you in and we decided what we'd do is load up our backpacks and hike up to Jones Park with Jason so we could figure out what to do. I stuffed my hiking pack full of food and clothes for Jason—he told me all he had with him was that knife—and I brought a book bag too, figuring I could carry up the heavy pack for Jason and leave it with him if he wanted to keep going and I'd bring the book bag home with me with anything he didn't need."

Matt shifted uncomfortably in his chair. "I still say we should have tried to persuade him to come back with us to face the music."

"I don't know," Russ said to him. "For weeks after that, I walked around terrified and I wasn't the one in trouble, except as an accessory."

"In any case," John continued, "while we got packed and took the Yellow Fellow up to the trailhead, Jason hiked up through the horse pasture above the school and up that front ridge, keeping off the Gold Camp Road so he wouldn't be spotted. He bushwacked up to Captain Jack's and then followed the trail west before cutting back over the ridge and down to the Seven Bridges Trail."

"By the time we got there," Matt said, "he was lying under a ponderosa, just about dead from exhaustion. That French bread Russ gave him was the only thing he'd eaten for days."

"So we shoved a sandwich in his face and pumped him full of water."

"And the first thing he asked was if you had called Manny," Matt recalled.

"Which, in the heat of the moment," John admitted, "I completely spaced out."

"So Jason wanted to go back down to the Cub, that curio shop by Helen Hunt Falls, and try to get a hold of Man from there."

"But I convinced him we couldn't hang around," John went on. "For one thing, we saw cop cars patrolling the Gold Camp Road on the way up. For another, it turned out to be one of those hazy August days when the clouds start to build early over the mountains and we wanted to get up to the cabin before the afternoon thunderstorms."

"So I promised Jason I'd get up first thing in the morning and hike back down to call your mom," Matt explained to May. "But he said it would probably be too late by then. And then, as it turned out, of course, I had to hike out first thing in the morning anyway to report him missing. So I called as promised."

"Matt called your Nana first," Deb explained to her. "After he told her it was an emergency, she gave him the number at the motel where your mother and I were staying, though she didn't know our real reason for going down there. He called just as we were walking out the door to go across the river to Juarez for the abortion."

May looked at Matt's sad, tired eyes. "So I guess I owe you my life."

"You owe Jason your life," he said quietly.

"What happened on the hike?" May asked John.

"Well, Jason was in pretty bad shape—exhausted, sore, dehydrated, complaining that he felt sick, running a temperature—so by the time we made it past the seventh bridge it was mid-afternoon. Early August is the peak of the monsoon season in Colorado so by then huge dark thunderheads had gathered over Almagre Mountain and lightning flashed every few seconds. Just about the time we got to the top of the ridge that separates North Cheyenne Cañon from Jones Park, the sky just opened up. Hailstones as big as marbles and so thick we couldn't see ten feet ahead started to pound us senseless. We tried to run but Jason had on pants three sizes too big and he kept tripping and falling. Lightning struck the ridge right after we got off of it, the thunderclap hitting us within a second of the flash and echoing through the mountains for what seemed like hours. Jason told us to just leave him and go on ahead but there was no way we could do that. By the time we got to Jones Park, we were all soaked to the skin, slogging through six inches of hail, and the rain was still coming down in buckets."

"Tell them about the cabin," Matt said.

"We thought our one saving grace would be the cabin, where we could build a fire and dry out. But when we got there, we discovered that vandals had ripped the shingles off the roof and pulled out the wood stove and dumped it in the trees. The roof, being nothing but slats, barely slowed down the rain and everything inside the cabin was as wet as everything outside."

"The only food I brought," Matt said, "was a couple more sandwiches, raw hamburger and bread for burgers, and bacon and eggs for breakfast. Without the stove, we couldn't cook anything."

"I tried to get Jason to eat a sandwich," John said, "but he was shaking so hard he couldn't swallow. All I had was a light cotton sleeping bag for him—that's all we had too—and we didn't have any sort of rain gear except some plastic bags that got ripped during the hike. So everything was soaked. And pretty soon it got dark. I brought candles but the wind and the rain put them out. So we just sat there on the bunks in the dark listening to Jason's teeth chatter, feeling the rain dripping down our necks, and watching the flashes of lightning through the skeleton of the cabin's roof."

"That's when I pointed out that we might as well get inside the sleeping bags, wet as they were, and try to get some sleep," Matt said.

"The bags were almost worse than nothing, cold and clammy and heavy," John recalled. "Jason started shaking so hard he rattled the wood of the bunk, saying over and over, 'Tom's acold. Poor Tom's acold.'"

"Tom who?" May asked. "Not Tom Huston."

"No," John said. "It was another of Jason's Uncle Willie references, in this case to Tom o' Bedlam in the scene on the moor in *King Lear*. He used some other lines from it as well as the night progressed, things like 'a dog in madness,' and 'Tom hath laid knives under his pillow.'"

"At one point he said something about being in the grave," Matt said.

"Oh, yeah," John remembered. "'Thou wert better in a grave than to answer with thy uncovered body this extremity of the skies,' and referring to himself as a 'poor, bare, forked animal.'"

"I thought he said 'fucked' animal," Matt said.

"How did he remember stuff like that?" May asked.

"Your father was a very intelligent guy," John told her. "And he loved Shakespeare."

For the first time it sank in to May that Jason truly was her father and that she could be proud of it. But she had to hear the end of the story. "So how did he disappear?"

John looked at Matt but Matt waved him off.

"Compared to Jason I was well rested and well fed and still I just about froze," John said. "I kept rubbing my legs together and rubbing my arms with my hands until I finally fell asleep."

"I did too," Matt admitted.

"But I don't think Jason ever so much as dozed off. Did you hear him get up?" John asked Matt.

"Not right away," Matt said. "But he crashed into something in the dark and that woke me up. I asked him what he was doing, afraid he might be getting delirious or something."

"That's right. I woke up at that point too," John remembered. "He said he had to go to the bathroom and I told him he could just pee into the root cellar, for all it mattered."

"And he said that if he did what he had to do in the root cellar, none of us would get any sleep."

"What did you think that meant?" John asked Matt.

"He'd been complaining about his stomach being upset so I thought he meant he had to take a dump, or maybe throw up."

"That's what I thought too. So I guess we both figured he'd just go out into the bushes, do what he had to do, and come back in."

"That may be what he intended," Matt pointed out.

"In any case," John went on, "we both must have fallen back to sleep. The next thing I knew the rain had stopped and it was starting to get light."

"Well, I heard something at the door while it was still dark," Matt said, "which I assumed was Jason coming back in and then I guess I must have dozed off again as well."

"When I woke up, I saw that Jason wasn't in his bag. I woke up Matt and we got up and started looking for him."

"The first thing we found," Matt said, "was bear claw marks on the door. That must have been the sound I heard."

"So then we freaked. We started looking for tracks in the hail and followed them a little way back down toward Bear Creek but the rain had melted and washed away the hail and the tracks along with it."

"We shouted ourselves hoarse calling to him," Matt remembered.

"After a while we went back to the cabin and looked around there on the chance he had come back but there was no sign of him."

"Do you think he hiked out?" May asked.

"He didn't even take the pack I brought for him," John said.

"The only thing missing was that knife he had," Matt said.

Everyone fell silent a moment. Finally, it was up to May to ask the obvious question: "Do you think he killed himself?"

Still no one spoke. They didn't even look at one another.

Deb broke the impasse by asking Matt, "You don't think he did, do you?"

"I don't know," Matt said. "I've never told anyone this but Jason, even when we were kids, used to talk about killing himself. I just took it for big talk from an unhappy boy but that night up in Jones Park, I really don't think he felt he had much to live for. Whether he could take his own life, though, I don't know. I still feel he probably died of exposure. When hypothermia takes over, people do completely irrational things. Lost in the dark, freezing to death, he might have wandered to some unlikely spot, curled up, and never woke up. Or got hit by lightning. And we know there was a bear up there that night."

"But you guys looked for him, right?" May asked.

"I stayed up there that day and came back up the next," John said. "Matt came back up too with the Search and Rescue people. We combed the woods. But without tracks to follow, it became just anybody's guess which way he went. As I tried to explain to you on our hike, it's impossible to search every square inch of the mountains."

"So you think he died that night?" May asked him.

"I honestly don't know," John admitted. "There is a more sinister explanation that I thought of a long time ago but never told anyone. It's possible that someone on that Search and Rescue team did find him. Some of those guys might have been working for some intelligence agency, for all we know, with instructions to find Jason and spirit him out of there. Remember that guy named Easy, who was in the helicopter when Jason's brother Steve got killed? He died too, just a few months before."

"That's getting pretty paranoid," Russ said.

"What do you think happened to my father?" May asked Russ, happy to mean Jason rather than Bill.

Russ thought about his response. "If you'd asked me that a week ago," he said, "I think I would have told you he probably died. But Matt and John both know that I long held out hope that he survived. In fact, I guess I've always believed that he did. He was an incredible guy. He may have walked out of there and just kept going. Started a new life for himself somewhere. For that matter, I think the fact that we gathered here tonight proves that he lives on in some respect. How many of you came here without any glimmer of hope that somehow Jason might show up too?"

No hands went up.

"But it was an unbelievable long-shot," Matt said.

"The night's not over," Russ countered.

"You did once say that improbable things happen," John said to Matt. "They just happen rarely."

"And this is a very special night," Deb pointed out. "Both for all of us here and for the world at large."

"I don't know," Matt said stubbornly. "The shape he was in, the kind of night that was— if he got out of there alive, it was a miracle."

"Miracles happen sometimes," May said to him. "I know there have been times in my life when I felt the hand of my guardian angel."

Matt looked at Deb and Deb looked away. They had been holding hands. Matt let go.

Deb turned to May. "Could you show me to the powder room?" she asked.

May turned around in her chair and pointed down the hall. "It's the third door on your left."

"Would you like to come with me?"

May thought about whether she had to go and then it occurred to her that Deb wasn't asking, she was suggesting. "Sure," she said, picking up her purse.

O   O   O

Crestwood's upstairs powder room featured amenities the employee's rest room in the basement lacked: two stalls, a row of vanity lights above the mirror, paisley wallpaper in rich hues of purple and green, even a small settee. Deb had hung her jacket on the coat rack while she washed her hands.

"That certainly is a beautiful dress," May said, admiring the way the fine fabric fit the contours of Deb's figure. She also noticed a small abrasion on Deb's collarbone, hidden earlier by the jacket.

Deb, seeing what May had noticed, glanced in the mirror.

"What happened?" May asked her.

"This?" she asked, touching the abrasion. "Just a little mishap at one of my charity events. Although it did cost me $10,000."

"You're kidding!" May said.

"It's a long story. Anyway, you mentioned something about a guardian angel a little while ago. What did you mean?"

"I assume Mom told you that I've pretty much made a mess of my life."

"She said you'd had some problems."

May snorted. "Did she mention jail?"

"I knew about that, yes."

"Anyway, a few times I got in over my head and somebody came to my rescue. It wasn't my parents. My mom wanted to teach me to get myself out the scrapes I got into and I knew I wouldn't get any help from my father — Bill, that is, although Jason certainly didn't help much either." It was May's turn for the sad smile. "I guess my grandmother must have kept an eye on me, pulling me out when I got in too deep."

"Nana?" Deb looked surprised. "Did you ask her about it?"

"Not really," May admitted. "I always figured she'd talk to me about it if she wanted to. Besides, I knew I could never pay her back."

"She loved you very much," Deb said. "And so did your mother, for that matter. But actually, neither of them was the guardian angel you mentioned."

"Then who was?"

Deb looked her in the eye and said, "I was."

"What?" May asked, stunned. "You mean when I was 15 and got arrested for vehicular homicide—"

"I hired that lawyer who got you off," Deb told her. "He got your DUI dropped last spring too. He also let me know when you were in Harborview in Seattle with hepatitis and he and I saw to it that you got better care."

May felt completely baffled but how could anyone but her guardian angel know about those things? "Why? Why would you do that?"

Deb put on her jacket. "I don't know how much your mom told you about me but I—" She hesitated. "I lost a baby just before your mom had you. I've never been able to have children of my own so I guess I kind of adopted you."

May stood gaping. "I don't know what to say," she confessed. "How can I ever thank you?"

"Oh, you don't owe me any thanks," Deb insisted. "What your mom and grandmother did, both in raising you and in having to live through your problems with you, deserves a lot more credit than anything I did."

"But it must have cost you thousands of dollars."

"Tens of thousands, actually. You have a penchant for expensive problems. But your folks did the hard work. I only spent money I could easily afford. I don't know if your mom told you this but I worked for Microsoft when they first broke onto the scene and I made enough money in ten years to retire."

May couldn't imagine having, much the less giving away, tens of thousands of dollars. "Did Mom know you helped me?"

Deb sighed. "Yes and no. You're right about your mom: she did want you to find your own way out of your scrapes. But she also saw dependence on money, which she had felt herself with her parents and then with Bill, as the source of many of her problems and didn't want to raise you that way. But the way I saw it, enough money for a good lawyer might solve some of your legal problems, and it did. I don't think, had she known, that she would have let me intervene, but I do think justice was served."

"So you never told her?"

"Actually, I did. I told her all about it the day she died."

"Oh." May did remember her mother and Deb arguing about something on the phone that day. "Well, why are you telling me this now?"

"Because I need your help."

It seemed incomprehensible that someone like Deb would come to May for help. But if she could help… "What can I do?"

"My husband is ill, as you know. In fact, it's more serious than we thought and he's going to need my help and attention more than ever."

"I'm sorry."

"So am I, believe me. Anyway, even though I am retired, I still take an active role in a number of charities." When she saw May glance toward her collarbone again, she added, "That particular charity is an exception. It looks like I'll be retiring from it all too soon. Anyway, I need someone I can trust who will work on my correspondence and answer the phone and schedule my appointments for me. I'm offering $40,000 a year to start, with full benefits."

"That sounds great," May said. "I wouldn't think you'd have any trouble finding someone for a job like that."

Deb smiled at her. "Your mother was right: you can be awfully obtuse at times."

May thought about it. "Wait a minute. You're not offering *me* the job, are you?"

"I thought I was."

"$40,000 a year?"

"Okay, $50,000. You drive a hard bargain. You'd have to move to Seattle, of course."

May's head spun. She had never made half that much. "But my daughter's here," she remembered. "My ex-husband has custody. I couldn't bear to be away from her."

"Don't you think the judge might feel more kindly disposed toward you if you have a $50,000-a-year job? And if you'd like to try to regain custody, I also know a very good lawyer who might be able to help you—again."

May felt dizzy. "I don't know what to say."

"Say you'll think about it. Let's rejoin the others. You and I can talk more about it tomorrow morning before Matt and I leave."

o   o   o

When they got back to the table, Russ was saying, "Maybe he stopped in Cheyenne. A high school would certainly have pencil and paper."

"And an envelope and a stamp?" Matt asked.

"We're trying to figure out when Jason wrote that letter," John explained to May and

Deb as they sat back down. "Did you bring it?"

"Sure," May said, digging through her purse and pulling out the envelope that contained the letter, the poem, the original of the Piñon Nuts pledge, and the photo. She took out the letter, unfolded it, and handed it to John.

"What's that?" Deb asked, looking at the poem May had unfolded with the letter.

"Did you ever see this?" May asked, showing it to her. "Mom did it as calligraphy once. About a month before she died she told me my father had written it. Of course I thought she meant Bill and that made no sense at all. But if she knew Jason was my father…"

"She knew," Deb assured her, reading the poem. "That's beautiful."

"Oh, Mother's Day is in May, isn't it?" it occurred to May.

"She named you after the month when you were conceived," Deb said.

"Oh, and the Uncle Willie he refers to in the letter must be Shakespeare," May realized, reading the last line of the poem, "'And love, whose month is ever May.'"

"A line, appropriately enough, from *Love's Labour's Lost*," John said. "But here it is," reading the letter. "See, he mentions Tom Huston. So he must have written it the next morning, right?"

"But look at the next paragraph," Matt said, leaning forward to read it too. "The line 'I assume Matt didn't get you in time.' If he's referring to my calling Manny down in Texas, he wouldn't have known that *I* was going to call until the afternoon, when we met him up on the trail."

"Could he have written it at the cabin?" Russ asked.

"Hardly," John said. "It was pitch black and everything was soaked. Besides, how could he mail it?"

"When was Nixon at the Broadmoor?" Matt asked.

"Who remembers?" John said. "That was 30 years ago. Sometime in August."

"What day of the week, though?" Matt asked. "Do you remember, Deb? When were you and Manny in El Paso?"

"You went to El Paso?" May asked Deb.

"Abortion was illegal here. We had to go to Mexico."

"Nana talked about El Paso just before she died," May said, thinking back. "She said Mom was upset over some boy when she came home. She must have been referring to Jason. To Dad," she added, trying that on to see how it felt. It felt pretty good.

"We went to El Paso," Deb recalled for Matt, "over the weekend. Because we scheduled the abortion for Monday morning."

"Well, look at this," Matt said. "At the top of his letter, Jason wrote 'thurs,' as in Thursday. But he wouldn't have known about Tom Huston on the Thursday *before* he died."

"Before he went to Jones Park with you, that is," Russ said, sounding a little smug. "Whether he died there is another issue."

"What are you saying?" May wondered, getting goosebumps.

John looked at her. "I'm not sure but it looks like this is proof that somehow Jason survived that night."

Matt still looked at the letter. "What about what's above the 'thurs'? What does the word 'chinook' signify?"

"Beats me," John said. "When I first read it I just thought it meant he wrote it on a windy day."

"Chinook winds don't come in August, though," Matt pointed out. "They come in late winter. Deb, remember when I used to have to go over to Clarkston, Washington, twice a month?"

"For that salmon study, right?"

"Well, just across the Snake River, near Lewiston, Idaho, is the Nez Perce Tribal Center, where I picked up that book about Chief Joseph and the Nez Perce tribe's incredible flight from the U. S. Army. The entire band—hundreds of men, women, and children and over a thousand horses—fought off and eluded the best soldiers of the Army for nearly three months and 1600 miles, only to be stopped on the north slope of the Bear Paw range, just 30 miles short of the Canadian border and freedom."

"I remember seeing that on a PBS special," John mentioned. "But I guess I don't see the relevance here."

"See this line 'I will fight no more forever'?" Matt asked, pointing to Jason's letter. "That's what Chief Joseph, 'the old chief,' said when he surrendered. The closest town to that final battlefield is Chinook, Montana."

"What are you saying?" May asked, confused.

"I think he's saying," Russ said, "that this may mean your father made it at least as far as Chinook, Montana, on his flight to Canada and freedom."

John reread that part of the letter. "And this line: 'Our futures lie beyond the borders of this kingdom.' Jason had to cross the border into Canada while, he thought at least, Manny had to cross the border into Mexico."

"But Mom didn't cross the border," May said.

"You were her future," Deb said to her.

"Ooo, I didn't catch this before either," John said, still studying the letter. "See the words he repeats three times? Try, try, try, nix, nix, nix, on, on, on. Shrink it down and he's saying, 'Try Nixon.' Which, of course, the Senate would have done if Nixon hadn't resigned. And the FBI reference and Tom Huston," John said, looking up. "Jason knew he was in real trouble."

"Could I see that?" Deb asked.

John handed the letter to her but said, "Who's the 'Quaker SOB' he talks about?"

"Nixon," Russ said. "Tricky Dick was a Quaker, believe it or not."

"I think I know what this line refers to," Deb said. "'Nature abhors a vacuum.' When they do a D-and-C abortion, they usually use a suction device."

"Was he anti-abortion then?" May asked, feeling very odd talking about a procedure that might easily have ended her life almost before it started.

"He was certainly anti *this* abortion," Deb said. "Although he seems to have accepted Mandy's decision."

"Did you catch his French?" Matt asked his wife, reading over her shoulder.

"Yes," Deb said. "*Bon chance, bon ami.*"

"I wondered about that," May said. "What does it mean?"

"It means 'Good luck, good friend'," Matt translated.

"Also, some of Mandy's closest friends referred to her as Amy," Deb added.

"She didn't tell me that," May said, wondering how many other things about her mother she would learn from Deb.

"Actually," Matt said, looking at the letter again, "the most interesting line of all is at the end. 'Maybe a tomorrow will come to me. Maybe at the end of time, maybe just the century.' The century ends in a few minutes, folks."

Once again, they all fell silent. So many surprises had come to May already this evening that she didn't know what to expect. Miracles do happen once in a while. For just a moment she listened for Jason's footsteps. But she could only hear a few late carousers down in the lounge and, coming up the elevator shaft, the sound of Scott cleaning up the kitchen. "Figures," May thought to herself. "My life just doesn't work that way." After all, a few minutes ago Deb had explained away all of May's previous miracles.

Then, before anyone spoke, they did hear solitary footsteps reaching the top of the stairs, turning their direction. May could tell by the look on the other faces that they too had entertained the idea that Jason might somehow appear. Sitting at the end of the four-top table, she had her back to the door. As she watched the expectant faces, she saw Matt, Deb, and John puzzle over the face of the man who had walked in and Russ recognize with a smile an old friend.

So it came as something of blow when she spun around, half expecting to see her long-lost father, and found only Eric Van Deutch, looking 70, tired, and happy, carrying a bottle of Champagne in an ice bucket and a fistful of cocktail glasses.

"We didn't want you folks to think we forgot about you up here," Eric said, setting the ice bucket on the table. "The hour approaches! How are you, Russell? It's been many years."

Russ stood to shake his hand. "It's great to see you, Eric. I think I speak for everyone when I say that you and Lucy and your staff put on one of the all-time classic New Year's Eve feasts for us. How's your night been?"

"It's been pretty good," Eric said. "As you know, we found ourselves a little short-handed tonight but the people who spent the last few hours of the millennium working, including May here, really came through for us. It wasn't quite as busy as we expected but this isn't a late-night place anyway. Most of our customers left for other destinations. And some, with this beautiful, clear weather, left just to watch the fireworks on the Peak."

"That's what Jason and Mandy did 30 years ago," Deb pointed out, taking Matt's hand again. "We might not be here otherwise."

"A lot of people are just staying home this New Year's Eve," John observed. "I wonder how many of them are thinking, Tonight's the night, the end of an era. The Day of Judgment is at hand."

"After all," Russ said, "where do you want to meet your Maker? People are doing it on their own turf, at home with loved ones. As am I," he added, looking around at his friends. He pulled the Champagne from the ice and read the label. "Perrier-Jouët Belle Epoque. Very nice! Will you join us?" he asked Eric.

"No, thanks," Eric said, with a dip of his head. "I should get back to Lucy for midnight. Enjoy! The Champagne's on the house."

After Eric left with profuse thanks on both sides, John chuckled. "I don't know about the rest of you but I thought for a minute there that we would see Jason come through that door. But who are we fooling? Does anybody really believe that, even if Jason did survive, he remembered our pledge to get together tonight?"

"That's true," May agreed reluctantly, carefully refolding the letter and the poem, putting them back in the envelope with the pledge and the photo and setting it on Russ's satchel. "After all, if my mom hadn't died, I never would have found this stuff. How many of you would have remembered this without seeing the Piñon Nuts pledge?"

Again, no hands went up.

"It is nice to know he survived the night," Matt said. "But even if our guesses about this vague letter are right, we only know that he survived a few more days. It's still true that nobody's seen or heard from him in 30 years."

"Maybe so," Russ said, wrapping his napkin around the top of the Champagne bottle and easing out the cork. "But assuming he made it to Canada and is still alive and kicking out there somewhere, what do you suppose he's up to?"

"What do you think?" May asked him.

"I think he would have stuck to his first love, music," Russ said as the cork popped free. "Maybe he changed his name to Dog Walker and toured with the Beagles, making enough that now he's retired and living in the south of France."

"Or," John added with a grin, "maybe he could never persuade George Harrison to join the Beagles, so he went berserk, broke into Harrison's mansion yesterday morning with that same knife…"

"Yeah, right," Matt said, holding out his Champagne glass to Russ. "I don't think he'd ever make much of a living playing music. Jason was nobody's fool. Like the rest of us, he would have realized early on that, unless you're really good or really lucky, you never strike it rich in show business. I think he went back to school and became a respected botanist, wandering through the woods and unraveling the mysteries of the universe."

"The Lone Ranger's dead, you know," John pointed out.

"What do you mean?" Matt asked.

"Clayton Moore, the guy who played the Lone Ranger on television, died on the 27th," John explained.

"Okay, smarty pants," May said to him. "What do you think he did?"

John thought about it. "I think he probably followed in his Uncle Willie's footsteps. First and foremost, he was a writer."

"What do you think, May?" Deb asked. "You're his daughter, after all."

May watched Russ fill her glass from the flower-painted Champagne bottle. "You know, it doesn't really matter to me what he might be doing. Maybe, like me, he's just an average person working an average job somewhere. I just wish he could have been here with us tonight. I'm sure he would have loved to see all of you. I know it's been the most wonderful night of *my* life."

A commotion broke out downstairs. "It must be midnight!" John cried. "Happy New Year, everybody!"

They raised their glasses. "To Jason!" Russ proposed and it was unanimous. From the lounge downstairs came the strains of "Auld Lang Syne," and they sang along:

> Should old acquaintance be forgot and never brought to mind?
> Should old acquaintance be forgot and days of Auld Lang Syne?
> For Auld Lang Syne, my dear, for Auld Lang Syne
> We'll drink a cup of kindness yet for Auld Lang Syne

"Obviously, the answer is no," Russ said, when the kissing and hugging and hand-shaking faded and the glasses stood empty. "Old acquaintance shouldn't be forgot."

"Some acquaintance, though," Deb said, putting her hands on Matt's shoulder, "is getting pretty old."

Matt looked very tired but he smiled. "See what I saved you from, Jacques?" he said to John. "She's worn me down to a stump."

John looked fondly at Deb. "There, but for the gracelessness of God, go I," he said to Matt.

Russ chuckled as he pushed back his chair. "Well, we'd better get out of here and let the fine employees of Crestwood finish up. It's been quite a night though."

"That it has, my friend," John said, putting his arm around Russ's shoulders. "That it has."

Deb and May helped Matt stand. As they walked out of the room, he said, "I think I better use the restroom before we go."

"We'll meet you downstairs," Deb told him. "Or do you want me to wait here?"

"No, I'll be fine. You go ahead."

"Well, this was great, kids!" John said as they wended their way down the stairs toward the foyer. "What say we do this again in 30 years?"

"Oh, sooner than that," Deb said.

"I guess I could stand to see your ugly mugs in, say, another five years then," John countered.

"I'm not sure Matt can wait that long," Deb said to him as Russ leaned into the lounge to wave good-night to Lucy and Eric.

"What do you mean?" John asked, concerned, as was May, with the sober look on Deb's face.

"Russ, could you help me with my coat?" Deb asked.

Russ held Deb's coat for her. "Did I miss something?" he asked, seeing their expressions.

Deb took a deep breath. "I might as well tell you all right now. Matt didn't have walking pneumonia. He has prostate cancer."

"Oh, God, no!" John said.

Russ looked too stricken to respond.

May had thought all evening that Matt looked pretty ill but she hadn't expected this. She looked at Deb's dry eyes and steeled expression. Deb really would need her help.

"Why didn't you say something earlier?" Russ asked.

"Matt didn't want to spoil everyone's evening," Deb said. "He was afraid you'd all... well, look like you look right now."

"Is there anything we can do?" John asked.

"Tonight meant all the world to him," she said. "You don't know what he went through to make this trip."

"How bad is it?" Russ asked quietly as they heard Matt's slow steps coming down the stairs.

Deb put on a bright face for Matt's benefit. "I just don't think we should wait another five years," she said, sounding cheerful. "Come on, John. You could call more than once every couple of decades."

"See? I knew it," Matt said to John, letting go of the balustrade at the bottom of the stairs. "All these years, she's just been using me to get to you."

"Hey, the only reason I quit calling was because I knew I couldn't compete with you," John said, looking fondly at his old friend.

"We need to get you home, big fella," Russ said to Matt. "May, you really know how to throw a party. Let's do this again soon. I know a great little spot in the Village if you guys find yourselves back east sometime."

John hugged May and kissed her cheek. "Thanks for everything. We'll talk soon."

Deb kissed her as well. "And I'll call you in the morning. Do you work?"

"Not till 4:00."

"Give some thought to that offer, okay?"

"It won't require much thought," May said. She hugged Matt gently. "Thanks so much for coming all the way here when you weren't feeling well. I can't tell you how special you and Deb have made me feel."

"You are special," Matt assured her as they walked out the door.

"Drive carefully, John!" May called to them as they walked to the car. "Happy New Year, everybody!"

January 1, 2000
12:10 a.m.

Deb and Russ helped Matt into the back seat of the Outback while John got behind the wheel and started the engine. With a last wave to May, John pulled out onto Cresta and drove down the hill. For a while, no one spoke.

The news of Matt's prostate cancer certainly sobered John. All that he'd been through the last couple of months—the break-up of his marriage, Anne's disastrous involvement with Wayne Giles, the shake-up at the *Trail Gazette*—paled in comparison. He couldn't recall exactly why he hadn't phoned Deb and Matt in 20 years. He could always fall back on the one-size-fits-all, no-arguing-it excuse that everyone used at the end of the 20th Century: he'd just been too busy. Meanwhile, as he chased paper money around Estes, saw to every one of the girls' fleeting desires, and let television, Hollywood, and the Internet fill every peaceful nook and cranny with the clamor of the Information Age, real life and true friends quietly slipped away.

In the back seat, Matt and Deb sat very close, holding hands. Matt leaned to her and asked, "Did you ask her?"

"Mm-hmm," Deb said.

"What did she say?"

"She seemed interested."

"Did you dazzle her?"

Deb chuckled. "I made her a very tempting offer. I'll call her in the morning and we'll talk more about it."

"You made May some sort of offer?" John surmised as he drove down Cheyenne Boulevard past the 8th Street intersection near the site of May's car accident.

"I'm hoping to persuade her to move to Seattle to help me with my charities," Deb explained. "Matt and I are going to take a trip."

"Really?" Russ asked. "I mean, isn't that...?" He didn't finish his thought.

"You told them, didn't you?" Matt asked Deb.

"I thought they should know," Deb said. "I hope you don't mind."

"No, that's fine," Matt said. "Sorry to ruin the night for you guys."

"Well, the night turned out splendidly," Russ said. "But we're awfully sorry to hear this news. How long have you known?"

"Six weeks or so," Matt said.

"But you're going on a trip?" John asked.

"Matt's going in for some surgery next week," Deb said. "While he's recovering, we're going to fly down to Cancun and Costa Rica. He'll start regular treatments when we get back. I'm going to spend so much time with him that I'll need someone to help out. I'm hoping I can persuade May to take the job."

"That's a wonderful idea," John said. "May's really had a tough go of it lately, losing her mom and grandmother and everything."

"I've actually felt quite attached to her all along," Deb said. "It's time I started showing it."

"Anyway, Matt," Russ said, "we really appreciate your making this trip under those circumstances. It really took balls."

"Yes, it did," Deb said, kissing Matt, who had laid his head on her shoulder.

"Which is more than we can say for Jason, that son of a bitch," John pointed out. "I mean, we all braved hell and high water to make it here. He's the one who dropped the ball. I think he should be dismembered, like the pledge promised."

"And excommunicated too," Russ vowed. "I think we should all avoid talking to him for another 30 years. That'll show him."

"It is amazing to think he might still be alive and kicking," Russ said.

"It's amazing we're all alive and kicking," John said as he angled from Cheyenne Boulevard onto Tejon Street. "The last couple of months have been pretty rough."

Russ murmured his agreement. "Earlier, I heard Doris Kearns Goodwin mention the old Chinese curse: May you live in interesting times. It really feels like some of the turmoil of the end of the '60s has come back to haunt us at the end of the '90s. It would make a good book."

"Matt told me you were thinking of doing some writing," Deb said to Russ. "Maybe you should write about that."

"Me?" Russ scoffed. "Hell, I've got a restaurant to dig out of trouble and a baby on the way. Besides, I was planning a philosophy book, not a novel or a memoir. What about you, John? Aren't you an aspiring writer? What about your marijuana article for the paper?"

"That was mostly non-fiction and it pretty much went up in smoke when the paper sold," John said. "And now Susan's threatening to take me back."

"That's great!" Deb said.

"It is good," John admitted, pulling onto I-25 north toward Woodmen Valley where Deb's parents had moved. "I suppose there's no such thing as a perfect relationship but Susan and I make a good team regardless of our differences. And the girls look to us to learn how to be grown-ups so we better start acting like grown-ups. In any case, there's no way I could find the time to write a book. You know who ought to do it? That bastard Jason. Serve him right for not showing up."

"You know," Russ pointed out, "now that we know he survived, maybe we ought to try looking for him."

"Where in world would you start?" John asked.

"I don't know. You could search some databases in a hurry now, I suppose."

"Maybe he doesn't want to be found," Deb observed.

"Oh, I think the heat's probably died down after 30 years," Russ said.

"Yeah, but who knows what other kinds of situations he's gotten himself into since then?" John asked. "He was never one to let sleeping dogs lie."

"But it's not like he went out looking for trouble," Russ pointed out. "Trouble just seemed to find him."

"And his daughter seems to carry on that family tradition," John said. "Although she may be more of an instigator."

"But maybe we need people like that in our lives," Deb said, "to shake us out of our complacency."

"We wouldn't have gotten together if it hadn't been for the two of them," Russ admitted. "You know what song I've heard a lot on television commercials lately? 'Come Together.' Maybe it's something about the end of the millennium, or maybe the 20th anniversary of Lennon's assassination, but it certainly seems appropriate to the Piñon Nuts as well."

"Incidentally, Russ," Deb said, "I know everybody, especially May, was thrilled with that watercolor of Jason that Sylvia did. I hope you'll pass along our compliments to her."

"I sure—uh-oh," Russ said. "Where's my satchel?" He felt around on the floor of the car and next to his seat. "It's not back there, is it?" he asked Deb.

"I don't see it."

"Oh, jeez, I must have left it at the restaurant," Russ groaned.

"I'm sure they'll hold it for you," John assured him.

"But my flight tomorrow is at 9:30 and I doubt if anyone will get to the restaurant until 10:00 or so. Oh, God, Sylvia will kill me if I lose that. She had some other sketches on the pad too."

"I'm sure someone could ship it to you," John said.

"Sylvia would refuse to speak to me until she actually held that pad in her hands," Russ said. "God, I hate to ask this but could we go back for it?"

"Do you think anyone would still be there?" Deb asked.

"Oh, someone's bound to be there for a while after such a big night," Russ said. "We haven't been gone that long. Would you mind?" he asked John.

"It's no problem for me," John said. "But should I take you two home first?" he asked Matt and Deb, looking in the rear-view mirror.

Matt's tall, thin body rested against Deb. Quietly, she said, "He fell asleep a while ago. I'm not exaggerating when I say that being with you guys has been the best thing that's happened to him in the last couple of months. He may sleep through it but I'm sure he wouldn't mind."

"Let's do it," John said, turning on his blinker to take the Uintah exit so they could turn around.

"Thanks, John," Russ said. "You have no idea how much this will mean."

He seemed so relieved, in fact, that he sang a snatch of "We're On Our Way Home," an old Beatles song that they all knew so well they joined him for the chorus.

January 1, 2000
12:10 a.m.

May watched Deb and Russ help Matt into the back seat of the Outback while John got behind the wheel and started the engine. When Deb waved to her one last time, May waved back, wondering how many more ways Deb would change her life. She didn't go back inside until John pulled out onto Cresta.

With a sigh, she closed the heavy front door behind her and locked it. She went into the lounge and thanked Eric and Lucy for their confidence in her, all the while wondering if she wouldn't soon be giving them her notice. Just on a whim, she went through the solarium so she could take the elevator back upstairs to get her purse.

As the elevator door closed behind her, though, the door in front, to the kitchen, opened and she saw Scott waiting there with a bus cart.

"You're still here?" she asked him as he pulled the cart into the elevator.

"Almost done," he said as the door closed. "I just thought I'd clear your table upstairs, get the last of the dishes down to the dishwasher."

"I'll help you," she volunteered. "You must be beat."

"I may be old," he said, wiping some sweat from his cheek, "but I can still climb a hill without shifting gears. You're off the clock. You ought to go home to your daughter."

"Oh, I'm too excited to sleep anyway," she said. "I've had the most incredible night!"

The elevator stopped. "That's right," Scott said as he wheeled the cart out the door. "How did your party go?"

"Fantastic! I even got an unbelievable job offer," she told him. She knew she shouldn't talk too much about this, especially to fellow Crestwood employees, at least until she and Deb worked out the details but she felt like she had to tell someone or burst.

"Really?" he said as they got to the northwest bedroom. "Doing what?"

"Oh, helping one of my friends," she said proudly. "I'd have to move to Seattle, though."

"No kidding," he said, pushing the cart to the table. "I came here from Seattle a few months ago. In fact, I've been toying with the idea of moving back. It looks like we're both at one of those choice points in our lives. It's sad and exciting at the same time, isn't it?"

"Yes, it is," she said. Whether it stemmed from the closeness she felt from being with the Piñon Nuts or from his helping her see through Marcus, she found herself liking Scott. "Well, if you do, and if I do, maybe we should try to keep in touch."

"That would be great," he said, clearing the table. "What's your last name? I'll try to look you up."

"Mendoza," she said, thinking, though, even as she said it, that maybe Deb's lawyer could help her dump Paco's name. But what would she choose? Black? Walker? Anyway, "What's yours?" she asked, looking through her purse for something to write on.

"Free," he said. "Spelled like 'free.'"

That would explain his earlier remark about always being free, she thought as she wrote it down. Oh, Scott Free, she realized.

"What's this?" he asked from behind her.

She heard a heavy thump and turned around, alarmed. He had collapsed into a chair, his face ashen, his hands trembling. At first she thought he'd had a heart attack. Then she saw that his left hand held her envelope and his right hand held the photo of the Piñon Nuts which he had just taken from it. He looked at the old Polaroid with amazement and dismay.

On the table next to him sat the black satchel Russ must have forgotten. Suddenly a profound realization dawned on May. In the satchel was Sylvia's watercolor of Jason, which had looked so familiar to her earlier because, she now knew, it looked so much like Scott! Like him, she slumped limply into a chair.

For a few moments they just sat staring at one another in wordless astonishment.

"Wha—? Wha—?" he stammered at last. "Where did this come from?"

"Oh, my God!" she cried. "Are you Jason?"

"I don't know," he told her, looking genuinely lost. "I mean I… Well… But where did you get this? Were all these guys here?"

"Oh, no!" May lamented as she realized what had happened.

"Oh, they were, weren't they? Oh, God, no! I missed them, didn't I?"

"I don't believe this!" she cried, simultaneously overjoyed at finding him and devastated that he had missed the others. "This can't be happening!"

"But I checked the reservation book!" he insisted and then realized: "Oh, but you put it under your name, Mendoza. No wonder. Oh, Lord!" he groaned.

"So you've been here for months!" she exclaimed. "You remembered!"

"I've thought about this for years," he said, gazing fondly again at his old friends. "That's part of what drew me back here to Colorado, I guess. But I never *dreamed* they'd remember too after all this time."

"Well, they did," she said, thinking that his blue eyes looked the same as they had in Sylvia's watercolor: intelligent, ironic, timeless. "Why didn't you try to contact anybody?"

"I did, actually," he told her, taking off his toque to wipe his nearly-bald head. "None of the Piñon Nuts, or even a parent, is still in town, or at least in the phone book. I couldn't remember Manny's parents' first names and the phone book listed several Tyrees. I didn't want to just start calling people at random."

"But you could have done something!" she insisted.

"I guess it was kind of a test, too," he said. "I wasn't sure they'd want to see me again after all these years, to tell you the truth. I don't know how much you know about this but I left here under a big black cloud. I guess I wanted to see if any of them still remembered our old pledge. I mean, if they showed up on their own, it would prove to me that they genuinely wanted to see me, that they weren't just being polite. And then as tonight drew closer, I began to realize how absurd such a thing would be. I mean, it's been 30 years! I figured they probably just forgot about me."

"Well, obviously they didn't," she told him.

"Besides," he said, sounding a little defensive, "I *did* do something! When I came here to Russ's old place and found they'd turned it into a restaurant, I figured this would be the best place in the world to keep my eyes peeled for them. So I got a job as a cook. But then tonight rolled around and I got stuck filling in for Marcus and doing the salads too, and then I burned the ducks, so I never got time to get out of the kitchen to look around. You know, I put piñon nuts in the wild rice stuffing just for old times' sake. But it was such an unbelievable long shot anyway, I guess I just didn't think it was possible. And I assume they didn't try to find me either."

"Until tonight, we all thought you were dead!" she told him, flabbergasted that she had found him. "Everybody but Russ, maybe. What happened up in Jones Park, anyway? How did you get out of there?"

"They told you about all of that?" he said. "Oh, wow. What a night that was."

"They said you left the cabin with nothing but a knife."

"That's true," he said, gazing back over the years, looking disturbed by what he saw. "I guess I've blocked all of that out of my mind ever since. In fact, in a way I killed Jason Walker that night."

"What do you mean?"

Staring dismally into space, he said, "When I left the cabin with that broken knife I got at the Broadmoor, I fully intended to kill myself. I felt like everything I cared about was gone, except for those friends of mine, and having me around could only bring them trouble. So I staggered out of the cabin—God, I was sick!—and stumbled around through the rain, the hail covering the ground, the lightning so bright and so frequent that I had no trouble finding my way. I climbed up a ridge and found a big rock to sit on. I held up the metal blade of the knife to the clouds and just waited for God to strike me down, take the poor, pathetic remnants of me He had spared so far and be done with it."

When he stopped, lost in thought, she asked him what happened.

"Well, I got impatient," he said. "After a while, when the lightning kept striking all around but missing me, I figured God had left it up to me to perform this one last act. I turned the knife sideways and set the point just under my ribs. I took a deep breath and tried as hard as I could to quit shaking so I wouldn't screw up my suicide too. As I was hunched over like that with the knife blade poised to pierce my aching heart, just as I finally felt myself grow still, there came a brilliant flash of lightning. The light reflected from the wide notched blade of the knife and I had this sudden flash of realization. Just 24 hours before, it actually crossed my mind to try to throw that same notched knife blade into President Nixon's heart. But I didn't. I guess that sort of violence just isn't in my nature. I showed the man mercy. Why was I unwilling to show myself the same mercy?"

"What did you do?"

"I'm not really sure. As I said, I think I killed Jason Walker that night. It wasn't as though I spared myself. I came so close to dying that for all I knew, I *had* died. I became someone else. I was reborn. I veered into an alternate reality. I had a free life, to do with what I pleased. I still had the knife, after all. I could kill myself any time."

"Is that the same knife you showed me downstairs?"

"Yeah," he said. "I've cooked with it at home ever since, although this is the first time I've used it professionally. Whenever I look at it, it reminds me that I'm still on my free life."

"So you escaped."

"I just started walking, figuring I'd use up what legs I had left, and die hiking, if that was my destiny. I knew I couldn't go back. So I headed north toward Canada."

"Weren't you freezing?"

"I was at first but then the walking warmed me up. I still could see my way just by the lightning. The next morning the sun warmed me up as I headed down toward Manitou Springs. I was so hungry I was shaking the piñon trees to try to loosen a few nuts."

"Did it work?"

"Indirectly. I didn't get any piñon nuts but the sound attracted some hikers just starting up the Barr Trail who thought I might be a bear. Anyway, they fed me and gave me a spare jacket. So I just kept going, heading north. Over the next few days I ran into people along the way who gave me rides and meals and a place to crash."

"So you did make it to Canada."

"Yeah. How did you know?"

"Matt figured it out from your letter."

"Letter?"

"This one," she said, taking the envelope and pulling out the letter. She handed it to him.

"Oh, my God! She kept it!" he said, looking at the folded notebook paper. "I wrote this just before I crossed the border, to reassure Manny that I did survive and that I wouldn't come back to mess up her life anymore. I just couldn't bear to leave her hanging. Look. See where it says 'scot free'? That's where I came up with the name. I used it as a stage name playing music up in Canada. Then, four years later when Nixon resigned and Gerald Ford issued an amnesty for draft dodgers, I came back to the States. I traveled around the Northwest playing music as Scott Free until I moved back to Colorado last summer. But that's a long story. You'd have to read my memoirs."

"That's right, you told me you were writing, didn't you?" May asked, her mind having trouble sorting all this out.

He snorted. "It's only a couple dozen pages. And the best one, but one that I couldn't bear to write, was the one I just told you. Anyway, how did this whole thing come about? Was this Manny's doing?"

"In a way," May said wistfully.

"I really did try to get a hold of her," he said. "I even called Bill Black, this guy she used to be involved with. I don't know what I would have done if I found Amanda there but luckily Bill's married to some exotic dancer. So anyway, Man was here then? How is she?"

"Oh, I'm so sorry to have to tell you this," she said, tears welling up in her eyes. "She died last August."

His spirits, which had revived when he saw the letter, crumbled. His eyes, too, filled with tears and he slumped forward, putting his face in his hands.

May leaned forward and put her hand on his knee. "If it's any consolation, I know she thought about you until the end."

"How did she die?" he asked through his hands.

"She was killed in a glider accident," she said softly. "She got caught in a thunderstorm and crashed on Pikes Peak."

He began to sob. "Oh, God, I'm such a fool," he moaned. "Man's dead and all my friends have come and gone. Why did I have to come back here? Why couldn't I let sleeping dogs lie?"

She reached over and stroked his head, and then put her arm around his quaking shoulders. "It's not your fault," she whispered to him. "You did what you could. At least you tried."

After a while, he gathered himself a little, grabbing one of the napkins from the table to wipe his eyes and nose. He heaved a couple of sobbing sighs.

"I'm sorry," he said to her. "I just wasn't prepared for this."

"I wasn't either," she assured him.

Blinking away his tears, he sat back up and looked at her. "You know," he said, looking embarrassed, "this is probably going to sound like a really stupid question. I mean, obviously you're quite involved in all this, but I guess I don't know how. Are you the daughter of one of the Piñon Nuts?"

May realized just how obtuse she could be. In the excitement it had never crossed her mind to properly introduce herself.

"Actually," she told him, "I'm the daughter of two of the Piñon Nuts."

He cleared his eyes and looked at her. "That's why you remind me of someone! You're

Manny's daughter, aren't you?"

She nodded.

"Oh, I'm so glad she didn't marry Bill Black."

"Actually, she did. But I'm not his daughter."

He shook his head in bewilderment. "Then who…?"

She fell to her knees on the floor and wrapped her arms around his legs and hugged him. Looking up at him with tears in her eyes, she said, "I'm *your* daughter."

His mouth dropped open. He took her face in his hands and gazed at her in disbelief. "It's not possible! Is it?"

"Matt called Mom just in time," she told him. "I'm your baby angel."

With an indescribable look of joy mixed with grief, he held out his arms to her. She wrapped herself around him and hugged him so hard she almost crushed him.

Finally he pulled her away from him. "How can this be? Let me look at you. You're so beautiful, so strong! How can you possibly be my daughter? And now you have a daughter of your own!"

"Oh, Jason!" she gushed. "Dad! Oh, wait'll you meet Libby!"

"I'm a grandfather," he realized, shaking his head in disbelief.

"John said he thought Libby had your hair."

"She's the one!" he said, rubbing his bald head. "So you and John are friends?"

May felt a pang when she thought about South Park but she said, "You wouldn't believe it. Just two months ago he and I took an incredible hike up near Estes where he lives."

"A hike? Then you really are a Walker!"

"Yes, I am!" she declared, but added, "I have done my share of stumbling through the dark, though. I've got a long way to go to catch up with you."

"What do you mean?"

"Just in terms of being enlightened or whatever."

He laughed. "Oh, I don't know that I'm in front of anyone on that path. Seeking enlightenment is like chasing your shadow. Either enlightenment is already an inherent part of you or it's forever beyond your grasp."

"Oh, I wish you could have been up here for the Gathering!"

"Oh, well," he said philosophically. "I've always known that you can either cook a great meal or eat a great meal, but it's really hard to do both. Besides, maybe we'll get a second chance if we both move up to Seattle. Who are you going to help up there, anyway? Matt?"

May knew she couldn't break the news about Matt to him right now. "Matt and Deb actually."

"They got married!? That's great! I tried looking them up in the phone book once when I first moved there but they must have an unlisted number. How are they doing? And how's Russ?"

Out the window May saw car headlights pull into the drive. She looked again at Russ's satchel sitting on the table. "You know something?" she said. "I have a feeling you can ask them yourself."

"That can't really be them, can it?" he asked, looking out the window.

"It's John's car," she told him, picking up the forgotten satchel. "The question is, how are we going to tell them about this?"

He put his arm around her. "Together."

...O...O...O...O...

June 1, 2000

So this is what alternate reality looks like.

Sorry if that whole thing sounded disingenuous in light of subsequent events but Ed and I talked it over and figured that alternating the memoirs with the text made the most sense. I tried to rearrange them for the best fit to what follows, which worked better with some than with others.

I certainly couldn't have put this together in so short a time without everyone's frank and lucid help. If I hadn't had such a great story ready-made, a book like this would have taken years to write.

Clear Eye had the balls to go through with the orchiectomy. His lovely doting wife has blossomed in the role of Grandma. My daughter (yikes!) works below decks on the S. S. McCleary, becoming an indispensable member of the crew. I spend a lot of time here myself, attacking those pesky blackberry vines when the writing stumps me.

The Cough Man is still high in Estes, having reached an uneasy peace at home. Yes, Santa, this year there will be no Virginia.

The Tweakmaster, his Window Syl, and that long-gone slanted L are in their second trimester, all doing fine. Buzz tells me that, if I'm ever out there and the boss okays it, he and Christine will let me sit in with the band.

Last but not least, it is a certain someone's second birthday today so we're having a little party. (Come a little closer: I hear there's a bow on a little pony out in the barn.)

What's next for me? God knows. Maybe a little road work, a few more gigs. It doesn't really matter. Home is where the heart is.

But, hey, they're calling me to dinner. Besides, my fingers are tired and your eyelids are beginning to droop. But did I ever tell you about the time I—

What's that, Uncle Willie? "Puck off"? Nuts. Nuff said.

> *If we shadows have offended,*
> *Think but this, and all is mended —*
> *That you have but slumb'red here*
> *While these visions did appear.*
> *And this weak and idle theme,*
> *No more yielding but a dream...*